John H. C...
Champa...

S0-ABN-028

THE BORZOI

Turgenev

SMOKE

FATHERS AND SONS

FIRST LOVE

ON THE EVE

RUDIN

A QUIET SPOT (THE BACKWATER)

THE DIARY OF A SUPERFLUOUS MAN

THE BORZOI

Turgenev

Translated from the Russian by

HARRY STEVENS

Foreword by SERGE KOUSSEVITZKY

Introduction by AVRAHM YARMOLINSKY

1950
NEW YORK : ALFRED A. KNOPF

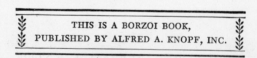

THIS IS A BORZOI BOOK,
PUBLISHED BY ALFRED A. KNOPF, INC.

Copyright 1950 by Alfred A. Knopf, Inc. All rights reserved. No part of this book may be reproduced in any form without permission in writing from the publisher, except by a reviewer who may quote brief passages in a review to be printed in a magazine or newspaper.

Published simultaneously in Canada by McClelland & Stewart Limited

Manufactured in the United States of America

FIRST EDITION

I SHALL SAY BRIEFLY THAT I AM, ABOVE ALL, *a realist and chiefly interested in the living truth of the human face; to everything supernatural I am indifferent, and I do not believe in absolutes and systems; I love freedom more than anything else, and so far as I can judge I am sensitive to poetry. Everything human is dear to me, Slavophilism is alien, and so is all manner of orthodoxy.*

TURGENEV

Foreword

THE VERY NAME of Ivan Sergeevich Turgenev suggests a great Russian epoch, one illuminated by high aspirations and made electric by an extraordinary upsurge in the intensity and productivity of cultural and literary forces. It can truly be called the most glorious and glowing epoch in the history of Russian thought and art.

Of the constellation that brightened the literary firmament of nineteenth-century Russia, the star of Turgenev has proved both universal and lasting. His words do not hold the shattering impact and revelation of Tolstoy's or the prophetic power and penetration of Dostoyevsky's. Turgenev does not pound upon and break open the closed door of Destiny. He merely stands by, listens intently, observes closely. An inimitable master painter, he has at his command the rich, subtle palette of the Russian language, which he knows perfectly and the beauty of which he explores to its deep roots and manifold sources.

Page after page we traverse with Turgenev the long gallery of his masterpieces. He unfolds before us the Russian nature and way of life. He reveals the Russian peasant, the serf on the threshold of liberation. He paints with infinite care, understanding, and insight the portrait of the Russian woman. With him we meet Russians of all classes and social standings, from the older landowners to the young intellectuals. In his writing we feel the rising ferment of the new generation, the conflict, the brutal break with old traditions, the inescapable inner quest.

Foreword

Today, when the door of Destiny has been flung open upon old Russia, we look searchingly with Turgenev through the dense curtain of smoke. With him we still question the future.

SERGE KOUSSEVITZKY

Introduction

TURGENEV: A REVALUATION

In his student years Turgenev, who was slow in discovering his true medium, broke into print with some verse. Then he tried his hand at writing for the stage. Although he made at least one permanent contribution to the Russian repertory with *A Month in the Country*, his interest in drama did not persist. He grew to dislike his plays and he kept his poems out of his collected works: a poem, like an oyster, was worthless, he said, if it was less than perfect. The allegories, fantasies, and lyrical pieces that make up the work of his old age, *Poems in Prose*, are examples of a hybrid genre lacking both the form and the substance of poetry.

In his late twenties he published several romantic stories, which passed unnoticed. His work began to attract attention only when he started publishing serially, under the general title *A Hunter's Notes*, better known as *A Sportsman's Sketches*, short pieces ranging from sketches with a factual slant to more formal stories. They are held together by the device of presenting them as accounts of the narrator's experiences during his excursions in pursuit of game. Turgenev wrote many of them abroad, where he had gone to be close to Pauline Viardot, the prima donna with whom, on her first visit to Russia, he had fallen desperately and permanently in love. His great reputation dates from the publication of the *Sketches* in book form in 1852, when he was a man of thirty-four.

The work owed its great initial success in part to the fact that it was taken as an attack on serfdom, the abolition of which was then a burning issue. It is hardly an abolitionist tract, however. Turgenev abominated serfdom, but he was not a crusader by temperament and could no more engage in propaganda than he could walk on his head. In half the pieces the dangerous subject is not touched upon at all. It may be noted that when the book was in the writing the author inherited from that domineering dowager, his mother, fifteen thousand acres and two thousand male "souls," and that un-

Introduction

til the Emancipation he remained the owner — an uneasy one, it is true — of what his friend Herzen called "baptized property." It is certain, nevertheless, that the book did materially help to create an atmosphere hostile to the perpetuation of serfdom and may, indeed, have played a part in disposing the Emperor in favor of the peasant reform.

The movement against Russian serfdom is a battle long ago. Yet after the lapse of a century *A Sportsman's Sketches* still makes uncommonly good reading. It has the evergreen freshness of a classic. An outdoor, wholesome book, it is written out of an intimate knowledge of and sensitiveness to the natural scene, its shapes and colors, its sounds and odors. Felicitously these pages evoke the landscape Turgenev knew best, that of central Russia, where the forest gives way to the grasslands. It is a landscape with figures. The author's main concern here, as in the bulk of his 'work, is with human beings. In all these respects it represents the lineaments of his later work.

With the publication of *A Sportsman's Sketches* in book form, Turgenev decided that he had come to the close of a period of his life as an author and must strike out in a new direction. "I am done with extracting the triple essence of human character," he wrote to a friend, "pouring it into small bottles: 'Sniff it, please, gentle reader, uncork it and sniff it; it has the Russian bouquet, hasn't it?' Enough, enough!" He must adopt a new manner. He must put his mind to a studied piece of work on a large scale, a novel. But was he capable of "something great and calm"? He knew he couldn't tell until he tried.

In the thirty years that were left him he did produce several long narratives that are usually classed as novels. At the same time he continued to write short pieces. He curbed an inclination to flippancy and a weakness for odd characters, but his manner underwent a less clearly discernible change than his matter. Men and women of the people practically disappeared from his fictions, except as accessory figures, kept well in the background. True, the very year *A Sportsman's Sketches* was published he wrote two peasant tales. One, which Carlyle pronounced the most pathetic story in the world, is the widely anthologized *Moomoo,* an account of the miseries of a gentle giant of a serf, deaf and dumb, almost a symbolical figure. Turgenev never again focused his attention on simple villagers, except to add to *A Sportsman's*

Introduction

Sketches, many years later, a piece about a peasant woman reduced by an accident to little more than a living corpse, yet accepting her bleak lot with a meekness and fortitude more than human. Henceforth he was to draw his models from the middle class: members of the gentry and people whom education had raised above their unprivileged status.

A distillate of character continues to be the main ingredient of the thirty-odd stories he was to write. In one of his few public addresses Turgenev elaborated a theory of personality, the gist of which was that mankind consists of Hamlets and Don Quixotes, or, more exactly, of persons in whom the hamletic and the quixotic elements are mixed in varying proportions. This view of human nature was useful to him in the construction of his characters, though a healthy instinct kept him from applying the formula with mechanical rigidity. Of course, his best creations refuse to be pigeonholed. Himself a man with a hamletic strain in his make-up, he satisfied his urge to project men and more especially women of the opposite temper. Yet it is significant that even his strong characters are not shown as having realized their ends. Either they die young, with their work undone, or their achievements are merely mentioned as a thing of the future.

A variant of the hamletic type appears in an early narrative that was not included in *A Sportsman's Sketches: The Diary of a Superfluous Man*. This is a characteristic piece of writing, though it does not show the author at his best. Like so many of his tales, it is a story of frustration and failure, enveloped in an atmosphere damp with pathos. Indeed, pathos is the earmark of Turgenev's art. The diarist is defeated in love and, as a victim of consumption, he is defeated in a more elementary, biological sense. Both he and his lucky rival are unworthy of the young heroine. Woman's superiority to man was a belief at which Turgenev arrived early in life. The theme of woman's moral supremacy haunts him as a recurrent dream haunts the mind. It is present in *A Quiet Spot*, which offers in passing a glimpse of the confined, uneventful, leisurely existence of the provincial gentry. It is a tale of unrequited passion, a love story, like nearly all of Turgenev's fictions.

Nothing so fascinates him as does this force welling up from the irrational depths of the soul. Now it floods the heart with "the gay terror" of impending happiness. Now its enchantment creates a new personality. It can clothe the world in glory, it can give a

Introduction

man wings, but it can also act on him like a disease. It "seizes a human being as a hawk does a chick." It may exalt or crush the finer instincts. Be it good or evil, Turgenev's preoccupation with it is not in terms of sensuality but of sentiment. And never does he show fulfillment. He is content to paint the dawn and occasionally the afterglow of love.

His particular delight is to celebrate the secret inception and first stirrings of young love, all compact of expectation and foreboding. Thus in *First Love* he succeeds in capturing the bliss and torment of a schoolboy passion, seen retrospectively in that mood of melting nostalgia to which he not seldom yields. The most striking backdrop for the action here is what Russians call a "sparrow night" — a short summer night tremulous with heat lightning, which is peculiarly appropriate to the mood of the piece. Memories of a dead love are also the substance of *Asya*. This charming story revolves about a rather likable youth who, like so many of Turgenev's male characters, is lacking in ardor and tenacity. At the psychological moment he fails to respond to the feeling he has aroused in the moody, passionate heroine. Fate intervening, their first embrace is also the last — a situation that recurs in Turgenev's work. The youth thus misses his chance of happiness. The story might take as its epigraph the remark of a character in one of Turgenev's later novels: "Man is weak, woman is strong, chance is all-powerful."

The pleasant young man with a fatal flaw in his make-up reappears in that rather mawkish tale, *Torrents of Spring*. He falls in love with an angelic, ravishingly beautiful girl, but ignominiously betrays her by allowing himself to be seduced by a hardly more credible predatory siren. Although his enslavement lasts only a few years, his life is permanently blighted. Like the protagonist of *Asya*, he is doomed to drag out the existence of a lonely old bachelor. It is tempting to relate this emphasis on joyless celibacy to a personal predicament of the novelist's. Because of his lifelong attachment to Pauline Viardot, the exact nature and history of which will probably never be known, he had no family of his own, and, moreover, was an expatriate during the last twenty years of his life. He had an illegitimate daughter by one of his mother's laundresses, but she did not live with him. The situation nourished his self-pity and the sense of unfulfillment that shadows his pages.

Introduction

Other stories of his dwell on the irrationality and the power of love. That it is the most unfathomable of life's mysteries is the conclusion reached by the narrator in *A Hapless Girl*, a somber, melodramatic tale with a tragic finale. The familiar thesis is illustrated more successfully in *The Brigadier*, which, in spite of its meanderings, has the verisimilitude of a case history. In a totally different genre is his last story, *Clara Milich*. An unconventional young actress falls in love with a backward, characterless youth and, when he spurns her, poisons herself. Dead she succeeds, where alive she failed: the ghost takes possession of Aratov. Turgenev was never more emphatic in assigning the active role in the relationship to the woman. Aratov dies (of "a fever complicated by inflammation of the heart") with a blissful smile on his lips, his fingers clutching a strand of his phantom bride's hair. His last words are that love is stronger than death. Turgenev would have been glad to believe this, but his work offers abundant evidence that he did not.

In quite a few of his stories everyday life is invaded by the supernatural. Like Hawthorne, he is careful to leave a loophole for a natural explanation, yet the impression these narratives are apparently intended to leave is that there are more things in heaven and earth than are dreamt of in positivist philosophy. Turgenev kept circling about the occult and peering beyond the gates of the unknown. But he was a man of realistic temper, secular, sober, skeptical. His spectral tales are the nadir of his art. In almost all of them only the creaking machinery of the supernatural is present. An admirable reporter, he could seldom write convincingly about matters outside the range of his experience.

One turns with relief from these apparitions and prophetic dreams, from mesmerism and Oriental magic, to the clear-eyed, bitter realism of *A King Lear of the Steppes*. Equally compelling is that fine character study, *Old Portraits*. One of Turgenev's last stories, it is based on memories of his early years. Indeed, a reminiscential strain pervades many of his shorter narratives. Thus *Old Portraits* evokes the charm of the placid past when the foundations of the ancestral order were still firm, but does not gloss over its horrors. The story ends on a note harsher than any sounded in the peasant tales. A serf, a gay little fellow who is made much of as an accomplished dancer, comes into the possession of a master who goads him cruelly. One day the gentle soul splits his owner's skull with an ax. "Those were good old days — but let's be done with them," are the closing words.

A King Lear of the Steppes may be classed as a novelette, and *Torrents of Spring* comes closer to the proportions of a novel. Turgenev himself dignified by that name only six of his tales, all written between 1855 and 1876: *Rudin, A House of Gentlefolk, On the Eve, Fathers and Sons, Smoke,* and *Virgin Soil.* Henry James, who admired Turgenev this side idolatry and whose work shows traces of his influence, considered his finest novel to be *On the Eve.* There is much to be said for this estimate. *Virgin Soil* is ampler and *Fathers and Sons* has passages of greater depth than those in any other of Turgenev's novels, but structurally it is less satisfactory and the total effect of it does not measure up to that of individual scenes, so that the whole is less than the sum of its parts.

Turgenev's method, generally, is to concentrate on one or more crucial episodes and to report briefly the antecedent and subsequent developments that serve to round out the cycle of the lives involved. As a rule the stories are told by an omniscient narrator, the author or another. Objective though he is, he can never keep himself completely out of the picture. Now and then he offers an obtrusive generalization or puts in a gnomic remark. Rarely, however, does he introduce a character who functions as his mouthpiece. Exceptions are the argumentative Potugin in *Virgin Soil* and Uvar Ivanovich, the penetrating old glutton who acts as a tongue-tied choragus in *On the Eve.* Turgenev practically never explores the sensibilities of his characters through the consciousness of an observer, the author's alert but not all-knowing deputy. The action is usually slight and takes place within a short period of time. There is no concern for suspense. The design is simple, its dominant principle being antithesis: the strong woman versus the weak man, the pure virgin versus the Jezebel, the idealist versus the philistine. Except for *Virgin Soil,* these novels give the impression of expanded short stories. They argue a shortness of breath on the author's part. Can it be that Turgenev's genius, like Chekhov's after him, was most at home with the minor form? He himself seems to have thought so. "Who looks for a novel in the epic sense of the word," he once remarked, "needn't come to me. . . . No matter what I write, it will always be a series of

Introduction

sketches." Fortunately, there is room for novels that are not epic in character.

As might be expected, "the great constringent relation between man and woman" plays an important part in the novels, as it does in the rest of Turgenev's work. Here, as nearly everywhere else, he dwells on the romance of love, rather than passion or durable affection. Even in *Fathers and Sons*, a novel of ideas, it has a prominent role. Arkady's entanglement with the two sisters is delineated with all the delicacy and understanding of which Turgenev was capable in dealing with young lovers. Alone in *Virgin Soil* is the love motif somewhat muted. It is paramount in *A House of Gentlefolk*. Steeped in pathos, the story of Liza and Lavretzky is framed to illustrate the evanescence of happiness, which is no sooner grasped than it escapes. With this theme goes another motif dear to Turgenev's heart: the melancholy wisdom of renunciation. Time was when countless hearts were wrung for the sorrows of this ill-fated pair. In our dry-eyed age few tears are likely to be shed over a heroine who takes the veil to expiate the sin of having fallen in love with another woman's husband, whom she had mistaken for a widower, and over a hero who accepts this decision without protest. Yet though some of these pages have a faded look, it is not difficult to surrender to the art with which the progress of the brief romance is traced in this finely wrought period piece. In *Rudin* the love affair serves as a test of the protagonist, "a man of words, but not of deeds," a test that he ignominiously fails. The involvement here is the familiar one of a high-hearted girl with a weakling of a man.

There are in these novels specimens of conventional girlhood and motherhood, "emancipated" members of the sex, one or two aged harpies and delightful old ladies, and several wicked women: the promiscuous creature who is Lavretzky's wife; the seductive society belle of easy morals who nearly captures Litvinov (in *Smoke*); the unscrupulous wife of Nezhdanov's employer (in *Virgin Soil*). Unique in Turgenev's gallery is the undersexed lady of the beautiful shoulders (in *Fathers and Sons*) through whom Bazarov learns that love is not all a matter of physiology. The center of the stage, however, is usually occupied by a lovely woman of exceptional moral stature, who has the wisdom of the heart as well as of the mind. It is to her that the novels owe their special fragrance and sometimes their meaning. She appears in various guises,

Introduction

all having a family resemblance. These spiritual sisters are idealistic creatures with an intense nature controlled by a firm will. Their stories, which are paralleled in the shorter narratives, form a legend of good women, as true in love as Chaucer's, but with no Cleopatras or Medeas among them.

The most vital example of the type is Yelena (in *On the Eve*). Before our eyes this dreamy girl turns into a woman, single-minded, intransigent, faithful unto death and beyond. She has the bearing of an Antigone. That she should give herself to her lover before their marriage (a bold stroke for so Victorian a novelist) and start with her husband for the hardships and dangers of an alien land might be put down to nothing more unusual than the impulsiveness of a romantic girl deeply in love. But when her husband dies before they reach their destination, the young widow knows neither despair nor confusion. She does not weakly return to her people and her own country. Instead, she resumes her journey to the savage Balkans, resolved to carry on the work to which her husband had dedicated himself: the freeing of his countrymen from the Turkish yoke.

Yelena throws in her lot with a militant Bulgarian nationalist. She plays Ruth to her Insarov's Naomi. For Russia had not bred — not yet — fit mates for her kind: her suitors had been a mercurial artist, a timid pedant, and a soulless bureaucrat. In *A House of Gentlefolk* Liza too is wooed by a young official who is a shallow, self-seeking worldling. But she does meet a Russian who is all but worthy of her. Among philistines and scoundrels, fools and toadies, the author places in a prominent position not only hamletic characters like Rudin and like Nezhdanov (in *Virgin Soil*), but also men of the type of Lavretzky. These members of a gentry that has had its day are honest, well-intentioned, sensitive, and, at least potentially, useful citizens, but they are no towers of strength. Rising head and shoulders above them are only Insarov, the dedicated soul who lives for a cause, Solomin (in *Virgin Soil*), a man of broad social vision and firm purpose, and, of course, Bazarov. The "nihilist" is Turgenev's greatest achievement in portraiture. His impulses and opinions, his crudities and faults, are as unmistakably his own as his long face and green eyes and make him wholly credible. He has a masculinity, a directness and vigor, almost unique in Turgenev's male characters. Rudin, like Lavretzky, can be fully understood only in the context of his age and country. As a projection of the radical temperament, Bazarov, though profoundly Russian and clearly a man of the fifties, has universal validity.

The times favored "engaged" literature; they demanded of the author that he embrace his age and contribute to its self-knowledge. The public looked for guidance to writers of fiction and expected to find in their works an echo of its fears and hopes, a confrontation of the *Zeitgeist*. Though his natural bent was toward the intimate rather than the public theme — he protested that he had no *"politisches Pathos"* and that "to a man of letters politics is poison" — Turgenev tried to live up to these expectations. His novels, unlike his shorter narratives, show a concern for the political questions of the day. The ultimate relevance of the short stories is one of personal morality. They carry no social message, fly no programmatic flag. They have to do with individuals in their private capacity, confronting problems of the inner life and meeting their separate fates. The protagonists of the novels, on the contrary, have a social dimension. These are pages from the history of Russia during the middle decades of the last century, when the country was in the throes of the revolutionary change from a serf economy to one based on free labor.

Thus *Rudin* reflects a phase in the development of the Russian intellectual. The hero's failure on the personal level, in his relationship with Natalia, is seen as symbolic of the inadequacy of the generation to which he, and his creator, belonged: "the idealists of the thirties." Scions of the gentry, nurtured for the most part in a hothouse atmosphere of German romantic literature and philosophy, they were volubly devoted to the good, the true, and the beautiful. But they were apt to be strangers in their own country, rootless men, unfit for action and incapable of feeling, given as they were to an excess of self-analysis. Before the story comes to an end, the author makes a valiant if rather lame attempt to arouse our sympathy for Rudin. The man, he argues, has high moral standards, and his rhetoric, since it can kindle the young with enthusiasm for lofty principles, is a power for good. And the poor devil comes to a quixotic end — an afterthought of Turgenev's, the account of Rudin's death on a barricade in revolutionary Paris appearing only in the second edition of the tale, several years after it was first published.

A man of Rudin's stripe appears in *A House of Gentlefolk*,

Introduction

which is also set in the forties. This "Poltava Demosthenes," however, is a wholly subsidiary figure. The leading character, Lavretzky, is not a seedy, declassé intellectual, but the owner of many "souls" and broad acres, an agreeable, cultivated, well-intentioned man. For a few rapt hours he had believed that he would mend his broken life with the aid of Liza's love. We catch our last glimpse of him when, after a lapse of years, he returns, a lonely, aging man, to the scene of his brief bliss. Yet he faces existence with a serenity born of renunciation: he has given up hope of personal happiness and learned to find contentment in useful work. The moral of the tale is not without faint social overtones. Attention is called to the fact that Liza, whose character had been formed by her peasant nurse, talks to a villager without a trace of condescension. In managing his estates Lavretzky, whose mother had been a serf, has at heart not only his own interests but also those of his peasants. It is in character that, in an argument with Liza's odious suitor, he should demand reverence for the moral values (*pravda*) cherished by the Russian masses.

On the Eve opens on a summer's day in 1853. Before it closes, the guns have spoken, and Russia is in the midst of a war, the end of which will usher in the period of great reforms. Living up to its title, the novel reflects the anticipatory spirit of the years that opened into the stormy sixties. This is something other than the atmosphere of futility dominating *Rudin* and the aura of nostalgic melancholy enveloping *A House of Gentlefolk*. Insarov dies without striking a blow in the fight for which his life had been a preparation. Yelena, his widow, goes off to carry on his work and is lost to view. The story ends on a mournfully meditative note. Nevertheless this novel breathes the tonic air of promise. To the contemporary reader it was both a reproach addressed to a remiss generation and a pledge that the time was near when Russia would breed men, like the Bulgarian, possessed by the will to fight for the freedom of their own country. It was more than a pledge: Yelena became the model for the young women who in the next generation were to lay down their lives for the revolution.

The promise held out in *On the Eve* is to some extent fulfilled in *Fathers and Sons*. Like not a few youths of the late fifties, Bazarov, the young medico on whom the novel turns, holds to the philosophy of "nihilism." This is puerile when it is not brutish, and moreover is at variance with his own thoroughly decent instincts. Like Insarov, a plebeian by birth, he typifies the *raznochintzy* (commoners) who were beginning to enter the ranks of the intelligentsia, previously limited to members of the privileged classes. What is more essential, he is a rebel, a destroyer, a revolutionary by temperament, with all of a revolutionary's intolerance, all his scorn of finicky sentiments and moral scruples. When he declares: "We mean to fight," it is clear that his kind will pull no punches. Science of the crudely materialistic, utilitarian sort has his fanatical allegiance. Since it cannot offer him a program of social action, he has no political ax to grind and is content to hit out at the modes of thought and behavior associated in his mind with the genteel tradition that he abominates. It may be surmised, however, that the "fight" is to be not only against the "principles" and shams of an aristocratic culture, but against the very foundations of the society that supports it. Not its ostensible theme, the conflict between the generations, but the emergence of democratic radicalism is the heart of the book.

In the novels considered thus far, particularly the last two, the private difficulties of the characters are seen against the larger predicament of the country itself, of this vast, dark, inert Russia. Whence will salvation come? Turgenev's answer in *Smoke* is that of a good European who knew no other remedy for the ills of society than "the homeopathy of science and civilization." Only slow, patient, "pedagogical" activity conducted at the grass-roots level can help. The Russians must learn the rational methods, the habits of industry and efficiency that have produced the civilization of the West. And it behooves them to be humble. The diatribes of Potugin, Turgenev's mouthpiece, against patriotic self-complacency make timely reading in days when Russia, under official stimulus, is indulging in an unparalleled orgy of national pride. For all his European sympathies, Turgenev, as a Russian classic, has not been put on the Index. It is heartening to reflect that his writings, along with those of other Russian authors in the liberal tradition, are exerting their humanizing influence at home.

The message of *Smoke* is underscored by its satire. Gall drips from a pen usually so temperate. Animus is directed against two sets in the Russian summer colony at Baden: on the one hand, the titled aristocrats yearning for the fleshpots of serfdom (the action

Introduction

is laid in the year following the Emancipation), and, on the other, the lunatic fringe of the radical camp. The reactionaries, with their stupidity and illimitable egoism, and the fire-eaters, ridden by a doctrinaire fury, are shown as brothers under the skin, equally alienated from the people. Not that the *mystique* of populism, whether of the Slavophil or the socialist variety, could be acceptable to Turgenev, the least doctrinaire of men. The rights of the individual were paramount with him.

The Westernist credo and the political caricature are dovetailed, with incomplete success, into a love story, a tragic variant of which will appear several years later as *Torrents of Spring*. The satire is heavy-handed, the love story convinces. In spite of its title, which of course refers to Litvinov's meditation on the insubstantiality of all things human, *Smoke* is by no means another monument to futility. And this not only because the novelist allows his hero eventually to rebuild his personal life and engage in honorable, useful work, thus, for once, providing a happy ending. Litvinov is one of those competent, practical, public-spirited men who, being pioneers of civilization, are Russia's hope, and, Turgenev suggests, their number is growing. Finally, there is the boon of Emancipation. Litvinov, at last returning to his estates, finds disorder and confusion. Yet above the troubled waters of Russian life "moved, like the spirit of God, freedom."

Virgin Soil, the last of the novels, is the most explicitly political of the lot. It deals with the inchoate revolutionary movement of the late sixties. The two young people who are the central characters are drawn together by a community of ideals that they mistake for love. Marianna's devotion to the populist cause is depicted with the feeling with which Turgenev usually celebrates the personal relation. She is a virginal creature, pure-hearted and dauntless, ready to die for her convictions. Nezhdanov, on the other hand, is another variation on the hamletic theme, a frustrate and divided soul, involved in revolutionary action only through adventitious circumstances and eventually losing faith in it.

In the end Marianna finds her true mate in Solomin. It is upon the strong plebeian shoulders of men like this hard-headed, hard-working engineer, the author implies, that the future of Russia rests. Like the conspirators who consider him one of their own, he hates the decaying feudal class and the equally predatory bourgeoisie that is bound to supplant it. But he does not share his comrades' belief in the imminence of the agrarian revolution. "A gradualist from below," anticipating the Fabians, he envisages a long, peaceful preparatory process of an essentially educational character. The epigraph to the book speaks of the necessity of tilling virgin soil with a plow that cuts deep. Turgenev meant not violence, but enlightenment. The lesson offered here is the same as that of *Smoke*. And again the beneficiaries of the existing order, whether frankly reactionary or hiding behind a spurious progressivism, are given no quarter. On the other hand, some of the freaks and crackpots who plot peasant uprisings and actually precipitate an ill-starred miniature *Putsch*, are treated with a certain amount of affection. In no other piece of fiction does Turgenev so unmistakably show his democratic sympathies.

The weakness of the novel is apparent when it is contrasted with Dostoevsky's work on virtually the same theme: *The Possessed*. This book, born of fear and wrath, in spite of its distortions gets at the heart of the matter in revealing the possibilities of perversion in the process of revolution. It is clear that the subject is alien to Turgenev. Just as in some of his stories there is the mechanics of the supernatural without its atmosphere, so here we have the apparatus of conspiracy without its animating spirit. Here as elsewhere the fine passages tend to redeem the feebler part of the book. Turgenev properly finds in a sense of injury, inferiority, and failure a mainspring of the revolutionary temper. Paklin, the unhappy fellow traveler, is one of the novelist's most subtly conceived characters. The factual side of the movement is depicted with more accuracy than might be expected, considering that the author was an expatriate who got his information about underground activities at second hand.

Looking back on his novels, Turgenev wrote in 1880, three years before his death: ". . . I strove, within the limits of my power and ability, conscientiously and impartially to represent and incarnate in appropriate types both what Shakspere called 'the body and pressure of the time' and the rapidly changing countenance of educated Russians, who have been the predominant object of my observations." The artist speaks here in the accents of the memoirist or the social historian. Indeed, their procedure was not uncongenial to Turgenev. Some of the pieces in *A Sportsman's Sketches* straddle the borderline between fact and fiction. *The Brigadier* contains the text of a letter that Turgenev had found among his mother's papers. As one reads the long dossier-like digressions in his novels, one feels that a first-rate biographer was lost in him. "Every line I have ever written," he told an American visitor, "has been inspired by something that has actually happened to me or come within my observation." He had the huntsman's eye and ear, as well as a prodigious memory upon which he leaned heavily. He insisted that he discovered rather than invented his characters, drawing them only after they had, in the Russian phrase, "calloused his eyes." George Moore acutely observed that Turgenev's imagination was illuminative rather than creative. Naturally, he transmuted the empirical data with which he worked, and at some point in the process of composition the unconscious put its hand to the wheel. Indeed, he asserted that he wrote *Fathers and Sons* almost in a trance, so that he was sometimes surprised at what came from his pen.

The body of his work is of unquestionable documentary and cognitive value. Within its confines the student will find much that is flesh of the flesh and bone of the bone of "the strangest and most wonderful people in the world," as Turgenev in an expansive moment described his compatriots. To open his books is to enter a lost world under the guidance of one of its inhabitants. Over it hangs a breath of decay. Perhaps for that reason he tends to hark back to his early years, when it was less rickety, and to carry-overs from an even more remote past. *Old Portraits*, as also the eighteenth-century vignette, a miniature masterpiece, in *Virgin Soil*, shows how skillful Turgenev could be in animating amiable fossils. But, for all his nostalgia, nothing was further from his mind than the wish to turn the clock backward. The existing order is doomed, he knows, but a better society lies within man's grasp. All that is needed to obtain the conditions of justice and freedom is persevering work carried on in an atmosphere of enlightenment.

To a generation that has seen what ours has seen there is something unreal about pages that imply the meliorist position dictated by the liberal's faith in reason and science. Turgenev has little to say about the evil in the heart of man. He does, however, convey a sense of Fate's malfeasance in some of his most memorable scenes: that, for instance, of Insarov's end in Venice, and particularly the description of Bazarov's death, one of the cruelest as it is also one of the tenderest things in literature. Charac-

Introduction

teristically enough, this powerful, ruthlessly veracious passage is not allowed its full force. It ends on a pietistic note that rings hollow. Turgenev has his lapses of taste. Reading *First Love*, for example, one of his best stories, is an experience similar to that of walking along a firm road with a fine view and suddenly stepping into a boggy place.

In a kind of credo that he set down in 1875 at the request of a friend, he wrote: ". . . I am, above all, a realist and chiefly interested in the living truth of the human face." A modern reader is apt to find Turgenev's realism not sufficiently penetrating, a little bloodless, rather timid. He tends to be too explicit. His habit of leaving no loose ends in his narratives gives them a look of spinsterish tidiness. He sees each character in detail, he scans the features, he looks into the heart. The rest of the anatomy is largely neglected. How these men and women came to be what they are is not shown, but reported in factual digressions on which his imagination had not gone to work. He keeps his nose too close to the evidence to permit the vision of far-off things. There is pity in his pages, but no terror. They are the product of an empirical, not a metaphysical mind. Here is an intelligence that does not soar or dive, and if it thus avoids risks, it also misses opportunities for discovery.

One returns to his work for the sake of observing characters sometimes subtly, almost always firmly drawn, against an appropriate background. Here are a few full-length portraits, and any number of neat sketches, intriguing cartoons, and delicate line drawings. One recognizes the nicety of his insights into human feelings and foibles, yields to the moods he creates, senses, too, even when one is strange to them, the beautiful authenticity of his settings. He has the power to conjure up the genius of a place, to give the very breath and being of a moment in a moonlit garden, on a country road, in a room of a dilapidated manor house smelling of kvass, apples, and leather. The scene of practically all his writings is rural or semi-rural. Rusticity is his element. He prefers the diffused light of the outdoors to the theatrical glare of spots. His dramas are played out against a background of earth and sky that has the charm of a Corot and the fine fresh detail of a Constable. What he wrote as a young man remained true to the end: "I should prefer to contemplate the precipitous movements of a duck's wet foot as it scratches the back of its head

Introduction

on the edge of a marsh, or the long and glistening drops of water slowly falling from the muzzle of a motionless cow that has just drunk from a pond in which she stands knee-deep, rather than all that the cherubim can behold in the heavens." Occasionally, however, Turgenev betrays a certain unease in the presence of nature. He asks whether men feel at a loss before her because her completeness mocks their insufficiency. Or he reflects somberly that she maintains her equilibrium in indifference to man's imbalance. But he is not at home with abstractions, is not given to dialectics, and falls back readily into a stasis of resignation or appreciation.

Whatever his attitude, the felicity of Turgenev's style is something that even a mediocre translation must suggest. The dialogue, except in the admirable interchange of his peasants, may be too literary; but the narrative and descriptive passages are couched in a prose never startling, yet both precise and emotional, moving with an ease and grace that has the effect of a cool music. The writing flows along smoothly, and is punctuated by the deliberate simile rather than the flashing metaphor.

Realist though he is, the lyric touch comes naturally to Turgenev. Exploration, analysis, are not his forte. The thinking of this confirmed rationalist is apt to be fraught with feeling. As often as not, he swings between a mild elation and a gentle melancholy. The tone of his fictions is often elegiac. They dwell on "the agitated sadness of expectation in the young, the impassive sadness of regret in the old." When Turgenev touches upon personal annihilation and the transience of all by which the human spirit lives, he strikes the chord of despair, but he does not hold it. If happiness is an illusion, he implies, it is an ineradicable one. Life may be a brief interval between two darknesses, but it admits virtue and beauty. Does the universe care nothing for them? Turgenev cannot contemplate them without an emotion which his art, at its best, renders contagious.

AVRAHM YARMOLINSKY

Contents

THE BORZOI

Turgenev

Smoke

1866

I

AT four o'clock in the afternoon of August 10, 1862 very many people were assembled outside the famous Konversations-haus in Baden-Baden. The weather was beautiful; the trees in their leafy green, the light-tinted houses of the cozy little town, the undulating hills — all things were festively arrayed with an overflowing munificence beneath the rays of the benignant sun; all things wore a blind, trustful, and pleasant smile; and the same vague but happy smile roved over the human faces, whether old or young, ugly or handsome. Even the figures of the Parisian *lorettes*, with their blackened eyebrows and powdered faces, did not mar the general impression of obvious complacency and ex-ultation; and the varicolored ribbons, the feathers, the golden and steely sparkles on hats and veils, involuntarily called to mind the vivacious shimmer and gentle play of spring flowers and irides-cent wings. Though, truly, the dry, guttural rattle of the French patois, which was to be heard everywhere, could neither replace the twittering of birds nor compare with it.

Everything followed its appointed course, however. The or-chestra in the pavilion played a potpourri from *Traviata*, a Strauss waltz, or the Russian ballad *Tell Her*, which the obliging con-ductor had given an instrumental arrangement. The same well-known figures were crowded round the green baize tables in the Casino, and they all wore the stupid and avaricious, half-amazed, half-indignant, but essentially rapacious expression that is con-ferred on even the most aristocratic features by the gambling fever. The same rather corpulent and over-fashionably dressed landowner from Tambov, with the same incomprehensible, con-vulsive haste, goggling his eyes, leaning his chest against the table, and paying no attention even to the croupiers' frigid sneers, scat-tered the golden louis d'ors with a perspiring hand over all the four corners of the roulette table at the very moment they

3

shouted: *"Rien ne va plus,"* and so robbed himself of all hope of winning anything, even if his number did turn up. But that did not prevent his waxing indignant the very same evening as he fawned on Prince Coco, one of the well-known leaders of the court opposition. This was the Prince Coco who in the presence of the Emperor, in Princesse Mathilde's salon at Paris, had remarked so pithily: *"Madame, le principe de la propriété est profondément ébranlé en Russie."* As usual, our charming compatriots of both sexes gathered at the "Russian tree," *à l'arbre russe.* They came up with an air of sumptuous, fashionable negligence and greeted one another majestically, with an easy elegance, just as one would expect of creatures who are at the highest level of contemporary culture. But when they met and sat down, they had not the slightest idea what to say to one another, and resorted to empty inanities, or to the hackneyed, highly impudent, and very flat witticisms of a certain Frenchman, a played-out ex-littérateur who wore Jewish shoes on his miserable little feet and had a miserable little beard on his odious face. This buffoon and gasbag passed on to them, *à ces princes russes,* all kinds of filth from old copies of *Charivari* and *Tintamarre;* and they, *ces princes russes,* gurgled with grateful laughter, as though involuntarily admitting both the overwhelming superiority of the foreign wit and their own complete inability to think of anything amusing. And yet here in Baden-Baden was gathered almost all the *"fine fleur"* of our society, "all the nobility and leaders of fashion." Here was our incomparable dilettante Count X, a profoundly musical personality, who was said to "execute" ballads so divinely, but who in reality could not tell one note from another without haphazardly poking his forefinger on the keys, and who sang more like a second-rate gypsy or a Paris barber. Here, too, was our captivating Baron Z, that jack-of-all-trades: writer and administrator, orator and card-sharper. Here, too, was Prince Y, the friend of religion and the people, who once upon a time, in the blessed era of liquor licenses, had made an enormous fortune by selling cheap brandy with thorn-apple juice added; and the brilliant General O. O., who had conquered something or other, had suppressed something or other, but had no idea what to do with himself or even how to introduce himself; and R. R., an amusing fat fellow who regarded himself as a very ailing and a very intelligent man, but who was as healthy as a bull and as stupid as a block. . . . This R. R. was

4

almost the last in our day to preserve the tradition of the lions of
the forties, the era of *A Hero of Our Time* [1] and Countess Vorotinskaya. He had preserved the habit of rocking on his heels as he
walked, and *"le culte de la pose"* (it is not possible even to write
that in Russian), and an unnatural slowness of movement, and a
drowsy majesty of expression on his immobile, injured-looking
face, and the habit of interrupting someone else's remark with a
yawn, of diligently examining his own fingers and toes, laughing
through his nose, suddenly pulling his hat from the back of his
head down over his eyebrows, and so on. Here were gathered
even the statesmen, the diplomats, the aces with European reputa-
tions, the men of counsel and intelligence, who thought that the
Golden Bull was issued by the Pope, and that the English "poor-
tax" was a tax on the poor.

Here, finally, were the zealous but bashful devotees of the ca-
mellia, the young society lions with superb partings down the
backs of their heads, with splendid hanging side-whiskers, and
dressed in real London clothes; young lions whom, apparently,
nothing could prevent being just as vulgar as the notorious French
windbag. But our own home produce is not in the vogue, and
when the Frenchman was not available the Countess Sh., the well-
known arbiter of fashion and the *grand genre*, whom evil tongues
nicknamed "Czaritsa of the Wasps" and the "Medusa in a Bonnet,"
preferred to turn to certain Italians, Moldavians, and American
"spiritualists," dashing secretaries of foreign embassies, and Germans with effeminate but prudent faces, etc., who were to be
found in the town. The Countess's example was followed by
Princess Babette, the same Princess in whose arms Chopin died
(it is estimated that in Europe there are a good thousand ladies in
whose arms he gave up the ghost). And by Princess Annette, who
would captivate everybody but for the fact that occasionally a
simple village washerwoman peers through the society mask quite
suddenly, like the smell of cabbage amid the subtlest of ambergris.
And by Princess Rachette, who had suffered such a terrible misfortune: her husband had been given an important position and
suddenly, *Dieu sait pourquoi*, the head of the town had arrived
and stolen twenty thousand rubles of government money. And by
the risible Princess Zizi and the lachrymose Princess Zozo. All
these ladies ignored their fellow countrymen, and treated them

[1] A novel by the poet Lermontov, published in 1840. (Tr.)

rather unkindly. . . . We, in our turn, will take no more notice of them, these charming ladies, and will leave the celebrated tree round which they are sitting in such expensive but tasteless toilets. And may the Lord send them relief from their gnawing boredom!

2

A few steps away from the "Russian tree," at a little table outside the Weber Café, was sitting a handsome man almost thirty years of age, of average height, rather spare and swarthy, with a strong, attractive face. Leaning forward and resting both hands on a cane, he was sitting quietly and unaffectedly, like a man who could not imagine that anyone might notice him or take any interest in him. He slowly gazed about him with large and expressive hazel eyes, shot with yellow, sometimes narrowing them against the sunlight, then suddenly staring after some passing eccentric-looking figure, while a swift, almost childlike smile touched his thin mustaches, lips, and square, prominent chin. He was dressed in a loose coat of German cut, and a gray soft hat was drawn half down over his high forehead. At first glance he gave the impression of being an honest and efficient, rather self-confident young fellow, such as are often met in the world. He appeared to be resting after long continued labors and was all the more artlessly enjoying the picture spread before him because his thoughts were far away, and moreover they circulated, those thoughts, in a world not at all resembling the one surrounding him at that moment. He was Russian; his name was Grigory Mikhailovich Litvinov.

We need to make his acquaintance, and so we shall have to say a few words about his past, which had been quite simple and straightforward.

The son of a retired old-time official of merchant descent, he had been brought up not in a town, as one would have expected, but in the country. His mother was a noblewoman, educated in a "school for young ladies of noble birth," a very kind and very exalted being, yet not without character. She was twenty years younger than her husband, and had re-educated him, so far as she could; she had dragged him out of his official circle into that of a landowner, had tamed and softened his robust, caustic temper. Under her influence he began to dress tidily and behave decently, and gave up swearing; he began to have respect for learning and the learned, although, of course, he never picked up a book, and did his very best not to degrade himself. He even began to walk more quietly and to talk in a languid tone, and more and more about exalted subjects, though this cost him no little effort. "Ah, you ought to be flogged!" he sometimes thought, but aloud he said: "Yes, yes, that is . . . of course; that is the question." Litvinov's mother put her house also on a European basis; she spoke to the servants in the second person plural, and at dinner never allowed anyone to eat so much that he wheezed. As for her estate, neither she nor her husband was able to do anything with it; it suffered from long neglect; but it was of considerable extent, with all kinds of appendages, forests, and a lake. At one time a large factory, founded by the zealous but unmethodical master, had stood beside the lake; in the hands of some swindling merchant it had prospered, but it had gone to utter ruin under the administration of an honest entrepreneur from Germany. Mme Litvinova was satisfied, if only because she did not squander her fortune and did not run into debt. Unfortunately, she could not boast of her health, and she died of consumption in the very year her son entered the Moscow University. He did not complete the course, owing to certain circumstances (the reader will learn about them later), but slipped away into the country, where he lounged about for some time without anything to do, with no connections, almost without acquaintances. Owing to the unfriendliness of the noblemen of his county, who were permeated not so much with the Western theory of the noxious nature of "absentee landlordism" as the homebred conviction that "your own shirt is nearer to your body," in 1855 he was called up for service and all but died of typhus in the Crimea, where he spent six months in a dugout on the shore of the Putrid Sea without seeing a single "Ally." Next he was elected to the local government service for some time, of course not without experiencing some unpleasantness, and, after residing on his estate for a while, developed a taste for farming. He realized that his mother's estate, which was badly and sluggishly managed by his senile old father, did not yield one tenth of the income it could yield, and that in experienced and expert hands it could be transformed into a gold mine. But he also realized that experience and knowledge were precisely what he lacked — and he went abroad to study agronomy and technology, to learn the A B C of farming. He spent more than four years in Mecklenburg, Silesia, and Karlsruhe; he visited Belgium and England, worked conscientiously, and acquired knowledge. All this did not come easily to him, but he endured the ordeal to the end. And now, confident of himself, of his future, of the benefit he would bring to his fellow countrymen, and maybe even to the whole country, he was preparing to return home. For in every letter his father wrote he called him back with desperate adjurations and entreaties; the old man was completely overwhelmed by the emancipation of the peasants, the allocation of the prescriptive rights over the land, the redemption transactions, by all the new order, in a word. . . . But in that case why was he in Baden?

He was in Baden because any day now he was expecting the arrival of his second cousin and fiancée, Tatiana Petrovna Shestova. He had known her almost from childhood and had spent the spring and summer with her in Dresden, where she had taken up residence with her aunt. He sincerely loved, he deeply respected his young kinswoman, and when he had completed his hard, preparatory work and was making ready to enter on a new career, to begin active and not state service, he proposed to her, asking her as the woman he loved, as his comrade and friend, to unite her life with his, for weal and woe, for labor and for repose, "for better, for worse," as the English say. She consented, and he went off to Karlsruhe, where he had left his books, his things, his papers. . . . But then why is he in Baden? you will ask again.

He was in Baden also because the aunt who had brought up Tatiana, Kapitolina Markovna Shestova, an old maid of fifty-five, a very good-natured and honest but eccentric creature, a free spirit, all aglow with the fire of self-sacrifice and self-renunciation, an *esprit fort* (she had read Strauss — truly, in secret from her niece), and a democrat, a mortal opponent of society and the aristocracy, could not resist the temptation of taking at least one look at that very society in such a fashionable place as Baden. . . . Kapitolina Markovna did not wear a crinoline and had her white hair cut short, but luxury and glitter secretly agitated her, and she found it pleasant and sweet to revile and scorn them. . . . So why not give the good old lady that pleasure?

But Litvinov was so tranquil and frank, he looked about him so self-confidently, because his life stretched quite clearly before him, because his destiny was determined. And he was proud of that destiny and rejoiced in it as the work of his own hands.

3

"Well, I never! So there he is!" a squeaky voice suddenly sounded right in his ear, and a puffy hand shook him by the shoulder. He raised his head and saw one of his few Moscow acquaintances, a man named Bambayev, a decent though rather empty sort, no longer young, with cheeks and nose as flabby as though soft-boiled, disheveled, greasy hair, and a flabby, corpulent body. Always without a farthing and always in raptures over something or other, Rostislav Bambayev roamed vehemently but aimlessly over the face of our long-suffering mother earth.

"Now this is what we call a meeting!" he repeated, goggling his bloated little eyes and sticking out his swollen little lips, above which his dyed whiskers bristled absurdly and ineptly. "Hurrah for Baden! They all crawl here like cockroaches. How did you get here?"

(Bambayev addressed Litvinov in the second person singular, as he did absolutely everybody and everything in the world.)

"I arrived three days ago."

"Where from?"

"Why, what do you want to know for?"

"What for? But wait a bit, wait a bit. Perhaps you don't know who else has arrived. Gubariov! Himself, in person! That's who is here! He arrived from Heidelberg yesterday. You know him, of course?"

"I've heard of him."

"Is that all? Really! We'll take you along to see him in a moment, this very minute! Not know such a man! And that reminds me that Voroshilov — But wait, I don't think you know him? I have the honor to introduce you to each other. You are both savants! And he is more, he's a phœnix! Kiss each other!"

At this, Bambayev turned to a handsome young man with a fresh and rosy but already serious face who was standing beside him. Litvinov rose and, of course, did not kiss, but exchanged a slight bow with the "phœnix" who, judging by his standoffish attitude, was not altogether pleased at this unexpected introduction.

"I said 'phœnix,' and I do not withdraw the word," Bambayev went on. "Go to Petersburg, to the —nd corps, and look at the roll of honor: what is the first name you see? Voroshilov, Semion

Yakovlevich! But Gubariov, Gubariov, my boys! That's the man we must hurry along to, hurry we must! I absolutely worship that man! And not I alone; everybody without exception worships him. The work he is writing now, on — on — on —"

"What is it about?" Litvinov asked.

"About everything, my boys, it's a kind of — you know: Buckle — only more profound, more profound. . . . In it everything will be settled and clarified once for all."

"But have you read it?"

"No, I haven't, and really it is a secret and shouldn't be made public; but you can expect everything of Gubariov, everything! Yes!" Bambayev sighed and folded his arms. "Now if we only had two, or say three, more heads like his in Russia, ah, if that were possible! My God! I'll tell you one thing, Grigory Mikhailovich; no matter what you have been doing recently — and I don't know what you ever do — no matter what your convictions — and I don't know them either — in him, in Gubariov, you'll find something to learn from. Unfortunately, he isn't staying here long. We must profit by the occasion, we must go and see him. Come on, come on!"

A passing dandy with little red curls and a blue ribbon on his low hat turned and, smiling sarcastically, stared at Bambayev through his monocle. Litvinov was vexed.

"What are you shouting for," he said, "as though you were calling a bloodhound to a trail? I haven't dined yet."

"What does that matter? We can have dinner at once at Weber's — the three of us. . . . Splendid! Have you enough money to pay for me?" he added in an undertone.

"I expect I have; only I really don't know —"

"Please don't go on; you'll thank me afterward, and he will be delighted. Ah, my God!" Bambayev interrupted himself. "They're playing the finale from *Ernani*. What a joy! . . . '*A som—mo Carlo* . . .' But that's just like me! In tears in a moment! Well, Semion Yakovlevich! Voroshilov! Shall we go?"

Voroshilov, who was still standing motionless and stiff, retaining his rather proud dignity of bearing, significantly dropped his eyes, knitted his brows, and muttered something between his teeth . . . but did not refuse. Litvinov thought: "Well, why not? I've got time for the visit. I've plenty of time." Bambayev took his arm, but first he beckoned with his finger to Isabella, the well-known

Smoke

flower-girl of the Jockey Club, thinking he would buy a nosegay from her. But the aristocratic flower-girl did not stir; and indeed why should she for a gentleman whom she had never seen before even in Paris, who was without gloves and was wearing a stained velveteen jacket, a varicolored cravat, and patched boots? Then Voroshilov beckoned to her. For him she came. Choosing a tiny bunch of violets from her basket, he gave her a gulden. He thought such munificence would astonish her, but she did not even raise an eyebrow, and when he turned away she contemptuously writhed her lips to reveal her clenched teeth. Voroshilov was dressed very smartly, even exquisitely, but the Parisian girl's experienced eye at once discerned that his toilet, his figure, even his gait, which bore the signs of premature military training, were lacking in genuine, thoroughbred "chic."

Taking a table in Weber's main hall and ordering dinner, our acquaintances engaged in conversation. Bambayev loudly and fervently expatiated on Gubariov's exalted destiny; but he soon lapsed into silence and, breathing and chewing noisily, tossed off glass after glass. Voroshilov drank and ate little, with a reluctant air, and, after questioning Litvinov concerning the nature of his occupations, began to express his own opinion — not so much about these studies as on various "problems" in general. . . . He suddenly grew animated, and tore along like a mettlesome horse, spiritedly and sharply enunciating every syllable, every letter, like a dashing young cadet at a final examination, and vigorously but awkwardly waving his arms. As no one interrupted him, with every moment he grew more garrulous, more glib; he might have been reading a dissertation or a lecture. The names of the latest scientists, with the addition of the date of birth or death of every one of them, the chapter heads of brochures only just published, and a mass of names, names, names poured rapidly from his tongue, evidently to his own great satisfaction, as could be seen by his flaming eyes. It appeared that Voroshilov was contemptuous of everything old and esteemed only the cream of education, the latest, the foremost viewpoint of science; to mention, even though ineptly, the book of some Dr. Sauerbengel on Pennsylvanian prisons or yesterday's article in the *Asiatic Journal* on the Vedas and Puranas (he pronounced the word *Jernul*, though of course he did not know English) gave him genuine pleasure, amounting to felicity.

Litvinov listened to him and listened, and simply could not make out what was really his special subject. At one moment he was talking about the part the Celtic tribes had played in history; then he was carried back into the ancient world and was discoursing on the Egyptian marbles; he excitedly commented on the sculptor Onatas, who had lived before Phidias, whom, however, he transformed into Jonathan and thus for a moment gave all his argumentation a kind of Biblical or perhaps American tint; now he suddenly jumped to political economy and called Bastiat a fool and blockhead, "as bad as Adam Smith and all the physiocrats." "The physiocrats!" Bambayev whispered after him. "Aristocrats?" In passing, Voroshilov brought an expression of astonishment to Bambayev's face by a perfunctory and parenthetical remark about Macaulay as an out-of-date writer whom knowledge had already superseded. And as for Gneist and Riehl, he announced that they were only worth mentioning, and shrugged his shoulders. Bambayev also shrugged his shoulders. "And all this poured out all at once, without rhyme or reason, in the presence of strangers, in a café," Litvinov meditated, looking at his new acquaintance's fair hair, light eyes, and white teeth (he was especially embarrassed by those large, sugary teeth, and those hands with their awkward movements). "And he never smiles; yet he seems to be quite a good fellow and extremely inexperienced. . . ." Voroshilov quieted down at last; his voice, youthfully ringing and hoarse like a young cock's, broke a little. . . . And then Bambayev began to declaim poetry and again all but burst into tears, which made a scandalous impression on an adjacent table occupied by an English family, who sat giggling at one another. At a second table two *lorettes* were dining with some very old buck in a lilac peruke. The waiter brought the bill; the friends paid.

"Well," Bambayev exclaimed, rising heavily from his seat, "now for a cup of coffee and quick march! And yet there it is, there is our Russia," he added, halting at the door and almost rapturously pointing his soft red hand at Voroshilov and Litvinov. "And what is she like?"

"Yes, Russia!" Litvinov thought; but Voroshilov, who had already restored the concentrated look to his face, smiled condescendingly and clicked his heels a little.

Some five minutes later they were all climbing the stairs of the hotel where Stepan Nikolaevich Gubariov was staying. A tall lady, of graceful figure, wearing a little hat with a short black veil, came briskly down the same staircase and, seeing Litvinov, suddenly turned to him and halted as though struck with astonishment. Her face momentarily flamed and then as swiftly paled beneath the fine net of the lace. But Litvinov did not notice her, and she ran down the broad stairs even more briskly than before.

4

"Let me introduce Litvinov, a very decent fellow, a Russian spirit," Bambayev exclaimed as he led Litvinov up to a man of small size and the appearance of a landowner, with unbuttoned collar, a short jacket, gray morning pantaloons, and slippers, who was standing in the center of the light, well-furnished room. "And this," he added, turning to Litvinov, "this is he, the man himself, d'you understand? I mean Gubariov, in short."

Litvinov fixed inquisitive eyes on "the man himself." At first sight he found nothing unusual in him. He saw a gentleman of respectable and rather stupid exterior, big-browed, big-eyed, with a thick neck and an oblique and downward glance. This gentleman smirked, muttered: "Mmmm — yes — this is a good — very pleasant . . ." raised his hand to his face and, at once turning his back on Litvinov, paced several times up and down the carpet, waddling slowly and queerly, as though moving by stealth. He had the habit of continually walking to and fro, occasionally tugging at and combing his beard with the ends of his long, brittle nails. Besides Gubariov there were two other people in the room. One was a lady about fifty years of age, wearing a shabby silk dress. She had an amazingly mobile face as yellow as a lemon, short black hairs on her upper lip, and swift little eyes that looked ready to dart out of their sockets. The other was a thickset man sitting huddled in a corner.

"Well, my dear Matriona Semionovna," Gubariov began, turning to the lady and evidently not considering it necessary to introduce Litvinov to her, "what was the story you had begun to tell us?"

The lady, who was named Matriona Semionovna Sukhanchikova, was a widow, childless, not at all rich, and for two years now had been wandering from country to country, began to speak at once with a peculiar, vehement enthusiasm:

"Well, and so he calls on the Prince and says to him: 'Your

Excellency, you are in such a rank and in such a position, what would it cost you to alleviate my lot? You cannot but respect the purity of my convictions! And in our day is it possible to persecute anyone for his convictions?' And what do you think the Prince, that educated, highly placed dignitary, did?"

"Well, what did he do?" Gubariov said, meditatively lighting a cigarette.

The lady drew herself up and stretched her bony right hand before her with the index finger extended:

"He summoned his lackey and told him: 'Take that coat off this man at once and keep it for yourself. I give it to you.' "

"And the lackey took it off?" Bambayev asked, with a gesture of astonishment.

"He took it and kept it. And that was done by Prince Barnaulov, a well-known plutocrat, a magnate, entrusted with special authority, a representative of the government! And what else may we expect after that?"

All Mme Sukhanchikova's puny body shook with indignation, her face was contorted with spasms, her consumptive breasts heaved convulsively beneath her shapeless corset; of her eyes one may not even speak, they darted from side to side so rapidly. But they were always darting, no matter what she talked about.

"A scandal, a crying scandal!" Bambayev exclaimed. "There is no punishment fit for it!"

"Mmm — mmm. . . . Rotten from top to toe," Gubariov remarked, even now not raising his voice. "It isn't punishment — here a different measure — is necessary."

"But really, is it true?" Litvinov asked.

"Is it true?" she retorted. "Why, one may not even think of doubting it, n-n-n-not even think —" She pronounced the last word with such force that she writhed. "I was told the story by a most trustworthy man. Why, you know him, Stepan Nikolaevich — Yelistratov Kapiton. He himself heard it from eyewitnesses, from eyewitnesses of this disgusting scene."

"Which Yelistratov?" Gubariov asked. "The one that was in Kazan?"

"That's the one. I know somebody spread a story about him that he had taken money from some contractor or distiller or something. But who spread the story? Pelikanov! And can anyone

Smoke

believe Pelikanov, when everybody knows he's nothing but a spy?"

"But pardon me, Matriona Semionovna," Bambayev intervened, "I am a friend of Pelikanov. Why do you call him a spy?"

"Because that's what he is — a spy!"

"But wait, pardon —"

"He's a spy, a spy!" the lady shouted.

"But he isn't, he isn't; wait a bit; I'll tell you something," Bambayev shouted in his turn.

"A spy, a spy!" she declared.

"No, no! Now, Tenteleev, he's another story!" Bambayev bawled at the top of his voice.

Mme Sukhanchikova was momentarily silent.

"I have authentic information," he went on in his ordinary tone, "that when the Third Department [1] sent for that man, he crawled at the feet of Countess Blazenkrampf and whined and whined: 'Save me, speak for me!' But Pelikanov never let himself descend to such turpitude."

"Mmm — Tenteleev . . ." Gubariov muttered, "that — that needs to be noted."

She contemptuously shrugged her shoulders.

"They're both excellent!" she said. "But I know an even better story about Tenteleev. As everybody knows, he was a terrible tyrant to his people, though he also pretended to be an emancipator. And one day he was sitting with acquaintances in Paris, and suddenly Madame Beecher Stowe walked in — you know her, *Uncle Tom's Cabin.* Tenteleev is a terribly conceited man, and he asked the host to introduce him. But as soon as she heard his name: 'What?' she said, 'he dares to make the acquaintance of the author of *Uncle Tom?*' And she slaps his cheek! 'Get out!' she says, 'this minute!' And what do you think? He picked up his hat, tucked in his tail, and slipped off."

"Well, I think that's exaggerated," Bambayev remarked. "She certainly did say 'Get out!' to him, that's a fact; but she didn't slap his face."

"She did slap his face, she did slap his face!" she repeated with convulsive intensity. "I don't talk rubbish. And you're a friend of people like that!"

[1] The Czarist secret police. (Tr.)

"Excuse me, excuse me, Matriona Semionovna, I never claimed that Tenteleev was any friend of mine; I was talking about Pelikanov."

"Well, if it isn't Tenteleev, it's someone else; Mikhniov, for instance."

"And what has he done?" Bambayev asked, already feeling intimidated.

"What? Do you say you don't know? On the Voznesensky Avenue he shouted for all the world to hear that all the liberals ought to be put in prison. And then some old colleague of his high-school days, poor of course, goes up to him and says: 'Can I have dinner with you?' And he answers: 'No, you can't; I've got two counts coming to dinner today — clear off!' "

"But that's a slander, I tell you!" Bambayev began to howl.

"A slander — a slander? To begin with, Prince Vakhrushkin, who also had dinner with your Mikhniov — "

"Prince Vakhrushkin," Gubariov sternly intervened, "is my cousin. But I don't allow him to call on me. . . . There's no need even to mention him."

"Secondly," Sukhanchikova continued, humbly bowing her head in Gubariov's direction, "Praskovia Yakovlevna told me herself."

"Now you've found someone to appeal to! She and that Sarkizov, they're the biggest fabricators of all."

"Well, you'll pardon me!" she retorted. "Sarkizov's a liar, I agree; he took the brocade pall off his dead father, I shall never stop to argue about him. But Praskovia Yakovlevna — what a comparison! Remember how nobly she parted from her husband! But you, I know you're always ready — "

"Now, enough, enough, Matriona Semionovna," Bambayev interrupted her. "Let's drop this filthy gossip, and we'll soar to the empyrean. I'm a man of the old school. Have you read *Mlle de la Quintinie*? It's really delightful! And it just fits your principles."

"I no longer read novels," she replied dryly and curtly.

"Why not?"

"Because this is not the time for them. I've only one thing in my head now: sewing-machines."

"What machines?" Litvinov asked.

"Sewing, sewing; we must provide all women, every one of them, with sewing-machines, and form a society. Then they will

16

all earn their own bread, and in an instant they'll become independent. Otherwise they will never achieve their emancipation. That is an important, a very important social problem. We had an argument about it with Boleslav Stadnitsky. Boleslav Stadnitsky is a wonderful character, but he has a terribly frivolous outlook on these matters. He always laughs — the fool!"

"In due time they will all be called to account, from each will it be exacted," Gubariov declared slowly, in an admonitory or maybe prophetic tone.

"Yes, yes," Bambayev reiterated, "it will be exacted; precisely, it will be exacted. But tell me, Stepan Nikolaich," he added, lowering his voice, "is the work moving?"

"I am collecting the materials," Gubariov replied, knitting his brows. Turning to Litvinov, whose head was beginning to spin with this collection of unknown names, this frenzy of slander, he asked: "What are you engaged in?"

Litvinov satisfied his curiosity.

"Ah! natural sciences, in other words. That is useful, as training; as training, not as an aim. The aim now should be — mm — should be — different. Pardon me for asking, but what opinions do you hold?"

"What opinions?"

"Yes. I mean, to be precise, what are your political convictions?"

Litvinov smiled.

"To be precise, I haven't any political convictions."

At these words the thickset man sitting in the corner suddenly raised his head and stared at Litvinov attentively.

"How do you mean?" Gubariov said with strange moderation. "You haven't yet thought about it, or you've already grown tired?"

"How can I put it? It seems to me that it is still early for us Russians to have political convictions or to imagine we have them. Note that I give the word 'political' the meaning that belongs to it by right, and that — "

"Aha! One of the immature," Gubariov interrupted him in the same mild tone. Going up to Voroshilov, he asked him: "Have you read the brochure I gave you?"

Voroshilov, who, to Litvinov's surprise, had not said a word since his arrival, but had only wrinkled his brows and rolled his eyes significantly (it was his custom either to make a speech or to be silent), Voroshilov threw out his chest in military fashion and, clicking his heels, nodded affirmatively.

"Well, and what do you think? Were you satisfied?"

"So far as the main bases are concerned, I am. But I don't agree with the conclusions."

"Mmm. . . . But Andrei Ivanich recommended that brochure to me. You must expound your doubts to me later."

"Would you like them in writing?"

Gubariov was obviously surprised; he had not expected this question. But after a moment's thought he said:

"Yes, in writing. And, by the way, I ask you also to state your conceptions — in regard to — in regard to the association."

"Would you like me to do so according to Lassalle's method or that of Schulze-Delitzsch?"

"Mmm — according to both. The point is, you understand, that for us Russians the financial aspect is particularly important. And, of course, the co-operative working gang — as the core. . . . All that will have to be taken into account. It needs to be gone into thoroughly. And so, too, with the question of the peasants' allocation of land."

"But tell me, Stepan Nikolaich, what is your view of the amount of land each peasant should have?" Voroshilov asked in a tone of respectful delicacy.

"Mmm. . . . But what of the peasant community?" Gubariov remarked profoundly. Nibbling at a tuft of beard, he fixed his eyes on a table leg. "The community — d'you understand? That is a great word! And then what do those conflagrations mean — those — those governmental measures against secular Sunday schools, reading-rooms, periodicals? And the peasants' refusal to sign the statutory documents? And finally, all that's happening in Poland? Don't you see where all this is leading to? Don't you see that — mm —that we — we need now to fuse with the people, to find out — find out their opinion?" He was suddenly possessed by an oppressive, almost malevolent agitation; he turned livid and breathed heavily, but even now he did not raise his eyes and continued to chew his beard. "Don't you see . . ."

"Yevseev is a scoundrel!" Mme Sukhanchikova suddenly let fly, as Bambayev told her something, speaking in an undertone in deference to his host. Gubariov turned sharply on his heels and again waddled about the room.

Smoke

More visitors began to arrive; toward the end of the evening quite a number of people had gathered. Among them was the Mr. Yevseev whom Sukhanchikova had referred to so harshly; she talked very amicably with him and asked him to see her home. And there was a man named Pishchalkin, who made an ideal arbitrator, one of those men of whom, perhaps, Russia has particular need: to wit, narrow-minded, with little knowledge and no talent, but conscientious, patient, and honest. The peasants of his patrimony all but prayed for him, and he treated himself very deferentially, as though he were someone worthy of respect. Other arrivals included several young officers, who had dashed into Europe on short leave and were delighted at having the opportunity, of course with all prudence and always bearing the regimental commander in mind, to play with fire in the form of intelligent and even rather dangerous people. Two scraggy little students from Heidelberg came hurrying in; one of them did nothing but look about him contemptuously, the other laughed spasmodically — both felt very awkward. Immediately after them a little Frenchman, one of the so-called *"p'tites gens,"* insinuated himself; he was rather dirty, rather badly off, and rather stupid. He was renowned among his colleagues, the *commis voyageurs,* because Russian countesses fell in love with him; but he himself was more concerned with the possibility of getting a free dinner. The last to appear was Tit Bindasov, who was a turbulent *Bursch* to look at, but who in reality was a hard-headed wealthy peasant and a skinflint, in his speech a terrorist, a policeman by vocation, and the friend of Russian merchants' wives and Parisian *lorettes;* he was bald, toothless, and drunk. He arrived very flushed in the face and unhappy, declaring that he had paid his last kopek to that "scoundrel Benazet," though in reality he had won sixteen guldens. . . .

In a word, quite a crowd of people assembled. Very remarkable was the respect with which all the visitors turned to Gubariov as their mentor or head; they laid their doubts before him, submitted them to his judgment. And he replied — with bellows, with tugs at his beard, rolling his eyes or uttering desultory, insignificant remarks, which were at once caught up as pronouncements of the very highest wisdom. He himself rarely intervened in the discussions; on the other hand, all the others zealously exercised their lungs. More than once three or four were shouting together for ten minutes on end, and they were all satisfied and they all understood. The talk went on till past midnight and was distinguished, as usual, by the abundance and variety of subjects discussed. Mme Sukhanchikova talked about Garibaldi, about someone named Karl Ivanovich, who had whipped his servants, about Napoleon III, about female labor, about the merchant Pleskachev, who was known to have worn out twelve working women and in return had received a medal with the inscription "For service," about the proletariat, about the Georgian Prince Chukcheulidzeve, who had shot his wife out of a cannon, and about the future of Russia. Pishchalkin also talked about the future of Russia, about the licensing system, about the meaning of nationality, and how most of all he hated the mean and base. Voroshilov was suddenly carried away: in one breath, almost choking, he mentioned Draper, Firkhov, Mr. Shelgunov, Bische, Helmgoltz, Star, Stour, Reymont, John Miller the physiologist and John Miller the historian (obviously confusing them), Taine, Renan, Mr. Shchapov, and then Thomas Nash, Peel, and Green.

"And what birds are they?" Bambayev muttered in astonishment. "Predecessors of Shakspere, bearing the same relationship to him as the foothills of the Alps to Mont Blanc!" Voroshilov answered trenchantly. And he, too, touched on the future of Russia.

Bambayev also talked about the future of Russia, and even described it in iridescent colors, but he was especially transported at the thought of Russian music, in which he saw something "ah, tremendous!" In proof of this he struck up a ballad by Varlamov, but was soon interrupted by a general shout that "He is really singing the '*Miserere*' from *Il Trovatore*, and making a horrible mess of it."

Under cover of the tumult one of the officers abused Russian literature, another quoted some moderate verse from the periodical *Iskrá*. But Tit Bindasov put things even more simply: he declared that all these rogues and swindlers ought to have their teeth knocked out and be done with it, not, however, defining who "these rogues and swindlers" were. The smoke of the cigars grew asphyxiating; everybody was hot and uncomfortable, they all went hoarse, all eyes were bleary, the sweat poured down like rain from every face. Bottles of cold beer appeared and were emptied in a moment. "What was it I was just saying?" said one. "But whom was I arguing with just now, and what were we arguing about?" asked another. Amid all this hubbub and smoke Gubariov strolled about indefatigably, still waddling, and muttering in his beard, now listening to somebody's remark with one ear thrust forward, now putting in a word of his own. And everybody involuntarily felt that he, Gubariov, was indeed the mother of them all, that here he was the host and the leading figure. . . .

Toward ten o'clock Litvinov developed a severe headache and left quietly and unnoticed, taking advantage of a sudden outburst of general shouting. Mme Sukhanchikova had recalled some further injustice committed by Prince Barnaulov: he had all but ordered someone's ear to be bitten off.

The fresh night air nestled gently against Litvinov's inflamed face, flowed in a perfumed stream between his parched lips. "What is all this?" he thought as he walked along the dark avenue. "What have I just been present at? Why have they come together? What were they shouting for, cursing for, letting themselves go for? What is the point of it all?" He shrugged his shoulders and made his way to Weber's, obtained a newspaper, and asked for an ice. The newspaper contained a great deal about the Roman problem,[1] and the ice was not at all nice. He was on the point of going home when a stranger in a hat with a broad brim came up to him and, saying in Russian: "I hope I'm not disturbing you?" sat down at his table. Only then did Litvinov, looking more closely at the man, recognize him as the stolid gentleman who had skulked in one corner of Gubariov's room and had looked at him so attentively when the talk turned to political convictions. This gentleman had not opened his mouth all the evening. Now, as he sat down opposite Litvinov and removed his hat, he gave him a friendly and rather embarrassed look.

5

"Mr. Gubariov, in whose room I had the pleasure of seeing you this evening," he began, "did not introduce me to you; and so, if you will allow me, I shall introduce myself: I am Potugin, a retired court councilor;[2] I served in the Ministry of Finance, in St. Petersburg. I hope you will not consider it strange — I don't usually

[1] The question of the inclusion of Rome (held by the Vatican) in the newly born Kingdom of Italy. (Tr.)

[2] Seventh class in the Czarist civil-service hierarchy. (Tr.)

make a habit of striking up such a sudden acquaintance — but in your case — "

At this point he stopped short and asked the waiter to bring him a glass of kirschwasser. "To give me courage," he added with a smile.

Litvinov looked more closely at this last of all the new faces whom he had had to meet during the day, and at once thought: "He's not the same as the others."

Certainly he was not the same. Opposite Litvinov, fingering the edge of the table with thin, small hands, sat a broad-shouldered man, with a bulky body on short legs, a drooping, curly head, very intelligent and very sad little eyes beneath thick eyebrows, a large, well-proportioned mouth, bad teeth, and that purely Russian nose which has been nicknamed "potato-nose"; a man awkward and even a little uncouth to look at, but certainly out of the ordinary. He was dressed negligently; an old-fashioned type of coat hung about him like a sack, and his cravat had slipped to one side. His sudden trustfulness not only did not seem intrusive; on the contrary, secretly Litvinov was flattered by it: it was quite obvious that this man was not in the habit of forcing himself on strangers. He made a queer impression on Litvinov: he aroused a feeling of respect, and sympathy, and an involuntary feeling of compassion.

"I really am not disturbing you?" he repeated in a soft, rather hoarse and weak voice, which could not have better accorded with his whole figure.

"Of course not," Litvinov protested. "Indeed, I am very glad."

"Really? Well, and I'm glad too. I have heard a great deal about you; I know what you are studying and what your intentions are. It's a good purpose. But you didn't talk at all this evening."

"Well, you, too, said very little, I think," Litvinov remarked.

Potugin sighed.

"Others talked rather a lot. I listened. Well, what do you think?" he added after a little silence, amusingly raising his eyebrows. "Did you like our Tower of Babel?"

"That's just the word: Babel. You've put it perfectly. I continually felt like asking them what they were making such a hubbub about."

Potugin sighed again.

"That's just the point, they themselves don't know. In the old days people would have said: 'They are blind instruments of higher purposes'; but these days we use rather more pungent epithets. And note that really I have no intention whatever of condemning them; I would go farther and say they are all — or at any rate almost all — splendid people. Concerning Madame Sukhanchikova, for instance, I certainly know a great deal that is to her credit: she gave her last farthing to two poor nieces. Even if we assume that a desire to show off a little, to pose a little, had its part in that deed, still you must agree that it is a remarkable self-sacrifice for a woman who herself is not rich! And about Mr. Pishchalkin there is no need to speak: the peasants of his estate will undoubtedly present him with a silver bowl shaped like a watermelon some time or other, and possibly an icon with a representation of his particular angel. And even if in his speech of thanks he tells them that he does not deserve such honor, he will be telling an untruth: he does deserve it. Your friend, Mr. Bambayev, has a marvelous heart. Truly, like the poet Yazikov, who, they say, sang the praises of debauchery while sitting over a book and drinking water, he possesses an enthusiasm that is not really directed toward anything; but all the same it is enthusiasm. And Mr. Voroshilov is also one of the best. He, and all the people of his school, the people of the roll of honor, are, so to speak, assigned as orderlies to science, to civilization, and even their silences are eloquently phrased; but he is still so young! Yes, yes, they are all splendid people, but in the last resort they all amount to nothing; the victuals are of the finest quality, but for goodness' sake don't taste the dish!"

Litvinov listened to Potugin with growing astonishment; all the style, all the turns of his unhurried yet self-confident speech revealed both an ability and a desire to talk.

And truly Potugin both liked and knew how to talk; but he talked as a man whom life had succeeded in robbing of some of his self-esteem; he waited with philosophic calm for the right opportunity, for a kindred spirit.

"Yes, yes," he began again, with the queer, not painful, but despondent humor peculiar to him, "it is all very strange. And there's something else I ask you to note. When ten Englishmen, for example, come together, they at once begin to talk about the submarine telegraph, about the paper-tax, about a method of dressing rats' skins — in other words, about something positive, definite. If ten Germans come together, well, of course, then

Schleswig-Holstein and the unity of Germany are the subject of conversation. If ten Frenchmen come together, the talk inevitably touches on cultivated strawberries, no matter how they begin. But if ten Russians meet, the question that at once arises — you have had an opportunity to be convinced of this today — is that of the meaning, the future, of Russia, and it is all discussed in very general outline, beginning with Leda's egg, inconclusively, hopelessly. They chew and chew over that unfortunate problem like children chewing indiarubber; there's no taste in it, nor object. And, of course, they always have a smack at the rotten West. It's very queer, you know, it beats us in every respect, does the West — yet it's rotten! And it wouldn't be so bad if we really did despise it, but that is all talk and lies. We swear at it and abuse it, but its opinion is the only one we value, and fundamentally it is the opinion of Parisian idiots. I have an acquaintance, a decent fellow, seemingly, the father of a family, and no longer young; he was depressed for several days because in a Paris restaurant he asked for *une portion de bifteck aux pommes de terre*, and a genuine Frenchman at once shouted: '*Garçon, bifteck pommes!*' My friend burned with shame; and he's been shouting '*Bifteck pommes*' and instructing others to do the same ever since. Even the *lorettes* are amazed at the reverential tremor with which our young steppe creatures enter their shameful drawing-rooms. . . . My God! our youngsters think, but where am I? With Anna Deslions herself!"

"Please tell me," Litvinov asked, "what do you think is the reason for Gubariov's undoubted influence on all those who surround him? Not his talents, not his abilities, surely?"

"Oh no, oh no! He hasn't anything of that sort. . . ."

"Then is it his character?"

"He hasn't any character either, but he has considerable willpower. As is well known, we Slavs generally are not rich in that quality and we call 'Pass' to it. Mr. Gubariov wanted to be the head, and they have all recognized him as the head. What else would you expect? The government has freed us of feudal dependence, for which we have to thank it; but the habits of serfdom are too deeply ingrained in us: we shan't get rid of them so quickly. Always and everywhere we need a master; usually that master is a living thing, but sometimes it is some so-called tendency that takes possession of us. . . . Now, for instance, we have all entered into a conspiracy in regard to natural sciences. . . . Why and by force of what arguments we subscribe to the conspiracy is obscure; evidently it is just our nature. But the main thing is that we must have a master. Well, and now we have got one; and that means he is ours, and we spit on all the rest! We're perfect slaves! With both slavish pride and slavish humiliation. A new master has been born — down with the old! It was Yakov, and now it is Sidor; knock Yakov down and throw yourselves at Sidor's feet! Remember how many escapades we have indulged in along those lines! We talk of negation as our distinguishing quality; but we do not negate as a free man would, smiting with his sword, but like a lackey hitting with his fist; and besides, in all probability he even uses his fists on the master's orders. Well, but we are a soft people too: it isn't difficult to take charge of us. And that is how Mr. Gubariov has become the master; he has pecked and pecked at one point and pecked his way through. People see a man with a good opinion of himself, believing in himself, and giving orders — that's the main thing, that he gives orders; so he must be right, and he must be obeyed. All our schisms, our Onufriev movement and Akulinov movement, were based on this very principle. The man with the stick is the man to pick."

Potugin's cheeks flushed and his eyes filmed, but, strange to say, his speech, bitter and even malevolent, did not sound splenetic, but rather sorrowful — with a true, sincere sorrow.

"How did you come to know Gubariov?" Litvinov asked.

"I've known him a long time. And note one other strange feature about us: a certain writer, say, who all his life in prose and verse had denounced drunkenness and decried the licensing system, suddenly bought not one but a couple of wineries and rented a hundred taverns — and that's quite all right! Anyone else would be wiped off the face of the earth, but no one even reproaches him. And so with Mr. Gubariov: he's a Slavophil, and a democrat, and a socialist, and anything you like, but his estate was and still is run by his brother, a master of the old breed, the kind that used to be called 'dentistes.' [1] And the same Madame Sukhanchikova who makes Madame Beecher Stowe slap Tenteleev on the face all but crawls to Gubariov. Yet the only thing in his favor is that he reads sensible books and is always trying to achieve profundity. What

---

[1] A jocular term for advocates of a hard-fist policy in regard to the peasants. (Tr.)

gift of speech he has you were able to judge for yourself this evening; and we have to thank God that he talks little and only shrivels up. For when he is in the mood and opens his heart, then even I, a patient man enough, cannot stand it. He begins to banter and to tell dirty stories — yes, yes, our great Mr. Gubariov tells dirty stories and laughs filthily as he tells them. . . ."

"Are you so patient?" Litvinov said. "I assumed the contrary. . . . But may I ask your name and patronymic?"

Potugin sipped a little of the kirschwasser.

"My name is Sozont — Sozont Ivanich. They gave me that beautiful name in honor of a relative who was an archimandrite, and that is all I owe to him. I, if I may dare to express myself so, am of a priestly generation. And as for your doubts in regard to my patience, they are beside the mark: I am patient. I served twenty years under my own blood uncle, the active state councilor Irinarkh Potugin. You don't happen to know him?"

"No."

"On which I congratulate you. Yes, I am patient. But 'let us return to the beginning,' as my worthy spiritual brother, the martyred archpriest Avvakum, says. I am amazed at my compatriots, my dear sir. They are all in a state of gloom, they all go about with long faces, and at the same time they are all filled with hope, and at the least thing they go into a rage. Take the Slavophils, for example, among whom Mr. Gubariov reckons himself; very fine people, but all the selfsame mixture of despair and enthusiasm; they all live for some undefined future. Everything will be, will be. There is nothing to show yet; and for a whole ten centuries Russia has produced nothing of her own, either in administration, or in law, or in science, or in art, or even in crafts. . . . But wait, be patient: everything will be. But why will it be, you may be inquisitive to know. Because we, you know, we educated people — are trash; but the people — oh, it's a great people! You see that peasant overcoat? That's where everything will come from! All other idols are destroyed, so let us believe in the peasant coat. Well, but supposing the coat betrays us? No, it will not betray us; you read Kokhanovskaya and then you'll see! Really, if I were a painter I would paint this picture: an educated man standing before a peasant and bowing low to him. 'Cure me,' he is saying, 'little father peasant, I am perishing with disease.' And the peasant, in his turn, bows low to the educated man. 'Teach me,' he is saying, 'little father and master, I am perishing of ignorance.' And of course neither of them gets anywhere. But it would only be necessary to effect a real reconciliation — not only in words — and to learn a little from our elder brothers, to see what they have invented, better than we could and before we could!*Kellner, noch ein Gläschen Kirsch!* Don't think I am drunk, but alcohol loosens my tongue."

"After what you have just said," Litvinov remarked with a smile, "there is no point in my asking to what party you belong, and what is your opinion of Europe. But allow me to make one comment. You have just said that we ought to study and borrow from our elder brothers. But how is it possible to borrow without taking into account the climatic conditions, the soil, the local and national peculiarities? My father, I remember, ordered an iron winnowing-machine that was particularly recommended. It was in fact a very good machine, but what happened? For a full five years it stood in a shed without being used, until it was replaced by a wooden American one, which was much more suited to our way of existence and to our habits, as all the American machines are generally. You mustn't take over things haphazardly, Sozont Ivanovich."

Potugin raised his head.

"I didn't expect such an objection from you, my dear Grigory Mikhailovich," he began after a moment. "Who is forcing you to take things over haphazardly? Why, you borrow other people's ideas not because they are other people's, but because they are of use to you. Accordingly, you think it over and you choose. And as for results — you need not be so anxious; they will have their own peculiarity as the result of those same local, climatic, and other conditions you have mentioned. You just offer good food, and the national stomach will digest it in its own fashion; and with time, when the organism has grown strong, it will provide 'its own' juice. Take our language just as an example. Peter the Great flooded it with thousands of foreign words — Dutch, French, and German. These words expressed conceptions that it was necessary for the Russian nation to become acquainted with. Without philosophizing or standing on ceremony, Peter poured these words *en masse*, tubs and barrels of them, into our belly. Certainly, at first the result was something monstrous, but then that very process of digestion which I have just explained to you began. The conceptions were grafted on and assimilated; the foreign forms were gradually sweated out, the language found something to replace them within its own womb. And now your humble servant, quite a mediocre stylist, undertakes to translate any page you like from Hegel — yes, yes, from Hegel — without using a single non-Slavonic word. What happened with the language will happen, we are entitled to hope, in other things also. The whole question is whether the nature is strong. And our nature is all right, it will stand it: that wasn't the cause of all the trouble. Only people suffering from nervous ailments, and nations that are weak, need be afraid for their health, for their independence; just as only the empty-minded can exult till they foam at the mouth because we, you see, are Russian. I take a lot of care for my health, but I never go into raptures over it; I'd feel ashamed."

"All that is true, Sozont Ivanich," Litvinov began in his turn; "but why must we necessarily be subjected to such tests? You yourself admit that at first something rather monstrous came of it! Well, but supposing that monstrosity were to remain? And besides, it has remained, you know that yourself."

"Only not in the language — and that means a great deal! But I didn't make our people; it is not my fault that it is condemned to pass through such a school. 'The Germans have developed on right lines,' the Slavophils shout; 'give us, too, a sound development!' But where are you to get it, when the very first historical step taken by our tribe, of inviting a prince from overseas to rule them, was already an unsound step, an abnormality, and that same abnormality is repeated in every one of us right down to this day? Every one of us, at least once in his life, has indubitably said to something foreign, not Russian: 'Come and rule and lord it over me!'

"I am ready, perhaps, to agree that if we deposit a foreign substance in our own body, we can never know for certain in advance what it is we are depositing; a piece of bread or a piece of poison! But then it is a well-known fact that you never go from worse to good through the better, but always through the worse — and in medicine poison can be beneficial. Only blockheads and foxes consider it decent to point triumphantly to the poverty of the peasants after their emancipation, to their increased drunkenness since the abolition of the private liquor licenses. Through the worse to the better!"

Potugin passed his hand over his face.

Smoke

"You asked me my opinion of Europe," he began again. "I am amazed at her and extremely devoted to her elements, and don't in the least think it necessary to conceal the fact. Long since — no, recently — for some time now, I have ceased to be afraid to express my convictions — just as you didn't have any misgivings about telling Mr. Gubariov your manner of thought. I, thank God, have ceased to reckon with the conceptions, views, and habits of the person with whom I am talking. I know nothing fundamentally worse than that unnecessary cowardice, that contemptible complaisance, which makes some important official of ours ingratiate himself with some poor little student who is quite insignificant in his eyes, and almost play with him, and fuss around him like a little dog. Well, presumably that sort of official behaves like that out of a desire for popularity, but why should the likes of us, independent and educated, twist and prevaricate? Yes, yes, I am a Westerner, I am devoted to Europe. I mean, to put it more exactly, I am devoted to its cultured standards, to those same cultured standards at which our people poke such delightful fun these days — its civilization — yes, yes, that word is still better. And I love it with all my heart, and I believe in it, and I have and will have no other belief. That word: civ-i-li-za-tion" (Potugin distinctly and emphatically pronounced every syllable), "is both comprehensible, and clean, and sacred; but all the rest, the nationality, say, and the glory, stinks of blood. . . . Let them go."

"Yes, but Russia, Sozont Ivanich, your country — do you love her?"

Potugin passed his hand over his face.

"I love her passionately, and I hate her passionately."

Litvinov shrugged his shoulders.

"That is an old song, Sozont Ivanich, that is a platitude."

"Well, and what of it? Is it the worse for that? Fancy being frightened of that! A platitude! I know many good platitudes. For instance: freedom and order — that is a well-known platitude. Why, do you think it is better as we have it: hierarchy and disorder? And besides, aren't all those phrases which intoxicate the young heads so much — the contemptible bourgeoisie, the *souveraineté du peuple*, the right to work — aren't they all platitudes too? And as for love, inseparable from hate — "

"That's Byronism," Litvinov interrupted him, "the romanticism of the thirties."

29

"Pardon me, you are mistaken; the first to point to such a mingling of feelings was Catullus, the Roman poet Catullus,[1] two thousand years ago. I quoted it from him, because I know a little Latin as the result of my spiritual origin, if I may venture to put it in that way. Yes, I both love and hate my Russia, my strange, dear, rotten, precious country. Now I have abandoned her: I had to give myself a bit of an airing after sitting for twenty years in an official chair, in an official building. I have abandoned Russia, and here I am very comfortable and happy; but I shall go back soon, I feel that. Garden soil is good, but you can't grow cloudberries on it!"

"You're happy, you're comfortable, and I, too, like being here," said Litvinov, "and I came here to study; but that doesn't prevent my seeing such things as that, for instance." He pointed to two passing *lorettes*, with several members of the Jockey Club grimacing and lisping around them, and to the Casino, packed to its doors, despite the lateness of the hour.

"But who told you that I'm blind to it?" Potugin caught him up. "You'll excuse me, but your remark reminds me of the triumphant way in which our unfortunate little periodicals pointed to the defects of the British military administration, as shown up by the *Times*, during the Crimean War. I myself am not an optimist, and I do not take any rosy view of everything human, of all our life, of all this comedy with a tragic ending. But why ascribe solely to the West something that maybe is rooted in our very human nature? That Casino is repulsive, I agree; but our own home-grown swindling, is it any more attractive? No, my dear Grigory Mikhailovich, let us be more humble and more quiet. A good pupil sees his teacher's mistakes, but is respectfully silent about them; for those very mistakes act to his benefit and set him on the right road. But if you really do want to wag your tongue about the rotten West, there's Prince Coco jogging along over there; I expect that in fifteen minutes at the green table he has lost the hard-won, extorted rents of a hundred and fifty families; his nerves are all in rags. And yet I saw him in Marx's today turning over the pages of a brochure by Veuillot. . . . He will make an excellent conversational companion for you!"

---

[1] *"Odi et amo. Quare id faciam, fortasse requiris.*
Nescio: sed fieri sentio et excrucior."
Catullus, Book LXXXVI.

"But one minute, one minute," Litvinov said hurriedly, seeing that Potugin was rising from his seat. "I know Prince Coco very little, and of course I prefer to talk with you — "

"I am very grateful to you," Potugin interrupted him, rising and bowing, "but I have already had a rather long conversation with you, or rather I have done all the talking, while of course you have mentally noted that a man always feels awkward and con-science-stricken when he does all the talking. Especially when it is their first conversation: 'Behold and see what manner of man I am,' so to speak. To our next pleasant meeting. . . . But, I repeat, I am very glad to have made your acquaintance."

"But wait a moment, Sozont Ivanich, tell me at any rate where you live and whether you intend to stay here long?"

Potugin seemed to shrink a little.

"I am remaining in Baden another week or so, but in any case we can meet here at Weber's, or at Marx's. Or if not, then I'll call on you."

"All the same, I ought to have your address."

"Yes, but there's one difficulty: I'm not alone."

"Are you married?" Litvinov asked abruptly.

"No, for goodness' sake — why ask such absurdities? . . . But I have a girl with me."

"Ah!" Litvinov said with a courteous twist of the lips, as though apologizing; and he looked down.

"She's only six years old," Potugin went on. "She's an orphan, the daughter of a certain lady — a very good acquaintance of mine. It would be better for us to meet here. Good-by."

He clapped his hat on his curly head and walked away swiftly; his figure showed up more clearly once or twice as he passed beneath the bracket gas lamps that dimly lit the road leading to the Lichtentaler Allee.

6

"A strange fellow!" thought Litvinov as he walked back to his hotel. "A strange fellow! I shall have to look him up!" He entered his room; a letter lying on the table caught his eyes. "From Tania!" he thought, and rejoiced prematurely: it was from his father in Russia. He broke the heavy, crested seal and began to read. . . . A strong, very pleasant and familiar scent caught his attention. He looked round and saw a large bouquet of fresh heliotrope in a glass of water at the window. He bent over them in some astonishment, touched them, breathed in their perfume. . . . Something seemed to quicken in his memory, something very remote . . . but he could not think exactly what it was. He rang for the boots and asked him where the flowers had come from. The man replied that they had been brought by a lady who didn't wish to give her name, but said that he, "Herr Zluitenhoff," would certainly guess who she was by these flowers. Again Litvinov had a vague recollection of something. . . . He asked what the lady looked like. The man explained that she was tall and beautifully dressed, but had a veil over her face.

"Probably a Russian countess," he added.

"Why do you think so?" Litvinov asked.

"She gave me two guldens," the man replied, and smirked.

Litvinov dismissed him and stood for a long time in a reverie before the window. But at last he gave it up and turned back to the letter from his father. It contained all his usual complaints; he declared that no one would take the grain even as a gift, that the servants had got completely out of hand, and that in all probability the end of the world would come before long. "Would you believe it," he wrote, "they cast the evil eye on my last coachman, the little Kalmuck — d'you remember him? — and the man would surely have been done for, and I had no one to drive me, but, thank goodness, some decent people gave me some advice and suggested sending the patient to Ryazan, to a priest well known for his cures of the evil eye and spells; and the treatment certainly couldn't have been a greater success, in confirmation of which I enclose a letter from the priest himself, as a document." Litvinov read this "document" with interest. It stated that:

"The yardman Nikanor Dmitriev succumbed to an illness not susceptible to medical science, as it was due to evil people; but the real cause of it was the man Nikanor himself, because he had not kept his promise to a certain maiden, and so through certain people she had made him good for nothing, and if in these circumstances I, the priest, had not announced that I would help him, he would have perished completely, like a cabbage caterpillar; but I, trusting in the All-Seeing Eye, became the support of his life, though how I accomplished this is a secret; but I ask Your Excellency to see that in future this maiden does not resort any more to such evil

Smoke

elements, and it will do no harm even to threaten her, otherwise she may again have an evil influence upon him."

Litvinov was lost in thought over this document; it brought to him a breath of the remote and isolated steppe, the impenetrable gloom of a life moldered and fusty, and it seemed remarkable that he had read this letter in Baden of all places. Meanwhile midnight had long passed; he got into bed and blew out the candle. But he could not sleep; the faces he had seen, the speeches he had heard, kept turning and circling, strangely interweaving and jumbling in his burning head, which ached terribly from the tobacco smoke. Now he thought he heard Gubariov's bellow and saw his downcast eyes with their dull and obstinate gaze; now suddenly those same eyes flamed and danced, and he recognized Mme Sukhanchikova, heard her crackling voice, and involuntarily repeated softly after her: "She slapped his face, she slapped his face"; now Potugin's awkward figure rose before him, and for the tenth, the twentieth time he recalled every word he had said; now, like a jack-in-the-box, Voroshilov sprang up in his close-fitting coat, which enveloped him like a new uniform; and Pishchalkin sagely and gravely nodded his perfectly trimmed and undoubtedly well-intentioned head; and Bindasov shouted and cursed, and Bambayev exulted lachrymosely. . . .

But, above all, that perfume, that persistent, importunate, sweet, heavy perfume did not give him any rest, but pervaded the room more and more strongly in the darkness, and more and more insistently reminded him of something that he simply could not define. . . . It occurred to him that the scent of flowers in a bedroom at night is detrimental to the health, and he rose, groped his way to the bouquet, and carried it into the other room; but even then the exhausting perfume penetrated to him on his pillow, under the blanket, and he turned over fretfully from side to side. Now a fever was beginning to steal upon him; a priest, "a master against enchantments," ran twice across his head, in the form of a very lively hare with a beard and pigtail, and Voroshilov, sitting in the enormous plume of a general's helmet, as though in a bush, began to twitter like a nightingale in front of him . . . when suddenly he raised himself in the bed and, throwing up his hands, exclaimed: "Surely it isn't *she*? It can't be!"

But in order to explain this exclamation we have to ask the indulgent reader to go back with us several years. . . .

33

7

At the beginning of the fifties the numerous members of a family belonging to the princely Osinin line were living at Moscow in very straitened circumstances, almost in poverty. They were true, not Tatar-Georgian, but pure-blooded princes, descendants of Rurik; their name is often mentioned in Russian annals during the times of the first grand dukes of Moscow, who consolidated the Russian lands. They owned very extensive patrimonies and many estates, were paid more than once for their "labors and blood and injuries," they sat in the boyars' Duma, one of them was even granted the right to the honorable title of "vich." But they fell into disgrace for a hostile plot in "sorcery and calumny," they were ruined "terribly and endlessly," they were stripped of their honors, they were exiled to remote spots. The Osinins crashed and never recovered, never regained their power; in the course of time their disgrace was removed and even their "little palace at Moscow" and their "chattels" were returned to them, but all to no avail. Their line grew poor and "impoverished," it did not recover either under Peter or under Catherine, and, continually declining and growing more petty, it now included estate administrators, wineshop-owners, and district police officers among its members. The Osinin family to which we have referred consisted of a husband, a wife, and five children. They resided near Sobaka Square, in a one-story wooden house with a small boarded front porch facing the street, green lions at the gate, and other noble devices, and only just managed to make ends meet, owing money to the grocer and quite often without wood or candles in the winter. The Prince himself was a sluggish and rather stupid man, at one time handsome and a fop, but now completely gone to pieces. Not so much out of respect for his name as a mark of attention to his wife, who had been a maid of honor, he had been given one of the Moscow traditional stewardships with a small salary, a queer name, and nothing to do; he never interfered in anything, and did nothing but smoke from morning till evening, never changing out of his dressing-gown, and always groaning. His wife was a sickly and bad-tempered woman, continually worried over domestic troubles, the placing of the children in state educational institutions, and the maintenance of her Petersburg connections; she simply could not get used to her position and her retirement from the court.

During his residence in Moscow, Litvinov's father had made Osinin's acquaintance, had had occasion to do him certain services, and once had made him a loan of three hundred rubles. Litvinov himself, while a student, often called on the Osinins; it happened that his apartment was not far from their house. But it was not their proximity that attracted him, not the poor comforts of their mode of life that allured him; he began to call on the Osinins regularly when he fell in love with their eldest daughter, Irena.

She was then a little past her seventeenth birthday; she had only just left the young ladies' institute, from which her mother had withdrawn her after some unpleasantness with the headmistress. The unpleasantness arose over the circumstance that at the public graduation celebration Irena was to have addressed the patron with some verses of welcome in French, but immediately before the function she was set aside in favor of another girl, the daughter of a very rich liquor licensee. The Princess could not stomach this affront, and even Irena did not forgive the headmistress her injustice; she had been dreaming of how, with all eyes on her, the center of attraction, she would rise and say her verses, and how Moscow would talk about her afterward. . . .

And she was right, Moscow would certainly have talked about Irena. She was a tall and graceful girl, with virgin breasts and angular shoulders, a pale, velvety complexion unusual for her age and as clear and smooth as porcelain, and thick, fair hair with very distinctive mingled darker and lighter strands. Her features were exquisitely, almost artificially regular and had not entirely lost the artless expression of early youth. But the deliberate movements of her beautiful neck, and her smile, a rather abstracted or rather weary smile, suggested that she was a highly strung young lady; and the very outlines of her fine, faintly smiling lips and her small, aquiline, rather firm nose expressed a self-willed and passionate quality — a quality dangerous both for others and for herself. Astonishing, truly astonishing were her eyes, which were a very dark gray shot with green, with a languishing look, and unsually long, like those of Egyptian goddesses, with radiating lashes and boldly sweeping brows. There was a strange expression in those eyes: they seemed to be attentively and thoughtfully looking out from an infinite depth and distance. At the institute Irena had had the reputation of being one of its most intelligent and capable pupils, but also of possessing an uncertain, ambitious character and a mischievous head. One class mistress prophesied of her that her passions would ruin her — *"vos passions vous perdront"* — whereas another class mistress chided her for her coldness and insensibility and called her *"une jeune fille sans cœur."* Her friends found her proud and secretive, her brothers and sisters were afraid of her, her mother did not trust her, and her father felt awkward when she fixed her mysterious eyes on him; but in both father and mother she inspired a feeling of involuntary respect, not because of her qualities, but because of the peculiar, vague expectations that she aroused in them, for no obvious reason.

"You'll see, Praskovia Danilovna," the old Prince said to his wife one day, removing his pipestem from his mouth; "our Irinka will yet mend over fortunes."

The Princess grew angry and told her husband that he had *"des expressions insupportables,"* but then she was lost in thought and repeated through her set teeth:

"Yes, and she should mend them well!"

Irena enjoyed almost unlimited freedom in her parents' house. She was not spoilt, the rest of the family even felt rather hostile to her; but they did not thwart her, and that was all that mattered to her. . . . At times, during some unusually humiliating scene — a shopkeeper arriving and shouting, for all the world to hear, that he had grown tired of calling for his money, or their own servants turning to swear at their masters to their face: "What sort of princes are you when you yourselves are tightening your belts with hunger?" — Irena would not even stir an eyebrow and would sit motionless, with an unpleasant smile on her moody face. But her parents found that very smile more painful than any reproaches, and they had a feeling of guilt, of innocent guilt, toward this creature, who from the very day of her birth had seemed to have a right to wealth, to luxury, to devotion.

Litvinov fell in love with Irena as soon as he saw her (he was only three years older than she), but for a long time he could not gain even her attention, still less any return of his feelings. Her conduct toward him was stamped with hostility, as if he had done her some injury, and though she would not reveal the reason, she could not forgive him. He was then too inexperienced and young to realize what might be hidden beneath this hostile, almost contemptuous harshness. There were times when, forgetting his lessons and exercise books, he would sit in the cheerless reception room of Osinin's house and would take surreptitious looks at Irena, while his heart slowly and mournfully sank, grew heavy with its load. But she seemed to be angry, or bored; she would rise and walk about the room, would gaze at him coldly, as if at a table or chair, would shrug her shoulders and fold her arms. Or, even when talking to him, she would deliberately avoid looking at him all the evening, as though refusing him even that charity. Or, finally, she would pick up a book and fix her eyes on it, without reading it, while she knitted her brows and bit her lips, or would suddenly ask her father or brother in a loud voice: "What is the German for 'patience'?" He attempted to break free of the enchantment in which he was tormented, and struggled incessantly like a bird caught in a snare. He left Moscow for a week. . . .

He all but went out of his mind with yearning and ennui and was quite thin and ill when he called on the Osinins again. . . . Strange to relate, Irena also had grown perceptibly thinner during those few days, her face had gone yellow, her cheeks were hollow . . . but she greeted him with even greater chilliness, with almost malevolent unconcern, as though he had even added to the secret injury he had done her. . . .

She tormented him thus for a couple of months. Then everything changed in a single day. As though it had flamed up in a conflagration, or had sped like a thunder cloud, love took possession of her. One day — he remembered that day for long after — he was sitting by the window in the Osinins' reception room and gazing unthinkingly out into the street, and he felt chagrin and ennui and contempt for himself, and he could not stir. . . . He felt that if a river had been flowing just beneath the window he would have thrown himself into it with horror, but without regret. Irena seated herself not far away and was strangely silent and very still. For some days now she had not spoken to him at all, nor, for that matter, did she speak to anybody. She sat all the time with her head in her hands, as though bewildered, and only occasionally gazed slowly about her.

At last this chilly languor grew too much for Litvinov: without taking his leave of her, he rose and began to look for his hat. "Stay!" he suddenly heard a quiet whisper. His heart trembled.

He did not recognize Irena's voice at once: there was an unusual note in that single word. He raised his head and was petrified: she was looking at him graciously, yes, graciously. "Stay," she repeated, "don't go. I want to be with you." She lowered her voice still more. "Don't go — I ask you." Completely at a loss, not fully realizing what he was doing, he went to her and held out his hands. . . . She at once gave him both hers, then smiled, and her face flamed. She turned away and, still smiling, left the room. . . .

A few minutes later she returned with her younger sister, looked at him once more with that long and gentle gaze, and made him sit beside her. . . . At first she could not say a word: she only sighed and blushed. Then she began shyly to question him concerning his studies, a thing she had never done before. During the evening she apologized to him again and again for failing to appreciate him before and assured him that now she was completely changed; she astonished him by displaying an unexpected tendency toward republicanism (at this period of his life he worshipped Robespierre and would not have dreamed of censuring Marat), and within a week he knew that she loved him. Yes, he remembered that first day for long after. . . .

Nor did he forget those that followed — those days when, still striving to doubt and fearing to believe, with a sinking feeling of rapture, almost of fear, he realized how his unexpected happiness had sprung to birth, had grown and, invincibly sweeping away everything before it, had come flooding at last. Now they experienced those luminous moments of first love, moments that are not fated to be repeated, and that, indeed, should not be repeated in one and the same life. Irena suddenly became as obedient as a lamb, as soft as silk, and endlessly kind. She began to give her younger sisters lessons — not on the piano, she was not a musician, but in French and English. She went through their schoolbooks with them and took her share in running the home. Everything amused her, everything interested her; she would chatter away without cease, or would be sunk in a speechless tenderness. She made various plans, gave herself over to endless speculation about what she would do when she married Litvinov (they had not the least doubt that they would be married), how together they would begin — "To toil?" Litvinov suggested. "Yes, to toil," she repeated, "to read . . . but most of all to travel." She particularly wanted to leave Moscow as soon as possible, and when he pointed out that he had not yet finished his university studies, she always, after thinking a little, replied that he could finish in Berlin or — somewhere abroad. She made little attempt to moderate the expression of her feelings, and so her attitude to Litvinov did not remain a secret from the Prince and Princess. They were not exactly delighted, but, taking all the circumstances into account, they did not consider it necessary to impose their veto at once. Litvinov's fortune was considerable.

"But his family, his family! . . ." the Princess remarked.

"Well, of course, there's the question of family," the Prince answered. "But, after all, he is not entirely outside the nobility; and the main thing is that in any case Irena will not listen to us. Have you ever known her not to do what she wished? *Vous connaissez sa violence!* And besides there is nothing definite yet." So the Prince reasoned, but he at once mentally added: "Madame Litvinova — is that all? I expected more."

Irena took complete possession of her future bridegroom, and he readily delivered himself into her hands. It was as though he had fallen into a whirlpool, as though he had lost himself. . . . It was both frightening to him and sweet; and he did not regret anything, and did not spare anything. To ponder on the meaning, on the duties of married life, on whether he, so irrevocably subjugated, could be a good husband, and what kind of wife Irena would make, and whether their mutual relations were sound — these were questions he could not enter into. His blood began to burn, and he knew one thing only: that he must follow her, must go with her, henceforth and without end, and then come what come may!

But despite his complete lack of resistance and her excess of impulsive tenderness, none the less the affair did not proceed without certain misunderstandings and upsets. One day he hurried to her straight from the university, in an old coat and with ink-stained hands. She rushed to meet him with her usual endearing welcome, but stopped short.

"You haven't any gloves," she pronounced deliberately, at once adding: "Pah! What a — student you are!"

"You're too sensitive, Irena," he remarked.

"You're — a real student," she repeated, *"vous n'êtes pas distingué."*

Turning her back on him, she left the room.

Truly, an hour later she implored him to forgive her . . . In general she readily punished and reproached herself in his presence. But, strange to say, often, all but weeping, she reproached herself with evil motives that she did not possess, and obstinately denied her real defects. Another time he found her in tears, with her head resting on her hand, her curls fallen over her back. When, thoroughly alarmed, he asked the reason for her sorrow, she silently pointed her finger to her breast. He involuntarily shivered. "Consumption!" the thought flashed through his head, and he seized her hand.

"Are you ill?" he asked in a quivering voice (they had already begun to use the intimate second person singular to each other on serious occasions). "If so I'll go at once for a doctor —"

But Irena did not allow him to finish. She stamped her foot with vexation.

"I am quite well — but this dress — don't you really understand?"

"What's the matter — that dress — ?" he said in perplexity.

"What is the matter? Why, that I haven't any other, and it is old and disgusting; and I am forced to put on this same dress every day — even when you — even when you" (here she corrected the pronoun to the plural) "come. . . . In the end you will cease to love me, seeing me in such a slovenly state!"

"Really, Irena, what are you saying! That dress is very nice! . . . I am particularly fond of it because you were wearing it the first time I saw you!"

She flushed.

"Please, Grigory Mikhailovich, don't remind me that I hadn't another dress even then."

"But I assure you, Irena Pavlovna, that it suits you charmingly."

"No, it is disgusting, disgusting," she declared, pulling nervously at her long, soft curls. "Oh, this poverty, poverty, this darkness! How can one escape from this poverty! How emerge, how emerge from the darkness!"

He did not know what to say and half turned away.

Suddenly she jumped up from her chair and put both hands on his shoulders.

"But you do love me, don't you? You love me?" she uttered, bringing her face close to his; and her eyes, though still filled with tears, began to sparkle with the gaiety of happiness. "You love me even in this disgusting dress?"

He flung himself down on his knees before her.

"Ah, love me, love me, my dear, my savior!" she whispered, bending down to him.

So the days passed, the weeks went by, and although no formal explanations had been entered into, although Litvinov still delayed with his formal request, not, of course, by his own desire, but in expectation of Irena's command (she remarked one day that they were both absurdly young, they must add at least a few more weeks to their age), yet everything was moving toward the denouement, and the immediate future was being delineated more and more clearly. When suddenly an event occurred that dissipated all these presumptions and plans like dust on a road.

8

During that winter the court visited Moscow. One function followed another; the time came for the usual great ball in the Palace of the Nobility. The news of this ball, though in the form of an announcement in the *Police Gazette*, reached the little house on Sobaka Square. The Prince was the first to raise the alarm; he at once decided that he must go in any case and must take Irena with him, that it would be unforgivable to lose the opportunity to see Their Majesties, that the blue-blooded nobility was even under a kind of obligation to do so. He maintained his opinion with a degree of fervor that was quite foreign to him; the Princess agreed with him to some extent and only sighed over the expenses; but Irena was resolutely opposed to the idea.

"It's quite unnecessary, I shall not go," she replied to all her parents' arguments. She grew so vehement under obduracy that the old Prince decided to ask Litvinov to try to persuade her and to point out to her, among other "reasons," that it was not seemly for a young lady to be unsociable, that she ought "to have this experience too," that, as matters stood, no one ever saw her. Litvinov undertook to put these "reasons" to her. Irena gazed at him fixedly and attentively, so fixedly and so attentively that he was embarrassed. Playing with the ends of her belt, she calmly said:

"Do you desire this? You?"

"Yes — I think so," he replied hesitantly. "I agree with your father. . . . And besides why shouldn't you go — to see people and to be seen?" he added with a little laugh.

"To be seen," she slowly repeated. "Well, good, I'll go. Only, remember that you yourself desired this."

"That is, I — " Litvinov began.

"You yourself desired it," she interrupted him. "And I have one other condition: you must promise me that you will not be present at the ball."

"But why not?"

"It is my wish."

He flung out his hands.

"I submit. . . . But, I confess, it would be very delightful for me to see you in all your magnificence, to be a witness of the impression you will surely make. . . . How proud I would be of you!" he added with a sigh.

Irena smiled. "All my magnificence will consist of a white gown; and as for the impression — well, in a word, that is how I want it to be."

"Irena, you seem to be angry."

She smiled again.

"Oh no! I am not angry. Only you — " (she fixed her eyes on him, and it seemed to him that never before had he seen such an expression in them). "Perhaps it is necessary," she added in an undertone.

"But, Irena, you do love me?"

"I love you," she replied with almost a solemn seriousness, and gave his hand a strong, vigorous squeeze.

All the following days Irena was diligently occupied with her toilet, her coiffure. On the eve of the ball she felt unwell; she could not sit still, and she shed a tear or two in solitude. So long as Litvinov was present she seemed to wear a fixed smile . . . for that matter, though she was as affectionate to him as ever, she was abstracted, and looked at herself in the mirror from time to time. On the actual day of the ball she was very taciturn and pale, but calm. At nine in the evening Litvinov arrived to take a look at her. When she came out to him in a white tarlatan gown, with a chaplet of small blue flowers in her slightly fluffed-up hair, he gasped, so beautiful and majestic, even beyond her years, did she seem to him. "Yes, she has grown since this morning," he thought. "And what a carriage! What a lot birth does mean, after all!" She stood with arms hanging loosely, without a smile and without affectation, looking resolutely, almost boldly, not at him, but into the distance, straight before her.

"You are just like a legendary princess," he said at last. "But no; you are like a general before the battle, before victory. . . . You would not permit me to attend this ball," he continued, while she still stood motionless, apparently not listening to him, but following some other, inner voice. "But you will not refuse to accept these flowers from me and take them with you?"

He gave her a bouquet of heliotrope.

She threw him a swift glance, raised her hand, and, suddenly seizing one end of the chaplet adorning her head, she said:

"Would you like me to? Say only the word and I will tear off all this and remain at home."

Litvinov's heart beat madly. Her hand was already pulling at the chaplet. . . .

"No, no, why should you?" He restrained her hurriedly, in an outburst of grateful and generous feelings. "I am not an egotist. Why restrict your freedom — when I know that your heart — "

"Well, then, don't come near me, you'll crease my gown," she said hastily.

He was disconcerted.

"But you'll take the bouquet?" he asked.

"Of course. It is very nice, and I am very fond of that perfume. *Merci*. . . . I shall keep it in memory — "

"Of your first coming out," Litvinov remarked; "of your first triumph."

Irena looked across her shoulder at herself in the mirror, slightly bending her figure.

"And am I really so very beautiful? You're not prejudiced?"

He broke into enthusiastic praises. But she was no longer listening to him. Raising the bouquet to her face, she again gazed into the distance with her strange, seemingly deepened and dilated eyes. Sent fluttering by a gentle breath of air, the ends of the fine ribbons lifted a little from her shoulders, like wings.

The Prince appeared, wearing a crimped peruke, a white cravat, a faded black frock coat, and with the ribbon of the order of St. Vladimir in his buttonhole. He was followed by the Princess in a silk figured gown of old-fashioned cut. With that fussy severity which mothers resort to in the attempt to conceal their agitation, she arranged her daughter's dress at the back: in other words, she quite unnecessarily shook out the folds of her gown. A four-seated hired coach, harnessed to two shaggy nags, crawled up to the porch, with its wheels squeaking and scrunching through the drifts of unswept snow, and a conceited lackey in an incredible livery jumped down from the box and reported with a swagger that the carriage was ready. . . . After blessing the children who were to be left for the night, and wrapping themselves in their furs, the Prince and the Princess went to the door: Irena, in a thin, short mantle — how she hated that mantle already! — silently followed them. Litvinov, who saw them off, hoped to receive one farewell glance from her; but she seated herself in the carriage without turning her head.

About midnight he walked past the windows of the Palace of the Nobility. The innumerable candles of the enormous chandeliers shone like points of light through the crimson curtains, and all the square, which was crowded with equipages, was filled with the dashing, festive, challenging sounds of a Strauss waltz.

Next day Litvinov called on the Osinins about one o'clock. He found only the Prince at home, and was at once informed that Irena had a headache, that she was in bed and would not get up until evening, and that, after all, such an upset was not in the least surprising after her first ball.

"*C'est très naturel, vous savez, dans les jeunes filles,*" the Prince added in French, which somewhat astonished Litvinov, who at the same moment noticed that he was not in his dressing-gown as usual, but in a coat. "And besides," Osinin continued, "how could she avoid being unwell after yesterday's occurrences?"

"Occurrences?" Litvinov murmured.

"Yes, yes, occurrences, occurrences, *de vrais événements.* You cannot imagine, Grigory Mikhailovich, *quel succès elle a eu!* All the court noticed her. Prince Alexandr Fiodorovich said that her place was not here, and that she reminded him of the Duchess of Devonshire — you know, that — well-known — And old Blazenkrampf declared for all to hear that Irena was *la reine du bal* and expressed the desire to be introduced to her. He introduced himself to me, too; I mean, he told me he remembered me as a hussar and asked where I was serving now. He's highly amusing, is the Count, and such an *adorateur du beau sexe!* But what was I saying? My Princess — she, too, was not given any peace; Natalia Nikitishna herself talked with her — and what else? Irena danced *avec tous les meilleurs cavaliers;* they even put me in an awkward position — awkward. I even lost count. Will you believe it? — they all walked round us in crowds; during the mazurka they all wanted to dance only with her. When he learned that she was a Muscovite, one foreign diplomat said to His Majesty: 'Sire!' he said, '*décidément c'est Moscou qui est le centre de votre empire!*' And another diplomat added: '*C'est une vraie révolution, Sire*'; *révélation* or *révolution* — something of that sort. Yes — yes — it — it — I tell you, it was something extraordinary."

"Yes, but how about Irena Pavlovna herself?" asked Litvinov, whose hands and feet had been going colder and colder all the time the Prince was speaking. "Did she enjoy herself, did she seem satisfied?"

"Of course she enjoyed herself, and as if she wouldn't be satisfied! And, by the way, you know you never can understand her all at once. Everybody said to me yesterday how amazing it was, *jamais on ne dirait que mademoiselle votre fille est à son premier bal*. Among other things Count Reizenbach — of course you know him — "

"No, I don't know him at all and never have."

"He's my wife's first cousin — "

"I don't know him."

"He's wealthy, a court chamberlain, he lives in Petersburg, he's a man of affairs, he has everybody dancing attendance on him in Livonia. Hitherto he has ignored us — and I'm not the sort to chase after people. *J'ai l'humeur facile, comme vous savez.* Well, to get back to him. He sat down with Irena, talked to her for a quarter of an hour, no more, and afterward said to my Princess: '*Ma cousine*,' he said, '*votre fille est une perle; c'est une perfection*; everybody is congratulating me on having such a niece. . . .' And then I saw him go up to — an important personage and speak to her, while he went on gazing at Irena . . . and the personage looked, too. . . ."

"And so Irena Pavlovna will not leave her room all day?" Litvinov asked.

"No; she has a bad headache. She asked us to greet you on her behalf and to thank you for your bouquet, *qu'on a trouvé charmant*. She needs the rest. . . . My Princess has gone to pay some visits . . . and I myself am, as you see — "

The Prince began to cough and fidget, as though he had difficulty in finding anything further to say. Litvinov picked up his hat, said that he had no intention of hindering him and would call later to inquire about Irena's health, and withdrew.

Turgenev

A few paces from the Osinins' house he saw an elegant two-seated carriage standing close to a policeman. With a negligent air a liveried footman, as elegant as the carriage, bent down from the box and asked the policeman, a local Finn, where Prince Pavel Vasilievich Osinin lived. Litvinov glanced into the carriage: inside it was a middle-aged man wrapped in sables, with a lined and arrogant face of florid complexion, a Grecian nose, and evil lips: by all the signs an important dignitary.

9

Litvinov did not keep his promise to call later; he realized that it would be better to postpone his visit till the following day. When, about twelve o'clock, he entered the only too well-known reception hall, he saw the younger princesses, Victorina and Cleopatrina. He greeted them, then asked whether Irena Pavlovna was better and could he see her.

"Dear Irena has driven somewhere with Mamma," Victorina replied; though she lisped, she was less bashful than her sister.

"What do you mean — driven somewhere?" he repeated after her, and something quietly began to quiver in the very depths of his breast. "Surely — surely — surely at this time of day she ought to be occupied with you, giving you your lessons?"

"Dear Irena will not be giving us lessons any more," Victorina replied. "Not any more," Cleopatrina repeated after her.

"But is your papa at home?" Litvinov asked.

"Papa is not at home either," Victorina said. "But Irena isn't well: she cried all night, all night."

"Cried?"

"Yes, cried — so Yegorovna told me, and her eyes were so red, and they were so swollen — "

Litvinov paced the room once or twice, shivering a little as though with the cold, then returned to his apartment. He experienced a sensation similar to that which takes possession of a man when he looks down from a lofty tower: all his internals sank, and his head swam slowly and sickeningly. He felt a dull bewilderment, though his thoughts went scurrying like mice; he was conscious of a vague horror and mute expectation and a peculiar, almost malevolent curiosity; there was the bitterness of unshed tears in his choking throat, an attempt at a vacuous smile on his lips, and in his heart a meaningless, aimless supplication. . . . Oh,

46

how cruelly and humiliatingly infamous it all was! "Irena doesn't want to see me," the thought persistently recurred to his mind; "that is quite clear. But why doesn't she? What could have happened at that unfortunate ball? And how could such a sudden change be possible? So abruptly — " (Human beings are constantly witnessing the fact that death comes abruptly, but they can never get accustomed to this abruptness, and think it senseless.) "She does not give them any message for me, she does not wish to give me any explanation. . . ."

"Grigory Mikhailich!" a tense voice sounded right by his ear.

He started, and saw his man with a note in his hand. He recognized Irena's writing. . . . Even before he unsealed the note he had a presentiment of disaster and sank his head on his chest and hunched his shoulders, as though protecting himself against a blow.

At last he plucked up courage and tore the envelope open. On the small sheet of paper inside were the following words:

Forgive me, Grigory Mikhailich! Everything is over between us; I am going to Petersburg. It is terribly hard for me, but the deed is done. Evidently, it is my fate — but no, I have no wish to justify myself. My presentiments have come true. Forgive me, forget me; I am not worthy of you.

Irena

Be magnanimous: do not try to see me.

Litvinov read these six lines and sank slowly onto the sofa as though someone were pushing him in the chest. He dropped the note, picked it up, read it again, whispered: "To Petersburg," dropped it again, and let it lie. He was even possessed by a feeling of tranquillity; with hands flung behind him he even adjusted the cushion to his head. "People crushed to death don't struggle," he thought; "as it came, so it has gone again. . . . It is all quite natural, I always expected it. . . ." (He was lying to himself; he had never expected anything of the sort.) "Wept? . . . She wept? . . . What did she weep for? After all, she didn't love me! However, it is all understandable and in keeping with her character. She, she is not worthy of me. . . . You don't say so!" (He smiled bitterly.) "She herself did not know what power lurked within her, and once she had been convinced of its effect at the ball, how could she be satisfied with an insignificant student? . . . That is all quite understandable."

But then he remembered her tender words, her smiles, and those eyes, those unforgettable eyes, which he would never see again, eyes that lit up and melted if they happened to meet his eyes; he remembered her swift, timid, burning kiss — and he suddenly burst into sobbing. He sobbed convulsively, frenziedly, rancorously, with his face turned to the sofa, and so sobbing and panting, with frantic satisfaction, as though seeking to tear himself and everything around him to pieces, he beat his inflamed face against the cushion, chewed the material. . . .

Alas! the gentleman whom Litvinov had seen in the carriage the previous day was Princess Osinin's cousin, the court chamberlain and man of fortune Count Reizenbach. Observing the impression Irena made on highly placed personages, and at once realizing "*mit etwas Accuratesse*" what advantages could be derived from this circumstance, the Count, being an energetic man as well as a toady, at once formulated his plan. He decided to act swiftly, in Napoleonic fashion. "I'll take that remarkable young lady into my home at Petersburg," he deliberated. "I'll make her my heiress, damn it, though not to all my fortune. It so happens that I haven't any children, and she is my niece, and my Countess is bored with being alone. . . . Life is always more pleasant when there's a pretty face in the reception hall. . . . Yes, yes; that's it; *es ist eine Idee, es ist eine Idee!*" He would have to dazzle, to bemuse, to astound her parents. . . . "They haven't anything," he continued his meditations as he sat in the carriage on his way to Sobaka Square, "so I don't expect them to be obstinate. They're not so sensitive as all that. I could give them a lump sum, for that matter. But how about her? She will agree too. Honey is sweet — she had a taste of it yesterday. Granted that this is a whim on my part; well, let them have the benefit of it — the fools. I shall tell them my conditions, and they must decide. And if not, I'll take another; an orphan — still more convenient. Yes or no, twenty-four hours to decide, *und damit Punctum.*"

When the Count presented himself to the Prince, he used these very words; he had advised him the night before, at the ball, of his intention to call. It does not seem worth while enlarging to any extent on the consequences of this visit. The Count was not mistaken in his calculations: the Prince and Princess were not

Smoke

obstinate and accepted a sum of money, and Irena did agree before the time limit had expired. It was not easy for her to break off her relations with Litvinov; she loved him and, having sent him the note, she all but took to her bed, and wept incessantly, went thin and yellow. . . . But, none the less, a month later the Princess carried her off to Petersburg and installed her with the Count, entrusting her to the protection of the Countess, who was a very good woman, but had the mentality of a hen and looked like a hen.

Litvinov threw up his studies at the university and went to live with his father in the country. Little by little his wound healed. At first he had no news whatever of Irena, and indeed he avoided all talk of Petersburg and Petersburg society. Then gradually rumors began to circulate concerning her: not evil rumors, but strange; she was the subject of common gossip. The name of Princess Osinina, was surrounded with an aureole of general report, was remarked upon with peculiar emphasis, and began to be mentioned more and more even in provincial circles. It was mentioned with curiosity, with respect, with envy, as the name of Countess Vorotinskaya had once been mentioned. Finally the news was spread that she had married. But Litvinov paid hardly any attention to this latest report: by then he was betrothed to Tatiana.

Now the reader probably understands exactly what he recalled when he exclaimed: "Surely not?" And so we return to Baden and take up the thread of our interrupted story.

10

Litvinov fell asleep very late and did not sleep long; the sun had only just risen when he got out of bed. Visible from his windows, the crests of the shadowed hills showed humidly blood-red against the clear sky. "It ought to be fresh beneath the trees," he thought. He hurriedly dressed, glanced abstractedly at the bouquet, which had opened still more exuberantly during the night, took his stick, and set off to walk beyond the Old Castle to the well-known Cliffs. The morning clasped him in its strong and quiet caress. Bravely he breathed, bravely he moved; the health of youth played in his every tiny vein; the earth itself seemed to be conferring more resilience on his lightly striding legs. With every step he grew more free, more gay; he walked in the dewy shade, over the coarse sand of the paths, by the firs, all the tips of which were edged with the brilliant green of the vernal shoots. "How glorious

49

it is!" he told himself from time to time. Suddenly he heard familiar voices: he looked up and saw Voroshilov and Bambayev coming toward him. The sight was so jarring that, like a pupil escaping from a teacher, he started to one side and hid behind a bush. . . . "Creator!" he implored, "carry my compatriots past!" One can only assume that at that moment he would have given any sum to ensure that they did not see him. . . . And in fact they did not see him. The Creator carried his compatriots past. Voroshilov, talking in a voice as self-satisfied as any cadet's, was explaining to Bambayev the various "phases" of Gothic architecture, while Bambayev only mooed approvingly. Evidently Voroshilov's lecture on the "phases" had already lasted a long time, and the good-natured enthusiast was beginning to be bored. Biting his lip and stretching his neck, Litvinov listened to the retreating footsteps for quite a while; the guttural and nasal tones of the edifying speech continued to reach him for a long time; at last all sounds died away. He sighed, emerged from his ambush, and walked on.

For some three hours he wandered about the hills. Sometimes he left the path and went leaping from stone to stone, occasionally slipping on the smooth moss. Sometimes he sat down on a piece of rock beneath an oak or beech and thought pleasant thoughts, to the unceasing whisper of the little streams overgrown with bracken, the reassuring rustle of the leaves, the ringing song of a solitary black thrush. A light and pleasant drowsiness stole over him, seemed to envelop him from behind, and he dozed off. . . . But suddenly he smiled and looked about him; the gold and green of the forest, the forest air, were borne gently to his eyes — and he smiled again and closed them again. He felt that he would like some breakfast, and he made his way to the Old Castle, where for a few kreutzers one can get a glass of good milk and coffee. But he had not even had time to seat himself at one of the small white tables scattered about the platform before the castle when he heard the heavy snorting of horses, and three carriages appeared and discharged quite a large company of ladies and gentlemen.

Though they were all talking French, Litvinov at once recognized them as Russian — just because they were talking French. The ladies' toilets were distinguished by an artificial elegance; the gentlemen were wearing morning coats — spick and span morning coats, but tight-fitting and with fitted waists, which is not exactly usual in our day — shot gray pantaloons, and very glossy town hats. Each of these gentlemen had a low-hanging black tie, which tightly clasped his neck, and there was a military quality in the bearing of all. They were, in fact, military men; Litvinov had lighted upon a picnic of young generals, members of high society and of considerable weight. Their importance was indicated in all their mannerisms: their air of restrained jauntiness, their pleasantly dignified smiles, the tense abstraction of their gaze, the effeminate shrug of their shoulders, the way they swayed their bodies and bent their knees; it was indicated by the very tone of their voices, such a tone as they might have used to express their affable and loathsome thanks to a crowd of underlings. All these officers were superlatively washed, shaved, and saturated with a perfume peculiar to the genuine courtier and guardsman, a blend of finest cigar smoke and subtle patchouli. And every one of them had courtiers' hands, white and large, with nails as strong as ivory; they all had gleaming mustaches and sparkling teeth, and their fine skin was flushed with crimson on their cheeks and was bluish at the chin. Some of these young generals were playful, others thoughtful; but they all bore the stamp of exquisite propriety. Each one seemed to be profoundly conscious of his own worth, of the importance of his future role in the state, and bore himself both easily and with stern restraint, with just a touch of that mettle, that "damn it all" which so naturally develops during travels abroad.

After seating themselves noisily and elegantly, the company summoned the bustling waiters. Litvinov hastened to finish his glass of milk, paid his bill, and, clapping on his hat, was just slipping past the generals' picnic. . . .

"Grigory Mikhailich," came a woman's voice. "Don't you recognize me?"

He involuntarily halted. That voice — that voice in past days had made his heart beat all too rapidly. . . . He turned and saw Irena.

She was sitting with her arms folded over the back of a chair that she had drawn away from a table. Smiling, with her head cocked a little to one side, she gazed at him with a welcoming, almost joyous look.

He recognized her at once, though she had changed since he had last seen her, ten years ago, and though the girl he had known was transformed into a woman. Her slender figure had developed and blossomed, the contours of her once angular shoulders now recalled those of the goddesses depicted on the ceilings of ancient Italian palaces. But her eyes had remained the same, and it seemed to Litvinov that they looked at him just as they had in that long past time in that small Moscow house.

"Irena Pavlovna — " he said uncertainly.

"So you recognized me? How glad I am, how glad — " She stopped, reddened slightly and drew herself up. "This is a very pleasant meeting," she continued in French. "Let me introduce you to my husband. Valérien, this is M'sieur Litvinov, *un ami d'enfance;* and this is Valerian Vladimirovich Ratmirov, my husband."

One of the young generals, perhaps the most exquisite of them all, rose from the table and bowed to Litvinov with unusual courtesy. But his colleagues knitted their brows a little, or rather not so much knitted their brows as withdrew for a moment each into himself, as though protesting in advance against any rapprochement with some civilian outsider; while the other ladies present deemed it necessary to narrow their eyes a little and to smile, and even to adopt a look of astonishment.

"You — have you been long in Baden?" General Ratmirov asked, attitudinizing in rather an un-Russian fashion and obviously not knowing what to talk about to a friend of his wife's childhood.

"Not long," Litvinov answered.

"And are you intending to stay for long?" the courteous general continued.

"I haven't yet decided."

"Ah! That is very pleasant — very."

The general was silent. Litvinov also said nothing. They both held their hats in their hands and, smirking and bending their bodies forward, looked at each other's eyebrows.

"Deux gendarmes, un beau dimanche," a shortsighted and rather yellow-faced general began to sing, of course in a falsetto voice — we have never yet come across a Russian nobleman who did not sing falsetto. This general wore an expression of permanent irritability, as though he could not forgive himself his own exterior. Among them all, he alone had no resemblance whatever to a rose.

"But why don't you sit down, Grigory Mikhailich?" Irena said at last.

Smoke

Litvinov complied and sat down.

"I say, Valérien, give me some fire," [1] said another general, also young, but already corpulent, with immobile eyes looking as though fixed on space, and thick, silky whiskers, in which he slowly buried his snow-white fingers.

Ratmirov handed him a silver match-box.

"*Avez-vous de papiros?*" one of the ladies asked; she could not roll her "r's" properly.

"*De vrais papelitos, Comtesse.*"

"*Deux gendarmes un beau dimanche,*" the shortsighted general again struck up, all but grinding his teeth.

"You simply must call on us," Irena was saying to Litvinov meanwhile. "We are staying at the Hôtel de l'Europe. I am always at home from four to six. It's such a long time since we saw each other."

Litvinov glanced at Irena; she did not lower her eyes.

"Yes, Irena Pavlovna, it is a long time. Not since Moscow."

"Since Moscow, since Moscow," she said slowly. "Come and see me; we'll have a talk and recall the old times. But you know, Grigory Mikhailich, you haven't changed much."

"Really? But you have changed, Irena Pavlovna."

"I've grown older."

"No. That's not what I wanted to say — "

"Irène?" a lady who was wearing a yellow hat on her yellow hair said interrogatively, after a preliminary whisper and giggle with the gentleman sitting beside her. "Irène?"

"I have grown older," Irena continued without answering her, "but I have not changed. No, no, I haven't changed in the least."

"*Deux gendarmes un beau dimanche!*" was now heard again. The irritable general could remember only the first line of the well-known ballad.

"It still stings, Your Excellency," the corpulent general with the whiskers said in a loud voice, probably alluding to some amusing story known to all the beau monde. Laughing a curt, wooden laugh, he again fixed his eyes on space. All the rest of the company also laughed.

"What a sad dog you are, Boris!" Ratmirov remarked in an undertone. He spoke in English and pronounced the name Boris in the English fashion.

---

[1] In English in the original. (Tr.)

"Irène?" the lady in the yellow hat called a third time. Irena turned swiftly to her.

"*Eh bien, quoi? Que me voulez-vous?*"

"*Je vous le dirai plus tard,*" the lady replied in a finicky tone. Despite her quite unattractive appearance, she continually minced her words and grimaced. Some wit had said of her that she "*minaudait dans le vide.*"

Irena knitted her brows and impatiently shrugged her shoulders.

"*Mais que fait donc Monsieur Verdier? Pourquoi ne vient-il pas?*" one lady exclaimed with that drawling emphasis which is a peculiarity of the Great Russian accent, but which the French find unbearable.

"*Ah, voui, ah voui, Msie Verdie, Msie Verdie,*" groaned another lady, who obviously originated directly from Arzamas.[1]

"*Tranquillisez-vous, mesdames,*" Ratmirov intervened. "*Monsieur Verdier m'a promis de venir se mettre à vos pieds.*"

"He-he-he!" The ladies began to play with their fans.

A waiter brought several glasses of beer.

"*Bayrisch bier?*" asked the general with the whiskers, deliberately speaking in a deep tone and pretending to surprised. "*Guten Morgen.*"

"Tell me! Is Count Pavel still there?" one young general coldly and languidly asked another.

"Yes," the other replied as coldly. "*Mais c'est provisoire.* Serge is in his place, they say."

"Aha!" the first general muttered through set teeth.

"M'yes!" the second hissed through his teeth.

"I cannot understand," began the general who had struck up the song, "I cannot understand what made Pavel attempt to justify himself, to make all kinds of excuses. . . . After all, he had squeezed the merchant a bit, *il lui a vait rendre gorge.* . . . But what of it? He may have had his reasons."

"He was afraid — of charges in the press," someone snorted.

The irritable general flared up.

"Well, that's the last word! The press! Charges! If it depended on me, I'd allow that press of yours to print only the taxes on meat or bread, and advertisements for the sale of furs or boots."

"And noblemen's estates for auction," Ratmirov put in.

---

[1] A small provincial town of central Russia, famous for its geese. (Tr.)

"Maybe, in the present circumstances . . . But what a conversation for Baden, *au Vieux Château!*"

"*Mais pas du tout! Pas du tout!*" the lady in the yellow hat lisped. "*J'adore les questions politiques.*"

"*Madame a raison,*" another general with an extremely pleasant and rather girlish face intervened. "Why should we avoid these questions — even in Baden?" With these words he looked at Litvinov courteously and gave him a condescending smile. "An honest man should never and in no circumstances betray his convictions. Isn't that so?"

"Of course," the irritable general replied, also throwing a look at Litvinov and, it seemed, obliquely rebuking him. "But I don't see the necessity — "

"No, no," the condescending general interrupted in his previous mild manner. "Our friend Valerian Vladimirovich just mentioned the sale of noblemen's estates. Well, and isn't that a fact?"

"But in any case it is impossible even to sell them now, no one wants them!" the irritable general exclaimed.

"Maybe — maybe. And for that very reason it is necessary to proclaim the fact — that mournful fact — at every step. We are ruined — excellent; we are impoverished, that is not to be disputed; but we, the large landowners, all the same we represent an element — *un principe*. It is our duty to maintain that principle. *Pardon, madame,* I think you have dropped your handkerchief. When a certain obscurity, so to speak, dominates even the highest minds, we must point, must with humility point" (the general extended his finger), "point out to the citizen with our finger the bottomless pit into which everything is rushing. We must warn him, we must say with respectful firmness: 'Turn, turn back. . . .' That is what we ought to say."

"But it isn't possible to go right back," Ratmirov remarked thoughtfully.

The condescending general only smirked.

"Right back; right back, *mon très cher*. The farther back, the better."

The general again glanced politely at Litvinov. Litvinov could stand no more.

"But surely we haven't to go right back to the days of state anarchy, Your Excellency?"

"Yes, even so far! I express my opinion without ambiguity; everything that has been done must be redone — yes — redone."

"And the 19th of February?" [1]

"And the 19th of February, in so far as that is possible. *On est patriote ou on n' l'est pas.* 'But how about freedom?' they say to me. Do you think the people find this freedom sweet? You ask them —"

"You try," Litvinov retorted, "you try to take that freedom from him —"

"*Comment nommez-vous ce monsieur?*" the general whispered to Ratmirov.

"But what are you talking about?" The corpulent general, who evidently played the role of the spoilt child in this society, suddenly began to speak. "Still about the press? About the quill-drivers? Allow me, I'll tell you an incident I had with a quill-driver — it was extraordinary! I was told that *un folliculaire* had written a pasquil about me. Well, of course, I immediately put him under arrest. They brought the fellow along. 'My friend,' I said, 'how do you dare, you *folliculaire*, to write pasquils about me? I suppose your patriotism conquered you?' 'It did,' he said. 'Well,' I said, 'and do you like money, *folliculaire*?' 'I do,' he said. Then, my dear sirs, I gave him the knob of my stick to smell. 'And do you like that, my angel?' 'No,' he says, 'I don't like that.' 'But you take a good smell of it!' I said; 'my hands are quite clean.' 'I don't like it,' he said, 'and that's sufficient.' 'But I, my soul,' I said, 'I like it very much, only not for myself. Do you understand this allegory, my treasure?' 'I understand,' he said. 'Well, now you be a good boy in the future, and here's a silver ruble for you; clear out and bless me day and night.' And the *folliculaire* departed."

The general laughed, and everybody again laughed after him, all except Irena, who did not even smile, but gazed at the narrator moodily.

The condescending general shook Boris by the shoulder.

"You invented all that story, my dear friend. I should like to see you threatening anybody with a stick. Why, you don't even own a stick. *C'est pour faire rire ces dames.* Just for the sake of talking! But that is not the point. I have just said that we need to

---

[1] Emancipation of the serfs, February 19 (old style), 1861. (Tr.)

go right back. Understand me aright. I am not an enemy of so-called progress; but all these universities and seminaries and elementary schools, these students, these priests' sons, these independent educated classes, all this small fry, *tout ce fond du sac, la petite propriété, pire que le prolétariat*" (the general spoke with an effeminate, almost debilitated voice), "*voilà ce qui m'effraie* — that is where it is necessary to come to a stop — and to stop them." (He gave Litvinov another gracious look.) "Yes, it is necessary to come to a stop. Don't forget that no one ever wants anything, or asks for anything, in our country. Local government, for instance — does anyone ask for it? Do you indeed ask for it? Or you? Or you? Or you, *mesdames*? As it is, you already govern not only yourselves, but all the rest of us" (the general's handsome face lit up with a diverting smile). "My dear friends, why run like a hare? Democracy is glad of you, it flatters you, it is ready to serve your ends . . . but remember it is a two-edged sword. Then surely it is better the old way, the former way — that is far more reliable. Don't allow the rabble to show off their intelligence, but trust in the aristocracy, in which alone is strength. . . . Really, it will be better so. But progress — I myself have nothing against progress. Only don't give us just lawyers, and barristers, and a crowd of officials from the zemstvos,[1] and then there's the question of discipline; above all, don't touch the discipline. But you can build bridges, and embankments, and hospitals, and why not light the streets with gas?"

"Set fire to Petersburg on all four sides, there's your progress!" the irritable general hissed.

"Ah, I see you're in a bad temper," the corpulent general said, lazily swaying. "It would be a good idea to make you attorney general. But in my view, *avec Orphée aux enfers le progrès a dit son dernier mot.*"

"*Vous dites toujours des bêtises*," the lady from Arzamas giggled.

The general assumed a dignified look.

"*Je ne suis jamais plus sérieux, madame, que quand je dis des bêtises.*"

"M'sieur Verdie has already made that same remark more than once," Irena observed in an undertone.

"*De la poigne et des formes!*" exclaimed the corpulent general.

---

[1] Provincial local government organizations. (Tr.)

57

"De la poigne surtout. And that can be translated: politely, but with the first in the teeth!"

"Ah, you're a joker, an incorrigible joker!" the condescending general took him up. "Mesdames, please do not listen to him. He would not hurt a fly. He is content to devastate hearts."

"But, all the same, you're wrong, Boris," Ratmirov began, exchanging glances with his wife. "A joke's a joke, but that's exaggeration. Progress is a manifestation of social life, that is what we mustn't forget; it is a symptom. We must follow it, must watch it."

"Why, yes," the corpulent general retorted, and wrinkled his nose. "We understood that you are aiming at the statesmen!"

"Not at all at the statesmen. What have the statesmen to do with it? But the truth has to be admitted."

Boris again thrust his fingers into his whiskers and fixed his eyes on space.

"The social life is very important, because in the development of the nation, in the destinies, so to speak, of the fatherland — "

"Valérien," Boris interrupted authoritatively, *"il y a des dames ici.* I hadn't expected this of you. Or do you want to be elected to a committee?"

"They're all dissolved now, thank God!" the irritable general observed, and once more began to sing: *"Deux gendarmes, un beau dimanche. . . ."*

Ratmirov raised his batiste handkerchief to his nose and gracefully said no more; the condescending general repeated: "A joker, a joker!" But Boris turned to the lady who was grimacing at empty space and, without lowering his voice, not even changing the expression on his face, began to ask her when she would "crown his flame," because he loved her madly and was suffering extraordinarily.

As this conversation proceeded, Litvinov had felt more and more awkward. His pride, his honest, plebeian pride, rose in indignant revolt. What was there in common between him, the son of a petty official, and these military Petersburg aristocrats? He loved everything that they hated, he hated everything they loved; he saw that all too clearly, he felt it with all his being. He thought their jokes flat, their tone intolerable, their every movement false; in the very gentility of their speech he sensed a revolting contempt — and yet he seemed abashed by them, by these people, these enemies. . . . "Pah! How beastly! I am a constraint on them, they think me funny!" the thought went through his head. "So why am I staying here? I'll go, I'll go at once!" Irena's presence could not detain him; she, too, awakened unhappy feelings in him. He rose from his chair and began to take his leave.

"You're going already?" Irena said. But after a moment's thought she made no attempt to insist on his staying and only persuaded him to promise that he would certainly call on her. General Ratmirov bowed to him with his previous exquisite courtesy, shook his hand, accompanied him to the edge of the platform. . . .

But Litvinov had hardly turned the first bend in the road when a sudden burst of laughter broke out behind him. This laughter had no connection with him, but was aroused by the long expected M'sieur Verdier, who unexpectedly came onto the platform in a Tyrolean hat and a blue blouse, and riding an ass. But the blood rushed to Litvinov's cheeks, and he felt bitter: as though wormwood were gluing his compressed lips together. "Contemptible, ignoble people," he muttered, not realizing that the few moments he had spent in their company gave him no cause to express himself so strongly. And it was into this world that Irena, she who had been his Irena, had fallen! In it she circled, she lived, she reigned, for it she had sacrificed her own dignity, the finest feelings of her heart. . . . Evidently that was as it should be; evidently she was not worthy of a better fate! How he rejoiced that she had not thought of questioning him on his intentions! He would have had to tell her in front of "them," in "their" presence. . . . "Not for anything! Never!" he whispered, taking a deep breath of the fresh air and all but running down the road leading to Baden. He thought of his fiancée, of the dear, kind, good Tatiana; and how pure, how noble and true she seemed to him! With what unfeigned tenderness he recalled her features, her words, her very habits . . . with what impatience he awaited her arrival!

The swift walk soothed his nerves. When he returned to his hotel he sat down at a table and picked up a book, but abruptly dropped it, even shivered. . . . What had happened to him? Nothing had happened to him, but Irena — Irena — his meeting with her suddenly seemed astonishing, strange, extraordinary. Was it possible? Had he met and talked with that same Irena? . . . And why was it that the repulsive, worldly impress that was so firmly stamped on all those others was not noticeable in her? Why did he imagine that she seemed to be bored, or sad, or oppressed with her position? She was in their company, but she was not an enemy. And what could have made her turn to him and so cordially invite him to see her?

Litvinov gave a start. "Oh, Tania, Tania!" he exclaimed passionately; "you alone are my angel, my good genius, you alone do I love and will love forever. I shall not call on her. She can do what she likes! Let her amuse herself with her generals!"

He turned again to his book.

I I

He turned to his book, but he did not read. He left the hotel, strolled about for a while, listened to the music, watched the gaming in the Casino for a time, then returned to his room and again attempted to read — all quite aimlessly. The time seemed to drag past very sluggishly. Pishchalkin, the well-intentioned arbitrator, dropped in and sat on for a good three hours. He talked, he explained, he posed problems, expatiated in turn first on exalted subjects, then on practical subjects, and finally spread such an air of boredom around him that poor Litvinov all but howled. Even among people of the highest morality, who are well known as experts in this regard, Pishchalkin had no rivals in the art of inducing boredom, a yearning, chilly, hopeless, and endless boredom. The very sight of his close-cropped and sleekly greased hair, his light and devitalized eyes, his genteel nose, aroused an involuntary feeling of despondency, while his deliberate, sleepy, baritone voice seemed a chosen instrument for giving persuasive and lucid expression to such platitudes as that two and two are four, and not five or three; that water is wet, and virtue laudable; that a private individual needs credit for financial operations just as much as the state, and the state just as much as a private individual. And with all this he was an excellent man! But then, that is in the very nature of human destiny in Russia: our excellent people are such bores! Pishchalkin departed; he was replaced by Bindasov, who immediately, with great impudence, demanded a loan of a hundred guldens. Litvinov gave it to him, though he was far from interested in Bindasov, and really loathed him and knew perfectly well that he would never get his money back; and yet he had need of it himself. "Then why did he give it to him?"

the reader will ask. The devil knows why! The Russians are great fellows for that sort of thing too. Let the reader set his hand on his heart and recall how many of his own actions have had no other reason whatever. But Bindasov did not even thank Litvinov: he asked for a glass of Affentaler (the red wine of Baden) and left without wiping his lips, and brazenly clattering with his boots. And how vexed Litvinov was with himself, as he stared after the departing peasant miser's golden mane!

Late in the afternoon he received a letter from Tatiana, informing him that she could not arrive in Baden for another five or six days as her aunt was not well. This news had an unpleasant effect on Litvinov: it added to his mortification. And he went to bed early, feeling very down in the mouth.

The following day proved to be no better than its predecessor, and perhaps was even a little worse. From early morning Litvinov's room was inundated with his compatriots; Bambayev, Voroshilov, Pishchalkin, the two officers, the two Heidelberg students, all arrived at once and somehow or other did not depart till dinnertime, though they soon said all they had to say and were obviously bored. They simply did not know what to do with themselves and, once in Litvinov's room, they were "stranded" there, as one says. At first they discussed the fact that Gubariov had gone back to Heidelberg, and declared that everybody ought to go and visit him there. Then they philosophized a little and touched on the Polish question. Then they turned to the discussion of gaming, of *lorettes*, then to telling scandalous stories. Finally the conversation meandered into consideration of athletes, fat men, and gluttons. The time-worn stories about Lukin, the deacon who ate thirty-three herring at one sitting, the Uhlan Colonel Izyedinov, famous for his corpulence, and the soldier who broke a bullock's bone against his forehead were all brought out into the light of God's day, and of course they were followed by out-and-out lies. Pishchalkin himself told with a yawn of how he had known a woman in Malorussia who on her death had been found to weigh nearly a thousand pounds, and of a landowner who ate three geese and a sturgeon for breakfast. Bambayev suddenly went into ecstasies and announced that he himself felt that he could devour a whole sheep, "of course with the trimmings," while Voroshilov retailed some story concerning a comrade of his, a cadet athlete, so utterly absurd that they were all struck dumb, sat in silence, stared at one another, then reached for their hats and departed. Left alone, Litvinov thought he would devote some time to study. But it was just as though his brains were addled; he could not do anything sensible, and the evening also was wasted.

He was getting ready for breakfast next morning when someone knocked at his door. "Lord," he thought, "some of yesterday's friends again," and called, not without a shiver:

"Herein!"

The door was quietly opened, and Potugin entered the room.

Litvinov was extremely delighted to see him.

"Now, this is really pleasant," he said, vigorously shaking his unexpected guest's hand. "Thank you indeed! I would have called on you without fail, but you wouldn't tell me where you are staying. Please sit down and put your hat somewhere. Do sit down."

Potugin made no answer to Litvinov's warm remarks, but stood shifting from foot to foot in the middle of the room and only smiled and shook his head. Litvinov's cordial welcome obviously moved him, but his face had a rather embarrassed expression.

"There's — a little misunderstanding —" he began, not without some hesitation. "Of course, I am always pleased . . . but as a matter of fact I — I have been sent to you."

"That is, you mean," Litvinov said in a mournful tone, "that you wouldn't have called on me of your own choice?"

"Oh no, please don't think that! . . . But I — I don't think I would have ventured to trouble you today if I had not been asked to call on you. In a word, I have a message for you."

"May I ask from whom?"

"From someone you know, from Irena Pavlovna Ratmirova. You promised to call on her two days ago, and you haven't been."

Litvinov stared at him in bewilderment.

"Are you acquainted with Madame Ratmirova?" he asked.

"As you see."

"And well acquainted?"

"I am her friend to some extent."

Litvinov made no comment.

"May I ask you," he said at last, "whether you know why Irena Pavlovna would like to see me?"

Potugin went across to the window.

"Up to a point I do. So far as I can judge, she was very glad to meet you, and, well, she desires to renew her previous relationship."

"Renew," Litvinov repeated. "Excuse me if I seem lacking in modesty, but may I further ask you whether you are aware of the nature of that relationship?"

"No, as a matter of fact, I am not. But I assume," Potugin added, suddenly turning to Litvinov and smiling at him amiably, "I must assume that it was a very good relationship. Irena Pavlovna was full of your praises, and I had to give her my word that I would bring you to her. Will you go?"

"When?"

"Now — this minute."

Litvinov only threw out his hands.

"Irena Pavlovna," Potugin continued, "thinks that that — how can I put it? — that milieu, perhaps, in which you saw her two days ago could hardly have been particularly agreeable to you. But she told me to say that the devil is not so black as he is painted."

"Hm. . . . Does that saying apply expressly to that — milieu?"

"Yes — and more generally."

"Hm. . . . Well, but how about you, Sozont Ivanich? What is your opinion of the devil?"

"I think, Grigory Mikhailich, that in any case he is not what he is made out to be."

"Is he better?"

"Whether better or worse is difficult to decide, but he is not what people think. Well, shall we go, then?"

"But first sit down for a little while. I confess that it seems somewhat strange to me — "

"What does, I dare to ask."

"That you, you in particular, have become a friend of Irena Pavlovna's."

Potugin ran his eyes over himself.

"In view of my figure, and my position in society, it is truly difficult to believe. But, you know, Shakspere said: 'There are more things in heaven and earth, Horatio — ' and so on. And besides, life is not fond of joking. Here is a comparison for you: you are looking at a tree, and there is no wind; how can a leaf on a lower branch manage to touch a leaf on an upper branch? It simply cannot. But then a storm arises, everything is shifted from its place, and the two leaves touch."

"Aha! So there was a storm!"

"Of course! Can you get through life without them? But away with philosophy! It's time we were going."

Even now Litvinov hesitated.

"Oh, Lord!" Potugin exclaimed with a comical grimace. "What is wrong with the young people these days! A very charming lady invites them to call on her, sends express couriers for them, and yet they stand on ceremony! Here's your hat. Take it, and *'vorwärts!'* as our friends the passionate Germans say."

For a moment or two longer Litvinov stood irresolutely, but he ended by picking up his hat and leaving with Potugin.

12

They went to one of the finest hotels in Baden and asked for Mme Ratmirova, the general's wife. The porter first asked their names, then at once replied: *"Die Frau Fürstin ist zu Hause."* He himself conducted them through the hotel, knocked at the door of the suite, and reported their arrival. *"Die Frau Fürstin"* received them at once. She was alone; her husband had gone to Karlsruhe to see a highly placed dignitary, a man of "influence," who was passing through that town.

Irena was sitting at a small table, doing some frame embroidery, when Potugin and Litvinov entered the room. She briskly threw the needle aside, pushed away the table, and rose; her face wore an expression of unfeigned satisfaction. She was wearing a morning gown that fitted closely to the neck; the beautiful contours of her shoulders and arms were revealed through the light material; her carelessly braided hair had come undone and had fallen low over her slender neck. She threw a swift glance at Potugin, whispered: *"Merci,"* and, holding out her hand to Litvinov, gently reproached him for his forgetfulness. "And an old friend, too," she added.

He began to apologize. *"C'est bien, c'est bien,"* she said hurriedly. With gentle force she took his hat from him and made him sit down. Potugin also sat down, but at once got up again, saying that he had urgent business to attend to and that he would drop in after dinner. He began to bow his way out. Irena threw him another swift glance and nodded to him cordially, but did not detain him. As soon as he had disappeared behind the portiere, she turned to Litvinov with impatient vivacity.

"Grigory Mikhailich," she began in Russian in her soft and musical voice, "we're alone at last, and I can tell you that I am very glad of our meeting, because it — it enables me — " (she looked straight into his face) "to ask your forgiveness."

Litvinov involuntarily started. He had not expected such a rapid onslaught. He had not expected that she herself would turn the conversation to talk of the old times.

"Forgiveness — for what?" he muttered.

Irena crimsoned.

"For what? . . . You know for what," she said, and turned a little away from him. "I did you a wrong, Grigory Mikhailich — although, of course, it was my fate" (he recalled her letter) "and I do not repent . . . it would be too late in any case. But, meeting you so unexpectedly, I said to myself that we simply must become friends, simply must . . . and I would be greatly upset if that did not come about. . . . And I think that in order to achieve that friendship I must explain everything to you without delay and once for all, so that there will not afterward be any — *gêne*, any awkwardness; once for all, Grigory Mikhailich. And you must tell me you forgive me; otherwise I shall presume that you are feeling — *de la rancune. Voilà!* Perhaps it is a great deal for me to ask, because you've probably forgotten it all long ago; but all the same, do tell me you forgive me."

She said all this speech without taking breath, and he noticed that tears, real tears, were glittering in her eyes.

"But really, Irena Pavlovna," he hurriedly began, "aren't you ashamed to apologize, to ask forgiveness? . . . It is all a thing of the past, it is gone like a stone into water, and I can only wonder that you, amid all the splendor that surrounds you, could still retain a memory of the obscure companion of your first youth. . . ."

"Does that surprise you?" Irena said quietly.

"It moves me," he retorted, "because I simply could not imagine — "

"But even now you haven't told me you forgive me," she interrupted.

"I am sincerely glad that you are happy, Irena Pavlovna, and with all my heart I wish you all the best that the world can give. . . ."

"And you don't remember the wrong I did you?"

"I remember only those wonderful moments that I once owed to you."

She held out both hands to him. He squeezed them strongly and did not let them go at once. . . . At that gentle touch something that for long had been nonexistent secretly stirred in his heart. Once more she looked straight into his face; but this time she smiled. . . . And he for the first time looked directly and fixedly at her. He again recognized features once so dear, those deep eyes with their extraordinary lashes, and the mole on the cheek, and the special way the hair lay above the brow, and her habit of pleasantly and amusingly twisting her lips and very slightly twitching her eyebrows; he recognized them all — all. . . . But how beautiful she had grown! What enchantment, what strength there was in the youthful femininity of her body! And no rouge, no cerise, nor pencil, nor powder, nothing artificial at all on the fresh, clean face. . . . Yes, she certainly was beautiful!

He fell into a reverie. . . . He was still gazing at her, but his thoughts were far away — she noticed it.

"Well, that's splendid," she said in a loud voice. "Now my conscience is at rest, and I can satisfy my curiosity."

"Curiosity?" he repeated, as though he did not understand.

"Yes, yes — I simply must know what you have been doing all this time, and what your plans are. I want to know everything — what, when, how — everything, everything. And you must tell me the truth, because I warn you I have never lost sight of you — so far as was possible. . . ."

"You did not lose sight of me — there — in Petersburg?"

"Amid all the splendor that surrounded me, as you put it just now. Yes, exactly; I did not lose sight of you. We'll talk later about that splendor, but now you must tell me all that has happened to you, a full story, a long story. No one will interrupt us. Ah, how marvelous it will be!" she added, gaily sitting down and attitudinizing a little in an armchair. "Well, now begin."

"Before I start to tell my story, I must thank you," Litvinov began.

"What for?"

"For the bouquet of flowers I found in my room."

"What bouquet? I don't know anything about it."

"What?"

"I tell you I don't know anything about it. . . . But I'm waiting — waiting for your story. . . . Ah, how clever Potugin was to bring you!"

Litvinov pricked up his ears.

"Have you been acquainted with Mr. Potugin long?" he asked.

"Quite a long time . . . but begin your story."

"And do you know him well?"

"Oh, yes!" Irena sighed. "There are particular reasons. . . . You have heard of Eliza Belskaya, of course — the one that died such a terrible death two years ago? . . . Ah, of course, I had forgotten that you do not know our stories. . . . It is fortunate, fortunate that you do not. Oh, *quelle chance!* At last, at last I have met one man, a living man, who doesn't know anything about us. And one can talk to him in Russian, and though it is a stupid language, still it is Russian and not that everlasting, cloying, repellent Petersburg French!"

"And Potugin, you say, was in contact with — "

"It is very painful for me even to recall it," she interrupted. "Eliza was my best friend in the institute; and later, in Petersburg, we were always seeing each other. She confided all her secrets to me; she was very unhappy, she suffered a great deal. Potugin behaved perfectly in the affair, like a true knight! He sacrificed himself. Only then did I appreciate his true worth. But we've gone off at a tangent again. I am waiting for your story, Grigory Mikhailich."

"But my story cannot interest you in the least, Irena Pavlovna."

"That is not for you to decide."

"Remember, Irena Pavlovna, it is ten years since we saw each other, a whole ten years. How much water has flowed under the bridges since then!"

"Not only water, not only water!" she repeated, with a peculiar, bitter expression. "That is just why I want to hear about you."

"And besides, to tell the truth, I cannot imagine where to begin."

"At the beginning. From that very moment when you — when I went off to Petersburg. You left Moscow then. . . . Do you know, I have never been back to Moscow since."

"Really?"

"At first it was quite impossible. And later, when I married — "

"Have you been married long?"

"Four years."

"Haven't you any children?"

"No," she answered curtly.

Litvinov was silent for a moment.

"And until you were married you lived all the time with, what was his name, Count Reizenbach?"

She looked at him fixedly, as though wishing to discover why he had asked this question.

"No — " she said at last.

"So your parents — By the way, I haven't even asked you about them. How are they?"

"They are both well."

"And still living in Moscow?"

"Still living in Moscow."

"And your brothers and sisters?"

"They're all doing well; I have provided for them all."

"Ah!" He glanced at her from under knitted brows. "In reality, Irena Pavlovna, it is not I but you who should tell the story, if only — "

He suddenly pulled himself up and was silent.

Irena raised her hands to her face and twisted her engagement ring on her finger.

"And why not? I do not refuse to," she said at last. "Some day — perhaps. . . . But first you — because, you see, although I watched you, I know almost nothing about you, but as for me — well, you have certainly heard enough about me. Isn't that so? For you have heard about me, haven't you?"

"Irena Pavlovna, you have occupied too prominent a position in the world not to cause some talk — especially in the provinces, where I was, and where every rumor is believed."

"But did you believe those rumors? And what did they say?"

"I have to admit, Irena Pavlovna, that very few of them came to my ears. I lived a very solitary life."

"Why do you say that? You were in the Crimea, in the general levy, weren't you?"

"Do you know even that?"

"As you see. I told you I have watched you."

68

Smoke

Litvinov could not help being astonished again.

"But why should I bother to tell you what you know already?" he said in an undertone.

"In order — in order to do what I ask. For I do ask you, Grigory Mikhailich."

He bowed his head and began. . . . He began a little incoherently, in general outlines, to tell her his simple adventures. He often stopped and looked at her interrogatively: perhaps she had heard enough? But she insistently demanded that he should continue and, throwing her hair back behind her ears, propping her head on the chair arm, seemed to be listening to every word with the utmost attention. An outsider looking at her and following the expression of her face might, perhaps, have thought that she was not listening at all to what Litvinov said, but was only buried in contemplation. . . . But it was not Litvinov she was contemplating, though he grew embarrassed, and reddened beneath her persistent gaze. Before her arose a whole life, another life — not his, but her own.

He did not finish, but lapsed into silence, constrained by an unpleasant feeling of increasing awkwardness. This time Irena did not say anything to him, did not ask him to go on. Pressing her palm to her eyes as though tired, she slowly leaned back against the chair and was still. He waited a little; then, realizing that his visit had already lasted more than two hours, he reached for his hat. Suddenly the swift stride of thin patent-leather boots sounded in the next room; preceded by the same exquisite perfume, blended of nobility and the guards, Valerian Vladimirovich Ratmirov entered.

Litvinov rose from his chair and exchanged bows with the handsome general. But Irena unhurriedly took her hand from her face and, looking coldly at her husband, said in French: "Ah! So you're back already! But what is the time, then?"

"It will soon be four o'clock, *ma chère amie*, and you're not dressed yet. The Princess will be waiting for us," the general replied. Elegantly inclining his tightly clothed figure toward Litvinov, he added with the almost effeminately playful tone peculiar to him: "Evidently your kindly guest has helped you to kill the time."

At this point the reader will allow us to impart some information concerning General Ratmirov. His father was the natural —

What are you thinking? You are not mistaken, but that is not what I wanted to say — the natural son of an aristocratic magnate of the Alexandrine period and a pretty little French actress. The magnate introduced his son into society, but did not leave him any fortune, and this son (the father of our hero) also failed to achieve a fortune: he died with the rank of colonel and the status of chief of police. A year before his death he married a beautiful young widow who had had to resort to his protection. Valerian Alexandrovich, his son by the widow, was appointed through patronage to the *corps des pages*. He attracted the attention of the authorities, not so much by his successes in study as by his splendid bearing, excellent manners, and good conduct (though he was subjected to everything that students in state military institutions were subjected to at that time), and entered the guards. He made a brilliant career, thanks to the modest cheerfulness of his disposition, his grace in dancing, his masterly horsemanship as orderly at parades — usually on a horse he had never ridden before — and, finally, to some special gift for establishing familiarly respectful relations with higher officers, for a pensively endearing, almost forlorn subservience, with an admixture of vague liberalism, as light as gossamer. . . . This liberalism, however, did not prevent his flogging fifty peasants in a rebellious Byelorussian village to which he was sent to suppress a revolt. He had an attractive and unusually youthful appearance; sleek, ruddy, lithe, and clinging, he enjoyed amazing success with the ladies; the aristocratic old women simply raved about him. Prudent by habit, taciturn by calculation, like an industrious bee extracting the juice from even the meanest of flowers, General Ratmirov continually moved in the highest circles. He was without morals, had the reputation of being efficient though there was no evidence of it, had a nose for people and an understanding of circumstances, but most of all he possessed an unswervingly firm desire for his own good; and at last he saw all roads open before him. . . .

Litvinov smiled forcedly, but Irena only shrugged her shoulders.

"Well," she said in the same cold tone, "did you see the Count?"

"Of course I saw him. He commanded me to convey his greetings to you."

"Ah! And is he just as stupid as ever, your patron?"

Smoke

General Ratmirov did not answer and only laughed a little in his nose, as though indulgent to the temerity of feminine judgment. Kindly adults respond to children's absurd tricks with exactly the same laugh.

"Yes," Irena added, "the stupidity of your Count is only too obvious; and I think I have seen enough in my time."

"You sent me to him yourself," the general snarled. Turning to Litvinov, he asked him in Russian: "Are you taking the Baden waters?"

"I enjoy good health, thank God," Litvinov answered.

"That is much the best," the general continued, smiling amiably. "And besides, nobody comes to Baden for the cure. But the waters here are very effective, *je veux dire, efficaces;* and anyone who suffers, as I do for instance, from a nervous cough — "

Irena rose swiftly to her feet. "We shall see you again, Grigory Mikhailich, and soon, I hope," she said in French, contemptuously interrupting her husband's speech; "but now I must go and dress. That old Princess is unbearable with her everlasting *parties de plaisir,* where there is nothing whatever to do except get bored."

"You are very disparaging today," her husband muttered, and he slipped into the other room.

Litvinov went toward the door. . . . Irena stopped him.

"You have told me all the story," she said, "but have kept the chief thing a secret."

"What are you referring to?"

"They say you are engaged?"

He flushed to his ears. He had in fact deliberately said nothing about Tania; but now he felt terribly vexed, first that Irena knew about his forthcoming marriage, and secondly that she seemed to be charging him with a desire to conceal that marriage from her. He simply did not know what to say, and she did not remove her eyes from him.

"Yes, I am getting married," he said at last, and went at once.

Ratmirov returned to the room.

"Well, why aren't you dressing?" he asked.

"Go by yourself; I have a headache."

"But the Princess — "

Irena measured her husband with a look from head to foot, turned her back on him, and went to her room.

71

13

Litvinov was far from satisfied with himself; he felt as though he had lost at roulette or had broken his word. An inner voice told him that as a fiancé, as a man with a sense of responsibility and no longer a boy, he should not have yielded either to the prick of curiosity or to the seduction of memories. "Much need I had to go!" he deliberated. "On her part it is only coquetry, a whim, caprice. . . . She's bored, she's sick of everything, she's clutched at me . . . a gourmet suddenly has a fancy for some black bread . . . well, and very nice too. But what did I go for? Is it possible that I — do not feel contempt for her?" It cost him some effort to pronounce the word "contempt," even mentally. "Of course, there is no danger whatever in it, nor can there be," he continued his deliberations. "After all, I know whom I'm dealing with. But, all the same, one shouldn't play with fire. . . . I shan't set foot in her place again." He did not dare to think or else he was not yet conscious of how beautiful she had seemed to him and how strongly she had moved him.

That day also dragged by idiotically and interminably. At dinner he found himself sitting next to a portly *belle-homme* with dyed whiskers, who sat without speaking and only puffed and goggled his eyes. . . . He suddenly hiccuped, however, and proved to be a fellow countryman, for he remarked angrily in Russian: "But I said it wasn't wise to eat the melon!" Nor did anything of a consoling nature happen during the evening. Under Litvinov's very eyes Bindasov won a sum four times as large as the amount he had borrowed, yet he not only did not return his debt, but he even stared threateningly right into Litvinov's face, as though to penalize him even more just because he had seen him win.

Next morning another horde of compatriots poured into his room. He managed at last to get away from them and, setting off into the hills, first ran into Irena — he pretended not to recognize her and walked swiftly past — then into Potugin. He would have stopped to talk, but Potugin did not give him any encouragement. He was holding the hand of a smartly dressed little girl with fluffy, lint-white curls, large black eyes in a pale, sickly little face, and that peculiar, imperative, and impatient expression that spoilt children wear. Litvinov spent a couple of hours in the hills

Smoke

and returned home along the Lichtentaler Allee. . . . A lady in a blue veil, who was sitting on a bench, briskly rose and came up to him. . . . He recognized Irena.

"Why are you avoiding me, Grigory Mikhailovich?" she said in the uncertain tone that indicates a heart in turmoil.

He was embarrassed. "I avoid you, Irena Pavlovna?"

"Yes, you — you. . . ."

She seemed agitated, almost angry.

"You are mistaken, I assure you."

"No, I am not mistaken. This morning — when we met — do you think I didn't see that you recognized me? Will you say you didn't recognize me? Will you?"

"Really I — Irena Pavlovna — "

"Grigory Mikhailovich, you are not a deceitful man, you always told the truth; tell me, tell me, you did recognize me, didn't you? You deliberately turned away, didn't you?"

He glanced at her. Her eyes were glittering with a peculiar glitter, but behind the fine mesh of her veil her cheeks and lips were of a deathly pallor. The expression of her face, the very sound of her impetuous whisper, was so invincibly mournful, imploring. . . . He could not keep up the pretense any longer.

"Yes — I recognized you," he said, not without effort.

She gently shivered and gently dropped her hands.

"Why didn't you come and speak to me?" she whispered.

"Why didn't I — why?" He turned off the path; she silently followed him. "Why?" he repeated yet again, and his face suddenly flamed, and a feeling akin to anger clutched at his chest and throat. "You — you ask that, after all that has happened between us? Not now, of course, not now, but there — there — in Moscow."

"But you see we decided, but you promised — " Irena began.

"I promised nothing. You must forgive the harshness of my words, but you ask the truth, so judge for yourself: to what can I ascribe your — I do not know what to call it — your persistence if not to coquetry — which I admit I find incomprehensible — or a desire to see how far you still have power over me? Our roads have parted so completely! I had forgotten it all, I had got beyond all that pain long since, I had become quite a different man; and you are married, are happy, at least superficially, you enjoy an enviable position in the world; then what is the purpose, what is

73

the object of this new approach? What am I to you, or you to me? We cannot even understand each other now, we have nothing whatever in common now, neither in the past nor in the present! Especially — especially in the past!"

He uttered all this speech hurriedly, jerkily, without looking at her. She did not stir and only held out her hands a little toward him from time to time. She seemed to be imploring him to halt and listen to her. But at his last words she slightly bit her lower lip, as though suppressing a feeling of acute and sudden pique.

"Grigory Mikhailich . . ." she began at last in a more composed voice, and she walked still farther away from the path, to avoid occasional strollers.

He followed her.

"Grigory Mikhailich, believe me: if I imagined that I still had the least power over you, I would rather avoid you. If I did not do that, if I decided, despite — despite my former guilt, to renew my acquaintance with you, it is because — because — "

"Why?" he asked almost roughly.

"Because," Irena replied with sudden strength, "it has now become too intolerably, unbearably stifling for me in that world, in that enviable position you have spoken of. Because, having met you, a living man, after all those dead dolls — you saw specimens of them three days ago, at the *Vieux Château* — I rejoiced as though I had found a spring in the desert. But you call me a coquette and are suspicious of me, and repulse me under the pretext that I really was to blame in regard to you, and even more in regard to myself."

"You chose your own lot, Irena Pavlovna," he said moodily, still not looking at her.

"I did, I did — nor do I complain, I have no right to complain," she said hurriedly, and apparently his very harshness gave her secret comfort. "I know that you must condemn me, nor do I attempt to justify myself. I only want to explain my feeling to you, I want to convince you that I am far from coquetry now. . . . I behave like a coquette with you! Why, there's no sense in it. . . . When I saw you, all the good, the youthful in me was awakened . . . the time when I had not yet chosen my lot, all that lies back in that happy period, beyond the past ten years."

"But now you really must forgive me, Irena Pavlovna! So far

as I know, the happy period of your life began from the very moment when we parted. . . ."

She raised her handkerchief to her lips.

"That is a very cruel thing to say, Grigory Mikhailich; but I cannot be angry with you. Oh no, that time was not happy, not for happiness did I leave Moscow; not one minute, not one second of happiness have I known — believe me, no matter what others may tell you. If I had been happy, could I talk to you as I am talking now? . . . I repeat, you do not know what those people are. . . . You see, they understand nothing, they have no feeling for anything, they haven't even any mind, *ni esprit, ni intelligence,* but only cunning, and a certain flair. Why, fundamentally music, and poetry, and art are all equally alien to them. . . . You will say that I myself was rather indifferent to all that; but not to such an extent, Grigory Mikhailich — not to such an extent! It is not a woman of society that stands before you now — you have only to glance at me — no lioness — that is what I think they call us — but a poor, poor creature, who, in very truth, is deserving of pity. Don't be astonished at my words — I am not concerned about pride now! I extend my hand to you as a beggar — do realize that clearly — as a beggar. . . . I ask for alms," she added suddenly with an involuntary, irresistible outburst. "I ask for alms, but you — "

Her voice betrayed her. He raised his head and looked at her. She was breathing rapidly, her lips were quivering. His heart suddenly began to pound, and his feeling of anger disappeared.

"You say our roads have separated," she went on. "I know you are marrying according to your inclination, and you have now drawn up a plan to cover all your life. Yes, that is all true, but we haven't grown alien to each other, Grigory Mikhailich, we can still understand each other. Or do you suppose that I have grown quite unfeeling, that I have sunk completely into that mud? Ah, no, please don't think that! Let me unburden my soul, I ask you, if only in the name of those former days, if you do not want to forget them. Let your response be such that our meeting shall not have been in vain: that would be very bitter; as it is, it will not last long. . . . I do not know how to say what I want to say, but you will understand me, because I ask little, very little — only a little sympathy, only that you will not repulse me, but will let me unburden my soul. . . ."

She was silent; tears had sounded in her voice. She sighed, and timidly, with a sidelong, questioning gaze, looked at him, held out her hand to him. . . .

He slowly took that hand and feebly squeezed it.

"Let us be friends," Irena whispered.

"Friends," he repeated thoughtfully.

"Yes, friends . . . but if that is too great a demand, then let us at least be good acquaintants. . . . Let us be simply as if nothing had ever happened."

"As if nothing had ever happened . . ." he again repeated her words. "You just told me, Irena Pavlovna, that I do not want to forget the former days. . . . Ah, but supposing I cannot forget them?"

A blissful smile flickered across Irena's face and at once vanished, to be replaced by an anxious, almost frightened expression.

"Be like me, Grigory Mikhailich, remember only the good. But, above all, give me your word now — your word of honor — "

"What for?"

"Not to avoid me — not to grieve me unnecessarily. . . . You promise? Tell me!"

"I promise."

"And you will drive all unpleasant thoughts out of your head?"

"Yes. . . . But all the same I give up trying to understand you."

"It isn't even necessary to understand — yet wait a little and you will understand me. But you promise?"

"I have already said yes."

"Well, thank you. But beware, I am accustomed to believing you. I shall expect you today, or tomorrow; I shall not leave the hotel. But now I must leave you. The Duchess is coming along the avenue. . . . She has seen me, and I cannot avoid speaking to her. . . . *Au revoir.* . . . But give me your hand, *vite, vite. Au revoir.*"

Giving his hand a strong squeeze, Irena went toward a woman of middle age and majestic appearance who was walking heavily along the sandy path, accompanied by two other ladies and a liveried, extremely good-looking lackey.

"*Eh bonjour, chère madame,*" the lady said as Irena respectfully curtsied to her. "*Comment allez-vous aujourd'hui? Venez un peu avec moi.*"

Smoke

"Votre Altesse a trop de bonté," Litvinov heard Irena's ingratiating voice.

14

He allowed the Duchess and all her suite to proceed for some distance; then he, too, emerged into the avenue. He could not be quite certain of his feelings: he felt ashamed, and even afraid, and his self-esteem was flattered. . . . The unexpected explanation with Irena had taken him by surprise; her burning, hurried words had passed over him like a threatening shower. "All these society women are queer," he thought; "they've got no sense of logic . . . and how they are perverted by the milieu in which they live, and the infamy that they themselves are conscious of! . . ." To be exact, he did not think this at all, but only mechanically repeated these hackneyed phrases, as if by doing so he hoped to rid himself of other, more frightening thoughts. He realized that it was not advisable to indulge in serious reflection at the moment, that if he did in all probability he would be bound to upbraid himself, and he walked along with loitering steps, almost forcing himself to pay attention to whatever he met. . . . He suddenly noticed that he was level with a bench, noticed someone's legs, ran his eyes upward over them. . . . The legs belonged to a man sitting on the bench and reading a newspaper. The man was Potugin. Litvinov let fall a muffled exclamation. Potugin laid the newspaper on his knees and gazed at him fixedly, without a smile; and Litvinov gazed at Potugin also fixedly and also without a smile.

"May I sit down beside you?" he asked at last.

"Certainly; I shall be delighted. Only I warn you: if you want to carry on conversation with me now, don't get angry; at present I am in a very misanthropic mood, and I have an exaggeratedly unpleasant view of everything."

"I don't mind, Sozont Ivanich," Litvinov said, dropping on the bench; "in fact, it is very much how I feel. . . . But why are you in this mood?"

"In reality I have no right to be annoyed," Potugin began. "I've just been reading in this newspaper about the draft bill for the transformation of the judicial system in Russia, and I note with genuine satisfaction that we, too, have at last got some sense and intelligence and are no longer intending to attach a home-grown tail to pure and clear European logic, under the pretext of our independence, nationality, or originality. On the contrary, we are taking a good foreign thing in its entirety. No more making isolated concessions to the peasantry. . . . Now we are to settle the general question of landownership! Truly, truly, I ought not to be annoyed; but, unfortunately for me, I ran into one of our Russian natural prodigies and had a talk with him; and these natural prodigies and self-educated people will give me cause for anxiety even in the grave!"

"Who was this natural prodigy?" Litvinov asked.

"Why, there's some gentleman running about Baden who regards himself as a musical genius. 'I,' he says, 'of course, am nothing, I am a cipher, for I haven't studied; but I have incomparably more melodies and more ideas than Meyerbeer.' To begin with, I ask, and why didn't he study? And secondly, even without mentioning Meyerbeer, the most insignificant German flautist who modestly whistles his part in the worst of German orchestras has twenty times as many ideas as all our rough diamonds; only the flautist keeps these ideas to himself and doesn't brag about them in the land of Mozarts and Haydns. But our rough diamond strums a little waltz or a ballad, and then you see him with his hands in his pantaloons and his mouth twisted contemptuously; 'I,' he says, 'am a genius!' And it's just the same in painting, and in everything else. Oh, these natural prodigies — I've had enough of them! And everybody knows that they are boasted of only in those countries where there is neither genuine science, something that has passed into the people's flesh and blood, nor genuine art. Surely it is time to put an end to all this bragging, this common lumber, together with all the well-known phrases to the effect that in Russia no one ever dies of hunger, and road travel is the fastest in the world, and that we can do everything better than anyone else? They sicken me with their impudent talk about the ability of the Russian character, with their 'instinctive genius,' with their Kulibin. . . . But where is that ability, for goodness' sake, gentlemen? It's nothing but the fuddled talk of a man half asleep, or else it's a bestial cunning. Instinct! There they've found something to boast about! Catch an ant in the forest and carry it a mile from its nest, and it will find its own way home. Man cannot do anything like that, but does that mean that he is lower than an ant? Instinct, even if it be of the highest genius, is un-

worthy of man. Reason — simple, healthy, everyday reason — that
is our clear achievement, our pride; reason never plays such tricks,
and that is why everything is guided by it. But as for Kulibin,
who, without knowing anything about mechanics, constructed
some perfectly monstrous clock — I'd order that clock to be exhibited on a pillory. Look, good people, I'd say, and see how
things should not be done. In this case Kulibin himself is not to
blame, but all the same his work is rubbish. People praise Telush-
kin for his daring and agility because he climbed the Admiralty
Needle [1] — let them; why not praise him? But that doesn't justify
us in shouting: 'Look how he has shown up the German archi-
tects! And what good are they? All they do is take our money.
. . .' He didn't show them up at all; but afterward a forest of
timber had to be raised round the Needle for it to be mended in
quite an ordinary manner. For God's sake, don't encourage us
Russians to think that anything can be achieved without study!
No; you can have as much brains as you like, but study, study
from the A B C up! Otherwise be quiet and sit still with your
tail tucked under you! Pfooh, it's made me go quite hot!"

Potugin took off his hat and fanned himself with his handkerchief.

"Russian art," he began again, "Russian art! . . . I know the
Russian resilience, and I know the Russian impotence too; but
I'm sorry, I've never come across Russian art. For twenty years
continuously they did homage to that inflated nullity Briullov,[2]
and imagined that we, too, had developed a school, and that it
would be even purer than all others. . . . Russian art, ha-ha-ha!
ho-ho!"

"But all the same, pardon me, Sozont Ivanich," Litvinov remarked, "so you don't accept Glinka?"

Potugin scratched himself behind his ear.

"You know, exceptions only prove the rule; but even in this
case we couldn't refrain from bragging! Nobody would bother
to deny that, for instance, Glinka was certainly a remarkable
musician, whom only circumstances, both internal and external,
prevented from being the founder of Russian opera. But no, how
can one stop there! Now he must be raised to the rank of *général
en chef*, the *Oberhofmarschall* in the musical field; and not only

[1] An architectural feature of the Admiralty in Petersburg. (Tr.)
[2] Famous eighteenth-century Russian painter. (Tr.)

that, but other nations have got to be depreciated: they've got nothing in the least like it, and then they ask us to admire some 'mighty' home-grown genius whose works are nothing but a miserable imitation of second-rate foreign composers — and the second-rate especially, for it is easier to imitate them. Nothing in the least like it! Oh, beggarly idiot barbarians, for whom there is no such thing as succession in art, and artists are something on the lines of Rappot: the foreigner can lift two hundredweight with one hand, but our man can lift four hundredweight! Nothing in the least like it? But I venture to tell you that the following memory is always with me: Last spring I was visiting the Crystal Palace near London. As you know, this palace contains a kind of exhibition of everything human inventiveness has achieved, it is an encyclopedia of humanity, that has to be admitted. Well, I walked, I walked past all these machines and weapons, and the statues of great men; and I thought then: if an order were to be issued that when any nation disappears from the face of the earth everything that that nation has invented must disappear from the Crystal Palace — our Little Mother, the true-believing Russia, could sink into the bottomless pit, and the darling's disappearance would not disturb a single little nail, not a single little pin. Everything would remain quite undisturbed in its place, because even the samovars, and the bast shoes, and the yoke, and the knout — all those celebrated products of ours — were not of our invention. It would be impossible to make such an experiment even with the Sandwich Islands; their inhabitants have invented boats and spears, and the visitors to the exhibition would notice their absence. That is a slander, that is too harsh, you may say. . . . But I say, to begin with, that I don't know how to censure with a smile; and secondly, that evidently it is impossible for anyone to look not only the devil, but even himself straight in the eye; and in Russia it isn't only the children that like lullabies. Our old fables reached us from the East, our new ones we have taken over from the West, but we still go on talking about independent Russian art! Other brave fellows have even discovered a Russian science: why, twice two are four in Russia too, and for some reason it is more clever there."

"But wait a moment, Sozont Ivanich," Litvinov exclaimed, "wait a moment! After all, we, too, are sending something to the universal exhibitions, and surely Europe is acquiring something from us?"

"Yes, raw stuff, raw materials. And note, my dear sir: to a large extent that raw material of ours is good only because it is conditioned by other wretched circumstances. Our bristles, for instance, are long and hard because our pigs are of poor quality; our hides are solid and thick because the cows are miserable specimens; the lard is rich because it is rendered down half with the meat. . . . For that matter, why should I expatiate to you on that subject? You're studying technology, you ought to know it all better than I. Inventiveness, they tell me! Russian inventiveness! Our landowner gentry complain bitterly and suffer losses because we haven't any satisfactory grain-driers which would save them the necessity of putting the shocks in drying-barns, just as they did in the time of Rurik.[1] Those drying-barns are terribly unprofitable, just like bast shoes and bast matting, and they're always catching fire. The landowners complain, but we're still without grain-driers. And why are we? Because the Germans don't need them; they thresh their grain damp, and so they don't worry about inventing them, while we — are unable to! Unable to — and that's the end of it. No matter how much you need them! From this day onward I promise myself that whenever some rough diamond or self-taught specimen is exposed to me, I shall say to him: 'Stop, my worthy sir, but where is the grain-drier? Let us have it!' But how can he? Now, if it's a case of picking up some old, well-patched shoe that has long since dropped off the foot of a Saint-Simon or a Fourier and of reverentially setting it on our head, treating it as a sacred relic — that we can do; or of scribbling a little article on the historical and modern significance of the proletariat in the chief cities of France — that, too, we can do. But I once suggested to some writer and political economist like your Mr. Voroshilov that he should name me twenty towns in that same France, and do you know what came of it? The result was that in his despair the political economist finally mentioned Mont-Fermelle, probably remembering Paul de Kock's novel. And now I have just remembered the following story. I was making my way through a forest with a gun and a dog one day — "

"Are you a hunter, then?" Litvinov asked.

[1] Varangian founder of Novgorod principality, died A.D. 873.

"I shoot a bit. I was making my way to a marsh after snipe; some other hunters had told me about this marsh. I looked and saw a fellow as fresh and pithy as a shelled nut, sitting in a glade outside a small hut. There he was sitting and smirking, what at, goodness knows. And I asked him: 'Where's the marsh around here, and are there any snipe in it?' 'Certainly, certainly'; he began to sing immediately, looking just as if I had given him a ruble. 'With great pleasure; the marsh is first-class, and as for all kinds of wild birds — my God, there is an excellent abundance.' I set off, but not only did I not find any wild birds, but even the marsh had long since dried up. Well, tell me for mercy's sake, why does the Russian tell lies? Why should a political economist lie, and about a wild bird, too?"

Litvinov did not answer and only sighed sympathetically.

"But you start talking to that same political economist," Potugin went on, "about the most difficult tasks of social science, only in generalities, without adducing any facts — whir! he soars like a bird, like an eagle. But on one occasion I managed to catch one such bird: as you will see, the decoy I used was well and truly visible. I was talking with one of our present-day 'young hopefuls' about various questions, as they put it. Well, he was very angry, as usual; and among other things he rejected marriage with a simply childish obstinacy. I put forward various arguments . . . but it was like beating your head against a wall! I could see there was no way of getting at him at all. And then I had a happy thought! 'Permit me to say,' I began — you always have to talk respectfully to young hopefuls — 'that I am amazed at you, my dear sir; you are interested in natural sciences, yet so far you have given not the slightest consideration to the fact that all the carnivorous animals and beasts of prey, all animals and birds that have to go out to catch their prey, work hard to supply living food for themselves and their children . . . but you include man among such creatures, don't you?' 'Of course I do,' the young hopeful retorted, 'man generally is nothing but a carnivorous animal.' 'And a beast of prey,' I added. 'And a beast of prey,' he confirmed. 'Well said!' I declared. 'Well then, I am surprised you haven't noticed that all such creatures live in monogamy?' The young hopeful started. 'What's that?' 'Why, it's quite true. Think of the lion, the wolf, the fox, the hawk, the kite; and besides, what else could they do? You try to think. It's difficult enough even for the two of them to feed the children.' My young hopeful was lost in thought. 'Well,' he said, 'in that case man must not copy the animals.' At that I called him an idealist, and then he was annoyed! He all but wept. I had to comfort him and promise that I would not betray him to his comrades. To earn the name of idealist — is that easy to bear? That's the whole point, that our young people of today have gone wrong in their calculations. They imagine that the time of the former, obscure underground work has passed, that it was all right for their old fathers to burrow like moles, but that for us such a role is humiliating, we shall act aboveground, we shall act — My dear fellows! Not even your children will act. But wouldn't it be as well for you to go on burrowing, burrowing in the tracks of your fathers?"

There was a brief silence.

"I, dear sir, am of the opinion," Potugin began once more, "that we are not obliged to civilization only for knowledge, art, and laws, but that the very feeling of beauty and poetry develops and comes into force under the influence of that same civilization, and that so-called popular, naïve, unconscious creation is absurd rubbish. Even in Homer one can already perceive the traces of a refined and rich civilization; even love is ennobled by it. The Slavophils would willingly hang me for such a heresy if they were not such tender-hearted creatures; but, all the same, I stand by my guns, and no matter how much they regale me with Madame Kokhanovskaya [1] and 'swarm in peace,' I shan't take even a sniff at that *triple extrait de moujik russe,* because I don't belong to higher society. From time to time that society has to reassure itself that it is not in the least Frenchified, and in fact this literature *en cuir de Russie* is specially written for it. You try reading the most trenchant, the most 'popular' parts of *Swarm* to one of the common people — the real sort — he'll think you're informing him of a new attack upon fraud or hard drinking. I repeat, without civilization there is no poetry. Do you want to get a clear idea of the poetic ideal of the uncivilized Russian? Glance through our folk poems, our legends. I won't adduce the fact that in them love is always the result of magic, of a love-potion, is produced by a 'philter' and is even called a spell, an enchantment. Nor do I adduce the fact that among all the European and Asiatic literatures our

[1] Pseudonym of Nadezhda Stepanova Sokhansky (1825-84), Russian writer of stories of the provincial gentry. (Tr.)

so-called epic literature alone (alone, mark you) failed to produce (if we leave Ivan and Tania out of account) any typical loving couple; not that the Holy Russian hero always opens his acquaintance with his 'destined future' by beating her on her white body 'mercilessly,' and as the result 'the female sex lives as a hireling.' I shall not stop to discuss all that, but I do take the liberty of drawing your attention to the magnificent specimen of youth, the *jeune-premier*, as he was delineated in the imagination of the primitive, uncivilized Slav. Here he comes, the *jeune-premier*; he has made himself a fur coat of marten skins stitched down all the seams; his belt is fastened right up under his armpits; his fingers are covered with gloves; the fur collar is turned up above his head, you can't see his ruddy face from the front, nor his white neck from the back; his little cap rides over one ear, and on his feet are morocco-leather boots, with toes like awls, and pointed heels — round the point of the toe you can roll an egg, under the heels a sparrow can flutter and fly. And this youngster walks with mincing little steps, that celebrated 'elegant' gait with which our Russian Alcibiades, Churilo Plenkovich, produced such an astonishing, almost medicinal effect on the old women and young girls; the very same gait with which that cream, that flower of Russian elegance, that *nec plus ultra* of Russian taste, our native waiter, even today minces so inimitably with all his joints loose. I am not joking when I say that our artistic ideal is a baggy jauntiness. A fine picture, isn't it? With plenty of material in it for painting, for sculpture? And what of the beauty who captivates the youth, and who has 'as much blood in her face as if she were a hare'? However, I rather think you are not listening to me?"

Litvinov started. It was true that he had not been listening to Potugin; he was thinking, persistently thinking about Irena, about his last meeting with her. . . .

"Excuse me, Sozont Ivanich," he began, "but I want to ask you again my previous question about . . . about Madame Ratmirova."

Potugin folded his newspaper and thrust it into his pocket.

"You want to know again how I made her acquaintance?"

"No, not that; I should like to have your opinion — of the role she played in Petersburg. What was that role really?"

"To tell the truth, I don't know what to say, Grigory Mikhailich. I became quite friendly with Madame Ratmirova — but quite

Smoke

by accident and not for any length of time. I did not even look into her world, and what went on there remained unknown to me. Certain things were talked about in my hearing, and, as you know, in Russia slander is prevalent not only in democratic circles. For that matter, I was not curious. I see, however," he added after a brief silence, "that you are interested in her."

"Yes; we have had a couple of very frank talks. But I still ask myself: is she sincere?"

Potugin looked down. "When she is interested she is sincere, like all passionate women. Her pride also sometimes prevents her telling lies."

"But is she proud? I rather would say she is capricious."

"As proud as a demon; but that is nothing."

"It seems to me she exaggerates sometimes . . ."

"That, too, is nothing; she is still sincere. But, in any case, whom would you go to for truth? The very finest of these ladies is depraved to the marrow of her bones."

"But, Sozont Ivanich, remember, didn't you yourself say you were her friend? Wasn't it you yourself who took me to her almost by force?"

"And what of it? She asked me to bring you; and I thought: 'Well, why not?' But I really am her friend. She isn't lacking in some good qualities: she is very kind, I mean generous; I really mean that she gives others what she herself has no absolute need of. But, after all, you should know her just as well as I do."

"I knew Irena Pavlovna ten years ago; but since then — "

"Ah, Grigory Mikhailich, what are you suggesting? Does the human character change? What we are in the cradle, we are in the grave. Or, perhaps — " at this point Potugin huddled into himself still more — "perhaps you are afraid of falling into her hands? That certainly — But then, you can't avoid falling into someone's hands."

Litvinov smiled forcedly. "Do you think so?"

"You just can't. Man is weak, woman is strong, chance is all-powerful, to reconcile oneself to a colorless existence is difficult, completely to forget oneself is impossible . . . and then come beauty and sympathy, and warmth and light — how can you resist? And you run like a child to its nurse. Well, and afterward, of course, come cold and gloom, and emptiness — as usual. And it ends with your getting unaccustomed to everything, you cease to understand anything. In the beginning you will not understand how anyone can love; but afterward you will not understand how it is possible to live."

Litvinov stared at Potugin and thought that he had never met a man more lonely, more friendless — more unhappy. On this occasion he was not diffident, he was not formal; utterly morose and pale, with his head on his chest and his hands on his knees, he sat motionless and only smiled a despondent smile. Litvinov felt sorry for this poor, splenetic eccentric.

"Among other matters," he began in an undertone, "Irena Pavlovna mentioned a certain close acquaintance of hers, whose name was, I think, Belskaya or Dolskaya — "

Potugin glanced at Litvinov.

"Ah!" he said gruffly. "She mentioned her — well, and what of it? However," he added, yawning unnaturally, "it's time I was getting home, to dinner. I must ask your pardon."

He jumped up from the bench and strode away briskly before Litvinov had time to utter a word. . . . His pity was replaced by a feeling of vexation, with himself, of course. Immodesty of any kind was not natural to him; he had simply wanted to express his sympathy. But the result had been rather like an inept innuendo. With secret discontent in his heart he returned to his hotel.

"Depraved to the marrow of her bones," he thought a little later . . . "but as proud as a demon! She, this woman who all but goes down on her knees to me — proud? Proud, and not capricious?"

He tried to drive Irena's picture out of his head, but he could not. And so he did not even attempt to think of his fiancée; he felt sure that that picture would not give way today. He decided that, without worrying himself any more, he would await the denouement of all this "strange history." The denouement could not be delayed, and he had not the least doubt that it would be quite harmless and natural. So he thought, but meanwhile it was not only Irena's picture that would not leave him: all her words passed successively through his memory.

A waiter brought him a note; it, too, was from Irena.

"If you are doing nothing this evening, come and see me. I shall not be alone; I shall have guests, and you will see our circle, our society, at even closer quarters. I very much want you to see them, I think they will display themselves in all their glory. And it is important that you should know the kind of air I breathe. Do come; I shall be glad to see you, and you will not be bored" (she had wanted to write: "bored with me"). "Prove to me that our talk today has once for all made any misunderstanding between us impossible. Your devoted, I."

Litvinov put on his frock coat and made his way to Irena's hotel. "It is all very trivial," he mentally repeated as he went, "and I can take a look at them — why shouldn't I? It will be interesting." A few days previously these same people had aroused a different feeling in him: they had aroused a feeling of indignation.

He walked at a rapid pace, with his hat pulled down over his eyes, with a tense smile on his lips. And Bambayev, who was sitting outside Weber's café, pointed him out in the distance to Voroshilov and Pishchalkin and exclaimed enthusiastically: "D'you see that man? He's a stone! He's a rock! He's granite!"

15

He found quite a large number of guests already arrived. Three of the generals at the picnic — the fat, the irritable, and the condescending one — were sitting at a card-table in a corner. They were playing dummy whist, and no words in any human language could convey the seriousness with which they dealt, took tricks, led with clubs, led with diamonds . . . they were true statesmen! Leaving it to the independent professions, to the bourgeoisie, to indulge in the stories and facetious remarks customary at cards, the generals uttered only the most indispensable words. The stout general did, however, allow himself to roll out energetically between two deals: *"Ce satané as de pique!"* Among the visitors Litvinov recognized ladies who had been present at the picnic; but there were others he had not previously seen. One of them was so old that she looked as though she would fall to pieces at any moment; she wriggled her bare, horrible, dark-gray shoulders and, covering her mouth with her fan, gave Ratmirov languid looks with her already quite dead eyes. He danced attendance on her: in high society she was greatly respected as the last surviving lady in waiting of the Empress Catherine. By the window, dressed as a shepherdess, sat Countess Sh., "the Princess Wasp," surrounded with young people; among them was the celebrated, rich, handsome Finikov, distinguished from the rest by his haughty bearing, perfectly flat cranium, and his soullessly animal facial expression, worthy of a khan of Bokhara or a Roman Heliogabalus. Another lady, also a countess, known by the brief name of Lise, was talking to a long fair-haired pale-faced "spiritualist"; beside them stood a gentleman, also pale and long-haired, who laughed meaningly. This gentleman also believed in spiritualism, but in addition he engaged in prophecy and on the basis of the Apocalypse and the Talmud foretold all kinds of amazing events. None of these events ever came to pass, yet he was never disconcerted, but continued to prophesy. At the piano was that same natural prodigy who had moved Potugin to such indignation; he played chords with an abstracted hand, *d'une main distraite*, and looked about him. Irena was sitting on a divan between Prince Coco and Mme X, a once well-known beauty and all-Russian wit, who had long since been transformed into a worthless toadstool and gave off a scent of vegetable oil and stale poison. When Irena saw Litvinov she flushed, rose, and, when he went across to her, squeezed his hand firmly. She was wearing a black crepe gown with hardly perceptible gold ornamentation; her shoulders were of an unpolished marble whiteness, and her face, also white beneath the momentary crimson wave that flooded over it, breathed with the exultation of beauty, and not only of beauty: a repressed, almost a mocking joy shone in her half-closed eyes, fluttered round her lips and nostrils. . . .

Ratmirov came up to Litvinov and, after exchanging the customary greetings, which were not, however, accompanied by his usual playfulness, introduced him to two or three ladies, including the old ruin, the Princess Wasp, and Countess Lise. . . . They received him quite favorably. He did not belong to their little circle . . . but he was quite, in fact very handsome, and the expressive features of his youthful face aroused their interest. He was not capable of retaining that interest, however; he was not accustomed to society and felt embarrassed; and now the stout general also fixed his eyes on him. "Aha! the partridge, the freethinker!" that immobile, heavy gaze seemed to be saying, "so he's come crawling into our circle, with a 'give me your hand.' " Irena came to Litvinov's rescue. She arranged matters so neatly that he found himself in a corner by the door, a little behind her. Whenever she spoke to him she had to turn round, and each time she turned he delighted in the beautiful curve of her gleaming neck,

he drank in the subtle scent of her hair. The expression of gratitude, profound and still, did not pass from her face; he could not
but recognize that it was indeed gratitude that those smiles, those
glances expressed, and he himself was seething with the same feeling, and he felt conscience-stricken, and blissful, and horrified.
. . . And at the same time she seemed continually to be saying:
"Well, what do you think of them? What are they like?" Litvinov caught that unspoken question even more clearly whenever
one of the company said or committed some banality; and that
happened more than once during the evening. On one occasion
even she could not restrain herself, and she laughed outright.

Countess Lise, a highly superstitious lady who was drawn toward all things supernatural, talked to her heart's content with
the fair-haired spiritualist about Home,[1] turning tables, self-
playing concertinas, and so on, and ended by asking him whether
any living creatures were affected by magnetism.

"Certainly, one such creature does exist," Prince Coco joined
in from some distance away. "You know Milvanovsky, of course.
He was put to sleep in my presence, and he even snored. Dear,
dear!"

"You are very naughty, *mon prince;* I am talking about real
animals, *je parle des bêtes.*"

"*Mais moi aussi, madame, je parle d'une bête. . . .*"

"Real animals are affected, too," the spiritualist intervened. "For
instance, crabs; they are very nervous and easily go into a catalepsy."

The Countess was amazed.

"What? Crabs? Really? Ah, now, that is extraordinarily interesting! I'd like to see that! M'sieur Luzhin," she added, turning to
a young man with a face as stony as that of a new doll and wearing a stony collar (he boasted that he had irrigated that same
face and that same collar with sprinkles of water from Niagara
and the Nubian Nile, but he could never remember anything of
all his travels and was fond only of Russian puns). "M'sieur Luzhin, be so kind as to get us a crab."

M'sieur Luzhin smirked. "Quick or only quickly?" he asked.

The Countess did not understand him. "*Mais oui,* a crab," she
repeated, "*une écrevisse.*"

"What? What's that? A crab, a crab?" Countess Sh. sternly

[1] D. D. Home (1833–86), a well-known medium of the period. (Tr.)

intervened. She was vexed by the fact that M'sieur Verdier was absent; she could not understand why Irena had not invited that most charming of Frenchmen. The ruin, who had long since lost all understanding of anything — and besides, she was very deaf — only tossed her head.

"*Oui, oui, vous allez voir.* M'sieur Luzhin, please — "

The young traveler bowed, went out, and returned very quickly. He was followed by a waiter who, smiling all over his face, was carrying a dish on which a large black crab was visible.

"*Voici, madame,*" exclaimed Luzhin; "now we can proceed to the 'cancer' operation. Ha-ha-ha!" (Russians are always the first to laugh at their own witticisms.)

"He-he-he!" Prince Coco responded in the capacity of patriot and patron of all native products.

(We ask the reader not to be astonished and not to be indignant; who can vouch for himself that if he were sitting in the parterre of the Alexandrinsky Theater in Petersburg and carried away by its atmosphere, he would not clap an even feebler pun?)

"*Merci, merci,*" the Countess said. "*Allons, allons, Monsieur Fox, montrez-nous ça.*"

The waiter placed the dish on a small round table. The guests started into gentle movement; several necks were craned; only the generals at the card-table preserved an imperturbable solemnity of attitude. The spiritualist tousled his hair, knitted his brows, and, approaching the table, began to make passes; the crab raised itself, fell back, and extended its claws. The spiritualist repeated and accelerated his movements; the crab continued to raise itself.

"*Mais que doit-elle donc faire?*" asked the Countess.

"*Elle doit rester immobile et se dresser sur sa queue,*" Mr. Fox replied with a strong American accent, convulsively shaking his fingers over the dish. But the magnetism did not act, the crab continued its movements. The spiritualist announced that he was not in a good mood and moved away from the table with a dissatisfied air. The Countess began to console him, assuring him that similar failures had sometimes occurred even with Mr. Home. . . . Prince Coco confirmed her words. The expert on the Apocalypse and the Talmud surreptitiously went across to the table and, swiftly but vigorously jabbing his fingers toward the crab, also tried his luck, but unsuccessfully: no signs of catalepsy appeared. Then the waiter was summoned, and he was ordered to carry out the crab, which he did with his former broad smile; his snorts as he shut the door behind him were audible in the room. . . . When he told the story in the kitchen, there was a good deal of laughter *über diese Russen.* The natural prodigy, who during the experiments on the crab had continued to play chords, keeping to minor tones, as after all it was impossible to know what effect anything would have — the natural prodigy played his invariable waltz and, of course, received the most flattering approbation.

Carried away by a feeling of rivalry, Count X, our incomparable dilettante (see Chapter 1), "sang" a chansonette of his own invention, entirely stolen from Offenbach. Its playful refrain, consisting of the words *"Quel bœuf? Quel bœuf?"* sent almost all the ladies' heads swaying to right and left; one even began to groan faintly, and the irresistible, inevitable word *"Charmant," "Charmant!"* flew from mouth to mouth. Irena exchanged glances with Litvinov, and once more that repressed, derisive expression flickered round her lips. . . .

But it began to play even more definitely a little later, it even acquired a malicious nuance, when Prince Coco, that representative and defender of the nobility's interests, took it into his head to expound his views to the spiritualist and, naturally, at once brought into action his celebrated phrase about the profound disturbance of the principle of property in Russia, during which, of course, the democrats also received a basting. The spiritualist's American blood was aroused; he began to argue. The Prince, as is proper, at once started to shout at the top of his voice, and instead of providing any proofs incessantly repeated: *"C'est absurde, cela n'a pas le sens commun!"* The wealthy Finikov took to making audacious remarks, without regard for persons; the Talmudist began to scream, even Countess Sh. grated. . . . In a word, there was almost as much idiotic hubbub as there had been at Gubariov's; perhaps the only difference being that here there was no beer and tobacco smoke, and everybody was wearing better clothes. Ratmirov tried to restore silence (the generals expressed their dissatisfaction, and Boris was heard to exclaim: *"Encore cette satanée politique!"*), but the attempt was a failure. A dignitary who was present, one of the gently persuasive kind, took it on himself to present *le résumé de la question en peu de mots,* and suffered defeat. To tell the truth, he mumbled and re-

peated himself so much, he was so obviously incapable of either
listening to or understanding objections, and so obviously did not
really know what *la question* was, that it was impossible to expect
any other result. And then, to make matters worse, Irena stealthily instigated and poisoned the disputants against one another,
looking round at Litvinov occasionally and nodding slightly to
him. . . . But he sat as though enchanted, heard nothing, and
only waited for those splendid eyes to glitter again before him,
and for that pale, delicate, evil, delightful neck to gleam once
more. . . . It all ended with the ladies rising in revolt and demanding that the quarrel should end. . . . Ratmirov asked the
dilettante to repeat his chansonette, and the natural prodigy played
his waltz. . . .

Litvinov remained till past midnight and was the last to leave.
During the evening the conversation had touched upon many
subjects, diligently avoiding anything in the least interesting. Having ended their majestic game, the generals majestically joined in
the conversation; the influence of these statesmen was felt at once.
The talk turned to the Parisian demimonde celebrities, whose
names and talents appeared to be very well known to all the company, to Sardou's latest play, About's novel, and Patti in *Traviata*.
Someone suggested a game of *"au secrétaire,"* but it was not a success. The answers were insipid and not without grammatical er-
rors; the stout general related how he had once answered the
question *"qu'est ce que l'amour?"* by saying it was *"une colique
remontée au cœur,"* and immediately burst into his wooden laugh;
the ruin gave him a swinging tap on the hand with her fan; this
violent movement caused a lump of cerise to fall from her brow.
The withered toadstool began to recall the Slavonic dukedoms
and the necessity for Russian Orthodox propaganda beyond the
Danube, but, obtaining no response, she spluttered and faded out.
Most of the conversation was about Home; even the "Princess
Wasp" told of how hands had slipped over her, and how she had
seen them and put her own ring on one of them.

Irena certainly had cause for exultation: if Litvinov had paid
even more attention than he did to all the talk, he would not have
carried away a single sincere word, a single useful thought, a
single new fact from all its incoherent and lifeless babble. No
enthusiasm was to be detected even in the shouts and exclamations; even in the denials no passion was to be felt; only from time

Smoke

to time, behind the mask of pseudo-civic indignation, or pseudo-contemptuous indifference, a tearfully whimpering fear of every possible kind of privation was to be detected, and several names that posterity will not forget were uttered with a grinding of teeth. . . . And beneath all this lumber and rubbish there was not one drop from a living stream! What outworn, what unnecessary nonsense, what empty trifles occupied all these heads, these souls; and not only during this one evening, not only in society, but at home also, during every hour of every day, throughout all the breadth and depth of their existence. And, in the last resort, what boorishness! What inability to understand everything on which human life is based, everything with which it is adorned!

As she said good-by to Litvinov, Irena again squeezed his hand and significantly whispered: "Well, what do you think? Are you satisfied? Have you seen enough? Is it good?" He did not answer and only made a low, calm bow.

Left alone with her husband, Irena was about to go to her bedroom. . . . He halted her.

"*Je vous ai beaucoup admirée ce soir, madame,*" he said, lighting a cigarette and leaning on the mantelpiece. "*Vous vous êtes parfaitement moquée de nous tous.*"

"*Pas plus cette fois-ci que les autres,*" she replied unconcernedly.

"How do you wish that to be understood?" he asked.

"As you like."

"Hm. *C'est clair.*" Cautiously, with a catlike movement, he brushed off the ash of his cigarette with the long nail of his index finger. "Yes, that reminds me! That new acquaintance of yours — what is his name? — Mr. Litvinov should have the reputation of being a very intelligent man."

At the mention of Litvinov, Irena turned sharply.

"What are you trying to say?"

The general smiled.

"He never says a word — evidently he's afraid of compromising himself."

Irena also smiled, only not at all like her husband.

"Better to be silent than to talk — as others talk."

"*Attrapé,*" he said with feigned humility. "Joking apart, he has a very interesting face. Such a — concentrated expression . . . and his bearing generally — yes." The general adjusted his tie and with head thrown back gazed at his own mustaches. "I should

93

think he is a republican, like that other friend of yours, Mr. Potugin. Now, there's another of your speechless sages."

Irena slowly raised her eyebrows above her dilated, gleaming eyes, while she compressed and very slightly twisted her lips. "What is the point of your saying all this, Valerian Vladimirich?" she remarked in a sympathetic tone. "You're only firing into the air. . . . We're not in Russia, and nobody is listening."

He shuddered.

"That is not only my opinion, Irena Pavlovna," he began with a suddenly guttural voice. "Others also consider that this gentleman looks like a *Carbonero*." [1]

"Really? And who are these others?"

"Why, Boris, for instance."

"What? And did he have to express his opinion?"

Irena wriggled her shoulders as though flinching from the cold and gently ran the tips of her fingers over them.

"He — yes, he — he too. Allow me to put it to you, Irena Pavlovna, that apparently you are angry. And you know yourself that anyone who gets angry — "

"I am angry? What about?"

"I don't know; perhaps you were unpleasantly affected by the remark I permitted myself to make just now concerning — "

He hesitated.

"Concerning?" she repeated interrogatively. "Ah, please, without irony, and quickly! I'm tired, I want to get to bed." She picked up a candle from the table. "Concerning — ?"

"Why, again concerning that same Mr. Litvinov. As there is now no doubt that you are greatly interested in him . . ."

Irena raised the hand holding the candlestick, so that the flame was level with her husband's face, and gazing into his eyes attentively, almost with curiosity, suddenly burst into laughter.

"What's the matter with you?" he asked, frowning.

She did not stop laughing.

"But what is all this?" he repeated, and he stamped his foot.

He felt that he was insulted, cut to the quick, yet at the same time the beauty of this woman who was confronting him so easily and boldly involuntarily dumbfounded him — she tormented him.

[1] Originally, a member of an early nineteenth-century Italian secret society of democratic and republican principles; later used as a label for any subversive or even progressive movement. (Tr.)

Smoke

He beheld all her charm; even the rosy gleam of her shapely nails on the slender fingers firmly gripping the dark bronze of the heavy candlestick — even that gleam did not escape his notice . . . and the feeling of injury ate even more deeply into his heart. But Irena went on laughing.

"What? You? You're jealous?" she said at last. Turning her back on her husband, she left the room. "He's jealous," he heard her say through the door, and she laughed again.

Ratmirov stared morosely after his wife — even at that moment he could not but observe the enchanting harmonious grace of her figure, of her movements — and, putting out his cigarette with a vigorous blow on the marble mantelshelf, he flung it far from him. His cheeks suddenly turned pale, his chin quivered convulsively, and his eyes dumbly and bestially wandered over the floor, as though looking for something. . . . All semblance of refinement vanished from his face. It must have worn a similar expression when he slaughtered the Byelorussian peasants.

But Litvinov went home to his room and, sitting on a chair before the table, took his head in both hands and remained so, motionless, for a long time. He got up at last, opened the table drawer, and, picking up his document case, took Tatiana's portrait out of an inner pocket. Her face, distorted and, as is usual, aged by the photograph, gazed at him mournfully. Litvinov's fiancée was a girl of Great Russian blood, fair, rather full, and with somewhat heavy features, but with an amazing expression of good nature and modesty in her intelligent, light-brown eyes, and with a delicate white brow on which a ray of sunlight seemed to lie permanently. For long he did not remove his eyes from the portrait; then he gently put it away and once more clutched his head with both hands. "It's all over!" he whispered at last. "Irena! Irena!"

Only now, only at that moment did he realize that he was irrevocably and insanely in love with her, had loved her from the day of that first meeting with her in the Old Castle, that he had never ceased to love her. But how astonished he would have been, how utterly incredulous, how he would even have laughed, perhaps, if anyone had told him so a few hours ago!

"But Tania, Tania! My God! Tania! Tania!" he repeated remorsefully; yet even then Irena's picture rose before him in her black, almost mourning clothes, with the radiant silence of victory on her white marble face.

16

Litvinov did not sleep all night and did not undress. He felt greatly oppressed. As an honest and just man, he realized all the meaning of obligation, of sacred duty, and would have considered it shameful to be casuistic with himself, with his weakness, with his delinquency. At first a torpor took possession of him; for a long time he could not rid himself of the obsessive oppression of one invariable, half-conscious, vague sensation. Then he was seized with horror at the thought that the future, his almost conquered future, was again enveloped in gloom, that his house, his solidly built, only just erected house had suddenly rocked. . . . He began to upbraid himself mercilessly, but at once put a stop to his outbursts. "What pusillanimity!" he thought. "This is not the moment for reproaches; now I must act. Tania is my fiancée, she believed in my love, my honor; we are united forever, and we cannot, we must not be parted." He vividly recalled all Tatiana's virtues, he mentally turned them over and catalogued them; he tried to quicken in himself a feeling of fondness and tenderness. "There is only one thing left for me to do," he thought again, "I must hurry, hurry at once, not waiting for her arrival, must hurry to meet her; even if I suffer, even if I am tortured with Tania — that is incredible — but in any case even to consider it, even to take it into consideration, is out of the question. I must do my duty, even if I die after!" "But you haven't any right to deceive her," another voice whispered to him, "you haven't any right to conceal from her the change that has occurred in your feelings. Perhaps when she learns that you have fallen in love with another, she will not wish to become your wife." "Rubbish! Rubbish!" he objected; "that's just sophistry, contemptible cunning, false scruples. I have no right not to keep my plighted word, that's the point. Well, excellent. . . . Then I must go away from Baden without seeing Irena. . . ."

But at this his heart sank, he turned cold, physically cold; a momentary shiver ran over his body, his teeth chattered quietly. He stretched himself and yawned, as though in a fever. Not pondering further on that last thought, smothering that thought, turning from it, he began to be astonished and wonder how he could again — again have fallen in love with that perverted, worldly creature, in all her repellent, inimical milieu. He attempted to ask himself: "But wait, are you sure you have fallen in love with her?" and only dismissed the very question. He was still feeling amazement and incomprehension when before him, as though out of a soft, scented mist, emerged an enchanting face; radiant lashes were raised; gently, and irresistibly, bewitching eyes pierced into his heart, and a voice sounded sweetly, and gleaming shoulders, the shoulders of a young princess, enveloped him in their freshness and voluptuous fire. . . .

Toward morning a decision matured at last in Litvinov's soul. He proposed to travel that same day to meet Tatiana; he would see Irena for the last time, would tell her — if there were no other way out — all the truth, and then part from her forever.

He put his things in order and packed them, waited till twelve o'clock, then went to her. But at the sight of her half-curtained windows his heart sank — he could not summon up sufficient spirit to enter the hotel. He walked up and down the Lichtentaler Allee several times.

"Our respects to Mr. Litvinov!" a derisive voice suddenly sounded behind him from the height of a swiftly moving dog-cart. He raised his eyes and saw General Ratmirov sitting beside Prince M., a well-known sportsman and amateur of English equipages and horses. The Prince was driving, and the general leaned over the side and bared his teeth, raising his hat high above his head. Litvinov bowed to him, and at the same moment, as though submitting to a secret command, went at a run to Irena.

She was at home. He sent a messenger to report his arrival; he was received at once. When he entered, she was standing in the middle of the room. She was wearing a morning blouse with broad, open sleeves; her face, as pale as yesterday, but not as fresh as yesterday, showed signs of weariness; the languid smile with which she welcomed her guest defined this expression even more clearly. She held out her hand to him and gave him a kindly but abstracted look.

"Thank you for coming," she said in a mournful voice, and dropped into a chair. "I am not quite well today; I spent a bad night. Well, what have you to say about yesterday evening? Wasn't I right?"

He sat down.

"I've come to you, Irena Pavlovna—" he began.

She momentarily straightened up and turned to him; she fixed her eyes on him.

"What is the matter with you?" she exclaimed. "You're as pale as a corpse, you are ill. What is wrong?"

He was disconcerted.

"With me, Irena Pavlovna?"

"Have you had some bad news? Some misfortune has occurred, tell me, tell me. . . ."

He in turn stared at her.

"I haven't had any bad news," he said, not without effort, "but a misfortune has indeed occurred, a great misfortune—and it is that which has brought me here."

"A misfortune? What is it?"

"Why—that—"

He tried to go on—and could not. He only clenched his hands until the fingers cracked. Irena leaned forward and seemed to turn to stone.

"Ah! I love you!" the words burst at last in a muffled groan from his breast, and he turned away, as though wishing to hide his face.

"What, Grigory Mikhailich, you—" She, too, could not finish her sentence. Leaning against the back of the chair, she raised both hands to her eyes. "You—love me?"

"Yes—yes—yes . . ." he repeated harshly, turning his face more and more away from her.

There was complete silence in the room; a butterfly that had flown in beat its wings and struggled between the curtain and the window.

He was the first to speak.

"There, Irena Pavlovna," he began, "there is the misfortune that has—struck me, that I should have foreseen and avoided if I hadn't fallen at once into the whirlpool just as I did in that former Moscow time. Evidently it pleased fate once more to compel me, and once more through you, to endure torments that, one would have thought, should never have been repeated. . . . Not without reason did I resist—try to resist; but there, what is to be will be. . . . But I tell you all now in order to put an end more quickly to this — this tragicomedy," he added with a new outburst of ruthlessness and shame.

He was silent again; the butterfly was still beating and fluttering. Irena did not take her hands from her face.

"And you are not deluding yourself?" her whisper came from behind those white, apparently bloodless hands.

"I am not deluding myself," he replied in a toneless voice. "I love you as I have never loved anyone but you. I do not intend to upbraid you: that would be too absurd. I do not intend to emphasize that perhaps none of this would have happened if you yourself had behaved differently with me. . . . Of course, I alone am to blame, my self-reliance has been my undoing. I am justly punished, and you could not expect this in the least. Of course, you did not realize that it would have been far safer for me if you had not been so ardently conscious of your guilt — your ostensible guilt toward me, and had not wished to expunge it . . . but what is done cannot be undone. I only wanted to explain my situation to you: it is difficult enough as it is. . . . At least, there will not be any misunderstanding, as you say; and the frankness of my confession, I hope, will diminish the feeling of offense that you cannot but have."

He spoke without raising his eyes; but even if he had glanced at Irena he could not have seen what was occurring in her face, for she did not remove her hands. Meanwhile, if he could have seen he certainly would have been astonished: fear and joy were expressed in that face, and a blissful exhaustion, and alarm; the eyes hardly glittered beneath the drooping lids, and a deep, spasmodic breathing chilled the parted, apparently thirsting lips. . . .

He waited a moment, in expectation of some response, some sound. . . . Nothing!

"There is only one thing left to me," he began again. "I must go away; I have come to say good-by."

Irena slowly dropped her hands to her knees.

"But I remember, Grigory Mikhailich," she began, "that — that person of whom you spoke to me, she should be coming here? Aren't you expecting her?"

"Yes; but I shall write to her . . . she will stop somewhere on the road — at Heidelberg, for instance."

"Ah! At Heidelberg — yes — that is a good place. . . . But all

99

this must derange your plans. Are you sure, Grigory Mikhailich, that you are not exaggerating, *et que ce n'est pas une fausse alarme?*"

She spoke quietly, almost coldly, with brief pauses, and looking away to the window. He did not answer her last question.

"Only why did you say something about my being offended?" she continued. "I am not offended – oh, no! And if either of us is to blame, then in any case it is not you; not you alone. . . . Recall our last conversation, and you will be convinced that not you are to blame."

"I never had any doubt of your magnanimity," Litvinov said through set teeth. "But I wish to know: do you approve of my intention?"

"To go away?"

"Yes."

She continued to look away from him.

"For one moment I thought your intention premature . . . but now I have thought over what you have just said . . . and if you are sure you are not mistaken, then I think you should go away. That will be better — better for us both."

Her voice grew softer and softer, and her very speech grew slower and slower.

"Certainly, General Ratmirov might notice —" he began.

Her eyes dropped again, and a strange expression flickered round her lips — flickered and faded.

"No. You haven't understood me aright," she interrupted him. "I was not thinking of my husband. Why should I? There would be nothing for him to notice. But I repeat: separation is necessary for both of us."

Litvinov picked up his hat, which had fallen to the floor.

"It's all over," he was thinking, "I must go." "And so now I have only to say good-by to you, Irena Pavlovna," he said aloud; and he suddenly felt afraid, as though he were about to pronounce sentence on himself. "It remains only for me to hope that you will not think badly of me — and that if at any time we —"

She again interrupted him:

"Wait, Grigory Mikhailich, don't say good-by to me yet. That would be too hasty."

Something quivered inside him; but at once, and with re-doubled force, a corrosive bitterness took possession of his heart.

"But I cannot remain!" he exclaimed. "What for? Why continue this exhausting ordeal?"

"Don't say good-by to me yet," Irena repeated. "I must see you once more — another dreary parting like that one in Moscow? No, I do not want that! You may go now; but you must promise me, must give me your word of honor, that you will not go away without seeing me once more."

"Do you wish that?"

"I demand it. If you go away without saying good-by to me I shall never, never forgive you; do you hear? Never! It is strange!" she added, as though to herself; "I simply cannot realize that I am in Baden — I continually have the feeling that I am in Moscow. . . . Go!"

He rose.

"Irena Pavlovna," he said, "give me your hand."

Irena shook her head.

"I told you I do not wish to say good-by to you . . ."

"I am not asking it in farewell. . . ."

She was about to hold out her hand, but for the first time since his confession she glanced at him — and drew her hand back.

"No, no," she whispered, "I will not give you my hand. No — no. Go!"

He bowed and went. He had no idea why she had refused him that last friendly handshake. . . . He could not know what she feared.

He went; but she dropped back into the chair and again covered her face with her hands.

17

He did not return home; he went off into the hills and, plunging into the heart of the forest, flung himself face-downward on the earth and lay there for about an hour. He did not suffer, did not weep; he simply went oppressively and exhaustingly numb. Never before had he felt anything like it: he had an unbearably nagging and gnawing sensation of emptiness, emptiness in himself, in everything around him, everywhere. . . . Neither of Irena nor of Tatiana did he think. He felt only one thing: the blow had fallen, and life was severed like a cable, and he was being dragged forward and caught up by something unknown, yet cold. At times he felt that a whirlwind had swept him away, and he was conscious of the rapid beating and disorderly blows of its somber wings. . . . But his resolution did not waver. To remain in Baden — that was unthinkable. Mentally he had already left; he was already sitting in the thundering and smoky carriage and fleeing, fleeing into the mute, dead distance.

He raised himself at last and, leaning his head against a tree, remained still; only with one hand, himself not noticing what he was doing, did he seize the upper frond of some bracken and swing it measuredly. The sound of approaching steps brought him out of his torpor; two charcoal-burners with great sacks over their shoulders were making their way along the steep track. "Time to go!" he whispered, and followed the charcoal-burners down into the town, then turned aside to the railway station and sent a telegram to Tatiana's aunt, Kapitolina Markovna. In this telegram he informed her of his plan for immediate departure from Baden and proposed to meet her at the Schrader Hotel in Heidelberg. "To end, to end it at once," he thought; "there's no point in postponing it till tomorrow."

Then he went into the Casino. With dull curiosity he stared two or three players in the face, noted Bindasov's odious nape and Pishchalkin's irreproachable features in the distance, and, after standing a few moments under the colonnade, went, unhurriedly, to Irena. Not in the grip of a sudden, involuntary attraction did he go to her: having decided to leave, he also decided to keep his given word and to see her once more. Unnoticed by the porter, he entered the hotel, went up the stairs without meeting anyone, and did not knock at the door, but mechanically pushed at it and entered the room. Irena was sitting in the room, in the same chair, in the same dress, in exactly the same position as three hours before. . . . It was obvious that all that time she had not moved from her seat, had not even stirred. She slowly raised her head and, seeing Litvinov, shuddered from head to foot and clutched at the chair arm.

"You frightened me," she whispered.

He gazed at her in speechless amazement. The expression of her face, of her faded eyes, astounded him.

She smiled forcedly and tidied her fallen hair. "It's nothing — to tell the truth, I don't know — I think I must have fallen asleep here in my chair."

Smoke

"Excuse me, Irena Pavlovna," he began, "I came in without warning. . . . I have called to do that which you insisted I should do. As I am leaving today —"

"Today? But I think you told me you first wanted to write a letter —"

"I have sent a telegram."

"Ah! You found it necessary to hurry. And when are you leaving? At what time, I mean?"

"At seven in the evening."

"Ah! At seven o'clock! And you've come to say good-by?"

"Yes, Irena Pavlovna, to say good-by."

She was silent.

"I must thank you, Grigory Mikhailich. It must have been far from easy for you to come."

"Yes, Irena Pavlovna, it was very far from easy."

"Life generally is far from easy, Grigory Mikhailich; what do you think?"

"It depends on who it is, Irena Pavlovna."

She was again silent, as though in a reverie.

"You have proved your friendship by coming," she said at last. "I thank you. And I must say I approve of your intention to put an end to everything as quickly as possible — because any delay — because — because I, that same I, whom you accused of coquetry, whom you called a comedienne — that, I think, is what you called me —?"

She swiftly rose and, seating herself in another chair, huddled and pressed her face and hands against the edge of the table. . . .

"Because I love you . . ." she whispered through her clenched fingers.

He fell back as though someone had struck him in the chest. She grievously turned her head away, as though wishing in turn to hide her face from him, and rested it on the table.

"Yes, I am in love with you — I love you — and you know it."

"I? I know it?" Litvinov said at last. "I?"

"Well, but now you see," she continued, "that you really must go, that you must not delay — both for us and for me there must be no delay. That is dangerous, that is fearful. . . . Good-by," she added, starting impetuously out of her chair. "Good-by!"

She took a few steps in the direction of the door of her room and, stretching out her hand behind her, hurriedly passed it

103

through the air, as though wishing to meet and squeeze Litvinov's hand. But he stood as though rooted to the floor, far off. . . . She once more said: "Good-by, forget!" and rushed out without looking back.

He was left alone, but he could not come to his senses. He collected himself at last, went swiftly to her room door, called her name once, twice, thrice. . . . He already had his fingers on the handle . . . Ratmirov's ringing voice floated up from the hotel veranda.

Litvinov pulled his hat down over his eyes and went down the stairs. The elegant general was standing in front of the porter's box and explaining to him in bad German that he wished to hire a carriage for all the following day. Seeing Litvinov, he again raised his hat unnaturally high and again expressed his "respects." He was obviously making fun of him, but Litvinov was not concerned with that. He hardly replied to Ratmirov's bow. On reaching his room, he halted before his trunk, which was already packed and locked. His head was whirling, his heart was quivering like a violin string. What was he to do now? And could he have foreseen this?

Yes, he had foreseen it, no matter how incredible it seemed. It had stunned him like a thunderclap, but he had foreseen it, though he did not dare to admit it. He had known nothing for certain, however. Everything inside him was tangled and confused; he had lost the thread of his own thoughts. He remembered Moscow, he remembered how then, too, "it" had come upon him like a sudden storm. He panted; exultation, yet an exultation that was joyless and hopeless, tore and burdened his breast. Not for anything in the world would he have agreed that the words Irena had said should not have been uttered. . . . But what of it? Even so, those words could not change the decision he had made. He did not vacillate any more than before, and he held firmly, like an anchor dropped overboard. He had lost the thread of his own thoughts . . . truly; but his will was still for the moment his, and he disposed of himself as though he were some other, subordinated person.

He rang for the waiter, ordered him to bring his account, reserved a seat in the evening omnibus; he deliberately cut off all his ways of retreat. "And then afterward you can die if you like," he declared, as he had during the past sleepless night; he particularly liked that phrase. "And then afterward you can die if you like," he repeated, slowly pacing backward and forward about the room. And only occasionally did he involuntarily close his eyes and cease to breathe, when those words, those words of Irena's, burst into his soul and scorched it with fire. "Evidently you don't fall in love twice," he thought. "Another life has entered into yours, you have let it in — and never shall you rid yourself of that poison until the end, never shall you snap those threads! True; but what does that prove? Happiness. . . . As if that is possible? You love her, let us assume — and she — she loves you. . . ."

But now he again had to take himself in hand. Like a traveler on a dark night who sees before him a tiny light and, afraid of losing his road, does not remove his gaze from that light for a moment, so Litvinov continually concentrated all the strength of his attention on one point, on one end. To present himself to his fiancée, and not even, strictly speaking, to his fiancée (he tried not to think of her), in that room of the Heidelberg hotel — that was what faced him steadfastly, like a guiding light. What would happen after he did not know, nor did he want to know. . . . One thing was beyond doubt: he would not come back. "After that you can die if you like," he repeated for the tenth time, and glanced at his watch.

Six fifteen! How long he still had to wait! He again took to pacing backward and forward. The sun declined to its setting, the sky flushed above the trees, and a crimson half-light streamed through the narrow windows into his darkened room. Suddenly he had the feeling that a door was opened behind him quietly and swiftly, and was as swiftly closed again. . . . He turned; at the door stood a woman, wrapped in a black mantilla. . . .

"Irena," he exclaimed, and opened his arms wide. . . .

She looked at him and fell into his arms.

Two hours later he was sitting on the sofa in his room. The trunk was standing in one corner, open and empty, and on the table, among things scattered untidily, lay a letter from Tatiana, which he had only just received. She wrote that as her aunt's health was completely restored, she had decided to hasten her departure from Dresden, and that, apart from unforeseen obstacles, they would both arrive at Baden at twelve o'clock next day, and they hoped he would come and meet them at the railway station. He had already reserved an apartment for them in his hotel.

He sent a note to Irena that same evening, and her answer came the next morning. "Whether a day later, or a day earlier," she wrote, "it was inevitable. But I repeat to you what I said yesterday: my life is in your hands, do with me as you wish. I do not desire to constrain your freedom, but you must know that if necessary I will abandon everything and follow you to the ends of the earth. We shall see each other tomorrow, shall we not? Your Irena."

The last two words were written in a large and bold, resolute hand.

18

Among the people who gathered on the railway-station platform just before twelve o'clock of August 18 was Litvinov. A few minutes previously he had seen Irena: she was sitting in an open carriage with her husband and another, elderly gentleman. She caught sight of Litvinov, and he noticed that she saw him; her eyes momentarily darkened, but she at once hid from him behind her parasol.

Since yesterday a strange transformation had occurred in him: in all his appearance, in his movements, in the expression of his face; and he himself felt that he was a different man. His self-confidence had vanished, his calm had vanished also, and his respect for himself; nothing was left of his previous mental poise. His recent ineffaceable impressions had veiled all else. An unprecedented feeling, strong, sweet—and evil, had taken charge of him; a mysterious guest had made his way into the sanctuary and occupied it, and had lain down in it silently, but throughout all its extent, like the master of a new house. Litvinov was no longer ashamed, he was afraid—and at the same time a desperate audacity had flamed up within him. The captured and the conquered are acquainted with that blend of antagonistic feelings; nor is it unknown to the thief, after his first robbery. Litvinov too was conquered, conquered suddenly . . . and what had become of his integrity?

The train was several minutes late. His weariness passed into a tormenting yearning; he could not stand still and, quite pale, he pushed and rubbed shoulders with the crowd. "My God," he thought, "if only another twenty-four hours . . ." His first glance at Tania, Tania's first glance — that was what was terrifying him, that was what he had to face, and the sooner the better. . . . And afterward? But afterward — let come what may! . . . He no longer made any decision, he no longer answered for himself. Yesterday's phrase morbidly flickered through his head. . . . And this was how he was meeting Tania. . . .

At last there was a long-drawn-out whistle, a heavy, steadily rising roar was heard, and the locomotive appeared, slowly steaming round a bend in the track. The crowd rushed to meet it, and Litvinov followed the crowd, dragging his feet like a man condemned. Faces, ladies' hats began to emerge from the cars, a white handkerchief fluttered at one window — Kapitolina Markovna was waving to him. . . . It was the end: she had seen Litvinov, and he recognized her. The train came to a halt. He rushed to the door and opened it; Tatiana was standing beside her aunt; smiling brightly, she held out her hand.

He helped them both to alight, said a few words of greeting, unfinished and vague, and at once began to fuss about, began to collect their tickets, their traveling bags, their rugs, ran to find a porter, called a carriage; other people fussed all around him, and he was glad of their presence, their hubbub and shouts. Tatiana stepped a little aside and, not ceasing to smile, calmly waited for him to complete his hurried arrangements. Kapitolina Markovna, on the contrary, could not stand still; even now she could not believe that at last she had reached Baden. She suddenly cried: "But how about the parasols? Tania, where are the parasols?" not noticing that she had them firmly tucked under her arm. Then she began to take a loud and prolonged farewell of another lady, with whom she had made acquaintance during the journey from Heidelberg to Baden. This lady was none other than the Mme Sukhanchikova already known to us. She had been to Heidelberg for the adulation of Gubariov, and had returned with "instructions." Kapitolina Markovna was wearing a rather queer, varicolored mantelet and a round traveling hat shaped like a mushroom, beneath which her close-cut white hair was breaking loose untidily; short and gaunt, she was flushed with the journey and talked in Russian with a penetrating singsong voice. . . . She at once attracted everybody's attention.

At last Litvinov seated her and Tatiana in the carriage and placed himself opposite them. The horses set off. Now questions began to be asked, hands were again shaken, there were mutual smiles, greetings. . . . He breathed more easily: the first moments had passed without event. Evidently Tania had not been disturbed by anything unusual in him; she looked at him just as openly and trustfully, blushed just as pleasantly, laughed just as good-naturedly. At last he himself decided to look, not sidelong and fleetingly, but directly and fixedly at her; hitherto his eyes had not been under his command. An involuntary tenderness took possession of his heart: the unperturbed expression of that honest, open face reacted on him like a bitter reproach. "So you have come here, poor girl," he thought, "you whom I have so long awaited and called, with whom I wanted to pass all my life to the end; you have arrived, you believed me . . . but I — but I — I — " He bowed his head. But Kapitolina Markovna would give him no opportunity for meditation; she plied him with questions.

"What is that building with the columns? Where is the gambling casino? Who is that coming? Tania, Tania, look, what crinolines! But now who is that? I should think most of them are Frenchwomen from Paris, aren't they? Lord, what a hat! Can you find everything here, as in Paris? Only I suppose everything is terribly dear? Ah, what an excellent, intelligent woman I have met! You know her, Grigory Mikhailich; she told me she had met you when visiting a certain Russian, who also is extremely intelligent. She has promised to call on us. The way she disposes of all these aristocrats — it's simply marvelous! Who is that gentleman with gray whiskers? The King of Prussia? Tania, Tania, look, that's the King of Prussia. No? It isn't the King of Prussia? The Dutch Ambassador? I can't hear, the wheels are making so much noise. Ah, what marvelous trees!"

"Yes, auntie, they are marvelous," Tania agreed; "and how green and cheerful everything is here! Isn't it, Grigory Mikhailich? . . ."

"Very cheerful," he replied through set teeth.

The carriage drew up outside the hotel. Litvinov led the two travelers to the suite reserved for them, promised to come back in an hour, and returned to his room. The enchantment, which had momentarily lost its power, possessed him again immediately he entered. Here, in this room, since yesterday Irena reigned;

everything spoke of her visit. . . . He again felt himself her slave. He took out her handkerchief, which he had hidden at his breast, and pressed his lips to it; and oppressively burning memories spread through his veins in a subtle poison. He realized that this time there was no return, no alternative; the mournful fondness Tatiana aroused in him melted like snow in fire, and his contrition died away — died away so completely that even the agitation within him was lulled, and the possibility of dissimulation, which occurred to his mind, did not arouse his indignation. . . . Love, Irena's love — that was now his right, his law, his conscience. . . . The prudent, common-sense Litvinov did not even think of how he was to extricate himself from his position, of which he felt even the horror and infamy quite lightly and almost, as it were, objectively.

Before an hour had passed, a waiter called at his room with a message from the newly arrived ladies: they asked him to join them in the hall. He followed the messenger down and found them already dressed in outdoor clothes and hats. They both expressed the desire to go out and see Baden at once; fortunately the weather was excellent. Kapitolina Markovna especially was burning with impatience; she was even a little downcast when she learned that it was not yet the hour for the fashionable parade outside the Konversationshaus. Litvinov took her by the arm, and an official promenade began.

Tatiana walked at her aunt's side and looked about her with tranquil curiosity; Kapitolina Markovna continued her interrogations. The sight of the roulette tables, the stately croupiers, whom, if she had met them in another place, she would certainly have taken for ministers of state, the sight of their nimble rakes, the gold and silver piles on the green cloth, the gambling old women and the painted *lorettes* reduced Kapitolina Markovna to a state of impotent frenzy; she quite forgot that she ought to be indignant and only stared, stared her eyes out of her head, shuddering occasionally at some new exclamation. . . . The whir of the ivory ball in the roulette bowl penetrated to her very marrow — and only when she found herself in the fresh air did she summon up sufficient strength, after emitting a profound sigh, to call the game of chance an immoral invention of aristocratism. A fixed, unpleasant smile appeared on Litvinov's lips; he spoke spasmodically and sluggishly, as though he were angry or bored. . . . But now he turned to Tatiana and was inwardly disconcerted: she was looking at him attentively, with an expression that suggested she was asking herself what impression he was making on her. He hastened to nod to her; she answered with a nod and again stared at him interrogatively, with some straining of her gaze, as though he were standing much farther from her than he was in reality. Litvinov conducted his ladies away from the Konversationshaus and, avoiding the "Russian tree," beneath which his compatriots were already in session, led them toward the Lichtentaler Allee. Even before he entered the avenue he saw Irena in the distance.

Accompanied by her husband and Potugin, she was coming toward him. He turned as white as a sheet; but he did not slacken his pace, and as he drew level with her he silently made a low bow. She also bowed to him pleasantly, but coldly; she ran her eyes swiftly over Tatiana as she glided past. . . . Ratmirov raised his hat high in the air, Potugin muttered something.

"Who is that lady?" Tatiana suddenly asked. Until that moment she had hardly opened her lips.

"That lady?" Litvinov repeated. "That lady? She is Madame Ratmirova."

"Russian?"

"Yes."

"Did you make her acquaintance here?"

"No; I've known her a long time."

"How beautiful she is!"

"Did you notice her toilet?" Kapitolina Markovna intervened. "Ten families could be fed for a whole year on the money her laces alone must have cost. Was that her husband walking with her?" She turned to Litvinov.

"Yes."

"He must be terribly rich?"

"I really don't know; I don't think so."

"And what is his rank?"

"He's a general."

"What eyes she has!" Tatiana said. "There is a strange expression in them: thoughtful, and piercing — I have never seen such eyes before."

Litvinov did not reply; he imagined that he again felt Tatiana's

Smoke

interrogative gaze fixed on his face. But he was wrong; she was looking down at her feet, at the sand of the path.

"My goodness! Who is that monster?" Kapitolina Markovna suddenly exclaimed, pointing to a low gig in which a red-haired and snub-nosed woman in unusually sumptuous finery and lilac stockings was insolently sprawling.

"That monster! Why, that is the well-known Mam'selle Cora."

"Who?"

"Mam'selle Cora — a Parisian — celebrity."

"What? That pug dog? But she's hideously ugly."

"Evidently that doesn't matter."

Kapitolina Markovna only gave it up.

"Well, your Baden!" she said at last. "But can we sit here on this bench? I'm feeling rather tired."

"Of course we can, Kapitolina Markovna — that is what the benches are put there for."

"The Lord knows! They say there are benches on the Paris boulevards too, but it isn't proper to sit on them."

Litvinov made no reply to her; only now did he realize that two paces away was the very spot where he and Irena had held that fateful, decisive conversation. Then he remembered that he had noticed a small rose-colored patch on her cheek as she passed. . . .

Kapitolina Markovna dropped on the bench. Tatiana sat down beside her. Litvinov remained standing on the path; between him and Tatiana — or did he only imagine it? — something was being accomplished . . . unconsciously and gradually.

"Ah, she's a buffoon, a buffoon," Kapitolina Markovna declared, commiserately shaking her head. "Now, if _her_ toilet were to be sold, one could feed not ten, but a hundred families. Did you see the diamonds beneath her hat, on that red hair of hers? Diamonds in daytime, what d'you think of that!"

"Her hair isn't really red," Litvinov remarked. "She dyes it red; that's the fashion now."

Kapitolina Markovna again gave it up and was even lost in thought.

"Well," she said at last, "we haven't reached such a scandalous state of affairs at Dresden yet. For, after all, it is farther from Paris. You're of the same opinion, aren't you, Grigory Mikhailich?"

III

"I?" he answered, and wondered: "What is she talking about?"
"I? of course — of course. . . ."

But at that moment unhurrying steps were heard, and Potugin approached.

"Good day, Grigory Mikhailich," he said, smiling and nodding.

Litvinov at once seized him by the arm.

"Good day, good day, Sozont Ivanich. I, I think I saw you here just now with — just now, in the avenue."

"Yes, it was I."

Potugin bowed respectfully to the seated ladies.

"Let me introduce you, Sozont Ivanich. My very good friends, relatives, only just arrived in Baden. Ladies, this is Potugin — Sozont Ivanich, a fellow countryman of ours, also visiting Baden."

Both ladies rose a little from their seats. Potugin repeated his bows.

"This is a real *rout*," Kapitolina Markovna began in a faint voice. The good-natured old maid felt a little diffident, but above all she tried to preserve her dignity. "Everybody regards it as a pleasant duty to visit Baden."

"Baden is certainly a pleasant place," Potugin replied, looking sidelong at Tatiana. "A very pleasant place is Baden."

"Yes, only it is too aristocratic, so far as I can judge. I and my niece have been living in Dresden all this time — Dresden's a very interesting town; but here it is a real *rout*."

"She likes that word," thought Potugin.

"You are absolutely right in that remark," he said aloud; "but then, the surrounding country is very striking, and the situation of the town is almost incomparable. Your companion especially should appreciate that. Don't you think so, madame?" he added, turning to speak directly to Tatiana.

Tatiana raised her large, clear eyes to him. She seemed to be puzzled to know what he wanted of her and why Litvinov had introduced her, on the very day of their arrival, to this stranger, who, however, had an intelligent and kindly face and looked at her with a welcoming and friendly air.

"Yes," she said at last, "it is very good here."

"You must visit the Old Castle," Potugin went on. "I advise you particularly to make an excursion to the Yburg."

"The Saxon Switzerland — " Kapitolina began.

A sudden burst of trumpets echoed along the avenue; the Prussian military band from Rastatt (in 1862 Rastatt was still a fortress of the German Confederation) had begun its weekly concert in the pavilion. Kapitolina Markovna rose at once.

"Music!" she said. "*Music à la Conversation!* . . . We must go there. It's four o'clock now, isn't it? I suppose society is beginning to assemble?"

"Yes," Potugin replied, "this is the most fashionable hour for society, and the music is excellent."

"Then there's no point in waiting — come, Tania!"

"Will you permit me to accompany you?" Potugin asked, to Litvinov's no little astonishment; it did not occur to him that Irena had sent him.

Kapitolina Markovna simpered.

"With the greatest of pleasure, M'sieur — M'sieur — "

"Potugin," he himself prompted her, and offered her his arm.

Litvinov gave his arm to Tatiana, and the two couples made their way toward the Konversationshaus.

Potugin continued to discuss various questions with Kapitolina Markovna. But Litvinov walked along without uttering a word, and only smiled a couple of times without cause and feebly pressed Tatiana's arm. There was falsity in those squeezes, to which she made no response, and he was conscious of that falsity. They did not convey any reciprocal assurance of the close union of two mutually devoted souls, as in the past; they only temporarily took the place of the words that he could not find. This taciturnity which had developed between them increased and was established firmly. Tatiana again looked at him attentively, almost fixedly.

The same relationship was continued outside the Konversationshaus, around the little table at which they all seated themselves, with the sole difference that because of the bustle of the crowd and the thunder and crash of the music, Litvinov's silence seemed more understandable. Kapitolina Markovna let herself go completely, as one says; Potugin could hardly keep pace with her in his attempts to satisfy her curiosity. Fortunately for him, among the mass of passers-by appeared the gaunt figure of Sukhanchikova, with her everlastingly darting, glittering eyes, Kapitolina Markovna at once recognized her, called her over to the table, and asked her to sit with them. And then a verbal storm set in.

Potugin turned to Tatiana and began to talk to her in a low, soft voice, with a kindly expression on his face, slightly inclined toward her. And she, to her own astonishment, answered him easily and freely. She found it pleasant talking to this casual acquaintance, this stranger, whereas Litvinov continued to sit motionless, with the same fixed and unpleasant smile on his lips.

Dinnertime arrived at last. The music died away, the crowd began to thin. Kapitolina Markovna took a tender farewell of Sukhanchikova. Immense was the respect she had conceived for her, though she afterward told her niece that "that person" was very malicious, but that on the other hand she knew everything about everybody. And certainly sewing-machines ought to be introduced as soon as the wedding had been celebrated. Potugin bowed his good-by to them all; Litvinov saw his ladies home.

At the entrance to the hotel he was handed a note; he stepped aside and hurriedly tore open the envelope. On a small scrap of vellum paper were the following words, written in pencil: "Come this evening at seven o'clock for one minute, I implore you. Irena." He thrust the note into his pocket and, turning round, smiled again — at whom? And why? Tatiana was standing with her back to him.

They had dinner at the general table. Litvinov sat between Kapitolina Markovna and Tatiana and strangely came to life, talked a great deal, told stories, poured out wine for himself and the ladies. He behaved in such a free and easy manner that a French infantry officer from Strasbourg, with an imperial and mustaches à la Napoleon III, who was sitting opposite them, was able to intervene in the conversation and even ended with a toast à la santé des belles Moscovites! Dinner over, Litvinov conducted both the ladies to their rooms and, after standing a moment with knitted brows at the window, abruptly announced that he must leave them for a short time to attend to a business matter, but would certainly return by the evening. Tatiana said nothing, turned pale, and lowered her eyes. Kapitolina Markovna was in the habit of sleeping after dinner. Tatiana knew that Litvinov was aware of her aunt's habit, and she had expected that he would take advantage of it, that he would remain, as he had not had a minute alone with her since her arrival, had not had any intimate talk with her. And now he was going out! How was she to take that? And altogether his behavior all day . . .

Smoke

He hurriedly withdrew without waiting for objections. Kapitolina Markovna lay down on the sofa and, after groaning and sighing once or twice, went off into a tranquil sleep; but Tatiana retired to a corner and sat down in an armchair, her hands firmly folded over her breast.

19

Litvinov walked briskly up the stairs of the Hôtel de l'Europe. . . . A girl about thirteen years old, with a crafty little Kalmuck face, who evidently was on the lookout for him, stopped him, saying in Russian: "This way, please; Irena Pavlovna will come in a minute." He stared at her in astonishment. She smiled, repeated: "Please, please," and led him into a small room opposite Irena's bedroom, a boxroom filled with traveling bags and trunks. Then she disappeared, quietly shutting the door. Before Litvinov had time to look about him the same door was swiftly flung open and Irena appeared in a rose-colored evening gown, with amber in her hair and at her neck. She rushed to him, seized both his hands, and stood for several moments speechless; her eyes sparkled and her breast heaved, as though she had been running uphill.

"I could not receive — you there," she began in a hurried whisper. "We're just going to a dinner engagement; but I simply had to see you. . . . That was your fiancée, wasn't it, whom I saw you with today?"

"Yes, that was my fiancée," he said, emphasizing the word "was."

"Well, then, I wanted to see you for one minute, in order to tell you that you should consider yourself absolutely free, that all that happened yesterday should not change your decisions in the least. . . ."

"Irena!" he exclaimed, "why are you saying this?"

He said these words in a loud voice. They throbbed with supreme passion. She involuntarily closed her eyes for a moment.

"Oh, my dear!" she continued in a still quieter whisper, but with uncontrollable fervor, "you don't know how much I love you; but yesterday I only paid my debt, I effaced my former guilt. . . . Ah! I could not give you my youth, much as I wished to; but I imposed no obligations on you, and so there was no promise from which I had to absolve you, my dear! Do as you

115

wish; you are as free as the air, you are bound in no way, understand that; you must understand that!"

"But I cannot live without you, Irena," he interrupted her in a whisper. "Since yesterday I am yours forever and always. . . . Only at your feet can I breathe. . . ."

He tremulously pressed his face against her hands. Irena gazed at his bowed head.

"Well, then know also," she said, "that I, too, am ready for anything, that I, too, shall spare no one and nothing. As you decide, so will it be. I, too, am forever yours — yours."

Someone knocked cautiously at the door. She bent over him and whispered yet again: "Yours. . . . Good-by!" Litvinov felt her breath on his hair, the touch of her lips. When he straightened up she was no longer in the room; but her gown rustled in the corridor, and in the distance he heard Ratmirov's voice: *"Eh bien? Vous ne venez pas?"*

Litvinov sat down on a large trunk and hid his face in his hands. A feminine scent, fine and fresh, enveloped him . . . Irena was holding his hands in her hands. "This is too much — too much," he was thinking. The girl entered the room; smiling again in response to his anxious glance, she told him:

"Please go, while . . ."

He rose and left the hotel. There could be no thought of his returning to his own hotel at once: he must recover his tranquillity. His heart was beating protractedly and unevenly inside him; the earth seemed to be gently stirring beneath his feet. He made his way once more to the Lichtentaler Allee. He realized that the decisive moment had come, that it had become impossible to procrastinate any longer, to dissemble, to avert his face, and that he must clear up the position with Tatiana. He imagined how she was sitting there and not stirring, and waiting for him . . . he had a presentiment of what he would tell her. But how to set about it, how to begin? He dismissed all his sound, well-arranged, well-ordered future; he knew that he was flinging himself head over heels into depths into which he should not even have glanced . . . but that did not disturb him. That question was settled. But how to go before his judge? And if it had been indeed a judge that awaited him — an angel with a flaming sword — it would have been easier for his sinful heart . . . but as it was, he himself must plunge the knife. . . . Infamous! But to turn back, to renounce the other, to take advantage of the freedom he was offered, which was recognized to be his — No! Rather die! No, he did not want that gelid freedom, but preferred to be flung down into the dust, so long as those eyes beamed with love over him. . . .

"Grigory Mikhailich," someone's mournful voice called, and someone's hand lay heavily on him.

He looked round, not without alarm, and recognized Potugin.

"Excuse me, Grigory Mikhailich," Potugin began with his usual grimace. "Perhaps I disturbed you. But seeing you in the distance, I thought — But if you don't want me — "

"On the contrary, I am very glad," Litvinov said through set teeth.

Potugin walked along at his side.

"A beautiful evening," he began; "so warm! Have you been out long?"

"No, not long."

"But there, why do I ask? I saw you come out of the Hôtel de l'Europe."

"So you followed me?"

"Yes."

"Have you something to say to me?'

"Yes," Potugin repeated almost inaudibly.

Litvinov halted and looked at his uninvited companion. Potugin's face was pale, the eyes absent; a former, ancient sorrow seemed to be revealed in his distorted features.

"And what exactly is it you wish to say to me?" Litvinov said slowly, and again walked on.

"Well, if you don't mind — one minute. If it's all the same to you, let's sit on this bench. It will be more convenient here."

"This is all rather mysterious," Litvinov said, sitting down beside him. "You don't seem to be yourself, Sozont Ivanich."

"No, I'm all right; and there's nothing mysterious about it, either. I simply wanted to communicate to you — the impression your fiancée made on me. She is your fiancée, isn't she? Well, in a word, the young lady to whom you introduced me today. I must say that in all my life I have never met a creature of a more pleasant temperament. She has a golden heart, and a truly angelic soul."

He said all this with the same bitter and afflicted air, so that even Litvinov could not help noting the strange contradiction between the expression on his face and the words he was saying.

"You are quite right in your estimate of Tatiana Petrovna," Litvinov began; "though I have to express my astonishment, first that you know my relations with her, and secondly that you have divined her character so quickly. She has, indeed, an angelic soul. But permit me to ask whether that is what you wanted to talk to me about."

"It is impossible not to recognize her character immediately," Potugin replied, and he seemed to be evading the last question. "You have only to take one look into her eyes. She is deserving of every possible happiness on earth, and enviable is the lot of the man who is destined to give her that happiness! One must hope that he will prove worthy of such a part."

Litvinov frowned a little.

"Excuse me, Sozont Ivanich," he said; "I must admit I find our conversation decidedly unusual. . . . I should like to know: do your words refer to me?"

Potugin did not answer at once; evidently he was struggling with himself.

"Grigory Mikhailich," he began at last, "either I have been completely mistaken in you or you are capable of listening to the truth, no matter whence it comes and beneath no matter what opaque integument it is presented. I said just now that I saw where you had come from."

"Why, yes, from the Hôtel de l'Europe. And what of it?"

"But I know whom you saw there!"

"What?"

"You saw Madame Ratmirova."

"Well, yes, I called on her. And what further?"

"What further? You, the fiancé of Tatiana Petrovna, you have been meeting Madame Ratmirova, whom you love — and who loves you."

Litvinov momentarily rose from the bench; the blood rushed to his head.

"What is this?" he said at last in an exasperated, choking voice. "A bad joke? Spying? Please explain."

Potugin gave him a despondent look.

"Ah! Don't be offended at my words, Grigory Mikhailich; and you certainly cannot offend me. That was not my object in wanting this talk with you, and joking is far from me at this moment."

"Maybe, maybe. I am prepared to believe in the purity of your intentions; none the less I take the liberty of asking you by what right you interfere in the domestic affairs, in the private life, of another man, and on what basis you so self-confidently put forward your — invention as the truth."

"My invention! If I had invented it, you would not have been angry. And as for the truth, I have never yet heard of anyone asking himself whether he has any right to stretch out a hand to a drowning man."

"I humbly thank you for your solicitude," Litvinov fierily retorted. "Only I have no need of it whatever, and all those phrases about the ruin prepared by society ladies for inexperienced youths, about the immorality of high society, and so on, I regard simply as phrases, and even in a sense I feel contempt for them. And so I ask you not to lift your saving hand, but calmly to let me drown."

Potugin again raised his eyes to Litvinov. He was breathing with difficulty, his lips were quivering.

"But look at me, young man," the words at last burst from him, and he beat himself on the chest. "Do I really look like a commonplace, self-satisfied moralist, like a sermonizer? Don't you really understand that I would not let fall one word, would not give you any right to reproach me with something that is absolutely repellent to me, with immodesty, with impertinence, simply out of commiseration for you, no matter how strongly I felt you deserved it? Don't you really see that this is quite a different question, that the man talking to you has been shattered, destroyed, completely annihilated by the very same feeling, that he wants to save you from the consequences of that feeling, which you have — for — for the very same woman?"

Litvinov fell back a pace.

"Is it possible? What did you say? You – you — Sozont Ivanich? But Madame Belskaya — that child . . ."

"Ah, don't question me — believe me! It is a dark, a terrible story, and I shall not stop to tell it to you. I hardly knew Madame Belskaya. That child is not mine, but I took everything on myself — because — because *she* wished it, because it was vital to *her*. Why should I be here, in this loathsome Baden of yours? And, finally, do you really assume, could you even for one minute imagine, that I decided to warn you out of sympathy for you? I am sorry for that good, kind girl, your fiancée; but really, what is your future, what does either of you matter to me? . . . No, I am afraid for her — for her."

"That does you honor, Mr. Potugin," Litvinov began, "but as, in your words, we are both in the same position, why don't you read similar admonitions to yourself, and why shouldn't I attribute your fears to another feeling?"

"In other words, to jealousy, you wish to say? Ah, young man, young man, shame on you to shuffle and palter, shame on you not to understand what bitter woe is now being spoken through my lips! No, you and I are not in the same position! I, I am an old, ludicrous, completely harmless eccentric. . . . And you? But why talk about it? Not for one second would you agree to take on yourself the role that I play, and play with gratitude! And jealousy? A man does not feel jealousy who has not even the least hope, and this would not have been the first time I had been forced to experience that feeling! I am only afraid — afraid for her, understand that. Could I have expected, when she sent me to you, that the feeling of guilt that she admitted she possessed would carry her so far?"

"Pardon me, Sozont Ivanich, you seem to know — "

"I know nothing, and I know all. I know," he added and turned away, "I know where she was yesterday. But there is no restraining her now: like a thrown stone, she must roll down to the bottom. I would be an even greater madman if I imagined that my words would halt you at once — you, whom such a woman — But enough of that. I could not compel myself to do otherwise, that is my only excuse. And besides, how is one to know, and why not try? Perhaps you will think better of it, perhaps some word of mine will penetrate into your soul; you do not wish to ruin both her and yourself and that innocent, noble creature. . . . Oh, don't get angry, don't stamp your foot! What have I to fear? Why should I stand on ceremony? It is not jealousy that speaks in me now, not chagrin. I am ready to fall at your feet, to implore you — But in any case, good-by. Don't be afraid, this will all remain a secret. I wish you well."

Potugin strode off along the avenue and quickly disappeared in the oncoming dusk. . . . Litvinov did not detain him.

Smoke

"A terrible, a dark story . . . " Potugin had said to Litvinov, and had not been willing to tell him that story. . . . We, too, shall touch on it in only a few words.

Some eight years previously Potugin's ministry had temporarily posted him to assist Count Reizenbach. It was summertime. Potugin traveled with documents to the Count's summer residence outside the town and spent days on end in this fashion. At that time Irena was living in the Count's house. She had never felt any contempt for people of lowly position; at any rate, she was not hostile to them, and the Countess more than once remonstrated with her because of her excessive Moscow familiarity. Irena soon recognized that this modest official, enveloped in a tightly buttoned, uniform frock coat, was an intelligent man. She frequently and readily talked to him . . . and he — he fell in love with her passionately, deeply, secretly. . . . Secretly! So *he* thought. The summer passed; the Count ceased to have need of outside help. Potugin lost sight of Irena, but he could not forget her. Some three years later he quite unexpectedly received an invitation from a certain lady of medium quality, whom he knew only slightly. At first this lady had difficulty in saying what she had in mind, but after making him swear to keep everything he heard a profound secret, she proposed to him that — he should marry a certain young lady who occupied a prominent position in the world and for whom marriage had become a necessity. The lady hardly dared to hint at the chief figure in the drama, and she at once promised him money — much money. Potugin did not take offense, his astonishment mastered his feeling of indignation, but, needless to say, he flatly refused. Then the lady handed him a note addressed to him — from Irena. "You are a noble and kind man," she wrote, "and I know you will do anything for me; I ask this sacrifice of you. You will save a creature who is dear to me. Saving her, you will save me too. . . . Don't ask: 'How?' I would not venture to address myself to anyone else with such a request, but to you I stretch out my hand and say: 'Do this for me.'" Potugin thought it over, and said that for Irena Pavlovna he was certainly ready to do a great deal, but he would like to hear her ask him with her own lips. The interview took place that same evening; it did not last long, and no one else knew of it except the lady who acted as intermediary. Irena was now no longer living with Count Reizenbach.

"Why did you think of me in particular?" Potugin asked her. She was about to expatiate on his good qualities; but she suddenly stopped.

"No," she said, "I must speak the truth to you. I knew, I know, that you love me; and that is why I ventured . . ." And she told him everything.

Eliza Belskaya was an orphan; her relations disliked her and hoped to gain her inheritance . . . she was faced with ruin. In saving her, Irena was in reality doing a service to the one who had been the cause of it all, and who now himself had become very dear to her, to Irena. . . . Potugin, not saying a word, gazed long at Irena, and agreed. She burst into tears and, streaming with tears, flung herself round his neck. He, too, broke into tears; but their tears were for different reasons. Now everything was prepared for a secret marriage, a powerful hand removed all the obstacles. . . . But an illness supervened . . . and during it a daughter was born, and during it the mother — took poison. What was to be done with the child? From the same hands, from the hands of Irena, Potugin took her into his charge.

A terrible, dark story. . . . Pass on, reader, pass on!

More than an hour elapsed before Litvinov could bring himself to return to his hotel. He was quite close to it when he suddenly heard steps behind him. It seemed that someone was persistently following him, walking more quickly when he accelerated his pace. As he passed beneath a street lamp he looked back and recognized General Ratmirov. In a white cravat and a dandyish unbuttoned topcoat, with a string of stars and crosses on a gold chain dangling from the buttonhole of his frock coat, the general was returning from the dinner, alone. His gaze, directly and arrogantly fixed on Litvinov, expressed such contempt and such hatred, all his bearing conveyed such a resolute challenge, that Litvinov considered it his duty to turn, reluctantly, to meet him, to turn and face a "scene." But as the general drew level with Litvinov his face changed in a moment: he adopted his customary look of playful elegance, and one hand in a pale lilac glove raised his gleaming hat high above his head. Litvinov silently raised his hat, and each went his way.

"He must have noticed something," Litvinov thought. "If it had been someone else," the general thought.

Smoke

Tatiana was playing piquet with her aunt when Litvinov entered their room.

"But I must say you're a fine specimen, my boy!" Kapitolina Markovna exclaimed, flinging her cards on the table. "Our very first day, and you vanish for the whole evening! We waited for you, and waited, we swore and swore — "

"I didn't say anything, aunt," Tatiana remarked.

"Well, we all know your meekness! Shame on you, my dear sir, and a fiancé, too!"

Litvinov awkwardly made his apologies and sat down at the table.

"Why have you stopped playing?" he asked after a brief silence.

"There's a fine thing! She and I are playing cards because we're bored, because we've nothing else to do. . . . But now you've arrived."

"If you would like to listen to the evening music," he said, "I will take you with the greatest of pleasure."

Kapitolina Markovna looked at her niece.

"If you'd like to go, auntie, I'm ready," Tatiana said. "But wouldn't it be better to stay at home?"

"That's an idea! We'll drink tea in our fashion, Moscow fashion, with a samovar; and we'll have a good talk. We haven't had a proper chat yet."

Litvinov gave orders for tea to be brought, but the good talk failed to develop. He felt a continual pricking of conscience; no matter what he said, he felt continually that he was playing the hypocrite and that Tatiana guessed. Yet no change was to be observed in her; she behaved just as unconstrainedly . . . only, not once did her gaze rest on Litvinov; it rather seemed to slip over him condescendingly and timorously. And she was paler than usual.

Kapitolina Markovna asked her if her head ached.

At first she was about to reply that it did not, but, thinking better of it, she said: "Yes, a little."

"It's the journey," Litvinov remarked, and he even went red with shame.

"The journey," Tatiana repeated, and her gaze again slipped over him.

"You must have a rest, Tania dear."

"In any case, I'll be going to bed soon, auntie."

On the table lay a copy of the *Guide des voyageurs*. Litvinov began to read aloud a description of the environs of Baden.

"That's all very well," Kapitolina Markovna interrupted him, "but one thing we mustn't forget. They say that linen is very cheap here, and it would be as well to buy some for the dowry."

Tatiana looked down.

"We've plenty of time, auntie. You never think of yourself; but you simply must get yourself a dress. Look what fine clothes everybody wears here."

"Oh, my soul, why should I? I'm not one of the smart set. That would be all right if I were as beautiful as that acquaintance of yours, Grigory Mikhailich — what is her name?"

"What acquaintance?"

"Why, the one we met today."

"Ah, that one!" Litvinov said with hypocritical indifference, and he again felt loathing and shame for himself. "No!" he thought; "it is impossible to go on like this."

He was sitting close to his fiancée; and only a few inches away from her, in his side pocket, was Irena's handkerchief.

Kapitolina Markovna went into the other room for a minute.

"Tania — " he said with an effort. It was the first time he had used that affectionate name all day.

She turned to him.

"I — have something very important to say to you."

"Ah! Have you really? When? Now?"

"No, tomorrow."

"Ah! Tomorrow. Well, all right."

An infinite pity momentarily filled his soul. He took Tatiana's hand and kissed it humbly, like a guilty child. Her heart stood still for a moment, and that kiss did not give her any joy.

That night, about two o'clock, Kapitolina Markovna, who was sleeping in the same room as her niece, suddenly raised her head and listened.

"Tania!" she called, "are you crying?"

Tatiana did not answer at once.

"No, auntie," her gentle voice called back at last. "I've got a touch of catarrh."

Smoke

20

"Why did I say that to her?" Litvinov thought next morning as he sat in his room, by the window. He shrugged his shoulders irritably; he had made that remark to Tatiana precisely in order to cut off all his ways of retreat. On the windowsill lay a note from Irena: she summoned him to visit her at twelve o'clock. Potugin's words came to his mind again and again; they sounded like an ominous, though feeble, underground rumble. He grew angry, but simply could not rid himself of them. Someone knocked at the door.

"*Wer da?*" Litvinov asked.

"Ah, so you're at home! Open the door!" he heard Bindasov's deep, hoarse voice.

The door handle was shaken.

Litvinov went pale with fury.

"I'm not at home," he said sharply.

"What d'you mean, not at home? What sort of game is this?"

"I tell you I'm not at home; clear off!"

"What a pleasant reception! And I'd come to borrow a little money," Bindasov snorted.

None the less he departed, clattering his heels as usual.

Litvinov all but rushed out after him, so strong was his desire to twist the brazen-faced fellow's neck. The events of the last few days had played on his nerves; a little more and he would burst into tears. He drank a glass of cold water, locked all the drawers of the furniture without knowing why, and went to see Tatiana.

He found her alone. Kapitolina Markovna had gone out to do some shopping. Tatiana was sitting on the sofa and holding a book in both hands; she was not reading it, and hardly even knew what it was about. She did not stir, but her heart beat violently in her breast, and the white collar round her neck quivered visibly and measuredly.

Litvinov was embarrassed. . . . None the less he sat down beside her, greeted her, and smiled; and she silently smiled back at him. She had inclined her head to him when he entered, nodding politely, but not with warmth — and had not looked at him. He held out his hand to her; she gave him her chilly fingers, at once released them, and turned back to her book. Litvinov felt that to begin the conversation with trivialities would only be insulting her. She, as usual, was demanding nothing, but all her attitude was saying: "I am waiting, I am waiting. . . ." He must keep his promise. But — though he had thought of nothing else almost all night — he had not prepared even the first, preliminary remarks and had no idea at all how to break this cruel silence.

"Tania," he began at last, "I told you yesterday that I have something important to tell you" (when alone with her at Dresden he had begun to talk to her in the second person singular, but now such intimacy was quite unthinkable). "I am ready, only I ask you in advance not to make a scene and to rest assured that my feelings for you — "

He stopped. His breath failed him. Even now she did not stir and did not look at him; she only gripped the book more firmly than before.

"Between us," he went on without finishing the previous sentence, "between us there has always been complete frankness. I respect you too much to palter with you. I want to prove to you that I can appreciate the loftiness and freedom of your soul, and although I — although of course — "

"Grigory Mikhailich," Tatiana began in an even voice, and all her face was suffused with a deathly pallor. "I will come to your aid. You have ceased to love me, and you don't know how to tell me so."

He involuntarily started.

"But why — ?" he said almost inaudibly, "how could you think — ? I really don't understand — "

"Well, isn't it true? Isn't it true? Tell me! Tell me!"

She turned all her body toward him; her face, with the hair flung back, drew near to his face, and her eyes, which for so long had not looked at him, were now fixed on his eyes.

"Isn't it true?" she repeated.

He did not say a word, did not utter a sound. He could not have lied at that moment, even if he had known that she would believe him and that his lie would save her. He was not even able to endure her gaze. He did not say a word, but now she no longer had need of an answer. She read that answer in his very silence, in those guilty, downcast eyes — and she threw herself back and dropped the book. . . . Even until that moment she had had doubts, and Litvinov realized that; he realized that

Smoke

she had still doubted, and realized how infamous, how utterly infamous was all that he had done!

He flung himself down on his knees before her.

"Tania," he exclaimed, "if only you knew how hard it is for me to see you in this situation, how terrible it is for me to think that it is I — I! My heart is torn asunder; I don't recognize myself. I have lost myself and you, and all. . . . Everything has been shattered, Tania, everything! Could I ever have expected that I — I would strike such a blow at you, my best friend, my guardian angel? . . . Could I ever have expected that you and I would see each other in such circumstances, would spend together such a day as was yesterday?"

Tatiana tried to rise and leave the room. He restrained her by the hem of her dress.

"No, listen to me just one more minute. See, I am down on my knees before you. But it is not for pardon that I have come to ask — you cannot and you should not pardon me. I have come to tell you that your friend is lost, that he is falling into an abyss and does not wish to drag you down with him. . . . But as for saving me — no, not even you can save me. I myself would thrust you away. . . . I am lost, I am lost irrevocably."

She gazed at him.

"You are lost?" she said, as though she did not fully understand him. "You are lost?"

"Yes, Tania, I am lost. All the past, everything that is precious, everything for which I have lived hitherto, is lost to me. Everything is destroyed, everything is wrested from me, and I know not what awaits me in the future. You have just said that I have ceased to love you. . . . No, Tania, I have not ceased to love you; but another, a terrible, irresistible feeling has come upon, has come over me. I resisted as long as I could. . . ."

Tatiana rose; her brows drew together; her pale face darkened. Litvinov also got up.

"You have fallen in love with another woman," she began, "and I guess who it is. We met her yesterday, didn't we? . . . Well, then! I know what is left for me to do now. As you yourself say that this feeling in you is immutable." (She paused for a moment: perhaps she still hoped that he would not let that last word pass without protest; but he said nothing.) "It remains for me to return you — your word."

He bowed his head, as though humbly receiving a well-deserved blow.

"You have every right to be indignant with me," he said. "You have every right to reproach me with pusillanimity — with deceit."

She looked at him again.

"I have not reproached you, Litvinov, I do not accuse you. I agree with you: the most bitter truth is better than what occurred yesterday. What sort of life would ours be now!"

"What sort of life will mine be now!" came a mournful response in Litvinov's soul.

Tatiana went toward the door of the bedroom.

"I ask you to leave me alone for a little while, Grigory Mikhailich. We shall see each other again, we shall talk more about it. It has all been so unexpected. I must gather a little strength . . . leave me . . . spare my pride. We shall see each other again."

And, having said these words, she swiftly retreated and locked the door behind her.

He went out into the street like a man in a fog, as though stunned; an obscure and oppressive feeling was implanted in the very depths of his heart; a man who has committed a murder must feel a similar sensation. Yet at the same time he felt lighter, as though he had at last thrown off a hateful burden. Tatiana's magnanimity had shattered him, he was vividly conscious of all he had lost . . . and what of it? His contrition was mingled with chagrin; he was passionately drawn to Irena, as to his sole remaining refuge — and he was annoyed with her. For some time past and with every day his feelings had grown continually stronger and more confused; this confusion tormented, irritated him; in this chaos he was lost. He desired just one thing: to come out at last on a road, no matter what; anything rather than go on circling in this meaningless twilight. Positive minds like Litvinov's should not be carried away by passion; it violates the very meaning of their life. . . . But nature does not concern herself with logic, with our human logic; she has her own, which we do not understand and do not recognize until it passes over us, like a wheel.

When he parted from Tatiana, Litvinov had only one thought in mind: to see Irena; and he went to her hotel. But the general was at home — so, at least, the porter told him — and he did not want to go up, did not feel capable of dissimulation; and he wandered off to the Konversationshaus. On this occasion Litvinov's inability to dissemble was felt personally by both Voroshilov and Pishchalkin, who happened to fall in with him; in an outburst of candor he told the one that he was as empty as a drum, the other that he bored him stiff. It was a good thing that Bindasov did not turn up, for then there would certainly have been a *"grosser Skandal!"* Both the young men were dumbfounded; Voroshilov even asked himself whether an officer's honor did not call for satisfaction — but, like Gogol's Lieutenant Pirogov, he appeased himself with *Butterbrot* in a café. In the distance Litvinov saw Kapitolina Markovna fussily running in her motley mantle from shop to shop. . . . He felt conscience-stricken at the sight of the good, funny, noble old lady. Then he remembered Potugin and yesterday's conversation. . . . But now something breathed on him, something intangible, yet indubitable; the waft could not have been more elusive if it had come from a falling shadow, yet he felt at once that it was Irena approaching. In very deed, she appeared a few paces away, arm in arm with another lady; their eyes met immediately. She must have noticed something unusual in Litvinov's expression: she halted before a shop selling innumerable tiny wooden clocks of Black Forest manufacture and summoned him to her with a movement of the head. Pointing to one of these little clocks, inviting him to admire the attractive clockface with a painted cuckoo above it, she said, not in a whisper, but in her usual voice, as though continuing a phrase she had begun — it was less likely to attract others' attention:

"Come in an hour's time, I shall be at home alone."

But now the well-known ladies' man M'sieur Verdier flew up to her and went into raptures over the *feuille morte* color of her gown, and her low-fitting Spanish hat, drawn right over her brows. . . . Litvinov vanished in the crowd.

21

"Grigory," Irena said to him two hours later as she sat beside him on the sofa with both her hands on his shoulder, "what is the matter with you? Tell me now, quickly, while we're alone."

"The matter with me?" Litvinov said. "I am happy, happy, that is what is the matter with me."

She looked down, smiled, and sighed.

"That is not an answer to my question, my dear."

He was lost in thought.

"Well, then, you must know — since you absolutely demand it" (she opened her eyes wide and started back a little), "today I have told my fiancée everything."

"Everything? Did you mention my name?"

Litvinov was decidedly astonished.

"Irena, for goodness' sake, how could you ever think that I — "

"Well, forgive me — forgive me. But what did you say?"

"I told her I didn't love her any more."

"Did she ask why?"

"I did not conceal from her that I had fallen in love with another woman and that we must part."

"Well — and what did she say? Did she agree?"

"Ah, Irena! What a wonderful woman she is! She is all self-sacrifice, all magnanimity!"

"I believe it, I believe it. . . . In any case, there was nothing else she could do."

"And not a single reproach, not a single bitter word did she say to me, to a man who has spoiled all her life, deceived her, deserted her pitilessly. . . ."

Irena examined her nails.

"Tell me, Grigory — did she love you?"

"Yes, Irena, she loved me."

She was silent for a moment, adjusting her dress.

"I admit," she began, "that I don't quite understand why you took it into your head to tell her."

"You don't understand why, Irena? Surely you didn't want me to lie, to dissemble to her, to that pure soul? Or did you suppose — "

"I didn't suppose anything," she interrupted. "I have to admit I thought little about her — I haven't the capacity to think of two people at once."

"That is, you mean to say — "

"Well, and what next? Is she going away, this pure soul?" she interrupted him a second time.

"I haven't the least idea," he replied. "I have to see her again. But she will not remain here."

"Ah! Pleasant journey!"

"No, she will not remain. For that matter, I, too, am not thinking of her now. I am thinking of what *you* said to me, of what *you* promised me."

Irena looked at him with knitted brows.

"Ingrate! Aren't you satisfied yet?"

"No, Irena, I am not satisfied. You have made me happy, but I am not satisfied, and you understand why."

"You mean, I — "

"Yes, you understand why. Remember your words, remember what you wrote to me. I cannot share you with another; no, no, I cannot agree to the miserable role of a secret lover. I have thrown not only my own life, but another life, too, at your feet, remorselessly and irrevocably. But on the other hand I believe, I am firmly convinced, that you, too, will keep your promise and unite your fate with me forever. . . ."

"You want me to run away with you? I am ready" (he exultantly pressed his lips to her hands), "I am ready, I do not go back on my word. But have you yourself thought about the difficulties — have you prepared the means?"

"I? I haven't had time to think of anything yet, or to prepare anything. But say only the word, give me permission to act, and before a month has passed — "

"A month! In a fortnight we are traveling to Italy."

"Even a fortnight is sufficient for me. Oh, Irena! You seem to be receiving my proposal coldly, perhaps to you it seems only a dream. But I am not a boy, I am not accustomed to comforting myself with dreams; I know what a terrible step it is, I know what responsibility I am taking on myself. But I do not see any other way out. Think: to do this I have to sever all connections with the past forever, so that I shall not become notorious as a contemptible liar in the eyes of that girl whom I have sacrificed to you!"

Irena abruptly drew herself up, and her eyes began to glitter.

"Well, you must forgive me, Grigory Mikhailich! If I make the decision, if I run away, then I run away with a man who has done this for me, just for me, and not in order to prevent his lowering himself in the opinion of a phlegmatic young lady who hasn't blood, but water and milk, *du lait coupé*, in her veins! And one other thing I tell you: I have to confess this is the first time I have been told that the man whom I favor is worthy of commiseration, is playing a miserable role. I know a still more miserable role: the role of a man who does not know what is occurring in his own soul!"

Litvinov drew himself up in his turn.

"Irena — " he began.

But she suddenly pressed both her palms to her brow and, vehemently flinging herself on his chest, embraced him with unwomanly strength.

"Forgive me, forgive me," she said in a quivering voice, "forgive me, Grigory! You see how spoilt I am, how loathsome, how jealous, how evil! You see how much I need your help, your indulgence! Yes, save me, wrest me out of this abyss, before I have completely perished! Yes, let us flee, let us flee from these people, from this world, into some distant, beautiful, free country! Maybe your Irena will at last become more worthy of those sacrifices you are making for her! Don't be angry with me, forgive me, my dear — and know that I will do all you order, I will go wherever you lead me!"

Litvinov's heart leaped up. She clung to him more strongly than ever with all her young and supple body. He bent over her perfumed, disordered hair, and in his intoxication of gratitude and exultation he hardly dared to caress it with his hand, hardly touched it with his lips.

"Irena, Irena," he declared, "my angel . . ."

She suddenly raised her head and listened. . . .

"That's my husband's steps — he's gone into his room," she whispered. She promptly moved away and seated herself in a chair. Litvinov was about to rise. "But where are you going?" she continued in the same whisper. "Stay! As it is, he suspects you. Or are you afraid of him?" She did not take her eyes off the door. "Yes, it is he; he will be coming in here in a minute. Tell me some story, be talking to me." Litvinov could not think of anything at once and remained silent. "You're not going to the theater tomorrow, are you?" she said aloud. "They're playing *Le Verre d'eau;* it's an old-fashioned play, and Plessis grimaces terribly. . . . It's just as though we're in a fever," she added, lowering her voice. "We can't go on like this; we must think it over thoroughly. I must warn you that all my money is in his hands; *mais j'ai mes bijoux.* We'll go to Spain, would you like that?" She raised her voice again. "Why do actresses always get so stout? Look at Madeleine Brohan, for instance. . . . Oh, do say something, don't sit there silent. My head is swimming. But you must not have any doubt of me. . . . I shall let you know when to come tomorrow. Only there was no need for you to have told that young lady — Ah, *mais c'est charmant!*" she exclaimed suddenly and, laughing nervously, tore the flounce of her dress.

"May I come in?" Ratmirov asked from the other room.

"Of course — of course."

The door opened, and the general appeared on the threshold. He frowned when he saw Litvinov, but he bowed to him; in other words, he swayed the upper part of his body.

"I didn't know you had a visitor," he said. "*Je vous demande pardon de mon indiscrétion.* So you're still finding amusement in Baden, M'sieur — Litvinov?"

Ratmirov always pronounced Litvinov's name with a slight pause, as though he always forgot, but immediately recalled it. He thought that this trick, and that of exaggeratedly raising his hat on meeting Litvinov, would sting him.

"I am not bored here, *M'sieur le général.*"

"Really? But I'm terribly tired of Baden. We're leaving here soon, aren't we, Irena Pavlovna? *Assez de Bade comme ça.* By the way, I won five hundred francs for you today."

Irena coquettishly held out her hand.

"Then where is it? Give it to me. For pin-money."

"It's mine, it's mine. . . . But are you going, M'sieur — Litvinov?"

"Yes, I am going, as you can see."

Ratmirov again swayed his body.

"To our next pleasant meeting!"

"Good-by, Grigory Mikhailich," Irena said. "But I shall keep my promise."

"What promise? May I be so inquisitive?" her husband asked.

She smiled.

"No, it's something — between us. *C'est à propos du voyage — où il vous plaira.* Do you know Stahl's compositions?"

"Ah! Of course, of course, I know them. Very nice drawings."
Ratmirov seemed to be on good terms with his wife: he spoke
to her in the second person singular.

22

"It is better not to think, really it is!" Litvinov assured himself
as he strode along the street and felt that a tumult was again
rising within him. "The question's decided. She will keep her
promise, and now all I have to do is to take all the necessary
steps. . . . But she seems to have doubts. . . ." He shook his
head. Even to himself his own intentions were presented in a
strange light; they looked strained and improbable. It is impossible
to worry for long over one and the same thought: it gradually shifts its position, like the little pieces of glass in a kaleido-
scope; as you watch, the pictures you see change completely.
Litvinov was mastered by a feeling of profound weariness. . . .
If he could only rest for a little hour. . . . But Tania? He shook
himself and, no longer stopping to deliberate, humbly wandered
home, with the sole thought that today he was being tossed like
a ball from one to the other. . . . No matter; he must put an
end to it. He returned to the hotel and just as humbly, almost
senselessly, without hesitation or delay, went to Tatiana.

Kapitolina Markovna came forward to meet him. As soon as
he looked at her he realized that she knew everything: the poor
old maid's eyes were swollen with tears, and her reddened face,
framed in fluffy white hair, expressed fear and anxious indignation, grief, and unbounded astonishment. She was on the point
of rushing to him, but she stopped at once and, biting her
quivering lips, looked at him as though she wanted to plead
with him, and kill him, and assure herself that it was all a dream,
a lunacy, an impossible business, wasn't it?

"And so you — you've come, you've come," she began. . . .
That same moment the door from the next room was flung wide
open, and Tatiana, translucently pale, but calm, entered with a
light step.

She quietly put one arm round her aunt and seated her beside
herself.

"And you sit down too, Grigory Mikhailich," she said to Litvinov, who had remained standing at the door, as though lost. "I am
very glad to have this further meeting with you. I have told

auntie your decision, our joint decision; she completely shares it and approves it. . . . Without mutual love there cannot be happiness; mutual respect alone is insufficient" (at the word "respect" Litvinov involuntarily cast down his eyes), "and it is better to part earlier than to repent later. Isn't that so, auntie?"

"Yes, of course," Kapitolina Markovna began; "of course, my dear Tania, anyone who does not know how to appreciate you — who has decided —"

"Auntie, auntie," Tatiana interrupted her, "remember what you promised me. You yourself have always told me: 'the truth, Tatiana, the truth above all — and freedom.' Well, but the truth isn't always pleasant, nor is freedom; otherwise what merit would we possess?"

She gently kissed Kapitolina Markovna on her white hair and, turning to Litvinov, continued:

"Auntie and I have decided to leave Baden — I think it will be easier so for all of us."

"When are you thinking of going?" he asked thickly. He recalled that Irena had only recently used these very same words.

Kapitolina Markovna was about to speak first, but Tatiana restrained her with a gentle touch on the shoulder.

"Probably soon, very soon."

"And may I ask where you are intending to go?" he said in the same tone.

"First to Dresden, and then probably to Russia."

"But what do you need to know for now, Grigory Mikhailich?" Kapitolina Markovna exclaimed.

"Auntie, auntie!" Tatiana again intervened. There was a brief silence.

"Tatiana Petrovna," he began, "you can understand what painfully difficult and mournful feelings I must be experiencing at this moment. . . ."

Tatiana rose.

"Grigory Mikhailich," she said, "don't let us talk about that. Please! I ask you, if not for your sake, then for mine. I knew you before yesterday, and I can well imagine what you must be feeling now. But what is the point of talking, why make things worse?" (She stopped; it was obvious that she was waiting to master the agitation rising within her, to choke back the tears starting to her eyes; and she succeeded.) "Why aggravate a wound that cannot be healed? Let us leave it to time. But now I have one request of you, Grigory Mikhailich; if you will be so good, I'll give you a letter in a moment. Take this letter to the post yourself, it is rather important, and auntie and I haven't the time now. . . . I shall be very grateful to you. Wait just a minute — I'll be back."

At the door Tatiana turned and looked anxiously at Kapitolina Markovna; but her aunt was sitting so seriously and sedately, with such a stern expression in her knitted brows and tightly pressed lips, that she only nodded to her and went out.

The door had hardly closed behind her, however, when all the look of seriousness and sternness vanished from Kapitolina Markovna's face. She rose, ran across to Litvinov on tiptoe, and, crouching down and trying to look into his eyes, began to speak in a quivering, tearful whisper.

"My God!" she said, "Grigory Mikhailich, what is this? Surely it's a dream? *You* are rejecting Tatiana, you have ceased to love her, you are betraying your word! You are doing this, Grigory Mikhailich, you, in whom we all put our hopes as in a rock! You? You? You? You, our dear Grigory? . . ." She paused. "Why, you'll kill her, Grigory Mikhailich," she continued without waiting for an answer, and the tears rolled in tiny drops down her cheeks. "Don't take any notice of the fact that she is putting a good face on it; you know her character, she never complains. She is not sparing herself, and so others should spare her! She has just been telling me: 'Auntie, we must preserve our dignity!' But what has dignity to do with it when I know she will die, will die. . . ." Tatiana made a noise with a chair in the other room. "Yes, I know she will die," the old woman hurried on even more quietly. "And what could have happened? Someone has bewitched you, surely? Only the other day you were writing her the tenderest of letters, weren't you? And, in the last resort, can an honest man behave like this? You know I am a woman without any prejudices, *un esprit fort*, and I have given Tania a similar upbringing; she, too, has a free soul. . . ."

"Auntie!" Tatiana's voice sounded from the other room.

"But one's word of honor — that is a duty, Grigory Mikhailich. Especially for people with your, with our rules of conduct! If we are not going to recognize our duty, what is left to us? That may not be repudiated just out of personal caprice, without

any regard for what it means to someone else! It is disgraceful
— yes, it is a crime. What sort of freedom is that?"

"Auntie, come here, please," they heard again.

"One minute, my dear, one minute." Kapitolina Markovna
seized Litvinov by the hand. "I see you are angry, Grigory Mikhailich." ("I? I angry!" he wanted to exclaim, but he was tongue-
tied.) "I don't want to make you angry, oh, my goodness, no!
How could I? On the contrary, I want to ask you: come to your
senses while there is still time, don't ruin her, don't ruin your own
happiness, she will still believe in you. Grigory dear, she will
believe you, nothing is lost yet; you see, she loves you as no
one else ever will love you! Leave this hateful Baden-Baden, we'll
go away together; only free yourself of this magic, and, above all,
have pity, have pity. . . ."

"Now, auntie," Tatiana called with a hint of impatience in
her tone.

But Kapitolina Markovna did not hear her.

"Say only yes," she said to Litvinov, "and I'll manage the
rest. . . . Well then, at least nod your head! Nod just one little
once, like this!"

It seems that Litvinov would gladly have died at that moment,
but he did not utter the word "yes," nor did he nod his head.

Tatiana appeared, with the letter in her hand. Kapitolina Markovna at once started back from Litvinov and, turning her face
away, bent low over the table as though examining the accounts
and papers lying on it.

Tatiana went to Litvinov.

"Here is the letter I mentioned to you," she said. "You will
go to the post at once, won't you?"

He raised his eyes. Before him, in very deed, stood his judge.
Tatiana seemed taller, more harmoniously proportioned; the face
that had beamed with unusual beauty was set majestically, stat-
uesquely; her breast did not stir, and her gown, of one color
and as close-fitting as a chiton, fell in straight, long, marble folds
to her feet, which it concealed. She gazed directly before her,
at Litvinov alone; and even her gaze, level and cold, was the
gaze of a statue. In it he read his sentence. He bowed, took the
letter from the hand rigidly extended toward him, and left
without saying a word.

Kapitolina Markovna rushed to Tatiana, but she avoided her

embrace and lowered her eyes; a flush spread over her face, and with the words: "Well, now quickly!" she returned to the bedroom. Kapitolina Markovna followed her, hanging her head.

The letter that Tatiana had entrusted to Litvinov was addressed to one of her Dresden friends, a German woman who had small furnished apartments to let. He dropped the letter in the box, and had the feeling that with that little scrap of paper he had dropped all his past, all his life, into a grave. He walked out of the town and wandered a long time over the narrow tracks running between the vineyards; as though it were the buzzing of an importunate summer fly, he could not rid himself of a constant feeling of self-contempt: he had played a very unenviable role in this last meeting. . . .

But when he returned to the hotel and, some little time later, inquired after his ladies, he was informed that the moment he went out they gave orders for a carriage to take them to the station and left by the post train for an unknown destination. Their things had been packed and their accounts paid since morning. It was obvious that Tatiana had asked Litvinov to take the letter to the post in order to get rid of him. He tried to find out from the porter whether the ladies had left any note for him, but the man replied in the negative and was even astonished; it was obvious that he, too, thought there was something strange and suspicious in this sudden departure from a suite taken for a week. Litvinov turned his back on the man and locked himself in his room.

He did not leave it till the following day. A large part of the night he spent at his table, writing and tearing up what he wrote. . . . Dawn was coming when he finished his labor: it was a letter to Irena.

23

Here is what he wrote in his letter to Irena:

My fiancée left yesterday; we shall never see her again. . . . I don't even know for certain where she will reside. With her she has taken all that hitherto has seemed desirable and precious to me; all my assumptions, my plans, my intentions have vanished with her; even my labors have gone by the board, my prolonged work has been reduced to nothingness, all my studies are without sense and purpose; that is all dead; since yesterday my I, my former I, is dead and buried. I clearly feel that, see it, know it. . . . And I do not regret it in the least. Not for the sake of complaining have I written of this to you. . . . Is it for me to complain when you love me, Irena? I only wanted to tell you that of all that dead past, of all those enterprises and hopes — turned to smoke and dust — just one has remained living and inviolable: my love for you. Apart from that love I have nothing and am left with nothing; to call it my sole treasure would be inadequate; I am entirely in this love, that love is all I; in it is my future, my calling, my holy of holies, my country! You know me, Irena, you know that all phrase-mongering is alien and repellent to me, and no matter how strong the words in which I attempt to express my feelings, you will not suspect their sincerity, you will not think them exaggerated. It is not a boy who is stammering unconsidered vows to you, in an outburst of momentary rapture, but a man tested by the years — who simply and straightforwardly, all but with horror, is expressing that which he has recognized to be the undoubted truth. Yes, your love has changed everything for me — everything, everything!

Judge for yourself; can I leave this everything in another man's hands? Can I allow him to have the disposal of you? You, you will belong to him; all my being, the blood of my heart will belong to him — but I myself — where am I, what am I? To one side, a spectator — a spectator of my own life! No, that is impossible, impossible! To share, to share clandestinely in something without which my life has no reason for existence, or even possibility of existence — that is falsehood and death.

I know what a great sacrifice I am demanding of you, without any right to do so; and besides, what can confer any right to a sacrifice? But not out of egotism am I acting so: it would be easier and lighter for an egotist not to raise this question at all. Yes, my demands are heavy, and I shall not be surprised if they frighten you. You hate the people with whom you have to live, you are oppressed by society; but have you strength enough to throw aside that society, to trample on the crown with which it has crowned you, to arouse social opinion, the opinion of those hateful people, against you? Question yourself, Irena; do not undertake a burden you cannot carry. I do not want to reproach you, but remember: already once you have been unable to resist the temptation. I can give you so little in exchange for what you will lose! So listen to my final words: if you do not feel capable even tomorrow, even today, of leaving all and following me — you see how boldly I speak, how I do not spare myself — if you are frightened by the unknown of the future, by alienation, and loneliness, and human censure, if, in a word, you do not have confidence in yourself: then tell me so frankly and without procrastination, and I will go. I shall go with tormented soul, but I shall bless you for your truth. But if you, my beautiful, radiant empress, have really fallen in love with such a petty and obscure man as I, and are really ready to share his destiny — well, then give me your hand, and we shall set out together on our difficult road! Only, do realize that my decision is beyond doubt: all or nothing! That is mad — but I can do no other; I cannot, Irena! I love you too much.

Your
G. L.

Litvinov himself was not much pleased with this letter; it did not quite accurately and exactly express what he wanted to say; clumsy expressions, bombast, bookish turns had found their way into it, and of course it was no better than many other letters that he had torn up. But it happened to be the last he wrote, and in any case the main thing was said; and tired, tormented as he was, he did not feel capable of writing anything more. In addition, he did not possess the gift of expounding his thoughts in a literary fashion, and, as always in such cases, he fussed over every syllable. His very first letter was probably the best of all: it poured more fervently from his heart. Whether this was so or not, Litvinov sent his missive to Irena.

She replied in a brief note:

Come to me today [she wrote]; *he will be away all day. Your letter has greatly agitated me. I think and think — and my head swims with thoughts. Things are very difficult for me, but you love me, and I am happy. Come.*

Your
I.

She was sitting in her room when Litvinov entered. He was shown in by the same thirteen-year-old girl who had watched for him at the stairs on a previous occasion. On the table before Irena lay an open semicircular box containing lace; with one hand she was abstractedly turning the lace over; in the other she held his letter. She had only just ceased weeping: her eyelashes were wet and her eyelids swollen; on her cheeks were the traces of unwiped tears. He halted at the door; she did not notice his arrival.

"Are you crying?" he said in astonishment.

She started, passed her hand over her hair, and smiled.

"Why are you crying?" he repeated. She silently pointed to his letter. "Is that how it — " he said slowly.

"Come here and sit down," she said; "give me your hand. Why, yes, I have been crying. Why are you surprised? Is *this* so easy?" She again pointed to the letter.

Litvinov sat down.

"I know that it is not easy, Irena. I myself said so in my letter. . . . I understand your position. But if you believe in the meaning of your love for me, if my words have convinced you, you must also understand what I feel now at the sight of your tears. I have come like a man awaiting sentence, and I wait: what shall I be told? Death or life? Your answer decides all. Only don't look at me with such eyes. They remind me of your former, Moscow eyes."

She suddenly flushed and turned away, as though she herself felt something awkward in her gaze.

"What made you say that, Grigory? Aren't you ashamed? You wish to know my answer — but can you have any doubt of it? You are embarrassed by my tears — but you haven't understood them. Your letter, my friend, sent me into a reverie. In it you write that my love for you has changed everything, that even your former studies must now remain without application; but I ask myself, can a man live only by love? Won't it bore him in the end, won't he desire activity, and won't he upbraid the thing that has lured him away from it? That is the thought that frightens me, that is what I am afraid of, and not what you assumed."

Litvinov looked at her closely, and Irena looked closely at him, as though each of them wanted to penetrate farther and more deeply into the soul of the other, farther and more deeply than can be achieved or than can be revealed by words.

"There is no reason for you to be afraid of that," he began; "I must have expressed myself stupidly. Boredom? Inactivity? In face of the new powers that your love gives me? Oh, Irena, believe me, in your love is all my world, and I myself cannot yet foresee all that may develop out of it!"

She grew thoughtful.

"And where shall we go?" she whispered.

"Where? We can talk about that later. But so — so you agree, you agree, Irena?"

She gazed at him. "And you will be happy, Grigory?"

"Oh, Irena!"

"You will never regret anything? Never?"

She bent over the box of laces and began to turn them over again.

"Don't be angry with me, my dear, for occupying myself with this rubbish at such a moment. I have to go to a ball a certain lady is giving. I have been sent these pieces of rag, and I must choose today. Ah, it is terribly hard for me!" she suddenly exclaimed, and she set her face against the edge of the box. The tears once more began to well from her eyes. . . . She turned away; otherwise the tears might have fallen on the lace.

"Irena, you're crying again," he said anxiously.

"Why yes, again," Irena replied. "Ah, Grigory, don't torture me, don't torture yourself! . . . We shall be free! What matters it that I am crying! Why, I myself, do I understand why I am crying? You know, you have heard my decision, you are sure that it will not be changed, that I agree to — how did you put it? — to all or nothing. . . . What else do you want? We shall be free! What is the point of these mutual chains? You and I are one now, you love me, I love you; have we nothing else to do but cross-examine each other for our opinions? Look at me; I didn't want to vaunt myself before you; not by a single word have I hinted that perhaps it is not so easy for me to trample on my duties as a wife . . . and I do not delude myself, I know that I am a criminal, and that *he* would be entitled to kill me. Well, and what of it? We shall be free, say I. Today is ours, all eternity is ours."

She rose from her chair and looked Litvinov up and down, faintly smiling and narrowing her eyes, and with her arm, bare to the elbow, brushing back from her face a long tress on which two or three tears were glittering. A rich lace neckerchief slipped from the table and fell to the floor, beneath her feet. She scornfully trod on it.

"Or do I not please you today? Have I grown more ugly since yesterday? Tell me, have you often seen a more beautiful hand? And this hair? Tell me, do you love me?"

She caught him with both hands, pressed his head to her breast; her comb jingled and dropped out, and her falling hair enveloped him in a perfumed and gentle wave.

24

Litvinov walked up and down his room in the hotel, his head sunk thoughtfully on his breast. Now he was faced with the transition from theory to practice, with seeking the means and ways for the flight, for removal to unknown countries. . . . But, strange to say, he was thinking not so much about these means and ways as whether the decision on which he had so obstinately insisted had actually, indubitably been taken. Was the final, irrevocable word spoken? But, after all, Irena had said to him at their parting: "Act, act, and when everything is ready, only let me know in advance." It was settled! Away with all doubts. . . . He must set to work. And he set to work — for the time being — to cogitate.

First and foremost the question of money. He found that in cash he had 1,328 guldens and 2,855 French francs; not a considerable sum, but sufficient for immediate needs. And when they arrived he must write at once to his father to send as much as possible; he could sell a forest, part of the estate. . . . But on what pretext? . . . Well, a pretext would be found. True, Irena had spoken of her *bijoux*, but they must not be taken into consideration at all; they would be of service, who knows, for a rainy day. In addition he had a good Genevan semi-chronometer, for which he could get — well, at least four hundred francs. He went to his banker and inquired in ambiguous terms whether it would be possible to have a loan, if necessary. But the bankers in Baden are a badgered and cautious lot, and in response to such circumlocutions they immediately adopt an evasive and drooping look, for all the world like a field flower that has had its stalk cut by a scythe; though some of them laugh bravely and boldly in your face, as if enjoying your innocent little jest. To his own

143

shame, Litvinov even tried his fortune at roulette, and even (oh, ignominy!) put a taler on number thirty, which corresponded to his age. He did this with a view to enlarging and rounding off his capital; and certainly, though he did not enlarge it, he rounded it off by getting rid of the surplus twenty-eight guldens.

The second question, also of no little importance, was that of a passport. But for a woman a passport is not so obligatory, and there are countries where they are not required at all. Belgium, for instance, or England. In the last resort one can even get a non-Russian passport. He gave very serious thought to all this; his resolution was strong, and without the least vacillation. But meanwhile, against his will, despite his will, thoughts anything but serious, almost comic, emerged and tinged his meditations, just as though his very enterprise were a joking matter, and no one had ever run away with anybody in real life, but only in comedies and novels, and perhaps somewhere in the provinces, in some Chukhlom or Sizran province, where, according to one traveler's statements, the people even vomit to relieve their boredom. Here he called to mind how one of his friends, the retired cornet Batsov, carried off a merchant's daughter in a hired carriage with bells, first making the parents drunk, and his bride-to-be too; and how afterward it transpired that it was they who had tricked him and all but caught him into the bargain. Litvinov grew extremely angry with himself for having such inept reminiscences; and as he recalled Tatiana, her abrupt departure, all that sorrow and suffering and shame, he at once felt all too deeply that what he had brought about was by no means a joking matter, and that he was profoundly right when he told Irena that for his own very honor there was no other way out. . . . And again at her very name something corrosive momentarily, with a pleasurable pain, entwined itself round his heart and was still.

He heard the sound of horses' hoofs behind him. He stepped aside. . . . Irena, on horseback, overtook him; the corpulent general was riding with her. She recognized Litvinov, nodded to him, and, striking her horse's flank with the whip, put it into a gallop, then suddenly shook loose the reins and gave the animal its head. Her dark veil streamed in the wind. . . .

"*Pas si vite! Nom de Dieu! Pas si vite!*" the general shouted, and galloped after her.

Smoke

Next morning Litvinov had only just returned from his banker, with whom he had had another talk about the playful inconstancy of the Russian rate of exchange and the best means of sending money abroad, when the porter handed him a letter. He recognized Irena's writing and, not breaking the seal at once — for some reason an unpleasant presentiment awoke within him — he went to his room. This is what he read (the letter was written in French):

My dear! I have thought all night about your proposal. . . . I shall not try to temporize with you. You were frank with me, and I shall be frank. I cannot flee with you, I haven't the strength to do it. I feel how guilty I am in regard to you; my second guilt is even greater than my first — I despise myself, my pusillanimity, I burden myself with reproaches; but I cannot transform myself. In vain do I tell myself that I have destroyed your happiness, that you are now quite justified in regarding me as only a frivolous coquette, that I myself offered, I myself gave you solemn promises. . . . I am horrified, I hate myself; but I cannot behave otherwise; I cannot, I cannot. I do not wish to justify myself, I shall not try to persuade you that I was carried away — all that means just nothing. But I want to tell you and to repeat, and repeat yet again: I am yours, yours forever; dispose of me as you wish, when you wish; unconditionally and unreservedly I am yours. . . .

But to run away, to leave everything — No! No! No! I implored you to save me, I myself hoped to blot out everything, to burn up everything as in a fire. . . . But evidently there is no salvation for me; evidently the poison has penetrated too deeply into me; evidently one cannot breathe this air for many years without having to pay for it! I long hesitated whether to write this letter to you, it is terrible to think of the decision you may make, my only hope is in your love for me. But I considered that it would be dishonest on my part not to tell you the truth — the more so as you may already have begun to take the first steps toward the fulfillment of our plan. Ah! It was beautiful, but unrealizable. Oh, my friend, regard me as an empty, feeble woman, despise me, but do not abandon me, do not abandon your Irena! . . .

Turgenev

I am not strong enough to give up this world, but neither can I live in it without you. Soon we shall be returning to Petersburg; come there, live there, we shall find you an occupation, your past labors will not be wasted, you will find a useful application for them. . . . Only live near me, only love me as I am, with all my weaknesses and defects, and know that no other heart will ever be so tenderly devoted to you as the heart of your Irena. Come quickly to me, I shall not have a moment's rest until I see you.

Your, your, your
I.

The blood struck at Litvinov's head like a hammer, then slowly and heavily sank into his heart; and there it petrified like a stone. He reread the letter and then, completely exhausted, as on that previous occasion in Moscow he fell on the sofa and lay still. A dark abyss suddenly enveloped him on all sides, and he gazed into that abyss senselessly and desperately. And so, once more, deceit — no, worse than deceit — falsehood and vulgarity. . . . And life shattered, everything torn up by the roots, from its very depths, and that sole thing at which it was still possible to clutch — that last support — also in fragments!

"Follow us to Petersburg," he repeated with bitter inward laughter; "we'll find you an occupation there." . . . "I suppose they would appoint me as a clerk in charge of an office section. And who are these 'we'? That was her past speaking. There we have that secret, that hideous thing of which I have no knowledge, but which she had attempted to blot out and to burn up as if in fire! There we have that world of intrigues, secret connections, the story of the Belskayas, the Dolskayas. . . . And what a future, what a beautiful role awaits me! To live near her, to visit her, to share with her the depraved melancholy of a fashionable lady who is oppressed and bored by society, but cannot exist outside its circle; to be a domestic friend of her and, of course, His Excellency . . . until — until the whim has passed, and the plebeian friend loses his piquancy, and that fat general or some Mr. Finikov replaces him — now, that is possible and pleasant and perhaps useful . . . she herself speaks of a useful application of my talents, doesn't she? — but our design is unrealizable! Unrealizable! . . ."

Smoke

Sudden gusts of frenzy swept over Litvinov's soul like the momentary gusts of wind before a storm. . . . Every expression in Irena's letter aroused his indignation, her very assurances of the immutability of her feelings affronted him. "It cannot be left like this," he exclaimed at last. "I shall not allow her to play so pitilessly with my life. . . ."

He jumped up and seized his hat. But what could he do? Rush to her? Answer her letter? He stopped and let his hands drop.

Yes: what was to be done?

Had he not himself presented her with this fatal choice? It had fallen otherwise than as he wished — any choice is liable to that misfortune. She had changed her decision, truly; she herself had been the first to declare that she would abandon everything and follow him, that also was true. Yet she did not deny her guilt: she openly called herself a weak woman. She did not wish to deceive him, she had been deceived in herself. . . . What could he object to in that? At the least she was not dissembling, was not temporizing . . . she was frank with him, ruthlessly frank. Nothing had compelled her to reveal her attitude at this moment, nothing had prevented her lulling him with promises, and procrastinating, and leaving everything in uncertainty right down to the departure — the departure with her husband for Italy! But she had ruined his life, she had ruined two lives! . . . Little was lacking, surely!

But in regard to Tatiana it was not Irena who was guilty; he was guilty, he alone, and he had no right to wash his hands of the responsibility that his guilt had laid on him like an iron yoke. . . . That was all true; but now what was there left to do?

He again flung himself on the sofa; and again the moments fled by dark and dull and traceless, with a consuming speed.

"But why not submit to her?" the thought flashed through his head. "She loves me, she is mine, and in our very attraction for each other, in that passion which, after so many years, has forced its way to the surface with such power, is there not something inevitable, irresistible, like a law of nature? To live in Petersburg — why, shall I be the first to have been placed in such a situation? And besides, where could she and I find shelter? . . ."

He was sunk in thought, and Irena's image quietly rose before him as it had been impressed forever in his latest memories. . . .

But not for long. He aroused himself and with a new outburst of indignation thrust away even those memories, even that enchanting image.

"You are giving me to drink from a golden goblet," he exclaimed; "but there is poison in your drink, and your white wings are soiled with filth. . . . Away! To remain here with you, after I — have driven away, driven away my future bride — that would be dishonorable, dishonorable!" He clenched his fists bitterly, and another face, with the imprint of suffering on its set features, with unspoken reproach in its farewell gaze, emerged from the depths. . . .

For long did he continue to torture himself; for long, like a difficult patient, his lacerated mind tossed restlessly. . . . He quieted down at last; at last he came to a decision. From the very first moment he had had a presentiment of that decision; it had appeared to him first as a distant, hardly perceptible point amid the whirlwind and gloom of his inward struggle; then it had begun to draw ever nearer and nearer, and it ended by driving like an icy steel blade into his heart.

Once more he dragged his trunk from the corner, once more, unhurrying, and even with a dull, meticulous care, he packed all his things, rang for the waiter, settled his account, and sent a note in Russian to Irena. It read as follows:

I don't know whether your guilt is greater toward me than before; but I do know that this blow is far stronger. . . . This is the end. You tell me: "I cannot," and I also repeat to you: I cannot do — what you desire. I cannot and I do not wish to. Don't answer this. You are not capable of giving me the only answer I would accept. I am leaving tomorrow morning by the first train. Good-by, be happy. . . . I don't suppose we shall ever see each other again.

All that day Litvinov remained in his room. Was he waiting for anything? God knows! About seven in the evening a lady in a black mantle, with a veil over her face, twice approached the entrance to his hotel. She drew back a little to one side and gazed into the distance, then she suddenly made a resolute gesture and went to the entrance yet a third time. . . .

"Where are you going, Irena Pavlovna?" A tense voice sounded behind her.

She turned round with a convulsive, hasty movement. Potugin ran up to her.

She halted, thought a moment, then rushed to him, took him by the arm, and drew him aside.

"Take me away, take me away," she demanded, panting.

"What is the matter with you, Irena Pavlovna?" he muttered in bewilderment.

"Take me away," she repeated with redoubled strength, "if you don't want me to remain forever — there!"

He humbly bowed his head, and they both hurried away.

Early next morning Litvinov was all ready for his journey when into his room walked Potugin himself.

He came up to him without speaking and squeezed his hand without speaking. Litvinov also said nothing. They both had long faces, and they both vainly tried to smile.

"I have come to wish you a good journey," Potugin said at last.

"But how do you know that I am going away today?" Litvinov asked.

Potugin looked round him at the floor. "It has become known to me — as you see. Our last conversation has now had such a strange result — I did not wish you to depart without expressing my sincere sympathy."

"You sympathize with me now — when I am going away?"

Potugin looked at Litvinov mournfully. "Ah, Grigory Mikhailich, Grigory Mikhailich," he began with a brief sigh, "this is not the time for that sort of thing, for such subtleties and hair-splittings. You, so far as I have been able to observe, are rather indifferent to our native literature, and so perhaps you have never heard of Vaska Buslaev?"

"Of whom?"

"Vaska Buslaev, a Novgorod hero — in Kirsh Danilov's anthology."

"What Buslaev?" Litvinov said, somewhat puzzled by such an unexpected turn in the conversation. "I've never heard of him."

"Well, it doesn't matter. But this is what I wished to draw your attention to. Vaska Buslaev took his Novgorod people on a pilgrimage to Jerusalem, and there, to their horror, bathed his naked body in the sacred waters of the river Jordan, because he believed 'neither in sneeze, nor in dream, nor in any feathered fowl,' and then this logical Vaska Buslaev climbed Mount Tabor, and on top of this mountain lay a large stone, over which all sorts of people had vainly attempted to jump. Vaska also wanted to try his fortune. And on the way he came across a skull, a human head; he kicked it with his foot. Well, and the head said to him: 'What are you kicking for? I knew how to live, I know how to roll in the dust — and the same will happen to you.' And it was right: Vaska jumped over the stone, and would have jumped clean over it, but he caught his heel and broke his head. And here I may remark that it would not be a bad thing if my friends the Slavophils, who are so fond of kicking all kinds of dead heads and rotten nations, were to pause to reflect over that legend."

"But what is the point of all this?" Litvinov at last interrupted him impatiently. "It's time I was off, you must excuse me."

"Why, just this," Potugin answered, and his eyes lit up with such a friendly feeling as Litvinov had not even expected of him; "just this, that you have not kicked aside a dead human head, and so, perhaps, because of your goodness, you may succeed in jumping over the fatal stone. I shall not keep you any longer, only permit me to embrace you in farewell."

"I shall not even try to jump," Litvinov said, as he and Potugin kissed three times; and with the dreary feelings that overfilled his soul was mingled a fleeting commiseration for this lonely wretch. "But I must go, I must go. . . ." He flung himself about the room.

"Would you like me to carry something?" Potugin offered his services.

"No, thank you very much; don't trouble, I can manage. . . ." He put on his cap and picked up his bag. "And so, you say," he asked, even as he stood at the door, "you have seen her?"

"Yes, I have."

"Well — and how is she?"

Potugin was silent for a moment. "She waited for you yesterday — and she will be waiting for you today."

"Indeed! Well, then tell her — No, there's no need, no need to say anything. Good-by — good-by!"

"Good-by, Grigory Mikhailich. . . . Let me say one more word to you. You still have time to listen: you have over half an hour before your train leaves. You will return to Russia. There you will — in the course of time — be active. . . . So allow an old chatterbox — for I, alas, am a chatterbox and nothing more — to give you some parting advice. Every time you have to turn to a task, ask yourself: are you serving civilization — in the exact and strict meaning of the word — are you carrying through one of its ideas, has your labor that educative, European character which alone is beneficial and fruitful in our day, in our country? If so, then go boldly forward: you are on the right road, and your work is blessed! God be thanked! You are not alone now. You will not be a 'sower of the wilderness'; laborers — pioneers — have come into being now in our country too. . . . But you have no time for this at the moment. Good-by, do not forget me!"

Litvinov went down the stairs at a run, flung himself into the carriage, and drove to the station without looking back once at the town where so much of his personal life was left. . . . He seemed to yield himself to a wave: it caught him up, carried him off, and he firmly decided not to resist its tow . . . he renounced all other manifestation of will.

He was already entering the car.

"Grigory Mikhailich — Grigory — " he heard an imploring whisper behind him.

He shuddered. Surely not Irena? Yes, it was she. Wrapped in her maid's shawl, with a traveling hat on her untended hair, she was standing on the platform and looking at him with faded eyes. "Turn back, turn back, I have come for you," said those eyes. And how much, how much they promised! She did not stir, she had no strength to add a word; everything in her, even the disorder of her dress, everything seemed to be pleading for mercy. . . .

Litvinov could hardly keep his feet, he all but rushed to her. . . . But the wave to which he had surrendered had its way. . . . He jumped into the car and, turning, pointed Irena to the seat beside him. She understood him. The time had not yet passed. Only one step, one movement, and two forever united lives would be tearing into an unknown distance. . . . While she hesitated, there was a loud whistle, and the train began to move.

Litvinov threw himself back in his seat. But Irena went with staggering steps to a bench and fell on it, to the great amazement of a petty diplomat who had happened to wander into the station. He did not know Irena well, but he was deeply interested in her and, seeing her lying apparently unconscious, he thought that she had suffered *"une attaque de nerfs."* And so he considered it his duty, the duty *d'un galant chevalier,* to go to her aid. But his amazement grew far greater when, at the first word he said to her, she suddenly rose, thrust away the proffered hand, and, running into the street, in a few seconds disappeared in the milky mist that is so common in the Black Forest climate during the first days of autumn.

26

We happened one day to go into the hut of a peasant woman who had only just lost her only, deeply loved son, and, to our no little surprise, found her absolutely tranquil, all but cheerful. "Don't trouble her," said her husband, who evidently noticed my surprise; "she is 'ossified' now." And Litvinov also was "ossified." During the first few hours of his journey a similar tranquillity came upon him. Completely annihilated and hopelessly unhappy, none the less he rested, rested after the alarms and torments of the past week, after all the blows that one after another had fallen on his head. They had shaken him all the more strongly because he was not created for such storms. Now it was as though he hoped for nothing and tried not to remember, most of all not to remember; he was traveling to Russia — he had to go somewhere! But he now made no assumptions concerning himself. He did not recognize himself; he did not understand his conduct, it was as though he had lost his real "I," and altogether he had little part at all in that "I." Sometimes it seemed to him that he was carrying his own corpse, and only the rare bitter spasms of irremediable spiritual pain that fled through him reminded him that he was still concerned with life. At times it seemed to him incomprehensible that a man — a man! — could allow a woman, and love, to have such influence over him. . . . "Shameful weakness!" he whispered; and brushed his greatcoat and settled himself more comfortably into his seat, as though saying: "Now the old is ended, we begin a new — minute"; and he only smiled bitterly and was amazed at himself.

He turned to looking out of the window. The day was gray and raw; it was not raining, but the mist still held, and low clouds veiled all the sky. The wind was blowing to meet the train; whitish billows of steam, sometimes singly, sometimes mingled with other, darker billows of smoke, tore in an endless string past the window beside which he was sitting. He began to watch that steam, to watch that smoke. Winding incessantly, rising and falling, whirling and clinging to the grass, to the bushes, as though grimacing, lengthening and melting, cloud after cloud was carried past . . . it unceasingly changed and remained the same . . . a monotonous, hurrying, boring game! Sometimes the wind changed, the road curved — the whole mass suddenly disappeared and immediately after was to be seen through the opposite window; then once more the enormous tail was flung across, and once more it veiled his view of the broad Rhineland plain. He watched and watched, and a strange reverie came upon him. . . . He was sitting alone in the car; no one disturbed him. "Smoke, smoke," he repeated several times; and abruptly everything seemed to be smoke — everything, his own life, Russian life, everything human, but especially everything Russian. "It is all smoke and vapor," he thought. "Everything seems to be incessantly changing, everywhere there are new pictures, phenomena speed after phenomena, but in essence everything is the same and still the same; everything is hurrying, hastening somewhere — and everything vanishes without a trace, without achieving anything; another wind blows — and everything is flung to the opposite side, and there too the same incessant, anxious, and unnecessary game goes on." He recalled much that had been accomplished before his eyes, with thunders and tumults, of recent years . . . "smoke," he whispered, "smoke." He remembered the burning arguments, the jostles and shouts in Gubariov's room, in other people's rooms, of people highly and lowly placed, foremost and rearmost, old and young people . . . "smoke," he repeated, "smoke and vapor." He recalled, finally, that celebrated picnic, he recalled other judgments and speeches of other statesmen, and even everything that Potugin had preached . . . smoke, smoke, and nothing more. But his own strivings and feelings, and struggles, and dreams? He only shrugged his shoulders.

But meanwhile the train was speeding and speeding; already Rastatt, and Karlsruhe, and Bruchsal had been left behind; the hills on the right-hand side of the track first turned away, retreated into the distance, then drew near again, but now not so lofty, and more rarely covered with forest. . . . The train swung sharply to one side . . . and now they were at Heidelberg. The cars drew under the roof of the station; he heard the shouts of newsboys selling all kinds of periodicals, and even Russian papers. The travelers fidgeted in their seats or went out on the platform. But Litvinov did not leave his corner and continued to sit with his head sunk on his chest. Suddenly someone called him by name. He raised his eyes: Bindasov's face was thrust through the window, and behind him — or did he only imagine it? No, it was so: all the familiar faces from Baden: Mme Sukhanchikova, Voroshilov, and even Bambayev; they all moved toward him, and Bindasov bawled:

"But where's Pishchalkin? We were expecting him. But it doesn't matter; out you get, lazybones, we're all going to see Gubariov."

"Yes, brother, yes, Gubariov's waiting for us." Bambayev confirmed, pushing forward. "Out you get!"

Litvinov would have been angry but for the dead burden that lay on his heart. He glanced at Bindasov and turned away without speaking.

"I tell you Gubariov's here," Mme Sukhanchikova exclaimed, and her eyes all but popped out.

Litvinov did not stir.

"Now listen, Litvinov," Bambayev said at last, "there's not only Gubariov here; there's a whole phalanx of very outstanding, very intelligent young people, Russians, and they are all studying natural science, and they all have the finest of convictions. You might remain at least for their sake. For instance, here we've got a certain — oh dear! I've forgotten his name. But he's an absolute genius!"

"Oh, let him go, let him go, Rostislav Ardalionich," Mme Sukhanchikova intervened. "Let him go! You see the sort of man he is; and all his family are the same. He's got an aunt who I thought at first was traveling our road; but I came here with her two days ago — she had only just arrived in Baden and back she was flying again — and as we came along I began to question her. . . . Would you believe it, I couldn't get a word out of her arrogance! The loathsome aristocrat!"

Poor Kapitolina Markovna, an aristocrat! Had she ever expected such a disgrace?

But Litvinov still said nothing, and turned away and pulled his cap down over his eyes. The train started off at last.

Smoke

"But do say something at least in parting, you lifeless stone!" Bambayev shouted. "You can't go off like that!"

"You scum, you dolt!" Bindasov howled. The cars were moving faster and faster, and he could swear with impunity. "You curmudgeon! You slug! You beer-glass licker!"

Whether Bindasov had invented this last nickname on the spot or whether he had got it from others is not known; but evidently it delighted two of the very noble young men studying natural sciences who were standing beside him; for several days later it was printed in the Russian periodical sheet then being published in Heidelberg, under the headline: "*A tout venant je crache!*" or: "God does not give. A swine is never full." [1]

But Litvinov again repeated the word he had previously been uttering: smoke, smoke, smoke! "For instance," he thought, "there are more than a hundred Russian students in Heidelberg at present; they're all studying chemistry, physics, physiology — and don't want to hear of anything else. . . . But in five or six years' time there won't be fifteen students attending the courses given by the same celebrated professors. . . . The wind will change, the smoke will shift to the other side . . . smoke . . . smoke . . . smoke!" [2]

Toward nightfall he passed through Kassel. Together with the darkness, an unendurable yearning dropped like a kite on him, and he burst into tears, huddling into the corner of the car. Long his tears flowed without lightening his heart, corrosively and grievously lacerating him. But at that very moment Tatiana was in bed with a fever in one of the Kassel hotels, and Kapitolina Markovna was seated beside her.

"Tania," she said, "for God's sake let me send a telegram to Grigory Mikhailovich. Do let me, Tania!"

"No, auntie," she said, "there's no need, don't be alarmed. Give me some water; it will soon pass."

And she was right; a week later she was restored to health, and the two friends continued their journey.

---

[1] A historical fact. (Author's note.)

[2] Litvinov's presentiments were justified. In 1866 there were thirteen Russian students attending Heidelberg University during the summer term, and twelve during the winter term. (Author's note.)

Stopping neither in Petersburg nor in Moscow, Litvinov returned to his estate. He was alarmed when he saw his father, so feeble and decrepit had the old man grown. Old Litvinov was delighted to see his son, in so far as a man who has finished with life can delight in anything; he immediately handed over to him all his badly disorganized affairs, and, after creaking in the joints for a few more weeks, he departed this earthly course. Litvinov was left alone in the dilapidated wing of his house and, with a heavy heart, without hopes, without zeal, and without money, began to manage the estate. Husbandry in Russia is not a cheerful occupation, as all too many know; we shall not stop to enlarge on how bitter it proved to Litvinov. Of course there could be no thought of transformations and innovations; the application of the knowledge he had gained abroad was postponed for an indefinite period; necessity compelled him to live from day to day, to agree to all kinds of concessions, both material and moral. The new was accepted reluctantly, the old had lost all its strength; [1] the bungler clashed with the unscrupulous; all the shaken life was quaking like a marsh, and only the one great word "freedom" hovered like the Divine Spirit above the waters. Patience was required most of all, and patience not passive, but active, insistent, not without some knack, not without cunning for the moment. . . . In his mental and psychological state Litvinov found it doubly hard. Little desire to live was left in him. . . . So where was he to find desire for troubles and labors?

But a year passed, and after it another; a third began. The great idea was realized little by little, was transformed into flesh and blood; sprouts emerged from the scattered seed, and now no enemy — either open or secret — could trample it down. Litvinov himself, though he ended by giving a large part of his land to peasants on a fifty-fifty basis — in other words, reverting to impoverished, primitive husbandry — did manage to achieve something: he restored the factory, ran a tiny farm with five hired laborers, and from time to time had as many as forty working for him. He paid off the largest of the private debts. . . . And

[1] All the following passage refers to the emancipation of the peasants in 1861, and the consequent transference of land to them. (Tr.)

Smoke

his spirit grew strong within him; he again began to resemble the former Litvinov. True, a sorrowful, deeply hidden feeling never left him, and he grew quiet beyond his years, shut himself up in his narrow circle, severed all his former relations. . . . But his deathly indifference disappeared, and among the living he again moved and acted like the living. And the last traces of the enchantment that had possessed him also disappeared; all that had occurred in Baden seemed like something seen in a dream. . . .

But Irena? She, too, faded and disappeared, and Litvinov had only a vague sense of something dangerous beneath the mist that gradually enveloped her image. He had news of Tatiana from time to time; he knew that she had settled with her aunt on her small property, some hundred and fifty miles away, and lived quietly, rarely left home, and hardly ever had guests. But she was quiet and well. And one day, one beautiful day of May, he was sitting in his study and indifferently turning over the pages of the latest number of a Petersburg periodical when a servant entered and reported the arrival of his old uncle. This uncle was Kapitolina Markovna's cousin, and he had recently visited her. He had bought a property adjacent to Litvinov's and was transferring to it. He stayed with his nephew for days on end and told him a great deal about the life Tatiana was living.

The day after his departure Litvinov sent a letter to her, the first since their parting. He asked permission to renew their acquaintance at least in writing, and also wished to know whether he must forever abandon the thought of seeing her again. Not without anxiety he awaited the answer . . . it arrived at last. Tatiana responded favorably to his question. "If it occurs to you to visit us," she ended, "by all means, come; they say that even sick people find things easier together than separately." Kapitolina Markovna joined in greeting him. Litvinov was as delighted as a child; not for long nor for anything else had his heart beat so merrily. And suddenly everything seemed light and clear. . . . Just as, when the sun rises and disperses the darkness of night, a little breeze speeds with the sun's rays over the face of the resurrected earth. All that day Litvinov smiled and smiled, even when he went round his farm and gave orders. He at once began to prepare for the journey, and two weeks later he was on his way to Tatiana.

He drove quite slowly, along byroads, without any particular adventures except that the tire of one back wheel broke. A smith welded it and welded it, swore both at it and at himself, but gave it up in the end. Fortunately it transpired that even with a broken tire one can travel quite comfortably in Russia, especially over the "soft" — in other words, through the mud. On the other hand, he had two or three quite interesting meetings. At one postal station he came upon an arbitration congress,[1] and in the chair was Pishchalkin, who impressed him as being a Solon or Solomon, with such exalted wisdom were his speeches filled, with such unbounded respect did the landowners and the peasants regard him. . . . Even in appearance Pishchalkin had begun to look like an ancient sage; the hair had gone from his temples, but his face had filled out and had frozen into a kind of majestic jelly of quite unbridled virtue. He greeted Litvinov on his arrival "in my — if I may use such an ambitious expression — my own country," but at once went into a spate of well-intentioned feelings. But he did manage to communicate one piece of news — namely, concerning Voroshilov. The knight of the roll of honor had again entered the military service and had already found time to read a lecture to the officers of his regiment on "Buddhism" or "dynamism" or something of that sort — Pishchalkin did not well remember what.

At the next postal station some long time elapsed before fresh horses were harnessed into Litvinov's carriage — it was at dawn — and he dozed off as he sat in his seat. He was aroused by a voice that seemed familiar; he opened his eyes. . . .

Lord! Surely it wasn't Mr. Gubariov in a gray jacket and baggy pajama trousers, standing and swearing on the balcony of the postal house? . . . No, it was not Mr. Gubariov. . . . But what a striking resemblance! . . . Except that this gentleman had a mouth still wider and toothier, and the look of his gloomy eyes was still more ferocious, and the nose was bigger, and the beard thicker, and all the features even more heavy and repellent.

"The scou-oundrels! The scou-oundrels!" he said slowly and malevolently, opening wide his wolfish mouth. "The filthy little

[1] Part of the machinery for settling land disputes between landowners and their peasants, after 1861. (Tr.)

peasants! . . . There you have it—your boasted freedom . . . and you can't get horses! . . . The scou-oundrels!"

"The scou-oundrels! Scou-oundrels!" came a second voice through the door, and on to the balcony walked another—also in a gray jacket and baggy pajamas—and this time it was genuinely, undoubtedly, the real Mr. Gubariov himself, Stepan Nikolaevich Gubariov in person.

"The filthy peasants!" he went on in imitation of his brother (it transpired that the first gentleman was his elder brother, the *"dentiste"* [1] of the old school, who ran his estate). "They deserve a good hiding, that's what; a few punches in the face; that's the freedom they need . . . in their teeth. . . . How they talk! . . . The local head man . . . I'd show them. . . . And where is that M'sieur Roston? . . . Why doesn't he see to it? . . . It's his business, the drone . . . he never troubles himself. . . ."

"But I have told you again and again, brother," said Gubariov senior, "that he is good for nothing, he's just a drone, as you say! Only you would, for old time's sake . . . M'sieur Roston, M'sieur Roston! . . . Where have you got to?"

"Roston! Roston!" shouted the younger, the great Gubariov. "Give him a good shout, brother Dorimedont Nikolaich!"

"That's what I am doing, brother Stepan Nikolaich. M'sieur Roston!"

"Here I am, here I am, here I am!" came a hurried voice, and out of the house flew Bambayev.

Litvinov gasped. A well-worn Hungarian coat with holes in the sleeves flapped miserably about the unfortunate enthusiast; his features had not so much changed as twisted and drawn together; his terrified little eyes expressed servile fear and hungry subservience; but his dyed whiskers still bristled above his downy lips. From the height of the balcony the brothers Gubariov immediately and violently began to berate him. He halted below, in the mud, before them and, humbly bowing his back, attempted to appease them with a timid little smile, and crumpled his peaked cap in his crimson fingers, and fidgeted with his feet, and muttered that the horses would be coming in a minute. . . . But the brothers did not stop nagging until at last the younger man happened to cast a glance at Litvinov. Whether he recognized him, or whether he was shamed in the presence of a stranger, one

[1] See note, p. 25. (Tr.)

cannot say; he suddenly turned on his heels, like a bear, and, chewing his beard, waddled into the post station. The other brother at once lapsed into silence and, also turning like a bear, followed him. Evidently the great Gubariov had not lost his influence even in his native land.

Bambayev was about to wander in after the brothers. . . . Litvinov called him by name. He looked round, stared, and, recognizing Litvinov, rushed to him with outstretched hands. But on reaching the carriage he clutched at the door leaned his chest against it, and broke into a flood of tears.

"Enough, enough of that, Bambayev!" Litvinov said, bending over him and touching him on the shoulder.

But he went on sobbing. "You see — you see — you see what I've come to . . ." he muttered as he sobbed.

"Bambayev!" the brothers thundered from the house.

Bambayev raised his head and hurriedly wiped away his tears.

"Greetings, my dear fellow!" he whispered, "greetings and good-by! . . . Do you hear? They're calling me."

"Yes, but what fate has brought you here?" Litvinov asked. "And what does all this mean? I thought they were calling a Frenchman — "

"I'm their — domestic manager, their steward," Bambayev answered, cocking his finger at the house. "And I've become a Frenchman by way of a joke. What is one to do, brother! I've nothing to eat, I've spent my last farthing, and so willy-nilly you slip your head through the collar. And not through ambition."

"But has *he* been long in Russia? And how did he part from his former comrades?"

"Ah, brother! That's all put away now. . . . You see, the weather's changed. . . He simply threw out Matriona Sukhanchikova on her neck. In her grief she went to Portugal."

"Why to Portugal? What an idiotic idea!"

"Yes, brother, to Portugal, with the two Matrionovites."

"With whom?"

"With the Matrionovites: that's what the members of her party call themselves."

"Has Matriona Kuzminishna formed a party, then? And is it very numerous?"

"Why, it consists of just those two. But soon it will be six months since *he* returned here. Others were placed under surveillance, but not he. He is living in the country with his brother, and you should hear now — "

"Bambayev!"

"Coming, Stepan Nikolaich, coming! But you're flourishing and enjoying life, my boy! Well, and God be thanked! Where are you off to now? . . . I never thought, I never guessed — Do you remember Baden? Ah, that was a life! And, by the way, do you remember Bindasov too? Just imagine, he's dead. He became an excise official. And one day he began to quarrel in a pub, and they gave him one with a stick and split his head open. Yes, yes, difficult times have arrived! But I still say: Russia — ah, this Russia! Look even at that couple of geese: in all Europe you won't see anything like them! Real Arzamas geese!"

And after paying this last tribute to his incorrigible necessity to rhapsodize, Bambayev ran to the postal station, where his name had been shouted again, and not without some banging of fists.

Toward the end of that same day Litvinov drove into Tatiana's village. The small house in which his former fiancée lived stood on a hillock above a little river, in the midst of a recently laid-out garden. The house also was new, only recently built, and could be seen for a long distance across the river and fields. It was revealed to Litvinov's eyes nearly a couple of miles away, with its steep-roofed mezzanine floor, and a row of windows glowing crimson in the evening sun. Ever since the last posthouse he had felt a secret anxiety; but now he was simply filled with embarrassment, an embarrassment joyous but not without a touch of fear. "How will they welcome me?" he thought; "how shall I present myself? . . ." To occupy himself with something he fell to talking with his driver, a sedate peasant with a gray beard, who, however, had charged him for eighteen miles, whereas the distance was not fifteen. He asked him whether he knew the landowners named Shestovy.

"The Shestovys? Of course I know them! They're good ladies, there's no denying! They give us peasants medical treatment. It's the truth I'm telling. They're doctors! People go to them from all the district round. It's true. They even crawl. When someone falls ill, for instance, or has cut himself, or something, they go to them at once, and they at once give them fomentations, powders, or plasters, and it's of great help. And you can't imagine how the people show their gratitude; but they say they can't agree to taking anything; they don't do it for money. And they've started a school. . . . But that's a waste of time!"

All the time the driver was talking, Litvinov did not take his eyes off the house. . . . Now a woman in white came out on the balcony, stood there awhile, stood and then vanished. . . . "Surely it isn't she?" His heart leaped within him. "Hurry! Hurry!" he shouted to the driver; the man whipped up his horses. A few more seconds . . . and the carriage rolled through the open gates. . . . And Kapitolina Markovna was standing on the veranda and, quite beside herself, clapping her hands, was shouting: "I recognized him, I was the first to recognize him! It's he! It's he! . . . I recognized him!"

Litvinov jumped out of the carriage before the page who ran up could open the door, and hurriedly embraced Kapitolina Markovna, then rushed into the house, through the vestibule, into the hall. . . . Before him stood Tatiana, all blushes. She looked at him with her kindly, gracious eyes (she was a little thinner, but that suited her) and gave him her hand. But he did not take the hand; once more he fell on his knees before her. She had not expected that in the least and she did not know what to say, what to do. . . . The tears started to her eyes. She was alarmed, but all her face lit up with joy. . . . "Grigory Mikhailich, what are you doing, Grigory Mikhailich?" she said. . . . But he went on kissing the hem of her dress . . . and he remembered with emotion how he had gone down on his knees before her at Baden also. . . . But then—and now!

"Tania," he repeated, "Tania, have you forgiven me, Tania?"

"Auntie, auntie, what does this mean?" Tatiana turned to Kapitolina Markovna as she entered.

"Don't stop him, don't stop him, Tania," the good old woman answered. "You see: he has brought a contrite heart."

However, it is time to end. Besides, there is nothing to add; the reader will guess for himself. . . . But what of Irena?

She is just as charming as ever, despite her thirty years; young men without number fall in love with her, and even more would fall in love if — if . . .

Reader, would you care to come with us for a few moments

Smoke

to Petersburg, to one of the most important buildings in that city? Look! Before you is a spacious room, furnished, we do not say richly — that expression is too lowly — but seriously, representatively, imposingly. Are you conscious of a certain shiver of servility? Then know: you have entered a temple, a temple consecrated to the highest decorum, to abundantly loving virtue; in a word: to something not of this earth. What an occult, truly occult silence envelops you! The velvet portieres at the door, the velvet curtains at the windows, the fluffy, yielding carpet on the floor, all would seem to be predestined and adapted to the appeasement, to the amelioration of all coarse sounds and strong sensations. The sedulously suspended lamps inspire sedate feelings; a seemly scent suffuses the rather fusty air; even the samovar on the table hisses restrainedly and modestly. The mistress of the house, an important personage in the Petersburg world, talks almost inaudibly; she always speaks as if there were a difficult, all but dying patient in the room. In imitation of her the other ladies hardly even whisper; and her sister, who is pouring tea, moves her lips quite without making a sound, so that the young man sitting opposite her, who has happened to find himself in this temple of decorum, is bewildered to know what she wants of him, though she whispers to him for the sixth time: *"Voulez-vous une tasse de thé?"*

In the corners young, comely men are visible; a gentle aspiration shines in their gaze; imperturbably gentle, though surreptitious, is the expression on their faces; numerous marks of distinction gently glitter on their chests. The conversation also is of a gentle character: it is concerned with religious and patriotic matters, with F. N. Glinka's [1] "Mysterious Drop," the missions to the East, the monasteries and brotherhoods in Byelorussia. At rare intervals, softly treading over the soft carpet, liveried lackeys pass to and fro; their huge calves, enveloped in tight-fitting silk stockings, shiver noiselessly with every step; the respectful quiver of the sturdy muscles only deepens the general impression of splendid magnificence, splendid intentions, splendid veneration. . . . This is a temple! A temple!

"Have you seen Madame Ratmirova today?" one personage briefly asks.

[1] Russian soldier, author, and mystic poet (1786–1880). (Tr.)

Turgenev

"I met her today at Lise's," the mistress answers like an æolian harp. "I am sorry for her. . . . She has a malevolent mind — *elle n'a pas la foi.*"

"Yes, yes," the personage repeats, "it was Piotr Ivanich, I remember, who said of her, and said very truly, *qu'elle a — she has a malevolent mind.*"

"*Elle n'a pas la foi,*" the mistress's voice exhales like the smoke from incense. "*C'est une âme égarée.* She has a malevolent mind."

"She has a malevolent mind," the sister repeats with only her lips.

And that is why not all the young men are completely in love with Irena. . . . They are afraid of her — they are afraid of her "malevolent mind." Such is the stock phrase that has come into currency about her; in that phrase, as in all phrases, there is a grain of truth. And not only the young people are afraid of her; she is feared by their elders, and by the higher-placed persons, and even by the personages. No one else has such a gift for faithfully and subtly hitting off the ludicrous or the petty aspect of a character, no one else has such a power to stigmatize it so mercilessly in the unforgettable word. . . . And that word sears all the more painfully because it comes from fragrant, beautiful lips. . . . It is difficult to say what goes on in her soul; but among the crowd of her adorers rumor attaches the title of favorite to none.

Irena's husband is swiftly advancing along the road that the French call the path to glory. The stout general has surpassed him; the condescending general has been left behind. And in the same city in which Irena resides, our friend Sozont Potugin also resides; he rarely sees her, and she has no particular need to keep in touch with him. . . . The girl who was entrusted to his care died recently.

Fathers and Sons

1 8 6 1

I

WELL, Piotr, nothing to be seen yet?" asked a gentleman some forty years of age, bareheaded, and wearing a dusty coat and checkered pantaloons, as on May 20, 1859 he walked out on the low, small veranda of an inn on the X X X highroad; he addressed the question to his servant, a young and heavy-cheeked fellow with a very light down on his chin, and tiny, lackluster eyes.

The servant, who had a turquoise ring in his ear, pomaded hair of various hues, and respectful movements of the body — in a word, everything that distinguished a manservant of the later, more perfect generation — condescended to gaze along the road and replied: "Nothing to be seen, nothing at all."

"Nothing to be seen?" the master repeated.

"Nothing at all," the man replied a second time.

The gentleman sighed and sat down on the bench. We shall introduce the reader to him while he is sitting, gazing thoughtfully about, with his little legs tucked under him.

His name is Nikolai Piotrovich Kirsanov. Some ten miles from the inn he has a good estate of two hundred souls, or, as he puts it since he reached a land-rental agreement with his peasants and started a "farm," of thirty-five hundred acres of land. His father, a general on active service in 1812, semiliterate, a coarse but not really bad man, and a true Russian, had toiled and sweated all his life, first commanding a brigade, then a division, and had lived permanently in the provinces, where, owing to his rank, he played quite a considerable role. Like his elder brother, Pavel, of whom we shall be speaking later, Nikolai Piotrovich was born in the south of Russia, and until he was fourteen was educated at home, surrounded by inexpensive tutors, jaunty but servile adjutants, and other regimental and staff personalities. His mother, one of the

Kolyazin family, responded to the Christian name of Agathe while she was single, but was called Agafoklea Kuzminishna Kirsanova after she was married; she was the type of officer's wife known as "mother commander," wore extravagantly trimmed bonnets and rustling silk dresses, was always the first to go up to the cross in church, was a loud and garrulous talker, let the children kiss her hand each morning, blessed them at night — in a word, she lived a life of full content. As a general's son Nikolai Piotrovich — though he not only was undistinguished for his bravery, but even deserved to be called a little coward — was, like his brother, Pavel, to have entered military service; but he broke his leg on the very day the news of his commission arrived and, after lying two months in bed, was left "rather lame" for the rest of his life. His father gave him up in despair and allowed him to join the civil service. He carried him off to Petersburg as soon as he had reached the age of eighteen and entered him in the university. It so happened that just about then his brother joined a guards regiment as an officer. The two young men set up house together in one apartment, under the distant supervision of Ilia Kolyazin, an important official, their first cousin once removed on the mother's side. Their father returned to his division and his spouse and only occasionally sent his sons large sheets of gray paper folded in four, mottled with the secretary's flowing script. The last page of these fourfold sheets was adorned with the words "Piotr Kirsanov, Major General," industriously circumscribed with scrolls and flourishes. In 1835 Nikolai Piotrovich left the university with the degree of Bachelor, and in the same year General Kirsanov was placed on the retired list owing to an unsatisfactory military parade, and arrived with his wife to live in Petersburg. He intended to rent a house close to the Tauride Garden and had put his name down for membership in the English Club, but he died suddenly of a stroke. Agafoklea Kuzminishna soon followed him: she could not get accustomed to the lonely life of the capital; the misery of existence as a retired general's wife gnawed at her. Meantime, even while his parents were alive and to their no little chagrin, Nikolai Piotrovich succeeded in falling in love with the daughter of an official named Prepolovensky, the former owner of his apartment; she was a pleasant-looking and, as one says, a mentally developed girl: she read the serious articles in the "scientific" sections of the journals. He married her as soon as the period of mourning was past and, abandoning the post in the Ministry of Crown Lands that his father had obtained for him by pulling strings, he lived a blissful life with his Masha, first in a summer residence out of town near the Institute of Forestry, then in town, in a small and very comfortable apartment, with a clean staircase and a rather chilly reception room, and finally in the country, where he settled down completely and where his son, Arkady, was born soon after. The couple lived very well and quietly: they were hardly ever separated, they read together, played four-hand pieces on the piano, and sang duets; she planted flowers and supervised the poultry yard, he engaged in farming and occasionally went hunting, while Arkady grew and grew, also well and quietly. Ten years passed like a dream. In 1847 Kirsanov's wife died. He hardly withstood this blow, and went gray in a few weeks; he planned to go abroad, in order to get at least a little change — but then 1848 arrived. He was forced to return to the country and, after a rather prolonged period of inactivity, began to make changes in the running of the estate. In 1855 he took Arkady to the university; he lived three winters with him in Petersburg, going hardly anywhere and endeavoring to cultivate acquaintance with his son's youthful colleagues. He could not travel to Petersburg for Arkady's last winter, and so we see him in May 1859, now quite gray, rather stout, and a little bent in the back; he was waiting for his son, who, like himself earlier, had gained the degree of Bachelor.

Out of a sense of the proprieties, or possibly because he wanted to escape his master's eye, the servant went under the gateway and lit a pipe. Nikolai Piotrovich's head drooped, and he began to gaze at the rickety steps of the veranda; a large, speckled chicken decorously walked about it, firmly setting down its large yellow feet; a bedraggled kitten, delicately perched on the railing, watched the bird with animosity. The sun was burning hot. From the shady entrance to the inn came the smell of warm rye bread. Our Nikolai Piotrovich fell to dreaming: "My son . . . a Bachelor . . . dear Arkady . . . " the thoughts incessantly revolved in his head; he tried to think of something else, but those same thoughts returned again and again. He recalled his dead wife: "She didn't live to see it!" he whispered despondently. . . . A plump dove-gray pigeon flew down onto the road and hurriedly went to drink from a puddle by the well. Nikolai Piotrovich began to watch it, but now his ear caught the rattle of approaching wheels.

"I think they're coming," his man reported, diving out of the gateway.

Nikolai Piotrovich jumped up and gazed along the road. A tarantass drawn by a troika of hired horses appeared; in the tarantass could be seen the band of a student's peaked cap, the familiar features of a dear face.

"My dear Arkady! My dear Arkady!" Kirsanov shouted, and he ran, and he waved his arms. . . . A few moments later his lips were pressed to the young Bachelor's beardless, dusty, and sunburnt cheek.

II

"Let me brush myself down, Papa," Arkady said in a voice rather hoarse with the journey, but ringing with the tones of youth, as he gaily responded to his father's embraces. "I'll make you all dirty."

"That's all right, that's all right," Nikolai Piotrovich declared, smiling tenderly, and he brushed his hand once or twice over the collar of his son's topcoat and his own coat. "Now let me see you, let me see you," he added, stepping back. But he at once went with hurried steps toward the inn, calling: "This way, this way, and bring the horses quickly!"

Nikolai Piotrovich seemed to be far more moved than his son; he seemed even to be a little embarrassed, as though shy. Arkady halted him.

"Papa," he said, "let me introduce you to my good friend Bazarov, whom I have told you so much about in my letters. He has been so kind as to consent to stay with us."

Nikolai Piotrovich turned swiftly and, going up to a tall man in a long canvas coat with tassels, who had just climbed out of the tarantass, firmly squeezed his bare red hand, which the other man seemed reluctant to hold out to him.

"I'm sincerely glad," he began, "and grateful for your kind intention to visit us; I hope — may I know your Christian name and patronymic?"

"Yevgeny Vasiliev," Bazarov replied in an indolent but manly voice and, turning back the collar of his coat, revealed all his face to Nikolai Piotrovich's eyes. The face was long and lean, with a high forehead, a nose broad above and thin below, large, rather green eyes, and hanging side-whiskers of a sandy color; it was animated with a tranquil smile, and expressed self-confidence and intelligence.

"I hope, my dear Yevgeny Vasilich, that you will not be bored during your stay," Nikolai Piotrovich continued.

Bazarov's thin lips very slightly parted, but he made no answer and only raised his peaked cap. His ash-blond hair, long and thick, did not conceal the considerable protuberances of his ample cranium.

"Well, what do you think, Arkady?" Nikolai Piotrovich began again, turning to his son. "We'll have the horses harnessed up at once, shall we? Or would you like to rest?"

"We can rest at home, Papa; order them to be harnessed."

"At once, at once," his father took him up. "Hey, Piotr, d'you hear? See to things quickly, my lad!"

Piotr, who, being a perfect servant, did not come to kiss his young master's hand, but only bowed to him from a distance, again vanished through the gateway.

"I have the carriage here, but there is a troika of horses for your tarantass as well," Nikolai Piotrovich fussily said, while Arkady took a drink from an iron ewer brought by the mistress of the inn, and Bazarov lit a pipe and went up to the driver, who was unharnessing the horses. "But the calash has only two seats, and I don't know how your friend — "

"He'll ride in the tarantass," Arkady interrupted in an undertone. "Please don't stand on ceremony with him. He's a very fine fellow, and very unassuming in his ways, as you'll see."

Nikolai Piotrovich's coachman brought out the horses.

"Well, hurry up, thick-beard!" Bazarov said to the tarantass-driver.

"D'you hear that, Mitiukha?" remarked another driver who was standing close by with his hands thrust into the back slit of his sheepskin. "Did you hear what the gentleman called you? You're thick-bearded all right."

Mitiukha only dusted his cap and dragged the reins free of the sweating shaft-horse.

"Quicker, quicker, give him a hand, lads!" Nikolai Piotrovich exclaimed; "and you'll have something for vodka."

A few minutes later the horses were harnessed, the father and son took their seats in the calash, Piotr clambered on the box,

Bazarov jumped into the tarantass and rested his head against the leather cushion, and both the carriages rattled off.

III

"Well, and so you're a Bachelor at last and have come home," Nikolai Piotrovich said, touching Arkady now on the shoulder, now on the knee. "At last!"

"And how is Uncle? Quite well?" asked Arkady, who, despite the sincere, almost childish joy that possessed him, was anxious to turn the conversation as soon as possible from an emotional to a more matter-of-fact note.

"Yes, he's quite well. He wanted to come with me to meet you, but for some reason he changed his mind."

"And have you been waiting for me long?" Arkady asked.

"Why, about five hours."

"Good old Papa!"

Arkady energetically turned to his father and kissed him vigorously on the cheek. Nikolai Piotrovich laughed quietly.

"I have a fine horse ready for you!" he began; "you wait and see. And your room has been hung with wallpaper."

"And is there a room for Bazarov?"

"We can find one for him."

"Please, Papa, be nice to him. I can't tell you how much I value his friendship."

"You made his acquaintance quite recently, didn't you?"

"Yes."

"I thought I didn't see him last winter. What is he doing?"

"His chief subject is natural science. But he knows everything. Next winter he wants to study to be a doctor."

"Ah! So he'll be in the medical faculty!" Nikolai Piotrovich remarked, and then was silent for a moment or two. "Piotr," he added, pointing, "surely those are our peasants coming along?"

Piotr looked in the direction his master was pointing. Several peasants' carts drawn by unbitted horses were swiftly rolling along a narrow field track. Each cart carried a peasant, and many of them two, riding with their sheepskins flung wide open.

"That is so," Piotr observed.

"Where are they driving to? Into the town, surely?"

"They must be going to the town. To the pub," Piotr added contemptuously, and leaned a little toward the coachman, as

170

though appealing to him. But the coachman did not even stir: he was a man of the old school and did not share Piotr's more modern views.

"I've had a lot of trouble with the peasants this year," Nikolai Piotrovich went on, turning to his son. "They're not paying their rent. But what can you do?"

"Are you satisfied with your hired laborers?"

"Yes." Nikolai Piotrovich let the word filter through his teeth. "But they're getting at them, that's the trouble; and there's no real effort being made even yet. They ruin the harness. But they haven't done the plowing at all badly. With thorough threshing there will be flour enough. But I suppose you're not interested in the farm at the moment?"

"We haven't any shade anywhere, that's the pity," Arkady remarked, without replying to the last question.

"I have had a large awning fitted over the balcony on the north side," Nikolai Piotrovich replied, "and now we shall be able even to dine in the open."

"It will be rather like a holiday house . . . but anyhow, these are all details. What air we have here! How gloriously it smells! Really, I think that nowhere in the world does the air smell as it does in these parts! And the sky — "

Arkady suddenly stopped, threw an oblique glance over his shoulder, and lapsed into silence.

"Of course," Nikolai Piotrovich remarked, "you were born here; everything about it ought to seem more than usually good to you."

"But, Papa, it doesn't matter where a man is born."

"None the less — "

"Really, it doesn't matter in the least."

Nikolai Piotrovich looked sidelong at his son, and the calash had covered nearly half a mile before the conversation was renewed.

"I don't remember whether I wrote and told you," Nikolai Piotrovich began, "your former nurse, Yegorovna, has died."

"Really? Poor old woman! But is Prokofich still here?"

"Yes, and he hasn't changed in the least. He still grumbles away just the same as ever. In fact, you won't find any great changes at Marino at all."

"Have you still got the same steward?"

"Except that I have changed the steward. I decided not to keep any freed servants or any of the former domestic serfs, or at least not to entrust them with any positions involving responsibility." (With his eyes Arkady indicated Piotr.) *"Il est libre, en effet,"* Nikolai Piotrovich remarked in an undertone, "but then, he is a valet. I now have a steward from the burgher class; he seems to be an efficient fellow. I have agreed to pay him two hundred and fifty rubles a year. But by the way," Nikolai Piotrovich added, rubbing his forehead and eyebrows with his hand, a gesture that was always a sign of his inward embarrassment, "I just told you that you won't find any changes in Marino. That is not quite correct. I consider it my duty to warn you, though — "

He hesitated for a moment, then went on in French:

"A strict moralist would find my frankness out of place, but to begin with, the matter can't be concealed, and secondly, as you know, I have always observed special principles in regard to relations between father and son. For that matter, you, of course, will be quite entitled to condemn me. At my age — In a word, that — that girl, of whom I expect you have already heard — "

"Fenichka?" Arkady asked easily.

Nikolai Piotrovich went red.

"Please don't mention her name aloud. Why, yes — she is living with me now. I have accommodated her in the house — where there were two small rooms. But in any case everything can be changed."

"But why should it, Papa?"

"Your friend will be staying with us . . . it will be awkward."

"Please don't be anxious on Bazarov's account. He's above all that."

"Well, you of course — " said Nikolai Piotrovich. "The small wing of the house is unsatisfactory, that's the trouble."

"But please, Papa," Arkady took him up, "you appear to be apologizing; you ought to be ashamed."

"Of course I ought to be ashamed!" Nikolai Piotrovich replied, going redder and redder.

"Now, that's enough, Papa, quite enough, please let it drop!" Arkady said, smiling amiably. "He's apologizing for something!" he thought, and his soul was filled with a feeling of condescending tenderness for his good and gentle father, a feeling mingled with a sense of secret superiority. "Please drop it," he repeated yet again, involuntarily enjoying the consciousness of his own more advanced and free views.

Nikolai Piotrovich glanced at him from under the fingers of the hand with which he was still rubbing his forehead, and something plucked at his heart. But he at once rebuked himself.

"Well, here is the beginning of our land," he said after a long silence.

"And that is our wood ahead, isn't it?" Arkady asked.

"Yes, that is ours. Only I have sold it. It will be felled this year."

"Why did you sell it?"

"We needed the money; and besides, that land is to be handed over to the peasants."

"Who don't pay you their rent?"

"That is their business; but in any case they will pay some time or other."

"It's a pity about the wood," Arkady remarked, and began to look about him.

The district through which they were driving could not be called picturesque. Open field, unbrokenly open field stretched right away to the horizon, sometimes rising a little, then declining again; here and there small woods were visible, and gullies, with scanty and stunted scrub, wound in a manner reminiscent of the way they were represented on the ancient maps of Catherine's time. Here and there, too, were narrow streams with steep banks, and tiny ponds with crumbling dams, and little villages with low, tiny huts beneath gloomy, frequently tumbledown roofs, and crooked threshing-sheds with walls made of wattle and with yawning little gateways by abandoned threshing-floors, and churches, sometimes of brick with the stucco falling away, sometimes of wood with crosses awry and decayed burial-grounds. Arkady felt a little griping of the heart. As though of deliberate intent, all the peasants they fell in with were ragged, and were riding miserable little nags; wayside osier willows with hanging bark and broken branches stood like beggars in rags; emaciated, shaggy cows, looking as though gnawed to the bone, were greedily nibbling at the grass in the ditches. They seemed to have only just torn themselves away from menacing, death-dealing talons. And, evoked by the miserable aspect of these debilitated animals, a white phantom of joyless, endless winter with its blizzards, frosts, and snows arose in the midst of that spring day. "No," Arkady thought, "this is not a rich country, it does not suggest either affluence or industry; it cannot, it cannot be left like that, changes simply must be made . . . but how to effect them, how to set about it? . . ."

So Arkady meditated; but while he was meditating, spring came into its own. Everything around him was green shot with gold, everything broadly and gently undulated and shone beneath the gentle breath of the warming breeze — everything, the trees, the bushes, and the grass; everywhere the skylarks poured out endless, ringing streams of song; the pewits called as they hovered about the low-lying meadows or silently flitted from mound to mound; beautifully black, the rooks wandered amid the tender green of the still young and low spring crops; they were lost in the rye, which was already beginning to whiten; only rarely did their heads appear amid its smoky waves. Arkady gazed and gazed, and his meditations gradually faded, vanished. He flung off his greatcoat, and such a merry, such a youthful lad looked at his father that Nikolai Piotrovich embraced him once more.

"Not far now," the older man remarked. "As soon as we get to the top of that little hill the house will be in sight. We shall have a wonderful life together, Arkady; you'll help me on the farm, provided that doesn't bore you. Now we must come really close to each other, must know each other really well, mustn't we?"

"Of course," Arkady said; "but what a wonderful day it is today!"

"It is for your arrival, my dear boy. Yes, spring in all its glory. But, you know, I agree with Pushkin — you remember, in *Yevgeny Oniegin?*

> *To me how mournful is thy coming,*
> *Springtime, springtime, the time of love!*
> *How — "*

"Arkady!" Bazarov's voice came from the tarantass; "send me a match, I've nothing to light my pipe with."

Nikolai Piotrovich lapsed into silence, and Arkady, who had begun to listen to him not without a feeling of astonishment, yet not without sympathy, hurriedly took a silver matchbox from his pocket and sent Piotr with it to Bazarov.

"Would you like a cigar?" Bazarov shouted again.

"Send it along," Arkady replied.

Piotr returned to the calash and handed him the matchbox and a black cigar, which Arkady lit at once, spreading such a strong and acrid scent of well-seasoned tobacco that Nikolai Piotrovich, who had never smoked in all his life, involuntarily turned his nose away, though imperceptibly, in order not to upset his son.

Fifteen minutes later both carriages halted before the veranda of a new wooden house painted gray and covered with a red iron roof. This was Marino, also known as Novaya-Slobodka — the new settlement — or, as the peasants called it, One-man Hamlet.

IV

No swarm of domestics poured onto the veranda to meet their masters; only one girl, aged about twelve, appeared; she was followed out of the house by a lad who greatly resembled Piotr and was dressed in a gray livery jacket with white buttons adorned with armorial bearings, for he was Pavel Kirsanov's man. He silently opened the door of the carriage and unbuttoned the apron of the tarantass. Nikolai Piotrovich and his son, together with Bazarov, went through the dark and almost empty hall, where a young woman's face peered for a moment round one of its doors, and passed into the reception room, which was furnished in the latest style.

"So we're at home," Nikolai Piotrovich observed, removing his hat and shaking back his hair. "Now the chief thing is to have some supper and a rest."

"It certainly would not be a bad idea to have something to eat," Bazarov remarked, stretching himself, and he dropped on a divan.

"Yes, yes, let us have some supper, supper quickly." For no obvious reason Nikolai Piotrovich stamped his foot. "And here is Prokofich, just at the right moment."

Prokofich was a man of about sixty, white-haired, thin, and swarthy, in a brown frock coat with copper buttons, and with a rose-colored kerchief round his neck. He smirked, went to kiss Arkady's hand, and, after bowing to the guest, retired to the door and stood with hands folded behind his back.

"There he is, Prokofich," Nikolai Piotrovich began, "he's come back to us at last. . . . Well, what do you think of him?"

"He looks in the best of health," the old man declared, and he smirked again, but at once knitted his thick eyebrows. "Am I to lay the table?" he said meaningly.

"Yes, yes, please. But won't you go to your room first, Yevgeny Vasilich?"

"No, thank you, I don't need to. Only give orders for my small trunk to be taken to my room, and this garment can be put in there too," he added, taking off his light coat.

"Very good. Prokofich, take his coat." (Prokofich, who appeared to be amazed, took Bazarov's "garment" in both hands and, raising it high above his head, retreated on tiptoe.) "And how about you, Arkady, will you go to your room for a moment or two?"

"Yes, I must clean myself up," Arkady replied, and was about to go to the door; but at that moment a man of average height, dressed in a dark English suit, a fashionable low-cut cravat, and patent-leather shoes, entered the reception room. He was Arkady's uncle, Pavel Piotrovich Kirsanov. He appeared to be about forty-five years of age; his close-cut gray hair gleamed darkly like new silver; his face, choleric but unlined, unusually regular and pure, as though fashioned by a light and subtle chisel, revealed that at one time he had been remarkably handsome; his clear, black, rather elongated eyes were particularly fine. All the uncle's elegant and well-bred appearance retained a youthful harmony and that upward striving from the earth which a man almost entirely loses when he has passed the twenties.

Pavel Piotrovich took his beautiful hand with its long, rosy nails — a hand that seemed even more beautiful because of the snowy whiteness of his cuff, with its fastening of a single large opal — out of the pocket of his pantaloons and held it out to his nephew. Having accomplished this preliminary European handshake, he kissed him three times, Russian fashion; in other words, he touched his nephew's cheek three times with his perfumed mustaches, and pronounced:

"Welcome home."

Nikolai Piotrovich introduced him to Bazarov: Pavel Piotrovich bent his supple waist a little and smiled faintly, but did not give him his hand and even put it back in his pocket.

"I was beginning to think you would not arrive today," he said in a pleasant voice, affably swaying his body, twitching his shoulders, and displaying his splendid white teeth. "Did anything happen on the road?"

"Oh no," Arkady replied, "we were only delayed a little. But in consequence we are as hungry as wolves. Get Prokofich to hurry, Papa, and I'll be back in a moment."

"Wait, I'll come with you," Bazarov exclaimed, suddenly starting up from the divan. The two young men went out.

"Who is that?" Pavel Piotrovich asked.

"A friend of Arkady's, a very intelligent man, according to him."

"Is he going to stay with us?"

"Yes."

"That hairy man?"

"Why, yes."

Pavel Piotrovich drummed his nails on the table.

"I find that Arkady *s'est dégourdi*," he remarked. "I am glad he has returned."

They talked little at supper. Bazarov especially said almost nothing, but he ate a great deal. Nikolai Piotrovich told various incidents of his farming life, as he put it, discussed the forthcoming government measures, the committees, the deputations, the necessity of introducing machinery, and so on. Pavel Piotrovich slowly walked to and fro (he never ate supper), occasionally sipping from a glass filled with red wine, and still more rarely making some remark, or rather exclamation, in the nature of "Ah! Ehee! Hm!" Arkady told some of the latest Petersburg news, but he felt a little awkward — that awkwardness which a young man usually possesses when he has just ceased to be a child and has returned to a spot where everybody is used to seeing and regarding him as a child. He dragged out his talk unnecessarily, avoided the word "Papa," and even replaced it once by the word "Father," pronounced, truly, through his teeth; with excessive jauntiness he poured far more wine into his glass than he really desired, and drank it all. Prokofich did not take his eyes off him and only chewed his lips. After supper they all retired at once.

"But you have a rather eccentric uncle," Bazarov said to Arkady as he sat in a gown by his bed and sucked at a stocky pipe. "What elegance to find in the country, you know! Those nails of his, those nails! Why, you could send those nails to an exhibition!"

"Ah, but you don't know that he was a lion in his day," Arkady replied. "I'll tell you his story some time or other. He was really handsome, he turned the heads of all the women."

"You don't say! So it's all for old times' sake. Pity there's no one to captivate here. I stared and stared: at those amazing cuffs of his, looking just as though made of stone, and his chin so smoothly shaved. But you know it's ridiculous, isn't it, Arkady Nikolaich?"

"Maybe; but he really is a fine man."

"An archaic phenomenon! But your father's a great lad! He wastes his time reading poetry, and I don't suppose he's brilliant at farming, but he's a good sort."

"My father is a man with a golden heart."

"Have you noticed that he's shy?"

Arkady shook his head, as though he himself were never shy.

"It's an astonishing thing," Bazarov went on, "these old romantics. They develop their nervous system to the point of irritability, and so their equilibrium is disturbed. All the same, good night! I've an English washstand in my room, but the door won't fasten. Even so, that is something to be encouraged — English washstands; now that really is progress!"

Bazarov went out, and Arkady was overcome by a feeling of happiness. It is pleasant to fall asleep in your own house, on a familiar bed, under a blanket over which beloved hands have toiled, perhaps the hands of the nurse — those gracious, kindly, and unwearying hands. Arkady recalled his old nurse, Yegorovna, and sighed, and wished her "rest in peace." For himself he did not pray.

Both he and Bazarov soon dropped off, but other people in the house were a long time getting to sleep. His son's return had excited Nikolai Piotrovich. He got into bed, but did not put out the candles and, resting his head on his hand, thought long thoughts. His brother sat until well after midnight in his own room, in a broad leather armchair, before a hearth in which coal was faintly burning. Pavel Piotrovich did not undress, he only changed patent-leather shoes for red Chinese slippers without heels. He held the latest issue of *Galignani* in his hands, but he did not read; he stared fixedly at the hearth, where a flickering bluish flame died away and started up again. God knows where his thoughts wandered to, but they did not wander only in the past: the expression on his face was concentrated and morose, which is not the case when a man is occupied only with memories. But in a little back room the young woman named Fenichka sat on a large chest, in a blue dressing-jacket and with a white kerchief flung over her dark hair, sometimes listening, sometimes dozing, sometimes gazing at a half-open door, through which a child's cot could be seen and the regular breathing of a sleeping infant could be heard.

v

Next day Bazarov was awake and out of the house before anyone else. "Hm!" he thought as he looked about him, "not a very impressive spot!" When Nikolai Piotrovich had divided the land with his peasants, he had had to use nearly eleven acres of completely level and bare ground to make the new homestead. He built the house, the offices and farm buildings, made a garden, dug a pond and two wells; but the young trees did not do well, very little water gathered in the pond, and the well water proved to have a brackish taste. Only an arbor of lilac and acacias had flourished; the family sometimes drank tea and had dinner in it. In a few minutes Bazarov had traversed all the paths in the garden, had been in the cattle yard and the stable, had discovered a couple of yard boys, with whom he at once struck up an acquaintance, and went with them to a small marsh, about half a mile from the house, in search of frogs.

"What do you want frogs for, sir?" one of the boys asked him.

"Why, I'll tell you," answered Bazarov, who had the special gift of winning the trust of people of the lower orders, though he never encouraged them and treated them offhandedly. "I flatten out the frog and look to see what is happening inside it; and as you and I are also frogs, only we walk on two legs, I shall know what happens inside us too."

"But what do you want to know for?"

"In order not to make any mistake if you fall ill and I have to attend you."

"Are you a doctor, then?"

"Yes."

"Vaska, d'you hear, the gentleman says that you and I are frogs. That's queer!"

"I'm afraid of them — frogs, I mean," remarked Vaska, a bare-footed boy about seven years of age with hair as white as flax, who was wearing a gray Cossack-style jacket with standing collar.

"What is there to be afraid of? They don't bite, do they?"

"Now, step into the water, philosophers!" Bazarov told them.

Meanwhile Nikolai Piotrovich also had risen and gone off to Arkady, whom he found fully dressed. The father and son went onto the terrace beneath the shade of the awning; a samovar was already boiling on a table by the railing, between great bouquets of lilac. A girl, the same who had been the first to meet the arrivals on the veranda the evening before, appeared and said in a piping voice:

"Fyodosia Nikolavna is not very well and cannot come; she told me to ask you whether you will pour out tea for yourselves or is she to send Dunia."

"I'll pour it out myself, myself," Nikolai Piotrovich hurriedly replied. "How do you drink tea, Arkady, with cream or with lemon?"

"With cream," Arkady replied, and after a momentary silence said interrogatively: "Papa dear?"

Nikolai Piotrovich looked at his son in some embarrassment. "Well?" he said.

Arkady looked down.

"Forgive me, Papa, if my question seems out of place to you," he began, "but you yourself, by your frankness yesterday, call for frankness in me. You won't be angry?"

"Go on."

"You make me bold to ask you — Isn't it because — it isn't because I am here that Fen — that she won't come to pour out the tea, is it?"

Nikolai Piotrovich turned a little away from his son.

"It may be," he said at last, "she supposes — she is shy."

Arkady gave his father a swift look.

"There's no reason why she should be. To begin with, you know my way of thinking" (Arkady was delighted to say these words), "and secondly, I have no wish to be the least constraint on your life, on your habits. Besides, I am sure you could not make a bad choice; if you have allowed her to live under the same roof with you, then she is deserving of it; in any case, a son is not his father's judge, especially I, and especially a father like you, who have never imposed any restraints whatever on my freedom."

Arkady's voice trembled at first: he was conscious of all his magnanimity, but at the same time he realized that he was reading his father something in the nature of a homily; but a man is greatly affected by the sound of his own voice, and Arkady said the last wards firmly, and even with a certain flair.

"Thank you, Arkady," Nikolai Piotrovich said thickly, and his fingers again wandered over his eyebrows and forehead. "Your assumptions are quite correct. Of course, if this girl were not worthy — It is not a frivolous caprice. It is not easy for me to talk to you about it; but you understand that it was difficult for her to come here, with you present, especially on the first day after your arrival."

"In that case I shall go to her," Arkady exclaimed with a new access of magnanimous feeling, and he jumped up from the table. "I'll explain to her that she has no reason whatever to be shy with me."

Nikolai Piotrovich also rose.

"Arkady," he began, "do me the favor — how can you — There — I haven't warned you — "

But Arkady was already out of earshot and running from the terrace. Nikolai Piotrovich stared after him and dropped disconcertedly into his chair. His heart began to beat. As he sat there was he realizing that the relations between him and his son must in the future inevitably be strange, or was he conscious that Arkady could hardly have shown any greater respect for him if he had not touched on the matter at all, or was he reproaching himself for his weakness? It is difficult to say; all these feelings struggled within him, but in the form of sensations — and even they were far from clear; but the flush did not leave his face, and his heart beat.

He heard hurried steps, and Arkady returned to the terrace.

"We've made each other's acquaintance, Father," he exclaimed with an expression of gracious and kindly triumph on his face. "It is quite true Fyodosia Nikolavna isn't very well today and will come later. But why didn't you tell me I had a brother? I would have kissed him yesterday evening, just as I kissed him a moment ago."

Nikolai Piotrovich was about to blurt out some remark, was about to rise and open his arms. Arkady flung himself on his neck.

"What are you doing? Embracing again?" Pavel Piotrovich's voice sounded behind them.

Both father and son were equally glad of his appearance at that moment; there are certain situations that are very affecting, but which those who take part in them find rather trying.

"Why the surprise?" Nikolai Piotrovich said gaily. "At last I have lived to see Arkady home. I have not had time to take a good look at him since yesterday."

"I am not at all surprised," Pavel Piotrovich remarked. "Even I am not averse from embracing him."

Arkady went up to his uncle and again felt the light brush of his perfumed mustaches on his cheeks. Pavel Piotrovich sat down at the table. He was wearing an elegant morning suit of English cut, and his head was adorned with a little tarboosh. This tarboosh and the small, negligently tied cravat suggested the freedom of country life; but the tight-fitting collar of the shirt, which, to be sure, was not white, but colored, as it should be for the morning toilet, dug with its customary inflexibility into his clean-shaven chin.

"But where is your new friend?" he asked Arkady.

"He's gone out; he's in the habit of rising early and going off somewhere. The main thing is not to pay any attention to him; he doesn't like ceremony."

"Yes, that is evident." Pavel Piotrovich began unhurriedly to spread butter on his bread. "Is he going to stay with us for long?"

"As long as is convenient. He's come here on the way to his father."

"And where does his father live?"

"In our own province, fifty miles from here. He has a small estate there. He was formerly a regimental doctor."

"Ah, yes, yes, yes. I kept asking myself where I had heard the name of Bazarov before. Nikolai, I think I remember that there was a Dr. Bazarov in Father's division."

"I think there was."

"Exactly, exactly. So that doctor is his father? Hm!" Pavel Piotrovich wriggled his whiskers. "Well, and what exactly is Mr. Bazarov himself?" he asked with a drawl.

"What is Bazarov?" Arkady smiled. "If you like, uncle, I'll tell you just what he is."

"I shall be greatly obliged, nephew mine."

"He's a nihilist." [1]

"What?" Nikolai Piotrovich asked, but Pavel Piotrovich raised a knife with a piece of butter on its blade into the air and remained immobilized.

"He's a nihilist," Arkady repeated.

"A nihilist," Nikolai Piotrovich declared. "That is from the Latin *nihil*, or nothing, so far as I can judge; so the word means a man who — who recognizes nothing?"

"Rather say: who respects nothing," Pavel Piotrovich caught him up, and began again on the butter.

"Who approaches everything from a critical standpoint," Arkady remarked.

"But isn't that the same?" Pavel Piotrovich asked.

"No, it isn't. A nihilist is a man who does not bow to any authorities, who does not take any principle on trust, no matter with what respect that principle is surrounded."

"Well, and is that good?" Pavel Piotrovich interrupted him.

"It depends, uncle. It is good for some, and very bad for others."

"Really. Well, I can see that this is outside our province. We, the people of the older generation, we assume that without principles" (Pavel Piotrovich pronounced that last word evenly, in the French fashion, whereas Arkady, on the other hand, put the emphasis on the first syllable), "without principles taken, as you put it, on trust, it is impossible to move a single step forward, or to breathe. *Vous avez changé tout cela*, God grant you health and general's rank, but we shall only admire you, gentlemen — what did you call it?"

"Nihilists," Arkady distinctly declared.

"Yes. Formerly there were Hegelists, and now there are nihilists. We shall see how you will exist in a vacuum, in an airless expanse; but now, brother, please ring; it is time I had my cocoa."

Nikolai Piotrovich rang and called: "Duniasha!" But instead of Duniasha, Fenichka herself came onto the terrace. She was a young woman of twenty-three, with a clear white and soft skin, dark hair and eyes, crimson, childishly swollen lips, and delicate

[1] This word was coined by Turgenev. (Tr.)

little hands. She was wearing a neat cotton dress; a new azure triangular kerchief lay over her rounded shoulders. She brought a large cup of cocoa, and as she set it before Pavel Piotrovich she was completely abashed; the hot blood flooded in a crimson wave beneath the fine skin of her pleasant face. She lowered her eyes and halted by the table, resting lightly on the very tips of her toes. She seemed conscience-stricken at having come, and at the same time she seemed to feel that she had the right to come.

Pavel Piotrovich knitted his brows sternly, but Nikolai Piotrovich was confused.

"Good morning, Fenichka," he said between his teeth.

"Good morning," she replied in a voice not loud, but melodious, and, glancing sidelong at Arkady, who gave her a friendly smile, she quietly withdrew. She walked with a slight tendency to waddle, but it became her.

For a few moments there was silence on the terrace. Pavel Piotrovich began to sip his cocoa, but suddenly raised his head.

"And here is Mr. Nihilist coming to present himself to us," he said in an undertone.

He was right; Bazarov was coming through the garden, striding across the flower-beds. His canvas coat and pantaloons were soiled with mud; clinging marsh vegetation was wrapped round the crown of his old round hat; in his right hand he was carrying a small bag; in the bag something living was stirring. He came swiftly up to the terrace and, nodding his head, said:

"Good morning, gentlemen; pardon me for being late for tea; I'll be back in a minute; I must just put these prisoners in a safe place."

"What have you got, leeches?" Pavel Piotrovich asked.

"No, frogs."

'Do you eat them – or cultivate them?"

'For experiments," Bazarov said in an unconcerned tone, and went into the house.

"So he'll cut them up," Pavel Piotrovich remarked. "He doesn't believe in principles, but he believes in frogs."

Arkady gave his uncle a commiserative look. Nikolai Piotrovich surreptitiously shrugged his shoulders. Pavel Piotrovich himself felt that his witticism had fallen flat, and he began to talk about farming and the new steward, who the evening before had come to him to complain that one of the workmen was idling and had got out of hand. "That is the Æsop he is," he said in passing. "He always protested that he was a stupid man; he will live his day and will depart as stupid."

VI

Bazarov returned, sat down at the table, and hurriedly began to drink his tea. The two brothers gazed at him without speaking, but Arkady took stealthy glances first at his father, then at his uncle.

"Did you go for a long walk?" Nikolai Piotrovich asked at last.

"You have some marshland not far from here, by an ash grove. I started up five snipe; you can kill them, Arkady."

"You don't go hunting, then?"

"No."

"You yourself are studying physics, are you not?" Pavel Piotrovich asked in his turn.

"Yes, physics, and natural sciences generally."

"They say the Germans have had great successes recently in that field."

"Yes, the Germans can teach us a great deal in that respect," Bazarov answered carelessly.

Pavel Piotrovich had used the Russianized form of the word "Germans" instead of the original Slavonic word, with the intention of being ironic; but no one noticed it.

"Have you such a high opinion of the Germans?" Pavel Piotrovich asked with exquisite courtesy. He was beginning to feel a secret irritation. His aristocratic nature was revolted by Bazarov's completely free and easy manner. This doctor's son was not merely lacking in modesty; he even replied offhandedly and reluctantly, and there was something coarse, almost insolent, in the tone of his voice.

"Their scientists are an efficient lot."

"Yes, truly. But I suppose you haven't such a flattering opinion of Russian scientists?"

"I'm afraid you're right."

"That is very praiseworthy self-denial," Pavel Piotrovich remarked, straightening up and throwing his head back. "But how is it that Arkady Nikolaich has just told us you do not recognize any authorities? Don't you believe them?"

"Why should I trouble to recognize them? And what am I to believe? They tell me something to the point, I agree, and that's all there is to it."

"And do all Germans speak to the point?" Pavel Piotrovich said, and his face took on such a dispassionate, distant expression that he seemed to have departed beyond the clouds.

"Not all of them," Bazarov replied with a little yawn; evidently he had no desire to continue the verbal contest.

Pavel Piotrovich glanced at Arkady as though wanting to say to him: "Your friend is polite, you must admit."

"As for me," he said again, not without some effort, "I, sinful man that I am, do not feel any pity for the Germans. I will not say anything about the Russian Germans; we all know what they are like. But I have no liking even for the German Germans. Even in the old days they were all over the place; in those days they had — well, there was Schiller, and 'Gette,' wasn't it? My brother thinks very highly of them. . . . But now they are all chemists and materialists."

"A decent chemist is twenty times more useful than any poet," Bazarov interrupted.

"Really!" Pavel Piotrovich remarked, and slightly raised his eyebrows, as though dropping off to sleep. "So you do not recognize art, then?"

"The art of acquiring money, or no more hemorrhoids!" Bazarov exclaimed with a contemptuous sneer.

"Indeed! So that is your idea of a joke. And so you renounce everything? Granted. So you believe only in science?"

"I have already told you that I do not believe in anything; and what do you mean by science — science in general? There are sciences, just as there are crafts and professions; but there is no such thing as science in general."

"Very good! But with regard to other generally accepted conventions, do you hold to the same negative tendency?"

"What is this, a police inquiry?" Bazarov asked.

Pavel Piotrovich paled a little. Nikolai Piotrovich considered it advisable to intervene in the conversation.

"We'll discuss this subject with you in more detail some other time, my dear Yevgeny Vasilich; we shall ascertain your opinion, and we shall express our own. For my part I am very glad that you are studying natural science. I have heard that Liebig has made some remarkable discoveries concerning land fertilization. You may be able to help me in my agricultural work; you may be able to give me some useful advice."

"I am at your service, Nikolai Piotrovich; but how can we tackle Liebig? We have to learn the A B C first, only then can we turn to books; and so far we haven't even seen A for ourselves."

"Well, I see you are definitely a nihilist," Nikolai Piotrovich thought.

"Permit me none the less to turn to you if I require to," he added aloud. "But now, brother, I think it is time for us to go and have a talk with the steward."

Pavel Piotrovich rose from the table.

"Yes," he declared, not looking at anybody, "it is a misfortune to have lived five short years in the country, far from the great minds! You become such a perfect fool. You try not to forget what you were taught, but there — in a trice it transpires that all you have learned is nonsense, and you are told that sensible men no longer occupy themselves with such trifles, and that you are a backward nincompoop. But there is nothing to be done about it! Evidently the youngsters are wiser than we."

Pavel Piotrovich slowly turned on his heels and slowly left the terrace. Nikolai Piotrovich followed him.

"Tell me, is he always like that?" Bazarov unconcernedly asked Arkady as soon as the door closed behind the two brothers.

"Listen, Yevgeny, you treated him too harshly," Arkady remarked. "You've affronted him."

"Oh yes, I'll pamper them, these country aristocrats! Why, they're all self-esteem, with their habits of country lions and their foppery. He should continue his career in Petersburg, if that is what he is like. . . . But, in any case, I am not interested in him. Do you know I have found a quite rare specimen of the water beetle, *Dytiscus marginalis*? I'll show it to you."

"I promised to tell you his story," Arkady began.

"The story of the beetle?"

"Now, do stop it, Yevgeny. The story of my uncle. You'll see that he is not the man you imagine him to be. He is more deserving of pity than sneers."

"I don't dispute it; but how is it he has taken you in?"

"One must be fair, Yevgeny."

"What does that follow from?"
"But do listen. . . ."

And Arkady told him the story of his uncle. The reader will
find it in the next chapter.

VII

Pavel Piotrovich Kirsanov was educated first at home, like his
younger brother, Nikolai, and then in the *corps des pages*. Even
as a child he was distinguished by his remarkably handsome appearance, and in addition he was self-confident, a little derisive,
and amusingly splenetic — people could not help liking him. As
soon as he became an officer he was to be seen everywhere. He
was lionized, and he enjoyed himself, even played the fool, even
put on airs, but that, too, became him. Women lost their wits
over him, men called him a fop and secretly envied him. He
lived, as we have said, in one apartment with his brother, of whom
he was sincerely fond, though they were not in the least like
each other. Nikolai Piotrovich limped a little, had small features,
pleasant, but rather mournful small black eyes, and soft, thin
hair; he was always ready to be lazy, but just as ready to read, and
was afraid of society. Pavel Piotrovich never spent an evening
at home; he was famous for his daring and dexterity (he had made
gymnastics fashionable among the society youth) and read only
five or six French books. At the age of twenty-eight he was already a captain; a brilliant career awaited him. Suddenly everything was changed.

About that time a certain woman, who is not forgotten even
today, Princess R., made rare appearances in Petersburg society.
She had a well-bred and decorous but rather stupid husband, and
they had no children. She suddenly went abroad, suddenly returned to Russia, and altogether led a strange life. She was reputed to be a frivolous coquette, gave herself over enthusiastically
to all kinds of pleasure, danced till she dropped, laughed and
joked with young people, whom she received in a twilit reception hall before dinner, and at night wept and prayed, was never
able to rest, and often wandered about the room until dawn,
miserably wringing her hands, or sat, pale and cold, over a
psalter. Day came, and she was again transformed into a society
lady, she again paid visits, laughed, chattered, and literally threw
herself in the way of anyone who could provide her with the

least amusement. She was an amazing combination of physical characteristics: her tresses, of golden color, and as heavy as gold, fell below her knees, but no one would have called her a beauty; of all her features only her eyes were fine, and not even the eyes themselves — they were small and gray — but their look, swift and deep, was unconcerned to the point of audacity and thoughtful to the point of despondency — an enigmatic look. Something out of the ordinary shone in that look, even when her tongue was babbling the most empty of phrases. She dressed exquisitely. Pavel Piotrovich met her at a ball, danced a mazurka with her, during which she did not say one sensible word, and fell passionately in love with her. He was accustomed to triumphs, and once more he swiftly achieved his purpose; but the ease of the victory did not cool his ardor. On the contrary, he grew even more tormentedly, even more strongly attached to this woman, who, even when she yielded herself irrevocably, still seemed to retain something sacred and inaccessible, into which none could penetrate. What lurked in that soul, God knows! She seemed to be in the power of secret forces, unknown even to herself; they played with her as they wished; her little mind could not cope with their caprices. . . . All her conduct was a succession of incongruities: the only letters that could have aroused her husband's rightful suspicions were written to a man almost unknown to her; but her love was tinged with sorrow; she no longer laughed or jested with the man she had chosen, and listened to him and looked at him in bewilderment. Sometimes, very often quite suddenly, this bewilderment would pass into a frigid horror; her face acquired a dead and wild expression; she locked herself in her bedroom, and her maid, listening with one ear to the keyhole, could hear her bitter sobbing. Often, returning home after a rapturous meeting, Kirsanov felt within him that rending and bitter chagrin which rises in the heart after utter failure. "Yet what else do I want?" he asked himself, but his heart remained despondent. One day he gave her a ring with a sphinx carved on it.

"What is it," she asked, "a sphinx?"

"Yes," he answered, "and that sphinx is you."

"I?" she asked, and slowly raised her enigmatic gaze to him. "Do you know that that is very flattering?" she added with a faint smile; but her eyes still had that strange look.

It was hard for Pavel Piotrovich even when Princess R. loved him; but when she cooled in her feeling for him, and that happened quite quickly, he all but went out of his mind. He tormented himself and was jealous, would not give her any peace, and dragged after her everywhere; she grew tired of his importunate persecution, and she went abroad. Despite the requests of his friends, the exhortations of his higher officers, he went into retirement, and set off after the Princess; four years he spent in foreign countries, sometimes chasing after her, sometimes deliberately losing sight of her; he was ashamed of himself, he was furious at his own pusillanimity — but nothing was of avail. Her image, that incomprehensible, almost senseless, but enchanting image had been carved too deeply into his soul. At Baden he succeeded in renewing his former relations with her; it seemed that never before had she loved him so passionately. . . . But within a month it was all finished; the fire had flamed up for the last time, and it went out forever. Having a presentiment of the inevitable parting, he wanted at least to remain her friend, as if friendship with such a woman were possible. . . . She quietly left Baden, and thenceforth she persistently avoided him. He returned to Russia, tried to resume his old ways of life, but could not re-enter the old circles. With a poisoned soul he wandered from place to place; he still paid visits, he preserved all the habits of a man of society, he could boast of two or three new victories; but now he no longer expected anything remarkable either of himself or of others, and he did nothing. He grew old, went gray; to sit of an evening in the club, to be splenetically bored, to argue unconcernedly in bachelors' society, became a necessity to him, and that is a bad sign, as is well known. Of course he did not even think of marrying. Ten years passed in this way, drably, fruitlessly, and swiftly, terribly swiftly. Nowhere else does time speed past as in Russia; in prison, they say, it speeds even faster. One day, at dinner in the club, Pavel Piotrovich heard that Princess R. was dead. She had died in Paris, in a state verging on insanity. He rose from the table and walked a long time about the club rooms, halting, as though rooted to the ground, close to the card-players, but did not return home any earlier than usual. Some time later he received a packet addressed to him; it contained the ring he had given the Princess long before. She had drawn a cross over the sphinx and had given orders that he was to be told that the Cross was the solution.

This occurred at the beginning of 1848, just when Nikolai Piotrovich arrived in Petersburg after losing his wife. Pavel Piotrovich
had hardly seen his brother since Nikolai's retirement to the
country; Nikolai Piotrovich's wedding occurred during the very
early days of Pavel Piotrovich's acquaintance with the Princess.
On his return from abroad he had gone to his brother with the
intention of staying with him for a couple of months, admiring
his happiness; but he had remained only one week. The difference
between the two brothers' lives was too great. In 1848 this difference had greatly diminished: Nikolai Piotrovich had lost his
wife, Pavel Piotrovich had lost his memories; after the Princess's
death he tried not to think of her. But Nikolai was left with the
consciousness of a wisely spent life, his son was growing up before his eyes; Pavel, on the contrary, was a lonely bachelor and
was entering on that vague, crepuscular time, the time of regrets
that resemble hopes, of hopes that resemble regrets, when youth
has passed, but old age has not yet arrived.

That time was more difficult for Pavel Piotrovich than for
anyone else: having lost his past, he had lost all.

"I shall not invite you to Marino now," Nikolai Piotrovich said
to him one day (he had called his estate Marino in honor of his
wife); "you were bored there even when my wife was alive, and
now I think you would be eaten up with yearning there."

"Then I was still stupid and flighty," Pavel Piotrovich replied,
"but now I have sobered down, even if I have not grown any
wiser. Now, on the contrary, if you will allow me, I am ready to
settle down with you forever."

Instead of replying, Nikolai Piotrovich embraced him; but
after this conversation eighteen months passed before Pavel
Piotrovich decided to carry out his intention. On the other hand,
once he had settled down in the country he did not go away
again, not even during the three winters Nikolai Piotrovich spent
in Petersburg with his son. He began to read, mostly English
books; in fact, he ordered all his life in accordance with English
tastes; he rarely met his neighbors and went visiting only during
elections, and even then he was usually silent, only occasionally
irritating and alarming landowners of old-fashioned ideas with
his liberal ways, and not coming into any close contact with the
representatives of the new generation. Both the one and the other
group regarded him as arrogant; both groups respected him for

his distinguished, aristocratic manners, for the rumors of his conquests; because he dressed excellently and always stayed in the best room of the best hotel; because he always dined well, and once had even dined with Wellington and Louis-Philippe; because he always carried a silver dressing-case and a portable bath around with him; because he was always scented with some unusual, amazingly "noble" perfume; because he was a splendid whist-player and always lost; finally, he was also respected for his irreproachable integrity. The ladies considered him an enchanting melancholist, but he did not mix with the ladies.

"And so you can see, Yevgeny," Arkady said as he ended his story, "how unjustly you judge my uncle! I do not even mention the fact that he has more than once rescued my father from difficulties, has given him all his money — you may not know that the estate was not divided between them — but he is always glad to help anyone and, I must say, always stands up for the peasants; though it is true that when talking to them he frowns and sniffs cologne."

"That's obviously nerves," Bazarov interrupted.

"Maybe, but he has a very good heart. And he's far from stupid. What very good advice he has given me — especially — especially in regard to relations with women!"

"Aha! He's scalded his lips with his own milk, so he blows on another's. We know that trick!"

"Well, in a word," Arkady went on, "he is deeply unhappy, believe me; to feel scorn for him would be wicked."

"But who feels any scorn for him?" Bazarov retorted. "All the same, I say that a man who staked all his life on the card of woman's love, and who, when that card failed him, grew sour and let himself sink to being incapable of anything at all, is not a man, but a male animal. You say he is unhappy; you should know best; but he hasn't lost all his stupidity. I am confident that he seriously imagines himself to be clever because he reads *Galignani* and once a month saves a peasant from a flogging."

"But remember his upbringing, the times in which he has lived," Arkady remarked.

"Upbringing?" Bazarov took him up. "Every man should bring himself up — well, as I have, for instance. . . . And as for the times, why should I be dependent on them? Let them rather be dependent on me. No, brother, all that is simply wanton and empty! And what are these mysterious relations between man and woman? We physiologists know what those relations are. You study the anatomy of the eye: what is the cause of that enigmatic look, as you put it? It's all romanticism, nonsense, rottenness, art. Let's rather go and look at that beetle."

And the two friends went off to Bazarov's room, which was already pervaded with the scent of medicaments, mingled with the smell of cheap tobacco.

VIII

Pavel Piotrovich did not stay long to listen to his brother's conversation with the steward, who was a tall and gaunt man with a wheedling, consumptive voice and knavish eyes, and who replied to all Nikolai Piotrovich's remarks with "Of course, that is well known," and endeavored to represent the peasants as drunkards and thieves. The husbandry only recently set on a new course was creaking like an ungreased wheel, cracking like home-made furniture of unseasoned timber. Nikolai Piotrovich did not despair, but he sighed rather frequently and was lost in thought: he felt that without money his affairs would make no progress, and his money had almost all gone. Arkady had told the truth: Pavel Piotrovich had helped his brother more than once; more than once, seeing him struggling and racking his head, wondering how to get out of his difficulties, Pavel Piotrovich had slowly gone across to the window and, thrusting his hands in his pockets, had muttered through his teeth: *"Mais je puis vous donner de l'argent,"* and had given him money; but that day he himself had none, and he preferred to withdraw. The petty vexations of the farm made him feel miserable; moreover, it always seemed to him that Nikolai Piotrovich, despite all his fervor and industry, did not set about affairs in the right way, though he himself could not have pointed out just where his brother had gone wrong. "He is not sufficiently practical," he thought; "they fool him." Nikolai Piotrovich, on the other hand, had a high opinion of his brother's practical nature and always asked his advice. "I am soft and weak, I've spent my life in the lonely countryside," he used to say, "and you haven't lived so much among people for nothing, you know them well; you have an eagle eye." In reply

Pavel Piotrovich only turned away, but did not disillusion his brother.

Leaving Nikolai Piotrovich in his room, he went along the corridor separating the front from the back part of the house and, as he reached a low door, halted irresolutely, tugged at his whiskers, and knocked.

"Who's there? Come in," he heard Fenichka's voice.

"It is I," Pavel Piotrovich said, and opened the door.

Fenichka jumped up from the chair on which she was seated with her child and, handing the baby to a girl, who at once carried it out of the room, hurriedly adjusted her kerchief.

"Pardon me if I have disturbed you," Pavel Piotrovich began, without looking at her; "I simply wanted to ask you — I think they are sending to town today — to order them to buy some green tea for me."

"Very good," Fenichka replied; "how much do you wish them to buy?"

"Why, half a pound will be enough, I think. But I see you have made a change here," he added, looking about him with a swift glance, which also slipped over Fenichka's face. "Those curtains," he added, seeing that she did not understand what he meant.

"Yes, the curtains; Nikolai Piotrovich gave them to us; but they've been up a long time now."

"But then, I have not been here for a long time. It is very pleasant here now."

"Owing to Nikolai Piotrovich's kindness," Fenichka whispered.

"You are more comfortable here than in the other wing?" Pavel Piotrovich asked politely, but without smiling in the least.

"Of course."

"Whom have they put there in your place?"

"The laundresses are there now."

"Ah!"

He lapsed into silence. "Now he'll go," Fenichka thought. But he did not go, and she remained standing before him as though rooted to the ground, gently playing with her fingers.

"Why did you have your baby taken out?" Pavel Piotrovich said at last. "I am fond of children: let me see him."

Fenichka went quite red with embarrassment and pleasure. She was afraid of Pavel Piotrovich; he hardly ever spoke to her.

"Duniasha," she called, "bring in Mitya" (Fenichka spoke in the second person plural to everybody in the house, even the servants). "But wait a moment: we must dress him." She went to the door.

"But that doesn't matter," Pavel Piotrovich observed.

"I'll be back in a moment," Fenichka replied, and briskly left the room.

Now Pavel Piotrovich was left alone, and he looked about him with particular attention. The small, rather low room in which he was standing was very clean and cozy. It still smelt of the paint with which the floor had recently been painted, as well as of camomile and balm. Along the wall stood chairs with lyre-shaped backs; the late general had bought them in Poland, during a campaign. In one corner stood a little bed beneath a muslin canopy, beside an ironbound chest with a rounded lid. In the opposite corner a little lamp was burning before the large dark icon of Nicholas the Miracle-Worker; suspended from the halo by a red ribbon, a tiny marble egg hung on the saint's breast. Along the windowsills jars of last year's jam, carefully tied up, shed a green light; on their paper covers Fenichka herself had written "Gooseberry" in large letters; Nikolai Piotrovich was particularly fond of this kind of jam. A cage with a bobtailed siskin hung on a long cord from the ceiling; the bird chirruped and hopped about incessantly, and the cage rocked and quivered incessantly; hempseed fell with a quiet patter to the floor. On the wall between the windows, above a small cupboard, hung rather poor photographs of Nikolai Piotrovich in various positions, taken by a traveling artist; here, too, hung a photograph of Fenichka herself, a complete failure: an eyeless face smiled tensely in a dark little frame — it was impossible to distinguish anything else — and above Fenichka was General Yermolov in a Caucasian cloak, frowning sinisterly at distant Caucasian mountains from beneath a silk cowl for holding pins, which had fallen right over his brow.

Some five minutes passed; a rustling and whispering came from the other room. Pavel Piotrovich took a grease-stained book, an odd volume of Masalsky's *Sharpshooters*, from the cupboard and turned over several pages. . . . The door opened, and Fenichka entered with Mitya in her arms. She had dressed him in a little crimson shirt with a galloon at the neck, had combed his hair and wiped his face; he breathed deeply, struggled with all his body, and tugged with his little hands, as all healthy children do; but the elegant shirt obviously had an effect on him; all his chubby little figure expressed his satisfaction. Fenichka had tidied her own hair too and had arranged her kerchief better; but she could have remained as she was. And, in very deed, is there anything in the world more captivating than a young and beautiful mother with a healthy baby in her arms?

"What a chubby boy!" Pavel Piotrovich said in a condescending tone, and he tickled Mitya's double chin with the end of the long nail of his forefinger; the child fixed its eyes on the siskin and smiled.

"It's your uncle," Fenichka said, bending her head over the baby and gently shaking him, while Duniasha quietly set a lighted fumigating pastille on a kopek piece in the window.

"How many months is he now?" Pavel Piotrovich asked.

"Six months; it will soon be seven, on the 11th."

"Won't it be eight, Fyodosia Nikolavna?" Duniasha intervened a little shyly.

"No, seven; how could it be the eighth!" The child smiled again, fixed his eye on the chest, and suddenly clutched at his mother's nose and lips with all five fingers. "Naughty!" Fenichka said, without drawing her face away from his fingers.

"He is like my brother," Pavel Piotrovich observed.

"Who else should he be like?" Fenichka thought.

"Yes," he went on, as though talking to himself, "an undoubted likeness." He looked at Fenichka closely, almost sorrowfully.

"It's your uncle," she repeated, but now in a whisper.

"Ah! Pavel! So there you are!" They suddenly heard Nikolai Piotrovich's voice.

Pavel Piotrovich hurriedly turned round and knitted his brows; but his brother was looking at him so joyfully, so gratefully, that he could not but smile in reply.

"You have a splendid little fellow!" he pronounced, and looked at his watch, "but I dropped in here to see about some tea. . . ."

And, adopting an unconcerned expression, he at once left the room.

"Did he come here of his own accord?" Nikolai Piotrovich asked Fenichka.

"Yes; he knocked and came in."

"But Arkady hasn't been to see you again?"

"No. Don't you think I ought to transfer to the wing, Nikolai Piotrovich?"

"What for?"

"I think it might be better for the time being."

"N-no," Nikolai Piotrovich said hesitantly, and rubbed his forehead. "It should have been done earlier. . . . Good morning, tubby," he said with sudden vivacity, and, drawing close to the child, kissed him on the cheek; then he stooped a little and put his lips to Fenichka's hand, which showed as white as milk against Mitya's crimson shirt.

"Nikolai Piotrovich! What are you doing?" she stammered, and cast down her eyes; then she slowly raised them. Delightful was the expression of her eyes when she looked up from under her brows and smiled graciously and a little foolishly.

Nikolai Piotrovich had made Fenichka's acquaintance in the following manner. One day, some three years previously, he had had to spend the night at an inn in a distant county town. He was pleasantly struck by the cleanliness of the room he was given and the freshness of the bed linen; "surely a German woman must be the hostess here," he thought; but the hostess proved to be Russian, a woman about fifty years of age, neatly dressed, with an open, intelligent face and modest speech. He talked with her over the tea; he liked her very much. At that time Nikolai Piotrovich had only just entered into occupation of his new farm and, not wishing to keep serfs around him, was looking for hired servants; the innkeeper, for her part, complained of the few people who passed through the town, and of the difficult times. He proposed that she should come and work for him as housekeeper; she agreed. Her husband had died long before, leaving her with only one daughter, Fenichka. Some two weeks later Arina Savishna (as the new housekeeper was named) arrived with her daughter at Marino and settled in the wing. Nikolai Piotrovich's choice proved to be very satisfactory. Arina introduced order into the house. No one talked about Fenichka, who was then just past seventeen, and she was rarely to be seen: she lived very quietly, very modestly, and only on Sundays did Nikolai Piotrovich notice the delicate profile of her rather white face somewhere at one side in the parish church. Thus more than a year passed.

One morning Arina came to him in his room and, after bowing low, as usual, asked him whether he could help her daughter, as a spark from the fire had flown into her eye. Like all stay-at-homes, Nikolai Piotrovich tried his hand at doctoring and had even acquired a case of homeopathic remedies. He at once told Arina to bring in the sufferer. When Fenichka learned that the master had sent for her she was very frightened, but she came with her mother. Nikolai Piotrovich led her across to the window and took her head in both his hands. After closely examining her reddened and inflamed eye, he prescribed a lotion that he himself at once made up and, tearing his handkerchief to pieces, showed her how to bathe the eye. Fenichka listened to all he had to say and was about to go. "Kiss the master's hand, you little stupid," Arina told her. Nikolai Piotrovich did not give her his hand and, in his embarrassment, himself kissed her on her bowed head, on the parting. Fenichka's eye soon got better, but the impression she had made on Nikolai Piotrovich did not quickly pass. He was always calling to mind that pure, tender, timorously upturned face; he felt that soft hair beneath the palms of his hands, he saw those innocent, half-parted lips, behind which pearly little teeth gleamed humidly in the sunlight. He began to watch her more closely in the church, sought to fall into conversation with her. At first she avoided him, and one day, late in the afternoon, meeting him on a narrow path that walkers had made across a ryefield, she turned into the dense, tall rye, with its undergrowth of wormwood and cornflowers, so that he would not catch sight of her. He noticed her little head amid the golden entanglement of the rye, from which she was peering out like a little animal, and called to her graciously:

"Good afternoon, Fenichka! I don't bite."

"Good afternoon," she whispered, not emerging from her lair.

Little by little she began to grow accustomed to him, but she always remained timorous in his presence. Then suddenly her mother died of the cholera. Where was Fenichka to go? From her mother she had inherited a love of order, and sagacity and gravity; but she was so young, so entirely alone, Nikolai Piotrovich himself was so kind and modest. . . . There is nothing more to be said.

"So my brother just came in to see you?" Nikolai Piotrovich asked her. "He just knocked and came in?"

"Yes."

"Well, that is good. Let me give Mitya a swing."

And he began to throw the baby almost up to the ceiling, to the great delight of the infant and the no little anxiety of the mother, who, every time he flew up, stretched out her hands to his bare feet.

But Pavel Piotrovich returned to his exquisite room, with its walls hung with excellent paper of an extravagant color, with weapons arranged against a variegated Persian wall carpet, with walnut furniture, upholstered in dark green velveteen, with a Renaissance bookcase of old black oak, with bronze statuettes on the magnificent writing-desk, with a chimney hearth. . . . He flung himself on a divan, put his hands behind his head, and remained motionless, staring almost with despair at the ceiling. Whether because he wanted to conceal what was occurring in his face even from the walls or for some other reason, he rose and unfastened the heavy window curtains, then flung himself back on the divan.

IX

On that same day Bazarov also made Fenichka's acquaintance. He was walking about the garden with Arkady and explaining to him why certain of the trees, especially the oak saplings, had not taken root.

"What this place wants is more silver poplars and firs, and limes if you like, to consolidate the black earth. Now, this arbor has taken well," he added, "because acacias and lilacs are good children, they don't need attention. But there's somebody here."

Fenichka was sitting with Duniasha and Mitya in the arbor. Bazarov came to a halt, but Arkady nodded to Fenichka as if she were an old acquaintance.

"Who is that?" Bazarov asked him as soon as they had passed. "She's very good-looking!"

"But whom are you talking about?"

"You know whom: only one of them was good-looking."

Arkady, not without some embarrassment, briefly explained who Fenichka was.

"Aha!" Bazarov exclaimed, "evidently your father has good taste. I like your father, really and truly I do! He's a dog! But I must make her acquaintance all the same," and he turned back to the arbor.

"Yevgeny!" Arkady shouted after him in alarm; "be careful, for God's sake!"

"Don't get agitated!" Bazarov said; "we're used to mingling with people, we've known town life."

As he approached Fenichka he removed his hat.

"Let me introduce myself," he began with a courteous bow. "I am a friend of Arkady Nikolaich's, and a quiet sort of man."

Fenichka half rose from the bench and looked at him without speaking.

"What a wonderful baby!" Bazarov continued. "Don't be alarmed, I've never yet given anyone the evil eye. Why has he got such crimson cheeks? Is he cutting his teeth?"

"Yes," Fenichka said, "he's already cut four teeth, but now the gums are swollen again."

"Let me look — don't be afraid, I'm a doctor."

Bazarov took the child in his arms, and, to the surprise of both Fenichka and Duniasha, Mitya made no resistance whatever and was not frightened.

"I see, I see. . . . It's all right, everything's going well; he'll have good teeth. If anything should go wrong, let me know. And you yourself are quite well?"

"Yes, God be thanked."

"God be thanked — that's best of all. And you?" Bazarov added, turning to Duniasha.

Duniasha, a girl who was very strict in the house and very forward when out of the master's sight, only snorted for answer.

"Well, that's fine. And here is your hero!"

Fenichka took the child back into her arms.

"How quiet he was with you!" she said half aloud.

"All children are quiet with me," Bazarov replied. "I know the trick."

"Children can feel who is fond of them," Duniasha observed.

"That's just it," Fenichka confirmed. "Mitya, for instance, won't let anyone else take him at all."

"But would he come to me?" asked Arkady, who, after standing a little way off for a time, had now come into the arbor.

He held out his arms to take Mitya, but the child threw his head back and began to bellow, which greatly embarrassed Fenichka.

"He'll come some other time, when he's used to me," Arkady said indulgently, and the two friends went off.

"What is her name, by the way?" Bazarov asked.

"Fenichka — Fyodosia, that is," Arkady replied.

"And her patronymic? I must know that too."

"Nikolavna."

"*Bene.* What I like about her is that she doesn't get too embarrassed. Maybe others would condemn that in her. But how absurd! Why should she be embarrassed? She's the mother, and so she is within her rights."

"She is within her rights," Arkady observed, "but my father, now — "

"And he is within his rights," Bazarov interrupted.

"Well, no, I don't think so."

"Evidently you don't like the idea of an extra little heir!"

"Aren't you ashamed to impute such ideas to me?" Arkady replied heatedly. "That isn't why I regard my father as in the wrong; I consider he ought to marry her."

"Hm!" Bazarov calmly commented. "Well, we are magnanimous! So you still attach importance to marriage; I hadn't expected that of you."

The friends walked on a few paces without speaking.

"I have had a look at your father's farm," Bazarov began again. "The cattle are poor, and the horses worn out. The buildings too are half drunk, and the workmen look like a lot of embittered drones; and the steward is either a fool or a rogue, I haven't yet completely decided which."

"You're severe today, Yevgeny Vasilich."

"And the good little peasants are cheating your father all the time. You know the saying: 'A Russian peasant would gobble up God.' "

"I am beginning to agree with my uncle," Arkady observed; "you have a downright poor opinion of the Russians."

"How terrible! The Russian is only good in the sense that he, too, has a very poor opinion of himself. The important thing is that twice two are four, and nothing else matters in the least."

"Including nature?" Arkady said, thoughtfully gazing at the checkered fields, beautifully and softly lit up by the setting sun.

"Even nature doesn't matter, in the sense in which you mean it at this moment. Nature isn't a temple, but a workshop, and man is the workman in that workshop."

At that very moment the languid sounds of a violoncello reached them from the house. Someone was playing Schubert's *Expectation* with feeling, though with an inexperienced hand, and the suavely flowing melody spread like honey through the air.

"What is that?" Bazarov asked in astonishment.

"It's Father."

"Your father plays the cello?"

"Yes."

"But how old is your father?"

"Forty-four."

Bazarov abruptly burst into laughter.

"What are you laughing at?"

"What do you think! A man of forty-four, a *pater familias*, in N . . . province, playing a cello!"

Bazarov went on laughing; but this time, despite all his respect for his teacher, Arkady did not even smile.

X

Some two weeks passed. Life in Marino flowed on in its normal course: Arkady played the sybarite, Bazarov worked. Everybody in the house had grown accustomed to him, to his perfunctory manners, his monosyllabic and fragmentary remarks. Fenichka especially grew so used to him that one night she asked for him to be awakened as Mitya had convulsions; and Bazarov went and, half joking as usual, half yawning, sat with her a couple of hours and treated the infant. On the other hand, Pavel Piotrovich came to hate Bazarov with all the strength of his soul: he regarded him as arrogant, insolent, cynical, plebeian; he suspected that Bazarov had no respect for him, that he all but had contempt for him — for him, Pavel Kirsanov! Nikolai Piotrovich was rather afraid of the young "nihilist" and doubted whether his influence over Arkady was beneficial; but he was always ready to listen to him and was glad to be present at his physical and chemical experiments. Bazarov had brought a microscope with him, and he pored over it for hours at a time. The servants also grew attached to him, though he was always deriding them: they felt that none the less he was one of them, and not a master. Duniasha was never slow to giggle with him and gave him sidelong, meaning glances as she ran past "like a little quail." Piotr, who was an extremely ambitious and stupid man who went with his forehead always tensely furrowed, and whose only virtue was that he looked honest, could spell out words, and frequently brushed his coat — even he smirked and came to life as soon as Bazarov paid any attention to him; while the yard boys ran after the "doctor" like little dogs. Only old Prokofich did not like him, wore a morose look as he handed him food at the table, called him a "knacker" and a "knave," and declared that with his side-whiskers he was a real swine in a bush. In his own way Prokofich was just as much an aristocrat as Pavel Piotrovich.

The first days of June arrived, the finest days of the year. The weather was set fair; there was a distant threat of cholera again, but by now the inhabitants of N . . . province had grown accustomed to its visits. Bazarov rose very early and went off for two or three miles not for a walk — he could not endure excursions without a purpose — but to collect grasses and insects. Sometimes he took Arkady with him. They usually fell into some argument on the way back, and as a rule Arkady lost, though he talked more than his companion.

One day they were gone rather a long time; Nikolai Piotrovich went out into the garden to meet them and, reaching the arbor, suddenly heard swift steps and the two young men's voices. They were passing on the farther side and could not see him.

"You don't know Father well enough," he heard Arkady say.

Nikolai Piotrovich froze where he stood.

"Your father's a very good fellow," Bazarov pronounced, "but he's on the retired list, his song is sung."

Nikolai Piotrovich pricked up his ears. . . . Arkady made no answer.

"The man on the retired list" remained standing for a minute or two, then slowly went back home.

"The day before yesterday I saw him reading Pushkin," Bazarov continued meanwhile. "Do explain to him that that will never do any good. After all, he's not a boy: it's time he threw aside that nonsense. Wanting to be a romantic, in these days! Give him something useful to read."

"What would you give him?" Arkady asked.

"Why, I think Büchner's *Stoff und Kraft* to begin with."

"I think so too," Arkady remarked approvingly. *Stoff und Kraft* is written in a popular style."

"So that's what you and I are," Nikolai said to his brother as he sat in his room after dinner that same day; "we've been put on the retired list, our song is sung. Well, what of it! Perhaps Bazarov is right. But I must admit I find one thing very upsetting: I was hoping that now at least I would come into close and friendly relations with Arkady, but it appears I have been left behind, he has gone on ahead, and we cannot understand each other."

"But why has he gone on ahead? And how is he so greatly different from us?" Pavel Piotrovich exclaimed impatiently. "All this has been put into his head by that *signor*, that nihilist. I hate that wretched doctor; in my view he is simply a charlatan; I am confident that with all his frogs he has not achieved much even in physics."

"No, brother, don't say that; Bazarov is intelligent and knowledgeable."

"And what repellent conceit!" Pavel Piotrovich again interrupted.

"Yes," Nikolai Piotrovich remarked, "he certainly is conceited. But evidently you cannot get on without it. And there is one thing I don't quite understand. I seem to do everything to keep up with the times: I've established my peasants on their own land, I've started a farm, so that I am even regarded as a Red all over the province; I read, I study, I do everything I can to keep abreast of contemporary requirements — but they say my song is sung. And now, brother, I am myself beginning to think that it really is sung."

"Why are you?"

"I'll tell you why. Today I was sitting reading Pushkin. I remember, I happened to light on *The Gypsies*. Suddenly Arkady comes up to me, and silently, with such a look of kindly commiseration on his face, he takes the book away from me as gently as if I were a child and puts another, a German book, in front of me. Then he smiled and walked away, taking Pushkin with him."

"You don't say! And what book did he give you?"

"This one."

And Nikolai took the notorious work by Büchner, its ninth edition, out of the back pocket of his frock coat.

Pavel Piotrovich turned it over in his hands.

"Hm!" he snorted. "Arkady Nikolaevich is taking your education in hand. Well, and have you tried to read it?"

"I have."

"And what was the result?"

"Either I'm stupid or this is all rubbish. I suppose I must be stupid."

"But you have not forgotten your German?" Pavel Piotrovich asked.

"I understand it well enough."

Pavel Piotrovich again turned the book over in his hands and looked at his brother with wrinkled brows. They were both silent.

"Why, that reminds me," Nikolai Piotrovich began, evidently wishing to change the conversation; "I've had a letter from Kolyazin."

"From Matvei Ilich?"

"Yes. He has arrived at X X X to hold an inquiry into the province. He's an important person now, and he writes that he would like to see us, as we're relations of his, and he invites me and you and Arkady to the town."

"Are you going?" Pavel Piotrovich asked.

"No; and you?"

"I shall not go either. Highly necessary to drag some thirty miles to eat jelly! Mathieu wants to exhibit himself to us in all his glory; but he can go to the devil! He'll get enough incense from the provincial authorities, he can manage without ours. A very important rank, a privy councilor! If I had continued in the service, stupidly toiling and slaving, I would have been an adjutant general by now. But now you and I are on the retired list."

"Yes, brother; evidently it's time we ordered our coffins and folded our hands across our chests," Nikolai Piotrovich remarked with a sigh.

"Well, I shall not surrender so soon," his brother muttered. "We shall yet have a tussle with that doctor, I foresee that."

The tussle occurred the very same day, during the evening tea. Pavel Piotrovich went into the reception hall all ready for battle, irritable and resolute. He waited only for a pretext to fling himself on the enemy, but for a long time that pretext did not offer itself. Bazarov always said little in the presence of the "old Kirsanovs," as he called both brothers, and that evening he felt out of sorts and silently drank cup after cup of tea. Pavel Piotrovich was consumed with impatience; but at last his desires were realized.

The talk had turned to discussion of one of the neighboring landowners. "He's a rotter, a petty aristocrat!" Bazarov, who had met him in Petersburg, unconcernedly remarked.

"Allow me to ask you," Pavel Piotrovich retorted, and his lips began to quiver. "In your conception do the words 'rotter' and 'aristocrat' have the same meaning?"

"I said: 'petty aristocrat,'" Bazarov observed, lazily taking a gulp of tea.

"You did; but I assume that you have the same opinion about aristocrats as you have about petty aristocrats. I consider it my duty to inform you that I do not share that opinion. I dare to say that everybody knows me as a man of liberal views and a lover of progress; but for that very reason I respect aristocrats, true aristocrats. Remember, my dear sir" (at these words Bazarov raised his eyes to Pavel Piotrovich), "remember, my dear sir," he repeated harshly, "the English aristocrats. They do not yield one iota of their rights, and so they respect the rights of others; they demand the fulfillment of obligations in regard to themselves, and so they themselves fulfill *their* obligations. It was the aristocracy that gave England freedom and maintains it."

"I've heard that song lots of times," Bazarov retorted; "but what are you trying to prove by it?"

"My dear sir, I am trying to prove by *this* — " (When he grew angry, Pavel Piotrovich deliberately used a distorted form of the Russian for "this," though he knew very well that grammar did not recognize such forms. This idiosyncrasy was a last survival of the tradition of Czar Alexander's times. On the rare occasions when the bigwigs of those days talked in their native language, some of them used the form *"efto,"* others *"echto,"* instead of *"eto,"* as though indicating: we, you know, are true Russians, and at the same time we are the magnates, who are permitted to ignore the school rules.) "By *this* I am trying to prove that without a sense of one's own worth, without respect for oneself — and in an aristocrat those feelings are developed — there is no stable basis for the social — *bien public* — the social edifice. Personality, my dear sir — that is the chief thing; the human personality should be strong as a rock, for on it everything is built. I know very well, for example, that you are pleased to consider my habits, my toilet, my very neatness, as absurd; but they all arise from a feeling of self-respect, from a feeling of duty, yes, yes, of duty. I live in the country, in a quiet spot, but I do not let myself down, I respect the man in me."

"Pardon me, Pavel Piotrovich," Bazarov rejoined; "you say you respect yourself and you sit with folded hands; what benefit to the *bien public* is that? You could be entirely without respect for yourself and do exactly the same."

Pavel Piotrovich turned pale.

"That is quite a different question. There is no reason whatever why I should explain to you now why I sit with folded hands, as you take the liberty of expressing it. I only wish to say that aristocratism is a principle, and in our times only immoral or empty people can live without principles. I said that to Arkady the day after his arrival, and I repeat it to you now. Is that not so, Nikolai?"

Nikolai Piotrovich nodded.

"Aristocratism, liberalism, progress, principles," Bazarov said. "Just think, how many foreign — and useless — words! They are quite unnecessary to a Russian."

"And what does he need, in your opinion? To listen to you, one would think we were outside humanity, outside all its laws. Pardon me, the logic of history requires — "

"Yes, but what do we want that logic for? We shall manage without it."

"How shall we?"

"Why, we just shall. You, I hope, have no need for logic in order to put a piece of bread into your mouth when you're hungry. What do we need those abstractions for?"

Pavel Piotrovich threw up his hands.

"After that I fail to understand you. You are insulting the Russian people. I do not understand how you can avoid recognizing principles, rules. What is the motive of your actions?"

"I have already told you, uncle, that we don't recognize any authorities," Arkady intervened.

"We act by the force of what we recognize as beneficial," Bazarov declared. "At the present time rejection is the most beneficial of all things, and so we reject."

"Everything?"

"Everything."

"How? Not only art, poetry — but also — it is a terrible thing to say — "

"Everything!" Bazarov repeated with complete imperturbability.

Pavel Piotrovich stared at him. He had not expected that, and Arkady even reddened with pleasure.

"None the less, allow me," Nikolai Piotrovich began. "You reject everything, or, to express it more exactly, you pull down everything. But then surely it is necessary to build up too?"

"That isn't our business. First we must clear the site."

"The present state of the people demands that," Arkady added sententiously. "We must meet those demands, we have no right to give ourselves over to the satisfaction of our personal egotism."

Evidently this last phrase did not please Bazarov: it had a waft of philosophy — in other words, of romanticism — for Bazarov called philosophy also romanticism. But he did not consider it necessary to contradict his young pupil.

"No, no!" Pavel Piotrovich exclaimed in a sudden outburst, "I am not prepared to believe that you, gentlemen, have a perfect knowledge of the Russian people, that you are the representatives of its requirements, its strivings! No, the Russian people is not such as you represent it. It sacredly respects the traditions, it is patriarchal, it cannot live without faith — "

"I shan't try to dispute that," Bazarov interrupted, "I am even ready to agree that *in this respect* you are right."

"But if I am right — "

"And all the same it proves nothing."

"It proves precisely nothing," Arkady repeated with the assurance of an experienced chess-player who has foreseen an apparently dangerous move by his opponent and so is not in the least perturbed.

"How does it prove nothing?" the bewildered Pavel Piotrovich muttered. "So you will go against the whole of the people?"

"And what if we do?" Bazarov exclaimed. "The people assume that when there is thunder it is the prophet Elijah driving across heaven in his chariot. Well, and are we to agree with them? And besides they are Russian, and am I not a Russian too?"

"No, you are no Russian after what you have just said. I cannot recognize you as Russian."

"My grandfather plowed the land," Bazarov replied with haughty pride. "Ask any of your own peasants whom they more readily recognize as their fellow countryman, you or me. You don't even know how to talk with them."

"But you talk with them, yet at the same time you are contemptuous of them."

"What of it, if they are deserving of contempt? You reject my attitude, but who told you that my attitude is something quite fortuitous, that it is not evoked by that same national spirit in the name of which you rant so much?"

"So you think! Great need we have of nihilists!"

"Whether there is need of them or not is not for you to decide. After all, even you regard yourself as not without use."

"Gentlemen, gentlemen, no personalities, please!" Nikolai Piotrovich exclaimed, and he half rose.

Pavel Piotrovich smiled and, laying his hand on his brother's shoulder, forced him to sit down again.

"Don't be alarmed," he said. "I shall not forget myself, precisely because of my feeling of worth, which Mr. — which the doctor ridicules so severely. Excuse me," he went on, turning again to Bazarov, "you, perhaps, think that your teaching is something new? That is quite a vain idea. The materialism that you preach has been in circulation more than once before and has always proved bankrupt — "

"Another foreign word!" Bazarov interrupted. He was beginning to be annoyed, and his face went a coarse, coppery color. "To begin with, we preach nothing; that is not our habit."

"Then what do you do?"

"This is what we do. Formerly, not so very long ago, we said that our officials take bribes, that we had neither roads, nor commerce, nor an impartial judiciary — "

"Why yes, yes, you are the accusers; that is what that is called, I think. With many of your accusations I agree, but — "

"But then we realized that to talk, everlastingly only talk about our ulcers is not worth the labor, that it leads only to platitudes and doctrinairism; we saw that our sages also, the so-called advanced people and accusers, were good for nothing, that we were occupying our minds with rubbish, we were talking about art, about unconscious creation, about parliamentarism, about the bar, and the devil knows what else, when it was really a question of daily bread, when we were being smothered by the coarsest of superstitions, when all our corporations were going to smash simply because there was an insufficiency of honest people, when the very freedom the government was making so much fuss about would hardly be of any use to us, because our peasant is glad to rob himself just in order to get drunk in the pub."

"So," Pavel Piotrovich interrupted him, "so you were convinced of all this and decided that you yourselves would not do anything serious about it at any price."

"And we decided not to do anything about it at any price," Bazarov glumly repeated. He suddenly felt vexed with himself for expatiating so freely before this gentleman.

"But only revile everything?"

"And revile everything."

"And that is called nihilism?"

"And that is called nihilism," Bazarov again repeated, this time with especial insolence.

Pavel Piotrovich slightly narrowed his eyes.

"So that is the position!" he pronounced in a strangely calm tone. "Nihilism is to be our help in all misfortunes, and you, you are our saviors and heroes. Indeed! But why do you abuse others, even those very accusers? Are you not simply indulging in talk, like everybody else?"

"Whatever others may do, we do not commit that sin," Bazarov said through his teeth.

"So what, then? Are you doing something? Are you intending to act?"

Bazarov made no reply. Pavel Piotrovich began to tremble, but he mastered himself at once.

"Hm! To act, to break down — " he continued. "But how can you break down when you do not even know why you are doing it?"

"We break things down because we are a force," Arkady observed.

Pavel Piotrovich looked at his nephew and smiled wryly.

"Yes, and force does not render any account," Arkady pronounced, and drew himself up.

"Unhappy wretch!" Pavel Piotrovich roared; he was quite unable to restrain himself any longer; "if only you knew *what* you are supporting in Russia with your trivial sententiousness! Really, this would try the patience of an angel! Force! There is force in the savage Kalmuck and in the Mongol — but what use is it to us? To us civilization is precious, yes, yes, my dear sir; to us its fruits are precious. And tell me not that those fruits are insignificant; the wretchedest dauber, *un barbouilleur,* a dance pianist who gets five kopeks an evening, even they are of more use than you, because they are representatives of civilization, and not of the coarse Mongol force! You imagine yourselves to be advanced, but you ought to be sitting in a Kalmuck tent! Force! But do remember in the last resort, you forceful gentlemen, that there are only four and a half of you all together, while there are millions of these others, and they will not allow you to trample on their most sacred beliefs, they will crush you!"

"If they crush, then that's the road to go," Bazarov declared. "Only we shall see. There aren't so few of us as you assume."

"What? You seriously think that you can cope — can cope with the entire nation?"

"You know, all Moscow was set alight by a farthing candle," Bazarov replied.

"Yes, yes. First a pride almost satanic, then derision. That is what the youth are carried away by, that is what the inexperienced hearts of striplings surrender to. Look, there is one of them sitting beside you, and he is all but praying to you, enjoy the sight!" (Arkady turned away and frowned.) "And this infection has already been spread far and wide. I have been told that in Rome our artists never even set foot in the Vatican. They regard Raphael as all but a fool, because, they say, he represents authority; but they themselves are loathsomely impotent and barren, and they have no more imagination than will suffice for *A Girl at the Fountain,* say what you like! And even that girl is drawn atrociously. In your view they are splendid fellows, are they not?"

"In my view," Bazarov retorted, "Raphael also is not worth a brass farthing; and they are no better than he."

"Bravo! Bravo! Listen, Arkady — now, that is how the modern young people should talk! And what else could they do, think you, than follow you? Formerly young people had to study, they were not anxious to acquire the reputation of being ignoramuses, and so willy-nilly they worked. But now you only need say to them: 'Everything in the world is rubbish!' and the thing is done. The young people are delighted. And in very deed formerly they were simply blockheads, but now they have suddenly become nihilists."

"And now your boasted feeling of your own worth has betrayed you," Bazarov remarked phlegmatically, whereas Arkady flared up and his eyes glittered. "Our argument has gone too far — I think it would be better to bring it to an end. But I shall be ready to agree with you," he added as he rose, "when you present me with a single convention of our present-day existence, in family or social life, that does not call for complete and ruthless rejection."

"I shall provide you with millions of such conventions," Pavel Piotrovich exclaimed. "Millions! Why, take the peasants' community, for instance."

A frigid sneer twisted Bazarov's lips.

"Well, so far as the commune is concerned," he said, "you'd better talk with your brother about it. I think he has now learned by experience what the commune is: mutual responsibility, sobriety, and all that kind of thing."

"Then the family, the family, as it exists among our peasants!" Pavel Piotrovich cried.

"That question too, I think, it would be better for you not to analyze in detail. I expect you have heard of fathers sleeping with their daughters-in-law? Listen to me, Pavel Piotrovich, give yourself a couple of days — I don't think you'll find anything at once. Consider all our social strata, and think carefully over each of them, and meanwhile Arkady and I will — "

"Sneer at everything," Pavel Piotrovich caught him up.

"No, dissect frogs! Come along, Arkady; good-by, gentlemen."

The two friends went out. The brothers were left alone and at first only looked at each other.

"There!" Pavel Piotrovich began at last; "there you have our present-day youth! There they are — our heirs!"

"Heirs," Nikolai Piotrovich repeated with a despondent sigh. All through the argument he had sat like a cat on hot bricks, only taking stealthy, unhappy glances at Arkady. "Do you know what

I have just remembered, brother? One day I quarreled with our mother: she started to shout and wouldn't listen to me. . . . At last I told her that she couldn't understand me: we belonged to two different generations. She was terribly annoyed, but I thought: 'It can't be helped. It's a bitter pill, but it has to be swallowed.' And now our turn has come, and our heirs can say to us: 'You are not of our generation; swallow the pill.' "

"You are far too magnanimous and modest," Pavel Piotrovich objected. "I, on the contrary, am confident that you and I are far more right than these gentlemen, though perhaps we express ourselves in a rather old-fashioned way, *vieilli*, and we do not have that impertinent self-confidence. . . . And how bombastic this present-day youth is! You ask one of them: what wine would you like, red or white? 'I have the habit of preferring red,' he answers in a bass voice and with such a serious face, as if all the universe were watching him at that moment. . . ."

"Do you want any more tea?" Fenichka asked, putting her head in at the door. She could not bring herself to enter the reception room so long as she could hear the sound of arguing.

"No, you can tell them to take the samovar away," Nikolai Piotrovich replied, and he rose to meet her. Pavel Piotrovich vehemently said: "*Bon soir*" to him and went off to his own room.

XI

Half an hour later Nikolai Piotrovich went into the garden, to his favorite arbor. He was obsessed with mournful thoughts. For the first time he clearly realized what a gulf separated him from his son; he had a presentiment that with every day the gulf would grow wider and wider. So in vain had he spent the winters in Petersburg, in vain had he sat for days on end over the latest publications, in vain had he listened to the young people's conversations, in vain had he rejoiced to get in some remark amid their heady speeches. "My brother says we are right," he thought, "and, putting aside all conceit, it does seem to me that they are farther from the truth than we are; but at the same time I feel that they have something we do not possess, some advantage over us. . . . Youth? No: not only youth. Doesn't it consist in the fact that they have fewer traces of gentility than we?"

Nikolai Piotrovich let his head sink, and he passed his hand over his face.

"But to reject poetry?" he thought again, "to have no feeling for art, for nature . . ."

And he looked about him as though seeking to understand how anyone could have no feeling for nature. Evening was coming on; the sun had hidden behind a small ash grove lying half a mile away from the garden: the shadow of the trees stretched endlessly across the silent fields. A peasant was trotting on a little white horse over a dark, narrow track at the very edge of the grove; in vain did he ride in the shadow: he was clearly visible in every detail, even to the patch on his shoulder. It was pleasant to see the little horse's legs twinkling so distinctly. The rays of sunlight penetrated into the grove from the other side and, making their way through the trees, flooded the trunks of the ashes with such a warm light that they came to resemble pine trunks, while their foliage turned almost blue, and above it rose a pale blue sky, faintly flushed with the sunset. The swallows were flying high; the wind had completely died away; belated bees were sluggishly and drowsily humming in the lilac flowers; gnats were swirling in a column above a single outjutting branch. "My God, how good it is!" thought Nikolai Piotrovich, and his favorite verses were about to come to his lips; he recalled Arkady, *Stoff und Kraft*, and was silent, but he continued to sit, continued to give himself over to the mournful and joyous play of single thoughts. He liked to indulge in dreams: his country life had developed this capacity in him. Was it so long since he had sat dreaming as he waited for his son at the inn? But since then there had already been a change, relations that then were still uncertain were already defined . . . and in what manner! He recalled again his dead wife, but not as he had known her over many years, not as the domesticated, efficient housewife, but as a young girl with a slender waist, an innocently curious gaze, and a tightly twisted pigtail coiled above her childishly thin neck. He recalled how he had seen her the first time. He was still a student then. He had met her on the staircase of the apartment in which he lived, and, accidentally jostling against her, had turned and tried to apologize, but had only muttered: "Pardon, monsieur," and she had bent her head, smiled, and suddenly taken fright and fled. But at the turn of the stairs she had glanced swiftly up at him, had put on a serious look, and had blushed. And then the first shy visits, the half-words, the half-smiles, and the misunderstandings, and

the sorrow, and the raptures, and finally that panting joy. . . .
Where had they all fled? She had become his wife, he had been
happy as are few on this earth. . . . "But," he thought, "those
first sweet moments — why couldn't we live on in them with an
everlasting, undying life?"

He did not try to clarify his thought to himself, but he felt
that he wanted to retain that blessed time with something
stronger than memory; he wanted once more to feel that his
Maria was near him, to be conscious of her warmth and breath,
and he was even beginning to imagine that above him . . .

"Nikolai Piotrovich," Fenichka's voice sounded close at hand.
"Where are you?"

He started. He did not feel pain, or shame. He did not con-
cede even the possibility of comparison between his wife and
Fenichka, but he regretted that she had thought of coming to
look for him. Her voice at once reminded him of his gray hairs,
his age, his present existence. . . .

The enchanted world that he had already entered, which had
already emerged from the misty waves of the past, stirred — and
vanished.

"I'm here," he replied; "I'm coming, you go on." "There they
are, the traces of gentility," the thought flashed through his head.
Fenichka glanced into the arbor without speaking and disappeared; but he noted with surprise that while he had been dreaming, the night had come on. Everything was darkening and was
beginning to be still all around him, and past him slipped Fenichka's face, so white and small. He rose and was about to return to
the house; but his heart, softened with tenderness, could not be
still in his breast, and he began to walk slowly about the garden,
now thoughtfully looking down at his feet, now raising his eyes
to the sky, where the stars were already swarming and twinkling.
He walked about a great deal, almost until he was tired, but the
anxiety he felt, a kind of searching, indefinite, mournful anxiety,
was still not alleviated. Oh, how Bazarov would have laughed at
him, if he had discovered what went on within him during those
moments! Even Arkady would have condemned him. He, this
man of forty-four, an agriculturist and farmer, burst into tears,
causeless tears; and that was a hundred times worse than the cello.

Nikolai Piotrovich continued to walk about and could not
bring himself to go into the house, into that peaceful and cozy

nest which gazed at him so invitingly with all its lighted windows. He had no strength to part with the darkness, the garden, the feeling of the fresh air on his face, and that sorrow, that anxiety. . . .

At a turn in the path he was met by Pavel Piotrovich.

"What is the matter with you?" his brother asked him. "You are as pale as a ghost; you are not well; why don't you go to bed?"

Nikolai Piotrovich briefly explained his spiritual condition to him and walked away. Pavel Piotrovich walked to the end of the garden, and he, too, was lost in thought, and he, too, raised his eyes to the sky. But in those handsome, dark eyes was reflected nothing but the light of the stars. He had not been born a romantic, and his exquisitely dry and sensual soul, misanthropic in the French manner, was incapable of dreaming.

"Do you know what?" Bazarov said to Arkady that same night. "A magnificent idea has occurred to me. Your father mentioned today that he had received an invitation from that eminent relative of yours. Your father won't go; so let's both slip away to X X X; the gentleman invites you as well. You see the weather that's settled here; so we'll have a ride and see the town. We'll spend five or six days there and then come away!"

"And will you be coming back here?"

"No, I must go and see my father. You know he lives twenty miles from X X X. I haven't seen him for a long time, nor my mother; the old people need a little comfort. They're very good to me, especially Father; he's very amusing and I am their only son."

"And will you be staying with them long?"

"I don't think so. I'm afraid I shall be bored."

"And will you call here on the way back?"

"I don't know, I'll see. Well, what d'you think? Shall we go?"

"If you like." Arkady lazily remarked.

Inwardly he was greatly delighted by his friend's suggestion, but he considered it his duty to conceal his feelings. Not for nothing was he a nihilist.

Next day he drove with Bazarov to X X X. The younger people at Marino regretted their departure; Duniasha even burst into tears . . . but the old men breathed more easily.

XII

The town of X X X, to which our friends drove, was in charge of one of the younger type of governor, both progressive and despot, as is the case everywhere in Russia. During the first year of his administration he managed to fall out not only with the provincial marshal of the nobility — a retired captain of the guards, a horse-breeder, and a convivial fellow — but with all his own officials. The ensuing conflict finally grew to such dimensions that the ministry at Petersburg found it necessary to commission a man of trust to inquire into the entire affair on the spot. The authorities' choice fell upon Matvei Ilich Kolyazin, the son of the Kolyazin who at one time had had the brothers Kirsanov under his patronage. He, too, was one of the "younger men"; in other words, he had recently passed his fortieth birthday; but he had already made his mark among statesmen and wore a star on each breast. One was a foreign decoration, to be sure, and not of the best at that. Like the governor whom he had come to judge, he regarded himself as a man of progress and, though already a bigwig, was unlike the majority of bigwigs. He had the very highest opinion of himself; his vainglory knew no limits; but he bore himself simply, looked approvingly, listened indulgently, and smiled so benevolently that at the beginning of an acquaintance he could even pass for a "very fine chap." On important occasions, however, he could make the sparks fly, as the saying is. "Energy is indispensable," he would say at such times, *"l'énergie est la première qualité d'un homme d'état"*; none the less he was usually made a fool of, and any least experienced official could ride him. Matvei Ilich spoke with great respect of Guizot, and tried to give all and sundry the impression that he was not to be classified among the routine and backward bureaucrats, that he did not let a single important manifestation of social life pass unobserved. . . . He was good at all that kind of talk. He even followed, though truly with a negligent dignity, the development of contemporary literature — just as a grown man, meeting a procession of boys in the street, sometimes attaches himself to it. In reality Matvei Ilich was not greatly unlike those statesmen of Czar Alexander's times who, when preparing to spend an evening with Mme Svechina, who was living in Petersburg at the time, read a page from Condillac in the morning; only his manners were different, more modern. He was an accomplished courtier, a very sly fox, and nothing more; he had no understanding of affairs and no intelligence, but was capable of managing his own business; in that respect no one could put anything across him, and, after all, that is the main thing.

Matvei Ilich received Arkady with the benevolence proper to an enlightened dignitary, and we will say more, with jocosity. None the less he was astonished when he learned that the relatives he had invited had remained behind. "Your papa always was eccentric," he remarked, playing with the tassels of his superb velvet dressing-gown. And suddenly, turning to a young official in a very well-meant, tightly buttoned semi-uniform, he exclaimed with a preoccupied air: "Well?" The young man, who had been silent for so long that his lips had stuck together, half rose and gazed in bewilderment at his chief. But, having embarrassed his subordinate, Matvei Ilich paid no more attention to him. Our dignitaries generally are fond of embarrassing their subordinates; the methods they use in order to achieve this end are very varied. We may note in passing that the following method is much resorted to, "is quite a favorite," as the English say. A dignitary will suddenly cease to understand even the simplest of words and will go quite deaf. He asks, for instance: "What is today?"

They tell him very respectfully: "Today is Friday, Your Ex-ex-ex-cency."

"Well? What? What's that? What did you say?" the dignitary repeats tensely.

"Today is Friday, Your Ex-ex-ex-cency."

"How? what? What's Friday? Which Friday?

"Friday, Your E-e-e-e-cency, a day of the week."

"No-ow! Are you trying to teach me?"

After all, Matvei Ilich was a dignitary, though he regarded himself as a liberal.

"I advise you, my friend, to call on the governor," he told Arkady. "You understand, I advise you to do so not because I hold to the ancient idea that it is necessary to go and pay your respects to the authorities, but simply because the governor is an honest man; and besides I expect you would like to make the acquaintance of local society. . . . For you're not a boor, I hope? And he is giving a great ball the day after tomorrow."

"Will you be at the ball?" Arkady asked.

"He is giving it in my honor," Matvei Ilich declared almost commiseratingly. "Do you dance?"

"Yes, but only badly."

"That's unfortunate. There are some pretty girls here, and besides, a young man should be ashamed not to dance. But again I say that not because I am dominated by ancient ideas; I don't think at all that the mind should be in the feet, but Byronism is absurd, *il a fait son temps.*"

"But, uncle, it isn't at all because of Byronism that I — "

"I'll introduce you to the local ladies, I'll take you under my wing," Matvei Ilich interrupted him, and smiled conceitedly. "You'll like that, won't you?"

A servant entered and reported the arrival of the chairman of the criminal court, a honey-eyed old man with pursed lips, who was extremely fond of nature, especially on summer days, when, as he said: "every little bee takes a little consideration from every little flower." Arkady withdrew.

He found Bazarov in the inn where they had taken a room, and spent a long time persuading him to call on the governor. "It can't be helped!" said Bazarov at last; "in for a penny, in for a pound. We've come to have a look at the landowners, so let's look at them." The governor received the young men affably, but did not ask them to be seated and did not sit down himself. He was everlastingly fidgeting and hurrying; he had worn a tight-fitting semi-uniform and an extremely tight cravat since early morning, he had not had any proper food or drink, and he was continually issuing orders. In the province he was nicknamed Burdal, in allusion not to the well-known French preacher Bourdaloue, but to *burda*, the Russian word for bilge. He invited Kirsanov and Bazarov to attend the ball, and a couple of minutes later invited them again, now regarding them as two brothers and calling them both Kaisarov.

They were on their way home from the governor's when suddenly a little man in a Slavophil Hungarian hussar jacket jumped out of a passing droshky and, crying: "Yevgeny Vasilich," rushed to Bazarov.

"Ah, so it's you, Herr Sitnikov!" Bazarov remarked, continuing along the sidewalk. "What fate has brought you here?"

"Just imagine, quite an accident," the man replied. Turning to

Turgenev

the droshky, he waved his hand five times or so and shouted: "Follow us, follow us! My father has business here," he went on, jumping across the gutter, "and so he asked me. . . . I learned of your arrival today and have already been to call on you." (The two friends did, in fact, find a visiting-card waiting for them on their return to their room; it had crumpled corners and bore the name of Sitnikov, written in French on one side and in Slavonic script on the other.) "I hope you are not coming away from the governor's?"

"Then don't hope, we've come straight from there."

"Ah! In that case I'll go and call on him. . . . Yevgeny Vasilich, introduce me to your — to him."

"Sitnikov, Kirsanov," Bazarov snorted without halting.

"I am highly honored," Sitnikov began, falling in beside them, smirking, and hurriedly pulling off his excessively elegant gloves. "I've heard a great deal. . . . I am an old acquaintance of Yevgeny Vasilich and, I can even say, his pupil. I am obliged to him for my regeneration. . . ."

Arkady looked at Bazarov's pupil. A worried and stupid expression was imprinted on the small though pleasant features of his very smooth face; the little eyes, which looked as though they had been pushed in, had a fixed and anxious gaze, and he smiled anxiously, with a fleeting, wooden smile.

"Will you believe," he went on, "that when Yevgeny Vasilich said for the first time in my hearing that one should not recognize any authorities, I felt such exultation — as though I had come to maturity. Now, I thought, at last I have found a man! By the way, Yevgeny Vasilich, you simply must make the acquaintance of a certain local lady who is quite capable of understanding you and who will regard your visit as a real festival; I expect you have heard of her?"

"What is her name?" Bazarov said reluctantly.

"Kukshina, Eudoxie, Yevdoksia Kukshina. She's a remarkable character, *émancipée* in the true sense of the word, an advanced woman. Do you know what? Let us all go along to her now. She lives only a couple of steps away. We'll have breakfast there. I don't suppose you have breakfasted yet?"

"Not yet."

"Well, that's excellent. She's gone a different road from her husband, you know; she is dependent on no one."

"Is she good-looking?" Bazarov interrupted him.

"Nn-no, I can't say she is."

"Then what the devil are you asking us to go along to her for?"

"Now, you wag, you wag. . . . She'll bring out a bottle of champagne for us."

"Really! Now the practical man is evident. By the way, is your father still the local licensee?"

"Yes, he is," Sitnikov replied hurriedly, and squealed with laughter. "Well, are you coming?"

"I really don't know."

"You wanted to see the local people, so why not go with him?" Arkady observed in an undertone.

"But what about you, Mr. Kirsanov?" Sitnikov intervened. "You come too, we can't go without you."

"But how can all three of us drop in on her without warning?"

"That's all right. She's an eccentric sort."

"And there will be a bottle of champagne?" Bazarov demanded.

"Three!" Sitnikov exclaimed. "I'll guarantee that."

"What with?"

"My own head."

"Your father's purse would be better. But come on, then."

XIII

The small upper-class house in Moscow style in which Avdotia Nikitishna (or *Yevdoksia*) Kukshina lived was situated in one of the recently burned-down streets of the town of X X X (it is a well-known fact that our provincial towns are burned down every year). At the door, above a crookedly pinned visiting-card, was a bell handle, and in the porch the visitors were met by someone who might have been a servant, or perhaps a companion, in a cap — an obvious sign of the mistress's progressive trends. Sitnikov asked whether Avdotia Nikitishna was at home.

"Is that you, Victor?" a thin voice came from the next room. "Come in."

The woman in the cap at once vanished.

"I'm not alone," Sitnikov announced, spiritedly throwing off his hussar coat and revealing a coat like a sack or a Russian peasant coat. He gave Arkady and Bazarov a dashing look.

"It doesn't matter," the voice replied. "*Entrez!*"

The young men entered. The room in which they found themselves was more like a workroom than a reception room. Papers, letters, and stout issues of Russian periodicals, most of them with edges uncut, were lying about on dusty tables; the white butts of cigarettes were scattered everywhere. A lady, still young, fair-haired, rather disheveled, in a silk and not entirely tidy dress, with large bracelets on her short arms and a lace kerchief on her head, was reclining on a leather divan. She rose from the divan and, negligently drawing a short velvet coat lined with yellowing ermine fur round her shoulders, she drawled: "Good morning, Victor," and squeezed Sitnikov's hand.

"Bazarov, Kirsanov," he introduced them impetuously, in imitation of Bazarov.

"You are welcome," she replied and, fixing Bazarov with her round eyes, between which was a little red snub nose, she added: "I know you," and squeezed his hand too.

Bazarov's face clouded. There was nothing really hideous in this emancipated woman's tiny and insignificant figure, but her facial expression had an unpleasant effect on the observer. Involuntarily one wanted to ask her: "What is the matter — hungry? Or bored? Or shy? What are you all strung up for?" She, like Sitnikov, was everlastingly clawing at her soul. She talked and moved jauntily yet awkwardly; evidently she regarded herself as a good-natured and simple creature, and yet, no matter what she did, one continually had the impression that that was precisely what she did not want to do; everything she did seemed to be "on purpose," as children say; in other words, it was not simple, not natural.

"Yes, yes, I know you, Bazarov," she repeated. (She had the habit, common to many provincial and Moscow ladies, of calling a man by his surname from the first day of their acquaintance.) "Would you like a cigar?"

"We don't mind a cigar," said Sitnikov, who was already sprawled in an armchair, with one leg cocked up, "but how about some breakfast? We're terribly hungry; and tell them to bring in a bottle of champagne."

"You sybarite," Yevdoksia declared, and smiled. (When she smiled, she laid bare her upper gum above her teeth.) "Isn't that so, Bazarov, isn't he a sybarite?"

"I am fond of the comforts of life," Sitnikov pronounced gravely. "That doesn't prevent my being a liberal."

"Oh, but it does, it does!" Yevdoksia exclaimed; none the less she ordered her lady help to see about both breakfast and champagne. "What is your view on that?" she added, turning to Bazarov. "I am sure you share my opinion."

"Well, no," Bazarov objected; "a piece of meat is better than a piece of bread, even from the chemical aspect."

"Do you study chemistry, then? That is my passion! I have even invented a kind of mastic myself."

"A mastic? You?"

"Yes, I. And do you know what it is for? To make dolls' heads, so that they don't break. You see, I'm practical, too. But it isn't ready yet. I must read Liebig first. By the way, have you read Kislyakov's article on female labor in the *Moscow News*? Do read it. You are interested in the woman question, aren't you? And in schools too? What does your friend do? What are his Christian name and patronymic?"

Mme Kukshina let her questions *drop* one after another with delicate negligence, without waiting for the answers; spoilt children talk to their nurses in the same way.

"My name is Arkady Nikolaich Kirsanov," Arkady said. "And I am not doing anything."

Yevdoksia burst into a roar of laughter.

"Now, that's charming! Why aren't you smoking? Victor, you know, I am angry with you."

"What for?"

"I hear you have begun to praise George Sand again. She's a backward woman and nothing more! How can you compare her with Emerson! She has no ideas whatever on education, or physiology, or anything. I am sure she has never even heard of embryology, and in our day what can you do without that?" (Yevdoksia even threw out her hands.) "Ah, what an amazing article Yelisievich has written on that question! Now, he's a gentleman of genius!" (Yevdoksia always used the word "gentleman" instead of "man.") "Bazarov, sit down by me on the divan. You may not know it, but I am terribly afraid of you."

"Why are you? Forgive my curiosity."

"You are a dangerous gentleman; you're such a critic! Ah, my God! it's absurd of me, I talk like some steppe landowner woman. For that matter, I really am a landowner. I run my own estate and, just imagine, I have a drunkard for head man — an amazing type, exactly like Cooper's Pathfinder: there's something so forth-right in him! I have settled down finally here; it's an intolerable town, isn't it? But what can one do?"

"It's no worse than others," Bazarov observed unconcernedly.

"But they all have such petty interests, that's what makes it so horrible! I used to spend the winters in Moscow . . . but now my faithful consort, M'sieur Kukshin, lives there. And besides, Moscow today — I really don't know — it isn't what it was. I am thinking of traveling abroad; last year I was on the point of going."

"To Paris, of course?" Bazarov asked.

"To Paris and Heidelberg."

"Why Heidelberg?"

"Why, Bunsen is there, of course!"

To which Bazarov could find no reply.

"Pierre Sapozhnikov — do you know him?"

"No, I don't."

"But really, Pierre Sapozhnikov — he is always to be seen with Lydia Khostatova."

"I don't know her either."

"Well, he's undertaken to escort me. Thank God, I am free, I haven't any children — What did I say: *'Thank God'!* However, it's of no consequence."

Yevdoksia rolled a cigarette in her tobacco-stained fingers, ran her tongue along the edge, sucked at it, and lit it. Her lady help entered with a tray.

"Ah, here's breakfast! Would you like a bite of something? Victor, uncork a bottle; that's your department."

"Yes, that's mine, that's mine," Sitnikov mumbled, and again squealed with laughter.

"Are there any good-looking women here?" Bazarov asked as he drank his third glass.

"There are," Yevdoksia replied, "but they're all so empty-headed. For instance, *mon amie* Odintsova isn't at all bad-looking. Pity her reputation is rather — Not that that would matter, but she has no freedom of outlook, no breadth, nothing — of that sort. We have got to change the entire system of education. I've al-ready thought of that; our women are very stupidly brought up."

"You'll never do anything with them," Sitnikov retorted. "They're only deserving of contempt, and I do feel contempt for them, wholly and completely!" (The possibility of feeling contempt and expressing his contempt was the most pleasant feeling Sitnikov could have; he was especially fond of attacking women, not suspecting that within a few months he would be cringing before his own wife, simply because she was born Princess Durdoleosova.) "Not one of them would be able to understand our talk, not one of them is worthy of serious men like us talking about her!"

"But then there isn't any need for them to understand our talk," Bazarov observed.

"Whom are you talking about?" Yevdoksia intervened.

"Good-looking women."

"What? So you share Proudhon's opinion!"

Bazarov drew himself up haughtily. "I share no one's opinions; I have my own."

"Down with the authorities!" Sitnikov shouted, rejoicing at the opportunity to express himself strongly in the presence of a man to whom he toadied.

"But Macaulay himself — " Kukshina began.

"Down with Macaulay!" Sitnikov thundered. "Do you defend those petticoats?"

"Not the petticoats, but the rights of women, which I have sworn to defend to the last drop of my blood."

"Down — " But here Sitnikov stopped. "Well, I don't deny those rights," he declared.

"Ah, but I see you are a Slavophil."

"No, I am not a Slavophil, though of course — "

"Yes, yes, yes! You are a Slavophil. You are an adherent of the 'Rules of the Household.' [1] You should have a whip in your hand!"

"A whip is a good thing," Bazarov remarked; "only we have now reached the last drop — "

"Of what?" Yevdoksia interrupted.

"Of champagne, deeply respected Avdotia Nikitishna, of champagne, not of your blood."

"I cannot listen with equanimity when women are attacked," Yevdoksia continued. "It's terrible, terrible. Instead of attacking

---

[1] "Rules for Household Government," emphasizing the domination of the husband, which formerly circulated in manuscript among the common people of Russia. (Tr.)

them, you would do better to read Michelet's book *De l'amour*. That's a masterpiece! Gentlemen, we will now talk about love," Yevdoksia added, languidly letting her head fall back on the divan's crumpled cushion.

There was a sudden silence.

"But why talk about love?" Bazarov observed.

"You mentioned Odintsova just now. That is the name you said, I think? Who is this lady?"

"Charming, charming!" Sitnikov began to squeal. "I'll introduce you to her. She's intelligent, rich, and a widow. Unfortunately, she isn't sufficiently developed yet: she should make our Yevdoksia's closer acquaintance. I drink to your health, Eudoxie! Let's clink glasses! *'Et toc, et toc, et tin-tin-tin. Et toc, et toc, et tin-tin-tin!!'* "

"Victor, you're a madcap. . . ."

The breakfast went on for quite a long time. The first bottle of champagne was followed by a second, a third, and even a fourth. . . . Yevdoksia chattered away without stopping; Sitnikov echoed her. They talked a great deal about marriage, whether it was a prejudice or a crime, and how people were born, whether all identical or not, and what exactly individuality was. It ended at last with Yevdoksia, crimson with the wine she had drunk, and knocking her flat nails on the keys of an out-of-tune piano, beginning to sing in a hoarse voice first gypsy songs, then Seymour-Schiff's ballad "Drowsy Granada is dozing," while Sitnikov tied his head in a scarf and acted the dying lover when she came to the words:

> "And thy lips with mine
> Are fused in a burning kiss."

In the end Arkady could stand no more. "Gentlemen, this has grown rather like a madhouse," he observed aloud. Bazarov, who only rarely interjected a derisive remark — he was more occupied with the champagne — yawned noisily, rose, and, without taking leave of their hostess, went out with Arkady. Sitnikov jumped up to follow them.

"Well, now what do you say, what do you say?" he asked, dancing attendance on first one, then the other. "Didn't I tell you she was a remarkable personality? Now, that's the kind of woman we could do with more of! She is a highly moral phenomenon of her kind."

"And is that establishment of thy father also a moral phenomenon?" Bazarov remarked, pointing to a pub they were passing at that moment.

Sitnikov again squealed with laughter. He was deeply ashamed of his origin, and did not know whether to feel flattered or aggrieved by Bazarov's unexpected "thouing."

XIV

The governor's ball took place a few days later. Matvei Ilich was the genuine "hero of the celebrations." The provincial marshal announced to all and sundry that he was present entirely out of respect for Matvei Ilich, while the governor, even at the ball, even when standing still, continued to "issue orders." Matvei Ilich's benignity in his relations with others was only equaled by his majesty. He was gracious to all — to some with a nuance of fastidiousness, to others with a nuance of respect; he was expansive *en vrai chevalier français* in the ladies' company and incessantly laughed a large, resounding, and monotonous laugh, as is proper for a dignitary. Arkady he patted on the back and loudly called "little nephew"; Bazarov, who was attired in an old frock coat, he vouchsafed an abstracted but condescending glance out of the corner of his eye, and a vague but affable bellow in which the only intelligible sounds were "I . . . " and "mmm yes"; Sitnikov he gave one finger and a smile, but with his head turned away; even to Kukshina herself — who arrived at the ball without crinoline of any kind and wearing dirty gloves, but with a bird of paradise in her hair — even to Kukshina he said *"enchanté."* There was a very large crowd and there was no lack of gentlemen partners; the civilians mostly thronged the walls, but the military danced zealously, especially one of them, who had lived for some six weeks in Paris, where he had learned various devil-may-care exclamations in the style of *"zut," "Ah, fichtrrre," "pst, pst, mon bibi,"* and suchlike. He pronounced them perfectly, with genuine Parisian chic, yet he said *"si j'aurais"* instead of *"si j'avais,"* and *"absolument"* in the sense of "certainly"; in a word, he expressed himself in that Great-Russian French dialect which the French laugh at so much when there is no need for them to assure us that we talk their language like angels, *"comme des anges."*

Arkady was a poor dancer, as we know already, and Bazarov did not dance at all: they took up a position in one corner, where Sitnikov joined them. Putting a contemptuous smile on his face and letting fall venomous remarks, he looked about him insolently, and apparently felt genuine satisfaction. Suddenly his face changed and, turning to Arkady, he said, evidently in some embarrassment: "Odintsova has arrived."

Arkady looked round and saw a tall woman in a black gown standing at the entrance to the hall. She struck him by the dignity of her bearing. She carried her bare arms beautifully to set off her graceful figure; light sprigs of fuchsia fell beautifully from her gleaming hair to her sloping shoulders; her luminous eyes gazed calmly and intelligently — calmly was just the word, but not thoughtfully — from beneath a slightly beetling white brow, and her lips smiled a hardly perceptible smile. A gracious and gentle strength radiated from her features.

"Do you know her?" Arkady asked Sitnikov.

"Intimately. Would you like me to introduce you?"

"Please — after this quadrille."

Bazarov also turned his attention to Odintsova.

"Who is that person?" he said. "She is quite unlike any of the other women."

Sitnikov waited till the end of the quadrille, then led Arkady to Odintsova. But he could hardly have been intimately acquainted with her: he stammered as he spoke, and she gazed at him with some astonishment. None the less she smiled at Arkady when she heard his surname. She asked him if he wasn't the son of Nikolai Piotrovich.

"Yes, that is so."

"I have met your father twice, and I have heard a great deal about him," she continued. "I am very glad to make your acquaintance."

At that moment some adjutant flew up to her and asked her for a quadrille. She consented.

"Do you dance, then?" Arkady asked respectfully.

"Yes. But why should you think I don't? Or do I seem too old to you?"

"Oh, really, how could I — But in that case permit me to ask you for a mazurka."

She smiled indulgently.

"Very well," she said, and looked at Arkady not exactly patronizingly, but rather as married sisters look at very young brothers.

She was a little older than Arkady, for she had passed her twenty-ninth birthday; but in her presence he felt like a schoolboy, a young student, as though the difference in their ages was far greater. Matvei Ilich approached her with a majestic air and unctuous remarks. Arkady slipped aside, but he continued to watch her: he did not take his eyes off her even during the quadrille. She talked as unconstrainedly with her partner as with the dignitary; she rolled her head and eyes a little, and laughed quietly once or twice. Her nose was rather flashy, like almost all Russian noses, and her complexion was not perfectly clear; but even so, Arkady decided that he had never before met such a charming woman. The sound of her voice did not fade from his ears; even the folds of her gown seemed to be arranged round her differently, they fell more harmoniously and amply, and she moved with a very buoyant yet natural grace.

Arkady felt some bashfulness in his heart when, at the first sounds of the mazurka, he took his place beside his lady and prepared to enter into conversation, only to run his hand over his hair, finding not one word to say. But he was shy and agitated only for a few moments. Her composure was communicated to him: before fifteen minutes had passed he was talking easily about his father, his uncle, about life in Petersburg and in the country. She listened to him with polite sympathy, slightly opening and closing her fan; his chatter was interrupted when other male partners came to ask for her; Sitnikov, by the way, carried her off twice. She returned, sat down again, picked up her fan, and even her breast did not rise and fall more rapidly; but Arkady again began to chatter, completely absorbed in the happiness of finding himself close to her, of talking to her, of looking into her eyes, at her fine brow, at all her pleasant, serious, and intelligent face. She herself talked little, but knowledge of life was revealed in her words; from various of her remarks Arkady concluded that this young woman had already managed to feel and to think a very great deal. . . .

"Who was that you were standing with?" she asked him, "when Mr. Sitnikov led you to me?"

"Did you notice him, then?" Arkady asked in his turn. "Don't you think he has a very fine face? He is a friend of mine, named Bazarov."

He began to talk about "his friend."

He talked about him in such detail and with such enthusiasm that she turned toward him and looked at him attentively. Meanwhile the mazurka was nearing its end. Arkady felt regretful at having to part with his lady: he had so greatly enjoyed the hour or so he had spent with her! True, all that time he had felt continually that she was treating him indulgently, that somehow he ought to be grateful to her . . . but young hearts are not burdened by that feeling.

The music stopped.

"*Merci*," she said, rising. "You've promised to call on me; bring your friend with you. I shall be very curious to see a man who has the courage not to believe in anything."

The governor came up to her, announced that supper was ready, and with a preoccupied air gave her his hand. As she went out she turned to smile and nod to Arkady for a last time. He bowed low, gazed after her (how shapely he thought her waist, flooded with the gray shimmer of black silk!), and as he thought: "She has already forgotten my existence," he felt an exquisite humility in his soul. . . .

"Well?" Bazarov asked Arkady as soon as he returned to his friend in the corner, "satisfied? I've just been told by one gentleman that that lady is — oh, dear, dear! But that gentleman would appear to be a fool. Well, but what do you think, is she really — oh, dear, dear?"

"I don't quite understand that definition," Arkady replied.

"Really, now! What an innocent!"

"In that case I don't understand your gentleman. She is very nice, undoubtedly, but she behaves so coldly and severely that — "

"Still waters — you know!" Bazarov interrupted him. "You say she is cold. But that is just what gives the savor. You like ice cream, don't you?"

"Maybe," Arkady muttered, "I can't judge as to that. She wishes to make your acquaintance and asked me to take you along to see her."

"I can imagine how you described me! All the same, you did

well. Take me along. No matter who she may be, just a simple provincial lioness or an 'émancipé' like Kukshina, I haven't seen such shoulders as hers for a long time."

Arkady was rather jarred by Bazarov's cynicism, but, as often happens, he chided his friend with something a little different from the thing to which he objected.

"Why aren't you prepared to allow freedom of thought in women?" he said in an undertone.

"Because, dear brother, according to all my observations the only women who think freely are hideous."

There the conversation ended. The two young men left immediately after supper. Kukshina smiled after them with nervous malevolence, but not without some timidity; her self-esteem was deeply wounded by the circumstance that neither of them had paid any attention to her. She was the last to leave the ball, and at four in the morning she and Sitnikov danced a polka-mazurka in the Parisian manner. And with this instructive spectacle the governor's celebration came to its end.

XV

"We'll see what category of mammals this person belongs to," Bazarov said to Arkady next day as they went up the stairs of the hotel in which Mme Odintsova was staying. "My nose tells me that there is something not quite as it should be here."

"I am amazed at you!" Arkady exclaimed. "What? You, you, Bazarov, hold to that narrow-minded morality which — "

"Aren't you queer!" Bazarov interrupted him carelessly. "Don't you really know that in our dialect and for the likes of us 'not quite as it should be' means 'just as it should be'? It means that there's something in it to our advantage. Didn't you yourself say this morning that she had made a strange marriage? — though, in my view, to marry a wealthy old man is not in the least strange, but on the contrary is perfectly sensible. I don't believe the town rumors; but I like to think, as our cultured governor says, that they are justified."

Arkady did not answer; he knocked on the door. A young servant in livery led the two friends into a large room, furnished stupidly, like all the rooms in Russian hotels, but decorated with flowers. Soon Mme Odintsova herself appeared in a simple morning dress. By the light of the spring sunshine she seemed even younger. Arkady introduced her to Bazarov and with secret astonishment noted that he seemed to be embarrassed, whereas she remained perfectly composed, as she had been the previous evening. Bazarov himself felt that he was embarrassed, and he was chagrined. "Here's a fine thing; afraid of a woman!" he thought and, sprawling in his chair as negligently as Sitnikov, he began to talk with exaggerated jauntiness, while she did not remove her clear eyes from him.

Anna Sergeevna Odintsova was the daughter of Sergei Nikolaevich Loktiev, a notoriously handsome adventurer and gamester who, after keeping his head above water and causing a great sensation for fifteen years in Petersburg and Moscow, ended by being completely ruined and was forced to settle down in the country, where in any case he died soon after, leaving almost nothing to his daughters, Anna, aged twenty, and Katherine, aged twelve. Their mother, of Prince X's impoverished line, had died in Petersburg while her husband was still at the height of his career. After her father's death Anna's situation was very difficult. The brilliant upbringing she had received in Petersburg had not prepared her for the anxieties of estate management and domestic responsibilities or for quiet country existence. She knew absolutely no one in all the district, and she had no one with whom to take counsel. Her father had tried to avoid contact with the neighbors; he was contemptuous of them and they were contemptuous of him, each in their own fashion. She did not lose her head, however, and immediately sent for her mother's sister, Princess Avdotia Stepanovna X, a malicious and arrogant old woman who, on settling in her niece's house, at once took all the best rooms for herself, snorted and grumbled from morning till evening, and even when walking in the garden was accompanied by her sole serf, a glum-faced lackey in shabby pea-green livery with blue galloons and a tricorne. Anna patiently endured all her aunt's caprices, gradually set about her sister's education, and seemed to be reconciled to the thought of withering in her out-of-the-way house. . . . But fate had decided otherwise.

She chanced to be seen by a man named Odintsov, very rich, aged about forty-six, an eccentric, a hypochondriac, rather fat, heavy, and sour, yet neither stupid nor a bad man; he fell in love with her and offered her his hand. She consented to be his wife; he lived with her for six years and, on dying, left her all his fortune. For some twelve months after his death Anna Sergeevna did not leave her country home at all; then she went abroad with her sister, but stayed only in Germany; she grew miserable and returned to reside in her charming Nikolskoe, which was some twenty-five miles from the town of X X X. There she had a magnificent, excellently furnished house, and a beautiful garden with a conservatory — her husband had never denied himself anything. She visited the town very rarely, usually on business, and did not stay long. She was not liked in the province, there had been a terrible outcry over her marriage with Odintsov, all kinds of stories were told about her, people declared that she had helped her father in his swindling transactions, nor was it for nothing that she had traveled abroad, but out of the necessity to conceal certain unfortunate consequences. . . . "Do you realize what consequences?" the indignant narrators ended. "She has passed through fire and water," it was said of her; and a well-known wit of the province usually added: "and through copper tubes." [1] All these rumors reached her ears; but she took no notice of them; she had an independent and very resolute character.

She sat leaning against the back of her armchair, with one hand laid on the other, and listened to Bazarov. Contrary to his custom, he talked a great deal and obviously tried to interest his hostess, which greatly surprised Arkady. He could not make up his mind whether Bazarov had achieved his aim. It was difficult to judge from Anna Sergeevna's face what impression was made on her: it preserved one and the same expression, friendly but subtle; her fine eyes beamed with attention, but an imperturbable attention. Bazarov's affectation during the first few minutes of their visit had an unpleasant effect on her, like a bad smell or a harsh sound; but she at once realized that he felt embarrassed, which even flattered her. Only the trivial repelled her, and no one could have reproached Bazarov with trivialities. That day Arkady was astonished by one thing after another. He expected Bazarov to talk to her as though she were an intelligent woman, about his convictions and views; she herself had expressed the desire to hear a man "who has the courage not to believe in anything"; but instead he talked about medicine, about homeopathy, about

[1] "Through fire, water, and then copper tubes" — used of a slippery, artful person. (Tr.)

botany. It transpired that Mme Odintsova had not wasted her time in her seclusion: she had read several good books, and she expressed herself in correct Russian. She turned the talk to the subject of music, but, perceiving that Bazarov did not appreciate art, little by little she returned to botany, though Arkady was all ready to talk about the significance of folk melodies. She continued to treat him as a younger brother: apparently she appreciated his goodness and simplicity of youth — and that was all. For more than three hours the conversation went on, unhurriedly, yet varied and vital.

At last the two friends rose and began to take their leave. Anna Sergeevna looked at them graciously, extended her beautiful white hand to each of them in turn, and, after a moment's thought, said with an irresolute but pleasant smile:

"If you're not afraid of being bored, gentlemen, come and visit me at Nikolskoe."

"Why, of course, Anna Sergeevna," Arkady exclaimed. "I shall regard myself as particularly happy to."

"And you, M'sieur Bazarov?"

Bazarov only bowed — and Arkady was made to feel astonishment for a last time: he noticed that his friend blushed.

"Well?" he said to Bazarov when they reached the street, "are you still of the opinion that she is — oh, dear, dear?"

"Who can tell? You saw how she froze up!" Bazarov retorted. After a brief silence he added: "She's a duchess, an imperious person. She only needs a train to be carried behind her and a coronet on her head."

"Our duchesses don't talk Russian like that," Arkady remarked.

"She's been refashioned, my boy, she's tasted our bread."

"All the same she is enchanting," Arkady declared.

"Such a fine body!" Bazarov continued, "it ought to go at once to the anatomical theater."

"Stop it, for God's sake, Yevgeny! That talk is like nothing on earth."

"Now, don't be angry, you're too sensitive! I've said she's first-class. We'll have to go and visit her."

"When?"

"Well, say the day after tomorrow. What can we do here? Drink champagne with Kukshina? Listen to your relation, the

liberal dignitary? . . . We'll slip off the day after tomorrow. As
it happens, my father's little place isn't far from there. It's the
Nikolskoe on the — road, isn't it?"

"Yes."

"*Optime.* There's no point in hanging about. Only fools dally
— and wise men. I tell you it's a fine body!"

Two days later the two friends were driving along the road to
Nikolskoe. The day was clear and not too hot, and the well-fed
hired horses trotted along rapidly, gently waving their twisted
and plaited tails. Arkady gazed at the road and smiled, himself
not knowing why.

"Congratulate me!" Bazarov suddenly exclaimed; "today is
the 22nd of June, the day of my angel. We shall see how he looks
after me. They're expecting me home today," he added, lowering
his voice. "Well, they can wait a little longer, it isn't so important as that!"

XVI

Anna Sergeevna's country house stood on a rolling, open rise, a
little distance from a yellow brick church with a green roof,
white columns, and, above the main entrance, an alfresco painting,
representing *The Resurrection of Christ* in the Italian style. A
swarthy, helmeted warrior, prone in the foreground, was particularly remarkable because of his swelling contours. Beyond the
church a village extended in two long rows, with chimneys
rising here and there above straw roofs. The gentry's house was
built in the same style as the church, the style known to us as the
Alexandrine; this house, too, was painted yellow, and it, too, had
a green roof and white columns and a pediment with armorial
bearings. The provincial architect had erected both edifices with
the approval of the dead Odintsov, who could not endure any
empty and, as he expressed it, arbitrary innovations. On both
sides of the house were the dark trees of an old-world garden; an
avenue of close-pruned firs led to the main entrance.

In the vestibule our friends were met by two well-built
lackeys in livery; one of them immediately ran for the butler.
The butler, a stout man in a black frock coat, appeared at once
and led the guests up carpeted stairs into a separate room, which
was already furnished with two beds and all the appurtenances

Turgenev

of the toilet. It was evident that order reigned in the house, everything was clean, everything had a decorous odor, as in ministers' waiting-rooms.

"Anna Sergeevna requests you to present yourselves to her in half an hour," the butler reported, "and in the meantime have you any commands?"

"There will not be any commands whatever, my dear fellow," Bazarov replied, "except perhaps that you would be so kind as to bring us a glass of vodka."

"Very good," the butler replied, not without a touch of bewilderment, and he retired, his boots creaking.

"What a *grand genre*!" Bazarov observed, "that is what I think you call it? A duchess, and in every respect!"

"A fine duchess," Arkady retorted, "when at our first meeting she invites such distinguished aristocrats as you and me to call on her."

"Especially me, a future doctor, and a doctor's son, and a deacon's nephew. You know, of course, that I am a deacon's nephew? Like Speransky," [1] Bazarov added after a brief silence, with a twist of his lips. "But, all the same, she has indulged herself; oh, how this lady has indulged herself! Surely we ought to wear frock coats?"

Arkady only shrugged his shoulders, but he, too, felt a little embarrassment.

Half an hour later Bazarov and Arkady went down into the reception hall. It was a lofty, spacious room, furnished quite luxuriously, but without any particular taste. Heavy, expensive furniture stood in the usual starchy order along the walls, which were hung with brown wallpaper with a design in gold; Odintsov had ordered it from Moscow through his friend and agent, a wine merchant. Above the central divan hung a portrait of a flabby, fair-haired man — and it seemed to stare at the guests inimically. "That must be he *himself*," Bazarov whispered to Arkady and, wrinkling his nose, added: "Shall we clear out?" But at that moment their hostess entered. She was wearing a light *barège* gown; her hair, combed smoothly back behind her ears, conferred a maidenly expression on her pure, fresh features.

"Thank you for keeping your word," she began; "you will stay with me for a while, won't you? It really isn't bad here. I'll

[1] A Russian statesman of the early nineteenth century. (Tr.)

236

introduce you to my sister, she can play the piano well. To you,, M'sieur Bazarov, that is a matter of indifference; but you, M'sieur Kirsanov, like music, I think; in addition to my sister my old aunt is living with me, and sometimes one of our neighbors drives over to play cards; and that is all the society we have. But now let us sit down."

She uttered all this little speech very meticulously, as though she had learned it by heart; then she turned to Arkady. It transpired that her mother had been acquainted with his mother and had even been a confidante of her love for Nikolai Piotrovich. Arkady began to talk enthusiastically about his dead mother, but meanwhile Bazarov examined some albums. "How humble I have become!" he thought.

A handsome borzoi with a blue collar ran into the room, its nails tapping on the floor, and it was followed by a girl of about eighteen, black-haired and swarthy, with a rather round but pleasant face and small dark eyes. She was carrying a basket full of flowers. "And this is my sister, Katya," Odintsova said, nodding toward the girl.

The girl made a little curtsy, seated herself by her sister, and began to pick over the flowers. The borzoi, which was called Fifi, approached each guest in turn, wagging its tail, and thrust its cold muzzle into their hands.

"Did you pick all those yourself?" Mme Odintsova asked.

"Yes," Katya replied.

"And is auntie coming for tea?"

"Yes."

When Katya spoke she smiled very pleasantly, bashfully and openly, and looked up with an amusingly severe expression. Everything about her was still youthfully verdant: her voice, and the down all over her face, and her rosy hands with whitish little rings in the palms, and the very slightly raised shoulders. . . . She blushed incessantly and breathed hurriedly.

Mme Odintsova turned to Bazarov.

"You're looking at those pictures only out of politeness, Yevgeny Vasilievich," she began. "You're not really interested in them. Come and join us, and let us have an argument about something."

Bazarov approached.

"What do you command us to argue about?" he asked.

"Whatever you like. I warn you that I am a terrible arguer."

"You?"

"Yes, I. That seems to surprise you. Why does it?"

"Because, so far as I can judge, you have a calm and cold disposition, and discussion calls for enthusiasm."

"How have you managed to get to know me so quickly? To begin with, I am impatient and insistent, you had better ask Katya about that; and secondly, I very easily grow enthusiastic."

Bazarov looked at her.

"Maybe; you should know best. Well, so you would like to argue; very good. I have just been looking at the views of the Saxon Switzerland in your album, but you have just remarked that they cannot interest me. You said that because you do not think I have any artistic inclinations, and certainly I have none; but I found those views interesting from the geological aspect, from the aspect of mountain formation, for instance."

"Excuse me, but as a geologist surely you would rather turn to a book, to some special work, than to a picture."

"A picture shows me at a glance what it takes dozens of pages of a book to expound."

She was silent for a moment.

"And you really haven't the least touch of artistic feeling?" she said, resting her elbows on the table and by this very movement bringing her face closer to Bazarov. "But how do you manage without it?"

"But what does one need it for, if you will permit me to ask?"

"Why, if only to be able to recognize and study people."

Bazarov smiled.

"In the first place, to do that, one relies on vital experience; and secondly, I have to inform you that the study of individual personalities is not worth the labor. All people are like one another, in both body and soul; each of us has a brain, a spleen, a heart, and lungs, all constructed alike; and the so-called moral qualities are one and the same in all: the tiny variations are of no significance. One needs only a single human specimen in order to judge of all the others. People are like trees in the forest; no botanist will stop to study every birch separately."

Katya, who was unhurriedly matching flower to flower, raised her eyes to Bazarov in astonishment and, meeting his swift and

perfunctory look, flamed to her ears. Anna Sergeevna shook her head.

"Trees in a forest!" she repeated. "So in your view there is no difference between a stupid and an intelligent man, between good and evil."

"Yes, there is a difference like that between the sick and the healthy. The lungs of a consumptive are not in the same condition as yours and mine, though they are of identical construction. We know approximately what our physical maladies are caused by; but moral diseases are due to stupid upbringing, to all kinds of trash with which human heads are stuffed from childhood — to the monstrous state of society, in a word. Put society right, and there will not be any diseases."

Bazarov said all this with an air suggesting that meanwhile he was saying to himself: "Whether you believe me or not I don't care!" He ran his long fingers slowly over his side-whiskers, and his eyes darted from side to side.

"And do you consider," Anna Sergeevna said, "that when society is put right, there will no longer be any stupid or bad people?"

"At any rate, with a sound organization of society it will make no difference whatever whether a man is stupid or intelligent, bad or good."

"Yes, I understand; you mean they will all have one and the same spleen."

"Exactly so, madame."

She turned to Arkady.

"And what is your opinion, Arkady Nikolaevich?"

"I agree with Yevgeny," he replied.

Katya looked up at them from under knitted brows.

"You amaze me, gentlemen," Mme Odintsova declared; "but we will discuss the question with you again. Now I can hear auntie coming to tea; we must spare her ears."

Anna Sergeevna's aunt, Princess X, a rawboned little woman with features clenched like a fist and with staring, malignant eyes below a gray wig, entered and, hardly acknowledging the guests, dropped into a broad velvet armchair, in which only she was allowed to sit. Katya placed a stool beneath her feet; the old woman did not thank her, did not even glance at her, only fidgeted with her hands beneath the yellow shawl that covered almost all her puny body. The Princess liked yellow: even in her cap there were bright yellow ribbons.

"How did you rest, auntie?" Mme Odintsova asked, raising her voice.

"That dog here again," the old woman snorted in reply; noticing that Fifi had taken two irresolute steps in her direction, she cried: "Shoo! Shoo!"

Katya called Fifi and opened the door for her.

Fifi rushed out joyfully, hoping that she was to be taken for a walk. But, finding herself alone outside the door, she began to scrape and whine. The Princess frowned. Katya was about to go out.

"I think tea will be ready now," Mme Odintsova said. "Come, gentlemen; auntie, will you have some tea?"

The Princess rose from her chair without speaking and was the first to leave the room. Everybody followed her into the dining-room. At the table a page in livery noisily drew back an armchair, which also was sacred and was piled with cushions, into which the Princess dropped. Katya, who poured the tea, gave her the first cup, which was adorned with armorial bearings. The old woman put some honey into her cup (she considered it both sinful and extravagant to drink tea with sugar, though she herself never spent a kopek on anything) and suddenly asked in a hoarse voice:

"But what does Prince Ivan say in his letter?"

No one answered her. Bazarov and Arkady soon realized that nobody paid any attention to her, though everybody treated her with respect. "It's just the importance they attach to their princely line," Bazarov thought.

After tea Anna Sergeevna suggested a walk, but a fine rain began to fall, and the entire company, with the exception of the Princess, returned to the reception hall. Porfiry Platonich, the neighbor who was fond of playing cards, arrived. He was rather stout, rather gray-haired, with fingers rather stubby, as though they had been ground down, and a very polite and jocular man. Anna Sergeevna, who talked more and more to Bazarov, asked him whether he would like to try conclusions with them in an old-fashioned game of preference. Bazarov agreed, saying that he must prepare himself in advance for the country doctor's duties that awaited him.

"Beware!" Anna Sergeevna observed; "Porfiry Platonich and I will beat you hollow. And you, Katya," she added, "play something for Arkady Nikolaevich; he is fond of music, and we can listen too."

Katya reluctantly went over to the piano; and Arkady, though he did indeed like music, reluctantly went after her: he had the feeling that Anna Sergeevna was sending him away, and in his heart, as in that of any young man of his years, a vague and wearisome feeling, resembling the presentiment of love, began to work. Katya raised the lid of the piano and, without looking at Arkady, said in an undertone:

"And what shall I play for you?"

"Whatever you like," Arkady answered indifferently.

"What music do you like most?" Katya repeated, without changing her position.

"Classic," Arkady replied in the same tone.

"Do you like Mozart?"

"Yes, I like Mozart."

Katya selected Mozart's Sonata and Fantasia in C minor. She played very well, though somewhat meticulously and dryly. Fixing her eyes on the music and tightly pursing her lips, she sat motionless and upright, and only toward the end of the sonata did her face begin to burn and a tiny strand of unruly hair fell over her dark brow.

Arkady was particularly struck by the last part of the sonata, in which, amid the captivating merriment of a carefree refrain, there are sudden outbursts of such mournful, almost tragic sorrow. . . . But the thoughts aroused in him by Mozart's music had no reference to Katya. Looking at her, he only thought: "But, you know, this young lady doesn't play at all badly, and she herself isn't at all bad-looking."

When she had finished the sonata, Katya, without removing her hands from the keys, asked: "Have you had enough?" Arkady announced that he did not dare to burden her any more and began to talk to her about Mozart; he asked her whether she herself had chosen this sonata, or had someone recommended it to her? But Katya replied to him in monosyllables, she *concealed* herself, retired within herself. When this occurred with her it was long before she emerged again; at such times even her face took on an obstinate, almost stupid expression. She was not

Turgenev

exactly bashful, but distrustful, and she was rather afraid of the sister who had brought her up, a feeling that, of course, the sister did not suspect at all. Arkady ended by calling to Fifi, who had returned, and, to keep himself in countenance, began to stroke the dog on the head, smiling benevolently. Katya returned to her flowers.

But meanwhile Bazarov was fleeced. Anna Sergeevna played cards expertly, and Porfiry Platonich also could hold his own. Bazarov was left the loser, though not of any considerable sum, yet to an extent not exactly agreeable to him. Over the supper table Anna Sergeevna again turned the conversation to the subject of botany.

"We'll go for a walk the first thing in the morning," she told him. "I want you to tell me the Latin names of the wild flowers and their properties."

"What do you want to know the Latin names for?" Bazarov asked.

"Order is necessary in all things," she replied.

"What a marvelous woman Anna Sergeevna is!" Arkady exclaimed when he and his friend retired to their room.

"Yes," Bazarov replied, "she's a female with a brain. And she has seen the world, too."

"In what sense did you mean that, Yevgeny Vasilich?"

"In a good sense, in a good sense, my dear father, Arkady Nikolaich! I am confident that she also manages her estate excellently. But the miracle is not she, but her sister."

"What? That swarthy little creature?"

"Yes, that swarthy little creature. She is fresh, and untouched, and shy, and taciturn, and everything you could wish. Now there's somebody one could occupy oneself with. With her, what you plan, that you will accomplish; but the other, she's a sly vixen."

Arkady made no reply to Bazarov, and each of them went to sleep with his own thoughts.

Anna Sergeevna also thought about her guests that evening. She liked Bazarov because he was not of a flirtatious disposition, and for the very severity of his judgments. She saw in him some-

242

thing new, something she had never happened to meet before, and she was inquisitive.

Anna Sergeevna was quite a strange creature. Having no prejudices whatever, not even having any strong beliefs, she hesitated at nothing and never achieved anything. She was clearsighted in many respects, she was interested in many things, and nothing completely satisfied her; nor, in all probability, did she desire complete satisfaction. Her mind was inquisitive and indifferent at one and the same time; her doubts never faded into oblivion, and never grew into anxiety. If she had not been wealthy and independent she might have flung herself into battle, might have known passion. . . . But life was easy for her, though sometimes she was bored, and she continued to spend day after day never hurrying and only rarely getting excited. Rainbow tints sometimes glowed before her eyes, but she breathed easily when they faded, and she did not regret them. Her imagination traveled even beyond the limits regarded as permissible by the laws of ordinary morality; but even then her blood flowed as quietly as before in her enchantingly graceful and tranquil body. There were times when, stepping out of her perfumed bath, all warm and limber, she would dream of the insignificance of life, of its sorrow, of toil, and evil. . . . Her soul would be filled with a sudden audacity, would seethe with noble striving; but a draft would blow from a half-closed window, and Anna Sergeevna would huddle together, and complain, and be almost angry, and at such a moment the only necessity she felt was that that loathsome wind should not blow on her.

Like all women who have never succeeded in falling in love, she wanted something, not knowing exactly what. In reality she wanted nothing, though it seemed to her that she wanted everything. She could hardly endure her late husband (she had been calculating in her marriage, though probably she would not have consented to be his wife if she had not regarded him as a good man) and had developed a secret loathing for all men, whom she imagined only as slovenly, heavy and sluggish, impotently irksome creatures. Once, somewhere abroad, she had met a young, handsome Swede with a chivalrous expression and honest blue eyes beneath an open forehead; he made a strong impression on her, but that did not prevent her returning to Russia.

"A strange man, that doctor!" she thought as she lay in her sumptuous bed, on lacy pillows, beneath a light silk blanket. . . . From her father Anna Sergeevna had inherited some little of his love of luxury. She had been very fond of her sinful but good father, and he had worshipped her, had amiably joked with her as with an equal, and had confided in her completely, had taken counsel with her. She could hardly remember her mother.

"A strange man, that doctor!" she repeated to herself. She stretched herself, smiled, flung her arms behind her head, then skimmed through a couple of pages of a stupid French romance, let the book fall, and dropped off to sleep, all clean and cool, in clean and scented linen.

Next morning, immediately after breakfast, Anna Sergeevna set off to botanize with Bazarov and returned just before dinner; Arkady had not been anywhere and had spent about an hour with Katya. He did not feel bored with her, she herself offered to repeat yesterday's sonata to him, but when Anna Sergeevna returned at last, when he saw her — his heart momentarily stopped beating. . . . She was walking through the garden with a rather weary gait; her cheeks were crimsoned, and her eyes glittered more brightly than usual below her round straw hat. She was turning the slender stalk of some wild flower over and over in her hand, a light mantilla fell to her elbows, and the broad gray ribbons of her hat nestled against her breast. Bazarov was walking behind her, self-confidently and negligently, as always; but though the expression of his face was cheerful and even gracious, Arkady did not like it. Muttering through his teeth: "Good day," Bazarov went off to his room, while his companion abstractedly gave Arkady her hand and then she too walked past him.

" 'Good day,' " Arkady thought. "Is this the first time we have seen each other today, then?"

XVII

Time (as is well known) sometimes flies like a bird, sometimes crawls like a worm; but man feels especially happy when he does not even notice whether it is passing rapidly or quietly. That was exactly how Arkady and Bazarov spent fifteen days at Nikolskoe. This was due in part to the order that Mme Odintsova had introduced into her house and her life. She observed it strictly, and compelled others also to submit to it. Everything all through the day was done at a regular time. In the morning all the company gathered for tea punctually at eight o'clock; from tea to break-fast time everybody could do as he wished; the mistress herself was occupied with the steward (the estate was rented out to the peasants), with the butlers, with the head housekeeper. Before dinner the company again assembled for talk or for reading; the evening was devoted to a walk, to cards, to music; at half past ten Anna Sergeevna retired to her room, gave her orders for the following day, and went to bed. Bazarov did not like this measured, somewhat formal regularity of everyday life — "just as though you're running on rails," he declared; the liveried lackeys, the decorous butlers affronted his democratic feelings. He considered that, as matters had gone so far, the company should dine in the English fashion, in tail coats and white ties. One day he raised this question with Anna Sergeevna. Her atti-tude was such that anyone could express his views to her without circumlocutions. She listened to him to the end and observed: "From your viewpoint you are right — and perhaps in this respect I am a lady; but in the country it is impossible to live without order, you would be overcome with boredom," and she continued to go her own way. Bazarov snorted, but during their stay at Nikolskoe both he and Arkady found life so easy just because, among other things, everything in her house "ran as though on rails."

Meanwhile from the first day of their residence at Nikolskoe there was a change in the two young men. Bazarov, for whom Anna Sergeevna showed much predilection, though she rarely agreed with him, began to manifest an uneasiness he had never before displayed: he grew irritable quickly, spoke reluctantly, looked at the others angrily, and fidgeted in his seat as though something was worrying him. But Arkady, who now had decided that he himself was in love with Anna Sergeevna, began to give himself over to a quiet despondency. This despondency, however, did not prevent his growing intimate with Katya; it even helped him to enter into benevolent, friendly relations with her. "*She* does not appreciate me! So be it! . . . But here is a good creature who does not reject me," he thought, and his heart again tasted the joy of magnanimous feelings. Katya vaguely realized that in her company he was seeking consolation for something and did not deny either him or herself the innocent satisfaction of a half-bashful, half-trusting friendship. In Anna Sergeevna's presence they did not talk to each other: beneath her sister's keen gaze Katya always closed up; and, as is only proper for a man in love, when close to the object of his devotion, Arkady could not pay attention to anything else. But when alone with Katya, he was quite at ease. He felt that he had not the talents to interest Mme Odintsova; he grew shy and confused when left alone with her; and she did not know what to say to him: he was too young for her. On the other hand, with Katya Arkady was quite at home; he treated her with condescension and did not stop her telling him the impressions aroused in her by music, by the reading of novels, poems, and other such trifles, though he did not notice or did not realize that these trifles interested him also. For her part, Katya did not prevent his feeling sorrowful. Arkady felt at ease with Katya, Mme Odintsova with Bazarov; and so as a rule, after being together for a little while, the two couples went their own ways, especially when they were out for a walk. Katya *worshipped* nature, and Arkady was fond of it, though he would not have dared to confess the fact; but Mme Odintsova was rather indifferent to it, in which she was exactly like Bazarov. The almost constant separation of our two friends was not without its consequences: their relations began to change. Bazarov stopped talking to Arkady about Mme Odintsova and even stopped railing against her "aristocratic ways"; true, he continued to praise Katya as before and suggested only that her sentimental tendencies should be moderated; but his praises were hurried, his advice dry, and altogether he talked much less than formerly to Arkady; he seemed to avoid, seemed to be ashamed to meet him. . . .

Arkady noticed all these things, but he kept his observations to himself.

The real cause of all this "change" was the feeling Mme Odintsova inspired in Bazarov, a feeling that tormented and enraged him and that he would have denied immediately with contemptuous laughter and cynical abuse if anyone had even distantly hinted at the possibility of what was happening inside him. Bazarov was a great woman-chaser and devotee of feminine beauty, but love in the ideal sense, or, as he expressed it, the romantic sense, he called nonsense, an unforgivable stupidity; he regarded chivalrous feelings as something in the nature of a deformation or disease, and more than once expressed his surprise that Toggenburg [1] with all his minnesingers and troubadours had not been put away in a madhouse. "If you take a fancy to a woman," he used to say, "try to gain your end; but if you can't, well then, it's no matter, turn your back on her, the world is large enough." He had taken a fancy to Mme Odintsova, and the rumors spread about her, the freedom and independence of her thought, her undoubted predilection for him — everything appeared to be in his favor; but he soon realized that with her he would not "gain his end." To his own amazement, however, he found he had no power to turn his back on her. His blood began to burn as soon as he thought of her; he could easily have managed his blood, but something else had entered into it, which formerly he would never have tolerated, which he had always made fun of, and which stirred up all his pride. When talking to her he expressed his indifferent contempt for everything romantic even more than before; but when he was alone he angrily recognized the romanticism that was in himself. Then he went off into the forest and walked through it with great strides, breaking the branches that came in his way, and cursing half aloud both her and himself; or he climbed into the hayloft, into the coach-house, and, obstinately closing his eyes, forced himself to sleep, in which, of course, he was not always successful. Suddenly he imagined those undefiled arms some day twining around his neck, those proud lips responding to his kisses, those intelligent eyes tenderly — yes, tenderly — resting on his eyes, and his head whirled and he forgot himself for a moment, until indignation again flamed up within him. He caught himself thinking all kinds of "shameful" thoughts, as though he were being provoked by a demon. Sometimes it seemed to him that a change was occurring in her too, that something peculiar was revealed in the expression of her face, that, perhaps . . . But at this he usually stamped his foot or grated his teeth and shook his fist at himself.

Meanwhile Bazarov was not altogether wrong. He caught her imagination; he occupied it, she thought a great deal about him. In his absence she did not long for him, did not wait for him; but his arrival at once aroused her; she readily remained alone with him and readily talked with him, even when he made her

[1] Hero of Schiller's ballad of the same name. (Tr.)

angry or affronted her taste, her exquisite manners. She seemed
to desire to try him, and to plumb herself.

One day as he was walking with her in the garden, he abruptly
announced in a glum tone that he intended to travel on to see
his father soon. She turned pale, as though something had stabbed
at her heart, and had stabbed so violently that she was amazed,
and for long after she meditated on what it could mean. Bazarov
had informed her of his departure not with the intention of
trying her, of seeing what would come of it; he never "created."
That same morning he had had a meeting with his father's steward
and his own former servant, Timofeich. This Timofeich, who
was a shabby, brisk little old man with faded yellow hair, a red,
weatherbeaten face, and little tears in his shrunken eyes, and was
wearing a rather short coat of stout grayish-blue cloth belted
with a leather strap and had tarry boots on his feet, arrived
without warning to see Bazarov.

"Ah, old fellow, good morning!" Bazarov exclaimed.

"Good morning, Master Yevgeny Vasilich," the old man began,
and he smiled joyfully, so that all his face was wrinkled.

"What have you come for? I suppose they've sent you to fetch
me?"

"Why, of course not, master, how could they!" Timofeich
stammered (he remembered the strict injunction his master had
given him on his departure). "I was traveling to the town on the
master's business, and I had heard you were here, so I dropped
in on my way, just to take a look at you — otherwise how could
I have dared to trouble you?"

"Now, don't lie!" Bazarov interrupted him. "Is this your way
to the town?" Timofeich was disconcerted and did not reply.
"Is my father well?"

"Yes, praise be."

"And my mother?"

"And Arina Vlasievna, praise be to God."

"I suppose they're expecting me?"

The old man cocked his little head on one side.

"Ah, Yevgeny Vasilich, how could they help waiting for you?
Believe it or not, your parents' hearts are pining with looking for
you."

"Well, good, good! Don't make a song of it. Tell them I shall
be home soon."

"Very good," Timofeich answered with a sigh.

As he left the house, he clapped his peaked cap on his head with both hands, climbed into the wretched-looking light droshky he had left at the gate, and made off at a trot, but not in the direction of the town.

In the evening of the same day Mme Odintsova was sitting in her room with Bazarov, while Arkady was striding about the hall and listening to Katya's playing. The Princess had gone upstairs to her room; she never could endure guests, least of all these "new wild men," as she called them. In the best rooms she only sulked; but in her own room, in front of her maid, she sometimes exploded into such abuse that her cap danced on her head together with her wig. Mme Odintsova knew all about these outbursts.

"But how can you be intending to leave us?" she asked Bazarov. "What of your promise?"

He started.

"What promise?"

"Have you forgotten? You intended to give me a few lessons in chemistry."

"I can't help that! My father is waiting for me; I can't hang about any longer. And besides, you can read Pelouse and Frémy's *Notions générales de chimie;* it's a good book and clearly written. In it you'll find all you need."

"But remember you assured me that a book cannot take the place — I have forgotten how you expressed it, but you know what I am trying to say — do you remember?"

"I can't help that!" Bazarov repeated.

"Why go?" she said, lowering her voice.

He glanced at her. She had thrown her head against the back of the armchair and had folded her arms, bare to the elbows, over her breast. By the light of the single lamp, shielded with a shade of cut-out paper, she seemed more pale than usual. An ample white gown entirely enveloped her in its soft folds; the tips of her crossed feet were only just visible.

"But why remain?" Bazarov replied.

She turned her head a little.

"Why do you ask? Aren't you enjoying yourself here? Or do you think no one will miss you here?"

"I am convinced of that."

She was silent for a moment.

"You are wrong in thinking so. But, in any case, I don't believe you. You could not have said that seriously." He did not stir. "Yevgeny Vasilievich, why are you silent?"

"But what can I say to you? It is never worth regretting anybody, least of all me."

"Why do you say that?"

"I am a positive, uninteresting man. I don't know how to talk."

"You're fishing for compliments, Yevgeny Vasilievich."

"That is not one of my habits. Don't you really understand that the exquisite side of life, that side which you treasure so much, is inaccessible to me?"

She bit the corner of her handkerchief.

"Think what you like, but I shall be bored when you go."

"Arkady will remain," Bazarov remarked.

She shrugged her shoulders a little.

"I shall be bored," she repeated.

"You really will? In any case, you won't be bored for long."

"Why do you assume that?"

"Because you yourself told me that you are bored only when your order is violated. You have organized your life on such impeccably sound lines that there cannot be any room in it for boredom, or yearning — or any oppressive feeling whatever."

"And you find that I am impeccable — I mean, that I have organized my life so perfectly?"

"I should say! Why, for instance, in a few minutes ten o'clock will strike, and I know in advance that you will turn me out."

"No, I shall not turn you out, Yevgeny Vasilievich, you can remain. Open that window — I feel stifled, somehow."

Bazarov rose and pushed at the window. It at once flew open with a crash. He had not expected it to open so easily; moreover, his hand trembled. The dark, gentle night, with its almost black sky, its faintly rustling trees, and the fresh scent of the free, clean air, looked into the room.

"Lower that blind and sit down," she said. "I want to have a chat with you before your departure. Tell me something about yourself; you never talk about yourself."

"I endeavor to talk with you about useful subjects, Anna Sergeevna."

"You are very modest. . . . But I should like to know something about you, about your family, about your father, for whom you are abandoning us."

"Why is she using such words?" Bazarov pondered.

"All that is not in the least interesting," he said aloud, "especially to you. We are obscure people."

"But I, in your view, am an aristocrat?"

Bazarov raised his eyes to her.

"Yes," he said, with exaggerated harshness.

She smiled wryly.

"I see you know me very little, though you maintain that all people are alike and that it is not worth studying them. Some day I'll tell you the story of my life — but first you will tell me yours."

"I know you very little," Bazarov repeated. "Perhaps you're right; perhaps it is true that every man is an enigma. Take even you, for instance; you avoid society, you are oppressed by it — and you have invited two students to stay with you. Why do you, with your intelligence, with your beauty, live in the country?"

"What? What is that you said?" she interrupted vivaciously. "With my — beauty?"

Bazarov knitted his brows.

"It doesn't matter," he muttered; "I only wanted to say that I don't understand at all why you have settled down in the country."

"You don't understand that. But you have your own explanation for it, haven't you?"

"Yes. I suppose you remain permanently in one spot because you have spoilt yourself, because you are very fond of comfort, of convenience, and are very indifferent to everything else."

She smiled again.

"You completely refuse to believe that I am capable of having enthusiasms?"

He looked up at her from under his wrinkled brows.

"Out of curiosity, perhaps; but not in any other way."

"Indeed? Well, now I understand why you and I have come together; you see, you are just the same as I."

"We have come together — " Bazarov said thickly.

"Yes! — but I had forgotten that you want to go away."

He rose to his feet. The lamp burned dimly in the darkened,

perfumed, secluded room; occasionally the blind was blown back, and through it the stimulating freshness of night flooded, the mysterious whisper of night could be heard. She did not stir a single limb; but little by little a secret agitation took possession of her. . . . It was communicated to Bazarov. He suddenly realized that he was alone with a young, beautiful woman. . . .

"Where are you going?" she slowly queried

He made no answer and dropped into his chair.

"And so you consider me a calm, effeminate, spoilt creature," she continued in the same voice, not taking her eyes from the window. "But I know myself that I am very unhappy."

"You unhappy! Why? Surely you cannot attach any significance to worthless rumors?"

Her face clouded. She felt vexed that he had understood her in *that* way.

"I am not even amused by those rumors. Yevgeny Vasilich, and I am too proud to let them disturb me. I am unhappy because —because in me I have no desire, no wish, to live. You gaze at me distrustfully; you think: the one who is saying that is an 'aristocrat,' is all dressed in lace and is sitting in a chair of velvet. Nor do I conceal that I love all that you call comfort, yet at the same time I have little desire to live. Reconcile those contradictions as best you can. In any case, all this is romanticism in your eyes."

Bazarov shook his head.

"You are healthy, independent, wealthy; what else do you want? What is it you wish for?"

"What is it I wish for?" she repeated, and sighed. "I am very tired, I am old, I have the feeling that I have been living a very long time. Yes, I am old," she added, gently drawing the edges of her mantilla over her bare arms. Her eyes met Bazarov's eyes, and she reddened a little. "Behind me I have already so many memories: life in Petersburg, wealth, then poverty, then my father's death, marriage, then the journey abroad, everything in order. . . . Memories in plenty, but nothing to remember, and ahead, before me, is a long, long road, but no aim. . . . And I don't want to take the road."

"Are you so disillusioned?" Bazarov asked.

"No," she said deliberately, "but I am dissatisfied. I feel that if I could get strongly attached to something —"

"You would like to fall in love," he interrupted her, "but fall in love you cannot: there is your misfortune."

She turned to examining the sleeves of her mantilla.

"Am I really incapable of falling in love?" she said.

"I think so! Only I was wrong in calling that a misfortune. On the contrary, he to whom that happens is more deserving of commiseration."

"To whom what happens?"

"Falling in love."

"But how do you know that?"

"By hearsay," Bazarov answered angrily.

"You are being flirtatious," he thought, "you're bored and you're teasing me because you have nothing better to do, but I — " And in very deed his heart was beating violently.

"Moreover you are perhaps too exacting," he said, leaning all his body forward and playing with the fringes of his chair.

"Maybe. In my view, either all or nothing. A life for a life. You've taken mine, so give your own, without regret and without recall. Otherwise it is better not at all."

"Well," Bazarov remarked, "that is a just condition, and I am surprised that so far you — haven't found what you wished."

"But do you think it easy to give yourself wholly to anything at all?"

"It is not easy if you stop to consider and bide your time, and attach a price to yourself, if you value yourself, in other words; but it is very easy to give yourself without reflecting."

"How can one not value oneself? If I have no value whatever, who needs my devotion?"

"That is not my business; it is for someone else to decide what is my value. The main thing is to be able to give oneself."

She drew away from her chairback.

"You talk," she began, "as if you had experienced it all."

"Now you've said it, Anna Sergeevna; all this, you know, is outside my province."

"But would you be able to give yourself?"

"I don't know; I don't want to boast."

She made no comment, and Bazarov lapsed into silence. The sounds of the piano floated in from the reception hall.

"What is Katya playing so late for?" she remarked.

Bazarov rose.

"Yes, you're right, it is late, it's time you retired to rest."

"Wait, wait, what are you hurrying for? . . . I must say one word to you."

"What is it?"

"Wait a moment," she whispered. Her eyes rested on Bazarov; she seemed to be examining him closely.

He strode up and down, then suddenly drew near her, hurriedly said: "Good-by," squeezed her hand so hard that she all but cried out, and left the room. She raised to her lips her fingers, pressed together, blew on them, and suddenly, starting impetuously out of her chair, went with swift steps to the door, as though intending to call him back. . . . A maid entered the room with a carafe on a silver tray. Mme Odintsova halted, ordered her to go, sat down, and was again sunk in thought. Her braided hair unwound and fell like a dark snake over her neck.

The lamp burned for a long time after in Anna Sergeevna's room, and long she remained motionless, only occasionally running her fingers over her arms, which were gently nipped by the nocturnal cold.

But Bazarov, disheveled and morose, his boots wet with dew, retired to his bedroom some two hours later. He found Arkady at the writing-desk with a book in his hands, his jacket tightly buttoned,

"Haven't you gone to bed yet?" he said, as though annoyed.

"You sat a long time with Anna Sergeevna this evening," Arkady replied without answering his question.

"Yes, I sat with her all the time you and Katerina Sergeevna were playing the piano."

"I didn't play — " Arkady began, and said no more. He felt the tears starting to his eyes, and he had no desire to weep in front of his derisive friend.

XVIII

Next morning when Mme Odintsova came down for tea, Bazarov sat for some time bent over his cup, then suddenly glanced at her. She turned to him as though he had nudged her, and he had the impression that overnight her face had paled a little. She soon retired to her room and appeared again only for breakfast. The weather had turned rainy that morning, it was impossible to go for a walk. All the company assembled in the reception hall. Arkady picked up the latest number of a periodical and began to read aloud. The Princess, as was her habit, first looked her astonishment as though he were planning something unseemly, then angrily fixed her eyes on him; but he paid no attention to her.

"Yevgeny Vasilievich," Anna Sergeevna said, "come to my room, I want to ask you — You mentioned a certain textbook yesterday. . . ."

She rose and made her way to the door. The Princess looked about her with an expression indicating that she would like to say: "Look, look, how amazed I am!" and again fixed her eyes on Arkady; but he raised his voice and, exchanging glances with Katya, who was sitting beside him, continued his reading.

Mme Odintsova hurried to her room. Bazarov followed her briskly, not raising his eyes and only catching the fine rustle and swish of the silk dress gliding ahead of him. She dropped into the same chair in which she had sat the previous evening, and Bazarov took up his former position.

"Now what did you say that book was called?" she began after a brief silence.

"Pelouse and Frémy: *Notions générales* — " Bazarov replied. "However, I can also recommend Ganot: *Traité élémentaire de physique expérimentale*. In that work the drawings are more distinct, and altogether it — "

She stretched out her hand.

"Yevgeny Vasilievich, forgive me, but I did not ask you here to discuss primers. I wanted to continue our conversation of yesterday. You went so abruptly. . . . You won't be bored?"

"I am at your service, Anna Sergeevna. But just what was it you and I talked about yesterday?"

She threw him a sidelong glance.

"I think we were talking about happiness. I told you about myself. And, by the way, I have just mentioned the word 'happiness.' Tell me, why is it that even when we are enjoying something, music, for instance, a good evening, or a talk with congenial people, why does it all seem to be rather a hint at some immeasurable happiness existing somewhere than actual happiness, I mean such as we ourselves know? Why is that? But perhaps you never feel anything of the kind?"

"You know the saying: 'We pine for what is not,' " Bazarov replied. "And besides, you yourself said yesterday that you are discontented. But you are right, such thoughts never enter my head."

"Perhaps they seem absurd to you?"

"No, but they just don't come into my head."

"Do you mean that? You know, I should very much like to know what *you* think about."

"How? I don't understand."

"Listen, for some time I have been wanting to discuss something with you. There's no need for you to say — and you know it yourself — that you are no ordinary man; you are still young, you have all your life before you. What are you preparing yourself for? What future awaits you? I mean — what aim do you wish to achieve, where are you going, what is in your soul? In a word, who are you? What are you?"

"You astonish me, Anna Sergeevna. You know that I am studying natural sciences, but as for who I am — "

"Yes, who are you?"

"I have already informed you that I am a future provincial doctor."

Anna Sergeevna made a movement of impatience.

"Why do you say that? You yourself don't believe it. Arkady could answer me so, but not you."

"But what Arkady — "

"Stop! Is it possible that you would be content with such modest activity, and aren't you yourself always declaring that for you there is no such thing as medicine? You — with your ambition — a provincial doctor! You tell me that in order to evade me, because you do **not** trust me at all. But do you know, Yevgeny Vasilievich, that I could understand you: I myself have been poor and ambitious, like you; I, perhaps, have passed similar trials to yours."

"All that is very fine, Anna Sergeevna, but you must excuse me. I am not in the least in the habit of unburdening myself, and between you and me there is such a gulf — "

"What gulf? You will tell me again that I am an aristocrat? Enough, Yevgeny Vasilievich; I think I have told you — "

"Yes, and apart from that," Bazarov interrupted, "what pleasure is there in talking and thinking about the future, which to a large extent doesn't depend on us? If a chance occurs of doing something — excellent; but if it doesn't, at least you will be glad you haven't chattered unnecessarily beforehand."

"You call a friendly talk chatter? . . . Or, since I am a woman, perhaps you don't regard me as worthy of your trust? For you are contemptuous of us all, aren't you?"

"I feel no contempt for you, Anna Sergeevna, and you know that."

"No, I don't know anything — but let us assume that I understand your reluctance to talk of your future activity; but what is happening within you now — "

"Happening!" Bazarov repeated after her. "Anyone would think I was some state or society! In any case, it isn't at all interesting; and besides, can a man always proclaim aloud all that is 'happening' inside him?"

"But I don't see why you cannot speak out all that you have in your soul."

"Can *you*?"

"I can," Anna Sergeevna replied after a momentary hesitation. Bazarov bowed his head.

"You are more fortunate than I."

She looked at him interrogatively.

"As you wish," she continued, "but, all the same, something tells me that we have not come together for nothing, that we shall be good friends. I am confident that your — how shall I put it? — your feeling of tension, of reserve, will vanish in the end."

"But have you noticed any reserve in me — and how else did you put it? — any tension?"

"Yes."

Bazarov rose and went over to the window.

"And you would like to know the cause of this reserve, you would like to know what is happening inside me?"

"Yes," she repeated, with a still incomprehensible feeling of fear.

"And you won't be angry?"

"No."

"No?" Bazarov was standing with his back to her. "Then I tell you that I love you idiotically, madly. . . . Now you know what you have forced from me."

She extended both hands in front of her, but Bazarov was resting his forehead against the glass of the window. He was panting; all his body was obviously quivering. But it was not the quiver of youthful timidity, not the pleasant dismay of a first declaration that possessed him: it was passion, strong and oppressive, that was struggling within him — a passion resembling malice and, perhaps, akin to it. . . . She suddenly felt afraid of and sorry for him.

"Yevgeny Vasilich," she said, and involuntarily a tender note sounded in her voice.

He turned swiftly, flung a consuming gaze at her — and, seizing her by both hands, violently drew her to himself. . . .

She did not free herself at once from his embrace; yet a moment later she was standing far off in a corner, staring at him. He started toward her.

"You haven't understood me," she whispered with urgent fear. It seemed that if he took another stride she would cry out. . . . He bit his lips and left the room.

Half an hour later a servant handed her a note from Bazarov; it consisted of one single sentence: "Am I to go away today, or can I remain till tomorrow?"

"Why go away? I didn't understand you — you haven't understood me," she replied. But her own thought was: "I didn't understand myself either."

She did not appear until dinnertime, and she walked to and fro in her room continually, her hands behind her, occasionally halting before the window, or before the mirror, and slowly rubbing her handkerchief round her neck, on which she still seemed to feel a burning patch. She asked herself what had made her force him to be frank, as he had put it, and why hadn't she suspected anything? . . . "I am to blame," she said aloud, "but I could not anticipate this." She was lost in thought, and flushed when she remembered Bazarov's almost bestial face as he rushed to her. . . .

"Or?" she suddenly said, and halted, and shook her curls. . . . She saw herself in the mirror; her head thrown back, and the mysterious smile in the half-closed, half-opened eyes and lips, seemed at that moment to be telling her something at which she herself was abashed.

"No," she decided at last, "God knows where that would lead to, one cannot play with that, tranquillity is after all the best thing in the world."

Her tranquillity was not disturbed; but she was distressed, and even burst into tears once, herself not knowing why, but certainly not from any outrage she had suffered. She did not feel outraged: rather she felt guilty. Under the influence of various vague feelings, the consciousness of departing life, the desire for novelty, she had forced herself to go as far as a certain line, had forced herself to look across it — and had seen beyond it not even an abyss, but emptiness . . . or infamy.

XIX

Despite all her self-possession, despite all her freedom from prejudices, even Mme Odintsova felt awkward when she went into the dining-room for dinner. The meal passed quite satisfactorily, however. Porfiry Platonich arrived, and he told a number of stories; he had just returned from the town. Among other things, he reported that the governor, "Burdal," had ordered his officials on special commissions to wear spurs, in case he needed to send them anywhere in haste on horseback. Arkady conversed with Katya in an undertone and diplomatically waited on the Princess. Bazarov was obstinately and morosely silent. Once or twice Mme Odintsova looked at him — directly, and not surreptitiously — at his face, stern and jaundiced, with downcast eyes and the impress of contemptuous resolution in every feature, and thought: "No . . . no . . . no. . . ." After dinner she and all the company went into the garden. Noticing that Bazarov wanted to have a word with her, she took several steps aside and halted. He came up to her, though even now he did not raise his eyes, and said thickly:

"I must apologize to you, Anna Sergeevna. You cannot but be angry with me."

"No, I am not angry with you, Yevgeny Vasilich," she replied, "but I am distressed."

"So much the worse. In any case, I am punished sufficiently. My position, as you will probably agree, is most stupid. You wrote to me: 'Why go away?' But I cannot and do not wish to remain. Tomorrow I shall no longer be here."

"Yevgeny Vasilich, why are you — "

"Why am I going away?"

"No, that isn't what I wanted to say."

"You can't bring back the past, Anna Sergeevna . . . and

259

sooner or later this was bound to happen. Consequently, I must go away. I know of only one condition on which I could remain; but that condition will never arise. For, after all, you — forgive my presumption — you do not love me and never will love me, will you?"

His eyes glittered for a moment beneath his dark brows.

She did not answer him. "I am afraid of this man," the thought flashed through her head.

"Good-by," he said, as though he had guessed her thought, and he went back to the house.

Anna Sergeevna walked slowly after him and, calling to Katya, took her by the arm. She kept her sister at her side all day. She did not play cards, and laughed more and more, which was quite out of keeping with her pale and discomposed look. Arkady was bewildered, and watched her, as young people do watch; in other words, he continually asked himself: what does all this mean? Bazarov shut himself away in his room; however, he came down for tea. Anna Sergeevna felt like saying some kindly word to him, but she did not know how to open conversation with him. . . .

An unexpected event rescued her from her difficulty: the butler announced that Sitnikov had arrived.

It is difficult to convey in words how this young progressive fluttered like a quail into the room. Having resolved, with the intrusiveness peculiar to him, to drive into the country to visit a woman whom he hardly knew, who had never invited him to do so, but with whom, according to the information he had gathered, such intelligent and intimate acquaintances of his were staying, he was now stricken with timidity to his very marrow, and instead of uttering the apologies and greetings he had planned, he muttered some idiotic remark to the effect that Yevdoksia Kukshina had sent him to inquire into Anna Sergeevna's health, and that Arkady Nikolaevich also always spoke to him in terms of the greatest praise. At this word he began to stammer and was so disconcerted that he sat on his own hat. As no one turned him out, however, and Anna Sergeevna even introduced him to her aunt and sister, he soon recovered, and his tongue began to wag in fine style. We often find that our lives are helped by some trivial event: it slackens the overtautened strings and sobers down self-confident or self-forgetful feelings by reminding them of its own close kinship with them. With Sitnikov's arrival everything seemed to grow more dull, more empty — and more simple; every-body even ate a more hearty supper and retired to sleep half an hour earlier than usual.

"I can repeat to you now," Arkady said in bed to Bazarov, who also was undressed, "what you once said to me: 'Why are you so sad? You must have paid some sacred debt?'" For some time past a hypocritically free and easy bantering had been going on between the two young men, a trick that always indicates secret dissatisfaction or unexpressed suspicions.

"I'm going home to Father tomorrow," Bazarov announced.

Arkady raised himself and rested on his elbow. He was both surprised and, for some reason, glad.

"Ah!" he uttered. "And is that why you are sad?"

Bazarov yawned. "You'll know a lot, you'll be an old man."

"But how about Anna Sergeevna?" Arkady went on.

"What about Anna Sergeevna?"

"I mean to say: will she really let you go?"

"I haven't hired myself out to her."

Arkady lay thinking, and Bazarov got into bed and turned his face to the wall.

Several minutes passed in silence.

"Yevgeny!" Arkady suddenly exclaimed.

"Well?"

"I'll leave too when you go tomorrow."

Bazarov made no reply.

"Only I'll go home," Arkady continued. "We'll travel together as far as the Little Russian hamlets, and there you'll get horses from Fyodot. I'd be delighted to make your people's acquaintance, but I'm afraid of making them, and you, feel awkward. But you will come back to us afterward, won't you?"

"I have left my things with you," Bazarov replied, without turning over.

"But why doesn't he ask why I am going? And just as suddenly as he!" Arkady thought. "And, in fact, why am I going, and why is he going?" he continued his meditations. He could find no satisfactory answer to his own questions, and his heart was filled with something corrosive. He felt that it would be difficult for him to part from this life, to which he had grown so accustomed; but it would be strange to remain here by himself. "Something has happened between them," he mentally decided, "but why should I hang around her after he has gone? I shall only completely upset her and shall lose my last chance." He began to recall Anna Sergeevna in his mind; but then, little by little, other features obscured the young widow's beautiful face.

"I'm sorry about Katya too," Arkady whispered into his pillow, on which tears were dropping. . . . He suddenly flung back his hair and said aloud:

"What the devil did that fool Sitnikov turn up for?"

Bazarov first stirred in his bed, then gave utterance to the following:

"You're still stupid, brother, I can see that. The Sitnikovs are necessary to us. I — you get this into your head — I need blockheads like him. After all, it's not for the gods to bake the pots."

"Aha!" Arkady thought, and only now was all the bottomless abyss of Bazarov's self-esteem momentarily revealed to him. "So you and I are gods? Or rather you're a god, but perhaps I'm the blockhead, is that it?"

"Yes," Bazarov repeated moodily, "you're still stupid."

Mme Odintsova did not show any particular surprise when next day Arkady told her that he was leaving with Bazarov; she seemed abstracted and tired. Katya gazed at him silently and seriously, the Princess even crossed herself beneath her shawl, in such a way that he could not but notice it, while Sitnikov was completely flabbergasted. He had only just come down to breakfast in new and elegant attire, this time not of Slavophil design; the previous evening he had astonished the man assigned to him by the quantity of linen he had brought, and now abruptly his comrades were deserting him! He fidgeted a little with his feet, cast about like a hunted hare on the edge of a forest — and suddenly, almost fearfully, almost with a shout, announced that he, too, intended to depart. Mme Odintsova made no attempt to dissuade him.

"I have a very comfortable carriage," the unhappy young man added, turning to Arkady; "I can take you, and Yevgeny Vasilich can have your tarantass, so that it will be even more convenient."

"But of course not, it is quite out of your way, and it is a long distance to my home."

"It's nothing, nothing; I've lots of time, and besides I've got business in that direction."

"In regard to licenses?" Arkady asked, rather too contemptuously.

But Sitnikov was in such a state of despair that, contrary to custom, he did not even smile.

"I assure you my carriage is extremely comfortable," he muttered, "and there will be room for everybody."

"Don't upset M'sieur Sitnikov with a refusal," Anna Sergeevna said.

Arkady glanced at her and bowed meaningly.

The guests departed after breakfast. As she said good-by to Bazarov, Mme Odintsova held out her hand to him and said:

"We shall see each other again, shan't we?"

"As you command," Bazarov replied.

"In that case, we shall see each other again."

Arkady was the first to go out on the veranda; he climbed into Sitnikov's carriage. He was respectfully helped into the carriage by a butler, but he would gladly have struck him or burst into tears. Bazarov seated himself in the tarantass. When they reached the Little Russian hamlets, Arkady waited while Fyodot, the innkeeper, harnessed up the horses, and then, going over to the tarantass, with his former smile he said to Bazarov:

"Yevgeny, take me with you; I should like to go to your place."

"Get in!" Bazarov said between his teeth.

Sitnikov, who, whistling blithely, was strolling by the wheels of his carriage, only gaped as he heard these words; but Arkady callously took his things out of the carriage, seated himself beside Bazarov, and, bowing respectfully to his former fellow traveler, shouted: "Whip them up!" The tarantass rolled off and soon disappeared from sight. . . . Sitnikov, now completely confused, stared at his coachman; but the man was playing his whip above the tail of the side-horse. He jumped into his carriage and, thundering at two passing peasants: "Put your caps on, you fools!" drove off to the town, where he arrived very late, and where, next day, during his visit to Kukshina, he said some bitter things about those two "repulsive stuck-ups and boors."

When he got into the tarantass beside Bazarov, Arkady gave his friend a strong squeeze of the hand and for a long time did not utter a word. Bazarov appeared to understand and appreciate both the handclasp and the silence. He had not slept all the previous night, and he had not smoked, or eaten much at all, for several days past. His emaciated profile was gloomy and harsh beneath the cap clapped on his head.

"Well, brother," he said at last, "give me a cigar. . . . And have a look, is my tongue yellow?"

"Yes," Arkady replied.

"As I thought . . . and the cigar doesn't taste pleasant. The machine's gone wrong."

"You certainly have changed during the last few days," Arkady observed.

"It's nothing! We'll get over it. The only thing that troubles me is that my mother is much too tender-hearted: if you haven't grown a paunch, and if you don't eat ten times a day, she worries herself to death. But Father's all right, he's been everywhere himself, and he has feasted and starved. No, I can't smoke," he added, and he flung the cigar into the dust of the road.

"It's fifteen miles to your estate, isn't it?" Arkady asked.

"Yes, fifteen. But ask that sage," he pointed to the peasant, one of Fyodot's workmen, sitting on the box.

But the peasant replied: "Who knows? We don't measure by miles here," and continued to swear at the shaft-horse in an undertone for "kicking up his muzzle" — in other words, for throwing up his head.

"Yes, yes," Bazarov began again, "there's a lesson for you, my young friend, a very instructive example. Damn it all, how idiotic everything is! Every man hangs by a thread, an abyss may open beneath him at any moment, yet he must needs go on thinking all kinds of unpleasant things for himself, spoiling his whole life."

"What are you hinting at?" Arkady asked.

"I am not hinting at anything, I am saying openly that you and I have behaved very stupidly. What is there to explain? But I've already observed at the clinic that anyone who fulminates against his pain invariably triumphs over it."

"I don't quite understand you," Arkady remarked, "I hardly think you had anything to complain about."

"As you don't quite understand me, I'll expound the following to you: 'It is better to be a stone in the road than to let a woman take possession of so much as the tip of your finger.' That is all — " Bazarov all but pronounced his favorite word, "romanticism," but he refrained, and said: " — rubbish. You won't believe me now, but I tell you: you and I found ourselves in women's company, and we liked it; but to cut yourself off from such company is just like having a cold shower on a hot day. A man has no time to occupy himself with such trifles; a man should be raging, says the excellent Spanish proverb. Now, take you," he added, turning to the peasant sitting on the box, "you, wise man, have you a wife?"

The man turned his flat and watery-eyed face to the two friends.

"A wife, d'you say? Yes. How could I do without a wife?"

"Do you beat her?"

"The wife, you mean? All kinds of things happen. We don't beat them without cause."

"That's splendid. Well, but does she beat you?"

The peasant tugged at the reins.

"A fine thing to say, master. You can always have your joke." He was obviously offended.

"D'you hear that, Arkady Nikolaevich? Yet you and I have been thrashed. That's what it means to be educated people."

Arkady smiled forcedly, but Bazarov turned away and did not open his mouth again for the rest of the journey.

The fifteen miles seemed a full thirty to Arkady. But now at last the small village where Bazarov's parents lived came into sight on the slope of a rolling hill. Beyond it, amid a young birch grove, appeared a small country house beneath a straw-thatched roof. At the first hut in the village two peasants were standing with their hats on, swearing at each other. "You're a great swine," said one to the other, "but you're worse than a little pig." "And your wife is a witch," the other retorted.

"By the unconstraint of their forms of address," Bazarov observed to Arkady, "and by the playfulness of their turns of speech, you can judge that my father's peasants are not greatly oppressed. And there he is himself coming out on the porch of his habitation. So he must have heard the carriage bell. It's he all right, I recognize his figure. Ah, but how gray he's gone, poor devil!"

xx

Bazarov hung out of the tarantass, while Arkady stretched his head round his comrade's back and saw a tall, gaunt man, with tousled hair and a fine aquiline nose, and dressed in an old military tunic wide open at the chest, standing in the little porch of the house. He stood with feet set wide apart, smoking a long pipe and screwing up his eyes against the sun.

The horses came to a halt.

"So you've turned up at last," Bazarov's father said to him, continuing to smoke, though the pipe was trembling between his fingers. "Well, climb out, climb out, and we'll greet each other properly."

He embraced his son. "Yevgeny, my dear little Yevgeny," a woman's quavering voice was heard. The door was flung wide open, and on the threshold appeared a round little, short little old woman, in a white mobcap and a short, varicolored jacket. She groaned, stumbled, and would certainly have fallen if Bazarov had not supported her. Her swollen little arms were at once wound round his neck, her head nestled against his chest, and there was a silence. Only her convulsive sobbing was to be heard.

Old Bazarov breathed deeply and screwed up his eyes even more.

"Well, that's enough, that's enough, Arina, my dear! Stop it!" he said, exchanging glances with Arkady, who was standing motionless by the tarantass, while the peasant on the box even turned away. "That's quite unnecessary, do please stop it!"

"Ah, Vasily Ivanich!" the old woman murmured, "at last, my dear, I see my little one, my little Yevgeny . . . " and, without unclasping her arms, she drew her wet, tearstained, crushed, and beaming face away from Bazarov, gazed at him with beatific and absurd eyes, then fell on his chest again.

"Well, yes, of course, that's all in the nature of things," Vasily Ivanovich said, "only we'd better go into the house. Here's a guest arrived with Yevgeny. You mustn't mind," he added, turning to Arkady, and slightly scraping one foot, "you understand, it's just a woman's weakness and a mother's heart, you know. . . ."

But his own lips and eyebrows were twitching, and his chin was quivering — though he obviously was trying to master himself and to appear all but unconcerned. Arkady bowed.

"Come on, Mother, Father's quite right," Bazarov said, and led the feeble old woman into the house. Seating her in a comfortable armchair, he once more hurriedly embraced his father and introduced Arkady to him.

"I am very glad to meet you," Vasily Ivanovich declared, "only you mustn't expect too much; everything of ours is simple, on a military footing. Arina Vlasievna, do calm down, be so good; what is all this weakness for? Our guest will have a poor opinion of you."

"My goodness!" the old woman said through her tears, "I haven't the honor of knowing your name and patronymic."

"Arkady Nikolaich," Vasily Ivanovich prompted her in an undertone, with an important air.

"You must pardon a stupid old woman." She blew her nose and, bending her head first to the right, then to the left, she diligently wiped one eye, then the other. "You must forgive me. You see, I was beginning to think I would die without seeing my d-d-d-ear boy."

"Well, you have lived to see him, madame," Vasily Ivanovich retorted. "Taniushka" — he turned to a barefoot girl aged about thirteen, in a bright red cotton dress, who was shyly peeping round the door — "bring your mistress a glass of water, on a tray, d'you hear? And you, gentlemen," he added with a kind of old-fashioned playfulness, "allow me to invite you into a retired veteran's private room."

"Let me put my arms round you just one little once more, Yevgeny my dear," Arina Vlasievna groaned. Bazarov bent over her. "But what a handsome fellow you've grown!"

"Well, handsome or not," Vasily Ivanovich observed, "he's a man, as they say, *ommfe*.[1] But now, Arina Vlasievna, I hope that, having satiated your maternal heart, you will see about satiating your dear guests, because, as you know, you mustn't feed nightingales on fairy stories."

The old woman got up from the chair.

"The table will be laid this very minute, Vasily Ivanich. I'll run into the kitchen myself and order the samovar to be got ready, we'll have everything, everything. Why, I haven't seen him for three years, I've given him neither food nor drink, and is that easy to bear?"

"Well then, hurry up about it, mistress, and don't bring shame on yourself; and I ask you, gentlemen, to follow me. And here's Timofeich come to pay his respects to you, Yevgeny. He is glad too, I think, the old spaniel. Well? You are glad, aren't you, you old spaniel? Please follow me."

[1] Russian transliteration of the French *homme fait*.

Turgenev

And Vasily Ivanovich bustled on in front, scraping and shuffling in his patched slippers.

The entire house consisted of six tiny rooms. One of them, the one to which he led our friends, was called the office. A stout-legged table, littered with papers black with ancient dust, as though they had been sprinkled with soot, occupied all the space between two windows; on the walls hung Turkish weapons, knouts, sabers, two maps, anatomical charts, a portrait of Hufe-land,[1] a knot of hair in a black frame, and a diploma behind glass; a ragged leather divan with broken springs was placed between two enormous bookcases of Karelian birch; on the shelves was a disorderly crowd of books, boxes, stuffed birds, cans, and phials; in one corner stood a broken electrical machine.

"I warned you, my dear visitor," Vasily Ivanovich began, "that we live here, so to speak, in bivouac."

"Now stop it, what are you apologizing for?" Bazarov interrupted. "Kirsanov knows very well that you and I are not Crœ-suses, and that you haven't a palace. Where shall we put him, that's the question."

"Why, of course, Yevgeny, I've got a very nice little room in the wing; he'll be very comfortable there."

"So you've a little wing now?"

"Why, of course; where the bathhouse is," Timofeich intervened.

"Really it's next to the bathhouse," Vasily Ivanovich hastened to add. "And it's summertime now. . . . I'll run along at once and see about it; and meanwhile you bring their things in, Timofeich. Of course, Yevgeny, I put my room at your disposition. *Suum cuique*."

"Well, there you are! A very amusing old chap and one of the best," Bazarov added as soon as Vasily Ivanovich had gone out. "Just as much an eccentric as your father, only in a different way. And he talks an awful lot!"

"And your mother, too, seems to be a very fine woman," Arkady observed.

"Yes, she's quite a simple sort. You wait and see the dinner she gives us!"

[1] A prominent German physician (1762–1836). (Tr.)

"We weren't expecting you, master, and they haven't brought any beef," remarked Timofeich, who had just dragged in Bazarov's trunk.

"We'll manage without beef; what the eye doesn't see — Poverty is no crime, they say."

"How many souls does your father own?" Arkady suddenly asked.

"The property isn't his, but Mother's; I think there are fifteen souls."

"Twenty-two all together," Timofeich observed in a dissatisfied tone.

They heard the shuffling of slippers, and Vasily Ivanovich reappeared.

"In a few minutes your room will be ready to receive you," he exclaimed triumphantly, "Arkady — Nikolaich. That is your name, isn't it? An here is your servant," he added, pointing to a close-cropped lad in a blue out-at-elbow caftan and oversized boots who had entered with him. "His name's Fyodka. I repeat again, though my son forbids me, don't expect too much. However, Fyodka knows how to fill a pipe. You do smoke, of course?"

"I smoke cigars usually," Arkady replied.

"And very sensible on your part. I myself have a preference for cigars, but in these lonely parts it is extremely difficult to get them."

"Now, enough of playing the Lazarus," Bazarov again interrupted him. "You sit down here on the divan and let me have a look at you."

Vasily Ivanovich laughed and sat down. He had a strong facial resemblance to his son, only his forehead was lower and narrower, and his mouth rather wider, and he was always on the move, twitching his shoulders as though his coat were cutting into his armpits, blinking, coughing, and wriggling his fingers, whereas his son was distinguished by a negligent immobility.

"Play the Lazarus!" Vasily Ivanovich repeated. "Don't think, Yevgeny, that I want to win our guest's pity, so to speak, by appealing to the backwoods we live in. On the contrary, I am of the opinion that there is no such thing as backwoods for a thinking man. At least I endeavor, as far as possible, not to let any moss grow on me, as they say, not to lag behind the times."

Out of his pocket he pulled a new yellow foulard handkerchief, which he had managed to snatch up while running to Arkady's room, and waved it in the air as he went on:

"I say nothing of the fact that, for instance, not without sacrifices painful to myself, I have put the peasants on a rental basis and given them half of my own land. I regarded that is my duty, and in that case common sense itself commands, though other landowners do not even think of it. I am talking of science, of education."

"Yes; I see you have *The Friend of Health* for 1855," Bazarov remarked.

"An old comrade sends it to me," Vasily Ivanovich said hurriedly. "But we have some notion of phrenology, for instance," he added, talking, for that matter, more to Arkady and pointing to a small plaster-of-Paris head, divided into numbered parallelograms, standing on the bookcase. "Schönlein [1] has not remained unknown to us — nor Rademacher." [2]

"But do they still believe in Rademacher in X X X province?" Bazarov asked.

Vasily Ivanovich began to cough.

"In the province — Of course, gentlemen, you know better than we; and how can we hope to keep up with you? Why, you have come to take our places. Even in my day some humoralist named Hoffman,[3] or a Brown [4] with his vitalism seemed very absurd to us, but they too had made a noise in their time. You have found some new name to take Rademacher's place and to have your respect; but in twenty years they will be laughing at him too, probably."

"I tell you by way of consolation," Bazarov said, "that we now laugh at medicine altogether and do not respect anybody."

"How can you say that? Why, you want to be a doctor, don't you?"

"Yes. But the one doesn't hinder the other."

Vasily Ivanovich thrust his third finger into his pipe, where a little hot ash was still left.

"Well, maybe, maybe, I won't argue about it. After all, what

[1] German physician (1793–1864). (Tr.)
[2] German physician (1772–1849). (Tr.)
[3] German physician (1660–1742). (Tr.)
[4] Dr. John Brown (1735–88). (Tr.)

am I? A retired staff doctor, *volatou;* [1] and now I've dropped into agriculture. I served in your grandfather's brigade" — he turned again to Arkady. "Ye-es, ye-es, I've seen many things in my time. And the company I've kept, and the people I've been on respectful terms with! I, this same I whom you are pleased to see before you, I have felt the pulses of Count Witgenstein and Zhukovsky! [2] All the men in the Southern Army, after 1814, you understand" (here Vasily Ivanovich pursed his lips meaningly), "I knew them all through and through. But, after all, my work was not so important: a doctor should know his lancet, and that's enough! But your grandfather was a very estimable man, a real warrior."

"Confess that he was a fine tough old cudgel!" Bazarov remarked lazily.

"Ah, Yevgeny, the way you put things! Have a little pity! . . . Of course, General Kirsanov was not among those who — "

"Well, drop him!" Bazarov interrupted. "As we drove up I was delighted with your birch grove; it's grown splendidly."

Vasily Ivanovich brightened up.

"But wait till you see the garden I have now! I planted every tree myself. And there are fruits, and berries, and all kinds of medical herbs. You can be as clever as you like, you young people, but, all the same, old Paracelsus uttered the sacred truth: *in herbis, verbis et lapidibus* . . . after all, although, as you know, I have given up practicing, once or twice a week I have to shake up my old knowledge. They come for advice, and I can't throw them out on their necks. Sometimes poor people come for help. And there aren't any doctors in the district at all. Just imagine, one of our neighbors, a retired major — he gives treatment too. I inquire about him: has he studied medicine? They tell me: no, he hasn't studied, he does it more out of philanthropy. Ha ha, out of philanthropy! What? How? Ha ha ha!"

"Fyodka, fill my pipe!" Bazarov said harshly.

"But there is another doctor who came here to see a patient," Vasily Ivanovich went on in a kind of desperation, "and the patient was already *ad patres;* his man wouldn't let the doctor in and said he wasn't wanted any more. The doctor didn't expect that; he was disconcerted, and asked: 'Well, did the master hiccup

[1] *Voilà tout.*
[2] Russian poet (1783-1852). (Tr.)

before he died?' 'Yes, he hiccuped.' 'And did he hiccup a lot?' 'Quite a lot.' 'Oh well, that's good.' And off he went home. Ha ha ha!"

Only the old man laughed; Arkady set his lips in a smile. Bazarov simply pulled a long face. The talk continued in this fashion for about an hour; Arkady even had time to visit his room, which proved to be the bathhouse anteroom, but was very cozy and clean. At last Taniusha entered and reported that dinner was ready.

Vasily Ivanovich was the first to rise.

"Come along, gentlemen! Your magnanimous pardon if I have bored you. I expect my good mistress will satisfy you more than I can."

Though prepared in a hurry, the dinner was very good, and even plentiful; only the wine was not up to scratch, as they say; it was an almost black sherry, and had been bought by Timofeich from a merchant acquaintance in the town; it tasted perhaps of honey, perhaps of resin. And the flies, too, were a nuisance. In normal times a yard boy drove them off with a large green branch; but on this occasion Vasily Ivanovich sent him out, for fear of being condemned by the younger generation. Arina Vlasievna had found time to dress herself up; she had put on a high-standing cap with silk ribbons and a dove-blue shawl with arabesques. As soon as she saw her Yevgeny, she again burst into tears, but her husband did not have to admonish her: she herself quickly wiped away her tears, in order to avoid spotting the shawl. Only the young men ate; the master and mistress had had dinner long since. Obviously burdened with his unusual footwear, Fyodka waited on table, being helped by a hunchbacked woman with a masculine face, named Anfisushka, who performed the functions of housekeeper, poultry-keeper, and washerwoman. All dinnertime Vasily Ivanovich walked about the room and talked with a perfectly happy and even beatific air of the serious fears instilled in him by Napoleon III's policy and the confusion of the Italian problem. Arina Vlasievna did not pay any attention to Arkady and did not pick out the best bits for him; using her little fist to support her round face, on which the swollen, cherry-colored warts and moles on her cheeks and above her eyebrows conferred a very good-natured expression, she kept her eyes

Fathers and Sons

fixed on her son and sighed continually. She desperately wanted
to find out how long he had come home for, but she was afraid
to ask him. "Well, supposing he says two days," she thought,
and her heart sank. After the roast Vasily Ivanovich disappeared
for a moment and returned with an uncorked half-bottle of
champagne.

"Look!" he exclaimed; "though we do live in the wilds, when
we want to celebrate we know what to make merry with!" He
poured champagne into three goblets and a wineglass, proposed the
health "of our inestimable visitors," and tossed off his goblet in
one gulp, military fashion, and made Arina Vlasievna drink her
glassful down to the last drop. When the jams appeared, Arkady,
who could not endure anything sweet, none the less considered
it his duty to taste the four different kinds, only just made,
especially as Bazarov refused outright and at once lit a cigar.
Then tea, with cream and butter and cracknels, appeared on the
scene; then Vasily Ivanovich led them all into the garden, in
order to admire the beauty of the evening. As they passed a
bench he whispered to Arkady: "I like to philosophize in this
spot, gazing at the sunset; it befits a recluse. And there farther
along I have planted several trees beloved of Horace."

"And what trees are they?" Bazarov, who overheard him,
asked.

"Why—acacias, of course."

Bazarov began to yawn.

"I assume it is time for the travelers to retire to the embraces
of Morpheus," Vasily Ivanovich observed.

"In other words, time for bed," Bazarov took him up. "A very
sound observation. It certainly is time."

As he said good-night to his mother he kissed her on the forehead; but she embraced him and, behind his back, surreptitiously,
blessed him three times. Vasily Ivanovich saw Arkady to his
room and wished him "such an abundant repose as I enjoyed at
your happy age." And, in fact, Arkady slept excellently in his
bathhouse anteroom; it smelt of mint, and two crickets sopo-
rifically outchirruped each other behind the stove. Vasily Ivanovich went from Arkady to his office and, settling down on the
divan at his son's feet, made ready to have a chat with him; but
Bazarov at once sent him away, saying that he wanted to sleep.
But he did not fall asleep until dawn came. Staring with wide-

273

open eyes, he gazed malevolently into the darkness: the memories
of childhood had no power over him, and besides he had not yet
succeeded in escaping from his last bitter impressions. Arina
Vlasievna first prayed to her heart's content; then had a long,
long talk with Anfisushka. Standing as though rooted to the
ground before her mistress and fixing her one eye on her, in a
mysterious whisper the servant imparted all her observations and
ideas concerning Yevgeny Vasilievich. The old mother's head
absolutely swam with joy, with wine, with cigar smoke; her
husband tried to talk to her, but gave it up.

Arina Vlasievna was a genuine Russian noblewoman of the old
days; she should have been living two hundred years before, in
the Old Moscow times. She was very pious and sensitive, believed
in all kinds of signs and tokens, fortune-tellings, charms, and
dreams; she believed in simpletons, in house goblins, in wood
sprites, in unlucky encounters, in the evil eye, in popular remedies,
in Maundy Thursday salt, in the imminent end of the world; she
believed that if the candles do not go out during the service on
Easter Eve the buckwheat will be a fine crop, and that mushrooms
stop growing once a human eye has seen them; she believed that
the devil loves to be where there is water, and that every Jew
has a little bloody spot on his chest; she was afraid of mice, of
grass-snakes, frogs, sparrows, leeches, thunder, cold water, drafts,
horses, goats, red-headed people, and black cats and regarded
crickets and dogs as unclean creatures; she ate neither veal nor
pigeons, nor crabs, nor cheese, nor asparagus, nor Jerusalem
artichokes, nor hare, nor watermelons, because a cut watermelon
reminded her of the head of John the Baptist; and she could
never speak of oysters without a shudder; she loved eating — and
she fasted strictly; she slept ten hours a day — and never lay down
at all if Vasily Ivanovich had a headache; she had never read a
book, except *Alexis, or The Cabin in the Woods;* she wrote one
or at the most two letters a year, but she was expert at domestic
economy, in drying fruits and turning them into jam, though she
never touched anything with her own hands and altogether shifted
only reluctantly out of her seat. Arina Vlasievna was very kind
and, in her own way, by no means stupid. She knew that in this
world there were the gentlemen, who were there to give orders,
and the ordinary people, who were there to obey — and so she
was not revolted by the peasants' servility or by bows to the

ground; but she was gracious and modest in her treatment of inferiors, never let a beggar pass without a gift, and never condemned anybody, though she did sometimes like a little slander. In her youth she had been very good-looking, she had played the clavichord and could make herself understood a little in French; but during many years of wandering with her husband, whom she had married against her parents' will, she had gone various ways and forgotten both music and French. She loved and was inexpressibly afraid of her son. She left the management of their property to Vasily Ivanovich and never put her nose into anything: she sighed, waved him off with her handkerchief, and in her terror raised her eyebrows higher and higher as soon as the old man began to talk to her about impending changes and about his plans. She was mistrustful, always expecting some great misfortune, and burst into tears as soon as she thought of anything sad. . . . Women like her are already dying out. God knows whether one should be glad of that!

XXI

On getting out of bed Arkady opened the window, and the first object that struck his eyes was Vasily Ivanovich. Attired in a Bokharan dressing-gown belted with a handkerchief, the old man was zealously exerting himself in the garden. He noticed his young guest and, resting on his spade, exclaimed:

"I wish you health! How were you pleased to rest?"

"Excellently!" Arkady replied.

"But, as you see, I am like Cincinnatus: I'm hoeing up some late turnips. In these days that have come now — thank God for it! — every man must provide his nourishment with his own hands; it's no use relying on others: you must labor for yourself. And it transpires that Jean-Jacques Rousseau was right. Half an hour ago, my dear sir, you would have seen me in quite a different position. Into one peasant woman, who was complaining of being loose — that is in their language, but we call it dysentery, I — how shall I put it? — I poured opium; and out of another I pulled a tooth. I proposed etherization to her, only she wouldn't agree. All this I do gratis, *anamater*.[1] For that matter, it's nothing to me: you see I 'm a plebeian, a *homo novus* — not one of the hereditary nobles, not like my faithful spouse. . . . But wouldn't you

---

[1] *En amateur.*

like to come out here into the shade, to breathe in the morning freshness before tea?"

Arkady went out to him.

"Pleased to meet you yet again!" Vasily Ivanovich said, putting his hand military fashion to the greasy skull-cap that covered his head. "I know you are accustomed to luxuries, to pleasure, but even the great of this world do not abhor to spend a brief period beneath the shelter of the cottage."

"But really," Arkady exclaimed, "how am I one of the great of this world? And I am not accustomed to luxuries."

"Allow me, allow me," Vasily Ivanovich objected with an amiable smirk. "Though I am relegated to the archives now, I have knocked about the world a bit, I know a bird by its flight. I am a psychologist too in my own way, and a physiognomist. If I hadn't had that — I dare to call it — talent, I would have gone under long since; I, a little man, would have been rubbed out. I tell you without seeking to pay compliments; the friendship that I observe between you and my son makes me sincerely glad. I have just seen him; as is his custom, of which you are probably aware, he jumped out of bed very early and ran off to see the district. Pardon my curiosity: have you known my Yevgeny long?"

"Since last winter."

"I see. And allow me also to ask — but perhaps we could sit down? Allow me to ask, as a father, with all frankness: what is your opinion of my Yevgeny?"

"Your son is one of the most remarkable people I have ever met," Arkady replied enthusiastically.

Vasily Ivanovich's eyes suddenly opened wide and his cheeks faintly burned. The spade fell from his hand.

"And so you think — " he began.

"I am sure," Arkady broke in, "that a great future awaits your son, that he will bring fame on your name. I was convinced of that at our very first meeting."

"How — how did it happen?" Vasily Ivanovich was hardly able to get the words out. An exultant smile parted his broad lips and did not leave them again.

"You want to know how we came to meet?"

"Yes — and in general — "

Arkady began to tell, and to speak about Bazarov with even

greater fervor, with greater enthusiasm than on that evening when he had had the mazurka with Mme Odintsova.

Vasily Ivanovich listened to him, listened, blew his nose, rolled his handkerchief in both hands, coughed, rumpled his hair — and finally could not restrain himself any longer: he leaned toward Arkady and kissed him on the shoulder.

"You have made me perfectly happy," he said, without ceasing to smile; "I must tell you that I — worship my son; I won't say anything about my old woman: one knows what a mother feels. But I dare not express my feelings in his presence, because he doesn't like it. He is hostile to all effusive feelings; many people even condemn him for his hardness of disposition and see in it a sign of pride or lack of feeling; but people like him are not to be measured by the normal measures, don't you agree? For instance, others in his place would get all they could out of their parents, but he has never taken an unnecessary kopek, that is God's truth!"

"He's a disinterested, honest man," Arkady observed.

"Disinterested is just the word. But I, Arkady Nikolaich, not only worship him, I am proud of him, and all my ambition consists in hoping that in the course of time the following words will appear in his biography: 'The son of a simple army doctor, who, however, early realized his gifts and spared nothing to ensure his education — '" The old man's voice suddenly broke.

Arkady squeezed his hand.

"What do you think?" Vasily Ivanovich asked after a silence, "surely in a medical career he will not achieve the fame you prophesy for him?"

"Not, of course, in a medical career, though even in that sphere he will be one of our leading scientists."

"Then what in, Arkady Nikolaich?"

"That is difficult to say at this moment, but he will be celebrated."

"He will be celebrated!" the old man repeated, and buried himself in his thoughts.

"Arina Vlasievna ordered me to ask you to come to tea," Anfisushka said as she passed with an enormous dish of ripe raspberries.

Vasily Ivanovich started, and asked:

"And will there be iced cream with the raspberries?"

"There will."

"But make sure it really is cold! Don't stand on ceremony, Arkady Nikolaich, help yourself. Why doesn't Yevgeny come?"

"I'm here," Bazarov called from Arkady's room.

His father turned swiftly.

"Aha! You thought you would call on your friend; but you're too late, *amice*, and we've already had a long talk. Now we must go and have tea: your mother's summoned us. By the way, I want to have a talk with you."

"What about?"

"There's a peasant here who's suffering from icterus."

"Jaundice, you mean?"

"Yes, chronic and very obstinate icterus. I have prescribed centaury and hypericum, and made him eat carrots, and given him soda; but these are all *palliative* measures; it needs something more decisive. Though you laugh at medicine, I am sure you can give me valuable advice. But we'll have a talk about it later. Now let us go in to have some tea."

He nimbly jumped up from the bench and began to sing from *Robert:*

> *"One law, one law, one law I set myself;*
> *In joy — in joy — in joyousness to live."*

"Remarkable vitality!" Bazarov said as he turned from the window.

Noonday arrived. The sun scorched through a fine veil of serried, milk-white clouds. Everywhere there was silence; only the cocks called vigorously to one another in the village, arousing in all who heard them a strange sensation of drowsiness and boredom; and somewhere high in the summits of the trees the incessant squeak of a young hawk sounded in a lachrymose challenge. Arkady and Bazarov lay in the shadow of a small haystack, after spreading a couple of armfuls of dry and rustling, yet still green and scented grass to lie on.

"That aspen," Bazarov began, "reminds me of my childhood; it grows on the edge of a hole left from a brick shed, and in those days I was sure that that hole and aspen acted as a special talisman: I was never bored when I was near them. I did not understand then that the reason I was not bored was that I was a child. And now I am grown up, the talisman doesn't work."

"How long did you spend here all together?" Arkady asked.

"A couple of years without a break; then later we came here on visits. We lived a nomad life; we spent most of our time in towns."

"And has this house been standing long?"

"Very long. It was built by my grandfather, my mother's father."

"Who was he, your grandfather?"

"The devil knows. Some second-major. He served under Suvorov and was always telling the story of the crossing of the Alps. I expect he was lying."

"That explains why Suvorov's portrait is hanging in your reception room. But I like such little houses as yours, very old and very warm; and they have a peculiar scent of their own."

"It reminds me of shrine-lamp oil and melilot," Bazarov declared, yawning. "And the flies in these pleasant little houses — ! Pah!"

"Tell me," Arkady began after a brief silence, "you weren't treated harshly as a child?"

"You see the kind of parents I have: not at all strict."

"Are you fond of them, Yevgeny?"

"I am, Arkady!"

"They're very fond of you!"

Bazarov said nothing.

"Do you know what I am thinking?" he said at last, flinging his arms behind his head.

"I don't. What is it?"

"I am thinking my parents find life pretty good! At the age of sixty my father goes fussing around, talking about 'palliative' measures, curing people, playing the magnanimous gentleman to the peasants — in a word, he lives a merry life. And my mother is happy too: her day is so crammed with all kinds of occupations, with oh's and ah's, that she never has time to think of herself. But I — "

"And you?"

"But I am thinking: here am I lying under a haystack. . . . The narrow little spot I occupy is so tiny by comparison with all the rest of space where I am not and where nothing is concerned with me, and that part of time which I shall succeed in living is so insignificant in comparison with eternity, where I have never been and never will be — And yet in this atom, in this mathematical point, blood circulates, the brain functions, and even wants something. . . . What ignominy! What pettiness!"

"Allow me to observe that what you are saying applies to absolutely everybody — "

"You're right," Bazarov broke in. "I simply meant to say that they — my parents, I mean — are occupied and they don't worry about their own personal insignificance, it doesn't stink in their nostrils . . . but I — I feel only boredom and malice."

"Malice? But why malice?"

" 'Why?' Why do you ask? Have you forgotten, then?"

"I remember everything, but, all the same, I don't think you have any right to be annoyed. You're unhappy, I agree, but — "

"Ah, Arkady Nikolaevich, I see you conceive of love like all the modern young people: 'Cluck, cluck, cluck, little hen,' and as soon as the little hen begins to approach, God give you good legs! I'm not like that. But enough of this talk. What can't be helped is shameful to talk about." He turned on his side. "Aha! Look at that great little ant dragging that half-dead fly. Drag it along, brother, drag it along! Don't take any notice of its resistance, take advantage of the fact that you, as a living creature, do not have to yield to any feeling of compassion; you're not like us, who are self-humiliated."

"It's not for you to talk like that, Yevgeny! When did you humiliate yourself?"

Bazarov raised his head.

"That is the only thing I am proud of. I haven't humiliated myself, and so no dear little woman will ever humiliate me. Amen! Full stop! You won't hear another word from me on this subject."

The two friends lay for some time in silence.

"Yes," Bazarov began again. "A strange creature is man. As you look from outside and from a distance at the lonely life the 'fathers' live here, you wonder: what could be better? Eat, drink, and know that you are behaving in a very sound, very sensible fashion. But no: you're eaten up with yearning. You want to have contact with people, even if you curse them, so long as you can have contact with them."

"One needs so to arrange one's life that every moment in it is of significance," Arkady declared thoughtfully.

"Easy to say! Though at times the significant is false, it is always sweet; but then again one can be reconciled to the insignificant too. . . . But petty annoyances, petty annoyances — now, they're a real misfortune."

"Petty annoyances don't exist for a man, provided he isn't prepared to recognize them."

"Hm — what you have said is an *inverted platitude*."

"What? What do you mean by that?"

"Why, just this: to say, for instance, that education is beneficial is a platitude; but to say that education is detrimental, that is an inverted platitude. It seems to be more subtle, but essentially it is the same thing."

"Yes, but where is the truth, on which side?"

"Where? I answer you, like an echo: where?"

"You're in a melancholy mood today, Yevgeny."

"Really? The sun must have cooked me, and one shouldn't eat so many raspberries."

"In that case it wouldn't be a bad idea to have a nap," Arkady observed.

"By all means; only don't look at me: any man's face looks stupid when he's asleep."

"But aren't you quite unconcerned what people think of you?"

"I don't know what to say to that. A real man ought not to be concerned about it at all; a real man is the one who isn't thought about, but who has to be listened to or hated."

"Strange! I don't hate anybody," Arkady observed after reflection.

"But I hate so many people. You're a gentle soul, and spineless, how could you hate! . . . You're timid, you have little hope in yourself — "

"But have you any hope in yourself?" Arkady interrupted. "Have you any high opinion of yourself?"

Bazarov was silent.

"When I meet any man who stands up to my conception of things," he declared deliberately, "then I shall change my opinion of myself. Oh, to hate! You, for instance, said today as we were passing our head man Philip's hut — it's so beautifully kept and whitewashed — 'Now,' you said, 'Russia will achieve perfection when the very poorest peasant has a house like that, and every one of us should help to achieve that state.' But I hated that

Turgenev

poorest peasant, that Philip or Sidor, for whom I have got to wear myself out and who won't even say thank-you to me for it . . . and, in any case, what do I want his thanks for? Well, he'll be living in a whitewashed hut, but docks will be growing out of me; and then what?"

"No more of this, Yevgeny — listening to you talking today, one cannot but agree with those who reproach us with having no principles."

"You talk like your uncle. There aren't any such things as principles, you haven't even yet realized that! But there are sensations. Everything depends on them."

"How does it?"

"Why, like this. For instance, I, I hold to a negative trend, by virtue of my sensations. I find it pleasant to reject, my brain is arranged that way — and that's all there is to it! Why am I fond of chemistry? Why are you fond of apples? Also because of your sensations. It is all the same thing. Man will never penetrate deeper than that. Not everybody would tell you this, and even I shan't tell you a second time."

"Yes, but is honesty also a sensation?"

"I should say!"

"Yevgeny!" Arkady began in a miserable voice.

"Well? What? Don't you like it?" Bazarov broke in. "No, brother! Having decided to mow everything down, then mow yourself down too! . . . All the same, we have philosophized enough. 'Nature is singing the silence of sleep,' said Pushkin."

"He never said anything of the sort," Arkady declared.

"Then if he didn't say it, he ought to have in his capacity as poet. Which reminds me: he must have served in the army."

"Pushkin never was in the army!"

"Pardon me, but on every page of his you will find: 'To battle, to battle, for the honor of Russia!'"

"What are you making up all these stories for? Why, it's simply slander."

"Slander! Very serious, that! What a word to think of in order to frighten me! No matter how much you slander a man, he really deserves twenty times worse."

"Let's have a nap!" Arkady said in an annoyed tone.

"With the greatest of pleasure," Bazarov replied.

But neither of them could sleep. An almost inimical feeling had taken possession of the two young men's hearts. Five minutes later they opened their eyes and silently exchanged glances.

"Look," Arkady said suddenly, "a dry maple leaf has broken off and is falling to the ground; its movements are exactly like those of a butterfly in flight. Isn't it strange? The most mournful and dead thing resembles the most merry and living."

"Oh, my friend, Arkady Nikolaich!" Bazarov exclaimed; "one thing I ask you: don't talk beautifully."

"I talk as I can. And besides, that is despotism on your part. A thought came into my head, so why shouldn't I express it?"

"Yes; but why shouldn't I, too, express my thoughts? I consider that to talk beautifully is indecent."

"But what is decent? To abuse everything?"

"Ah, I see you are firmly resolved to follow in your uncle's steps. How that idiot would rejoice if he heard you!"

"What did you call Pavel Piotrovich?"

"I called him what he ought to be called: an idiot!"

"But that is intolerable!" Arkady exclaimed.

"Aha! The family feeling speaks," Bazarov said imperturbably. "I have noticed before how obstinately it persists in people. A man is prepared to renounce everything, to give up all kinds of prejudices; but to admit that his brother, who steals other people's clothes, for instance, is a thief — that is too much for him. And besides, when you come down to it, *my* brother, *mine*, yet not a genius — is that possible?"

"It was a simple feeling of justice that spoke within me and not a family feeling at all," Arkady retorted fierily. "But as you don't understand that feeling, as you haven't got that *sensation*, you cannot judge of it either."

"In other words, Arkady Kirsanov is too exalted for my under-standing; I bow and am silent."

"Please do stop, Yevgeny; we shall end by quarreling in earnest."

"Ah, Arkady! Do me the favor, let us have at least one really good quarrel — to the death, to annihilation."

"But then if we do, surely we'll end by — "

"By coming to blows?" Bazarov interrupted. "Well, what of it? Here in the hay, in such idyllic surroundings, far from the world and human gaze — that doesn't matter. But you will never master me. I shall seize you at once by the throat — "

Bazarov opened his long, cruel fingers. Arkady turned and jokingly prepared to resist. But his friend's face suddenly appeared so sinister, such a far from joking threat did he think he saw in the crooked smile of those lips, in those burning eyes, that he felt involuntary misgiving. . . .

"Ah, so that's where you've got to!" Vasily Ivanovich's voice sounded at that moment, and the old army doctor, wrapped in a home-made linen jacket and wearing a straw hat, also home-made, on his head, appeared above the young men. "I've been looking and looking for you. . . . But you've chosen an excellent spot and are devoting yourselves to a fine occupation. Lying on the 'earth,' and gazing up at 'heaven.' Do you know, there is a special significance in that!"

"I gaze up at heaven only when I want to sneeze," Bazarov snorted and, turning to Arkady, said in an undertone: "Pity he interfered."

"Now, no more of that," Arkady whispered, and surreptitiously squeezed his friend's hand. But no friendship will long survive such clashes.

"I look at you, my young friends," Vasily Ivanovich was saying meanwhile, shaking his head and resting his crossed hands on a cunningly twisted stick of his own fashioning, with the figure of a Turk for a knob, "I look, and I cannot but enjoy the sight. How much strength there is in you, youth in its finest blooming, abilities, talents! Absolutely — Castor and Pollux!"

"Now listen — he's gone right off into mythology!" Bazarov declared. "You can see at once that he was strong at Latin in his time. Why, I remember, you won a silver medal for composition, didn't you?"

"Dioscuri, Dioscuri!" Vasily Ivanovich repeated.

"But that's quite enough, Father, don't get sentimental."

"Just once in a lifetime one may" the old man murmured. "However, I didn't come to look for you, gentlemen, in order to pay you compliments, but in order, firstly, to report that we shall be having dinner soon; and secondly, I wanted to warn you, Yevgeny — you're a sensible man, you know what people are like, and you know what women are like, and so you will excuse — your mother wanted to have a church service to celebrate your homecoming. Don't imagine I am summoning you to be present at that service; it's already finished; but Father Alexei —"

"The parson?"

"Why, yes, the priest; he's going to — dine with us. I didn't expect that and didn't even advise — but somehow it happened — he didn't understand me. . . . And then — and Arina Vlasievna — But in any case he's a very good and sensible man."

"Why, he won't eat my share of dinner, will he?" Bazarov asked.

Vasily Ivanovich laughed. "Really, the things you say!"

"And I don't demand any more than that. I am ready to sit down at table with any man."

Vasily Ivanovich adjusted his hat.

"I was sure in advance," he said, "that you are above all prejudice. And, for that matter, I, an old man, in my sixty-second year, I, too, haven't any." (Vasily Ivanovich did not dare to confess that he himself had desired the service. He was just as devout as his wife.) "And Father Alexei was very anxious to make your acquaintance. You'll like him, you see. He isn't averse from a game of cards, and even — but this is between ourselves — smokes a pipe."

"All right, then; after dinner we'll sit down to a round of whist, and I'll strip him."

"He-he-he, we'll see! 'The old woman spoke for both.' "

"Why, you aren't still troubled by the old passion, are you?" Bazarov said with peculiar emphasis.

Vasily Ivanovich's bronze cheeks vaguely reddened.

"You ought to be ashamed, Yevgeny. What has been, has been. Well, yes, I am prepared to admit before *them* that I had the passion in my youth, truly; yes, and I paid for it too. But isn't it hot? May I sit down with you? I shan't be in the way, shall I?"

"Not in the least," Arkady replied.

With much groaning Vasily Ivanovich sat down on the hay. "Your present couch reminds me, gentlemen," he began, "of my military, bivouac life, of dressing-stations, also arranged somewhere beside a haystack, and thank God even for that." He sighed. "Much, very much, have I experienced in my time. For instance, if you like, I'll tell you a curious incident of the plague in Bessarabia."

"For which you were given the Vladimir cross?" Bazarov intervened. "We know, we know. . . . By the way, why aren't you wearing it?"

"Didn't I tell you I hadn't any prejudices?" Vasily Ivanovich muttered (he had ordered the crimson ribbon to be removed from his coat only the previous evening), and he began to tell them about the incident during the plague. "But look, he's fallen asleep," he suddenly whispered to Arkady, pointing to his son and winking good-naturedly. "Yevgeny, get up!" he added aloud. "Let's go to dinner."

Father Alexei, a man of full and imposing figure, with thick, carefully combed hair, and wearing an embroidered belt around a lilac silk cassock, proved to be a very astute and resourceful man. He himself hastened to shake Arkady's and Bazarov's hands, as though realizing in advance that they had no need of his blessing, and altogether he was perfectly self-possessed. He did not degrade himself, nor did he provoke others; he neatly joked at seminary Latin, and spoke in defense of his bishop; he drank two glasses of wine and refused a third; he accepted a cigar from Arkady, but did not smoke it at once, saying that he would take it home. He had one not altogether pleasant habit: from time to time he slowly and cautiously raised his hand in order to catch a fly on his face and sometimes crushed it in doing so. He sat down at the card-table with a moderate demonstration of satisfaction, and ended by stripping Bazarov of two rubles fifty kopeks in notes; in Arina Vlasievna's house there was no thought of anyone settling in silver.

She sat as before beside her son (she did not play cards), resting her cheek on her little fist as before, and got up only to order some more refreshments to be brought. She was afraid to fondle Bazarov, and he did not encourage her, did not provoke her to caresses; and besides, Vasily Ivanovich had advised her not to "disturb" him very much. "The young people are not fond of it," he told her (there is no need to say how excellent the dinner was that day; Timofeich in his own person had galloped off at break of dawn for some special Circassian beef; the head man had ridden in the opposite direction for turbots, ruffes, and crayfish; for mushrooms alone the peasant women had received forty-two copper kopeks). But Arina Vlasievna's eyes, inseparably fixed on Bazarov, expressed not only devotion and tenderness; they also revealed sorrow, mingled with curiosity and fear; they contained a kind of humble reproach.

Fathers and Sons

Bazarov, however, was not in the mood to analyze exactly what his mother's eyes expressed; he rarely turned to her, and then only with a brief question. Once he asked her for her hand "for luck"; she quietly laid her soft little hand on his rough, broad palm.

"Well," she asked after waiting a little, "hasn't it helped?"

"It's still worse," he replied with a careless smile.

"They're taking great risks," Father Alexei declared almost with commiseration, and he stroked his handsome beard.

"The Napoleonic principle, Father, the Napoleonic," Vasily Ivanovich retorted, and led an ace.

"And that brought him to St. Helena," observed Father Alexei, and he covered the ace with a trump.

"Would you like some currant juice, Yevgeny, my dear?" Arina Vlasievna asked.

Bazarov only shrugged his shoulders.

"It's no good!" he said to Arkady next day, "I'm leaving here tomorrow. I'm bored; I want to work, but I can't here. I'll go back to your village; I've left all my specimens there. At least I can shut myself away in your house. But here my father tells me: 'my office is at your service — no one will interfere with you,' but he himself won't leave me for a second. And besides, I feel conscience-stricken at shutting myself away from him. And my mother too. I hear her sighing on the other side of the wall, but if I go out to her, there's nothing I can say to her."

"She'll be very upset," Arkady said, "and he too."

"I'll come back to them."

"When?"

"Why, on my way to Petersburg."

"I'm especially sorry for your mother."

"What's that? Has she been treating you to berries?"

Arkady lowered his eyes.

"You don't know your mother, Yevgeny. She is not only a splendid woman, she is very intelligent, really and truly. This morning she talked to me for half an hour, and so much to the point, so interestingly."

"I expect she talked about me the whole time."

"You weren't the only one we talked about."

"Maybe; you can see better, you're outside it. If a woman can maintain a conversation for half an hour, that is a good sign at any rate. But I shall go all the same."

"It won't be easy for you to tell them this news. They're always wondering what we shall be doing in two weeks' time."

"Not easy! The devil provoked me into annoying Father today! The other day he ordered one of his peasant tenants to be whipped — and it was very sensible of him; yes, yes, don't look at me in such horror — it was very sensible, for the man is a terrible thief and drunkard; only Father hadn't expected that it would come to my ears, as they say. He was quite crestfallen, and now in addition I've got to upset him. . . . It can't be helped! The wound will heal."

Bazarov had said: "It can't be helped!" but the whole day passed before he could bring himself to inform Vasily Ivanovich of his intentions. Finally, as he was saying good-night to him in the office, he remarked with a prolonged yawn:

"Ah yes. I almost forgot to tell you. Order our horses to be sent to Fyodot tomorrow for a relay."

Vasily Ivanovich was amazed.

"But surely Mr. Kirsanov isn't going away?"

"Yes, he is; and I'm going with him."

Vasily Ivanovich spun round where he stood.

"You're going?"

"Yes . . . I've got to. Please give orders about the horses."

"Good . . ." the old man began to stammer, "for a relay — good — only — only — Why are you going?"

"I must drive over to his place for a short while. I'll come back here afterward."

"Yes! For a short while. . . . Good." Vasily Ivanovich pulled out his handkerchief and, blowing his nose, bowed down almost to the floor. "All right then — that — will be done. I did think you would be staying with us — longer. Three days. That, that, after three years, is rather short, rather short, Yevgeny!"

"But I tell you I shall soon be coming back. I must go."

"Must — oh well! You must do your duty above all. . . . Send the horses, then? Good. Of course, Arina and I hadn't expected this. She's asked a neighbor to let her have some flowers, she was intending to decorate your room." (He did not even mention that each morning at daybreak, standing with unstockinged feet in his slippers, he held a conference with Timofeich; with trembling hands taking out one torn banknote after another, he commissioned him to make various purchases, especially insisting on stocks of food and red wine, which, so far as he was able to observe, the young men greatly liked.) "The main thing is liberty; that is my rule — no one must be constrained — no — "

He stopped short and made toward the door.

"We'll see each other soon, really, Father."

But Vasily Ivanovich did not turn round, he only waved his hand and went out. On going to his bedroom he found his wife in bed and began to whisper his prayers, in order not to disturb her. But she did wake up.

"Is that you, Vasily Ivanovich?" she asked.

"Yes, it's me."

"Have you been with Yevgeny? Do you know, I'm worried: I wonder whether he sleeps well on the divan. I ordered Anfisushka to put your camp mattress and new pillows under him; I'd have given him our feather bed, but I know he doesn't like to sleep on anything soft."

"Don't you worry, mother, that's all right. He's comfortable. Lord, forgive us sinners," he continued his prayer in an undertone. Vasily Ivanovich spared his old wife; he did not feel like telling her that night the sorrow that awaited her.

Bazarov and Arkady drove off next day. From early morning everybody in the house was in the dumps; a utensil fell from Anfisushka's hands; even Fyodka was astonished, and ended by taking off his boots. Vasily Ivanovich fussed about more than ever; he was obviously screwing up his courage, he talked loudly and stamped with his feet, but his cheeks were sunken, and his gaze continually slipped past his son. Arina Vasilievna wept quietly; she would have been completely broken up and would have had no control over herself if her husband had not argued with her for a full two hours in the early morning. And when, after repeated promises to return in any case within a month, Bazarov tore himself at last out of the embraces restraining him and seated himself in the tarantass, when the horses started off and the carriage bell began to jingle and the wheels to turn, and now there was nothing to gaze after, and the dust had settled again, and Timofeich, all huddled and staggering as he went, wandered back into his little room; when the two old folk were left alone in their home, which suddenly seemed to cringe and grow decrepit, then Vasily Ivanovich, who at the porch only a few moments before had been bravely waving his handkerchief, dropped into a chair and let his head fall on his breast.

"He's deserted, deserted us," he began to stammer; "he's thrown us over; he was bored with us. I'm as lonely as a finger now, as lonely as a finger," he repeated several times, and each time he thrust his hand out in front of him with the index finger separate from the others.

Then Arina Vlasievna went over to him, rested her gray head against his gray head, and said: "It can't be helped, Vasily! Our son is a piece cut off the loaf. He's like an eagle: he wanted to come, so he flew here; he wanted to go, so he's flown away; but you and I are like mushrooms in a hollow stump, we sit side by side and never stir from our place. Only I shall always be the same to you forever, just as you will to me."

Vasily took his hands from his face and put his arms round his wife, his comrade; so tightly he had never embraced her in his youth; she comforted him in his sorrow.

XXII

Our friends drove to Fyodot's in silence, only rarely exchanging insignificant remarks. Bazarov was not altogether satisfied with himself. Arkady was not satisfied with him. Moreover, in his heart he felt that causeless sorrow which is familiar only to very young people. The coachman changed horses and, climbing onto the box, asked: "To the right or the left?"

Arkady started. The road to the right led to the town, and thence to his home; the road to the left led to Mme Odintsova's house.

He glanced at Bazarov.

"Yevgeny," he asked, "to the left?"

Bazarov turned away.

"What stupidity are you thinking of now?" he muttered.

"I know it's stupid," Arkady answered, "but where's the harm of it? It isn't as though it was the first time."

Bazarov pulled his peaked cap over his brow.

"As you like," he said at last.

"Take the left!" Arkady shouted.

The tarantass rolled off in the direction of Nikolskoe. But, having decided on a stupidity, the friends were still more obstinately silent than before, and even seemed to be angry.

By the very manner in which the butler met them on the veranda the two friends could guess that they had acted imprudently in yielding to the fantastic idea that had suddenly occurred to them. They were obviously not expected. They were left sitting for quite a long time and with quite idiotic physiognomies in the reception hall. Mme Odintsova came out to them at last. She greeted them with her usual amiability, but was astonished at their speedy return and, so far as one could judge from the deliberation of her movements and speech, was not overjoyed by it. They hastened to announce that they had only dropped in as they were passing and in four hours would be driving on, to the town. She confined herself to a faint exclamation, asked Arkady to greet his father in her name, and sent for her aunt. When the Princess appeared, she looked very sleepy, which made her scowling, aged face seem even more malevolent. Katya was not well, she did not leave her room. Arkady suddenly felt that he at least wanted just as much to see Katya as Anna Sergeevna. The four hours passed in meaningless desultory talk; Anna Sergeevna both listened and talked without smiling. Only at the very moment of parting did her former friendliness seem to stir in her soul.

"I've a touch of hypochondria now," she said, "but don't take any notice of it and come back again — I say that to you both — a little later."

Both Bazarov and Arkady replied with a silent bow, got into their carriage, and without making any further calls drove home to Marino, where they arrived safely the following evening. All the way neither of them even mentioned the name of Odintsova. Bazarov in particular hardly opened his mouth and gazed steadily to one side, away from the road, with a harsh concentration.

At Marino everybody was highly delighted to see them. His son's protracted absence had begun to alarm Nikolai Piotrovich; he cried out, kicked his feet about, and bounced on the divan when Fenichka ran in to him with shining eyes and announced the "young gentlemen's" arrival; even Pavel Piotrovich felt a little pleasant agitation and smiled condescendingly as he shook the returned wanderers' hands. Then there was talk and cross-questioning; Arkady talked more than Bazarov, especially after supper, which continued long past midnight. Nikolai Piotrovich ordered several bottles of porter only just arrived from Moscow to be brought in, and he himself made merry to such an extent that his cheeks went a raspberry color, and he laughed and laughed with rather a childish, rather a nervous laugh. The general excitement spread even to the servants. Duniasha ran to and fro like a lunatic and banged the doors constantly; and even at three in the morning Piotr was still trying to play a Cossack waltz on his guitar. The strings sounded mournfully and pleasantly in the still air; but with the exception of a brief preliminary *fioritura* nothing resulted from the cultured valet's efforts; nature had denied him musical talent as well as all others.

But meanwhile life was not proceeding altogether satisfactorily at Marino, and poor Nikolai Piotrovich was in a bad way. His worries over the farm were growing with every day — worries that were disconsolate, pointless. His troubles with the hired laborers were becoming intolerable. Some were demanding to be paid off or were asking for a raise, others went off after getting an advance; the horses were ailing; the harness vanished as though burned in a fire; work was done carelessly; the threshing-machine ordered from Moscow proved to be useless because of its weight; another broke down the first time it was used; half the cattle shed was burned down because a blind old woman, one of the servants, went in windy weather with a firebrand to fumigate her cow. True, the old woman declared that all the mischief arose because the master had taken it into his head to make some cheese and dairy produce never known before. The steward suddenly grew lazy and even began to get fat, as any Russian gets fat who has fallen into "money for jam." Catching sight of Nikolai Piotrovich from a distance, in order to demonstrate his zeal he would fling a piece of stick at a little pig that happened to run past, or threaten some half-naked lad, but, in any case, he spent most of his time asleep. The peasants placed on a tenant basis did not bring the rent at the dates fixed, and stole the timber. Almost every night the watchmen caught peasant horses grazing on the farm meadows, and sometimes brought them in by force. Nikolai Piotrovich would impose a monetary fine for the damage done to the meadow, but usually the affair ended with the horses being returned to their owners after being kept for a day or two on the

master's fodder. To complete the mischief, the peasants began to
quarrel among themselves; brothers demanded that their land
should be shared out among them, their wives could not live together in one house; a fight would suddenly flare up, and everybody suddenly started to his feet as though by command, everybody ran to gather in front of the office porch, went crawling to
the master, often with bleeding snouts, or drunk, and demanded
trial and punishment; there was uproar, howling, women's snivel-
ing squeals mingled with men's curses. Then it became necessary
to separate the warring parties, to shout oneself hoarse, knowing
in advance that in any case it was impossible to come to a just
decision. There were not sufficient hands for the harvest; so, with
the most innocent of faces, a neighboring freeholder arranged to
supply reapers at two rubles per four acres and cheated in the
most unconscionable manner; the Kirsanovs' own women charged
incredible prices for their labor, and meanwhile the grain was
falling out of the ear, and then they couldn't manage to get the
mowing finished, and then the council for widows and orphans
began to threaten and demand an immediate payment of interest
up to date. . . .

"I haven't the strength to keep up with it!" Nikolai Piotrovich
exclaimed in despair more than once. "I mustn't join in the fight
myself, and my principles won't allow me to send for the district
policeman, yet without the threat of punishment one cannot do
anything!"

"*Du calme, du calme*," Pavel Piotrovich remarked at this,
though he himself muttered, frowned, and tugged at his whiskers.

Bazarov kept away from all these "worries," and in any case it
was not for him, a guest, to intervene in other people's affairs. The
day after his arrival at Marino he set to work on his frogs, on his
infusoria, and chemical constituents, and was occupied with them
all the time. Arkady, on the other hand, considered it his duty, if
not to help his father, at least to appear as if he were ready to
help him. He listened to him patiently and once offered some
advice, not expecting it to be followed, but in order to show his
sympathy. He felt no antipathy to farm management; he even
thought with satisfaction of undertaking agricultural activity; but
at this time other ideas were swarming in his head. To his own
amazement, he was thinking continually of Nikolskoe; yet formerly he would only have shrugged his shoulders if anyone had

told him that he would be bored under the same roof as Bazarov. And under which roof? Under his parental roof! Yet he was in fact bored, and he felt drawn to get away. He thought of walking till he was tired, but that did not help. While talking to his father one day, he learned that Nikolai Piotrovich possessed several quite interesting letters that Mme Odintsova's mother had written to his wife, and Arkady gave him no rest until he had got hold of these letters, for which his father had to rummage through twenty different boxes and chests. When he gained possession of these half-crumbling papers, Arkady seemed to be more at rest, as though he saw before him the end toward which he should proceed. " 'I say that to both of you,' she said," he muttered to himself again and again. "I'll drive over, I'll drive over, damn it all!" But he recalled the last visit, the chilly reception, and his previous awkwardness, and he was troubled by a sense of misgiving. Yet the "chance it" of youth, the secret desire to try his fortune, to test his strength alone, without anyone's patronage, conquered at last. Only ten days after his return to Marino he again dashed off to the town on the pretext of desiring to study the organization of Sunday schools, and thence to Nikolskoe.

Continually urging on his driver, he sped there like a young officer into battle: he felt both afraid and gay, and impatience choked him. "The main thing is that one mustn't think," he assured himself. His hired driver proved to be a spirited sort; he came to a halt before every tavern, saying: "Just one?" or "Surely just one?" But on the other hand, having had "just one," he did not spare the horses. Now at last the high roof of the well-known house appeared. "What am I doing?" the thought suddenly flashed through Arkady's head. "Well, but you can't turn back!" The troika dashed along merrily; the driver whooped and whistled. Now the little bridge was thundering beneath the hoofs and wheels, now the avenue of clipped firs was approaching.

A rose-colored gown was glimpsed amid the dark green, a young face peered out from beneath the light fringe of a parasol. . . . He recognized Katya, and she recognized him. Arkady ordered the driver to pull up his galloping horses, jumped out of the carriage, and went to her.

"So it's you!" she said, and slowly all her face went crimson. "Let us go to my sister, she's here in the garden; she will be glad to see you."

Katya led Arkady into the garden. It seemed to him that the meeting with her was a particularly fortunate omen; he rejoiced to see her as though she were a sister. Everything had happened so excellently: no butler, and no announcing his arrival. At a turn in the path he saw Anna Sergeevna. She was standing with her back toward him. Hearing steps, she slowly turned round.

Arkady was at a loss for words, but her very first remark at once reassured him. "Good morning, runaway," she said in her even, gracious voice, and came to meet him, smiling and screwing up her eyes against the sun and the wind. "Where did you find him, Katya?"

"I have brought you, Anna Sergeevna," he began, "something that you don't in the least expect. . . ."

"You have brought yourself; that is the best of all."

XXIII

After seeing Arkady off with sarcastic commiseration and making it quite clear that he was not under any illusion as to the real object of his friend's journey, Bazarov withdrew completely into himself; he was possessed with a fever for work. He no longer quarreled with Pavel Piotrovich, especially as in his presence the older man adopted an excessively aristocratic demeanor and expressed his opinion more in sounds than in words. On one occasion Pavel Piotrovich did, indeed, enter into competition with the *nihilist* in regard to the question, then fashionable, of the rights of the Ostsee gentry.[1] But he suddenly stopped, after muttering with frigid courtesy: "However, you and I cannot understand each other; I, at any rate, do not have the honor of understanding you."

"I should say not!" Bazarov exclaimed. "Man is capable of understanding everything — how the ether throbs, and what goes on in the sun — but he is quite incapable of understanding how another man can blow his nose in a different manner from the way he blows his own."

"Well, is that a clever remark?" Pavel Piotrovich said interrogatively, and walked away.

He sometimes asked permission to be present at Bazarov's experiments, however, and once even set his face, scented and

[1] The "Baltic barons," of German origin and culture, had retained extensive privileges, which later were whittled down. (Tr.)

washed with excellent detergents, against the miscroscope in order to see how a transparent infusorian swallowed up a green
speck and fussily digested it with what appeared to be very nimble little fists situated in its throat. Nikolai Piotrovich visited Bazarov much more frequently than did his brother; he would have
gone every day to "learn," as he expressed it, if the anxieties of
the farm had not dragged him away. He was no constraint on the
young naturalist experimenter; he sat in a corner of the room and
watched attentively, occasionally allowing himself a cautious
question. During dinner and supper he tried to turn the conversation to physics, geology, or chemistry, as all other subjects, even
economic, not to mention political ones, might lead, if not to
clashes, at least to mutual dissatisfaction. Nikolai Piotrovich
guessed that his brother's hatred of Bazarov had not diminished
in the least. One insignificant incident, among many others, confirmed his assumption. Cholera began to make its appearance here
and there in the neighborhood, and even "removed" two people
from Marino itself. One night Pavel Piotrovich had quite a severe
attack. He suffered agonies all night, but did not resort to Bazarov's skill. And when next day Bazarov asked: "But why didn't
you send for me?" he replied, still very pale, but already carefully brushed and combed and shaved: "Why, I remember you
yourself said that you don't believe in medicine!" So the days
passed. Bazarov worked persistently and morosely. . . . But
meanwhile in Nikolai Piotrovich's house there was one being with
whom he did talk readily, even though not to unburden his soul.
That person was Fenichka.

He usually met her early in the morning, in the garden or the
yard; he did not call on her in her room, and she approached his
door only once, in order to ask him whether she should bathe
Mitya or not. She not only trusted him, not only was not afraid
of him, but was even more free and at ease in his presence than
with Nikolai Piotrovich. It is difficult to say why this was so;
perhaps because she unconsciously felt that Bazarov lacked all
the qualities of a nobleman, lacked all the superiority that both
attracts and repels. In her eyes he was both an excellent doctor
and a plain sort of man. When attending to her child she was unconstrained by his presence, and one day, when her head suddenly
swam and began to ache, she took a spoonful of medicine that he
administered. If Nikolai Piotrovich was present she behaved more

distantly, doing so not out of cunning, but from a feeling of propriety. She was more afraid of Pavel Piotrovich than ever before; he had been watching her for some time past, and would turn up unexpectedly, as though sprung out of the ground behind her back, in his English suit, with a fixed, keen gaze and his hands in his pockets. "He makes you go cold all over," Fenichka complained to Duniasha, and in reply the girl sighed and thought of another "unfeeling" man. Bazarov, quite unwittingly, had become the *ruthless tyrant* of her soul.

Fenichka liked Bazarov, but he liked her too. Even his face changed when he talked with her; it acquired a clear, almost kind expression, and with his usual negligence was mingled a jocular kind of attention. Fenichka grew more good-looking with every day. There is a time in young women's lives when they suddenly begin to blossom and unfold like summer roses; such a time had come in Fenichka's life. Everything conduced to this, even the prevailing July heat. Dressed in a light, white dress, she herself seemed whiter and lighter; she did not get sunburned, and the heat, from which she could not escape, slightly flushed her cheeks and ears and, pouring a gentle sluggishness into all her body, was reflected in the drowsy languor of her pretty little eyes. She was almost unable to work; her hands always slipped down to rest on her knees. She did hardly any walking and continually groaned and complained with amusing impotence.

"You should bathe more frequently," Nikolai Piotrovich said to her. He had arranged a large bathing spot, enclosed with canvas, in a pond that was not yet completely dried up.

"Oh, Nikolai Piotrovich, while I am getting to the pond I shall die, and as I come back I shall die. There isn't any shade at all in the garden."

"You're quite right, there isn't any shade," Nikolai Piotrovich replied, and he rubbed his eyebrows.

One day, about seven in the morning, as Bazarov was returning from a walk he found Fenichka in the long since faded, but still dense and green lilac arbor. She was sitting on the bench with a white kerchief flung over her head, as usual; beside her lay quite a heap of red and white roses still wet with dew. He greeted her.

"Ah! Yevgeny Vasilich!" she said, and she raised the edge of her kerchief a little to look at him, baring her arm to the elbow as she did so.

"What are you doing here?" Bazarov said, sitting down beside her. "Making posies?"

"Yes; for the breakfast table. Nikolai Piotrovich likes it."

"But it's a long time yet to breakfast. What a mass of flowers!"

"I've picked them now because later it will get hot, and it will be impossible to come out of the house. Now is the only time you can breathe. I've gone quite weak with this heat. I'm beginning to fear I shall fall ill."

"What an idea! Let me feel your pulse." Bazarov took her hand, felt for the regularly beating artery, and did not even bother to count the beats. "You'll live to be a hundred," he said, dropping her hand.

"Ah! God forbid!" she exclaimed.

"Why? Don't you want to live long, then?"

"But a hundred years! We had a granny eighty-five years old, and what a martyr she was! She was black in the face, deaf, and hunchbacked and was always coughing; she was only a burden to herself. And what sort of life d'you call that!"

"So it is better to be young?"

"Why, of course it is, isn't it?"

"But how is it better? Tell me!"

"How is it better? Why, now I am young I can do everything — I can go, and come, and carry, and I never have to ask anybody for anything. . . . What could be better?"

"And yet for me it is all the same whether I am young or old."

"How can you say that? It's all the same? What you're saying isn't possible."

"But you judge for yourself, Fyodosia Nikolavna, what good is my youth to me? I live alone, like a recluse. . . ."

"That depends entirely on you."

"Not entirely on me! If someone would only have pity on me!"

Fenichka gave Bazarov a sidelong look, but did not say anything.

"What is the book you have there?" she asked after waiting a moment or two.

"This? It is a scientific book, a difficult one."

"But are you always studying? And aren't you bored? As it is, I think you know everything."

"Evidently I don't know everything. You try reading a little of it."

"Why, I shan't understand a word. Is it a Russian book?" Fenichka asked, taking the solidly bound volume in both hands. "How thick it is!"

"Yes, it's Russian."

"All the same, I shan't understand a word."

"But I didn't give it to you for you to understand. I just wanted to watch you as you read. When you read, the end of your little nose wrinkles very charmingly."

Fenichka, who had begun to read in an undertone from the article "On Creosote" at which she had happened to open the book, laughed and dropped it — it slipped from the bench to the ground.

"I like to see you laugh, too," Bazarov remarked.

"Now, do stop!"

"I like to hear you talk. It's just like a little stream rippling."

Fenichka turned her head away.

"You are a one!" she said, fingering the flowers. "And why should you listen to me? You have had conversations with such intelligent ladies."

"Ah, Fyodosia Nikolavna! Believe me, all the intelligent ladies in the world are not worth your little elbow."

"Now! There's a thing to say!" Fenichka whispered, and she covered her arms.

Bazarov picked the book up from the ground.

"This is a medical book. Why did you throw it down?"

"Medical?" Fenichka repeated, and turned to him. "But do you know what? Ever since you gave me those drops, do you remember, Mitya sleeps so well! I can't imagine how to thank you; really, you are so good."

"But doctors have to be paid properly," Bazarov remarked with a smile. "Doctors are mercenary people, as you know."

Fenichka raised her eyes to Bazarov; they seemed even darker because of the whitish reflection that fell on the upper part of her face. She did not know whether he was joking or not.

"If you wish, we'll be very glad. . . . We shall have to ask Nikolai Piotrovich — "

"But you don't think I want money?" Bazarov interrupted her. "No, I don't want money from you."

"Then what?" Fenichka said.

"What?" Bazarov echoed. "Guess."

"I'm not a thought-reader!"

"Then I'll tell you; I want — one of those roses."

Fenichka laughed again and even made a gesture of surprise, so amusing did Bazarov's wish seem to her. She laughed, and at the same time she felt flattered. He gazed at her fixedly.

"Certainly, certainly," she said at last and, bending over the bench, began to sort out the roses. "Which would you like, red or white?"

"Red, and not too large."

She straightened up.

"Here you are," she said, but she at once drew back her outstretched hand and, biting her lips, looked toward the entrance to the arbor, then listened intently.

"What's the matter?" Bazarov asked. "Nikolai Piotrovich?"

"No. He has gone off to the fields . . . and besides, I'm not afraid of him — but Pavel Piotrovich, now — I thought — "

"What?"

"I thought that he was walking past. No, there's no one. Take it." Fenichka gave Bazarov the rose.

"Why are you afraid of Pavel Piotrovich?"

"He's always frightening me. It isn't so much what he says, but he looks so meaningly. And you don't like him either, do you? You remember, you were always arguing with him at one time. I don't even know what you argue about, but I see that you get him so tied up, and so — "

Fenichka showed with her hands how, in her opinion, Bazarov tied up Pavel Piotrovich.

Bazarov smiled.

"But if he were to get the better of me," he asked, "would you take my part?"

"How can I take your part? But, in any case, no one could get the better of you."

"Do you think so? But I know a hand that if it wished could twist me round its little finger."

"Whose hand is that?"

"But don't you really know? Just smell what a beautiful scent this rose you gave me has."

Fenichka stretched forward her little neck and put her face

close to the flower. The kerchief slipped from her head to her shoulders, to reveal a soft mass of black, gleaming, rather disheveled hair.

"Wait a moment, I want to smell it with you," Bazarov said. He bent over and kissed her vigorously on her parted lips.

She quivered, and pressed her hands against his chest; but she pressed feebly, and he was able to renew and prolong his kiss.

A dry cough came from behind the lilac. Fenichka immediately shifted away to the other end of the bench. Pavel Piotrovich appeared, bowed stiffly, said with malevolent gloominess: "So you're here," and went away. Fenichka at once gathered up all the roses and left the arbor. "Shame on you, Yevgeny Vasilich!" she whispered as she went. A tone of unfeigned reproach sounded in that whisper.

Bazarov recalled another recent scene, and he felt conscience-stricken and contemptuously chagrined. But he at once shook his head, ironically congratulated himself on his formal entry into the company of Céladons,[1] and went to his room.

Pavel Piotrovich left the garden and slowly made his way to the wood. He remained there quite a long time, and when he returned for breakfast Nikolai Piotrovich anxiously asked him whether he was well, so darkened was his face.

"You know I sometimes suffer from an excess of bile," his brother calmly answered.

XXIV

Two hours later he knocked on Bazarov's door.

"I must apologize for interrupting you in your scientific occupations," he began, seating himself in a chair by the window and resting both hands on a handsome stick with an ivory knob (he usually went about without a stick), "but I am compelled to ask you to afford me five minutes of your time — no more."

"All my time is at your service," replied Bazarov, over whose face a strange look passed as Pavel Piotrovich entered.

"Five minutes will be sufficient for me. I have come to put before you a certain problem."

"A problem? What is it?"

"Be so good, then, as to listen. At the beginning of your stay

[1] Céladon: a stock name for a courtly lover, from the name of the hero of the French romance *Astrée* by Honoré d'Urfé (1568–1625).

in my brother's house, before I denied myself the pleasure of conversing with you, I had the opportunity to hear your views on many subjects; but, so far as I remember, neither between us, nor even in my presence, was there ever any talk of duels, of duels generally. Permit me to inquire what your opinion is on that subject."

Bazarov, who had risen to meet him, sat down on the edge of the table and folded his arms.

"Well, my opinion is," he said, "that from the theoretical aspect a duel is ridiculous; from the practical aspect, however, it is another matter."

"In other words, you mean to say, if I have understood you aright, that no matter what may be your theoretical view of a duel, in practice you would not allow yourself to be insulted without demanding satisfaction."

"You have guessed my thoughts perfectly."

"Very good. I am very pleased to hear you say that. Your words save me from uncertainty."

"From indecision, you mean to say."

"That is just the same; I express myself in order to be understood; I — am not a seminary rat. Your words save me a certain mournful necessity. I have decided to fight a duel with you."

Bazarov's eyes started out of his head.

"With me?"

"Undoubtedly with you."

"But what about? Please inform me."

"I could give you a reason," Pavel Piotrovich began. "But I prefer to be silent in that respect. To my taste, you are superfluous here; I cannot endure you, I despise you, and if that is not enough for you —"

His eyes began to flash. Bazarov's eyes also flamed.

"Very good!" he drawled; "no further explanations are necessary. You have had the fantastic idea of testing your chivalrous soul on me. I could refuse you that satisfaction, but since things have gone so far —"

"I am deeply obliged to you," Pavel Piotrovich answered, "and I can hope now that you will accept my challenge, without compelling me to resort to methods of violence."

"In other words, speaking without allegories, to that stick?" Bazarov observed unconcernedly. "That is perfectly correct.

There is no necessity whatever for you to insult me. Nor is it altogether safe. You can remain a gentleman. I accept your challenge also like a gentleman."

"Excellent," Pavel Piotrovich said, and he stood the stick in one corner. "In a moment we'll have a few words to say concerning the conditions of our duel; but first I would wish to know whether you consider it necessary to resort to the formality of a small quarrel, which might serve as the pretext for my challenge."

"No, better without formalities."

"That is what I think. I also consider it irrelevant to enter into the real causes of our conflict. We cannot endure each other. What more does one require?"

"What more does one require?" Bazarov repeated ironically.

"As for the actual conditions of the duel, as we shall not have seconds — for where are we to get them?"

"Precisely, where are we to get them?"

"I have the honor to propose the following: we shall fight to-morrow morning, I suggest, at six o'clock, behind the grove, with pistols; at ten paces from the line."

"At ten paces? That is just; that is the distance at which we hate each other."

"We can make it eight," Pavel Piotrovich observed.

"We can; why not?"

"Each to fire twice; and against possible eventualities each is to have in his pocket a letter in which he blames himself for his end."

"Now, with that I do not entirely agree," Bazarov said. "It is just a little like a French romance, just a little improbable."

"Maybe. However, you must agree that it is unpleasant to be placed under suspicion of murder."

"I agree. But there is a means of avoiding that mournful charge. We shall have no seconds, but there can be a witness."

"Who, namely, if I may ask."

"Why, Piotr."

"Which Piotr?"

"Your brother's valet. He is abreast of present-day ideas, and he will perform his role with all the *comme il faut* requisite in such circumstances."

"I have the feeling that you are jesting, my dear sir."

"Not in the least. When you have considered my proposal, you will be convinced that it is marked by its common sense and simplicity. You cannot hide a needle in a sack, and I undertake to prepare Piotr for his role and to bring him to the battlefield."

"You are still jesting," Pavel Piotrovich declared, rising from his chair. "But after the amiable readiness to meet me that you have displayed, I have no grounds for objection. Well, so everything is arranged. By the way, you haven't any pistols, have you?"

"Why should I have pistols, Pavel Piotrovich? I am not a warrior."

"In that case I offer you mine. You can be assured that it is five years since I last fired them."

"That is very comforting news."

Pavel Piotrovich picked up his stick.

"After which, dear sir, it only remains for me to express my gratitude to you and to let you return to your occupations. I have the honor to take my leave."

"Till our next pleasant meeting, my dear sir," Bazarov said, showing out his guest.

Pavel Piotrovich had left the room, but Bazarov remained standing before the door. Suddenly he exclaimed: "Pah, the devil! How noble, and how idiotic! What a comedy we played! Trained dogs dance on their hind legs like that. But it was impossible to refuse him; why, if I had he would have struck me, and then — " Bazarov turned pale at the very thought; all his pride rose on its hind legs. "Then I would have had to strangle him like a kitten." He returned to his microscope; but his heart was profoundly disturbed, and the calm necessary to scientific observation had vanished. "He saw us this morning," he thought; "but did he really take this step for the sake of his brother? And over what a serious matter — a kiss! There's something else behind all this. Why, I suppose he isn't in love with her himself? Of course he is! That's as clear as daylight. What a tangle! Who'd have thought it! . . . It's bad!" he decided at last, "it's bad, whichever way you look at it. To begin with, I shall have to face a bullet, and in any case I shall have to go away; and then there's Arkady, and that ladybird, Nikolai Piotrovich. It's bad, bad."

Somehow the day passed unusually quietly and languidly. It was as though Fenichka did not exist: she remained in her little room like a mouse in its hole. Nikolai Piotrovich had a preoccupied air. It had been reported to him that rust had appeared in his wheat, a crop on which he particularly relied. Pavel Piotrovich oppressed everybody, even Prokofich, with his icy courtesy. Bazarov started to write a letter to his father, but tore it up and flung it under the table. "If I die," he thought, "they will hear about it; but I shan't die. I shall hang about this world a long time yet." He ordered Piotr to come to him on important business next morning as soon as day broke; Piotr got it into his head that Bazarov wanted to take him with him to Petersburg. Bazarov went to bed late, and all night he was tormented by disjointed dreams. . . . Mme Odintsova hovered around him, and she was his mother too; she was followed about by a kitten with black whiskers, and the kitten was Fenichka; but Pavel Piotrovich appeared to him in the guise of a great forest, which he had to fight none the less. Piotr awakened him at four o'clock; he at once dressed and went out with him.

The morning was glorious, fresh; little speckled clouds hung like fleeces in the pallidly clear azure; a fine dew was sprinkled over the leaves and the grass, and glistened with silver on the spider-webs; the moist, dark earth still seemed to retain the ruddy traces of the dawn; from all the sky poured the songs of skylarks. Bazarov reached the grove, sat down in the shade at the edge, and only then revealed to Piotr what service he expected from him. The educated valet was terrified to death; but Bazarov calmed him with the assurance that he would have nothing to do but stand some distance off and watch, and that he would not have to undertake any responsibility at all. "But meanwhile," he added, "think of the important role you will have to play!" Piotr flung out his hands, cast down his eyes, and, looking quite green, leaned against a birch.

The road from Marino wound round the little wood; on it lay a light dust, as yet untouched by wheel or foot. Bazarov involuntarily gazed along that road and tore up and chewed grass, but continually told himself: "How idiotic!" The morning chill made him shiver once or twice. . . . Piotr looked at him despondently, but Bazarov only smiled; he was not afraid.

The sound of horses' hoofs along the road came to their ears. . . . A peasant appeared round the trees. He was driving two hobbled horses before him, and as he passed Bazarov he looked at him with a strange look, not removing his hat, an omission that evidently troubled Piotr as a bad omen. "Now, that man also has risen early," Bazarov thought, "but at least he is going about his business; but we . . . "

"I think they're coming," Piotr suddenly whispered.

Bazarov raised his head and saw Pavel Piotrovich. Dressed in a light check jacket and snow-white pantaloons, he was walking swiftly along the road; under his arm was a box wrapped in green baize.

"Pardon me, I am afraid I have kept you waiting," he said, bowing first to Bazarov, then to Piotr, for whom he now felt some respect as a kind of second. "I did not wish to disturb my valet."

"It's quite all right," Bazarov replied. "We have only just arrived."

"Ah! So much the better!" Pavel Piotrovich looked about him. "There is no one in sight, no one will interfere. . . . Can we begin?"

"We can."

"I assume you do not require any further explanations?"

"I do not."

"Would you like to load them?" Pavel Piotrovich asked as he took the pistols from the case.

"No; you load them, and I will measure the paces. I have longer legs," Bazarov added with a smile. "One, two, three . . . "

"Yevgeny Vasilich," Piotr stammered with difficulty (he was shivering as if in a fever), "say what you like, I am going — "

"Four — five. Go then, friend, go away; you can even stand behind a tree and stop your ears, so long as you don't shut your eyes; but if anyone falls, run and pick him up. Six — seven — eight — " Bazarov halted. "Enough?" he asked, turning to Pavel Piotrovich, "or shall I add two more paces?"

"As you wish," Pavel Piotrovich said, inserting a second bullet.

"Well then, we'll add two more paces." Bazarov made a line on the ground with the toe of his boot. "And there's the line. But, by the way, how many paces is each of us to walk away from the line? That's an important question too. We didn't discuss it yesterday."

"I think, ten paces," Pavel Piotrovich replied, handing Bazarov both pistols. "Will you be so good as to choose?"

"I will be so good. But you must agree, Pavel Piotrovich, that our duel is extraordinary to the point of absurdity. Just look at our second's physiognomy."

"So you still feel like jesting," said Pavel Piotrovich. "I do not deny the strangeness of our duel, but I consider it my duty to warn you that I am intending to fight seriously. *A bon entendeur, salut!*"

"Oh, I haven't any doubt that we have decided to exterminate each other; but why not laugh and why not combine *utile dulci?* There, now: you talk to me in French, and I to you in Latin."

"I shall fire to hit," Pavel Piotrovich repeated, and took up his position. Bazarov for his part counted out ten paces from the line and halted.

"Are you ready?" Pavel Piotrovich asked.

"Absolutely."

"We can advance."

Bazarov slowly moved forward, and Pavel Piotrovich advanced toward him, with his left hand in his pocket and gradually raising the pistol barrel. . . . "He's aiming straight at my nose," Bazarov thought, "and how industriously he is screwing up one eye, the brigand! All the same, this is an unpleasant sensation. I shall fix my eyes on his watch-chain. . . ." Something whizzed sharply past Bazarov's ear, and at the same moment a shot rang out. "I heard it, so nothing has happened," the thought had time to flash through his head. He advanced once more and, without taking aim, pressed the trigger.

Pavel Piotrovich quivered a little and pressed his hand to his thigh. A thin stream of blood began to flow down his white pantaloons.

Bazarov threw his pistol away and went up to his opponent.

"Are you wounded?" he asked.

"You were entitled to bring me to the line," Pavel Piotrovich said, "and this is nothing. According to our conditions each has one more shot."

"Well, you'll excuse me, but that must be some other time," Bazarov replied, and put his arm round Pavel Piotrovich, who was turning pale. "Now I am no longer a duelist but a doctor, and my first task is to look at your wound. Piotr! Come here, Piotr! Where have you hidden yourself?"

"It's only a trifle — I don't need anyone's help," Pavel Piotrovich said deliberately, "and — we — must — again — " He was about to tug at his mustache, but his hand grew weak, his eyes rolled, and he lost consciousness.

"There's a fine thing! He's fainted! What on earth!" Bazarov involuntarily exclaimed as he lowered him to the grass. "Let's see what has happened." He took out his handkerchief, wiped away the blood, and groped around the wound. . . . "The bone is whole," he muttered between his teeth; "the bullet passed through at no great depth, only the muscle, the *vastus externus*, is torn. He'll be dancing again in three weeks! So it's a faint! Oh, I do like these nervous people! Why, look how thin his skin is!"

"Is he dead?" Piotr's quavering voice whispered behind his back.

Bazarov looked round.

"Go and get water quickly, friend, and he'll yet outlive both you and me."

But apparently this perfect servant did not understand his words, and he did not stir from the spot. Pavel Piotrovich slowly opened his eyes. "He's dying!" Piotr whispered, and began to cross himself.

"You're right — what a stupid physiognomy!" the wounded gentleman said with a forced smile.

"Go and get some water at once, damn you!" Bazarov shouted.

"There's no need. It was only a momentary *vertige*. . . . Help me to sit up . . . that's right . . . I only need to hold something against this scratch, and I shall walk home, or they can send a droshky for me. If you agree, the duel will not be renewed. You have acted magnanimously — today, only today, please note."

"There's no point in recalling the past," Bazarov retorted, "and as for the future, it is not worth racking one's brains over that either, because I intend to slip away at once. Let me bandage your leg now; your wound is not dangerous, but it will be best to stop the blood. But first we must bring this mortal back to life."

Bazarov shook Piotr by the shoulder and sent him off for a droshky.

"Listen now, don't frighten my brother," Pavel Piotrovich said to him; 'you're not to think of reporting this business to him."

Piotr dashed off; while he was gone for the droshky the two opponents sat on the ground and were silent. Pavel Piotrovich tried to avoid looking at Bazarov; even now he was not prepared to be reconciled to him; he was ashamed of his own arrogance, his failure, he was ashamed of all the things he had devised, though he felt also that it could not have ended in any more satisfactory manner. "At any rate he won't be hanging about here," he reassured himself, "and thanks for that." The prolonged silence grew heavy and awkward. They both felt uncomfortable. Each of them realized that the other understood him. To friends such a realization is pleasant, but it is highly unpleasant to people who are not friends, especially when they can neither have an explanation nor part company.

"I haven't bandaged your leg too tightly, have I?" Bazarov asked at last.

"No, it is quite all right, it is excellent," Pavel Piotrovich replied. After a momentary pause he added: "There is no way of deceiving my brother; we shall have to tell him we quarreled over politics."

"Very good," said Bazarov. "You can say that I cursed all Anglophils."

"That is an excellent idea. What do you think, what is that man thinking about us now?" Pavel Piotrovich went on, pointing to the same peasant who had driven the hobbled horses past Bazarov a few minutes before the duel, and who, as he returned along the road, "fussed" and removed his hat at the sight of the "gentlemen."

"Who is to know what he thinks?" Bazarov replied; "most probably he isn't thinking at all. The Russian peasant is the same mysterious stranger of whom Mrs. Radcliffe once said so much. Who can understand him? He doesn't even understand himself."

"So that is what you think!" Pavel Piotrovich began, but abruptly exclaimed: "Look what your stupid fool Piotr has done! Why, there is my brother galloping toward us."

Bazarov turned, and saw Nikolai Piotrovich's pale face as he came along in the droshky. He jumped out before it stopped, and rushed to his brother.

"What does this mean?" he said in an agitated tone. "Yevgeny Vasilich, pardon me, but what is all this?"

"It is nothing," Pavel Piotrovich replied, "there was no need to alarm you. I have had a little quarrel with Mr. Bazarov, and I have paid a little for it."

"But what was it all about, for God's sake?"

"It is difficult to explain. Mr. Bazarov spoke disrespectfully of Sir Robert Peel. I hasten to add that I alone am to blame for everything, and Mr. Bazarov conducted himself admirably. I challenged him."

"But you're bleeding, look at you!"

"But did you think I had water in my veins? This bloodletting will even be beneficial. Is that not so, doctor? Help me to get into the droshky, and do not let it depress you. I shall be well again tomorrow. That is right; excellent! You can start, coachman."

Nikolai Piotrovich walked behind the droshky; Bazarov was about to fall back. . . .

"I must ask you to attend to my brother," Nikolai Piotrovich said to him, "until another doctor can arrive from the town."

Bazarov nodded without speaking.

An hour later Pavel Piotrovich was lying in bed with an artistically bandaged leg. All the house was plunged into consternation; Fenichka was taken unwell. Nikolai Piotrovich surreptitiously wrung his hands, but Pavel Piotrovich laughed and joked, especially with Bazarov; he put on a thin batiste shirt, an elegant morning jacket, and a fez, did not allow the window blinds to be lowered, and divertingly grumbled about the necessity to abstain from food.

By nightfall, however, he was running a fever; his head began to ache. The doctor from the town arrived. (Nikolai Piotrovich paid no heed to his brother, and Bazarov himself wanted the doctor to be sent for; he had sat all day in his room, jaundiced and ill-tempered, and went only on the very shortest of visits to see the patient; once or twice he happened to fall in with Fenichka, but she turned and fled from him in terror.) The new doctor advised cooling drinks, but confirmed Bazarov's assurance that no danger whatever was to be anticipated. Nikolai Piotrovich told him that his brother had wounded himself through not taking precautions, to which the doctor replied: "Hm!" but on being given twenty-five silver rubles in cash he said: "You don't say so! That does happen quite often, I know."

No one in the house went to bed or undressed. From time to time Nikolai Piotrovich tiptoed in to his brother and tiptoed out again; Pavel Piotrovich was dozing; he groaned a little, said to him in French: "*Couchez-vous*," and asked for a drink. On one of these occasions Nikolai Piotrovich made Fenichka take him a glass of lemonade; Pavel Piotrovich gazed at her fixedly and drank every drop of the liquid. Toward morning the fever increased a little, and the patient was slightly delirious. At first he uttered incoherent remarks; then he suddenly opened his eyes and, seeing his brother anxiously bending over him, he said:

"But don't you agree, Nikolai, Fenichka has something in common with Nelly?"

"With which Nelly, Pavel?"

"How can you ask that? With Princess R. Especially in the upper part of her face. *C'est de la même famille.*"

Nikolai Piotrovich made no answer, but inwardly he was astonished at the vitality of such long-past feelings in his brother. "Coming up after all this time!" he thought.

"Ah, how I love that empty creature!" Pavel Piotrovich groaned, throwing his arms behind his head with a yearning movement. "I cannot endure that some insolent nincompoop should dare to touch . . ." he stammered a few moments later.

Nikolai Piotrovich only sighed; he had no suspicion of the person to whom these words really referred.

Bazarov called on him the next morning, at eight o'clock. He had already packed and had set free all his frogs, insects, and birds.

"You have come to say good-by?" Nikolai Piotrovich said, rising to meet him.

"Exactly."

"I understand, and I entirely approve. Of course, my poor brother is to blame, and for that he is punished. He has told me he placed you in a position in which it was impossible for you to do otherwise. I believe it was impossible for you to avoid that duel, which — which to some extent is explained only by the constant antagonism of your mutual views." (Nikolai Piotrovich was getting his words mixed.) "My brother is a man of the old school, fiery and obstinate. . . . Thank God that it has ended as it has. I have taken all necessary measures to avoid publicity. . . ."

"I shall leave you my address, in case any trouble arises," Bazarov remarked perfunctorily.

"I hope that trouble will not arise, Yevgeny Vasilich. . . . I am very sorry that your stay in my house has had such — such an end. It is all the more upsetting for me because Arkady — "

"I expect I shall see him," replied Bazarov, who was always provoked to impatience by any kind of "explanation" and "declaration." "In the contrary case, I ask you to greet him for me and to accept the expression of my regrets."

"And I ask . . ." Nikolai Piotrovich replied with a bow; but Bazarov went out without waiting to hear the end of his phrase.

Learning that Bazarov was leaving, Pavel Piotrovich expressed the wish to see him and shake his hand. But Bazarov remained as cold as ice; he realized that Pavel Piotrovich wanted to display his magnanimity. He did not have a chance to say good-by to Fenichka: he only exchanged glances with her from the window. He thought her face seemed mournful. "I suppose she'll be ruined," he said to himself. "Well, she'll get away, somehow." On the other hand, Piotr was so upset that he wept on Bazarov's shoulder, until he froze the valet with the question: "Aren't your eyes on a wet spot?" And Duniasha had to flee to the grove in order to conceal her agitation. The cause of all this unhappiness climbed into his cart and lit a cigar. And when, at a turn in the road, some two miles away, he had a last view of the Kirsanov estate, stretching in a single line, with its masters' new house, he only spat and, muttering: "Damned petty gentry!" wrapped himself more closely in his greatcoat.

Pavel Piotrovich soon began to mend; but he had to lie in bed for about a week. He endured his "captivity," as he expressed it, quite patiently, but he took a lot of trouble over his toilet and continually ordered the servants to sprinkle his room with eau de Cologne. Nikolai Piotrovich read magazines to him; Fenichka waited on him as before, brought him bouillon, lemonade, soft-boiled eggs, and tea; but a secret horror took hold of her every time she entered his room. Pavel Piotrovich's unexpected behavior had alarmed all the people in the house, but her above all the others; only Prokofich was not perturbed; he explained that in his time too the gentlemen had made holes in one another, "but only noble people among themselves; they'd have ordered such upstarts to be flogged in the stable for their insolence."

Conscience hardly troubled Fenichka at all; but the thought of the real cause of the quarrel tormented her at times; and Pavel Piotrovich, too, looked at her so strangely . . . so that even when she turned her back on him she felt his eyes on her. She went thin with the incessant inward anxiety and, as so often happens, grew even more attractive.

One day — it was in the morning — Pavel Piotrovich felt very well and shifted from his bed to the divan, and Nikolai Piotrovich, after inquiring after his health, went off to the threshing-floor. Fenichka brought a cup of tea and, setting it on a little table, was about to retire. Pavel Piotrovich called her back.

"Where are you off to in such a hurry, Fyodosia Nikolavna?" he began. "Have you something you must do, then?"

"No-o — ye-es. I've got to go and pour out the tea."

"Duniasha can do that without you; sit a little while with a sick man. And, by the way, I have something I want to talk about to you."

Fenichka silently sat down on the edge of an armchair.

"Listen," Pavel Piotrovich said, and he tugged at his whiskers. "I have long been wanting to ask you: you seem to be afraid of me?"

"I-I?"

"Yes, you. You never look at me, as though you hadn't a clear conscience."

Fenichka reddened, but she glanced at Pavel Piotrovich. Somehow he seemed strange, and her heart began gently to palpitate.

"But your conscience is clear, is it not?" he asked her.

"Why shouldn't it be clear?" she whispered.

"Is there not good reason? However, whom can you have wronged? Me? That is incredible. Other people here in the house? That also is not to be believed. Unless it be my brother? But then, you love him?"

"I love him."

"With all your soul, with all your heart?"

"I love Nikolai Piotrovich with all my heart."

"Is that true? Look at me, Fenichka" (it was the first time he had addressed her by this diminutive of her Christian name). ". . . You know, lying is a great sin!"

"I am not lying, Pavel Piotrovich. If I did not love Nikolai Piotrovich I wouldn't want to live."

"And you will never desert him for anyone else?"

"Whom else can I desert him for?"

"Are there so few! Why, there is that gentleman who has just left us."

Fenichka rose to her feet.

"Good Lord, Pavel Piotrovich, what are you torturing me for? What have I done to you? How can you say such things? . . ."

"Fenichka," Pavel Piotrovich said in a mournful tone, "you see, I saw —"

"And what did you see?"

"Why, there — in the arbor."

Fenichka reddened to her ears and the roots of her hair.

"But how am I to blame for that?" she uttered with difficulty.

Pavel Piotrovich half raised himself.

"You are not to blame? No? Not in the least?"

"I love only Nikolai Piotrovich in all the world, and I shall love him forever!" Fenichka said with sudden strength, though sobs rose in her throat. "But as for what you have seen, I shall say even at the Day of Judgment that I was not in the least to blame for it, and never have been, and it would be better for me to die here and now if I am to be suspected of such a thing, that to my protector, Nikolai Piotrovich, I —"

But now her voice betrayed her, and at the same time she felt Pavel Piotrovich seize and squeeze her hand. . . . She stared at him, and was petrified. He had gone even paler; his eyes were glittering and, most surprising of all, a single heavy tear rolled down his cheek.

"Fenichka!" he said in a peculiar whisper, "love, love my brother! He is such a good, kind man! Never betray him for anyone in the world, never listen to anyone's speeches! Think, what can there be worse than to love and not be loved! Never desert my poor Nikolai!"

Fenichka's tears dried, and her fear passed, so great was her astonishment. But what happened to her when Pavel Piotrovich, Pavel Piotrovich himself, pressed her hand to his lips, and so remained with his lips pressed to her hand, not kissing it, and only sometimes sighing convulsively. . . .

"Lord," she thought, "he isn't having a fit, is he?"

But at that moment all his past ruined life was quivering within him.

The staircase creaked under hurried steps. . . . He pushed her away and flung his head back on the pillow. The door opened — and Nikolai Piotrovich appeared, cheerful, fresh, ruddy. Mitya, as fresh and ruddy as his father, was dancing in only his little shirt at Nikolai's chest, clinging with bare little feet to the large buttons of his country coat.

Fenichka rushed to him and, twining her arms round him and their son, dropped her head on his shoulder. Nikolai Piotrovich was amazed: never before had the bashful and modest Fenichka caressed him in the presence of a third person.

"What is the matter?" he said, looking at his brother, and he handed Mitya to her. "You don't feel any worse?" he asked, going over to Pavel Piotrovich.

His brother buried his face in his batiste handkerchief.

"No — it is — it is nothing. . . . On the contrary, I feel very much better."

"You were in too much of a hurry to get onto the divan. Where are you going?" Nikolai Piotrovich added, turning to Fenichka; but she had already slammed the door behind her. "I thought I would bring you my hero to show to you; he was anxious to see his uncle. Why did she carry him off? All the same, what is the matter with you? Has anything happened between you here?"

"Brother!" Pavel Piotrovich solemnly pronounced.

Nikolai Piotrovich shivered. He suddenly had a feeling of dread, though he did not understand why.

"Brother," Pavel Piotrovich repeated, "give me your word that you will fulfill my one request."

"What request? Speak!"

"It is very important; as I understand it, on it depends all the happiness of your life. All this time I have pondered a great deal on what I want to say to you now. . . . Brother, fulfill your obligation, the obligation of an honest and a noble man, put an end to this scandal and evil example, which you, the finest of men, are setting!"

"What are you trying to say, Pavel?"

"Marry Fenichka. . . . She loves you; she — is the mother of your son."

Nikolai Piotrovich fell back a step and flung out his hands.

"Do you say that, Pavel? You, whom I have always regarded as an inflexible opponent of such marriages! You say that! But don't you really know that it is only out of respect for you that I have not done what you so rightly call my duty?"

"In that case your respect for me was wasted," Pavel Piotrovich retorted with a dreary smile. "I am beginning to think that Bazarov was right when he reproached me with aristocratism. No, dear brother, we have done enough posing and caring what the world thinks: we are old and humble now; it is time we laid aside all vanity. We shall simply, as you say, begin to do our duty; and, you see, we shall be given happiness into the bargain."

Nikolai Piotrovich rushed to embrace his brother.

"You have finally opened my eyes!" he exclaimed. "I knew I was right in always declaring that you are the kindest and wisest man in the world; but now I see that you are as sensible as you are magnanimous."

"Quieter, quieter," Pavel Piotrovich interrupted him. "Don't irritate the leg of your sensible brother, who when just under fifty fought a duel like any ensign. And so the question is decided: Fenichka will be my — belle-sœur."

"My dear Pavel! But what will Arkady say?"

"Arkady? He will be delighted, I should think. Marriage is not one of his principles, but on the other hand his feeling of equality will be flattered. And really why should there be castes in the dix-neuvième siècle?"

"Ah, Pavel, Pavel! Let me kiss you once more. Don't be afraid, I'll do it gently."

The brothers embraced.

"What do you think, should you not inform her of your intention at once?" Pavel Piotrovich asked.

"What is the hurry?" Nikolai Piotrovich objected. "Have you two had a conversation, then?"

"We two had a conversation? Quelle idée!"

"Well, that's all right. You get well first, and this matter will not be lost sight of, we must think it over well, take into consideration —"

"But you have decided, have you not?"

"Of course I have decided, and I thank you with all my heart. I shall leave you now; you must rest; any agitation is harmful to you. . . . But we'll talk about it again. You have some sleep, my dear brother, and God grant you your health again."

"What is he so thankful to me about?" Pavel Piotrovich thought when he was left alone. "As though it did not depend on him! But I, as soon as he is married, I shall go off somewhere, to Dresden or Florence, and shall live there until I die."

Pavel Piotrovich moistened his brow with eau de Cologne and closed his eyes. Lit up by the brilliant daylight, his handsome, emaciated head lay on the white pillow like the head of a corpse. . . . And, indeed, he was a corpse.

XXV

At Nikolskoe, in the garden, in the shadow of a tall ash, Katya and Arkady were sitting on a grassy bank; Fifi had made herself comfortable beside them, giving her long body that elegant contour which among hunters is called "hare's lair." Both Arkady and Katya were silent; he held a half-open book in his hands, while she was picking out the crumbs of white bread left in a basket and throwing them to a little family of sparrows that, with their peculiar cowardly impudence, were hopping and twittering right by her feet. A gentle breeze, whispering in the leaves of the ash, quietly shifted pale golden patches of light backward and forward, over the dark path and over Fifi's yellow back; a level shadow enveloped Arkady and Katya; only occasionally did a brilliant streak catch fire in her hair. They were both silent; but in the very way they were silent, in the way they were sitting side by side, a trustful friendship was revealed; each of them seemed not to be thinking of his or her companion, yet secretly was rejoicing in their proximity. Their faces, too, had changed since we last saw them: Arkady seemed to be more tranquil, Katya more animated and bolder.

"Don't you think," Arkady began, "that in Russian the ash is very well named? There is no other tree that rises so lightly and serenely into the air."[1]

Katya raised her eyes and said: "Yes"; but Arkady thought: "Now *she* won't reproach me with expressing myself *beautifully*."

"I am not fond of Heine," Katya began, indicating with her eyes the book Arkady held in his hands, "either when he laughs or when he weeps; I am fond of him when he is thoughtful and sad."

"But I like him when he laughs," Arkady remarked.

"That is because you still have traces of your former satirical tendencies." ("Former tendencies!" thought Arkady; "if Bazarov

[1] A play on words: *yasen*, ash; *yasno*, brightly, serenely. (Tr.)

were to hear that!") "You wait a little longer, and we shall change you completely."

"Who will change me? You?"

"Who will? Why, my sister; Porfiry Platonovich, whom you have already stopped quarreling with; my aunt, whom you escorted to church three days ago."

"But I couldn't refuse her! And as for Anna Sergeevna, you remember that she herself agreed with Yevgeny on many things."

"My sister was under his influence then, just as you were."

"Just as I was! Have you noticed, then, that I have now freed myself of his influence?"

Katya was silent.

"I know," Arkady continued, "that you never liked him."

"I cannot judge him."

"Do you know what, Katerina Sergeevna? Whenever I hear that reply I do not believe it. . . . There isn't a man alive on whom we cannot pass judgment! That is simply an excuse."

"Well, then I will say that he — it isn't that I don't like him, but I feel that he is alien to me, and I to him. . . . And you, too, are alien to him."

"Why am I?"

"How can I tell you? . . . He's a wild animal, and you and I are domesticated."

"Am I domesticated too?"

Katya nodded.

Arkady scratched himself behind his ear.

"Listen, Katerina Sergeevna: really, that's rather insulting."

"Why, would you like to be wild?"

"Not wild, but strong, and energetic."

"That is something you cannot hope for. . . . Your friend, on the other hand, doesn't want it, but it is in him."

"Hm! So you think he had great influence on Anna Sergeevna?"

"Yes. But no one can dominate her for long," Katya added in an undertone.

"Why do you think that?"

"She is very proud — that's not what I wanted to say — she greatly treasures her independence."

"But who doesn't?" Arkady asked. But the thought flashed through his head: "What is she getting at?" "What am I getting at?" flashed through Katya's head too. One and the same thoughts are incessantly occurring to young people who meet often and with cordial feelings for each other.

Arkady smiled and, shifting a little closer to Katya, said in a whisper:

"Confess that you are a little afraid of her."

"Of whom?"

"Of her!" Arkady repeated meaningiy.

"And are you?" Katya asked in her turn.

"I too; note that I said: 'I too!' "

Katya shook a threatening finger at him.

"That surprises me," she began; "never was my sister so well disposed toward you as she is now; much more than on your first visit."

"You don't say!"

"But haven't you noticed it? Aren't you pleased?"

Arkady sat thinking.

"How have I managed to win Anna Sergeevna's favor? Surely not by bringing her your mother's letters?"

"That was one thing, and there are other reasons too, which I shan't tell you."

"Why not?"

"I shan't tell you."

"Oh! I know you are very obstinate."

"Yes, I am obstinate."

"And observant."

Katya gave Arkady a sidelong look.

"Perhaps that annoys you? What are you thinking of?"

"I am wondering where you could have got that power of observation which you really do possess. You are so shy, so distrustful; you avoid everybody. . . ."

"I have lived a great deal alone; you can't help beginning to think about things then. But do I really avoid everybody?"

Arkady looked at her gratefully.

"All this is very fine," he went on, "but people in your position, I mean to say with your fortune, rarely possess that gift; it is as difficult for the truth to reach them as it is to reach a czar."

"But then, you see, I am not rich."

Arkady was astonished and did not immediately understand what she meant. "And of course she's right, the estate belongs entirely to her sister," the thought struck him. This thought was not unpleasant.

"How well you said that!" he observed.

"What do you mean?"

"You said it well; quite simply, without any sense of shame and without affectation. And I must say I think that anyone who knows and who says that he is poor must possess some special feeling, something rather like pride."

"Because of my sister's kindness I have never felt anything like that; I mentioned my fortune only because the question happened to come up."

"Truly; but confess that you, too, have a tiny bit of that pride I have just referred to."

"For example?"

"For example, I am sure you — forgive my question — you wouldn't marry a wealthy man?"

"If I loved him very much — no, I think even then I wouldn't."

"Ah! So you see!" Arkady exclaimed. After waiting a moment he added: "But why wouldn't you marry him?"

"Because of what even the song sings about the poor girl who married a rich man."

"Perhaps you want to domineer or — "

"Oh no! What for? On the contrary, I am ready to be submissive, except that inequality is oppressive. But to respect oneself and be submissive, that I understand; that is happiness; but a subjugated existence — no, I'd rather be as I am."

" 'I'd rather be as I am,' " Arkady echoed her. "Yes," he continued, "it is not for nothing that you are of the same blood as Anna Sergeevna; you are just as independent as she, only you are more secretive. I am sure that not for anything would you be the first to express your feelings, no matter how strong and sacred they were. . . ."

"But how could it be otherwise?" Katya asked.

"You are just as intelligent; you have just as much character as she has, if not more — "

"Please don't compare me with my sister," she hurriedly interrupted; "that is too much to my disadvantage. You seem to have forgotten that my sister is both beautiful and clever, and — you especially, Arkady Nikolaich, should not say such things, and with such a serious expression too."

"What do you mean by: 'you especially,' and why do you conclude that I am joking?"

"Of course you're joking."

"Do you think so? But supposing I am convinced of what I am saying? Supposing I consider that even now I haven't expressed myself strongly enough?"

"I don't understand you."

"You really don't? Now I see that I have overestimated your powers of observation after all."

"How?"

Arkady made no answer and turned away. Katya found a few more crumbs in the basket and began to throw them to the sparrows; but she swung her hand too violently, and they flew off without getting a peck.

"Katerina Sergeevna!" Arkady suddenly began, "I expect it is all one to you; but I tell you that I wouldn't exchange you either for your sister or for anybody else in all the world."

He rose and walked swiftly away, as though he had taken fright at the words that had burst from his lips.

But Katya dropped both hands and the basket on her knees and, turning her head, gazed long after Arkady. Little by little a crimson hue began to tinge her cheeks; but her lips did not smile, and her dark eyes expressed bewilderment and some other, at that moment still nameless feeling.

"Are you alone?" Anna Sergeevna's voice sounded beside her. "I thought you came into the garden with Arkady."

Unhurriedly Katya turned her eyes to her sister (elegantly, even exquisitely dressed, Anna Sergeevna stood on the path and tickled Fifi's ears with the tip of her open parasol) and unhurriedly she said:

"I am alone."

"I see that," her sister replied with a laugh; "so he must have gone to his room."

"Yes."

"Were you reading together?"

"Yes."

Anna Sergeevna took Katya by the chin and raised her face.

"You haven't quarreled, I hope?"

"No," Katya said, and gently removed her sister's hand.

"How solemnly you answer! I thought I would find him here

and was intending to ask him to come for a walk with me. He is always asking me to come. Some shoes have arrived for you from the town; go and try them on. I noticed yesterday that your others are quite worn out. You don't pay anything like enough attention to them, and yet you have such enchanting little feet! You have fine hands too — only they're rather large; so you must conquer with your feet. But you're not a flirt, I know."

Anna Sergeevna continued along the path, her beautiful dress rustling a little; Katya rose from the bank and, taking Heine with her, also went off — only, not to try on her shoes.

"Enchanting little feet," she thought as she slowly and easily walked up the stone steps of the terrace, which were burning hot in the sun. "Enchanting little feet, you say. . . . Well, and he will be down at those feet."

But immediately she felt ashamed, and she ran nimbly upstairs.

Arkady was walking along the corridor to his room when the steward overtook him and reported that Mr. Bazarov was sitting in his room.

"Yevgeny!" Arkady muttered almost in alarm. "Has he been here long?"

"He arrived this very minute and said that I wasn't to inform Anna Sergeevna about him, but ordered me to take him straight to you."

"I hope nothing has happened at home," Arkady thought. Hurriedly running up the stairs, he flung open the door. Bazarov's appearance at once reassured him, though a more experienced eye would probably have discovered signs of internal emotion in the unexpected guest's still energetic, but hollow-cheeked figure. With a dusty greatcoat over his shoulders, his cap on his head, he was sitting on the windowsill; he did not rise even when Arkady flung himself on his neck with noisy exclamations.

"Now this is unexpected! What fate has brought you here?" Arkady asked, fussing about the room like a man who imagines and wishes to show that he is delighted. "Everything is all right at home, they're all well, aren't they?"

"Everything is all right, but they are not all well," Bazarov said. "But don't make so much commotion, order them to bring me some kvass, and sit down and listen to what I have to tell you in a few but, I hope, quite strong words."

Arkady calmed down, and Bazarov told him about his duel with

Pavel Piotrovich. Arkady was greatly astonished and even saddened, but he did not deem it necessary to say so; he only asked whether his uncle's wound really was not dangerous and, receiving the reply that it was extremely interesting, only not in a medical sense, he smiled forcedly. But his heart felt horrified and somehow ashamed. Bazarov seemed to understand his feelings.

"Yes, brother," he said, "that is what happens through living with feudalists. You yourself become a feudalist and take part in knightly jousts. Well, and so I am on my way back to my 'fathers,'" he concluded, "and on the way I turned aside here — to tell you all this, I would say, if I did not regard a useless lie as stupid. No, I turned aside here — the devil knows why. You see, sometimes it is good for a man to take himself by the forelock and pull himself up like a turnip out of a bed; that is what I have accomplished during the last few days. . . . But I felt I wanted to take one more glance at all I have parted from, at the bed in which I was planted."

"I hope those words don't apply to me," Arkady said agitatedly; "I hope that you are not thinking of parting from *me*."

Bazarov gazed at him fixedly, almost piercingly.

"Does that upset you so very much? It seems to me that *you* have already parted from me. You are so fresh-looking and clean-looking — your affair with Anna Sergeevna must be going well."

"What affair have I with Anna Sergeevna?"

"Why, didn't you come on here from the town because of her, you fledgling? And by the way, how are the Sunday schools getting on in the town? Aren't you in love with her? Or have you begun to be mock-modest?"

"Yevgeny, you know I have always been frank with you; I can assure you, I can swear by God to you that you are mistaken."

"Hm! A new phrase!" Bazarov remarked in an undertone. "But you have nothing to get worked up about, it is a matter of complete indifference to me. A romantic would say: 'I feel that our roads are beginning to separate,' but I simply say that we have begun to pall on each other. . . ."

"Yevgeny —"

"My dear fellow, that is no misfortune; isn't there much else yet to pall on us in the world? But now I am thinking, shouldn't we say good-by? Ever since I was here I have been feeling filthy, just as though I had read too much of Gogol's letter to the Kaluga governor's wife. I may mention that I did not order the horses to be unharnessed."

"But, really, that is impossible."

"Why is it?"

"I don't speak of myself; it will be most discourteous to Anna Sergeevna, who certainly will wish to see you."

"Well, there you are mistaken."

"But, on the contrary, I am sure I am right," Arkady retorted. "And what are you dissembling for? Now the question has arisen, haven't you yourself come here because of her?"

"That, maybe, is true, but, all the same, you are mistaken."

But Arkady was right. Anna Sergeevna did want to see Bazarov, and through the butler she invited him to come to her. Bazarov changed his clothes before he went: it transpired that he had packed his new suit so that it was right to hand.

She received him not in the room where he had so unexpectedly declared his love to her, but in the reception hall. She amiably extended the tips of her fingers to him, but her face expressed an involuntary strain.

"Anna Sergeevna," Bazarov hurried to say, "above all else I must reassure you. Before you stands a mortal who has long since come to his senses, and who hopes that others have forgotten his stupidities. I am going away for a long time, and you will agree that though I am not a soft creature, it would be unpleasant for me to go with the thought that you think of me with loathing."

Anna Sergeevna sighed deeply, like a man who has just reached the summit of a lofty hill, and her face brightened with a smile. She again held out her hand to Bazarov and responded to the pressure of his hand.

"Who remembers the past, let him go hence," she said, "the more so as, to tell the truth, I, too, was to blame then, if not with my coquetry, then with something else. In a word: we will be friends as before. It was a dream, wasn't it? But who remembers dreams?"

"Who remembers them? And besides, love — is an affectation."

"Is it really? I am very glad to hear it."

So Anna Sergeevna said, and so Bazarov said; they both thought they were speaking the truth. Was the truth, all the truth, expressed in their words? They themselves did not know, and the author knows even less. But the conversation proceeded as though they absolutely believed each other.

Anna Sergeevna, among other things, asked Bazarov what he had done at the Kirsanov's house. He all but told her of his duel with Pavel Piotrovich, but refrained at the thought that she might think he was trying to win her interest, and replied that he had worked all the time.

"But I," said Anna Sergeevna, "first had an attack of hypochondria, God knows why, and I even planned to go abroad, just imagine! . . . Then that passed, your friend, Arkady Nikolaich, arrived, and I again fell into my groove, my true role."

"And what is that role, if I may ask?"

"The role of aunt, of preceptress, of mother, whatever you like to call it. By the way, do you know, I didn't understand your close friendship with Arkady Piotrovich very well before; I found him rather uninteresting. But now I have come to know him better, and I am convinced that he is intelligent. . . . But the main thing is that he is young, young — not like you and me, Yevgeny Vasilich."

"Is he still just as bashful in your presence?" Bazarov asked.

"But surely — " Anna Sergeevna began; but after a moment's thought she added: "Now he has grown more confiding, and he talks to me. Formerly he avoided me. For that matter, I for my part have not sought out his company. He and Katya are great friends."

Bazarov felt annoyed. "A woman cannot help being artful," he thought.

"You say he avoided you," he said with a cold smile. "But probably it was no secret to you that he was in love with you?"

"What? He too?" the words burst from her.

"He too," Bazarov repeated with a humble bow. "Do you mean to say you didn't know that, and that I've told you news?"

Anna Sergeevna cast down her eyes.

"You are mistaken, Yevgeny Vasilich."

"I don't think so. But perhaps I should not have mentioned it." ("But in future don't you be artful," he added to himself.)

"Why shouldn't you mention it? But I think that here also you are attaching too much importance to a momentary impression. I am beginning to think that you are inclined to exaggerate."

"We'd better not talk about it, Anna Sergeevna."

"Why not?" she retorted, but she herself changed the conversation to a different subject. Even now she felt awkward with Bazarov, though she had told him, and assured herself, that everything was forgotten. When exchanging even the simplest of remarks with him, even when joking with him, she felt a slight pang of fear. So people on board a steamship on the sea talk and laugh unconcernedly about one thing and another, as if they were on dry ground; but let the least hitch occur, let the least sign of something unusual be manifest, and at once a peculiar expression of alarm appears on all faces, testifying to the constant recognition of a constant danger.

Anna Sergeevna's talk with Bazarov did not continue much longer. She began to go into a reverie, to answer abstractedly, and finally suggested that they should go into the hall, where they found the Princess and Katya. "But where is Arkady Nikolaich?" the mistress asked. Learning that he had not been seen for more than an hour, she sent for him. He was not speedily found: he had made his way to the most remote part of the garden and, resting his chin on his folded arms, was sitting buried in thought. They were deep and serious, were those thoughts, but not sorrowful. He knew that Anna Sergeevna was sitting closeted with Bazarov, but he felt no jealousy as he had in the past; on the contrary, his face slowly lit up; seemingly he was amazed and delighted, and had decided on something.

XXVI

Mme Odintsova's late husband had not liked innovations, but he had allowed "some play of refined taste," and so had had an edifice in the style of a Greek portico of Russian brick erected in the garden, between the conservatory and the pond. In the rear, dead wall of this portico, or colonnade, six niches were made to hold statues that Odintsov had intended to order from abroad. These statues were to have represented *Isolation, Silence, Meditation, Melancholy, Bashfulness,* and *Sensibility*. One of them, the goddess *Silence*, with finger to her lips, had been brought to Nikolskoe and set up; but on the very same day the yard boys knocked her nose off, and although a neighboring plasterer undertook to give her a new nose "twice as good as the old," Odintsov had ordered her to be taken down and she was relegated to a corner of the threshing-shed, where she stood for many long years, arousing the superstitious horror of the peasant women. The front of the portico had long since been overgrown with dense bushes; only the capitals of the columns were to be seen above the pillars. It was cool inside the portico, even at noon. Since the time she had seen a grass-snake in it, Anna Sergeevna was not fond of visiting the spot; but Katya often went and sat on the large stone bench set up below one of the niches. Enveloped in coolness and shade, she read, worked, or gave herself over to that sensation of complete silence which is probably known to everybody, the charm of which consists in the barely conscious, mute observation of the broad stream of life incessantly rolling both around us and within us.

The day after Bazarov's arrival Katya was sitting on her favorite bench, and beside her Arkady was sitting once more. He had entreated her to go with him to the portico.

There was about an hour left to lunchtime; the dewy morn had already been succeeded by the burning day. Arkady's face retained its expression of the previous afternoon; Katya had a preoccupied air. Immediately after tea her sister had summoned her to her room and, after a preliminary caress, which always frightened Katya a little, had advised her to be more prudent in her behavior with Arkady, and especially to avoid conversations alone with him, as apparently they had been remarked upon by their aunt, and by all the house. In addition, the previous evening Anna Sergeevna had been out of spirits; and Katya herself had felt some embarrassment, as though she recognized her own culpability. When she yielded to Arkady's request she told herself that it was for the last time.

"Katerina Sergeevna," he began with a bashful jauntiness, "ever since I have had the happiness of living in the same house as you, I have talked much with you, and yet there is something that for me is a very important — question, which I have never yet referred to. You remarked yesterday that I had been changed here," he added, both catching and avoiding Katya's gaze, fixed on him interrogatively. "In fact, I have changed in many respects, and you know that better than anyone else — you, to whom essentially I am obliged for this change."

"I? Me?" Katya said.

"I am no longer the presumptuous lad that I was when I first arrived here," Arkady went on; "it is not for nothing that I have passed my twenty-third birthday; I still wish to be useful, I wish to devote all my powers to the truth; but I no longer seek my ideals where I sought them formerly; they present themselves to me as — much nearer. Hitherto I have not understood myself, I have set myself tasks that are beyond my strength. . . . Recently my eyes have been opened, thanks to a certain feeling. . . . I am expressing myself not quite clearly, but I hope that you will understand me. . . ."

Katya made no answer, but she ceased to look at him.

"I think," he began again, now in a more agitated tone, while above him amid the leaves of a birch a chaffinch lightheartedly sang its little song, "I think that it is the duty of any honest man to be completely frank with those — with those people who — in a word, with those who are near to him, and so I — I have the intention — "

But here Arkady's eloquence betrayed him; he stumbled, hesitated, and was forced into silence for a moment. Katya did not raise her eyes at all. It seemed as though she did not even understand what all this was leading to and was waiting for something.

"I foresee that I shall surprise you," Arkady began again, collecting his strength, "the more so as this feeling is connected to a certain extent — to a certain extent, note that — with you. Yesterday, I remember, you reproached me with lacking in seriousness," he went on, with the air of a man who has walked into a marsh and feels that with every step he is sinking more and more, yet still hastens forward, in the hope of wading out of it the sooner. "That reproach is often directed to — falls upon — young people, even after they have ceased to deserve it; and if I had more self-confidence — " ("Oh, help me, do help me!" he thought in despair, but still Katya did not turn her head) "if I could hope — "

"If I could be sure of what you are saying," Anna Sergeevna's clear voice sounded at that moment.

Arkady at once lapsed into silence, and Katya turned pale. Past the bushes covering the portico ran a path. Anna Sergeevna, accompanied by Bazarov, was walking along that path. Katya and Arkady could not see them, but they heard every word, the rustle of her dress, their very breathing. They took a few steps farther and then, as though of intent, halted right in front of the portico.

"Don't you see," Anna Sergeevna continued, "you and I blundered; neither of us is any longer in our first youth, especially I; we have seen life, we have grown tired; both of us — why should we stand on ceremony? — are intelligent; at first we interested each other, our curiosity was aroused — but then — "

"But then I played myself out," Bazarov caught her up.

"You know that was not the cause of our disagreement. But no matter how it was, we had no need of each other, that is the main thing; in us there was too much — how can I express it? — homogeneity. We didn't realize that at first. On the contrary, Arkady — "

"Do you have any need of him?" Bazarov asked.

"Enough, Yevgeny Vasilich! You say he is not indifferent to me, and I myself have always had the impression that he liked me. I know I am old enough to be his aunt, but I do not wish to conceal from you that I have begun to think of him more often. In that young and fresh feeling there is a charm — "

"The word 'fascination' is the one more commonly used in such cases," Bazarov interrupted her; a seething rancor could be distinguished in his calm but muffled voice. "Arkady was rather secretive with me yesterday and talked neither about you nor about your sister. . . . That is a serious symptom."

"He is just like a brother with Katya," Anna Sergeevna said, "and I like that quality in him, though perhaps I ought not to allow such intimacy between them."

"Is that the — sister speaking in you?" Bazarov drawled.

"Of course. . . . But what are we standing here for? Let us walk on. What a strange conversation we are having, aren't we? And could I have ever imagined that I should talk like this to you? You know I am afraid of you — and at the same time I confide in you, because essentially you are very good."

"To begin with, I am not at all good; and secondly, I have lost all meaning for you, and you tell me I am good. . . . That is exactly like laying a wreath of flowers at a dead man's head!"

"Yevgeny Vasilich, we have no power — " Anna Sergeevna began; but a wind blew up, set the leaves rustling, and carried her words away.

"But you are free," Bazarov said after a moment.

It was impossible to distinguish any more; the footsteps passed into the distance . . . everything grew silent.

Arkady turned to Katya. She was sitting in the same position, only her head hung still lower.

"Katerina Sergeevna," he said in a quivering voice and clenching his hands, "I love you forever and irrevocably, and I love nobody but you. I wanted to tell you that, to learn what you think and to ask your hand, because I, too, am not rich, and I feel that I am ready for any sacrifice. . . . You don't answer? You don't believe me? You think I am speaking frivolously? But remember these last few days! Haven't you surely long since realized that everything else — understand me aright — everything, everything else, has long since vanished without trace? Look at me, say one word to me. . . . I love — I love you . . . do believe me!"

Katya glanced at Arkady with a serious and luminous glance and, after a long reverie, hardly smiling, she said: "Yes."

Arkady jumped up from the bench.

"Yes! You said 'Yes,' Katerina Sergeevna! What does that mean? Does it mean that you realize I love you, that you believe me? . . . Or — or — I do not dare to finish — "

"Yes," Katya repeated, and this time he understood her. He seized her large, beautiful hands and, panting with rapture, pressed her to his heart. He could hardly stand on his feet and only uttered: "Katya, Katya . . . " but she innocently fell to weeping, and laughing at her tears. Anyone who has never seen such tears in the eyes of a beloved one cannot fathom to what extent, all overcome with gratitude and shame, a human being can be happy on earth.

Next day, early in the morning, Anna Sergeevna asked for Bazarov to come to her room, and with a forced laugh she handed him a folded sheet of writing-paper. It was a letter from Arkady: in it he asked for her sister's hand.

Bazarov read the letter swiftly, forcing himself to conceal the feeling of malicious pleasure that momentarily flamed up in his breast.

"There now," he said, "and you, I believe, no longer ago than yesterday were thinking that he loved Katerina Sergeevna with a brotherly love. But what do you intend to do now?"

"What do you advise me to do?" she asked, still laughing.

"Why, I think," Bazarov replied, also with a laugh, though he did not feel in the least cheerful and had no desire whatever to laugh, any more than she had, "I think you must give the young people your blessing. The match is good in every respect; Kirsanov's fortune is not too bad, he is his father's only son, and his father's a fine sort, he won't thwart it."

Mme Odintsova walked about the room. Her face went red and pale in turn.

"Do you think so?" she said. "All right, I don't see any obstacles. . . . I am glad for Katya — and for Arkady Nikolaich. Of course, I shall await his father's reply. I'll send Arkady himself to him. Well, and so it transpires I was right yesterday when I told you that we were both old people. . . . How is it I didn't have any idea of this? It amazes me!"

She again began to laugh, but at once turned away.

"The youth these days have grown very artful," Bazarov remarked, and he laughed too. After a momentary silence he spoke again. "Good-by. I wish for your sake that the affair may end in the happiest of ways; but I shall rejoice at a distance."

She turned swiftly back to him.

"Are you going away, then? Why shouldn't you remain *now*? Remain — it is cheerful talking to you — just as though one were walking on the edge of a precipice. First one feels nervous, and then courage comes from somewhere or other. Remain."

"Thank you for your invitation, Anna Sergeevna, and for your flattering opinion of my conversational powers. But I consider that I have already circled too long in a sphere alien to me. Flying fish can survive in the air for a certain time, but they soon have to slap back into the water; allow me also to flop back into my element."

She gazed at Bazarov. A bitter sneer twisted his pale face. "This man loved me!" she thought. She felt sorry for him, and she sympathetically held out her hand to him.

But he, too, understood her.

"No!" he said, and he fell back a pace. "I am a poor man, but I have never yet accepted alms. Good-by, and fare well."

"I am convinced that this is not the last time we shall meet," Anna Sergeevna declared with an involuntary gesture.

"All kinds of things happen in this world!" Bazarov replied; he bowed and went out.

"And so you've thought to build yourself a nest?" he said to Arkady that same day as he squatted down, packing his trunk. "Well, it's a good idea. Only you were sly unnecessarily. I expected you to take quite a different direction. Or perhaps it rather surprised you yourself?"

"I certainly wasn't expecting it when I left you," Arkady replied, "but are you yourself being sly now in saying it's 'a good idea,' as though I didn't know your views on marriage?"

"Ah, my dear friend," Bazarov declared, "how you express yourself! Do you know what I am doing? There's some room left in my trunk, and I am putting hay into it; and that happens in our life's trunk too: we'll fill it up with anything rather than have an empty place in it. Please don't be annoyed; I expect you remember what opinion I have always held of Katerina Sergeevna. Another young lady only gets the reputation of being intelligent because she sighs intelligently; but yours stands up for herself, and stands so firmly that she will take you, too, in hand — why, yes, and that's how it should be." He slammed down the lid and rose from the floor. "But now in parting I will repeat to you — because there is no point in deluding ourselves — we are parting forever, and you are conscious of that yourself . . . you have acted sensibly; you were not created for our bitter, caustic, solitary life. You haven't either audacity or malevolence, but you have youthful daring and a youthful fervor; that is no good for our affairs. The likes of you, a nobleman, cannot get any farther than a noble humility or a noble indignation, and they are both trivial. You, for instance, don't fight — and yet you imagine yourselves as brave young lads — but we want to fight. And then what? Our dust will make your eyes smart, our filth will soil you, and besides, you haven't grown up to our level, you cannot help admiring yourself, you find it pleasant to swear at yourself; but we find it boring — give us others; we need to smash others! You're a fine fellow; but all the same you're a rather soft liberal nobleman's son — *e volatou*,[1] as my parent puts it."

"Are you saying good-by to me forever, Yevgeny," Arkady said mournfully, "and you haven't anything else to say to me than this?"

Bazarov scratched the nape of his neck.

"I have, Arkady, I have something else; only I shan't say it, be-

[1] *Et voilà tout.*

cause it is romanticism — and that means using too much syrup. But you get married quickly; and you arrange your nest and have as many children as possible. They'll be clever, if only because they will be born in their time, not like you and me. Aha! I see the horses are ready. Time I was off! I have said good-by to everybody. . . . Well, what now? Shall we embrace?"

Arkady flung himself on the neck of his former preceptor and friend, and the tears started from his eyes.

"Such is youth!" Bazarov said calmly. "But I rely on Katerina Sergeevna. You see how quickly she will comfort you!"

"Good-by, brother!" he said to Arkady when he had climbed into the cart. Pointing to a pair of daws perching side by side on the stable roof, he added: "There you are! Learn from them!"

"What does that mean?" Arkady asked.

"What? Are you so weak in natural history, then, or have you forgotten that the jackdaw is a very respectable family bird? An example for you! . . . Good-by, signor!"

With a rattle of wheels the cart rolled away.

Bazarov had spoken the truth. In conversation with Katya that evening Arkady completely forgot his preceptor. He was already beginning to be subordinated to her, and Katya felt that and was not surprised. He was to drive to Marino the following day, to see his father. Anna Sergeevna did not wish to constrain the young people and only out of propriety did not leave them too long alone. She magnanimously made sure that they were not troubled with the company of the Princess, who had been reduced to a lachrymose fury by the news of the forthcoming marriage. At first Anna Sergeevna was afraid lest the spectacle of their happiness should prove too depressing to her, but quite the contrary occurred; far from depressing her, this spectacle interested and in the end moved her. Anna Sergeevna was both delighted and saddened at the realization. "Evidently Bazarov is right," she thought; "curiosity, only curiosity, and love of peace, and egotism. . . ."

"Children," she said aloud, "tell me, is love an affectation?"

But neither Katya nor Arkady even understood her. They shunned her company; the involuntarily overheard conversation could not be forgotten. Anna Sergeevna soon set them at rest, however. And that was not difficult for her: she was herself set at rest.

XXVII

The old Bazarovs were all the more delighted at their son's abrupt arrival because it was entirely unexpected. Arina Vlasievna was so overcome and went running about the house in such a fashion that Vasily Ivanovich likened her to a little partridge; the short tail of her rather short jacket did, indeed, give her a birdlike quality. But he himself only mooed and chewed the amber mouthpiece of his pipe and, clutching his neck with his hands, twisted his head, as though testing to see whether it was screwed on properly, then suddenly opened his mouth wide and laughed without making a sound.

"I have come to stay with you for a whole six weeks, old man," Bazarov said to him. "I want to work, so please don't get in my way."

"You'll forget what I look like, that is how much I shall get in your way!" Vasily Ivanovich replied.

He kept his promise. Accommodating his son in his office as before, he all but hid away from him, and saw that his wife did not make any unnecessary demonstrations of affection. "You know, mother," he said to her, "Yevgeny got rather fed up with us on his first visit; this time we must be wiser." Arina Vlasievna agreed with her husband, but she gained little by doing so, for she saw her son only at the table and was completely afraid to talk to him. "Dear Yevgeny," she would say, and before he could look round she was fingering the strings of her reticule and stammering: "It's nothing, nothing, I just — " and then she would go off to Vasily Ivanovich and, supporting her cheek on one hand, say to him: "My dear, how am I to find out what our dear Yevgeny would like for dinner today, cabbage soup or borsch?" "But why didn't you ask him yourself?" "Because he gets fed up with me!" For that matter, Bazarov himself soon ceased to put up resistance: the fever of work fled from him and was replaced by a yearning boredom and dull anxiety. In all his movements a strange weariness was revealed; even his step, once firm and impetuously bold, was changed. He ceased to go off for lonely walks and began to seek company; he drank tea in the reception room, wandered about the garden with Vasily Ivanovich and smoked with him "in silence"; and one day he asked after Father Alexei. At first Vasily Ivanovich was delighted with this transformation, but his joy did not last long.

"Yevgeny distresses me," he quietly complained to his wife; "it isn't that he is dissatisfied or angry, that wouldn't be anything to worry about; he is embittered, he's sad — that is the terrible thing. He's always silent; if only he'd scold you and me; he's getting thin, and the color of his face isn't at all satisfactory."

"Lord, Lord," the old woman whispered, "I'd put a holy charm round his neck, but he wouldn't allow me."

Several times Vasily Ivanovich attempted very cautiously to question his son about his work, his health, about Arkady. . . . But Bazarov replied reluctantly and perfunctorily and one day, noticing during a conversation that his father was gradually leading up to something, said to him in a vexed tone: "What are you hovering about me for, just as though you were on tiptoe? That is worse than your previous manner."

"Now, now, now, I'm not doing anything," poor Vasily Ivanovich hurriedly replied.

His political allusions provoked just as little response. One day he talked about the imminent emancipation of the peasants, about progress, hoping to arouse his son's sympathy; but Bazarov unconcernedly remarked: "Yesterday as I walked past the fence I heard the local peasant lads singing, and not one of the old folk songs, but bawling the ballad: 'The time so true is coming now, my heart is conscious of love.' . . . And there's your progress!"

Sometimes Bazarov went off to the village and, quizzical as usual, fell into conversation with one of the peasants. "Well," he would say to him, "tell me all about your views on life, brother; for you know they say all the strength and the future of Russia are in you, with you a new epoch in history will begin; you will give us a real language, and laws."

The peasant either made no answer at all, or said something such as: "But we can — also, because you see — look, for instance, how our share of the land is situated."

"You tell me about your mir system, your communal organization," Bazarov interrupted him. "And is it the same mir that stands on three fishes?" [1]

[1] A play on words: "Mir" = both the Russian peasants' village community and the world. (Tr.)

"Ah, sir, it's the earth that stands on three fishes," the peasant explained reassuringly, with a patriarchally good-natured melodiousness of voice. "But it is well known that the masters are against our mir — our community, that is; because you are our fathers. And the more sternly the master demands, the sweeter it is for the peasant."

After listening to one such speech Bazarov shrugged his shoulders contemptuously and turned on his heel, while the peasant wandered home.

"What did he talk to you about?" the man was asked by another peasant of middle age and a morose visage, who, standing at the door of his hut, had been distantly present at the conversation. "About the arrears, I suppose?"

"Why about the arrears, brother of mine?" the first peasant replied, and there was no longer any trace of patriarchal melodiousness in his voice, but, on the contrary, a brusque austerity. "Why, he babbled away; he just wanted to let his tongue wag. We all know he's one of the masters; can he understand anything?"

"Yes, how can he?" the other peasant answered, and, shaking their hats and pulling down their belts, they turned to consideration of their affairs and their needs. Alas! Bazarov, contemptuously shrugging his shoulders, the Bazarov who knew how to talk to the peasants (as he had boasted in his dispute with Pavel Piotrovich), this same self-confident Bazarov did not even suspect that in their eyes he was in fact something of a jackanapes.

In the end, however, he found an occupation. One day in his presence Vasily Ivanovich bandaged a peasant's injured leg, but the old man's hands shook and he could not manage the bandages; his son helped him, and after that he began to take part in his father's practice, while continuing to make fun of the remedies he himself recommended and of his father, who at once put them into practice. But Bazarov's sneers did not trouble Vasily Ivanovich in the least; they even gave him some comfort. Holding his greasy dressing-gown together over his belly with two fingers, and smoking his pipe, he listened with pleasure; and the more malicious his son's observations, the more amiably did the gratified father chuckle, displaying every one of his blackened teeth. He even repeated Bazarov's occasional stupid or senseless remarks and, for instance, for several days on end he inappropriately and incessantly exclaimed: "Well, that's a ninth affair!" simply because his son had used that phrase on learning that his father attended morning service. "Thank goodness he's free of his hypochondria!" he whispered to his wife; "the way he rapped back at me today, it was marvelous!" Furthermore, the thought that he had such an assistant filled him with pride. "Yes, yes," he said to some peasant woman in a peasant overcoat and a horned headdress as he handed her a glass of Huillard water or a box of ointment, "you, my dear, should thank God every minute of the day that I have my son staying with me; we're treating you by the most scientific and up-to-date method now, do you understand that? The Emperor of the French, Napoleon, even he hasn't got a better doctor." But the woman, who had come to complain that she had the stitch (for that matter, she herself could not have explained what she meant by these words) only bowed and slipped her hand into her bosom, where she was carrying four eggs wrapped in the end of a towel.

On one occasion Bazarov even extracted a tooth from a peddler selling piece-goods, and although the tooth was quite ordinary, Vasily Ivanovich preserved it as a rarity and showed it to Father Alexei, repeating again and again:

"Look at those roots! What strength Yevgeny has! The peddler rose right into the air. . . . I think he could send an oak flying out of the ground!"

"Very praiseworthy!" Father Alexei said at last, not knowing how to answer and how to get rid of the ecstatic old man.

One day a peasant from a neighboring village brought to Vasily Ivanovich his brother, who was sick with typhoid. The unfortunate wretch was dying as he lay face-downward on a bunch of straw in a cart; his body was covered with dark patches; he had long since lost consciousness. Vasily Ivanovich expressed his regret that no one had thought of resorting to the aid of medicine before and announced that there was no hope. In fact, the peasant did not get his brother back home alive: the man died in the cart.

Three days later Bazarov entered his father's room and asked whether he had any silver nitrate.

"I have; what do you want it for?"

"I need it — to cauterize a small cut."

337

"Whom for?"

"Myself."

"Yourself? What's all this about? What kind of small cut? Where is it?"

"Here, on my finger. I've been to the village that typhoid case came from, you remember? For some reason they decided to open him up, and I haven't had any practice in that for a long time."

"Well?"

"Well, so I asked the county doctor to let me do it; well, and I cut myself."

Vasily Ivanovich suddenly turned white and, saying not a word, ran to his office, returning at once with a small piece of silver nitrate in his hand. Bazarov was about to take it from him and go out.

"For the very God's sake," Vasily Ivanovich said, "let me do it myself."

Bazarov smiled wryly.

"You're always keen on practicing!"

"Please don't jest. Show me your finger. It isn't a big cut, truly. Does that hurt?"

"Squeeze harder, don't be afraid."

Vasily Ivanovich stopped.

"What do you think, Yevgeny, wouldn't it be better to cauterize it with a hot iron?"

"That should have been done before, but now even silver nitrate isn't much use to tell the truth. If I have infected myself, it's too late now."

"How — too late — " Vasily Ivanovich could hardly get the words out.

"I should say! Four hours and more have passed since I did it."

Vasily Ivanovich cauterized the cut a little more.

"But do you mean to say the county doctor didn't have any silver nitrate?"

"No, he hadn't!"

"How was that, for God's sake! A doctor, and he hasn't such an indispensable article?"

"You should see his lancets!" Bazarov said, and went out.

All the rest of that day and all the following day Vasily Ivanovich resorted to every possible pretext to enter his son's room;

and although he did not even mention the cut, but tried to talk of indifferent matters, he looked so insistently into his son's eyes and watched him so anxiously that Bazarov lost his patience and threatened to go away. Vasily Ivanovich promised not to disturb him, especially as Arina Vlasievna, from whom he had of course concealed the whole affair, began to worry him by asking why he didn't sleep and what had happened to him. For two whole days he kept up his spirits, though he was far from satisfied with the look of his son, whom he watched surreptitiously. . . . But at dinner on the third day he could restrain himself no longer. Bazarov sat with head hanging and did not touch a single dish.

"Why aren't you eating, Yevgeny?" he asked, looking as cheerful as possible. "I think the food is nicely cooked."

"I don't want it, and so I don't eat it."

"Haven't you any appetite? How is your head?" he added in a diffident tone. "Is it aching?"

"Yes. Why shouldn't it ache?"

Arina Vlasievna straightened up and began to listen.

"Please don't be angry, Yevgeny," Vasily Ivanovich went on, "but won't you let me feel your pulse?"

Bazarov half rose.

"I can tell you without feeling it that I have a temperature."

"And have you had any rigor?"

"Yes, I have. I'll go and lie down; and you make me some lime tea. I must have caught a chill."

"I thought I heard you, you were coughing during the night," Arina Vlasievna remarked.

"I've caught a chill," Bazarov repeated, and went out.

Arina Vlasievna set to work to make some tea of lime flowers, but Vasily Ivanovich went into the next room and silently clutched at his hair.

Bazarov did not get up again that day, and he passed all the night in a heavy, semi-oblivious doze. At about one in the morning, opening his eyes with an effort, by the light of a little lamp he saw his father's pale face bent over him and ordered him to go out; the old man obeyed, but at once returned on tiptoe and, half hidden behind the doors of the bookcase, kept a steadfast watch on his son. Arina Vlasievna also did not go to bed and, opening the door of the room a very little, from time to time crept in to listen to "how her dear boy was breathing" and to look at Vasily Ivanovich. She could see only his motionless, bowed back, but even that gave her some relief.

In the morning Bazarov attempted to get up; his head swam, the blood started from his nose; he lay down again. His father silently waited on him; his mother went in to him and asked him how he felt. He replied: "Better," and turned to the wall. Vasily Ivanovich waved his wife away with both arms; she bit her lip to avoid bursting into tears, and went out. Everything in the house seemed suddenly to darken; all faces grew longer, a dreadful silence settled; a garrulous cock was carried from the yard down to the village and for long could not understand why he had been treated so.

Bazarov continued to lie with his face turned to the wall. Vasily Ivanovich tried to talk to him about various things, but talking wearied him, and the old man sat silent in his armchair, only cracking his fingers occasionally. He went into the garden for a few moments, stood there like a statue, as though struck by unexpressed astonishment (a look of astonishment never left his face at all during these days), and returned to his son, trying to avoid his wife's questionings. At last she seized him by the arm and convulsively, almost threateningly, said: "But what is the matter with him?" At this he stammered and forced himself to answer with a smile, but, to his own horror, instead of a smile, from somewhere inside him a laugh burst forth. He had sent for the doctor as soon as dawn came. He considered it necessary to warn his son of this step, so that he would not be angry.

Bazarov suddenly turned over on the divan, stared at his father fixedly and dully, and asked for a drink.

Vasily Ivanovich gave him some water and took the opportunity to feel his forehead. It was burning.

"Old fellow," Bazarov began in a hoarse and slow voice, "I'm in a bad way. I'm infected, and in a few days you will be burying me."

Vasily Ivanovich staggered back as though someone had struck him on the legs.

"Yevgeny!" he stammered, "what are you saying! . . . God forbid! You've caught a chill—"

"Enough of that!" Bazarov unhurriedly interrupted him. "It's not permissible for a doctor to talk like that. I have all the symptoms of infection, you know that yourself."

"But where are the symptoms — of infection, Yevgeny? . . . Don't say that!"

"But what is this?" Bazarov said, and, raising the sleeve of his shirt, he showed his father the sinister, crimson spots that had come up under his skin.

Vasily Ivanovich shivered and went cold with fear.

"Let us assume," he said at last, "let us assume — even — even if there is something in the nature of — infection — "

"Pyemia," his son prompted him.

"Why, yes — in the nature of — an epidemic — "

"*Pyemia*," Bazarov repeated harshly and distinctly. "Or have you forgotten your primers already?"

"Well, yes, yes, as you wish. . . . All the same, we shall cure you."

"Well, you hope! But that's not the point. I did not expect to die so soon; that is a chance that, to tell the truth, is very unpleasant. Now you and Mother must both rely on the fact that you are deeply religious; here's an opportunity for you to put it to the test." He drank a little more water. "But I want to ask you one thing — while my head is under my control. Tomorrow or the day after, my brain, as you know, will apply to be retired. Even now I am not quite sure whether I am making myself clear. While I was lying here I had the impression that red dogs were running round and round me, but you were pointing at me as if I were a grouse. I feel just as though I were drunk. Do you understand me all right?"

"Why, Yevgeny, you are talking quite naturally."

"So much the better; you told me you have sent for the doctor. . . . You comforted yourself with that — now comfort me: send a messenger urgently — "

"To Arkady Nikolaich?" the old man interrupted.

"Who is Arkady Nikolaich?" Bazarov said, as though uncertain. "Ah, yes! that fledgling! No, don't trouble him: he's fallen among the daws now. Don't look astonished, I'm not delirious yet. But you send a messenger urgently to — Anna Sergeevna Odintsova; there's a landowner of that name. . . . Do you know of her?" (Vasily Ivanovich nodded.) "He's to say that Yevgeny Bazarov sends his greetings and informs her that he is dying. Will you do that?"

"I will do it. . . . Only is it possible that you should die, you,

Yevgeny? . . . Judge for yourself! Where will there be any justice after that?"

"That I don't know; but you just send the messenger urgently."

"I'll send him this minute, and I'll write a letter myself."

"No, why bother? Say that I sent my greetings, that is all that is necessary. But now I'll go back to my dogs. Strange! I want to fix my thoughts on death, but nothing comes of it. I see a kind of patch . . . and nothing else."

He again turned heavily to the wall; but Vasily Ivanovich left his room and, making his way to his wife's bedroom, crumpled to his knees before the icons.

"Pray, Arina, pray!" he groaned; "our son is dying."

The doctor, the same county doctor who did not have any silver nitrate with him, arrived and, after examining the patient, advised resort to waiting methods, and at once remarked on the possibility of Bazarov's getting well.

"But have you ever happened to see anyone in my condition who did *not* depart to Elysium?" Bazarov asked. Suddenly seizing the leg of a heavy table that stood by the divan, he shook it and shifted it from its place.

"There's strength for you, strength," he said; "it's still here, but I've got to die! . . . An old man has at least had time to get unused to life, but I — But you try to deny death. It denies me, and that's all! Who's that crying?" he added after a pause. "Mother? Poor Mother! Whom will you feed now with your amazing borsch? But you, Vasily Ivanovich, you, too, seem to be down in the dumps? Well, if Christianity is of no help, be a philosopher, a stoic, won't you? After all, you did boast that you were a philosopher, didn't you?"

"What sort of philosopher am I!" Vasily Ivanovich began to bawl, and the tears rolled down his cheeks.

Bazarov grew worse with every hour; the fever took a rapid course, as it usually does with surgical infection. He had not yet lost consciousness and understood what was said to him; he still struggled. "I don't want to be delirious," he whispered, clenching his fists, "that's just idiotic!" And he added at once: "Well, if you take ten from eight, what is left?" Vasily Ivanovich went about like a lunatic, suggested first one remedy, then another, and in the end did nothing but cover his son's legs. "Wrap in cold sheets . . . an emetic . . . mustard plasters to the belly . . . bloodletting," he said tensely. The doctor, whom he implored to remain, assented to everything he proposed, gave the sick man lemonade, and asked for a pipe and something "strengthening and warming" — in other words, vodka — for himself. Arina Vlasievna sat on a low bench by the door and only went from time to time to pray; a few days previously a hand mirror had slipped out of her hand and had been shattered, and she always regarded that as a bad sign; even Anfisushka did not know what to say to her. Timofeich had been sent to tell Mme Odintsova.

The night was far from good for Bazarov. . . . The high fever tormented him. Toward morning he felt easier. He asked Arina Vlasievna to comb his hair, kissed her hand, and drank a couple of sips of tea. Vasily Ivanovich cheered up a little.

"God be thanked!" he declared; "the crisis has arrived . . . the crisis has come."

"Pah, just think of that!" Bazarov remarked. "All that that word means! He's found it, said it: 'crisis,' and he's comforted. It's astonishing how much man believes in words. Tell him, for instance, that he's a fool and don't thrash him, and he's miserable; call him a wise man and don't give him a farthing, and he feels satisfied."

This little speech, which was reminiscent of Bazarov's former sallies, deeply affected Vasily Ivanovich.

"Bravo! Excellently said, excellently!" he exclaimed, pretending to clap his hands.

Bazarov smiled mournfully.

"Well, what do you think," he said, "has the crisis arrived or passed?"

"You're better, that's what I see, that's what makes me glad," Vasily Ivanovich replied.

"Well, that's excellent; there's never any harm in being glad. But have you sent to her, you know who?"

"Yes, of course."

The change for the better did not last long. The attacks of fever were renewed. Vasily Ivanovich sat beside Bazarov. The old man seemed to be racked by some peculiar torment. He made several times as if to say something — and could not.

"Yevgeny!" he said at last; "my son, my dear, my darling son!"

This unusual call had an effect on Bazarov. He turned his head a little and, evidently striving to fight his way through from beneath the burden of the oblivion weighing upon him, he said: "What is it, my father?"

"Yevgeny," Vasily Ivanovich continued, and he dropped on his knees beside his son, though Bazarov did not open his eyes and could not see him. "Yevgeny, you're better now; if God pleases, you will get well; but take this opportunity, comfort me and your mother, fulfill the duty of a Christian! I have something to say to you, it is terrible; but still more terrible — you see, it's forever, Yevgeny — you just think, how — "

The old man's voice broke, but a strange look passed over his son's face, though he continued to lie with closed eyes.

"I do not refuse, if that may comfort you," he said at last; "but it seems to me that there is no need for haste. You yourself say that I am better."

"You're better, Yevgeny, you're better; but who knows? After all, it's in God's will, and when you have done your duty — "

"No, I'll wait," Bazarov interrupted. "I agree with you that the crisis has arrived. But if you and I are mistaken, well, after all, they administer the rites to unconscious people."

"But please, Yevgeny — "

"I'll wait. But now I want to sleep. Don't disturb me."

And he laid his head in its previous place.

The old man rose, sat down in the armchair, and, resting his chin on his hand, began to bite his fingers. . . .

The rattle of a springed carriage, the rattle that is so peculiarly audible in the quietness of the countryside, suddenly struck his ear. Nearer, still nearer rolled the light wheels; now he could hear the horses snorting. . . . Vasily Ivanovich jumped up and rushed to the little window. A two-seated chaise, harnessed to a four-in-hand, drove into the yard of his house. Not stopping to think what it might mean, in an outburst of thoughtless joy he ran out on the steps. . . . A liveried lackey opened the door of the chaise; a lady wearing a black veil, and in a black mantilla, emerged from it. . . .

"I am Odintsova," she said. "Is Yevgeny Vasilich still alive? Are you his father? I have brought a doctor with me."

"Benefactress!" Vasily Ivanovich exclaimed, and, seizing her hand, pressed it convulsively to his lips, while the doctor Anna Sergeevna had brought with her, a little man in spectacles, German to judge by his face, slid unhurriedly out of the chaise. "He's still alive, my Yevgeny's still alive, and now he will be saved! Wife! Wife! . . . An angel has come to us from heaven. . . ."

"Lord, what is all this!" the old woman stammered as she ran out from the reception room. Having no idea whatever of what was happening, in the anteroom she fell at Anna Sergeevna's feet and began to kiss her dress like a madwoman.

"What are you doing! What are you doing!" Anna Sergeevna cried, but Arina Vlasievna did not listen to her, and Vasily Ivanovich only repeated: "An angel! An angel!"

"*Wo ist der Kranke?*" the doctor said at last, not without a touch of annoyance.

Vasily Ivanovich recovered his wits.

"Here, here, please follow me, *wertester Herr Kollege*," he added as his memory of the past came back to him.

"Eh!" the German pronounced, and bared his teeth in a sour smile.

Vasily Ivanovich led him into his son's room.

"A doctor come from Anna Sergeevna Odintsova," he said bending right down to the sick man's ear. "And she's here too."

Bazarov suddenly opened his eyes.

"What did you say?"

"I said Anna Sergeevna Odintsova is here and has brought a doctor to see you."

Bazarov ran his eyes round the room.

"She's here? . . . I want to see her."

"You shall see her, Yevgeny; but first we must have a talk with the doctor. I shall tell him all the history of the case, as Sidor Sidorich has gone" (Sidor Sidorich was the county doctor) "and we'll hold a little consultation."

Bazarov glanced at the German.

"Well, get the talk over quickly; only not in Latin, for I know the meaning of *jam moritur*."

"*Der Herr scheint des Deutschen mächtig zu sein?*" the new foster-child of Æsculapius began, turning to Vasily Ivanovich.

345

Turgenev

"*Ich — gabe —* We'd better talk Russian," the old man said.

"Ah, ah! so diss iss de diss iss — Please . . ."

And the consultation began.

Half an hour later Anna Sergeevna, accompanied by Vasily Ivanovich, entered the room. The doctor had managed to whisper to her that there was not the least hope of the patient getting better.

She glanced at Bazarov — and halted at the door, so struck was she by his inflamed, yet deathly face with its dull eyes fixed on her. She was simply terrified with a cold and exhausting terror; the thought that this was not the feeling she would have experienced if she had really loved him flashed through her head.

"Thank you," he said with difficulty, "I hadn't expected this. This is kind on your part. So we have seen each other again, as you promised."

"Anna Sergeevna has been so good," Vasily Ivanovich began.

"Father, leave us. Anna Sergeevna, will you allow — ? I think, now — "

With his head he indicated his outstretched, helpless body.

Vasily Ivanovich went out.

"Well, thank you," Bazarov repeated. "This is regal of you. They say czars also visit the dying."

"Yevgeny Vasilich, I hope — "

"Oh, Anna Sergeevna, let us speak the truth. I'm done for. I've fallen under the wheel. And it transpires that there was no point in thinking about the future. It's an old story, is death, but to every man it comes anew. So far I have not been a coward . . . and then unconsciousness will come, and *fuit!*" (He feebly waved his hand.) "Well, and what have I to say to you — that I loved you? That was entirely without meaning even before, and now far more. Love is a form, but my personal form is already disintegrating. Rather let me say — how wonderful you are! And now you stand there, so beautiful — "

Anna Sergeevna involuntarily shuddered.

"It's all right, don't be alarmed — sit there. . . . Don't come near me: my illness is infectious."

Anna Sergeevna swiftly crossed the room and sat down in the chair beside the bed in which Bazarov was lying.

"Great-hearted!" he whispered. "Oh, how close, and how

346

young, fresh, pure . . . in this loathsome room! . . . Well, good-by! Live long, that is the best of all, and enjoy it, while there is time. Look, what a hideous spectacle: a half-crushed worm, and still puffing itself up! And yet it also thought: 'I'll achieve a great deal in my life, I shan't die, why should I? I have a task; why, I'm a giant!' But now the giant's whole task is to die decorously, though it is nothing to do with anyone. . . . All the same, I shan't wag my tail."

Bazarov was silent and with his hand began to grope for his glass. Anna Sergeevna gave him some drink, not taking off her gloves, and breathing apprehensively.

"You will forget me," he began again, "the dead is no comrade for the living. My father will tell you what a man Russia is losing. . . . That's all nonsense, but don't disillusion the old fellow. What comfort they get out of a child — you know. And make a fuss over Mother. After all, you won't find such people as they in your great world, even if you look for them with a candle in daylight. . . . Russia needs me. . . . No, evidently she doesn't. And who is needed? She needs the cobbler, she needs the tailor, needs the butcher — he sells meat — the butcher — wait, I'm getting mixed up. . . . There is a forest here — "

He laid his hand on his brow.

Anna Sergeevna bent over him.

"Yevgeny Vasilich, I am here."

He at once took her hand and half raised himself.

"Good-by," he said with sudden strength, and his eyes gleamed with a last gleam. "Good-by. . . . Listen — after all, I didn't kiss you that time. . . . Blow on the fading lamp, and let it go out. . . ."

Anna Sergeevna set her lips to his forehead.

"And that suffices!" he said, and fell back on the pillow. "Now — darkness . . ."

Anna Sergeevna quietly went out.

"Well?" Vasily Ivanovich asked her in a whisper.

"He's fallen asleep," she answered almost inaudibly.

Bazarov was not fated to awaken again. Toward evening he became completely unconscious, and he died the next day. Father Alexei performed the rites of religion over him. When the extreme unction was administered, when the consecrated chrism touched his breast, one of his eyes opened, and apparently, at the

sight of the priest in his vestments, the smoking censer, the candle
in front of the icon, something akin to a shudder of horror was
momentarily reflected on his deathly face. But when at last he
breathed his final breath and a general wailing arose in the house,
Vasily Ivanovich was possessed by a sudden frenzy. "I said I
would start to complain," he shouted hoarsely, with flaming, distorted face, shaking a fist in the air, as though threatening someone; "and I shall complain, I shall complain." But Arina Vlasievna,
all in tears, hung on his neck, and they fell to the ground together.
"And so they lay side by side," Anfisushka afterward related in
the servants' room, "and hung their heads, just like lambs at
noontide."

But the noontide sultriness passes, and evening and night come
on, and then the return to the quiet refuge, where there is sweet
sleep for the tormented and weary. . . .

<h3 style="text-align:center">XXVIII</h3>

Six months had passed. It was a white winter, with the cruel
stillness of cloudless frosts, packed, scrunching snow, a rosy
hoarfrost on the trees, a pallidly emerald sky, caps of smoke
above the chimneys, billows of steam from momentarily opened
doors, the faces of people fresh as though nipped, and the fussy
trot of shivering little horses. The January day was now drawing
to its end; the evening chill clenched the motionless air still more
strongly, and the blood-red sunset swiftly faded. Lights were lit
in the windows of the house at Marino; Prokofich, in a black
frock coat and white gloves, with unusual solemnity was laying
the table for seven places. A week before, in the small parish
church, two weddings had been celebrated quietly and privately:
Arkady to Katya, and Nikolai Piotrovich to Fenichka; and on
this very day Nikolai Piotrovich was giving a farewell dinner
for his brother, who was going on business to Moscow. Anna
Sergeevna had departed for that city immediately after the wedding; she had been munificent to the young couple.

They all came to the table at three o'clock exactly. Mitya
also was accommodated; he now had a nurse in a brocade headdress. Pavel Piotrovich sat between Katya and Fenichka: the
husbands were placed beside their wives. Our acquaintances had
changed of recent months; they had all seemed to improve in

their appearance and had matured; only Pavel Piotrovich was thinner, which, however, conferred still more refinement and the air of the *grand seigneur* on his expressive features. . . . Fenichka, too, had changed. In a new silk gown, a broad velvet fillet for her hair, and a golden chain round her neck, she sat deferentially motionless, deferential to herself, to everybody around her, and smiled as though she were wanting to say: "You must excuse me, I'm not to blame." And not she alone — all the others smiled, and they, too, seemed to be apologizing; they all felt a little awkward, a little sad, and fundamentally very happy. Each waited on the others with amusing anticipation, as though they had all agreed to play out some good-natured comedy. Katya was the calmest of all: she looked about her trustfully, and one could see that Nikolai Piotrovich had already come to love her obliviously. Before the dinner ended he rose and, taking his glass in his hand, turned to Pavel Piotrovich.

"You are abandoning us — you are abandoning us, dear brother," he began; "of course, not for long; but all the same I cannot but express to you that I — that we — how much I — how much we — There is all the trouble, that we do not know how to make speeches. Arkady, you say it."

"No, Papa, I haven't prepared myself."

"But I have prepared myself very well! Simply, brother, allow me to embrace you, to wish you all the best, and a very speedy return to us!"

Pavel Piotrovich kissed them all, not excluding Mitya, of course; in Fenichka's case he also kissed her hand, which she did not yet know how to hold out properly, and, drinking a second glass, said with a deep sigh: "Be happy, my friends! Farewell!" [1]

This English epilogue passed unnoticed; but they were all moved.

"In memory of Bazarov," Katya whispered into her husband's ear, and clinked glasses with him. In answer Arkady squeezed her hand, but could not bring himself to propose this toast aloud.

And that, it would seem, is the end? But perhaps some of our readers would like to know what each of the persons we have

[1] "Farewell" is in English in the Russian text.

introduced is doing now, just now. We are prepared to satisfy them.

Anna Sergeevna recently married, not for love, but out of conviction, one of the coming Russian public figures, a very intelligent man, a lawyer, with strong practical sense, resolute will, and a remarkable gift of speech, a man still young, good, and as cold as ice. They are living in great harmony with each other, and will live, perhaps, to see happiness — perhaps to love. Princess X has died, to be forgotten from the very day of her death. The Kirsanovs, father and son, have settled down at Marino. Their affairs are beginning to mend. Arkady has become a zealous master, and the "farm" is already beginning to bring in a considerable income. Nikolai Piotrovich has been elected an arbitrator between the landowners and peasants and is laboring with all his powers; he is continually driving about his district; he makes long speeches (he holds to the opinion that the peasants have to be "explained to"; in other words, by the frequent repetition of one and the same words he reduces them to weariness); none the less, to tell the truth, he does not completely satisfy either the educated noblemen, who talk sometimes with chic, sometimes with melancholy, of "*man*cipation" (saying the "an" through their noses), or the uneducated noblemen, who unceremoniously curse "this muncipation." Both the one and the other group think he is too easy-going. Katerina Sergeevna has a son, called Kolia, while Mitya is already running about in great style and prattles away garrulously. After her husband and Mitya, Fenichka — Fyodosia Nikolavna, that is — worships no one more than Arkady's wife, and when Katya sits down at the piano she is quite happy to stay with her all day. Here we may well mention Piotr. He has gone quite wooden with stupidity and importance, he pronounces all his "ye's" as "yu's," but he too has married and received a goodly dowry with his bride. She was a town gardener's daughter, who had refused two good grooms simply because they didn't have a watch; but Piotr not only had a watch, he had patent-leather boots.

In Dresden, on the Brühl Terrace, between two and four o'clock, at the most fashionable hour for walks, you may meet a man of about fifty, now quite gray and seemingly suffering from the gout, but still handsome, exquisitely attired, and with that peculiar impress which is conferred only by long mingling with the higher levels of society. He is Pavel Piotrovich. From Moscow he traveled abroad for the benefit of his health and remained to reside in Dresden, where he is well acquainted with the English and with passing Russians. With the English he behaves simply, almost modestly, but not without dignity; they find him rather boring, but respect in him the "perfect gentleman." With the Russians he is freer, he gives vent to his spleen, jeers at himself and at them; but it all proves to be very pleasant in his case, and offhand and becoming. He holds to Slavophil views: it is well known that in high society that is regarded as *très distingué*. He never reads anything in Russian, but on his writing-table there is a silver ashtray in the shape of a peasant's bast shoe. Our tourists run after him a great deal. While *in temporary opposition*, Matvei Ilich Kolyazin majestically called on him when passing through Dresden on his way to the Bohemian waters; and the natives, whom, however, he rarely meets, all but worship him. No one can so easily and quickly obtain a ticket for the court *Kapelle*, the theater, and so on as *der Herr Baron von Kirsanow*. He still does as much good as he can; he still makes quite a stir, even today; it is not for nothing that he was once a lion; but he finds life oppressive — more oppressive than he himself suspects. It is worth taking a glance at him in the Russian church, as, leaning against the side wall, bitterly pursing his lips, he is lost in thought and for a long time makes no movement at all, then abruptly starts and almost imperceptibly crosses himself. . . .

Kukshina also has gone abroad. She is in Heidelberg now and is no longer studying natural sciences, but architecture, in which, according to her, she has discovered new laws. As before, she hobnobs with students, especially with the young Russian physicists and chemists with whom Heidelberg is filled, and who, at first astonishing the native German professors with their sober view of things, now astonishes those same professors with their absolute inactivity and utter laziness.

In Petersburg Sitnikov rubs shoulders with two or three such chemists, who are not able to distinguish oxygen from hydrogen, but who are filled with nihilism and self-esteem; and he is on nodding terms with the great Yelisevich. Sitnikov also is preparing to be great and, if we may accept his assurance, is continuing Bazarov's "work." They say someone recently thrashed him, but he did not let the debt go unpaid; in a certain obscure little article, printed in a certain obscure little journal, he hinted that the man who had thrashed him was a coward. He calls this irony. His father domineers over him as before, and his wife regards him as a little fool — and a man of letters.

There is a small village cemetery in one of the remote little districts of Russia. Like almost all our cemeteries, it has a mournful appearance: the ditches surrounding it have long since been overgrown; the gray wooden crosses have faded and rotted beneath their once painted roofs; the tombstones have all shifted, as though someone were pushing at them from below; two or three meager little trees barely provide a miserable shade; sheep wander unhindered over the graves. . . . But among those graves is one that no man touches, that no creature tramples on; only the birds settle on it and sing in the dawn. An iron fencing surrounds it; two young spruces are set one at each end; in this grave Yevgeny Bazarov is buried. It is often visited by two now decrepit old people, a husband and wife from the near-by village. Supporting each other, they go with leaden steps; they approach the fencing, drop and remain on their knees, and weep long and bitterly, and gaze long and fixedly at the speechless stone beneath which their son lies; they exchange a brief word, they brush the dust from the stone, and tend the branches of the spruce trees, and pray again, and cannot tear themselves away from this spot where they seem to be nearer to their son, to memories of him. . . . Surely their prayers, their tears, are not fruitless? Surely love, their sacred, devoted love, is not lacking in omnipotence? Ah no! No matter what passionate, sinful, turbulent heart is concealed in the grave, the flowers growing on it look at us serenely with their innocent eyes; not of eternal peace alone, of that great peace of "indifferent" nature do they speak to us; they speak also of eternal reconciliation and life everlasting.

First Love

1 8 6 0

THE GUESTS had long since departed. The clock struck
half past twelve. Only the host, Sergei Nikolaich, and Vladimir
Piotrovich were left in the room.

The host rang and ordered the servant to clear the supper table.

"Well, so it's agreed," he said, making himself more comfortable in his armchair and lighting a cigar. "Each of us undertakes
to tell the story of his first love. You begin, Sergei Nikolaich."

Sergei Nikolaich, a portly man with a fair, puffy face, first
looked at his host, then fixed his eyes on the ceiling. "I never had
a first love," he said at last. "I started with my second."

"But how could you have done that?"

"Quite simply. I was eighteen when I first began to chase after
a certain very attractive young lady; but I courted her exactly
as if it were nothing new for me at all, exactly as — I paid
court to others, later. To tell the truth, the first time I fell in love
— and the last — was at the age of six, with my nurse; but that was
very long ago, I have quite forgotten the details of our relations,
and even if I could remember them, who would be interested?"

"Well, what am I to say?" the host began. "There isn't much
of interest to tell about my first love either. I never fell in love
with anyone until I met Anna Ivanovna, my present wife; and
everything went like clockwork then: our fathers arranged our
betrothal, we very quickly fell in love with each other, and we
got married without delay. So my story can be told in very few
words. I confess, gentlemen, that when I raised this question of
first love I was relying on you, — I won't say old bachelors, and
yet you're not exactly young. Surely you'll amend matters for us
with some story, Vladimir Piotrovich?"

"It so happens that my first love was not exactly ordinary,"
Vladimir Piotrovich replied after some hesitation. He was about
forty years old, and had black hair streaked with gray.

"Ah!" The host and Sergei Nikolaich exclaimed in one voice.
"So much the better. . . . Tell us the story."

Turgenev

"With pleasure. . . . But no, I won't tell you the story; I am no good at telling stories, I make them either dry and short, or long-winded and untrue to life. But if you'll allow me I'll write down all I can remember and read it to you."

At first his two friends would not agree, but he insisted on having his way. Two weeks later they met again, and he kept his promise.

This is what he had written.

I

At that time I was sixteen; it happened in the summer of 1833.

I was living with my parents in Moscow. They had rented a house for the summer close to the Kaluga Gate, opposite the Nieskuchny Gardens. I was preparing to enter the university, but I worked very little and at my leisure.

No one put any restraints on my freedom. I did what I liked, especially after I had parted from my last tutor, a Frenchman who could never get used to the idea that he had fallen "like a bomb" (*comme une bombe*) into Russia, and who spent days on end lying in bed with a fierce expression on his face. My father treated me with negligent kindness; my mother paid hardly any attention to me, though I was her only child: she was preoccupied with other cares. My father, a man still young and very handsome, had married her for money; she was ten years older than he. She had a miserable life; she was always getting upset, always jealous, always angry — but never in my father's presence. She was terribly afraid of him, and he treated her sternly, coldly, distantly. I have never known any other man so artificially calm, self-assured, and autocratic.

I shall never forget the first few weeks I spent in that house by the Kaluga Gate. The weather was perfect; we moved out of town on May 9, St. Nicholas's Day. I went walking in our garden, or about the Nieskuchny Gardens, or out beyond the city gate, taking a book with me — Kaidanov's *Course*, for instance — but rarely opening it. I spent much of my time reciting poems, for I knew very many by heart. My blood was coursing through my veins, and I was melancholy, so delightfully and absurdly; I was always expecting something, always afraid of something, and I was astonished at everything, and always at the ready. My imagination played and danced continually around the same ideas, like swifts round a belfry at dawn. I was lost in thought, I sorrowed and even wept. But through the tears and through the sorrow inspired by some melodious poem, or by the beauty of the evening, a joyous feeling of youthful and effervescent life sprang up like grass in spring.

I had a saddle-horse. I saddled her myself and rode alone to some distant spot, the farther the better; I shook out the reins in a gallop and imagined myself a knight at a tourney (how merrily the wind blew in my ears!). Or, turning my face to the sky, I took its radiant light and azure into my soul.

I remember that in those days my mind hardly ever visualized the image of a woman, the apparition of woman's love, in any definite shape; but in all my thoughts, in all my feelings, lurked a half-recognized, bashful presentiment of something new, something inexpressibly sweet — something feminine.

This presentiment, this expectation, suffused all my being: I drew it in with my breath, it flowed through my veins in every drop of my blood . . . it was fated to have speedy realization.

Our house consisted of a large timber dwelling with a columned portico and two low wings; in the left-hand wing was a tiny manufactory of cheap wallpapers; I sometimes went there to watch a dozen thin and shock-headed, hollow-cheeked boys in greasy gowns, who jumped from time to time on the wooden levers that worked the square blocks of the press and so, with the weight of their puny bodies, stamped the patterns on the wallpaper. The small wing on the right was empty, but was to be rented. One day, three weeks or so after May 9, the shutters of this wing were thrown open, and women's faces appeared at the windows: a family had come to live there. I remember that same day at dinner my mother asked our butler who our new neighbors were, and, when he mentioned the name of Princess Zasiokina, remarked not without a touch of respect: "Ah, a princess!" then added: "She cannot be very well off."

"They arrived in three droshkies," the butler observed as he respectfully presented the dish. "They haven't a carriage of their own, and the furniture they brought is hardly worth mentioning."

"Maybe," my mother replied, "but all the same a princess is better."

My father gave her a frigid look; she said no more.

Certainly the Princess Zasiokina could not have been wealthy: the small wing she had rented was so tumbledown and tiny that anyone at all well off would never have agreed to live in it. However, I paid no attention to any of this conversation. The Princess's title made little impression on me: I had recently been reading Schiller's *Robbers*.

2

I had the habit of wandering about our garden every evening with a gun and taking pot shots at the rooks. I had long felt hatred for those prudent, rapacious, and cunning birds. On the day I have already spoken of I went off into the garden as usual and, after walking fruitlessly along all the avenues (the rooks recognized me and only cawed brokenly in the distance), I happened to approach the low fence separating our domain from the narrow strip of garden extending beyond and attached to the right-hand wing. I walked along with my head sunk on my breast. Suddenly I heard voices. I looked over the fence and was petrified: I saw a strange sight.

A few paces away, in a glade between bushes of green raspberry, was a tall, graceful girl in a striped, rose-colored dress and with a white kerchief on her head; four young men were pressing round her, and she was smacking each of them in turn on the forehead with those small gray flowers — I don't know their names, but they are well known to children: the flowers form small bags and burst with a pop when you strike them against anything hard. The young men thrust out their foreheads so readily, and there was something so charming, so imperative, so gracious, amusing, and pleasant in the girl's movements, that I all but cried out with amazement and delight, and I think I would have given everything else on earth for those enchanting fingers to strike me on the forehead too. My gun slipped to the grass, I forgot everything; my eyes were fixed on that graceful waist and neck and the beautiful hands, and the rather untidy, fair hair beneath the white kerchief, and that one half-closed, intelligent eye (I was watching her from the side) and those eyelashes and the tender cheek below them. . . .

"Young man! Now, young man!" I suddenly heard a voice right beside me. "Is it permissible to stare like that at strange young ladies?"

First Love

I trembled all over, I was put to confusion. Beside me, but beyond the fence, a man with close-cut black hair was standing and gazing at me with an ironical expression. The girl turned toward me at that same moment. I saw her large gray eyes in her vivid, animated face, and all that face suddenly began to quiver, to smile; her white teeth gleamed, her eyebrows were raised amusingly. I crimsoned, snatched up my gun from the ground, and, pursued by a ringing but not ill-natured laugh, ran to my room, flung myself on my bed, and covered my face with my hands. My heart was dancing within me; I felt deeply abashed and gay; I felt an agitation I had never known before.

After a rest I combed my hair, made myself tidy, and went downstairs to tea. The image of the young girl went before me; my heart ceased to dance, but it felt a pleasant twinge.

"What is the matter with you?" my father suddenly asked me. "Have you killed a rook?"

I felt like telling him everything, but I refrained and only smiled to myself. When I went to bed, for some unknown reason I spun round three or four times on one leg, greased my hair, got into bed, and slept like a log all night. In the early morning I woke for a moment, raised my head, looked around me rapturously, and fell off to sleep again.

3

"How can I make their acquaintance?" was my first thought the moment I awoke in the morning. I went out into the garden before tea, but did not go close to the fence and did not see anyone. After we had had tea I walked up and down the road in front of the house several times and took glances at the windows from this distance. . . . I thought I saw her face behind a curtain, and in my alarm I hurriedly retreated. "All the same, we must make their acquaintance," I thought as I wandered aimlessly over the sandy waste that extends beyond the Nieskuchny Gardens. "But how? That's the problem." I recalled the tiniest details of the previous day's meeting; for some reason I remembered very clearly how she had laughed at me. But while I was working myself up and making all kinds of plans, fate was already taking care of me.

While I was out, my mother received a letter from her new neighbor; it was on gray paper and sealed with a brown seal such

357

as is used only for postal notices and to seal the corks of cheap wine-bottles. This letter, which was written in illiterate terms and slovenly handwriting, asked my mother to extend her protection to the Princess: according to her, my mother was intimately acquainted with certain important people who had the fate of the Princess and her children in their hands, as she was involved in very serious judicial cases. "I adress myself to you," she wrote, "as one noble lady to another, and moreover it is a plesure for me to have this oportunity." In conclusion she asked my mother's permission for her to call. I found my mother in an unpleasant frame of mind: my father was not at home, and she had no one with whom to discuss the letter. It was impossible not to reply to a "noble lady," and a Princess at that, but how to reply my mother could not imagine. She thought it would not be correct to write a note in French, but she herself was not very good at Russian orthography, she knew that; and she was anxious not to compromise herself. She was delighted at my arrival and at once ordered me to go to the Princess and tell her in person that my mother was always ready to do Her Excellency any service that lay in her power, and to ask her to call at one o'clock. The unexpectedly rapid fulfillment of my secret desires both delighted and frightened me. But I did not reveal the confusion into which I was plunged, and first went to my room to put on a new coat and cravat, for when at home I still went about in a jacket and turn-down collar, though I was deeply mortified at having to wear them.

4

All my body trembling uncontrollably, I entered the close and unpleasant lobby of the Zasiokins' wing and was met by an old, gray-headed servant with a dark, copper-colored face, moody little pig's eyes, and such deep furrows on the forehead and temples as I had never seen in all my life. He was carrying a picked herring backbone on a tray; shutting the door leading to the other room with his foot, he asked abruptly: "What do you want?"

"Is the Princess Zasiokina at home?" I asked.

"Vonifaty?" a jarring feminine voice shouted from the other side of the door.

The servant silently turned his back on me, revealing that the back of his livery was badly worn and had a single rusty button stamped with an armorial bearing, and went off, after setting the tray on the floor.

"Have you been to the policeman?" the same voice asked. The servant muttered something. "What? Someone come? Our neighbor's son? Well, ask him in."

The servant returned to me. "Please go into the recption room," he said as he picked up the tray from the floor. I tidied myself and went in.

I found myself in a small and not very neatly arranged room with poor furniture that looked as though it had been set out in a hurry. A woman aged about fifty, straight-haired and plain-looking, in an old green dress and with a varicolored triangular worsted neckerchief round her neck, was sitting by the window, in an armchair with a broken arm. Her small black eyes were fixed on me.

I went up to her and bowed.

"Have I the honor of speaking to Princess Zasiokina?"

"I am Princess Zasiokina. And are you Mr. V.'s son?"

"That is so. I have called with a message from my mother."

"Please sit down. Vonifaty! Where are my keys? Have you seen them?"

I told the Princess my mother's answer to her note. As she listened she tapped her fat red fingers on the windowsill, and when I had finished she fixed her eyes on me once more.

"Very good; I shall call without fail," she said. "But how young you still are! How old are you, if I may ask?"

"Sixteen," I replied with an involuntary stammer.

The Princess took some greasy, scribbled papers out of her pocket, raised them right to her nose, and began to sort them over.

"A fine age!" she said suddenly, turning and fidgeting in her chair. "But please don't stand on ceremony. I have simple ways."

"Too simple," I thought, with involuntary squeamishness running my eyes over all her unsightly figure.

At that moment another door of the reception room was swiftly flung open and the girl I had seen in the garden the previous evening entered. She raised her hand, and a derisive smile flitted over her face.

"And this is my daughter," the Princess said, pointing to the girl with her elbow. "Zenia, my dear, this is the son of our neigh-

359

bor, Mr. V. What is your name, if I may ask?" She turned to me.

"Vladimir," I replied, rising, and stuttering in my agitation.

"And your patronymic?"

"Piotrovich."

"Indeed. I knew a chief of police once whose name was Vladimir Piotrovich too. Vonifaty! Don't look for the keys. I have them in my pocket."

The young girl was still gazing at me with the same smile, her eyes half-closed and her head cocked a little on one side.

"I've already seen M'sieur Voldemar," she began. (The silvery sound of her voice ran over me like a pleasant chilliness.) "You will allow me to call you that, won't you?"

"Please!" I stammered.

"Where did you see him?" her mother asked.

The young Princess did not reply. "Are you busy now?" she said, not taking her eyes off me.

"Not at all."

"Would you like to help me ball some wool? Come with me to my room."

She nodded to me and went out. I followed her.

In the room we entered the furniture was rather better and was arranged with greater taste. At that moment, however, I was not in a state to notice anything: I walked as though in a dream, and in all my being I felt an idiotically tense felicity.

The Princess sat down, picked up a skein of crimson wool, and, pointing me to a chair opposite her, carefully opened the skein and put it over my hands. All this she did without saying a word, with an amusing deliberation of movement and with the same bright and crafty smile on her slightly parted lips. She began to wind the wool onto a card folded double, and suddenly transfixed me with such a clear and swift glance that I involuntarily cast down my eyes. When her eyes, which usually were half-closed, were opened to their full extent, her face changed completely: it was as though light had flooded over it.

"What did you think of me yesterday, M'sieur Voldemar?" she asked, after a moment. "I expect you condemned me?"

"I — Princess — I didn't think anything — how could I?" I answered in some embarrassment.

"Listen!" she retorted. "You don't know me yet; I am exceed-

ingly strange; I always like to be told the truth. I heard that
you're sixteen, and I am twenty-one; you see I am much older
than you, and so you should always tell me the truth — and do as
I tell you," she added. "Look at me; why don't you look at me?"

I was still more embarrassed; none the less, I raised my eyes to
her. She smiled, only not with her previous, but with a different,
approving smile. "Look at me," she said, caressingly lowering her
voice. "I don't dislike being looked at. I like your face; I have
a feeling we shall be friends. And do you like me?" She added
craftily.

"Princess — " I began.

"To begin with, call me Zinaida Alexandrovna; and secondly,
what is this habit children" (she corrected herself) — "young
people have of not saying frankly what they feel? That's all right
for grown-ups. Now, you do like me, don't you?"

Though I found it very pleasant to have her talking to me so
frankly, none the less I was a little annoyed. I wanted to show her
that she was not dealing with a boy, and so, adopting as non-
chalant and serious an air as possible, I said: "Of course I like
you very much, Zinaida Alexandrovna; I have no intention of
concealing that."

She shook her head deliberately. "Have you a tutor?" she suddenly asked.

"No. I haven't had a tutor for a long time."

I was lying; it was not a month since I had parted with my
Frenchman.

"Oh; why, so I see; you're quite big, really."

She gently tapped my fingers. "Hold your hands straight."
And she set to work diligently to wind the wool.

I took advantage of the circumstance that she did not raise her
eyes and began to scrutinize her, at first surreptitiously, then
more and more openly. Her face seemed even more charming
than it had looked the previous evening, so fine, intelligent, and
pleasant was everything about it. She was sitting with her back to
the window, which was hung with a white blind; the sunlight,
filtering through this blind, flooded her fluffy, golden hair, her
innocent neck, her drooping shoulders and tender, untroubled
breast with soft light. I looked at her, and how dear and close
she grew to me! I felt that I had known her a very long time,
that I had never known anything and had never even lived until

Turgenev

I met her. . . . She was wearing a dark, rather shabby dress and an apron; I think I would willingly have caressed every fold in that dress and that apron. The toes of her shoes peered out from under her dress: I would have bowed myself down to those shoes in adoration. "And so I am sitting in front of her," I thought; "I have made her acquaintance. . . . What happiness — really, what happiness!" I all but sprang off the chair in my rapture, but I only kicked my feet a little, like an infant enjoying some treat.

I felt as good as a fish in water, and I would have remained in that room forever; I would never have left that spot.

Her eyelids slowly rose, and again her shining eyes beamed before me, and again she smiled.

"How you are staring at me!" she said slowly, and threatened me with one finger.

I crimsoned. . . . "She understands everything, she sees everything," the thought flashed through my head. "And how can she help understanding and seeing everything?"

Suddenly there was a tapping sound in the next room, and a saber clattered.

"Zenia!" the Princess called from that room. "Belovzorov has brought you a kitten."

"A kitten!" Zinaida exclaimed, and, rising impetuously from the chair, she flung the ball of wool onto my knees and ran out.

I also rose and, laying the skein and ball of wool on the window-sill, went into the reception room and halted in astonishment: in the middle of the room a tabby kitten was lying with her paws spread out, and Zinaida was on her knees before it, carefully raising its tiny head. Close to the Princess was a flaxen and curly-haired young hussar with crimson face and goggling eyes; he covered almost all the wall space between the two windows.

"How funny it is!" Zinaida declared. "And its eyes are not gray, but green; and what big ears it has! Thank you, Victor Yegorich! You are very kind!"

The hussar, whom I recognized as one of the young men I had seen the previous evening, smiled and bowed, clattering his spurs and jingling the chain of his saber.

"You were so kind yesterday as to say that you wanted a tabby kitten with large ears — and here it is! Your word is law!" He bowed again.

First Love

The kitten squealed faintly and began to sniff the floor.

"Oh, it's hungry!" Zinaida exclaimed. "Vonifaty! Sonia! Bring some milk."

A maid in an old yellow dress, with a faded kerchief round her neck, brought in a saucer of milk and set it before the kitten. The kitten trembled, screwed up its eyes, and began to lap.

"What a rosy little tongue it has!" Zinaida observed, bending her head down almost to the floor and gazing at the animal from one side, with her eyes right by its nose.

The kitten drank till it had had enough and then began to purr, finically lifting its paws. Zinaida got up and, turning to the maid, said in an indifferent tone: "Take it out!"

"In exchange for the kitten, your little hand!" the hussar said, grinning and drawing up all his powerful body, which was tightly constricted in his new uniform.

"Both hands!" Zinaida retorted, and held out her hands to him. While he was kissing them she looked at me across her shoulder.

I stood rooted to the spot and did not know whether I ought to smile, to say something, or keep silent. Suddenly through the wide-open door leading to the lobby I caught sight of our servant Fyodor. He made signs to me. I mechanically went out to him.

"What do you want?" I asked.

"Your mother has sent for you," he said in a whisper. "She is angry because you haven't come back with a reply."

"But have I been here so long, then?"

"An hour and more."

"An hour and more!" I involuntarily repeated. Going back to the reception room, I began to take my leave and scrape my feet.

"Where are you going?" the young Princess asked me, looking round the hussar's body.

"I must go home. So I am to say" — I turned to her mother — "that you will call on my mother at one o'clock."

"Yes, you tell her that, my boy."

She hurriedly picked up a snuffbox and took a pinch so noisily that I shuddered. "Yes, tell her that," she repeated, blinking tearfully and wheezing.

I bowed once more, turned, and left the room with the feeling of awkwardness in the back that a very young man always feels when he knows people are staring after him.

"But don't forget to come and see us, M'sieur Voldemar," Zinaida called, and she again burst into a laugh.

"What is she always laughing for?" I thought as I returned home with Fyodor, who said not one word to me, but followed me with a disapproving air. My mother scolded me and wondered what I could have been doing so long in that Princess's place. I did not tell her and went off to my room. I suddenly felt very sad. . . . I tried not to cry. . . . I was jealous of that hussar!

5

The Princess kept her promise and called on my mother, who did not take any liking to her. I was not present at their meeting, but at table my mother told my father that she thought Princess Zasiokina *une femme très vulgaire*, that she had grown very tired of the Princess's requests that she should intercede with Princess Sergei on her behalf, that she was always involved in lawsuits and affairs, *des vilaines affaires d'argent*, and that she must be a terrible intriguer. My mother added, however, that she had invited the Princess and her daughter to dine with us next day (when I heard the words "and her daughter," I bent my head over my plate), because, after all, she was our neighbor, and a Princess. To which my father said he remembered now what sort of lady she was: in his youth he had known the late Prince Zasiokin, who had been very well brought up, but had been an empty and quarrelsome fellow. In society he had been known as *"le Parisien,"* because he had lived many years in Paris; at one time he had been very wealthy, but he had gambled away all his fortune. And for some unknown reason, possibly for money — though in any case he could have made a better choice, my father added with a frigid smile — he married the daughter of some lawyer's clerk and then began to indulge in speculation and ruined himself completely.

"So long as she doesn't ask us to lend her money," my mother observed.

"That is extremely possible," my father said calmly. "Does she speak French?"

"Very badly."

"Hm! But that doesn't matter. I think you said you had invited her daughter too; someone has assured me that she is a very pleasant and well-educated girl."

"Ah! In that case she doesn't take after her mother."

"Nor her father!" my father retorted. "He was educated too, but stupid!"

Mother sighed and was lost in thought. My father said no more. During this conversation I felt very awkward.

After dinner I went into the garden, but without my gun. I had pledged myself not to go near the Zasiokin garden, but an irresistible force drew me that way — and not for nothing. When still some distance from the fence, I saw Zinaida. This time she was alone. She was holding a small book in one hand and was walking slowly along the path. She did not notice me.

I all but let her pass, but suddenly I stopped short and coughed.

She turned, but did not stop; with one hand she threw back the broad blue ribbon of her round straw hat, then she looked at me, quietly smiled, and fixed her eyes on her book again.

I took off my cap and hesitated for a moment, then turned away with a heavy heart. *"Que suis-je pour elle?"* I thought (God knows why) in French.

I heard familiar steps behind me. I looked round: my father was coming toward me with his swift and easy stride.

"Is that the young Princess?" he asked me.

"Yes."

"Do you know her, then?"

"I saw her this morning when I called on her mother."

My father halted and, turning sharply on his heels, walked back. As he drew level with Zinaida he bowed to her politely. She bowed in reply, not without a look of astonishment, and let her book fall. I saw her following him with her eyes. My father always dressed exquisitely, in his own original and simple manner; but never had his figure seemed more finely proportioned, never had he worn his gray hat more beautifully on his still quite thick, curly hair.

I thought of going to Zinaida, but she did not even glance at me. She picked up her book and walked away.

6

I spent all that evening and the following morning in a despondent torpor. I remember I tried to work, and picked up Kaidanov, but the scrawling lines and pages of that famous primer flickered before me in vain. Ten times in succession I read the sentence: "Julius Cæsar was distinguished by his martial courage"; I understood not one word and threw the book down. Before dinner I again greased my hair and put on my coat and cravat.

"What are you wearing them for?" my mother asked. "You're not a student yet, and goodness knows whether you'll pass the entrance examination. And it isn't so long since you had the jacket made for you. You mustn't stop wearing it altogether."

"We're having guests," I whispered almost in despair.

"What rubbish! What sort of guests do you call them?"

I had to submit. I exchanged my coat for the jacket, but I did not take off the cravat. The Princess and her daughter arrived half an hour or so before dinner; the older woman was wearing the green dress I had already seen, had thrown a yellow shawl round her shoulders, and had put on an old-fashioned bonnet with flame-colored ribbons. She at once began to talk about her promissory notes, complained of her poverty, and was "importunate," but did not stand on ceremony in the least: she took snuff just as nosily, and shifted and fidgeted on her chair just as freely. Apparently it did not even occur to her that she was a Princess. On the other hand, Zinaida behaved very correctly, almost haughtily, like a real princess. Her face wore a look of cold immobility and importance, and I did not recognize her, did not recognize her looks or her smiles, though in this new guise also she seemed beautiful to me. She was wearing a light *barège* dress with pale blue figurework; her hair fell in long curls at the side of her cheeks, in the English fashion; this coiffure suited the cold expression of her face. My father sat next to her at dinnertime and entertained her with his own distinctive, elegant, and imperturbable courtesy. Occasionally he glanced at her, and occasionally she glanced at him, but so queerly, almost inimically. They carried on conversation in French; I remember I was astonished by the purity of her pronunciation. At table the older Princess was just as unconstrained as before; she ate a great deal and praised the cooking. My mother was obviously depressed by her and replied with a mournful disdain; from time to time my father knitted his brows a little. My mother did not take to Zinaida either. "She's so haughty," she said next day. "And what has she got to be haughty about, *avec sa mine de grisette?*"

"Evidently you've never seen grisettes," my father remarked.

"And thank goodness for that!"

"Of course, thank goodness — only, how can you pass judgment on them?"

Zinaida did not pay any attention to me whatever. Soon after dinner the Princess took her leave.

"I shall hope to have your protection, Maria Nikolaevna and Piotr Vasilievich," she said in a drawling voice to my father and mother. "What can I do? There were days — but they have passed. And here am I, an Excellency," she added with an unpleasant laugh; "but what's the good of honor if you haven't any food for dinner?" My father bowed to her respectfully and accompanied her to the door of the lobby. I stood beside him in my tailless jacket and stared at the floor, as though condemned to death. Zinaida's treatment of me had completely overcome me. But imagine my surprise when, as she walked past me, with the old gracious expression in her eyes she hurriedly whispered: "Come along at eight o'clock, do you hear, without fail. . . ." I was astonished, but she was already departing, throwing a white scarf over her head as she went.

7

At eight o'clock exactly, wearing my coat and with my hair combed up at the front, I entered the lobby of the small wing that the Princesses occupied. The old servant stared at me glumly and rose reluctantly from the bench. Merry voices could be heard coming from the reception room. I opened the door and started back in amazement. The young Princess was standing on a chair in the middle of the room, holding out a man's hat in front of her; five men were crowded round the chair. They were trying to put their hands into the hat, but she raised it and shook it vigorously. When she saw me she cried: "Wait, wait! We have a fresh guest; he must be given a ticket too." Lightly jumping down from the chair, she took me by the lapel of my coat. "Come on," she said, "what are you waiting for? Messieurs, let me introduce you. This is M'sieur Voldemar, our neighbor's son. And these," she added, turning to me and pointing to the guests one after another, "are Count Malevsky, Dr. Lushin, the poet Maidanov, retired Captain Nirmatsky, and Belovzorov, the hussar you have seen before. Please be friends, and good friends."

I was so embarrassed that I did not even bow to anyone. Dr. Lushin I recognized as the same swarthy gentleman who had so ruthlessly put me to shame in the garden. I did not know the others at all.

"Count!" Zinaida continued, "write a ticket for M'sieur Voldemar."

"That is unfair," the Count objected in a slightly Polish accent. He was a very handsome and fashionably dressed man with black hair, expressive hazel eyes, a thin white nose, and a scanty mustache above a very small mouth. "He hasn't played forfeits with us."

"It's unfair," Belovzorov and the gentleman described as a retired captain both repeated. The captain was a man about forty years of age, hideously pockmarked, with hair as frizzy as a Negro's, rather stocky, bowlegged, and wearing a military jacket without epaulets, flung round his shoulders.

"Write a ticket, I tell you," the Princess repeated. "What do you call this, mutiny? M'sieur Voldemar is with us for the first time, and today the law does not apply to him. Stop grumbling and write a ticket; that is my wish."

The Count shrugged his shoulders but, humbly bowing his head, took the pen in his white, beringed hand, tore off a piece of paper, and began to write on it.

"At any rate, do let us explain to Mr. Voldemar what it is all about," Lushin said in a scoffing tone, "for he looks completely bewildered. You see, young man, we're playing forfeits. The Princess has had to pay a forfeit, and the one who draws the lucky ticket will have the right to kiss her hand. Did you understand what I said?"

I only glanced at him and continued standing as before. But the Princess jumped onto the chair again and shook the hat. All the men drew round her, and I with the others.

"Maidanov," she said to the tall young man with emaciated face, small, shortsighted eyes, and extraordinarily long black hair; "you, as a poet, should be magnanimous and surrender your ticket to M'sieur Voldemar, so that he has two chances instead of one."

But Maidanov shook his head and whirled his hair. I was the last to thrust my hand into the hat. I drew out a ticket and unfolded it. Lord, what did I feel like when I read the words: "A kiss!"

"A kiss!" I involuntarily exclaimed.

"Bravo! He's won!" Zinaida cried. "I am glad!" She got down

from the chair and looked into my eyes so lucidly and sweetly that my heart beat violently. "But are you glad?" she asked me.

"I?" I stammered.

"Sell me your ticket," Belovzorov suddenly said ineptly right in my ear. "I'll give you a hundred rubles for it."

I gave him such an indignant look that Zinaida clapped her hands, while Lushin exclaimed: "Good lad!"

"But," Lushin went on, "I, as the master of ceremonies, am bound to see that all the rules are observed. M'sieur Voldemar, go down on one knee. That is our custom."

Zinaida stood in front of me with her head bent a little to one side, as though to examine me the better, and dignifiedly stretched out her hand. My eyes went misty; I tried to go down on one knee, but fell down on both my knees; and so clumsily did I press my lips against her fingers that I scratched the tip of my nose with her nail.

"Enough!" Lushin cried, and he helped me to rise.

We went on playing at forfeits. Zinaida seated me beside her. The forfeits she thought of! In one case she had to represent a "statue," and she chose the ugly poet Maidanov as her pedestal; she ordered him to lie face-downward, and even to tuck his head into his chest. The merriment did not cease for one moment. I was a privately and soberly educated lad, brought up in a genteel, sedate home, and all this noise and racket, this unceremonious, almost violent gaiety, these unprecedented relations with strangers, went to my head. I was just as intoxicated as if I had drunk too much wine. I began to laugh and talk even louder than the others, so that even the old Princess, who was closeted in the next room with some lawyer's clerk summoned into conference with her, came out to stare at me. But I felt so happy that, as we say, I did not care a fig and took no notice of anyone's sneers and wry looks. Zinaida continued to show preference for me and did not let me leave her side. In one forfeit I had to sit beside her, our heads covered with the one silk kerchief: I was supposed to tell her my greatest secret. I still remember how close together our heads were in that stifling, translucent, scented veil, how in that twilight her eyes shone very mildly and very close to me, and her parted lips breathed on me hotly, and I saw her teeth, and her hair tickled and scorched me. I was silent; she smiled mysteriously and roguishly and whispered at last: "Well, and now what?" But I only went red and laughed and turned away, and could hardly get my breath. We grew tired of forfeits, so we began to play a game in which we all had to stand in a circle holding a string, while she was in the middle. And my goodness! What rapture I felt when I forgot what I was doing and she gave me a strong, sharp smack on my extended fingers! And how I tried after that to pretend that I was forgetting again! But she only teased me and would not smack my fingers, though I left them extended.

What else did we do in the course of that evening! We played the piano and we sang and we danced and we acted a gypsy encampment. Nirmatsky was dressed as a bear and given salt water to drink. Count Malevsky showed us card tricks and ended by shuffling the cards and dealing himself a hand that held all the trumps, at which Lushin "ventured to congratulate him." Maidanov recited parts of his poem "The Murderer" (this was at the height of the romantic period in our literature), which he proposed to publish in a black jacket with the title in blood red. We stole the hat off the knees of the lawyer's clerk and made him do the Cossack dance as ransom; we dressed old Vonifaty in a bonnet, while Zinaida put on a man's hat. I could not tell you all we did. Only Belovzorov withdrew more and more into one corner, morose and angry. At times his eyes were suffused with blood, he flushed and looked as though at any moment he would charge down on us and scatter us in all directions, like splinters. But the Princess looked at him and threatened him with her finger, and once more he skulked in his corner.

At last we were worn out. Zinaida's mother was now ready for anything, as she herself expressed it, and no amount of shouting disturbed her; but even she felt tired and wanted to rest. Supper was served at midnight, and consisted of a piece of old, dry cheese and some cold patties of chopped ham, which I thought more tasty than any meat pie; there was only one bottle of wine, and that bottle was queer: dark, with a swollen neck, and the wine inside it was a rose color; however, no one drank any of it. When I left I was weary and happy to the point of exhaustion; at parting Zinaida squeezed my hand firmly and again smiled enigmatically.

The night breathed heavily and humidly into my flaming face; a storm appeared to be gathering; black clouds were growing and crawling over the sky, visibly changing their smoky outlines. A breeze trembled restlessly in the dark trees, and somewhere beyond the horizon thunder seemed to be grumbling to itself angrily and hollowly.

I made my way to my room through the back entrance. My servant was sleeping on the floor, and I had to step across him. He awoke, saw me, and reported that my mother had been annoyed with me again and had wanted to send for me to come home, but my father had restrained her. (I never went to bed without saying good-night to my mother and asking her blessing.) But there was nothing to be done about it now!

I told my man that I would undress and get myself to bed and put out the candle. . . . But I did not undress and I did not lie down.

I sat down on a chair, and sat there for a long time as though enchanted. What I felt was so new and so sweet: I sat looking about me and not stirring, breathing slowly, and only silently laughing at my memories from time to time, then going cold at the thought that I was in love, that this was it, this was love. Zinaida's face silently floated before me in the darkness — it floated up, and did not float past — her lips still enigmatically smiling, her eyes looking at me a little sidelong, interrogatively, thoughtfully, and tenderly, as they had at our parting. At last I rose, tiptoed over to my bed, and cautiously laid my head on the pillow without undressing, as though afraid that by some abrupt movement I would disturb the feeling with which I was overflowing. . . .

I lay down, but I did not even close my eyes. I quickly noticed that pallid gleams of light were continually flickering across the room toward me. I half raised myself and glanced at the window. Its transom showed up distinctly against the mysteriously and mournfully glimmering panes. A thunderstorm, I thought; and I was right, it was a thunderstorm. But it was a very long way off, and no thunder was to be heard; only dull, long, sheet lightning lit up the sky incessantly; it did not flash so much as flutter and quiver like the wings of a dying bird. I got up, went across to the window, and remained standing there till dawn came. . . . The lightning did not cease for a moment; it was what the common people call a "sparrows' night." I gazed at the silent sandy plain, at the dark mass of the Nieskuchny Gardens, at the yellowish façades of distant buildings, which seemed to be quivering with every feeble flash. I gazed and could not tear myself away; that mute lightning, those temperate flashes, seemed to be in accord with the mute and secret emotions that were flaming up inside me. The dawn began to break; the sunrise drew on in crimson patches. As the sun approached, the lightning grew paler and less frequent; it flickered more and more intermittently, and finally ceased, overborne by the sobering and indubitable light of the oncoming day . . .

Within me, too, my own lightnings faded. I felt a great weariness and stillness. . . . But Zinaida's image continued to hover triumphantly over my soul. Only, that very image seemed to grow composed: like a swan flying up from the reeds of a marsh, it separated from the other, unpleasant shapes surrounding it and, as I dropped off to sleep, I fell once more at its feet in a valedictory and trustful adoration.

O gentle feelings, tender sounds, the benignity and assuagement of the deeply moved soul, the melting joy of love's first emotions — where are you now, where are you now?

8

When I went down to tea next morning, my mother scolded me, but not so much as I had expected, and made me tell her how I had spent the previous evening. I replied in few words, omitting many of the details and trying to make it all appear as innocent as possible.

"All the same, they are not people *comme il faut*," Mother remarked, "and there is no reason why you should go chasing after them, instead of preparing for your examination and keeping yourself occupied."

As I knew that my mother's anxiety about my occupations was confined to these few words, I did not think it necessary to protest. But after tea my father took me by the arm and, leading me into the garden, made me tell him all I had seen at the Zasiokins' the previous evening.

My father had a strange influence over me, and our relations, too, were strange. He took hardly any interest in my education and upbringing, but he never upset me, he respected my freedom, and, if I may put it so, he was even polite to me . . . only he never let me draw close to him. I loved him, I admired him, he seemed to me the perfect pattern of a man, and, upon my word, how passionately I would have become attached to him if I had not continually felt that he was thrusting me off! On the other hand, if he wished, with just one word, one gesture, he could suddenly win my unbounded confidence in him. My soul would lay itself bare, I would talk to him as if he were an understanding friend, or an indulgent tutor . . . and then, just as abruptly, he would abandon me, and he again thrust me off, kindly and gently, but none the less he thrust me off.

Sometimes a spirit of gaiety came over him, and then he was ready to sport and romp with me like a boy (he was fond of all vigorous physical movement). Once — only once — he caressed me so tenderly that I all but burst into tears. But his gaiety and his tenderness vanished without trace, and the intimacy that had sprung up between us afforded me no hope whatever for the future — I might have dreamed it. There were times when I would study his intelligent, handsome, lucid face . . . my heart would begin to quiver, and all my being would be vehemently drawn toward him. . . . He seemed to feel what was going on inside me, he would pat me casually on the cheek, and either would go off or would occupy himself with something, or would go quite set and cold, as he alone could, and at once I would shrink and go cold too. His rare outbursts of feeling for me were never to be evoked by my mute but intelligible entreaties; they always came unexpectedly. In later days, when I pondered on my father's character, I came to the conclusion that he had no time for me, or for family life; he was fond of something else, and thoroughly enjoyed that something else. "You yourself take all you can, but never put yourself in someone else's hand; belong to yourself: that is the whole art of life," he once said to me. On another occasion I, as a young democrat, ventured to reflect on freedom in his presence (that day he was "good," as I used to say, and at such times I could talk with him about anything). "Freedom," he repeated. "But do you know what it is that can give man freedom?"

"No, what?"

"Will; his own will; and it gives him power too, which is better than freedom. Know how to desire, and then you will be free, and you will command."

First and foremost my father wanted to live . . . and he did live. Perhaps he had a presentiment that he would not be able to enjoy the "art" of life for long: he died at the age of forty-two.

I told my father all about my visit to the Zasiokins. He listened to me half-attentively, half-abstractedly, sitting on a bench and drawing in the sand with the butt of his whip. Very occasionally he smiled, and looked at me brightly and amusingly, and encouraged me to go on by asking brief questions and making interjections. At first I could not bring myself even to mention Zinaida's name, but I could not restrain myself, and I began to refer to her. My father went on smiling. Then he was lost in thought; he yawned and rose to his feet.

I remembered that on leaving the house he had ordered his horse to be saddled. He was an excellent horseman and could control the very wildest of horses.

"Shall I ride with you, Papa?" I asked him.

"No," he replied, and his face adopted its usual indifferent and kindly expression. "Go for a ride by yourself if you like; and tell the coachman I'm not going."

He turned his back on me and walked away swiftly. I followed him with my eyes; he vanished through the gate. I saw his hat moving along above the fence; he turned in at the Zasiokins' gate.

He remained there over an hour, but then went off at once to town and did not return home till the evening.

After dinner I myself went to call on the Zasiokins! I found only the old Princess in the reception room. When she saw me she scratched her head under her cap with the end of a knitting-needle and suddenly asked me if I would write out a soliciting letter for her.

"With pleasure," I replied, and sat down on the edge of a chair.

"Only write in a large letters," she said as she handed me a dirty sheet of paper. "But could you do it today, my dear?"

"I'll write it out this very day."

The door leading to the next room was opened very slightly and Zinaida's face appeared in the opening; it was pale, thoughtful, and the hair was thrown back negligently. She stared at me with great, cold eyes and quietly closed the door again.

"Zenia, Zenia!" her mother called. But Zinaida did not answer. I took away the Princess's letter and sat over it all the evening.

First Love

9

My "passion" began from that day. I remember I felt rather as a man must feel who has just entered the Czar's service: I had ceased to be a boy; I was in love. I have said that my passion began from that day; I could add that my torments also dated from that day. In Zinaida's absence I languished; my mind was a blank, everything dropped out of my hands, and for days on end I thought tensely only about her. . . . I languished. . . . But I felt no better in her presence. I was jealous, I realized my insignificance, I stupidly sulked and stupidly fawned; and even so an irresistible power drew me to her, and every time I crossed the threshold of her room I felt an involuntary throb of happiness. She guessed at once that I was in love with her, nor did I think to conceal the fact; she made fun of my passion, played with me, petted and tormented me. It is sweet to be the sole source, the autocratic and irresponsible cause, of another being's greatest joys and deepest sorrows — and in Zinaida's hands I was as the softest wax. For that matter, I was not the only one in love with her: all the men who visited her home went crazy over her, and she kept them all in leading strings, at her feet. She found amusement in arousing their hopes, or their fears, in twisting them round her finger at her whim (she called this knocking people against one another), and they did not even think of resisting and readily submitted to her. In all her being, so vital and beautiful, was a peculiarly enchanting blend of cunning and unconcern, artificiality and simplicity, stillness and high spirits; everything she did, or said, her every movement, was invested with a light, subtle charm, a playful strength. Her face, too, was incessantly changing, and it played too; almost in the same instant it would express derision, thoughtfulness, and passion. The most varied of feelings, light and swift, sped momentarily over her eyes and lips, like the shadows of clouds on a sunny, windy day.

She had need of every one of her devotees. Belovzorov, whom she sometimes called "my animal" and sometimes simply "mine," would readily have thrown himself into the fire for her; though he could put no hope in his mental capacity or any other qualities, he was continually proposing to her, hinting that others only talked. Maidanov answered to the poetic elements in her soul: though he was rather cold, like almost all authors, he tensely assured her, and possibly himself too, that he worshipped her, he lauded her in innumerable poems and read them to her with an unnatural yet sincere rapture. She felt sympathy for him, and at the same time she rather made fun of him; she did not really believe him and, after listening to his effusions, made him read Pushkin, in order to clear the air, as she said. Dr. Lushin, mocking and cynical of speech, knew her better than did any of the others, and loved her more than any of the others, though he ran her down behind her back and to her face. She respected him, but she did not release him and sometimes took a particular, malignant pleasure in making him feel that he, too, was in her hands. "I am a coquette, I am heartless, I have an actress's nature," she said to him once in my presence. "Well, all right! Give me your hand; I'll stick a pin in it; you will feel shame in front of this young man, it will hurt you; but all the same, Mr. Self-righteous, you've got to laugh!" Lushin flushed, turned away and bit his lips, but finished by putting out his hand. She pricked him, and he did begin to laugh . . . and she laughed too as she pushed the pin in quite deep and looked into his eyes, which vainly tried to avoid her gaze.

Least of all could I understand the relations between Zinaida and Count Malevsky. He was good-looking, adroit, and intelligent, but even I, a sixteen-year-old lad, found something dubious, something false in him, and I was amazed that Zinaida did not notice it. But perhaps she did notice this falsity and was not repelled by it. Her unsatisfactory upbringing, her strange acquaintances and habits, her mother's constant presence, the poverty and disorder of the home — everything, beginning with the very liberty that this young woman enjoyed, and her consciousness of superiority to everybody around her, developed a half-contemptuous negligence and lack of squeamishness in her. There were times when it did not matter what happened — Vonifaty might come to report that there was no sugar in the house, some petty calumny would come out, or the guests would quarrel with one another — she only shook her curls, said: "It's all nothing," and was not worried in the least.

On the other hand, there were times when all my blood boiled as I saw Malevsky go up to her, his body swaying craftily, like a fox, and then elegantly lean on the back of her chair and whisper into her ear with a self-satisfied and ingratiating little smile, while she folded her arms on her breast, looked at him attentively, and she too smiled and gently swayed her head.

"What pleasure do you get out of seeing Monsieur Malevsky?" I asked her one day.

"But he has such handsome little mustaches!" she replied. "In any case, it's nothing to do with you."

"You mustn't think I'm in love with him," she said to me on another occasion. "No, I'm not. I cannot love a man like him, a man I have to look down at. I need someone who will break me. . . . But I shall never meet such a man, thank God! I shall never be caught by anyone; no, never!"

"So you will never fall in love?"

"But how about you? Don't I love you, then?" she said, and struck me on my nose with the end of her glove.

Yes, Zinaida was always making fun of me. For three weeks I saw her every day, and there was little that she did not do with me! She rarely called on us, and I did not regret this; in our house she was transformed into a young lady, into a young princess, and I shunned her. I was afraid of betraying myself in front of my mother, who was very unfriendly to Zinaida and watched us inimically. I was not so afraid of Father; he did not appear to notice me, and he talked only little with Zinaida, though when he did he talked with particular intelligence and meaning in his words. I stopped working, reading, I even stopped wandering about the district and riding. Like a beetle tied by one leg, I continually hovered about the home of my beloved; I think I would have remained there forever . . . but that was impossible: my mother grumbled at me, and sometimes Zinaida herself drove me away. Then I locked myself in my room or went off to the very end of the garden, climbed onto the ruins of a lofty stone conservatory, and, dangling my feet from the wall overlooking the road, sat there for hours and gazed and gazed, seeing nothing. Around me white butterflies lazily fluttered over the dusty nettles, a saucy sparrow settled not far away on a broken red brick and irritatingly chirruped, incessantly twisting and turning all its body and spreading wide its tail; the rooks, still distrustful of me, occasionally cawed as they sat high up on the bare crown of a birch tree, the sun and the wind played gently among the tree's supple branches, from time to time the sounds of the bells of the Donskoi Monastery floated calmly and despondently to

377

my ears; but I sat, gazed, listened, and was entirely filled with a nameless feeling that included all feelings: sadness, and joy, and presentiment of the future, and desire, and fear of life. But at that time I understood nothing of all this, and I could not have given a name to any of the feelings that possessed me, or else I would have given all of it just one name, the name of Zinaida.

But Zinaida went on playing with me, like a cat with a mouse. At one moment she would flirt with me, and I grew excited and melted like wax; the next instant she drove me away, and I did not dare to go near her, did not dare to glance at her.

I remember she was very cold to me for several days in succession; I grew quite diffident, and when I timidly went to call on them I tried to keep near the old Princess, even though just then she was scolding and shouting a great deal: she was in a bad way with her promissory notes, and she had already had to see the police twice.

One day I was passing the well-known fence in the garden when I happened to see Zinaida: she was sitting very still on the grass, resting her head on both hands. I tried quietly to retreat, but she suddenly raised her head and beckoned to me imperatively. I was petrified: at first I did not understand her gesture. She repeated it. I at once jumped over the fence and ran up to her joyfully; but she halted me with a look and pointed to the path two steps away from her. In my confusion, not knowing what to do, I went down on my knees at the edge of the path. She was so pale, and such a bitter sorrow, such profound weariness, was expressed in all her features that my heart sank and I muttered involuntarily: "What is the matter?"

She stretched out her hand, pulled up some weed, bit it, and threw it away, as far as she could throw it.

"Do you love me very much?" she said at last. "Do you?"

I made no answer; and besides, why should I answer?

"Yes," she said, looking at me as before. "That is true. Just the same eyes," she added, then was lost in thought and covered her face with her hands. "Everything has grown repulsive to me," she whispered. "I would go off to the end of the world; I cannot bear this, I cannot cope with it. . . . And what awaits me in the future? . . . Ah, it is hard for me. . . . My God, how hard!"

"Why is it?" I asked timidly.

She did not answer and only shrugged her shoulders. I remained on my knees, looking at her with deep despondency. Every word she uttered was a stab in my heart. I think that at that moment I would willingly have given my life if only she had ceased to grieve. I looked at her and, still not understanding why she was so depressed, I vividly pictured her coming suddenly, in an outburst of uncontrollable sorrow, into the garden and falling to the ground as though mown down. It was bright and green all around us; the wind was rustling among the leaves of the trees and occasionally swaying the long cane of a raspberry above Zinaida's head. Somewhere doves were cooing, and the bees were humming as they flew low over the scanty grass. Above us the sky was a gracious azure — but I felt so sad. . . .

"Say some poetry to me," she said in an undertone, and leaned on her elbows. "I like you to say poems. You sing them, but that's nothing, that's the way of youth, Say 'On the Hills of Georgia' [1] to me. Only sit down first."

I sat down and recited "On the Hills of Georgia."

" 'That my heart simply cannot help loving' " — Zinaida repeated the line. "That is where poetry is so good: it tells of something that is not, something that not only is better than the reality, but is even more like the truth. . . .'That my heart simply cannot cease loving.' It would like to, but it cannot." She was silent again and suddenly started and rose. "Let's go. Maidanov is with Mamma; he brought me his poem, but I left him. And now he is upset too — but it cannot be helped. You will find out some day — only don't be angry with me!"

She hurriedly squeezed my hand and ran off in front. We returned to the house. Maidanov began to read us his "Murderer," which had just been printed; but I did not listen to it. He shouted out his four-foot iambics in a singsong voice; the rhythms alternated and jingled like sleighbells, empty and loud; but I gazed continually at Zinaida and continually tried to fathom the meaning of her last words.

> *"Or is it that a secret rival*
> *Suddenly has conquered thee?"*

Maidanov exclaimed in a nasal tone, and my eyes met Zinaida's eyes. She let them drop and faintly blushed. I saw her blush, and I went cold with alarm. I had already felt jealous, but only at

[1] An eight-line, one-stanza poem by Pushkin. (Tr.)

that moment did the thought that she was in love flash through my head. "My God! She's fallen in love!"

10

Now I was really tormented. I racked my brains, I thought, and thought again, and watched her persistently, though as far as possible secretly. A change had occurred in her, that was evident. Now she went off for walks by herself, and long walks too. Sometimes she did not come out of her room when there were visitors, but sat there for hours. This had not formerly been her habit. I suddenly became — or thought I became — extremely observant. "Isn't it he? Or perhaps it is he?" I asked myself, anxiously considering one devotee after another. Secretly I thought Count Malevsky more dangerous than the others, though for Zinaida's sake I felt ashamed of admitting this possibility.

My powers of observation did not extend beyond my own nose, and my secrecy probably did not deceive anybody; at least, Dr. Lushin soon saw through me. By the way, he, too, had changed of late: he had grown thinner, and though he laughed just as much, his laugh was more hollow, evil, and curt; his previous light irony and exaggerated cynicism were replaced by an involuntary nervous irritability.

"What are you always dragging along here for, young man?" he asked me one day when he was alone with me in the Zasiokins' reception room. (The young Princess had not yet returned from a walk, and her mother could be heard on the mezzanine floor loudly scolding her maid.) "You ought to be studying and working while you are young; but you — what are you doing?"

"You don't know whether I work or not at home," I retorted, not without a touch of hauteur, but also in some embarrassment.

"What work is there to be done here? That's not what is worrying you. But I won't argue with you — at your age this is to be expected. Only your choice is far from commendable. Don't you see the kind of house this is?"

"I don't understand you," I remarked.

"You don't understand? So much the worse for you. I consider it my duty to warn you. People like me, old bachelors, may call here with safety, what can happen to us? We have been well steeled, nothing whatever can make any holes in us. But you've still got a delicate skin; and the air here is injurious to you, believe me. You may catch the infection."

"What do you mean?"

"What I say. Tell me, are you really well, even now? Are you in any normal state? Is what you are feeling of any value to you, any good to you?"

"Well, and what am I feeling?" I said, though in my heart of hearts I had to admit that he was right.

"Ah, young man, young man!" he went on in a tone of voice that suggested there was something very insulting to me in those two words. "What are you trying to be clever for? After all, thank God you still reveal in your face what is going on in your soul. But there, why talk? I myself would not come here if — " (he clenched his teeth) — "if I were not just as big a fool as you are. Only this is the thing that amazes me: how is it that you, with your intelligence, don't perceive what is happening all around you?"

"But what is happening, then?" I retorted, and I went tense with expectation.

The doctor looked at me with derisive commiseration.

"And I'm a fine one too," he said, apparently to himself. "Much need I have to say all this to him! In a word," he added, raising his voice, "I repeat: this atmosphere is not good for you. You like being here; but then, why shouldn't you? It is pleasant to smell the scents of a conservatory, only you cannot go and live in it. Now take my advice and go back to Kaidanov."

The Princess entered and began to complain to him of the toothache. A little later Zinaida returned.

"Now do scold her, doctor," her mother said. "All day she is drinking nothing but ice water, and is it really good for her, with her weak chest?"

"Why do you do that?" Lushin asked Zinaida.

"What harm is there in it?"

"What harm is there in it? You may catch a chill and die."

"Really? Surely not? And in any case, what of it? If that is the way I am to go."

"You don't say!" the doctor snorted. Zinaida's mother went out.

"You don't say!" Zinaida repeated. "Is life so cheerful, after all? Look around you. . . . Well, are you satisfied? Or do you think that I don't realize it all, don't feel it all? I enjoy drinking ice water, and can you seriously assure me that such a life is so worth while that it is not to be risked for a moment of enjoyment? . . . I won't speak of happiness."

"That's just it," Lushin remarked. "Caprice and independence: those two words sum up all your being, they express the whole of your character."

She laughed a nervous laugh.

"You've missed the post, doctor. You are not very good at observation, you're left behind. Put your spectacles on. I am not interested in caprices now; making a fool of you, making a fool of myself — how very cheerful! And as for independence — M'sieur Voldemar," she suddenly cried, stamping her little foot, "don't pull that melancholy face. I cannot stand it when people show me commiseration." She swiftly left the room.

"This atmosphere is bad for you, young man; very bad," Lushin said to me once more.

II

That evening all the usual guests were gathered in the Zasiokins' reception room; I was among them.

The conversation turned to Maidanov's poem. Zinaida praised it, and quite sincerely. "But do you know what?" she said to him. "If I were a poet I would choose other subjects. Perhaps it is all nonsense, but sometimes strange thoughts come into my head, especially when I am lying awake, before dawn, when the sky begins to turn rosy and gray. For instance, I would — You won't laugh at me?"

"No! No!" we all exclaimed with one accord.

"I would picture a whole company of young girls in a large boat on a quiet river at night," she went on, folding her hands over her chest and gazing to one side. "The moon is shining, and they are all in white and wearing garlands of white flowers, and they're singing something, a kind of hymn, you know."

"I understand, I understand; go on," Maidanov said in a meaningful and dreamy tone.

"Suddenly there is noise, and laughter, torches, tambourines on the bank. . . . It is a crowd of bacchantes running with singing and clamor. And here you have to describe the scene, Mr. Poet.

First Love

. . . Only I would like the torches to be crimson and smoking a great deal, and the bacchantes' eyes must be glittering beneath their garlands, and the garlands should be of a dark color. And don't forget the tigerskins and the goblets . . . and gold, lots of gold."

"But where is the gold to be?" Maidanov asked, throwing back his straight hair and dilating his nostrils.

"Where? On their shoulders, on their arms, on their legs, everywhere. They say that in ancient times the women wore gold bangles round their ankles. The bacchantes call to the girls in the boat to join them. The girls have stopped singing their hymn — they cannot go on with it — but they do not stir. The river carries them to the bank. And now, suddenly, one of them quietly rises. . . . This must be described very well: how she quietly stands up in the moonlight, and how her friends are afraid. . . . She has stepped over the edge of the boat, the bacchantes surround her, they dash off into the night, into the darkness. . . . Here you must describe the smoke as floating in great billows, and everything is confused. Only their shrieks are to be heard, and her garland is left lying on the bank."

She was silent. ("Oh, she has fallen in love indeed!" I thought again.)

"And is that all?" Maidanov asked.

"Yes," she replied.

"That cannot be the subject for a whole poem," he said seriously. "But I shall make use of your idea in a lyric."

"In the romantic genre?" Malevsky asked.

"Of course, in the romantic genre, the Byronic."

"But in my view Hugo is better than Byron," the young Count said with a negligent air. "He is more interesting."

"Hugo is a first-class writer," Maidanov retorted, "and my friend Tonkosheev, in his Spanish novel *El Trovador* — "

"Ah, that is the book with the question marks round the wrong way, isn't it?" Zinaida interrupted him.

"Yes, that's the way the Spaniards write it. I was about to say that Tonkosheev — "

"Now you'll start arguing about classicism and romanticism again," Zinaida once more interrupted him. "I'd rather have a game — "

"Of forfeits?" Lushin broke in.

"No, forfeits are boring; we'll play comparisons." (This was a game she herself had invented; some object was named, and each player tried to compare it with something else, and the prize went to the one who made the best comparison.) She went across to the window. The sun had only just set; long, crimson clouds were floating high in the heavens.

"What are those clouds like?" she asked, and went on without waiting for us to answer: "I think they are like those purple sails on Cleopatra's golden vessel when she sailed to meet Antony. Do you remember, Maidanov? You told me all about it recently."

Like Polonius in *Hamlet*, we all decided that the clouds did remind us of those very sails, and that not one of us could ever think of a better comparison.

"But how old was Antony then?" she asked.

"I'm sure he was a young man," Malevsky remarked.

"Yes, he was young" Maidanov confirmed in a tone of conviction.

"Pardon me!" Lushin exclaimed; "he was over forty."

"Over forty," Zinaida repeated, giving him a swift glance.

I went home soon after. "She's in love," my lips involuntarily whispered. "But with whom?"

12

The days passed. Zinaida grew more and more strange, more and more incomprehensible. One day I went to see her and found her sitting on a rush chair with her head pressed against the sharp edge of the table. She straightened up. . . . All her face was wet with tears.

"Ah! So it's you!" she said with a harsh, sneering smile. "Come here."

I went to her; she laid her hand on my head, suddenly seized my hair, and began to twist it.

"That hurts," I said at last.

"Ah! So it hurts, does it? But doesn't it hurt me? Doesn't it?" she repeated.

"Oh!" she cried out suddenly as she saw that she had torn out a thin strand of hair. "What have I done? Poor M'sieur Voldemar!"

She carefully straightened out the strand of hair, wound it round her finger, and twisted it into a little ring.

"I shall put your hair in a medallion, and I shall wear it," she said, while her eyes glittered with tears. "Perhaps that will comfort you a little. . . . But now good-by."

I returned home, to find an unpleasant situation awaiting me. My mother was having a scene with my father. She was reproaching him with something or other, but he, as usual, was coldly and courteously silent, and not long after, he drove off. I could not catch what my mother was saying, nor was I particularly interested. I remember only that afterward she sent for me to go to her room and talked in a very dissatisfied tone about my visits to the Princess, who, in her words, was *une femme capable de tout*. I kissed her hand (I always did that when I wanted to cut short the conversation) and went to my room. Zinaida's tears had baffled me completely. I simply did not know what to make of it all, and I, too, was ready to cry: after all, I was a child, despite my sixteen years. Now I no longer thought of Malevsky, though Bolovzorov grew more and more threatening every day and looked at the shifty Count like a wolf at a sheep. Indeed, I did not think of anything or anybody. I was lost in conjecture, and was always going off to lonely spots. I grew especially fond of the conservatory. I would climb up to the top of the high wall, would sit down, and go on sitting there, such an unhappy, lonely, and sorrowful lad that I began to feel sorry for myself. And how comforting did I find those mournful feelings, how I reveled in them!

Well, one day, as I was sitting on the wall, gazing into the distance and listening to the church bells, suddenly something passed over me . . . like a little breeze; not a shiver, but literally a waft, literally a sensation that someone was in the vicinity. . . . I looked down. Below me Zinaida was hurriedly walking along the road; she was in a gray dress and had a rose-colored parasol over her shoulder. She saw me, halted, and, throwing back the brim of her straw hat, raised her velvety eyes to me.

"What are you doing up there, so high?" she asked me with a strange smile. "Listen! You're always declaring that you love me; jump down here to me, if you really do love me."

She hardly had time to say the words before I flew down just as though someone had pushed me in the back. The wall was about fourteen feet high. I reached the ground on my feet, but the drop was so great that I could not keep my balance: I fell and lost consciousness for a moment. When I came to, without opening my eyes I felt that Zinaida was kneeling beside me. "My dear boy," she said as she bent over me, and an anxious tenderness sounded in her voice; "what made you do that, what made you do as I told you? . . . You see, I love you. . . . Get up."

Her breast rose and fell beside me, her hands touched my head, and suddenly — ah, what happened to me then! — her soft, fresh lips began to cover all my face with kisses . . . they touched my lips. . . . But then she must have guessed by the expression of my face that I had come round, though I had not opened my eyes, for, swiftly rising, she said: "Now get up, you madcap, you stupid! What are you lying in the dust for?" I got up. "Hand me my parasol," she said; "I dropped it somewhere. And don't stare at me like that. . . . What a stupid thing to do! You haven't hurt yourself, have you? I expect you've stung yourself in the nettles. Don't stare at me, I tell you. Oh, he doesn't understand a thing, he doesn't say a word," she added, as though to herself. "Go home, M'sieur Voldemar, and brush yourself off, and don't dare to follow me or I'll be angry, and then never again — "

She did not finish the sentence and briskly walked away, while I sat up in the road. My legs would not support me. The nettles had stung my hands, my back ached, and my head was swimming, but the feeling of bliss that I experienced at that moment has never visited me again. It was like a pleasant pain in all my limbs, and it was resolved at last in rapturous jumps and exclamations of joy. Truly, I was still a child.

13

I was so gay and proud all that day, I retained the feeling of Zinaida's kisses so vividly on my face, I remembered her every word with such shuddering rapture, I cherished my unexpected happiness so deeply that I began to feel frightened, I did not even wish to see her, the cause of these new sensations. I felt that now I could demand nothing more of fate, that now I ought to "sigh deeply for the last time, and die." On the other hand, when I went to call on the Zasiokins next day, I felt great embarrassment, which I vainly tried to conceal beneath a modest jauntiness, proper to a man who wishes to indicate that he can keep a secret. Zinaida received me very simply, without any sign of agitation; she only threatened me with her finger and asked whether I had

First Love

any bruises. All my modest jauntiness and mysterious secrecy vanished in a moment, and with it my embarrassment. Of course, I had not expected anything in particular, but Zinaida's calm was like a douche of cold water. I realized that in her eyes I was a child, and I felt very miserable. She walked backward and forward, smiling swiftly whenever she glanced at me; but her thoughts were far away, I saw that clearly. . . . "Shall I be the first to refer to yesterday?" I thought. "Shall I ask where she was off to in such a hurry, so that I can find out definitely? . . ." But I only dismissed the idea and sat down in a corner.

Belovzorov came in; I was glad to see him.

"I haven't found you a riding-horse, not a quiet one, yet," he began in a harsh tone. "Freitag says he has one, but I'm not sure about it. I'm afraid."

"What are you afraid of?" Zinaida inquired. "May I ask?"

"What am I afraid of? Why, you cannot ride yet. God preserve us from anything happening! And what is this mad idea that has suddenly come into your head?"

"Well, that's my business, M'sieur my animal. In that case I shall ask Piotr Vasilich." (My father's name was Piotr Vasilich, and I was surprised to hear her mention his name so lightly and easily, as though she was quite sure of his readiness to serve her.)

"So that's it?" Belovzorov retorted. "So it's with him that you want to go riding?"

"Either with him or with someone else, it makes no difference to you. In any case it won't be with you."

"Won't be with me?" Belovzorov repeated. "As you wish. What of it? I'll get you a horse."

"Only, listen, I don't want any old nag. I warn you that I want to gallop."

"Gallop by all means. But whom are you going to ride with? Malevsky, by any chance?"

"And why not, warrior knight? Now calm down," she added, "and don't flash your eyes. I'll take you with me too. You know what I think about Malevsky now — pooh!" She shook her head.

"You say that just to console me," he snorted.

Zinaida half closed her eyes. "Does it console you, then? Oh, oh, oh, you warrior!" she said at last, as though she could not think of anything else to call him. "And what about you, M'sieur Voldemar? Would you go riding with us?"

"I'm not fond of riding — with lots of other people," I muttered without raising my eyes.

"So you prefer it to be tête-à-tête? Well, the free has his choice, the saved has — paradise," she said, sighing. "Go and see what you can do, Belovzorov. I need a horse for tomorrow."

"All very well, but where are we to get the money?" her mother intervened.

Zinaida knitted her brows.

"I shan't ask you for it. Belovzorov will give me credit."

"He will, he certainly will," the Princess replied, and suddenly shouted at the top of her voice: "Dunia!"

"*Maman*, I have given you a bell to ring," Zinaida observed.

"Dunia!" the old woman called again.

Belovzorov took his leave; I went with him. Zinaida did not detain me.

14

Next morning I rose early, cut myself a stick, and went for a walk out beyond the city turnpike. I thought I would walk off my misery. The day was beautiful, bright, and not too hot; a cheerful, fresh breeze was roving over the earth, and it blew and played gently, stirring everything and disturbing nothing. I wandered a long time over the hills, through the forest; I did not feel happy — I had left home with the intention of giving myself over to dejection; but my youth, the fine weather, the fresh air, the pleasure of the swift walk, the delight of lying alone on the thick grass, all had their way: the memory of those unforgettable words, of those kisses, again forced itself upon my soul. It was pleasant to think that at all events Zinaida would have to admit my resolution, my heroism. . . . "She may find others better than I," I thought, "and let her! On the other hand, others only say they'll do a thing, but I do it. And what else couldn't I do for her!" My imagination began to run riot. I imagined how I would save her from the hands of enemies, how, all streaming with blood, I would wrest her from a dungeon, how I would die at her feet. I remembered a picture that hung in our reception room; it depicted Maleque Adèle carrying off Mathilde [1] . . . and at that very moment my attention was distracted by the

[1] The hero and heroine of *Mathilde*, by the French woman novelist Marie Cottin (1770–1807).

sight of a great spotted woodpecker, which fussily climbed the slender trunk of a birch and peered anxiously out from behind it, first to the right, then to the left, like a musician from behind the neck of his double-bass.

Then I began to sing: "Not white are the snows," and went on to a ballad well known at that time, "I wait for thee, whenas the playful zephyr"; then I began to declaim Yermak's apostrophe to the stars, from Khomyakov's tragedy of the same name; I would have tried my hand at writing something in a sentimental style, I even thought of the line that was to end the poem: "O Zinaida, Zinaida!" But nothing came of it. Meanwhile the dinner hour was approaching. I dropped down into a valley; a narrow, sandy path wound along it in the direction of the city. I followed this path. . . . The hollow drumming of horse-hoofs sounded behind me. I looked round, involuntarily halted, and removed my cap: my father and Zinaida were riding toward me, side by side. My father was saying something to her, leaning all his body across and resting his hand on her horse's neck. He was smiling. Zinaida was listening to him without speaking, her eyes strictly cast down and her lips compressed. At first I saw no one else, but some moments later Belovzorov appeared round a bend in the valley; he was in his hussar uniform, with a pelisse, and was riding a foaming black horse. The good horse shook its head, snorted, and fretted; the rider was continually reining it in and spurring it on. I stepped aside. My father gathered up his reins and drew away from Zinaida; she slowly raised her eyes to him, and they both set off at a gallop. . . . Belovzorov tore after them, his saber clattering. "He's as crimson as a lobster," I thought. "And she — why is she so pale? They've been riding all the morning, and yet she's pale."

I hastened my steps and arrived home just before dinnertime. My father, who had washed and changed his clothes, was already sitting by my mother's chair and reading a *feuilleton* from the *Journal des débats* to her in his even, musical voice. But my mother was only half listening; when she saw me, she asked me where I had been all day, and added that she did not like people going off God knows where and God knows with whom. I felt like replying: "I have been for a walk by myself"; but I looked at my father, and for some reason I kept silent.

During the next five or six days I hardly saw Zinaida at all; she pleaded that she was unwell, which, however, did not prevent the usual visitors from reporting for duty, as they themselves put it — all except Maidanov, who grew depressed and bored as soon as he had no chance to rhapsodize. Belovzorov sat moodily in a corner, red of face, his coat tightly buttoned up. An unpleasant smiled roved continually over Count Malevsky's thin features. The Count certainly had fallen out of favor with Zinaida and now waited diligently on the old Princess, even driving with her in a hired carriage to see the Governor General. This journey proved a failure, however, and even led to some unpleasantness for Malevsky; they reminded him of some incident or other in which he had been involved with road engineers, and he had to plead in his justification that at that time he was lacking in experience. Lushin called a couple of times every day, but did not remain long. I was a little afraid of him after our last talk, but at the same time I was genuinely drawn toward him. One day he went for a walk with me in the Nieskuchny Gardens; he was very good-natured and amiable, told me the names and properties of various herbs and flowers, and suddenly went off at a tangent and exclaimed, striking himself on the forehead: "But I, fool that I am, thought she was a flirt! Evidently it is pleasant to sacrifice oneself for others!"

"What are you trying to convey?" I asked him.

"I'm not trying to convey anything to *you*," he retorted vehemently.

Zinaida avoided me: my arrival always made an unpleasant impression on her, as I could not help noticing. She involuntarily turned away from me — involuntarily, that was what made it so bitter, what upset me most of all. But there was nothing I could do about it, and I tried to keep out of her sight and watched over her only from a distance, which was not always possible. As before, something incomprehensible was happening to her: her features changed, she changed altogether. One warm, still evening I was particularly struck by the change that had occurred in her. I was sitting on a low bench under a spreading elder bush; I was fond of this spot, for from it I could see the window of Zinaida's room. I was sitting there, and above my head amid the darkened foliage a little bird was fidgeting; a gray kitten, arching its back, cautiously stole into the garden, and the first May bugs were buzzing noisily in the air, which was still translucent, though the day was fading. I sat and gazed at the window and waited to see whether it would open. Yes, it did open, and Zinaida appeared at it. She was wearing a white dress, and she herself, her face, her shoulders, her arms, were all as white as a sheet. She stood a long time without stirring and gazed a long time fixedly from under her wrinkled brows. I had not realized that she could look like that. Then she clenched her fists, strongly, very strongly, shook her curls, and, nodding with an air of decision, slammed the window shut again.

Three days later I met her in the garden. I tried to slip away, but she herself stopped me.

"Give me your hand," she said with all her former kindness. "You and I haven't had a talk for a long time."

I glanced at her. Her eyes were beaming mildly, and her face was smiling, as though through a mist.

"Are you still unwell?" I asked her.

"No, it's all past now," she replied as she picked a small red rose. "I'm a little tired, but that will pass too."

"And will you be again as you were before?" I asked.

She raised the rose to her face, and I had the impression that the brilliant color of the petals was reflected in her cheeks. "Have I changed, then?" she asked.

"Yes, you have changed," I replied in a low voice.

"I have been cold to you, I know," she began. "But you shouldn't have taken any notice of it. . . . I could not be otherwise. But why talk about it?"

"You don't want me to love you, that's what it is," I exclaimed moodily in an involuntary outburst.

"You're wrong; do go on loving me, but not as before."

"How, then?"

"We shall be friends, that's how." She held out the rose for me to smell. "Listen; after all, I am much older than you. I could quite well be your aunt, really I could; or if not your aunt, then your elder sister. But you — "

"You regard me as a child," I interrupted her.

"Why, yes. you are a child, but a dear, good, intelligent child whom I love very much. Do you know what? From today I appoint you my page; and you must not forget that pages should never leave their mistresses' side. Here is the token of your new dignity," she added, putting the rose in my buttonhole. "A token of my favor."

"I have had other favors from you in the past," I muttered.

"Ah!" she said, and looked sidelong at me. "What a memory he has! Well, what if I did? I'm just as ready now."

And, bending toward me, she printed a pure, tranquil kiss on my forehead.

I only gazed at her; but she turned away and went toward the house, saying: "Follow me, my page." I followed her, continually in a muse. "Is this gentle and sober-minded girl the same Zinaida whom once I knew?" I thought. "Surely not?" Even her walk seemed more staid, and all her figure more majestic and harmonious.

But my goodness! With what new strength did my love flame up within me!

16

After dinner guests again gathered in the Zasiokins' reception room, and Zinaida came out to join them. All the company was present that had assembled on that first unforgettable evening. Even Nirmatsky dragged himself along. This time Maidanov was the first to arrive; he brought some new verse. We played forfeits again, but now they were lacking in the previous ingenuity, and there was not the former foolery and hubbub; the gypsy element had vanished. Zinaida set a new mood for our gathering. I sat beside her, as was my right as a page. Among other things she suggested that the one who drew a forfeit should tell a dream he had had. But this was not a success. The dreams proved either uninteresting (Belovzorov had dreamed that he fed his horse on carp, and that his mount had a wooden head) or unnatural, invented. . . . Maidanov treated us to a whole novel: it included graveyard vaults, and angels with lyres, and flowers that talked . . . and sounds coming from afar. Zinaida would not let him finish. "Now we have begun to make up stories," she said, "let each of us tell some story, only it must be really made up." It fell to Belovzorov to begin.

The young hussar was disconcerted. "I can't think of anything," he exclaimed.

"What nonsense!" Zinaida rebuked him. "Imagine, for instance,
that you are married, and tell us how you would spend the time
with your wife. Would you keep her locked in?"

"I would keep her locked in."

"And would you sit with her yourself?"

"Of course I would."

"Excellent. But supposing she got bored with all this and was
false to you?"

"I would kill her."

"But supposing she ran away?"

"I would go after her, and I would kill her just the same."

"Yes, but supposing I were your wife, what would you do
then?"

He was silent for a moment, then replied: "I would kill myself."

Zinaida laughed. "I see your song isn't a long one."

She herself drew the second forfeit. She gazed up at the ceiling
and was lost in thought. "Now listen to what I have made up,"
she said at last, "Imagine a magnificent palace, a summer night,
and a marvelous ball. The ball is being given by the young Queen.
Everywhere there is gold, marble, crystal, silk, lights, amber,
flowers, incense, all the whims of luxury."

"You're fond of luxury, aren't you?" Lushin interrupted.

"Luxury is beautiful," she retorted. "I am fond of all beautiful
things."

"More than fine things?" he asked.

"That is too subtle, and I don't understand it. Don't interrupt
me. And so, it is a magnificent ball. There are a large number
of guests, they are all young, fine, and brave, they are all madly in
love with the Queen."

"But aren't there any women among the guests?" Malevsky
asked.

"No — but wait, yes, there are."

"And they're all ugly?"

"They're all charming, but all the men are in love with the
Queen. She is tall and graceful . . . she has a small gold diadem
on her black hair."

I gazed at Zinaida, and at that moment she seemed so much
taller than the rest of us, and such lucid intelligence and such authority beamed from her white forehead, from her knitted brows,
that I thought: "You yourself are this Queen."

"They all crowd round her," she continued, "they all make her highly flattering speeches."

"But is she fond of flattery?" Lushin asked.

"How unbearable you are! You're always interrupting. . . . Who doesn't like flattery?"

"Just one last question," Malevsky interposed. "Has the Queen a husband?"

"I hadn't thought about that. No, why should she have a husband?"

"Of course," Malevsky caught her up; "why should she have a husband?"

"*Silence!*" Maidanov, who spoke French badly, exclaimed in French.

"*Merci*," Zinaida said to him. "And so the Queen listens to these speeches, she listens to the music, but her eyes are not on any of her guests. Six windows are open from top to bottom, from ceiling to floor, and beyond them is the dark sky with great stars, and the dark garden with great trees. The Queen is gazing into the garden. There, by the trees, is a fountain; in the dusk it shows up white, and long, very long, like an apparition. Through the talk and the music the Queen hears the quiet splashing of the water; she gazes and thinks: 'All you gentlemen are of noble birth, you are all intelligent, and wealthy, you crowd round me, you treasure my every word, every one of you is ready to die at my feet, I rule over you. . . . But there, by the fountain, by that splashing water, the one I love, the one who rules over me, is standing and waiting for me. He is wearing neither sumptuous attire nor precious gems; no one knows him, but he is waiting for me and is sure that I shall come. And I shall go to him, and there is no power that could halt me when I desire to go to him and remain with him, and to be lost with him there in the darkness of the garden, beneath the rustling of the trees, beneath the splashing of the fountain.'"

She was silent.

"Is this — all made up?" Malevsky asked craftily.

Zinaida did not even look at him.

"But, gentlemen, what would we do," Lushin suddenly asked, "if we were among those guests and knew about that fortunate one by the fountain?"

"Wait, wait!" Zinaida interrupted him. "I myself will tell you what each of you would do. You, Belovzorov, would challenge him to a duel; you, Maidanov, would write an epigram on him. But no, you don't know how to write epigrams; you would write long iambic verse about him, in the manner of Barbier,[1] and you would publish your poem in the *Telegraph*. You, Nirmatsky, would borrow from him. . . . No, you would lend him money at interest. You, Doctor — " She paused. "As for you, I don't know what you would do."

"In my capacity as court physician," he said, "I would advise the Queen not to give balls if she hadn't time for her guests."

"Perhaps you'd be right. But you, Count — "

"And I?" Malevsky asked, with his unpleasant smile.

"You would offer him a poisoned sweet."

Malevsky's face twisted a little in a grimace and looked Jewish for a moment, but he immediately burst into a roar of laughter.

"And as for you, Voldemar — " Zinaida continued. "But no more of this; let us play some other game."

"M'sieur Voldemar, in his capacity as the Queen's page, would hold her train as she ran into the garden," Malevsky observed venomously.

I flared up; but Zinaida swiftly laid her hand on my shoulder, rose a little in her seat, and declared in a voice that shook a little: "I have never given Your Excellency any right to be insolent, and so I must ask you to withdraw." She pointed to the door.

"Forgive me, Princess!" Malevsky muttered, turning pale.

"The Princess is right!" Belovzorov exclaimed, and he, too, rose.

"By God, I never expected you to take it like that," Malevsky added. "I don't think there was anything of that nature in what I said. . . . It never occurred to me to insult you even in thought. . . . Do pardon me."

Zinaida gave him a cold look and coldly laughed. "If you wish you can remain," she declared with a negligent gesture. "I and M'sieur Voldemar were angry over nothing. You find it pleasant to wound! May you enjoy it!"

"Forgive me!" Malvesky repeated yet again; and I, remembering Zinaida's gesture, thought again that even a real queen could not have pointed an audacious man to the door with greater dignity.

[1] Henri Auguste Barbier (1805–82) French poet known chiefly by his satirical poems *Iambic Verses*.

Turgenev

The game of forfeits did not continue for long after this little incident; everybody felt rather awkward, not so much because of what had happened as because of another, not altogether defined, yet oppressive feeling. No one referred to it, but each of us was conscious of it, both in himself and in his neighbor. Maidanov read his poems to us, and Malevsky praised them with exaggerated enthusiasm. "Isn't he anxious to show how kind he is!" Lushin whispered to me. We soon broke up. Suddenly Zinaida went into a reverie; the Princess sent in to say that she had a headache; Nirmatsky began to complain of his rheumatism.

I was a long time getting to sleep; I had been impressed by Zinaida's story. "Was she hinting at something, perhaps?" I asked myself. "And at whom, at what was she hinting? And if there really is something to hint at, how is one to decide? . . . No, no, it cannot be that," I whispered, turning over from one hot cheek to the other. But I remembered Zinaida's face as she told her story. I remembered the exclamation that had burst from Lushin in the Nieskuchny Gardens, the sudden changes in her behavior toward me, and I was lost in conjecture. "Who is he?" Those three words seemed to rise before my eyes, outlined in the darkness. I felt as though a low, sinister cloud were hanging over me, and I could feel its pressure and was waiting for it to burst any moment. Of recent times I had grown accustomed to a great deal, I had seen a great deal at the Zasiokins'. Their untidiness, the greasy candle-ends, the broken knives and forks, the glum old Vonifaty, the ragged maidservants, the manners of the old Princess herself — all this terrible existence no longer disturbed me. But I could not get accustomed to what I vaguely surmised was occurring in Zinaida now. "She's an adventuress," my mother had once said of her in my presence. An adventuress: my idol, my divinity! That term burned me, I tried to get away from it by burying myself in the pillow; I was indignant. . . . And at the same time what would I not have agreed to, what would I not have given, if I could have been that fortunate one at the fountain!

The blood began to burn and course through my veins. "The garden . . . the fountain," I thought. "I'll go into the garden." I briskly dressed and slipped out of the house. The night was

396

dark; the trees were only faintly whispering; a gentle cool
fell from the sky, the smell of parsley came from the garden. I
walked along all the paths; the quiet sound of my footsteps both
disconcerted and encouraged me. I halted, waited, and listened
to the heavy and rapid beating of my heart. At last I approached
the fence and leaned on the thin rail. Suddenly — or did I imagine
it? — a woman's figure flitted past a few paces away. I strained
my eyes into the darkness, I held my breath. What was that? Did
I hear footsteps, or was it again my heart beating? "Who is
there?" I stammered almost inaudibly. And what was that? A
suppressed laugh? Or the leaves rustling, or a sigh close to my ear?
I began to feel afraid. "Who is there?" I repeated still more
softly.

The air streamed past me for a moment; a fiery streak glittered
over the sky; a star fell: "Zinaida?" I wanted to ask; but the
words died on my lips. And suddenly everything grew profoundly still all around me, as often happens in the middle of the
night. Even the crickets ceased to chirrup among the trees; only a
window was noisily shut somewhere. I went on standing and
standing for a moment or two longer, then returned to my room,
to my cold bed. I felt a strange agitation, as though I had been to
keep an assignation and had been left waiting alone and had
passed by another's happiness.

17

Next day I saw Zinaida only for a second: she drove off somewhere in a droshky with her mother. On the other hand I saw
Lushin, who, by the way, hardly deigned to speak to me, and
Malevsky. The young Count smirked and began to talk to me
quite pleasantly. Of all the visitors to the Zasiokins' he alone had
been able to insinuate himself into our house and to find favor
with my mother. My father did not like him and treated him
with insulting courtesy.

"Ah, *monsieur le page!*" Malevsky began. "Very glad to meet
you. What is your excellent queen doing?"

His fresh, handsome face was so repellent to me at that moment, and he looked at me so contemptuously and playfully, that
I made no answer whatever.

"Are you still angry?" he went on. "How absurd! After all, it

397

was not I who called you a page, and pages are usually found in attendance on queens. But allow me to observe that you perform your duties badly."

"Why do I?"

"Pages should be inseparable from their sovereigns; pages should always know what their sovereigns are doing, they should even watch over them"; and he added, lowering his voice: "Day — and night."

"What do you mean?"

"What do I mean? I think I am expressing myself clearly enough. Day — and night. In the daytime it is easy enough; one can see in the daytime and there are people about. But at night — that is the time to expect trouble. I advise you not to sleep at night, but to watch, to watch with all your powers. Remember, in the garden, by the fountain at night — that is where one should be on guard. You'll be grateful to me."

He laughed and turned his back on me. Probably he did not attach any special importance to what he had said: he had the reputation of being fond of mystifying people, and boasted of his ability to take people in at the masquerades — a gift that depended a great deal on the almost unconscious hypocrisy that marked his character. He was only trying to tease me, but every word he said flowed like poison through my veins. The blood rushed to my head. "Ah, so that's it!" I said to myself. "Good! So I did not go into the garden for nothing. But it shall not be!" I exclaimed aloud and beat my breast with my fist, though to tell the truth I had no idea what it was that must not be. "Whether it is Malevsky himself that visits the garden," I thought (possibly he had said too much, and he was capable of such insolence), "or anyone else" (our garden wall was very low, and it was quite easy to climb over it), "it will be a bad lookout for anyone I come across. I don't advise anyone to fall in with me! I shall show all the world and her, the traitress" (so after all I did call her a traitress) "that I can take my revenge!"

I returned to my room, went to my writing-desk and took out a penknife I had recently bought, felt the sharp blades, and, with furrowed brows, with cold and concentrated resolution I thrust it into my pocket, as though such deeds were nothing surprising and my actions nothing new to me. My heart swelled angrily and went numb. I did not relax my displeasure or my

compressed lips all that day, and I walked backward and forward
with one hand in my pocket, clutching the heated knife and preparing myself for something terrible. These new and unprecedented feelings so greatly occupied and diverted me that, to
tell the truth, I thought very little about Zinaida. I was continually thinking of Aleko, the young gypsy: "Whither, my handsome youth?" "Lie down!" And then: "Thou art all spattered
with blood; oh, what hast thou done?" . . . "Nothing!" With
what a harsh smile did I repeat that word "nothing"! My father
was not at home, but my mother, who for some time past had
been in a state of almost speechless irritation, noticed my air of
doom, and at supper she said to me: "What are you sulking for
like a mouse in the groats?" In reply I only smiled at her condescendingly and thought: "If she only knew!" Eleven o'clock
struck; I went to my room, but I did not undress. I waited for
midnight; at last it, too, struck. "Time!" I whispered between my
teeth and, buttoning my coat right up and even rolling up my
sleeves, I went out into the garden.

I had already chosen the spot where I would keep guard. At
the end of the garden, where the fence separating our domain
from that of the Zasiokins' ended in the common wall, grew a
single fir; standing beneath its low, thick branches, I could have a
good view of all that happened around me, so far as the nocturnal darkness would permit. Here, too, was a little path, which
always seemed rather mysterious to me: it crawled like a snake
up to the fence, which at this spot showed signs that someone
had climbed over it, and led to a circular arbor of dense acacias.
I reached the fir, leaned against its trunk, and began to watch.

That night was as still as the night before; but there were fewer
clouds in the sky, and I could see the outlines of the bushes, and
even the taller flowers, more clearly. Those first few moments
of expectation were exhausting, almost frightening. I had not resolved on any step; I only pondered what action I should take.
Should I thunder out: "Where are you going? Stop! Confess or
die"? Or should I simply strike? Every sound, every rustle and
whisper, seemed significant, extraordinary. . . . I made ready.
. . . I leaned forward. . . . But half an hour passed; an hour
passed; my blood grew still and cool; I began to realize that I was
doing all this for nothing, that I was even rather ridiculous, that
Malevsky had been making fun of me. I abandoned my ambush

and walked right through the garden. As though of intent, not the least sound was to be heard anywhere; everything was at peace; even our dog was asleep, rolled into a ball by the wicket gate. I climbed onto the ruins of the conservatory, and before me I saw the far-stretching plain. I recalled my meeting with Zinaida and was lost in thought.

I started. . . . I thought I heard the creak of a door being opened, then the light crack of a twig snapping. In two bounds I was down from the ruins, and froze still. Swift, light, and cautious steps were clearly to be heard in the garden. They drew near to where I was standing. "Here he comes — here he comes at last!" rushed through my mind. I convulsively drew the knife out of my pocket, convulsively opened it; crimson sparks danced before my eyes, in my fear and anger the hair stirred on my head. The footsteps came straight toward me; I bent down, I strained to meet them. A man appeared. . . . My God! It was my father!

I recognized him at once, though he was wrapped from head to foot in a dark cloak, and his hat was drawn down over his face. He went past me on tiptoe. He did not notice me, though nothing concealed me; but I crouched and cowered so low that I think I must have been level with the ground. The jealous Othello ready to commit murder was suddenly transformed into a schoolboy. I was so frightened by my father's unexpected appearance that at first I did not even notice whence he had come or where he went. Only when everything was again still all around me did I straighten up and wonder: "What is father walking in the garden at night for?" In my fright I had dropped my pocketknife in the grass, but I did not even trouble to look for it: I felt deeply ashamed. I cooled down in a moment. But as I returned home, I went to my bench under the elder bush and glanced at the window of Zinaida's bedroom. The small, slightly convex panes showed as dim blue patches in the feeble light coming from the nocturnal sky. Suddenly their color began to change. Behind them — I saw it, I saw it clearly — the white blind was let down cautiously and quietly, was let down to the windowsill, and remained down, motionless.

"What is all this?" I said aloud, almost involuntarily, when I was back in my room once more. "A dream, chance, or — ?" The suppositions that suddenly came to my mind were so new and strange that I did not even dare to give myself over to them.

Next morning I woke with a headache. The agitation of the night before had gone. It was replaced by a dull bewilderment and grief that I had never known before, as though something within me had died.

"What are you looking like a rabbit with half its brain extracted for?" Lushin asked me when we met. At breakfast time I took surreptitious glances first at my father, then at my mother. He was calm, as usual, and she, as usual, was secretly irritable. I waited for him to talk to me in his amiable way, as sometimes he did. But he did not even caress me with his everyday, cold caress. "Shall I tell Zinaida everything?" I thought. " . . . After all, it doesn't matter now, it's all over between us." I went to see her, but not only did I not say anything to her about it, I did not even succeed in saying more than a word to her, much as I wished to. Her brother, a twelve-year-old student in a military school, had arrived from Petersburg for a holiday. Zinaida at once placed him in my charge. "Here you are, my dear Volodya" (it was the first time she had used this diminutive), "here is a companion for you. His name is Volodya too. Please be nice to him; he's still shy, but he has a kind heart. Show him the Nieskuchny Gardens, take him for walks, and take him under your protection. You will do that, won't you? You're kind, too." She graciously laid both hands on my shoulders, and I was completely overcome. This boy's arrival turned me also into a boy. I gazed silently at the lad, who stared at me just as speechlessly. Zinaida burst into laughter and pushed us toward each other. "Now give each other a hug, children." We gave each other a hug.

"Would you like me to take you into the garden?" I asked him.

"If you please," he replied in a hoarse, genuinely cadet voice. Zinaida laughed again. I did manage to observe that never before had she had such a charming color in her cheeks. I went off with the cadet.

In our garden was an old swing. I seated him on the thin board and began to give him a swing. He sat very still in his new little uniform of stout cloth, with broad gold lace galloons, and clung tightly to the rope. "But you should unbutton your collar," I said to him. "It's all right, we're used to it," he said, and cleared

his throat. He was like his sister; his eyes especially reminded
me of her. I enjoyed doing him a kindness, but meanwhile that
same corrosive sorrow was gnawing at my heart. "Now indeed
I am a child," I thought; "but yesterday — " I remembered where
I had dropped my penknife the night before and went and found
it. The boy asked me for it, broke off a stout stem of angelica,
carved a pipe from it, and began to pipe. Othello whistled a little,
too.

But then how he wept, that very same Othello, in Zinaida's
arms, when, seeking him out in a corner of the garden that evening, she asked him why he was so sad. My tears poured down
so torrentially that she was alarmed. "What's the matter with
you, what's the matter, Volodya?" she asked, and as I did not
answer and did not stop crying, she made to kiss my wet cheek.
But I turned away from her and whispered through my sobs: "I
know everything; why did you play with me? . . . What did
you need my love for?"

"I have done you wrong, Volodya," she said. "Ah, I have done
you great wrong," she said, and clenched her fists. "How much
there is in me that is stupid, dark, sinful! . . . But I am not
playing with you now; I love you — you don't even suspect why,
or how. . . . But all the same — what do you know?"

What could I say to her? She stood before me and looked at
me, and I belonged to her wholly, from my head to my feet, the
moment she looked at me. . . . Fifteen minutes later I was running races with her and her brother; I was no longer weeping, I
was laughing, though my swollen eyelids dropped tears with my
laughter; round my neck Zinaida's ribbon was tied instead of a
cravat, and I cried out with joy when I succeeded in catching
her by the waist. She did just as she liked with me.

19

I should find it difficult if I were made to tell in detail all that
happened to me during the week after my unfortunate nocturnal
expedition. It was a strange, feverish time, a kind of chaos in
which the most contradictory feelings, thoughts, suspicions,
hopes, joys, and sufferings eddied like a whirlwind. I grew afraid
to look into myself, if a sixteen-year-old boy can look into himself at all; I grew afraid to take stock of anything; I simply
hastened to get through the day till the evening. On the other

hand, I slept at night — the child's mental levity helped me there. I did not wish to know whether anyone loved me, and did not wish to confess to myself that no one loved me; I avoided my father, but Zinaida I could not avoid. I burned as though on fire in her presence; but what use was there in my knowing the sort of fire in which I burned and melted? — it was bliss for me to melt and burn so pleasantly. I gave myself over entirely to my sensations, and was cunning with myself, turning my back on my memories, and closing my eyes to what I anticipated ahead of me. . . . Without doubt this drain on me would not have continued for long in any case — a thunderclap ended it all with one stroke and flung me into a new path.

Returning toward dinnertime after a long walk one day, I was amazed to learn that I would be dining alone: my father had driven somewhere, and my mother was not well, did not want anything to eat, and had locked herself in her bedroom. By the servants' faces I guessed that something unusual had occurred. I did not dare to question them, but I had one friend, the young butler, Philip, a passionate lover of verse and an artist on the guitar, and I spoke to him. He told me there had been a terrible scene between my father and mother (and every word was heard in the maids' room; much of the quarrel was in French, but the maid Masha had lived five years with a sempstress from Paris, and she understood everything). My mother had charged my father with infidelity, with intimacy with the young lady next door; at first my father had denied everything, but then he had flared up and in his turn had said something very harsh, "apparently about their ages," at which my mother had burst into tears. My mother had also made mention of a promissory note of the Princess's that had been accepted, and she had spoken very unpleasantly about her and the young lady too. And then my father had used threats to her. "And all the trouble arose," Philip added, "over an anonymous letter; and no one knows who wrote it. Otherwise there would have been no reason for all this affair to come out at all."

"But really was there anything in it?" I said with difficulty, while my hands and feet turned cold and something began to quiver in the very depths of my breast.

Philip winked meaningly. "There was. You can't keep these things quiet, no matter how careful your father was this time.

After all, you have to hire a carriage or something . . . and then you can't manage without the servants."

I sent Philip away and collapsed on my bed. I did not sob, or give way to despair; I did not ask myself when and how all this had happened; I was not astonished that I had not already guessed, long since. I did not even rail against my father. What I had learned was beyond my power to bear: this sudden revelation shattered me. It was all over. All my flowers were torn up in one handful and lay around me, scattered and trampled.

20

Next day Mother announced that she was going back to town. In the morning my father had gone to her bedroom and had sat alone with her for a long time. No one heard what he said to her, but she did not cry any more; she grew calm, and asked for food — but she did not come downstairs and did not change her decision. I remember I wandered about all day; but I did not go into the garden, and did not look once at the Zasiokins' wing. But that evening I was witness of an astonishing incident: my father led Count Malevsky by the arm from the reception room to the lobby and, in our footman's presence, coldly told him: "Several days ago in a certain house Your Excellency was shown the door. I shall not give you any explanation now, but I have the honor to inform you that if you call on me again I shall throw you through the window. I do not like your handwriting." The Count bowed, clenched his teeth, bristled up, and disappeared.

Preparations were put in hand for our return to town, to our house in Arbat Square. In all probability my father himself no longer wished to remain in the country. But evidently he had persuaded Mother not to make a scene; everything was done quietly, unhurriedly; my mother even sent a servant to convey her respects and to express her regret that, as she was not at all well, she would not be seeing the Princess again before our departure. I roamed about as though crazy and only wanted it all to end as soon as possible. One thought never left my head: how could she, a young girl, and a Princess after all, resolve on such conduct, knowing that my father was not free, and when she could have married Belovzorov, for instance? What did she hope for? Why was she not afraid of ruining all her own future? "Yes," I thought, "this is love, this is passion, this is devotion"; and I recalled Lushin's words: to sacrifice oneself for others is sweet. I happened to see a white patch at one of the windows of the wing. "Surely that isn't Zinaida's face?" I thought. . . . Yes, it was her face. I could endure no more. I could not part from her without saying a last good-by to her. I seized a convenient moment and went to her home.

In the reception room the old Princess welcomed me with her usual unpleasant and negligent greeting.

"Why have your people taken flight so soon?" she said, thrusting snuff into both her nostrils. I looked at her and felt relieved. Philip's reference to a "promissory note" had been tormenting me. But she suspected nothing; at least, so it seemed to me then. Zinaida came in from the next room, in a black dress, her face pale, her hair unbound; she silently took me by the hand and led me out of the room.

"I heard your voice and came out at once," she began. "And was it so easy for you to desert us, you wicked boy?"

"I've come to say good-by to you, Princess," I replied, "and probably forever. You have heard that we are going away?"

She gazed at me fixedly.

"Yes, I have heard. Thank you for coming. I had begun to think I would not be seeing you. Don't think badly of me. I tormented you sometimes, but all the same I am not what you imagine me to be."

She turned away and leaned against the window.

"Really I am not. I know you have a bad opinion of me."

"I have?"

"Yes, you have — you have. . . ."

"I have?" I repeated sorrowfully, and my heart began to quiver as of old under the influence of her irresistible, inexpressible enchantment. "I? Believe me, Zinaida Alexandrovna, no matter what you did, no matter how much you tortured me, I would love you and adore you to the end of my days."

She turned swiftly to me and, opening her arms wide, took my head in her hands and impetuously and hotly kissed me. God knows whom that long, farewell kiss was seeking, but I greedily tasted of its sweetness, I knew that it would never be repeated. "Good-by, good-by . . . " I said again.

She tore herself away and went out. And I left the house. I am unable to convey the feeling with which I left. I would never wish it to be repeated, but I would regard myself as unfortunate if I had never known it.

We drove back to town. It took me a long time to cut myself off from the past, it took me a long time to settle down to work. My wound slowly healed; but really there was no bad feeling between my father and me. On the contrary, he seemed to grow even more in my eyes; let psychologists explain this contradiction as they wish. One day as I was walking along the boulevard, to my indescribable joy I ran into Lushin. I liked him for his direct and unhypocritical nature, and, besides, he was dear to me because of the memories he awoke within me. I rushed over to him. "Aha!" he said. "So it's you, young man! Let me have a look at you! You're still rather yellow, but I must say there isn't the former nasty look in your eyes. Now you look like a man, not a lapdog. Well, and what are you doing? Working hard?"

I sighed. I did not want to lie, but I was ashamed to tell the truth.

"Now, don't be afraid," Lushin went on, "don't be shy. The main thing is to live a normal life and not to give yourself over to distractions. For what good will they ever do you? No matter where the wave carries you, it is always bad; but a man may stand on stone so long as he stands on his own feet. I've got a bit of a cough, and Belovzorov — have you heard?"

"No, I haven't. What's happened?"

"Vanished without a trace; they say he's gone off to the Caucasus. There's a lesson for you, young man. And all because they're not capable of getting out in time, of breaking the net. But you appear to have escaped without damage. Now see that you don't get caught again. Good-by."

"I shan't be caught again," I thought. "I shall never see her again." But I was fated to see Zinaida once more.

21

My father went riding every day; he had a magnificent roan and sorrel English thoroughbred, untiring and wicked, with a long, slender neck and long legs; he was called Electric. No one but my father could ride him. One day Father came to me in a good humor — a mood I had not known him to be in for a long time. He was intending to go for a ride and was already wearing spurs. I asked him to take me with him.

First Love

"We'd do better at a game of leapfrog," he replied. "On your hack you'll never keep up with me."

"Yes I shall; I'll wear spurs too."

"Come on, then."

We set off. I had a little shaggy raven horse, strong in the legs and quite skittish; true, he had to gallop at full speed when Electric was put into a fast trot, but even so I was not left behind. I have never seen another horseman like my father; he sat his horse so beautifully and with such careless ease that it seemed as though the horse beneath him were conscious of it and proud of him. We rode along all the boulevards, and through the Dvichye Fields, jumped several fences (at first I was afraid to jump, but my father felt contempt for timid people, and I ceased to be afraid), rode twice across the River Moskva, and I was just thinking that now we would be returning home, especially as my father himself had noticed that my horse was tired, when suddenly he turned away in the direction of the Crimean Ford and galloped along the bank. I set off after him. Drawing up to a lofty pile of old beams, he swung himself nimbly out of the saddle, ordered me to dismount, and, giving me his horse's reins, said I was to wait for him here by the beams. Then he turned into a narrow lane and was lost to sight. I began to walk up and down along the bank, leading the horses and swearing at Electric, who would keep throwing up or shaking his head, snorting and neighing. And when I halted he dug his hoofs into the earth one after another, squealed, and bit my mount on the neck; in a word, he behaved like a spoilt thoroughbred. My father did not return. An unpleasant dampness rose from the river; a fine rain fell softly and sprinkled tiny dark spots over the idiotic gray beams, which I now found thoroughly boring as I wandered about in their vicinity. I began to feel anxious, but still my father did not return. Some policeman, a Finn, who was all gray too, and had an enormous shako, like a pot, on his head, and was armed with a halberd (what was a policeman doing on the bank of the River Moskva, I wondered), came along and, turning his elderly, furrowed face in my direction, asked me:

"What are you doing here with those horses, young sir? Give them to me, I'll hold them."

I did not reply; he asked me for some tobacco. In order to get away from him (moreover, I was on tenterhooks with im-

407

patience), I went several paces in the direction my father had taken, then walked along the little lane to its end, turned a corner, and stopped short. In a street some forty paces away, outside the open window of a small wooden house, I saw my father. He was standing with his back to me and leaning with his chest against the windowsill. Inside the house, half hidden by the curtain, a woman in a dark dress was sitting, talking to him. The woman was Zinaida.

I was petrified. I confess that I had had not the least expectation of what I saw. My first reaction was to turn and flee. "He will look round," I thought, "and I shall be done for." But a strange feeling, a feeling stronger than curiosity, stronger even than jealousy, stronger than fear, restrained me. I began to watch, I tried to overhear what they were saying. Apparently my father was insisting on something. Zinaida would not agree. I can see her face even now, mournful, serious, beautiful, and with an indescribable impress of devotion, sorrow, love, and a kind of despair — I cannot find another word for it. She spoke in monosyllables, did not raise her eyes, and only smiled, humbly and obstinately. In that smile alone did I recognize my former Zinaida. My father shrugged his shoulders and adjusted the hat on his head: a movement that was always a sign that he was getting impatient. Then I caught the words: *"Vous devez vous separer de cette . . ."* Zinaida drew herself up and stretched out her hand. . . . Suddenly before my eyes, something unbelievable occurred: my father impetuously raised his whip, with which he had been beating the dust out of the edge of his coat, and I heard a sharp blow on that arm bared to the elbow. I could hardly refrain from crying out. But Zinaida shuddered, gazed silently at my father, and slowly raised her arm to her mouth, then kissed the weal that showed livid across it. He threw his whip away and, running hurriedly up the steps of the veranda, burst into the house. Zinaida turned and, stretching out her arms, throwing back her head, also left the window.

My heart sinking with fear, possessed with a bewildered horror, I flung myself back and, running along the lane, all but letting go of Electric, returned to the riverbank. I could make nothing of what I had seen. I knew that my cold and restrained father sometimes had outbreaks of frenzy, yet I could not realize that I had just witnessed such an attack. But I felt at once that no matter how long I lived, it would never be possible for me to forget that movement, that look, that smile of Zinaida's; I felt that her image, this new image that had suddenly been revealed to me, was imprinted forever in my memory. I stared senselessly at the river and did not notice that tears were running from my eyes. "They beat her," I thought; "they beat her . . . beat her. . . ."

"Now what's the matter with you? Give me my horse!" I heard my father's voice behind me.

I mechanically gave him the rein. He sprang into the saddle. The animal was chilled, and he rose on his hind legs and took one bound of a good ten feet. But Father quickly had him under control; he drove the spurs into his flanks and struck him on the neck with his fist. "Pity I haven't got my whip!" he muttered.

I remembered how that same whip had whistled and the blow it had struck, and shuddered.

"What have you done with it?" I asked after a moment.

He did not reply, but galloped on ahead. I overtook him. I simply had to see his face.

"Have you been bored while I was gone?" he asked through set teeth.

"A little. But where have you dropped your whip?" I asked him again.

He gave me a swift look. "I haven't dropped it," he said; "I threw it away." He was lost in thought and his head sank on his breast. And then, for the first and probably for the last time, I saw how much tenderness and regret could be expressed in his stern features.

He galloped on once more, and this time I could not overtake him: I arrived home fifteen minutes after him.

"Now, that is love," I said to myself again as I sat that evening before my writing-desk, which was now beginning to be littered with exercise books and primers. "That is passion. How could one help revolting, how could one endure a blow from anyone, least of all from the dearest of all hands! But evidently you can, if you really love. . . . Yet I — I imagined . . ."

The past month had aged me considerably, and even to me my love, with all its agitations and sufferings, seemed something petty, and childish, and miserable by comparison with this other, this unknown something, at which I could hardly surmise and which frightened me, like a strange, handsome, but threatening face that one vainly tries to discern in the dusk.

I dreamed a strange and terrible dream that night. I thought I was entering a low, dark room. . . . My father was standing with a whip in his hand and stamping his feet; Zinaida was huddled in one corner, and there was a crimson line, not on her hand, but on her forehead. . . . And behind them both Belovzorov rose covered with blood, grinning with his white teeth and angrily threatening him.

Two months later I entered the university, and six months afterward my father died of a stroke, in Petersburg, to which city we had recently moved. A few days before his death a letter arrived from Moscow that greatly agitated him. . . . He went to ask my mother for something, and they say he even wept — he, my father! On the very morning of the day he had the stroke he began to write a letter to me in French. "My son," he wrote, "fear woman's love; fear that happiness, that poison. . . ." After his death my mother sent quite a large sum of money to Moscow.

22

Four years passed. I had just left the university and still had no real idea what I intended to do with myself, at what door to knock; for the time being, I was loafing about in idleness. One fine evening I met Maidanov at the theater. He had married and gone into the civil service; but I did not notice any change in him. He still went into raptures just as unnecessarily, and grew depressed just as suddenly.

"Do you know," he said to me, in passing, "Madame Dolskaya is here?"

"Which Madame Dolskaya?"

"Why, have you forgotten? The former Princess Zasiokina, whom we were all in love with, including yourself. Do you remember, in the house you had for the summer near the Nieskuchny Gardens?"

"Has she married Dolsky, then?"

"Yes."

"And she is here, in the theater?"

"No, I mean she's in Petersburg. She arrived a day or two ago. She is planning to go abroad."

"What sort of man is her husband?" I asked.

First Love

"A splendid fellow, and wealthy. He was a colleague of mine in Moscow. You understand that after that affair — you must know all about it" (he smiled significantly) — "it was not easy for her to make a match; there were consequences. . . . But with her intelligence everything is possible. Go and call on her; she'll be very glad to see you. She has grown even more beautiful."

He gave me Zinaida's address. She was staying in the Hôtel Demuth. Old memories began to quicken within me. . . . I promised myself that I would call on my former "passion" the very next day. But something else came along; a week passed, then another; and when I did at last go to the Hôtel Demuth and ask for Mme Dolskaya, I learned that she had died four days previously, quite suddenly, in childbirth.

Something seemed to strike at my heart. The thought that I could have seen her and did not see her, and now never would see her — that bitter thought pierced me with all the strength of irresistible reproach. "She's dead!" I repeated, staring stupidly at the porter. I slowly made my way into the street and went, not knowing whither. All the past came back and rose before me in a moment. And so that was how it had been resolved, that was what that young, burning, brilliant life, hurrying and agitated, had striven to achieve! As I thought this, I imagined those dear features, those eyes, those curls, in a narrow box, in the damp underground gloom, here, not far from me, who was still alive, and perhaps only a few paces from my father. . . . I thought all this, I strained my imagination; but meanwhile:

> *"From indifferent lips I heard news of her death,*
> *And indifferently listened I to it . . ."*

the words echoed in my soul. O youth! Youth! There seems to be nothing you cannot do, you would seem to have mastery over all the treasures of the universe, even sorrow is a comfort to you, even grief confers added beauty on your face, you are self-confident and audacious; you say: "I alone am alive, look at me." But with you, too, the days speed past and disappear without trace and without number, and everything within you vanishes, like wax in the sun, like snow. . . . And, maybe, all the secret of your charm consists not in the possibility that you can do anything, but in the possibility of thinking that you can do anything, consists just in the circumstance that you cast to the winds strength that you would not know how to use on anything else, in the circumstance that every one of us seriously regards himself as a spendthrift, seriously assumes that he has every right to say: "Oh, what would I have done if I had not wasted my time in vain!"

So too I. . . . How much I hoped for, how much I expected, what a rich future did I anticipate, even when I had only just carried out the momentarily returning apparition of my first love, accompanying it with a single sigh, a single pang of mourning.

But of all that I hoped, what has come to pass? And now that the evening shadows are already beginning to speed over my life, what is left to me more fresh, more precious than the memory of that swiftly passed, vernal thunder of my morn?

But in vain do I upbraid myself. Even then, in that thoughtless, youthful time, I did not remain deaf to the mournful voice that called to me, the solemn sound that reached me from beyond the grave. I remember, a few days after I had learned of Zinaida's death, I was drawn by my own invincible attraction to be present at the deathbed of a poor old woman who lived in our house. Covered with rags, lying on hard boards, with a sack beneath her head, she died painfully and wretchedly. All her life had been passed in one bitter struggle with everyday need; she had never known joy, she had never tasted the honey of happiness; one would have thought that she could not but rejoice at death, at its freedom, its peace. And yet so long as her decrepit body still resisted, so long as her breast still heaved beneath the icy hand that lay on it, so long as her last strength had not departed from her, that old woman went on crossing herself and whispering: "Lord, forgive me my trespasses. . . ." And only with the last spark of consciousness did the expression of fear and terror of her end fade from her eyes. . . . And I remember that there, beside that poor old woman's deathbed, I suddenly felt afraid for Zinaida; and I wanted to pray for her, for my father . . . and for myself.

On the Eve

1859

I

Ln the shadow of a lofty lime, on the bank of the River Moskva, not far from Kuntsevo, on one of the hottest days in the summer of 1853, two young men were lying on the grass. One of them, who appeared to be about twenty-three years old, and was tall, swarthy, with a sharp and rather crooked nose, a lofty forehead, and a restrained smile on his broad lips, was lying on his back and thoughtfully gazing into the distance, with his small gray eyes closed; the other was lying on his chest, resting his fair, curly head in both hands, and was also gazing into the distance. He was three years older than his comrade, but he seemed to be much younger; his mustache was only just sprouting, and a light down was curling on his chin. There was something childishly pretty, something attractively refined, about the small features of his fresh, round face, his gentle, hazel eyes, his handsome, swollen lips and white little hands. Everything about him was vivid with the happy cheerfulness of health and youth — the light-heartedness, the self-reliance, the pampered air, and the charm of youth. He shifted his gaze and smiled and supported his head, just as boys do who know that others enjoy looking at them. He was wearing a full white coat rather like a blouse; a blue kerchief was wrapped round his slender neck; a crumpled straw hat was flung down on the grass beside him.

By comparison his companion seemed an old man and, looking at his angular figure, no one would have thought that he, too, was enjoying himself, that he, too, was on top of the world. He was lying awkwardly; his large head, broad at the top, narrow at the base, was carried awkwardly on his long neck; there was awkwardness in the very position of his hands, of his body in its tight-fitting short black coat, his long legs with knees bent upward, like the hind legs of a dragonfly. Despite all this, one could not but recognize that he was a well-bred man; the impress of

413

"decency" was to be noted in all his clumsy being, and his face, plain and even rather funny to look at, bore the cast of thought and kindliness. His name was Andrei Piotrovich Berseniev; his comrade, the fair-haired young man, was Pavel Yakovlich Shubin.

"Why don't you lie on your chest, like me?" Shubin remarked. "It's much better that way. Especially when you raise your legs and knock your heels against each other, like this. You've got the grass right under your nose; if you get tired of looking at the landscape you can gaze at some pot-bellied little insect crawling up a blade of grass, or at an ant fussing about. Really, it is better that way. But you've adopted some pseudo-classic pose, neither one nor t'other, like a ballet dancer when she leans against a cardboard cliff. You just bear in mind that now you have every right to take life easy. It's no joking matter, your being third in the list of B.A.'s! Now take it easy, sir; stop straining yourself, relax your limbs!"

Shubin said all this speech through his nose, half lazily, half jokingly (the way spoilt children talk to family friends who bring them sweets). Not waiting for an answer, he went on:

"What astonishes me most of all in ants, beetles, and other respectable insects is their amazing seriousness; they run about with such an important air, just as though their life had some meaning! You just think there is a man, the lord of creation, a higher creature, looking at them, but they're not in the least interested in him. And not only that, but some mosquito will even sit on the lord of creation's nose and begin to use it for food. That's downright insulting. And yet, on the other hand, in what respect is their life any worse than ours? And why shouldn't they behave as though they were important, if we allow ourselves to behave as though we were? Well now, philosopher, solve me that problem! Why don't you speak? Well?"

"What?" Berseniev said, starting.

"What!" Shubin echoed him. "Your friend is expounding profound thoughts to you, and you're not listening to him."

"I was enjoying the view. Look how hotly those fields are shimmering in the sun!" (Berseniev hissed a little when pronouncing sibilants.)

"The color's been put on thick," Shubin replied. "It's nature, in a word!"

Berseniev shook his head.

"You should admire it all even more than I do. It's in your line: you're an artist."

"No; it is not in my line," Shubin retorted, setting his hat on the back of his head. "I'm a butcher; my business is concerned with meat, sticking meat together — shoulders, legs, and arms. But here there isn't any form, or any completeness, it's gone all ways — and you try catching it!"

"But even here there's beauty," Berseniev remarked. "By the way, have you finished that bas-relief?"

"Which one?"

"The child with the goat."

"To hell with it! To hell with it! To hell with it!" Shubin exclaimed in a singsong tone. "I went and looked at the real things, at the ancients, at antiquity, and then I smashed my rubbish. You point me to nature and say: 'There's beauty here too.' Of course, there is beauty in everything, there's beauty even in your nose, but one doesn't go chasing after just any sort of beauty. The ancients didn't chase after it; it itself entered into their creations, where from, God knows — from heaven perhaps. All the world belonged to them; but we don't have to spread ourselves so much: our arms are short. We cast the hook at just one little point, and then we watch. If it nibbles, splendid! But if it doesn't — "

Shubin stuck out his tongue.

"Wait a moment, wait a moment," Berseniev objected. "That is a paradox. If you don't have sympathy for nature, and don't admire it no matter where you meet with it, then it will not surrender to you in your art either. If a splendid view, a splendid piece of music, doesn't say anything to your soul — I mean to say, if you don't feel in sympathy with it — "

"Ah, you sympathizer!" Shubin burst out, and smiled at his own newly invented word, though Berseniev was lost in thought. "No, brother," Shubin continued, "you're a sage, a philosopher, the third Bachelor of Moscow University; it is a fearful matter to argue with you, especially for me, a student who didn't finish his studies; but this is what I say to you: outside my art, I am fond of beauty only in women — in girls; and for some time now even that — "

He turned over on his back and put his hands behind his head.

Several moments passed in silence. The stillness of the noonday heat oppressed the radiant and drowsy earth.

445

"Speaking of women," Shubin began again, "why doesn't someone take Stakhov in hand? Did you see him in Moscow?"

"No."

"The old man has gone quite crazy. He spends days on end sitting with his Avgustina Khristianovna; he gets terribly bored, but he still goes on sitting. They eye each other so idiotically — it's quite unpleasant to watch them. Now take him! What a family God has blessed that man with! But no, give him Avgustina Khristianovna! I know nothing more odious than her duck-like physiognomy. The other day I did a caricature of her in the Dantan [1] style; it turned out quite good. I'll show it to you."

"But, how about the bust of Yelena Nikolaevna?" Berseniev asked. "Are you getting on with it?"

"No, brother, I'm not. That face is enough to reduce you to despair. You look at it, and the lines are clean, severe, straight-forward; it wouldn't seem difficult to catch the likeness. But it doesn't come. . . . It no more yields to you than treasure falls into the hand. Have you noticed the way she sits when listening? Not a single feature stirs, only the expression of her gaze changes incessantly, and all her figure changes because of it. What do you advise a sculptor, and a bad one at that, to do in such a case? She's an extraordinary creature — a strange creature," he added after a brief pause.

"Yes; she's an extraordinary girl," Berseniev repeated after him.

"And she's Nikolai Artiomovich Stakhov's daughter! And then you try to build up an argument based on blood and the breed! Yet it is an amusing fact that she is his daughter; she looks like him; and she's like her mother, Anna Vasilievna, too. I respect Anna Vasilievna with all my heart — after all, she is my patroness; but she really is a chicken. Where did Yelena get that soul from? Who set that fire alight? There's another problem for you, philosopher!"

But the "philosopher" made no more reply than before. In general Berseniev did not err in the direction of loquacity, and when he did speak, he expressed himself awkwardly, jerkily, gesticulating unnecessarily. And now a special silence had settled in his soul, a silence akin to weariness and sorrow. He had recently moved out of town after long and difficult labor that had

---

[1] Jean Pierre Dantan (1800–69), French sculptor, noted in particular for his statuettes caricaturing contemporary celebrities. (Tr.)

occupied him for several hours every day. The inactivity, the mildness and purity of the air, the consciousness of an end achieved, the whimsical and casual conversation with his friend, the suddenly evoked image of a dear being — all these heterogeneous, yet for some reason congruous impressions blended within him into a single general feeling, which tranquilized him, and agitated him, and debilitated him. . . . He was a very highly strung young man.

Beneath the lime it was cool and still; the flies and bees that flew into the circle of its shadow seemed to hum more softly; the clean fine grass of emerald color, without any golden tinge, did not stir; the long stalks stood motionless, as though enchanted; the tiny clusters of yellow flowers hung as though dead on the lower branches of the lime. With every breath the delicate perfume penetrated into the very depths of the lungs, but the lungs gladly drew in that scent. In the distance, beyond the river, away to the horizon everything was sparkling, everything was burning; occasionally a breeze sped over the land and disintegrated and intensified the sparkle; a radiant haze quivered above the earth. No birds were to be heard; they do not sing in the hours of heat; but the crickets were chirruping everywhere and for anyone sitting in the cool, in the stillness, it was pleasant to hear this fiery sound of life; it made one feel drowsy and dreamy.

"Have you ever noticed," Berseniev suddenly began, helping out his remarks with movements of his hands, "what a strange feeling nature arouses in us? Everything in it is so full, so clear, I mean so satisfied with itself, and we understand that and enjoy it, and at the same time it always, at any rate in me, arouses a kind of disquiet, a kind of anxiety, even sorrow. What is the reason for that? Is it that in her presence, before her face, we are more strongly conscious of all our incompleteness, our lack of clarity, or is that satisfaction which is sufficient for her too little for us, but she hasn't any other, I mean to say she hasn't just what we need?"

"Hm!" Shubin replied. "I'll tell you, Andrei Piotrovich, why all this is so. You have described the sensations of a man who is lonely, a man who doesn't live, but only looks on and gushes. Why look on? You yourself begin to live, and you'll do fine. No matter how much you knock at nature's door, she never answers in intelligible words, because she is dumb. She will sound and whine like a string, but don't expect a song from her. Now, a living soul — that will respond, especially if it is a woman's. And so, my noble friend I advise you to provide yourself with a sweetheart, and all your yearning feelings will disappear at once. That is what we 'need,' as you put it. For that anxiety, that sorrow you talk about, is all simply a kind of hunger. Give your stomach real food, and everything will immediately settle down. Occupy your own position in space, be a body, my brother. And what is this 'nature' you mentioned, what did you drag it in for? You just listen: love — what a strong, burning word that is! Nature — what a cold, scholastic expression! And so" (Shubin began to sing) " 'Hurrah for Maria Pietrovna!' but no," he added, "not Maria Pietrovna, but it doesn't matter. *Vous me compre-nez.*"

Berseniev half raised himself and rested his chin on his folded arms.

"Why sneer?" he said, without looking at his comrade. "Why jeer? Yes, you are right: love is a great word, a great feeling. . . . But what love are you talking about?"

Shubin also half raised himself.

"What love? Oh, any love you like, so long as it is present. I confess to you that in my opinion there aren't any different kinds of love at all. Once you have fallen in love — "

"With all your heart," Berseniev took him up.

"Why, of course, that goes without saying: the heart isn't an apple, you can't share it out. Once you have fallen in love you are right. But I wasn't thinking of jeering. I have such a feeling of tenderness in my heart now, it is so softened . . . I only wanted to explain why nature, as you call it, has that effect on us. It is because it arouses a necessity for love in us and is not able to satisfy it. It quietly drives us into other, living embraces, but we don't understand and expect something from nature itself. Ah, Andrei, Andrei, how splendid is this sun, this sky! Everything, everything all around us, is splendid; and yet you are sad. But if at this moment you were holding a beloved woman's hand in your hand, if that hand and all that woman were yours, if you even looked with *her* eyes, felt not with your own solitary feelings but with *hers*, nature would not arouse sorrow in you, Andrei, and not anxiety, nor would you stop to observe its beauty. Nature itself would rejoice and sing, nature would echo your hymn, because then you would give it, would give that dumb thing, a tongue!"

Shubin jumped to his feet and strode backward and forward several times; but Berseniev bowed his head, and his face was suffused with a faint flush.

"I don't altogether agree with you," he began; "not always does nature hint to us of — love." (He paused before he uttered that word.) "She threatens us also: she reminds us of terrible — yes, of inaccessible secrets. Isn't it nature who must finally swallow us up, isn't she incessantly swallowing us up? In her is both Life and Death; and in her, Death speaks just as loudly as Life."

"In love too there is Life and Death," Shubin interrupted.

"And so," Berseniev continued, "when I stand, for instance, in a wood in springtime, in a green thicket, when I imagine I hear the romantic sounds of Oberon's horn" (he felt a little ashamed after saying these words), "isn't that, too — "

"The craving for love, the craving for happiness, and nothing more!" Shubin broke in. "I, too, know those sounds; I, too, know that emotion and expectation which comes upon the soul beneath the shadow of the forest, in its heart, or of an evening in the open field, when the sun is setting and the river is smoking with mist beyond the bushes. But from the forest, and from the river, and from the earth, and from heaven, from every little cloud, from every blade of grass I expect, I desire happiness; I feel its approach, I hear its call in everything. 'My god is a light and happy god!' That's how I once began a poem; you must admit it is a splendid first line, but I simply couldn't think of a second to follow it. Happiness! Happiness! So long as life has not passed, so long as all our members are under our control, so long as we are going not down, but up hill! Damn it all!" Shubin went on with sudden impetuosity, "we are young, we're not monsters, we're not stupid; we shall win happiness for ourselves!"

He shook his curly head and self-confidently, almost challengingly gazed up at the sky. Berseniev raised his eyes to him.

"So apparently there is nothing greater than happiness?" he said quietly.

"For instance?" Shubin asked, and paused.

"Why, for instance, you and I are young, as you say, we are decent people, granted; each of us wishes happiness for himself. . . . But is that word 'happiness' such as would unite, could set us both on fire, would compel us to give each other our hands? Isn't it an egotistic, I would even say a disuniting word?"

"But do you know any words that do unite?"

"Yes; there are quite a lot of them, too; and you know them."

"Come on, then! What are they?"

"Why, there's art for instance — as you're an artist — and one's country, science, freedom, justice."

"And love?" Shubin asked.

"Love, too, is a uniting word; but not that love you crave at the moment: not love that is enjoyment, but love that is sacrifice."

Shubin's face clouded.

"That's all right for the Germans; but I want to love for myself; I want to be number one."

"Number one," Berseniev repeated. "But it seems to me that to put yourself number two is all the assignment of our life."

"If everybody were to act on your advice," Shubin said, pulling a mournful face, "nobody on earth would eat pineapples: everybody would be leaving them for others."

"In other words, pineapples are not necessary; but you needn't be afraid, all the same: there will always be some who are glad to take even the bread out of other people's mouths."

The two friends were silent for a while.

"I met Insarov again the other day," Berseniev began. "I have invited him along to my place. I simply must introduce him to you — and to the Stakhovs."

"With Insarov do you mean? Oh yes, that Serb or Bulgar you told me about? That patriot? Has he put all these philosophic thoughts in your head?"

"Maybe."

"He's an unusual sort of individual, isn't he?"

"Yes."

"Intelligent? Talented?"

"Intelligent? — yes. Talented? I don't know, I don't think so."

"No? Then what is there remarkable about him?"

"You'll see. But now I think it's time we went. I expect Anna Vasilievna will be waiting for us. What time is it?"

"Three. Let's go. How stifling it is! This talk has set all my blood on fire. And you, too, had a minute — I'm not an artist for nothing: I notice everything. Confess, you are interested in a woman — ?"

Shubin tried to glance into Berseniev's face, but his friend turned away and walked out from under the lime tree. Shubin followed him, walking easily and gracefully on his small feet. Berseniev walked clumsily, raising his shoulders high as he went, and craning his neck; even so he seemed a more passable man than Shubin, more the gentleman, we would say, if that word were not so vulgarized among us.

2

The young men dropped down to the River Moskva and walked along its bank. A breath of freshness came from the water, and the quiet ripple of the tiny waves caressed the ear.

"I'd have another bathe," said Shubin, "but I'm afraid of being late. Look at the river: it's just as if it were beckoning to us. The ancient Greeks would see it as a nymph. But we are not Greeks, O nymph! We are thick-skinned Scythians."

"We have our own water-nymphs," Berseniev observed.

"Get away with your water-nymphs! What to me, a sculptor, is that brood of a terrified, chilly fantasy, those images born in the fetor of the peasant's hut, in the gloom of the winter nights? I need light, and space — ah, when, by God, shall I travel to Italy? When — "

"In other words, to Little Russia, you mean?"

"Shame on you, Andrei Piotrovich, to reproach me with that thoughtless stupidity, which, as it is, I already bitterly repent. Yes, truly, I behaved like a fool: Anna Vasilievna was very kind and gave me money for my journey to Italy, but I went off to the Ukrainians to eat boiled dumplings, and — "

"Please don't go on!" Berseniev interrupted.

"And all the same I say that that money was not wasted. I saw such remarkable types there, especially women. . . . Of course, I know there is no salvation outside Italy!"

"You will travel to Italy," Berseniev said, without turning to him, "and you will do nothing. You will only go on flapping your wings and never flying. We know you!"

"But Stavasseur flew — and not only he. But if I don't fly, it is because I must be a penguin and have no wings. I'm stifled here, I want to go to Italy," Shubin continued; "there's sun there, and beauty there. . . ."

At that moment a young girl in a broad straw hat, with a rose-

421

colored parasol over her shoulder, appeared on the path the friends were following.

"But what do I see? Here, too, beauty is coming to meet us! Greetings from a conquered artist to the enchanting Zoya!" Shubin suddenly cried, theatrically waving his hat.

The girl to whom this exclamation was addressed halted and threatened him with her finger. Letting the two friends come up to her, she said in a ringing little voice with a slight lisp:

"Why aren't you coming to dinner, gentlemen? The table is laid."

"What do I hear?" Shubin said, throwing out his hands. "Surely, you, ravishing Zoya, haven't decided to come and look for us in this heat? Is that what I am to deduce from your remark? Tell me: have you really? But no, don't pronounce that word: contrition will shatter me at once."

"Ah, do stop it, Pavel Yakovlevich," the girl retorted, not without a touch of annoyance. "Why can't you ever talk to me seriously? I shall be angry," she added, with a coquettish *moue*, pouting her little lips.

"Don't be angry with me, my ideal Zoya Nikitishna; you don't want to plunge me into a gloomy abyss of frenzied despair, do you? But I can't talk seriously, because I am not a serious man."

The girl shrugged her shoulders and turned to Berseniev.

"He's always like that: he treats me like a child; but I'm already past eighteen. I'm grown up now."

"Oh, God!" Shubin groaned, and turned up his eyes. But Berseniev smiled without speaking.

She stamped her little foot.

"Pavel Yakovlevich! I shall be angry! Hélène would have come with me," she continued, "but she remained in the garden. She was fearful of the heat, but I am not afraid of heat. Come on."

She went ahead of them along the path, her slender figure swaying a little with every step. And she threw the soft, long curls back from her face with one pretty little hand, clad in a black *mitt*.

The friends followed her (Shubin first silently pressed his hands to his heart, then raised them above his head), and a few moments later they came to one of the numerous summer residences that surround Kuntsevo. A small wooden rose-colored house with a mezzanine floor stood in the middle of a garden and seemed to be peeping out naïvely from the green of the trees. Zoya was the first to unlatch the wicket gate; she ran into the garden and cried: "I've brought the wanderers home!" A young girl with a pale and expressive face rose from a bench close to the path, and at the door of the house appeared a lady in a lilac silk gown. Raising her embroidered batiste handkerchief above her head as protection from the sun, she smiled languidly and half-heartedly.

3

Anna Vasilievna Stakhova, née Shubina, had been left a total orphan and the heiress to quite a considerable property at the age of seven. She had both very rich and very poor relations: poor on her father's side, rich on her mother's: the Senator Volgin, and the Princess Chikurasova. Prince Arkadion Chikurasov, who was appointed her guardian, sent her to the best boarding school in Moscow, and when she left the school the Prince took her into his own home. He kept open house and gave balls in the wintertime. Anna Vasilievna's future husband, Nikolai Artiomevich Stakhov, conquered her at one of these balls, where she was dressed in "a charming rose-colored dress with a coiffure of little roses." She kept that coiffure. . . . Nikolai Artiomevich Stakhov, the son of a retired captain who in 1812 had been wounded and appointed to a remunerative post in Petersburg, entered the junkers' school at the age of sixteen and went on to enlist in the guards. He was a handsome fellow, well built, and regarded as almost the best of the young men at the middle-class evening parties that he chiefly frequented; he had no entrée to high society. As a youth he was obsessed by two dreams: to become an aide-de-camp, and to marry with profit; he soon gave up his first dream, but held all the more strongly to the second. So he went to Moscow every winter. He talked French passing well and had the reputation of being a philosopher, because he did not live a gay life. Even when he was only an ensign he was fond of arguing obstinately about such questions as whether a man can visit all the parts of the globe in the course of his life, or whether a man can know what happens on the bottom of the sea — and always maintained the view that it was impossible.

Nikolai Artiomevich was past twenty-five when he "caught" Anna Vasilievna; he applied for retirement and went to the country to play the farmer. He soon grew tired of country life, and moreover the estate was rented out; he settled down in Moscow, in his wife's home. As a youth he had never played any games, but now he developed a passion for lotto and, when lotto was forbidden, for whist. He was bored at home; he happened to meet a widow of German origin and spent almost all his time with her. He had not come out to Kuntsevo for the summer of 1853; he had remained in Moscow, ostensibly in order to have the benefit of the mineral waters; but the truth was that he did not wish to part from his widow. For that matter, even with her he talked little, but even with her he argued about such subjects as the possibility of predicting the weather. Someone had once called him a *frondeur*, he liked the term very much. "Yes," he thought, self-satisfiedly pulling down the corners of his lips and swaying, "it isn't easy to satisfy me, you can't cheat me." Nikolai Artiomevich's *frondeurisme* was exemplified by the fact that if, for instance, he heard the word "nerves," he would say: "But what are nerves?" Or if someone in his presence mentioned the successes of astronomy, he would say: "But do you believe in astronomy?" When he wanted to confound his opponent completely, he said: "That's all talk." It has to be admitted that many people found (and still find) this kind of objection irrefutable. But he had no suspicion whatever that in letters to her cousin Feodolinda Peterzilius his German widow called him "*Mein Pinselchen.*"

Nikolai Artiomevich's wife, Anna Vasilievna, was a small and rather thin woman with fine features and a propensity for emotionalism and dejection. In the boarding school she had studied music and read novels, but later she gave them up entirely: she took to dressing herself in fine clothes, and gave that up too; she intended to occupy herself with her daughter's education, but then grew tired and put her in the hands of a governess; at last she was left with only one occupation, that of indulging in sorrow and mild agitation. In giving birth to her daughter, Yelena, she had ruined her health, and was unable to have any more children; Nikolai Artiomevich would hint at this circumstance in justification of his acquaintance with Avgustina Khristianovna. Her husband's infidelity greatly chagrined Anna Vasilievna; she was especially pained when by a trick he gave his German woman a pair of gray horses taken from Anna Vasilievna's own stud. She never reproached him to his face, but surreptitiously complained about him in turn to everybody in the house, even to her daughter. She did not like going out; she liked having guests and listening to gossip; when by herself she at once began to feel unwell. She had a very loving and tender heart: life soon wore her down.

Pavel Yakovlevich Shubin was the son of her second cousin. His father had been in the civil service at Moscow. His brothers had entered the cadet corps; he was the youngest, his mother's favorite, and was of delicate constitution: he remained at home. He was intended for the university, and they had difficulty in maintaining him at the high school. From early years he began to display a bent for sculpture; the weighty Senator Volgin saw one of his statues at his aunt's house (he was then sixteen) and announced that he intended to patronize the youthful talent. The sudden death of Shubin's father all but completely changed the young man's future. The Senator, the patron of talents, presented him with a bust of Homer, and nothing else; but Anna Vasilievna helped him with money, and, somehow or other, at the age of nineteen he entered the university, to study in the medical faculty. He had no interest whatever in medicine, but because of the number of students taking courses at that time, it was impossible for him to enter any other faculty; and, moreover, he hoped to study anatomy. But he did not finish studying anatomy; he did not go on to the second course and, without waiting for the examination, left the university with the intention of devoting himself exclusively to his vocation. He labored zealously, but spasmodically, wandered about the environs of Moscow, sculptured and drew portraits of peasant girls, made acquaintance with various persons, young and old, high- and low-flying, Italian molders and Russian artists, would not hear of attending an arts academy, and had no respect for any professor. He possessed a definite talent: he began to be known in Moscow. His mother, a Parisian by birth, of excellent family, a good and intelligent woman, taught him French, solicited and fussed for him day and night, was proud of him, and, dying of consumption while still young, asked Anna Vasilievna to take him into her care. He was then in his twenty-first year. Anna Vasilievna fulfilled his mother's last wish: he occupied a small room in the wing of her summer residence.

4

"Do come and have dinner, come on," Anna Vasilievna said in a pitiful voice, and they all went into the dining-room. "Sit by me,

Zoé," she said, "and you, Hélène, entertain the guest, and you, Paul, please don't be naughty and don't tease Zoé. I have a headache today."

Shubin again turned his eyes toward heaven; Zoé answered him with a half-smile. This Zoé, or, to be more precise, Zoya Nikitishna Muller, was a pleasant Russian-German girl with a slight cast, a little nose split at the tip, and tiny crimson lips; she was flaxen-haired, and inclined to be plump. She sang Russian ballads not at all badly, played various, sometimes gay, sometimes touching little pieces very correctly on the piano, and dressed with taste, but in a rather childish manner and altogether too neatly. Anna Vasilievna had taken her as a companion for her daughter and kept her almost entirely in attendance on herself. Yelena did not complain of this arrangement: she had no idea what to talk about to Zoya whenever she happened to be left alone with her.

The dinner lasted quite a long time; Berseniev talked to Yelena about university life, about his intentions and hopes; Shubin listened, was silent, and ate with exaggerated avidity, occasionally casting comically despondent glances at Zoya, who always responded with the same phlegmatic little smile. After dinner Yelena, Berseniev, and Shubin went into the garden; Zoya gazed after them and, slightly shrugging her tiny shoulders, sat down at the piano. Anna Vasilievna remarked: "Why don't you go out for a walk too?" but without waiting for an answer she added: "Play me something sad."

"*La Dernière Pensée de Weber?*" Zoya asked.

"Ah yes, something from Weber," Anna Vasilievna said, dropping into a chair; and tears appeared on her eyelashes.

Meanwhile Yelena had led the two friends into an arbor of acacias with a small wooden table in the middle and benches all around it. Shubin looked about him, bounced up and down several times, and then, whispering: "Wait a moment," he ran to his room, brought back a lump of clay, and began to mold a figure of Zoya, shaking his head, muttering, and laughing as he worked.

"Up to your old jokes again!" Yelena said, glancing at his work. Turning to Berseniev, she continued the conversation they had begun at the dinner table.

"The old jokes!" Shubin repeated. "It is an inexhaustible subject! Today particularly it is making me lose all patience."

"Why is it?" Yelena asked. "One would think you were talking about some wicked, unpleasant old woman. A very pretty young girl — "

"Of course," he interrupted her, "she is pretty, very pretty. I am sure any passer-by who glanced at her would infallibly think: 'Now, there is someone it would be excellent — to dance a polka with'; I, too, am sure she knows that, and that she likes it. . . . Then why all those bashful grimaces, that modesty? You know quite well what I am trying to say," he added. "But you're occupied with something else now."

Breaking up the model of Zoya, he began to knead and shape the clay hurriedly, and seemingly with a feeling of annoyance.

"And so you would like to be a professor?" Yelena asked Berseniev.

"Yes," he replied, thrusting his red hands between his knees. "That is my favorite dream. Of course I am fully conscious of all I still need in order to become worthy of such a high — I mean to say that I have not had enough preparation, but I hope to obtain permission to travel abroad; I shall spend three or four years there, if necessary, and then — "

He stopped, cast his eyes down, then gave her a swift glance and, smiling awkwardly, smoothed his hair. When he talked to a woman his speech grew still slower, and his hiss even more pronounced.

"Do you want to be a professor of history?" Yelena asked.

"Yes, or else philosophy," he added, lowering his voice, "if that is possible."

"He's already as strong as the devil in philosophy," Shubin observed as he carved deep lines in the clay with his nail. "What does he need to go abroad for?"

"And you will be perfectly satisfied with your position?" Yelena asked, resting her head on her hand and looking him straight in the face.

"Perfectly, Yelena Nikolaevna, perfectly. And what better vocation can a man have? You think, to follow in the steps of Timofei Nikolaevich — The very thought of such activity fills me with delight and embarrassment — yes, embarrassment, which — which arises from a realization of my own poor powers. My dead father gave me his blessing on my task — I shall never forget his last words to me."

"Your father died last winter, didn't he?"

"Yes, Yelena Nikolaevna, in February."

"They say," she went on, "that he left a remarkable work in manuscript; is that true?"

"Yes, he did. He was a marvelous man. You would have loved him, Yelena Nikolaevna."

"I'm sure of that. But what is the work about?"

"It is rather difficult, Yelena Nikolaevna, to tell you in few words what it is about. My father was a learned man, a Schellingist, he made use of expressions that are not altogether clear —"

"Andrei Piotrovich," Yelena interrupted him; "forgive my ignorance, but what does 'Schellingist' mean?"

He faintly smiled.

"A Schellingist is a follower of Schelling, the German philosopher, and Schelling's teaching consisted —"

"Andrei Piotrovich!" Shubin suddenly exclaimed, "for goodness' own sake! Surely you're not going to give Yelena Nikolaevna a lecture on Schelling? Spare her!"

"I had no intention of giving her a lecture," Berseniev muttered, and flushed. "I simply wanted —"

"But why not?" Yelena caught him up. "You and I are badly in need of lectures, Pavel Yakovlevich."

Shubin fixed his eyes on her and burst into unexpected laughter.

"And what are you laughing at?" she asked coldly and almost severely.

He lapsed into silence.

"All right, don't be angry," he said after a moment. "It's my fault. But really, what is the pleasure of talking about philosophy now, in such weather, beneath these trees? Let us rather talk about the nightingales and roses, about young eyes and smiles."

"Yes; and about French romances, and women's finery," Yelena continued.

"And finery too, if you like," he retorted, "if it is beautiful."

"If you like. But supposing we don't want to talk about finery? You call yourself a free artist, so why do you encroach upon other people's freedom? And allow me to ask why you attack Zoya if you think like that? She is just the right person to talk to about finery and roses."

Shubin suddenly flared up and rose from the bench.

"Ah, so that's it?" he began in an uncertain tone. "I understand your hint; you're sending me off to her, Yelena Nikolaevna. In other words, I'm not wanted here."

"I didn't even think of sending you off."

"You are hinting," he continued fierily, "that I am not worthy of any other society, that I am a good match for her, that I am just as empty, and absurd, and petty as that sugary little German girl? Isn't that so?"

Yelena knitted her brows.

"You didn't always speak of her like that, Pavel Yakovlevich," she remarked.

"Ah! A reproach! A reproach now!" Shubin exclaimed. "All right, I don't conceal the fact that there was a minute, exactly one minute, when those fresh, vulgar little cheeks — But suppose I felt like repaying you with reproaches and reminding you — Good-by," he suddenly added; "I am ready to talk nonsense."

And, bringing his hand down heavily on the head he had molded from the clay, he ran out of the arbor and went to his own room.

"What a child!" Yelena said as she gazed after him.

"An artist," Berseniev observed with a quiet smile. "All artists are like that. We have to forgive them their caprices. That is their right."

"Yes," Yelena objected, "but so far Pavel hasn't done anything to earn that right. What has he done so far? Give me your arm and let us walk along the avenue. He has interrupted us. We were talking about your father's work."

Berseniev took Yelena's arm and walked with her through the garden; but the conversation, which had been broken off too soon, was not renewed; he turned again to telling her what he thought of a professorial occupation and his future activities. He walked along quietly at her side, stepping awkwardly, awkwardly holding her arm, occasionally jostling her with his shoulder, and not once looking at her. But his words flowed easily, even if not quite freely; he expressed himself simply and correctly, and his eyes, slowly wandering over the trunks of the trees, over the shingle of the paths, over the grass, beamed with a gentle light of noble feeling, while his tranquil voice quivered with the joy of a man who realizes that he has an opportunity to express his opinions to someone dear to him. Yelena listened to him intently and, walking, half turned toward him, did not remove her gaze from his rather pallid face, from his eyes, friendly and modest, though they avoided meeting her eyes. Her soul unfolded, and something tender, true, and good seemed to be poured into her heart, or else to be growing within it.

5

Shubin did not leave his room again all day. It was quite dark, a moon almost at the full hung high in the heavens, the Milky Way was faintly glimmering, and stars were beginning to shine when Berseniev, after taking leave of Anna Vasilievna, Yelena, and Zoya, went up to his friend's room. He found the door locked, and he knocked.

"Who's there?" he heard Shubin's voice.

"It's Berseniev," he replied.

"What do you want?"

"Let me come in, Pavel; enough of your moods; you ought to be ashamed of yourself."

"I'm not in any moods, I'm asleep and I'm dreaming of Zoya."

"Please do stop it. You're not a child. Let me in. I want to talk to you."

"Haven't you had enough of talking to Yelena?"

"Stop it now, stop it; let me in!"

Shubin replied with an artificial snore. Berseniev shrugged his shoulders and went home.

The night was warm and seemed to be unusually silent, as though everything around were listening and watching; and Berseniev, encompassed by a motionless haze, involuntarily halted and also listened and watched. A light rustle, like the swishing sound of a woman's gown, arose occasionally in the crowns of the near-by trees and aroused in him a pleasant and awed sensation, a sensation half of fear. Tiny shivers ran over his cheeks, his eyes went cold with momentary tears; he felt that he must move quite inaudibly, must conceal himself, must steal along. A stiff little breeze blew against one side of him; he shuddered slightly and froze still where he stood. A drowsy beetle fell from a branch and struck the road with a thud; he quietly exclaimed: "Ah!" and halted again. But he began to think of Yelena, and all these fleeting sensations vanished at once; only the invigorating impression of the nocturnal freshness and the nocturnal walk was left; all his soul was occupied with the image of the young girl. As he walked along with head bowed, recalling her words, her questions, he thought he heard a scamper of swift footsteps behind him. He pricked up his ears: someone was running, someone was overtaking him; he could hear a panting breath. Suddenly, out of the black circle of shadow cast by a great tree, with no hat on his disheveled hair, his face quite pale in the light of the moon, Shubin emerged before him.

"I'm glad you came along this road." He uttered the words with difficulty. "I wouldn't have slept all night if I hadn't overtaken you. Give me your hand. You are going home, aren't you?"

"Yes."

"I'll go with you."

"But how can you go without a hat?"

"That's all right. I've taken off my cravat too. It's warm now."

The friends walked on a few paces.

"I was very silly today, wasn't I?" Shubin abruptly asked.

"Speaking frankly, yes, you were; I couldn't understand you. I have never seen you like that before. And why did you get so angry, for goodness' sake? Over what trifles!"

"Hm!" Shubin grunted. "That's how you put it; but I wasn't at all concerned with trifles. You see," he added, "I must mention to you that I — that — Think what you like of me — I — well, here goes! I am in love with Yelena."

"You're in love with Yelena?" Berseniev echoed him, and stopped.

"Yes," Shubin continued with studied negligence. "Does that surprise you? I'll tell you more. Until this evening I could hope that in time she would come to love me too. But today I have been convinced that I have nothing to hope for. She is in love with another."

"With another? But whom?"

"Who? You!" Shubin exclaimed and brought his hand down on his friend's shoulder.

"Me?"

"Yes, you!" Shubin repeated.

Berseniev fell back a step and stood still. Shubin gave him a keen look.

"And does that surprise you? You are a modest young man! But she loves you. On that score you can rest assured."

Turgenev

"What rot you're talking!" Berseniev said at last in a vexed tone.

"No, it isn't rot. But, by the way, what are we standing here for? Let's go on. It's easier when walking. I have known her long, and I know her well. I can't make any mistake. You are a man to her heart. There was a time when she liked me; but, to begin with, I am too frivolous a young man for her, while you are a serious creature, morally and physically you are a tidy person, you — wait, I haven't finished; you are a conscientiously moderate enthusiast, a true representative of those high priests of science which — no, not which — whom the middle class of the Russian nobility are so justly proud of! And secondly, the other day Yelena caught me kissing Zoya's arm!"

"Zoya's?"

"Yes, Zoya's. What else would you have me do? She has such beautiful shoulders."

"Shoulders?"

"Why yes, shoulders, arms, is there any difference? Yelena caught me in the midst of these free occupations after dinner, but before dinner she had heard me swearing at Zoya. Unfortunately, Yelena does not understand how natural such contradictions are. And then *you* turned up: you believe — what is it exactly that you believe? — you turn red, you are confused, you talk about Schiller, about Schelling (and she is always on the lookout for remarkable people), and so you have conquered. But I, poor wretch, try to jest and — and — meanwhile — "

He suddenly burst into tears, turned aside, sat down on the ground, and clutched at his hair.

Berseniev went over to him.

"Pavel," he began, "what does this childish behavior mean? For goodness' sake! What is the matter with you today? God knows what nonsense has found its way into your head, and now you're crying. Really, I can't help thinking that you're just acting."

Shubin raised his head. The tears glistened on his cheeks in the moonlight, but his face smiled.

"Andrei Piotrovich," he began, "you can think what you like about me. I am even ready to agree that I am hysterical; but believe me, I am in love with Yelena, and Yelena loves you. But, all the same, I promised to see you home, and I'll keep my promise."

He rose.

"What a night! Silvery, dark, youthful! How good everything is at this hour for anyone in love! How pleasant it is for them not to be asleep! Will you be able to sleep, Andrei Piotrovich?"

Berseniev made no answer and hastened his steps.

"Where are you hurrying to?" Shubin continued. "Believe my words, there will not be such another night as this in your lifetime, but at home Schelling waits for you. Truly, he has rendered you some service today. All the same, don't hurry. Sing, if you can, sing still louder; but if you don't know how to, take off your hat, throw back your head, and smile to the stars. They are all gazing at you, only at you; that is all the stars do, they just gaze at people in love — that is why they are so enchanting. For you are in love, aren't you, Andrei Piotrovich? . . . You don't answer me. . . . Why don't you answer?" Shubin spoke again. "Oh, if you feel that you are happy, then be silent, be silent! I chatter away because I am an unhappy wretch, I am unloved, I am the juggler, the artist, the buffoon; but what silent raptures would I drink in from these nocturnal streams, beneath these stars, beneath these diamonds, if I knew that I was loved! . . . Berseniev, are you happy?"

Berseniev remained silent and walked swiftly along the smooth road. Ahead, amid the trees, he glimpsed the lights of the little village in which he was living; all together it consisted of about ten small summer residences. At its very beginning, to the right of the road, under two spreading birches, was a grocer's shop; all the windows were already shuttered, but a broad stream of light fell fanwise through the open door on the trampled grass and struck upward over the trees, brightly illuminating the whitish under side of the dense foliage. A girl, who looked as though she might be a maid, was standing in the shop with her back to the road and bargaining with the shopkeeper; her rounded cheeks and slender neck were just visible beneath the crimson kerchief that she had flung over her head and was holding under her chin with one bare hand. The young men passed into the band of light. Shubin glanced inside the shop, halted, and called: "Annushka!" The girl hurriedly turned round, revealing her pleasant, rather broad, but fresh face with merry hazel eyes and black brows. "Annushka!" Shubin repeated. The girl stared at him, took alarm, and was put to confusion. Without completing her purchases, she ran down from the veranda, nimbly slipped past them, and, throwing momentary glances back, went across the road to the left. The shopkeeper, a corpulent man and, like all suburban small grocers, completely imperturbable, grunted and yawned after her. But Shubin turned to Berseniev with the words: "She — she — you see — I know a family here — and they have got — you mustn't think — " Without finishing his remarks, he ran off after the retreating girl.

"Do wipe your tears away, at any rate," Berseniev called after him, and could not restrain a laugh. But when he returned home, there was no cheerful expression on his face; he was no longer smiling. Not for one moment did he believe what Shubin had said to him, but his friend's words had made a deep impression in his soul. "Pavel's making fun of me," he thought; "but some day she will love. . . . Whom will she love?"

In Berseniev's room was a piano, small and not new, but with a soft and pleasant, though not quite pure tone. He sat down at it and began to play chords. Like all Russian nobles, in his youth he had learned music, and, like almost all Russian nobles, he played very badly; but he was passionately fond of music. To tell the truth, what he loved in it was not its art, not the forms in which it is expressed (symphonies and sonatas, even operas made him feel depressed), but its elements: he liked those sorrowful and sweet, aimless, and all-embracing feelings which are aroused in the soul by the combination and modulation of sounds. For more than an hour he remained seated at the piano, again and again repeating the same chords, awkwardly groping for new ones, pausing and letting the sounds fade on diminished sevenths. His heart was despondent within him, and more than once his eyes were filled with tears. He was not ashamed of them: he shed them in the darkness. "Pavel is right," he thought, "I have a presentiment that there will not be another evening like this." At last he rose, lit a candle, flung his gown around him, took down the second volume of Raumer's *History of the Hohenstaufens*, and, sighing once or twice, sedulously began to read.

6

Meanwhile Yelena had returned to her room; she seated herself before the open window and rested her head on her hands. It had become a habit of hers to spend some fifteen minutes sitting at the window every evening. During this time she communed with herself, rendered herself an account of the past day. She had recently passed her twentieth birthday. She was tall, her face was pale but swarthy, with large gray eyes under arched eyebrows surrounded with tiny freckles, a forehead and nose quite straight, a pursed mouth and rather pointed chin. Her dark-brown, braided hair fell low over her slender neck. In all her being, in the expression of her face, attentive and a little timorous, in the clear but inconstant gaze, in the smile, seemingly forced, in the quiet and uneven voice, was something nervous, electrical, something impetuous and hurried — in a word, something that could not please everybody, and that even repelled some people. Her hands were narrow and pink, with long fingers; her feet also were narrow; she walked swiftly, almost vehemently, bending a little forward. Her emotional life while growing up had been very peculiar; at first she had worshipped her father, then she had become passionately attached to her mother, and finally had grown cold to them both, especially to her father. Lately she had treated her mother as a sick old woman; but now she was grown up, her father, who had been proud of her so long as she had the reputation of being an unusual child, was beginning to be afraid of her and said that she was like some exalted republican woman. God knows which! Weakness angered her, stupidity annoyed her, a lie she could not forgive "forever and ever," her demands had no bounds, even her prayers were often mingled with reproaches. A man had only to lose her respect — and she pronounced judgment quickly, often all too quickly — and so far as she was concerned he ceased to exist. All impressions were imprinted vividly in her soul: life did not come easy to her.

The governess whom Anna Vasilievna engaged to "complete" her daughter's education — an education that, we may remark in parenthesis, the bored lady had not even begun — was a Russian, the daughter of a man who had been ruined through accepting bribes; this woman had been educated at the State Institute for young ladies, and was a very sensitive, kind, and mendacious creature; she had fallen in love from time to time, and had ended at the age of fifty (when Yelena had passed her seventeenth year) by marrying an officer, who at once abandoned her. This governess was very fond of literature, and herself wrote verse; she encouraged Yelena to read. But reading was not sufficient to satisfy the girl; ever since her childhood she had thirsted for ac-

Turgenev

tivity, for active well-doing; the beggars, the hungry, the sick interested her, disturbed her, tormented her; she saw them in her sleep, she questioned all her acquaintances about them; she gave alms solicitously, with involuntary seriousness, almost with tears. All oppressed creatures — the skinny yard dogs, the kittens condemned to death, the sparrows fallen from their nests, even insects and reptiles — found a protector and defender in Yelena; she fed them herself, she was not repelled by them.

Her mother did not hinder her; on the other hand, her father was very indignant with his daughter for her silly tender-heartedness, as he put it, and declared that it was impossible to move in the house for dogs and cats. "My dear Yelena," he would shout at her, "come quickly, a spider is sucking at a fly, come and release the poor wretch!" And the little Yelena, thoroughly upset, would run and release the fly and unstick its legs. "Well, now let it bite you, as you're so kind," her father would remark ironically; but she did not listen to him.

At the age of ten Yelena made the acquaintance of a beggar girl named Katya and went secretly to see her in the garden, took her dainties, gave her kerchiefs, and kopeks — Katya would not take toys. She sat down at her side on the dry ground, in a remote spot, behind a clump of nettles; with a feeling of joyous humility she ate the beggar girl's moldy bread, listened to her stories. Katya had an aunt, a wicked old woman, who often beat her; Katya hated her and was always saying that she would run away from her aunt, that she would live in God's liberty. Gazing fixedly at Katya, Yelena listened to these unknown new words with secret respect and fear, and then everything about the beggar girl — her black, swift, almost animal eyes, her sunburnt hands, her hoarse little voice, even her ragged clothes — seemed something special, all but sacred. When Yelena returned home she thought of beggars, of God's liberty, for long after; she thought of how she would cut herself a hazel stick and put on a pack and run away with Katya, how she would wander along the roads, wearing a chaplet of cornflowers; she had once seen Katya wearing such a chaplet. If any of her family entered the room while she was in this mood, she avoided them and looked unsociable. One day she ran through the rain to keep a meeting with Katya and soiled all her dress; her father saw her and called her a slut, a peasant girl. She flamed up — and she felt terrible and

436

marvelous inside. Katya often sang some half-wild soldiers' song; Yelena learned the song from her. . . . Her mother overheard her singing it and was highly indignant.

"Where did you learn that filth?" she asked her daughter.

Yelena only gazed at her and did not say a word: she felt that she would sooner let herself be torn to pieces than betray her secret, and she again felt terrible and pleasant inside. Her acquaintance with Katya did not continue for long, however; the poor girl wasted away with a fever and died after a few days' illness.

When Yelena heard of Katya's death, she was very miserable and for long could not sleep at night. The beggar girl's last words incessantly sounded in her ears, and she had the impression that she herself was being called. . . .

But the years passed and passed; swiftly and inaudibly, like waters under snow, Yelena's youth flowed past, in outward inactivity, in inward struggle and anxiety. She had no friend; of all the girls who visited the Stakhovs' home, she did not become intimate with a single one. She had never been oppressed by parental authority, but from the age of sixteen she became almost completely independent; she settled down to living her own personal life, but it was a solitary one. Her soul both flamed up and died away in loneliness; she struggled like a bird in a cage, yet there was no cage; no one constrained her, no one restrained her, yet she fretted and exhausted herself. Sometimes she did not even understand herself, was even afraid of herself. She regarded everything that surrounded her as either senseless or incomprehensible. "How can one live without love? But there is no one to love!" she thought, and she grew terrified at these thoughts, at these sensations.

At the age of eighteen she all but died of a malignant fever; her organism, naturally healthy and strong, was shaken to its foundations, and for a long time could not cope with the malady. The last traces of the illness disappeared at last, but her father still continued, not without exasperation, to talk about her nerves. Sometimes it seemed to her that she wanted something that no one else wanted, that no one else in all Russia had thought of. Then she grew more tranquil, even laughed at herself, spent day after day heedlessly; but suddenly something strong and nameless, which she did not know how to deal with, boiled up within

437

her, pleaded to be given vent. The storm passed, the weary, un-used wings were folded; but these outbursts were not without their consequences for her. No matter how much she tried to avoid revealing her inward turmoil, the yearning of an agitated soul was expressed even in her outward tranquillity, and her par-ents were often perfectly justified in shrugging their shoulders, in being astonished at and unable to understand her "peculiarities."

On the day our story began, Yelena remained at the window for longer than usual. She thought a great deal of Berseniev, of her talk with him. She liked him; she believed in the warmth of his feelings, the purity of his intentions. Never before had he talked with her as on this evening. She recalled the expression of his diffident eyes, his smiles; and she herself smiled and was lost in thought, but now not about him. She turned to gazing through the open window into the night. Long she gazed at the dark, low-hanging sky; then she rose, threw back the hair from her face with a toss of her head, and, herself not knowing why, stretched her bare, chilled arms out to it, out to that sky. Then she let them drop, fell on her knees before her bed, pressed her face to the pillow, and, despite all her efforts to resist the feeling that had overcome her, began to weep with strange, bewildered, yet burning tears.

7

Next day, at twelve o'clock, Berseniev set out for Moscow in a droshky returning to the city. He had to fetch some money from the post and to buy some books, and he wanted to take the op-portunity to see Insarov and have a talk with him. During his last conversation with Shubin it had occurred to Berseniev to in-vite Insarov out to his summer home. But he did not quickly find him: he had moved from his former apartment to another, which was not easy to discover. It was approached from the back yard of a hideous brick house built in the Petersburg style, between Arbat Square and Povarskaya Street. Vainly did Berseniev wan-der from one dirty entrance door to another, vainly did he call first for a yardman, and then for "someone — anyone." Even in Petersburg the yardmen endeavor to escape the notice of visitors, and in Moscow the position is much worse. No one responded to Berseniev's call; only an inquisitive tailor, in his waistcoat and with a bunch of gray threads on his shoulders, poked his bleary and unshaven face with one half-closed eye out of a high ventilator window; and a black hornless goat, which had clambered onto a dungheap, turned round, bleated miserably, and chewed its cud more dumbly than before.

A woman in an old mantle and patched boots took pity at last on Berseniev and showed him to Insarov's apartment. He found his friend at home. Insarov had rented a room from the very tailor who had watched so unconcernedly out of the ventilator window while he searched. It was a large, almost empty room with dark-green walls, three square windows, a tiny bed in one corner, a little leather sofa in another, and an enormous cage hung right up under the ceiling; at one time a nightingale had lived in this cage. Insarov came to meet Berseniev as soon as he entered, but did not exclaim: "Ah, so it's you!" or "Ah, my God, what fate has brought you here?" He did not even say: "Good morning," but simply squeezed Berseniev's hand and led him to the only chair in the room.

"Sit down," he said, and seated himself on the edge of the table.

"As you see, I am still in a muddle," he added, pointing to the pile of papers and books on the floor. "I haven't settled in properly yet. I haven't had time yet."

Insarov spoke Russian quite correctly, strongly and clearly enunciating every word; but his guttural, though pleasant voice somehow did not sound Russian. His foreign origin (he was a Bulgar by birth) was still more clearly revealed in his appearance: he was a young man, aged twenty-five, gaunt and with prominent veins, a sunken chest, and knotted hands; his features were sharp, his nose was hooked; he had bluish-black straight hair, a low brow, small, penetrating, deep-set eyes, and thick eyebrows; when he smiled, his fine white teeth were revealed for a moment behind the thin, hard, rather too clearly defined lips. He was dressed in a rather old but neat coat, buttoned right up.

"Why have you left your previous room?" Berseniev asked him.

"This is cheaper; it's nearer to the university."

"But it's vacation time now. . . . And what makes you want to live in the town in the summer? You should have rented a room in the country, once you had decided to move."

Insarov made no answer to this remark. He offered Berseniev a pipe, saying: "Excuse me, I haven't any cigarettes or cigars."

Berseniev lit the pipe.

"Now, I," he continued, "have rented a little house for myself near Kuntsevo. Very cheap and very comfortable. And I even have a spare room upstairs."

Insarov again made no reply.

Berseniev yawned.

"It even occurred to me," he began again, puffing out a fine stream of smoke, "that if, for instance, I could find someone — you, for instance, so I thought — who would like — who would agree to take my upstairs room — that would be fine! What do you think, Dmitry Nikanorich?"

Insarov gave him a swift look with his small eyes.

"You're suggesting that I should live with you in the country?"

"Yes; I have a spare room upstairs there."

"I am very grateful to you, Andrei Piotrovich, but I think my resources will not permit of it."

"What do you mean: they won't permit of it?"

"They will not permit of my living in the country. I cannot keep two places going."

"But, you see, I —" Berseniev began, and halted. "It wouldn't involve you in any additional expenses," he continued. "You could keep this room, I should think; and on the other hand out in the country living is very cheap, we might even be able to arrange for us to have dinner together, for example."

Insarov was silent. Berseniev began to feel awkward.

"At any rate, come out and see me some time," he began after a pause. "A stone's throw from me lives a family I should very much like you to meet. One of them is a simply marvelous girl, if you only knew, Insarov! And a certain close friend of mine, a man with great talent, also lives with them; I am sure you and he would be good friends." (The Russian is fond of entertaining, and if he hasn't anything else, he entertains with his acquaintances.) "Really, do come out some time. Or, even better, come and live with us out there; I really mean it. We could work together, and read. . . . You know, I am studying history and philosophy. And you are interested in those subjects. I have a lot of books too."

Insarov got up and walked about the room.

"May I ask," he inquired at last, "how much you pay for your house?"

"A hundred silver rubles."

"And how many rooms are there in it?"

"Five."

"So that, on that basis, one would have to pay twenty rubles for one room?"

"On that basis. Don't you see, I haven't any need of the room. It's simply standing empty."

"Maybe; but listen!" Insarov added with a resolute yet good-natured shake of the head; "I can only agree to accept your proposal if you agree to accept the amount it works out at. I am able to pay twenty rubles, especially as you say I shall economize on everything else."

"That goes without saying; but really I don't like taking all that amount."

"I will not do it otherwise, Andrei Piotrovich."

"Well, as you wish; only you certainly are obstinate!"

Insarov again made no answer.

The young men agreed on the day when Insarov was to transfer to the room. They called for the landlord; but at first he sent his daughter, a girl about seven years of age, who was wearing an enormous motley-colored kerchief on her head. She listened attentively, almost with horror, to all that Insarov told her and went out without saying a word. Immediately afterward her mother, far gone in pregnancy, appeared, also wearing a kerchief, but a tiny one. Insarov explained to her that he was going to live near Kuntsevo for the summer, but intended to keep the room in town and leave his things in her charge. The tailor's wife also seemed to take fright and retreated. Finally the landlord arrived; at first he seemed to understand everything perfectly, and only thoughtfully remarked: "Near Kuntsevo?" then suddenly as he opened the door, he shouted: "So you keep the room, then?" Insarov reassured him. "Because I have to know," the tailor repeated harshly, and vanished.

Berseniev returned home much satisfied with the success of his proposal. Insarov saw him to the door with an affable courtesy such as is rarely met with in Russia and then carefully took off his coat and set to work to arrange his papers.

That same evening Anna Vasilievna was sitting in her reception room and making ready to weep. Her husband was also in the room, as well as a certain Uvar Ivanovich Stakhov, Nikolai Artiomovich's uncle twice removed, a retired cornettist aged sixty, a man so corpulent that he could hardly move, with sleepy little yellow eyes and thick, colorless lips in a yellow, puffy face. Ever since his retirement he had lived permanently in Moscow on the interest from a small capital left him by his wife, a merchant's daughter. He did nothing at all, and it is doubtful whether he ever thought; certainly, if he did think, he kept his thoughts to himself. Only once in his life did he get agitated and display any activity, and that was when he read in the papers about some new instrument, a "counter-mortar," at the London Great Exhibition, and wished to subscribe for this instrument, and even inquired where he should send the money to and through what agency. Uvar Ivanovich wore an ample snuff-colored coat, and a white kerchief round his neck; he ate often and plentifully; and only at difficult moments — in other words, whenever he had to express some opinion — did he convulsively wriggle the fingers of his right hand in the air, running them first from the thumb to the little finger, then from the little finger to the thumb, and declaring with much effort: "It would be desirable — somehow — this . . . "

Uvar Ivanovich was sitting in an armchair by the window and breathing heavily. Nikolai Artiomovich was walking about the room with great strides, his hands thrust into his pockets; his face expressed dissatisfaction.

He halted at last and shook his head.

"Yes," he began, "in our time the young people were brought up differently. The young people did not permit themselves to be disrespectful to their elders." (He pronounced certain syllables nasally, like the French.) "But now I only look and wonder. maybe it is not *I* who am right, but *they*; possibly. But, all the same, I have my own view of things; I wasn't born a blockhead. What is your opinion, Uvar Ivanovich?"

Uvar Ivanovich only gazed at him for a moment and wriggled his fingers.

"Yelena Nikolaevna, for instance," Nikolai Artiomovich continued, "Yelena Nikolaevna I simply don't understand, and that's a fact. I am not sufficiently exalted for her. Her heart is so spacious that it embraces all nature, down to the smallest cockroach or frog; in a word, everything except her own father. Well, splendid; I know that and I don't bother any longer. Because all these nerves, and this erudition, and this soaring into the heavens, it's all beyond us. But Mr. Shubin — let us assume that he is an astonishing, an unusual artist, I don't argue about that; but to be disrespectful to his elder, a man to whom, after all, one may say, he is greatly indebted — that, I must confess, I cannot allow *dans mon gros bon sens*. By nature I am not exacting, no; but there is a limit to everything."

Anna Vasilievna rang agitatedly. A page entered.

"For some reason Pavel Yakovlevich hasn't come," she said. "Why doesn't he come when I send for him?"

Nikolai Artiomovich shrugged his shoulders.

"But what do you want to call him for, aft[...] mand that he should be sent for, I don't even [...]

"Why do you ask that, Nikolai Artiomov[...] you; he may have spoiled your course of tr[...] clear up the matter with him. I want to know how he could have presumed to displease you."

"I repeat that I do not demand any such thing. And what a fine idea — *devant les domestiques* — "

Anna Vasilievna reddened a little.

"You have no right to say that, Nikolai Artiomovich. I never — *devant — les domestiques* — Leave the room, Fiodiushka; and listen, bring Pavel Yakovlevich here at once."

The page went out.

"All this is not in the least necessary," Nikolai Artiomovich said between his teeth, and he again began to stride about the room. "I did not turn the conversation in this direction at all."

"Pardon me, Paul must apologize to you."

"Pardon me — what do I want his apologies for? And what are apologies? It's all words."

"Why do you ask 'What for'? He must be brought to reason."

"You bring him to reason yourself. He is more ready to listen to you. I have no complaint against him at all."

"Excuse me, Nikolai Artiomovich, you have been out of spirits from the first moment of your arrival today. Of recent days you

have even gone thinner in my very sight. I am afraid the course
of treatment is not doing you any good."

"My course of treatment is indispensable," Nikolai Artiomovich remarked; "my liver is out of order."

Shubin entered at that moment. He seemed tired. A faint,
slightly sarcastic smile was playing on his lips.

"Did you ask for me, Anna Vasilievna?" he said.

"Yes, of course I asked for you. Listen, Paul, this is terrible. I
am very dissatisfied with you. How can you show disrespect for
Nikolai Artiomovich?"

"Has Nikolai Artiomovich complained to you about me?"
Shubin asked, and looked at Stakhov with the same sarcastic smile
on his lips. Stakhov turned away and lowered his eyes.

"Yes, he has complained. I don't know what offense you have
committed against him, but you must apologize at once, because

re young we

er all? I don't de-
wish it."

Stakhov. "I
ch? He has upset
ch," he said
atment. I want to
d you in any

"You haven't in the least — on that matter," Nikolai Artiomovich retorted, still avoiding Shubin's gaze. "However, I willingly
forgive you, because, as you know, I am not an exacting man."

"Oh, that is not open to any doubt whatever," Shubin said.
"But allow me to be inquisitive: does Anna Vasilievna know
exactly what my offense was?"

"No, I don't know anything," Anna Vasilievna observed, and
craned her neck.

"Oh, my God!" Nikolai Artiomovich hurriedly exclaimed,
"how many times already have I asked, have I pleaded, how many
times have I said how much I dislike all these explanations and
scenes! At my age I come home, I want to rest — people talk
about the family circle, an *intérieur*, be a family man — and then
we have these scenes, these upsets. Not a moment's rest. Willy-
nilly you go off to the club or — or somewhere or other. A man
is a living thing, he has his physics, he has his requirements, but
here — "

And, without finishing the speech he had begun, he walked

swiftly out of the room and slammed the door. Anna Vasilievna gazed after him.

"To the club!" she whispered bitterly. "It's not to the club that you're going, you featherbrain! There's no one in the club to give horses to from one's own stud — and grays into the bargain! My favorite color. Yes, yes, you frivolous man," she added, raising her voice, "it's not to the club that you're going. But you, Paul," she continued, rising to her feet, "aren't you ashamed? You're not a child, I think. And now my head has started to ache. Where is Zoya, don't you know?"

"I think she's in her room upstairs. That prudent little vixen always hides in her hole at such times."

"Now, please, please!" Anna Vasilievna looked about her, searching for something. "Haven't you seen my glass of ground horseradish? Paul, do me a favor, in future don't make me angry."

"How could I make you angry, Auntie? Give me your little hand to kiss. But I saw your horseradish on the occasional table in your room."

"Daria is everlastingly leaving it about and forgetting it," Anna Vasilievna said, and retired, her silk gown rustling as she went.

Shubin was about to follow her out, but, hearing Uvar Ivanovich's deliberate voice behind him, he halted.

"That isn't what you — should have got, you puppy," the retired cornettist said haltingly.

Shubin went up to him.

"And what should I have got it for, most praiseworthy Uvar Ivanovich?"

"What for? You're young, so show more respect. Yes."

"Respect for whom?"

"For whom? You know whom. Sneering like that."

Shubin folded his hands on his chest.

"Ah, you, you representative of the choral element," he exclaimed, "you power of the black earth, you foundation of the social edifice!"

Uvar Ivanovich began to wriggle his fingers.

"Stop that, my boy, don't tempt me."

"Just look!" Shubin continued, "he's not by any means a young nobleman, apparently, but how much happy, childish faith there is concealed within him! More respect! Why, do you know, you

445

elemental man, what Nikolai Artiomovich is angry with me for?
He and I spent all this morning with his German woman; why,
today we sang 'Never leave me,' as a trio: you should have heard
us. That shakes you, I think. We sang, my dear sir, we sang —
well, and I got bored; I saw that things were going badly, a lot
of tender nothings were flying about. And I began to tease them
both. And with excellent results. First she grew angry with me,
and then with him. But then he grew angry with her and told
her he was happy only at home, and that he had a paradise there.
And she told him he had no morals. And I said to her '*Ach!*' in
German. He departed, and I remained. He came here, to paradise,
in other words, and got sick of paradise. And so he began to
grumble. Well, and now who do you think is to blame?"

"You, of course," Uvar Ivanovich retorted.

Shubin fixed him with his gaze.

"I venture to ask you, worthy knight," he began in a wheedling
tone, "did you deign to utter those enigmatic words in consequence of any exercise of your thinking capacities, or was it
under the inspiration of a momentary necessity to cause the disturbance of the air known as sound?"

"Don't tempt me, I say," Uvar Ivanovich groaned.

Shubin laughed and ran out.

"Hey!" Uvar Ivanovich called, a quarter of an hour later. "You
— a glass of vodka."

The page brought vodka and hors d'œuvres on a tray. Uvar
Ivanovich gently took the glass from the tray and gazed at it for
a long time with strained attention, as though not properly understanding what he had in his hand. Then he looked at the page
and asked: "Isn't your name Vaska?" Then he adopted an embittered air, drank the vodka, had a bite of hors d'œuvres, and
struggled to get his hand into his pocket to fish out his handkerchief. But the page took the tray and carafe back to their place
and ate the remnants of the herring, and even managed to drop
off to sleep, nestling down against his master's overcoat, while
Uvar Ivanovich still held the handkerchief in front of him on outspread fingers and gazed with the same strained attention first at
the window, then at the floor and the walls.

9

Shubin returned to his room in the wing and opened a book. Nikolai Artiomovich's valet stealthily entered and handed him a small triangular note, sealed with a large heraldic seal.

I hope [the note read] *that you, as an honest man, will not allow yourself to hint by so much as a word at a certain monetary transaction of which there was some talk this morning. You know my relations and my principles, the insignificance of the sum itself, and other circumstances; and, finally, there are family secrets that should be respected, and family peace is a sacred thing, overthrown only by* êtres sans cœur, *among whom I have no reason to include you! (Return this note.)*

N. S.

Shubin scribbled at the bottom in pencil: "Don't be alarmed, I haven't started picking handkerchiefs out of pockets yet," handed the note back to the valet, and returned to his book. But before long it slipped out of his hands. He gazed at the crimsoning sky, at two young, mighty pines standing apart from the other trees, thought: "In the daytime pines look bluish, but how magnificently green they are in the evening!" and went off to the garden, with the secret hope of meeting Yelena there. He was not mistaken. Her gown glimmered in front of him, on a path between bushes. He overtook her and, as he drew level, remarked:

"Don't look in my direction, I'm not worth it."

She gave him a momentary glance, momentarily smiled, and went on, deeper into the garden. He followed her.

"I ask you not to look at me," he began, "yet here I am making conversation with you: an obvious contradiction! But what of it? That's nothing new for me. I have just remembered that I haven't yet asked your pardon, as I should do, for my stupid behavior yesterday. You aren't angry with me, are you, Yelena Nikolaevna?"

She came to a standstill and did not answer him at once — not because she was angry, but her thoughts were far away.

"No," she said at last, "I am not angry in the least."

Shubin bit his lip.

"What a preoccupied — and what an indifferent face!" he murmured. "Yelena Nikolaevna," he continued, raising his voice, "allow me to tell you a little story. I had a friend; and that friend also had a friend, who at first behaved as a decent man should behave, but then he took to drink. Now, one day, early in the morning, my friend met him in the street (but I must tell you that by then they had ceased to be friends), met him and saw that he was drunk. My friend simply turned and walked away. But the other went up to him and said: 'I wouldn't be angry,' he said, 'if you didn't bow to me, but why turn your back on me? Possibly I drink out of sorrow. Peace to my ashes!'"

Shubin lapsed into silence.

"And is that all?" Yelena asked.

"That is all."

"I don't understand. What are you hinting at? You have just told me not to look in your direction."

"True, but now I have just told you how wrong it is to turn your back."

"But do I really — " Yelena began.

"But don't you really?"

She flushed a little and held out her hand to him. He squeezed it firmly.

"You appear to have caught me behaving badly," Yelena said. "But your suspicion is unjust. I did not even think of avoiding you."

"Granted, granted. But confess that at this minute you have thousands of thoughts in your head, not one of which will you confide to me. Well? I fear I have said the truth. Haven't I?"

"Possibly."

"But why won't you? Why?"

"My thoughts are not clear even to myself," Yelena declared.

"That's just when you should confide them to others," Shubin retorted. "But I will tell you what the trouble is. You have a poor opinion of me."

"I have?"

"Yes, you have. You imagine that everything about me is half pretense, because I am an artist; that I am incapable not only of achieving anything — and in that you are probably right — but even of having any genuine, profound feeling; that I cannot even weep sincerely, that I am a chatterer and gossip — and all because I am an artist. Well, what unhappy wretches, what God-forsaken people we must be in that case! For instance, I am ready to swear that you don't believe that I am really sorry."

"You're wrong, Pavel Yakovlevich, I do believe you're sorry, and I believe in your tears too. But I have the impression that your very sorrow amuses you, and your tears too."

Shubin trembled.

"Well, I see that, as the doctors put it, you are an incurable case, a *casus incurabilis*. I can only hang my head and submit. And yet, my goodness, is that really true, am I really always concerned only with myself, when such a soul is living so close to me? And to know that one can never penetrate into that soul, will never know why she is sad, why she is glad, what is passing in her mind, what she wants, where she is going. . . . Tell me," he said after a brief silence, "never, not for anything, not in any circumstances, would you fall in love with an artist, I suppose?"

Yelena gazed straight into his eyes.

"I don't think so, Pavel Yakovlevich; no."

"Which was to be demonstrated," Shubin said with comical despondency. "After which I assume that it would be better if I did not hinder your solitary walk. A professor would ask you: on the basis of what data did you say no? But I am not a professor, I am a child, you think; but remember that people don't turn their backs even on children. Good-by. Peace to my ashes!"

Yelena was about to detain him, but she thought for a moment and replied:

"Good-by."

Shubin went into the street. A little distance from the Stakhovs' house he met Berseniev. His friend was walking along briskly, his head bowed, his hat thrust on the back of his head.

"Andrei Piotrovich!" Shubin called.

Berseniev halted.

"Go on, go on," Shubin continued, "I only called to you, I won't detain you; and go straight to the garden, you'll find Yelena there. I think she is waiting for you — she is certainly waiting for someone. . . . You realize the strength of those words: she is waiting! But, brother, do you know one extraordinary circumstance? Just imagine, for two years now I have been living in the same house with her, I am in love with her; and only now, just this minute, have I, I will not say understood, but really seen her. I saw and was amazed. Please don't look at me with that pseudo-venomous smile, which hardly suits your grave features. Yes, I know, you are about to remind me of Annushka. What of it? I do not deny it. Annushka is just right for the likes of us. And so hurrah for the Annushkas and the Zoyas, and even the Avgustina Khristianovnas! You go along to Yelena now, and I shall go — to Annushka, do you think? No, brother, worse: to Prince Chikurasov. He is a certain Mæcenas of the Kazan Tatars, a kind of Volgin. Do you see this note of invitation, those letters: R.S.V.P.? Even in the country there is no peace for me. *Addio!*"

Berseniev listened to Shubin's tirade in silence and seemingly a little embarrassed on his behalf, then he went on into the yard of the Stakhovs' house. But Shubin did drive to see Prince Chikurasov, to whom he made caustically impertinent remarks with a very amiable air. The Mæcenas of the Kazan Tatars roared with laughter, the Mæcenas's guests smiled, but no one felt happy, and when they went their ways they were all in a bad temper. Thus a couple of gentlemen, casual acquaintances, who happen to meet in the Nevsky Prospekt, will suddenly bare their teeth at each other, honeyedly grimace with their eyes, their noses and cheeks, and then, the moment they have passed each other, will return to their former unconcerned or morose and almost always hemorrhoidal expressions.

10

Yelena welcomed Berseniev cordially, not in the garden, but in the reception room, and at once, almost impatiently, resumed the previous day's conversation. She was alone. Nikolai Artiomovich had quietly slipped off somewhere; Anna Vasilievna was lying upstairs with a damp bandage round her head; Zoya was sitting beside her, with her dress neatly adjusted and her little hands folded on her knees; Uvar Ivanovich was resting in the mezzanine room on a broad and comfortable divan, which had been given the nickname "self-sleep." Berseniev again made mention of his father: he held his memory sacred. We, too, will say a few words about him.

The owner of eighty-two souls, whom he gave their freedom before his death, one of the illuminati, an old Göttingen student, the author of a manuscript work entitled "On the Manifestations or the Prototypes of Spirit in the World" — a work in which Schellingism, Swedenborgianism, and republicanism were mingled in the most original manner — Berseniev's father took his son to Moscow when Andrei was still a boy, immediately after his wife's death, and himself attended to the lad's education. He prepared himself for every lesson, labored very conscientiously and quite unsuccessfully; he was a dreamer, a bookworm, a mystic; he talked with a stammer, in a thick voice, expressed himself obscurely and floridly, usually in metaphors, and avoided the company even of his son, whom he loved passionately. It was not surprising that his son only blinked his eyes at his father's lessons and made no progress whatever. The old man (he was close on fifty, he had married very late) realized at last that matters were not proceeding satisfactorily, and he placed his Andrei in a boarding school.

Andrei began to learn, but he did not escape from the parental oversight: his father visited him regularly and wearied the proprietor with his exhortations and conversations; the form masters too were oppressed by the uninvited guest: from time to time he brought them, they said, excessively learned books on education. Even the scholars began to feel awkward at the sight of the old man's swarthy and pockmarked face, his gaunt figure, always enveloped in a square-edged, gray frock coat. The scholars did not suspect that this morose, never smiling gentleman, with a crane's strut and a long nose, was deeply concerned and worried over each one of them almost as much as over his own son. One day it occurred to him to talk to them about Washington. "Youthful nurselings," he began, but at the first sounds of his queer voice the youthful nurselings scattered. The honest Göttingenite had a life anything but a bed of roses: he was always overborne by the course of history, by all kinds of problems and conceptions. When the young Berseniev entered the university, his father went with him to the lectures; but now the old man's health was beginning to betray him. The events of 1848 shook him to his foundations (it became necessary to rewrite all his book), and he died in the winter of 1853, before his son had passed out of the university, but not before he had congratulated him on his degree and blessed him in his dedication to learning. "I pass the torch on to you," he said to him two hours before his death. "I have held it as long as I could, nor do you let go of this torch until the end."

Berseniev had a long talk with Yelena about his father. He lost the awkwardness he had felt in her presence, and he did not hiss so much. The talk turned to the subject of the university.

"Tell me," Yelena asked him, "were there any remarkable men among your fellow students?"

Berseniev recalled Shubin's words.

"No, Yelena Nikolaevna, to tell you the truth, there was not one remarkable man among the whole lot of us. And why should there be? They say there was at one time a Moscow University! But not now. Now it is an educational institution, not a university. I felt awkward with my colleagues," he added, lowering his voice.

"Awkward — ?" Yelena whispered.

"But," Berseniev continued, "I must make one reservation. I know one student — though he is not in my year — he really is a remarkable man."

"What is his name?" Yelena asked with interest.

"Insarov, Dmitry Nikanorovich. He is a Bulgar."

"Not a Russian?"

"No, he is not a Russian."

"Then why is he living in Moscow?"

"He's come here to study. And do you know the reason why he is studying? He has one idea: the liberation of his country. His life, too, has been unusual. His father was quite a wealthy merchant in Tirnovo. Tirnovo is now a small town, but in former days it was the capital of Bulgaria, when Bulgaria was still an independent kingdom. He had his business in Sofia, and had connections with Russia; his sister, Insarov's aunt, is still living in Kiev; she is married to a senior history master in the local high school. In 1835, eighteen years ago now, a fearful crime was committed: Insarov's mother vanished without trace. A week later she was found with her throat cut."

Yelena shuddered. Berseniev paused.

"Go on, go on," she said.

"There were rumors that she had been ravished and killed by a high Turkish officer. Her husband, Insarov's father, discovered it was true and tried to have his revenge, but he only wounded the officer with his dagger. . . . He was shot."

"Shot? Without trial?"

"Yes. At that time Insarov was eight years old. He was left in the care of neighbors. His aunt learned of the fate of her brother's family and decided to have her nephew with her. He was taken to Odessa, and thence to Kiev. He lived twelve years in Kiev. That is why he speaks Russian so well."

"He does speak Russian?"

"Just like you and me. When he had passed his twentieth birthday (this was at the beginning of 1848), he decided to return to his country. He was in Sofia and Tirnovo, traveled all through Bulgaria, spent two years there, and learned his native language properly again. The Turkish government persecuted him, and probably during those two years he was exposed to great dangers. I once saw a broad scar on his neck, the trace of a wound, evidently; but he doesn't like talking about it. He, too, is taciturn in his way. I attempted to find out all I could by questioning him, but he wouldn't have it. He answers only in general terms. He is terribly obstinate. In 1850 he came back to Russia, to Moscow, with the intention of finishing his education, of making friends with the Russians, and then, when he leaves the university — "

"And what then?" Yelena interrupted.

"Whatever God wills. It is difficult to anticipate."

Yelena did not turn her eyes from Berseniev's face for a long time.

"You have deeply interested me with your story," she said. "What is he like in himself, your — what did you call him — Insarov?"

"How can I tell you? I don't think he is at all bad-looking. But you'll see him for yourself."

"Why shall I?"

"I shall bring him here to see you. He is coming to live in our village the day after tomorrow and will stay in my house."

"Really? But will he want to come and see us?"

"I should say so! He will be very glad."

"He is not proud?"

"He, proud? Not in the least. I mean, if you like, you can say he is proud, only not in the sense that you meant. For instance, he will never borrow money from anyone!"

"But is he poor, then?"

"Well, he isn't rich. When he went to Bulgaria he gathered together a few crumbs left from his father's fortune, and his aunt is helping him; but it is all a mere nothing."

"He must have a great deal of character, I should think," Yelena observed.

453

"Yes. He is a man of iron. And at the same time, as you'll see, there is something of the child in him, something sincere, with all his concentration and even secrecy. True, his sincerity is not our rubbishy sincerity, the sincerity of people who have absolutely nothing to conceal. . . . But you wait, I'll bring him along to see you."

"And he isn't shy at all?" Yelena again asked.

"No, he's not shy. Only selfish people are shy."

"But are you selfish, then?"

Berseniev was put to confusion and did not know what to say.

"You arouse my curiosity," Yelena continued. "But tell me, has he taken vengeance on that Turkish officer yet?"

He smiled.

"People take vengeance only in novels, Yelena Nikolaevna; and besides, in twelve years the officer may have died."

"All the same, Mr. Insarov has never said anything to you about it?"

"No, never."

"Why did he go to Sofia?"

"His father had lived there."

Yelena was lost in thought.

"To liberate his country!" she declared. "Those words are terrible even to pronounce, so exalted are they. . . ."

At that moment Anna Vasilievna entered the room, and the conversation was broken off.

A strange feeling agitated Berseniev when he returned home that evening. He did not repent of his intention to introduce Insarov to Yelena, he thought the profound impression made on her by his story of the young Bulgar was quite natural . . . hadn't he himself attempted to intensify the impression? But a secret and obscure feeling nestled in his heart; he was saddened with an unpleasant sorrow. None the less, this feeling of sorrow did not hinder his picking up the *History of the Hohenstaufens* and beginning to read it from the very page where he had ended the evening before.

II

Two days later Insarov, as he had promised, arrived at Berseniev's house with his luggage. He had no servant, but without any assistance he put his room in order, arranged the furniture, wiped away the dust, and washed the floor. He took a good deal of trouble over the writing-desk, which simply refused to go into the space he planned for it between the windows; but with the taciturn persistence that distinguished him he finally achieved his end. When he had finished, he asked Berseniev to accept ten rubles in advance and, equipped with a stout stick, set off to survey the neighborhood of his new habitation. He returned three hours later. When Berseniev invited him to share his meal, he answered that he would not refuse to dine with him today, but that he had already negotiated with the mistress of the house and in future would get his food from her.

"But really!" Berseniev protested, "you'll have rotten food; that woman has no idea whatever how to cook. Why don't you want to eat with me? We could share the expenses."

"My means do not permit me to eat as well as you do," Insarov replied with a calm smile.

There was something in that smile that did not allow of any opposition: Berseniev said no more. After dinner he suggested that he should take Insarov along to the Stakhovs; but his friend replied that he intended to devote the evening to correspondence with his Bulgars, and so would ask him to postpone the visit to the Stakhovs to some other day. Berseniev already knew the inflexibility of Insarov's will, but only now, when he was under the same roof, was he finally convinced that his friend never changed any decision he had made, just as he never procrastinated with the fulfillment of a promise once given. To Berseniev, as a root-and-stock Russian, this more than German accuracy seemed rather mad at first, and even a little absurd; but he soon grew used to it and ended by finding it, if not estimable, at least very convenient.

The day after his arrival Insarov rose at four in the morning, strode round almost the whole of Kuntsevo, bathed in the river, drank a glass of cold milk, and set to work. And he had no little work to do: he was studying Russian history, and law, and political economy, was translating Bulgarian songs and annals, was collecting materials on the Eastern question, was compiling a Russian grammar for Bulgarians, and a Bulgarian grammar for Russians. Berseniev went up to his room and talked to him about Feuerbach. Insarov listened to him attentively, made comments only rarely, but always to the point; from his comments it was evident that he was trying to decide in his own mind whether he needed to study Feuerbach or could manage without him. Berseniev then turned the conversation to the question of Insarov's activities and asked whether he wouldn't show him some of his finished work. Insarov read his own translation of two or three Bulgarian songs and invited his friend's opinion. Berseniev found the translation accurate, but not sufficiently vivid. Insarov took note of this remark. From the songs Berseniev went on to discuss the present-day position of Bulgaria, and then for the first time noted the transformation that was accomplished in Insarov at the very mention of his country: it was not that his face burned or his voice rose — no! But all his being seemed to acquire strength and to be driving impetuously forward, the outline of his lips grew sharper and more implacable, and a dull, inextinguishable fire glowed in the depths of his eyes. Insarov did not like to expatiate on his own journey to his country, but he readily talked to anybody about Bulgaria in general. He talked, deliberately, of the Turks, of their persecutions, of the misery and tribulations of his fellow citizens, of their hopes; a concentrated brooding over a single and long-possessed passion sounded in his every word.

"I am afraid," Berseniev was thinking, "that that Turkish officer has probably paid his account for the death of his father and mother."

Insarov had not quite finished when the door was opened and Shubin appeared.

He entered the room a little too jauntily and genially. Berseniev, who knew him well, at once realized that something had upset him.

"I introduce myself without ceremony," he began with a beaming and open expression on his face. "My name is Shubin, I am a friend of this young man here" (he pointed to Berseniev). "You are Mr. Insarov, aren't you?"

"I am Insarov."

"Then give me your hand and let us make each other's acquaintance. I don't know whether Berseniev has told you about me, but he has told me a great deal about you. Have you come to live here? Excellent! Don't be angry with me for staring at you so hard. I am a sculptor by profession, and I foresee that before long I shall be asking your permission to use your head as a model."

"My head is at your service," Insarov declared.

"What shall we do today?" Shubin began, abruptly sitting down on a low chair and resting both hands on his widespread knees. "Andrei Piotrovich, has Your Excellency any plan for this day? The weather's marvelous; there is a scent of hay and dry strawberry — just like drinking mother's milk. We'll have to do something. We'll show the new inhabitant of Kuntsevo all its innumerable beauties." ("But somehing has upset him," Berseniev continued to think.) "Well, what are you silent for, my friend Horatio? Open your prophetic lips. Shall we do something or not?"

"I don't know about Insarov," Berseniev remarked. "I think he was intending to work."

Shubin swung round in his chair.

"Do you want to work?" he asked with a sniff.

"No," Insarov replied. "I can devote today to a walk."

"Ah! Well, that's fine!" Shubin declared. "Come, my friend Andrei Piotrovich, cover your wise head with your hat and we'll go wherever our feet take us. Our feet are young, they can take us a long way. I know a filthy little tavern where we can get an abominable little dinner, but we shall be very merry. Come along."

Half an hour later they were all walking along the bank of the Moskva River. It transpired that Insarov possessed a rather weird, ear-flapped, peaked cap, which sent Shubin into not altogether natural raptures. Insarov walked unhurriedly and looked, breathed, spoke, and smiled with composure; but he had devoted that day to pleasure, and he thoroughly enjoyed it. "This is the way sensible lads go for walks on Sundays," Shubin whispered into Berseniev's ear. He himself played about a great deal, running on ahead, standing in the attitudes of famous statues, and turning somersaults on the grass; Insarov's composure seemed not to irritate him so much as provoke him to show off.

"What are you fidgeting like this for, Frenchman?" Berseniev remarked to him once or twice.

"Yes, I am a Frenchman, half a Frenchman," Shubin retorted; "but you keep to the middle path between jest and earnest, as a waiter once told me!"

The young men turned away from the river and went along a deep and narrow defile between two walls of tall, golden rye; a

Turgenev

bluish shadow fell on them from one of these walls; the radiant sun seemed to be slipping over the tips of the ears; the skylarks were singing, the quails calling; everywhere the grass showed green; a warm breeze rustled and lifted its blades, sent the little heads of the flowers swaying. After long wanderings, rests, and chatter (Shubin even tried to play leapfrog with some passing toothless little peasant, who smiled and smiled, no matter what the gentleman did with him) the young men found their way to the "filthy" little inn. The staff almost rushed each of them off his feet and certainly fed them on a very poor dinner, with trans-Balkan wine, which, however, did not prevent their thoroughly enjoying themselves, as Shubin had forecast; he himself was the most noisily merry of them all—and the least merry of them all. He drank the health of some "incomprehensible" but great Vene-line,[1] and the health of a Bulgarian king named Krum, Khrum, or Khrom, who had lived "almost in the days of Adam."

"In the ninth century," Insarov corrected him.

"In the ninth century?" Shubin exclaimed. "Oh, what happiness!"

Berseniev observed that even in the midst of his larks, sallies, and jests Shubin seemed to be putting Insarov through an examination, seemed to be putting out feelers while he himself was inwardly agitated. But Insarov remained as calm and serene as before.

At last they returned home, changed, and, in order not to depart from the program they had followed all day, they decided to go off that same evening to the Stakhovs'. Shubin ran on ahead to announce their coming.

12

"The hero Insarov will be presenting himself here in a minute!" he solemnly exclaimed as he entered the Stakhovs' reception room, which at that moment was occupied by only Yelena and Zoya.

"Wer?" Zoya asked in German. She always expressed herself in her native tongue when she was taken by surprise. Yelena drew herself up. Shubin looked at her with a playful smile on his lips. She felt vexed, but she did not say anything.

[1] Yurii Hutza Veneline (1802–39), a Bulgarian savant and active revolutionary nationalist. (Tr.)

458

"You heard," he repeated; "Mr. Insarov is coming here."

"I heard," she answered, "and I heard what you called him. I am amazed at you, really I am. Mr. Insarov has not even set foot in this house, yet, but you already consider it necessary to show off."

Shubin suddenly wilted.

"You're right, you're always right, Yelena Nikolaevna," he muttered; "but I didn't mean any harm, really I didn't. We've been out walking together all day, and I assure you he is an excellent fellow."

"I didn't ask your opinion on that question," Yelena declared, and she rose.

"Is Mr. Insarov young?" Zoya asked.

"He is one hundred and forty-four," Shubin answered spitefully.

The page announced the arrival of the two friends. They entered. Berseniev introduced Insarov. Yelena asked them to sit down and seated herself, but Zoya went upstairs; Anna Vasilievna had to be forewarned. They began a conversation, of no particular significance, like all first conversations. Shubin watched silently from one corner, but there was nothing to watch. In Yelena he observed the traces of restrained annoyance with him, Shubin — and that was all. He looked at Berseniev and Insarov and, as a sculptor, compared their faces. Neither of them, he thought, was particularly handsome. "The Bulgar has a characteristic, sculptural face; ah, now it has lit up well; the Great Russian is more suited for a painting: he has no lines, but he has a physiognomy. But I should think it would be possible to fall in love with both the one and the other. She doesn't love anyone yet, but she will love Berseniev," he mentally decided. Anna Vasilievna appeared in the reception room, and the conversation took a completely summer suburban-residence turn — the sort of conversation to be heard only in a summer suburban residence and not in the country. It was highly varied in regard to the multiplicity of subjects discussed; but brief, rather wearing pauses interrupted it every three minutes. During one of these pauses Anna Vasilievna turned to Zoya. Shubin understood the unspoken hint and pulled a wry face, but Zoya sat down at the piano and played and sang all her little pieces. Uvar Ivanovich showed himself round the door, but he wriggled his fingers and retreated. Then tea was brought in;

then all the company walked in the garden. It grew dark outside, and the guests departed.

In reality Insarov had made less impression on Yelena than she herself had expected, or, to put it more exactly, he had not made on her the impression she had expected. She liked his bluntness and freedom from constraint, and she liked his face; but all Insarov's personality, calmly firm and ordinarily simple, somehow did not accord with the picture that Berseniev's stories had left in her head. Though she herself did not suspect this, Yelena had expected something more "fatal." "But," she thought, "he has talked very little today; I'm to blame for that; I did not question him; we'll wait till another time . . . but he has expressive, honest eyes." She felt that she wanted not to admire him, but to give him her hand in friendship, and she was amazed: this was not what she had conceived such people as Insarov, "heroes," to be. This last word reminded her of Shubin, and even as she lay in bed she flared up and grew thoroughly angry.

"How did you like your new acquaintances?" Berseniev asked Insarov as they walked back home.

"I like them very much," Insarov replied, "especially the daughter. She must be a very fine girl. She is easily agitated, but in her case it is a good agitation."

"We must call on them frequently," Berseniev observed.

"Yes, we must," Insarov said, and uttered not another word until they reached the house. He at once shut himself up in his room, but a candle was burning there until long past midnight.

Berseniev had not had time to read a page of Raumer when a handful of fine gravel rattled against his window. He involuntarily started, opened the window, and saw Shubin, looking as pale as linen.

"Oh, you fidget! You moth!" Berseniev began.

"Sh-sh!" Shubin interrupted him; "I've come to you by stealth, like Max to Agatha.[1] I simply must say a couple of words to you alone."

"Then come into the room."

"No, that's not necessary," Shubin objected, and set his elbows on the windowsill. "It's gayer like this, more like Spain. To begin with, I congratulate you: your stock has risen. Your belauded

---

[1] Characters in Weber's opera *Der Freischütz*. (Tr.)

out-of-the-ordinary man has failed to pass the test. I can guarantee you that. But in order to prove my impartiality to you, listen: here is a formal description of Mr. Insarov. Talents none at all, poetry none at all, capacities for work enormous, memory immense, mind not varied and not profound, but healthy and vivid; dryness and strength, and even a gift of words, when it is a question of his (between you and me) very boring Bulgaria. Well, what do you say, am I unjust? One other remark: you will never be on terms of intimate friendship with him, and no one ever has been. I, as an artist, am repellent to him, of which I am proud. He is arid! Arid! But he may grind us all into dust. He is bound to his country — not like our empty vessels, who fawn on the people: 'Pour yourselves,' say they, 'into us, you living water.' On the other hand, his task is easier too, more comprehensible: he has only to turn out the Turks, a great work! But, thank goodness, these are all qualities that do not attract women. He has no fascination, no *charm;* not as you and I have."

"What have you dragged me into it for?" Berseniev muttered. "And you're wrong in everything else too; you're not in the least repellent to him, and he is on intimate terms with his fellow countrymen — that I know."

"That's another matter! To them he is a hero. But I have to confess that I have a different conception of heroes: a hero should not know how to talk. A hero bellows like a bull; but when he charges with his horns, walls crumble. And he himself should not know why he is charging, but should simply charge. But possibly heroes of a different caliber are needed in our day."

"Why does Insarov interest you so much?" Berseniev asked. "Surely you haven't run along here just in order to describe his character to me?"

"I have come here," Shubin began, "because I was very sad at home."

"You don't say! You don't feel like crying again, do you?"

"Laugh away! I have come here because I am ready to bite my own elbow, because I am eaten up with despair, with chagrin, with jealousy."

"Jealousy! Whom of?"

"Of you! Of him, of everybody. I am tormented by the thought that if I had understood her earlier, if I had set to work intelligently — But what's the use of talking? It ends with my always sneering, playing about, showing off, as she says, and then I shall hang myself."

"Hm, hang yourself! — you won't hang yourself," Berseniev remarked.

"Not on such a night as this, of course; but if we live till the autumn. Even on such nights people die, only they die of happiness. Ah, happiness! Every shadow a tree casts across the road seems to be whispering now; 'I know where happiness is. . . . Would you like me to tell you?' I would ask you to come for a walk, but now you are under the influence of prose. Sleep, and may you dream of mathematical figures! But my soul is being torn asunder. You, gentlemen, see that a man is smiling, and you think that that means life is easy for him; you can prove to him that he is contradicting himself, and that means he is not suffering. . . . Damn you all!"

Shubin walked swiftly away from the window. "Annushka!" Berseniev felt like calling after him, but he refrained: Shubin's face really was as white as a sheet. A minute or two later Berseniev even thought he heard sobbing; he rose and opened the window. Everything was quiet, only somewhere in the distance some passing peasant, it must have been, was trolling *The Steppe of Mozdok.*

13

During the first two weeks after Insarov had transferred to Kuntsevo he did not visit the Stakhovs more than four or five times, while Berseniev called on them every other day. Yelena was always glad to see him, they always fell into a lively and interesting conversation, yet he often returned home with a mournful look on his face. Shubin was hardly ever to be seen; he was working at his sculpture in a fever of activity: he either sat locked away in his room and dashed out of it in a blouse, smothered with clay, or he spent the day in Moscow, where he had a studio and where he was visited by models and Italian molders, by his friends and teachers. Not once did Yelena have the conversation with Insarov that she would have liked; when he was absent she made ready to question him about many things, but when he arrived she felt conscience-stricken at her preparations. Insarov's very composure disconcerted her; she felt that she had no right to force him to express himself, and she decided to wait. Even so, she felt that with his every visit, no matter how insignificant were the words exchanged between them, he attracted her more and more. But she did not happen to be left with him alone — and to draw close to another human being one needs to have at least one intimate talk with him. She talked a good deal to Berseniev about him. Berseniev realized that Insarov had caught her imagination, and rejoiced that his friend had not failed to pass the test, as Shubin had declared; fervently, down to the tiniest detail, he told her all that he knew about him. (It is often the case that when we are trying to please someone we talk about our friends in exalted terms, hardly ever suspecting that by so doing we are really praising ourselves.) And only rarely, when Yelena's pallid cheeks flushed a little and her eyes sparkled and dilated, did that unpleasant sorrow which he had already experienced pinch his heart once more.

One day Berseniev went to call on the Stakhovs at his usual time, at eleven in the morning. Yelena went out into the hall to meet him.

"Just imagine!" he began with a forced smile. "Our Insarov's disappeared."

"What? Disappeared?" Yelena asked.

"Just disappeared. He went out somewhere two evenings ago and hasn't been back since."

"Didn't he tell you where he was going?"

"No."

She dropped into a chair.

"He's probably gone off to Moscow," she said, attempting to appear unconcerned, at the same time wondering at her very attempt.

"I don't think so," Berseniev objected. "He didn't go alone."

"Then whom did he go with?"

"Two men, I should think fellow countrymen of his, called on him two days ago, before dinner."

"Bulgarians? Why do you think they were?"

"Why, because, so far as I could catch their conversation, they talked with him in a language I didn't know, but which was Slavonic. . . . Yelena Nikolaevna, you're always thinking that there is very little of the mysterious in Insarov; but what could be more mysterious than this visit? Imagine it! They went up to

his room, and they shouted and argued, and so savagely, angrily
— And he shouted too."

"He too?"

"He too. He shouted at them. They seemed to be complaining
about each other. And if you had only seen those visitors!
Swarthy faces, broad cheekbones, dull-looking, with hooked
noses, both of them over forty, poorly dressed, dusty, sweaty;
artisans in appearance — yet not artisans, and not gentlemen. . . .
Goodness knows what sort of people they were."

"And he went off with them?"

"Yes. He gave them some food and then went out with them.
The landlady told me that the two of them ate a whole huge pot
of groats. And they swallowed it down like wolves, as though
racing each other, she said."

Yelena faintly smiled.

"You see," she said; "it will all turn out to be something very
prosaic."

"I hope so! Only you were wrong in using that word. There
is nothing prosaic about Insarov, though Shubin swears there is."

"Shubin!" Yelena broke in, and shrugged her shoulders. "But
you must admit that those two gentlemen, gulping down
groats — "

"Themistocles also ate on the eve of the Battle of Salamis,"
Berseniev remarked with a smile.

"Yes; but on the other hand there was a battle the next day.
All the same, let me know when he returns," Yelena added, and
tried to change the conversation. But the conversation failed to
make headway. Zoya appeared and began to walk about the room
on tiptoe, to indicate that Anna Vasilievna had not yet waked up.

Berseniev took his leave.

That same evening Yelena received a note from him. "He has
returned," he wrote to her, "sunburnt and dusty up to his eyebrows. But why and where he went I don't know; perhaps you
could find out?"

"Perhaps I could find out!" Yelena whispered. "Does he talk
to me?"

14

Next day, about two o'clock, Yelena was standing in the garden
before a small shed, where she was rearing two yard puppies.

(The gardener had found them abandoned under the fence and had brought them to the young lady, for the washerwomen had told him that Yelena took pity on all animals and beasts. He was not mistaken in his calculations. She gave him twenty-five kopeks.) She glanced into the shed, saw that the puppies were alive and well, and that fresh straw had been put down for them, turned round, and all but cried out: straight along the avenue Insarov was coming, alone.

"Good afternoon," he said, coming up to her and removing his cap. She noticed that he had, as Berseniev said, become deeply sunburnt during the last three days. "I wanted to bring Andrei Piotrovich, but he was delayed; so I set off without him. There's no one in the house; everybody's asleep or gone out, so I came here."

"You seem to be apologizing," Yelena answered. "That is quite unnecessary. We are all very glad to see you. . . . Let us sit down here on this bench, in the shade."

She sat down. He seated himself beside her.

"I gather you have been away from home during the past day or two?" she began.

"Yes," he answered; "I went off. . . . Did Andrei Piotrovich tell you?"

He looked at her, smiled, and began to play with his cap. When he smiled he blinked rapidly and pouted his lips, which gave him a very good-natured look.

"I expect Andrei Piotrovich also told you that I went off with some — monsters of men," he said, continuing to smile.

Yelena was a little disconcerted, but she at once felt that she must always speak the truth to Insarov.

"Yes, he did," she said decisively.

"And what did you think of me?" he asked her abruptly.

Yelena raised her eyes to him.

"I thought," she declared — "I thought that you always know what you are doing, and that you are not capable of doing anything bad."

"Well, and thank you for that. You see, it's like this, Yelena Nikolaevna," he began, turning and drawing close to her in a confiding manner; "there is a little family of our people here, and among us there are some who are poorly educated; but they are all steadfastly devoted to the common cause. Unfortunately, we cannot manage without quarrels. But they all know me and trust me, and so they asked me to go and settle a quarrel. And I went."

"Far from here?"

"I traveled some forty miles, to Troitsa. Some of our people are living there too, by the monastery. At any rate, my labor was not in vain: I settled the question."

"And was it difficult for you?"

"Yes. One was very obstinate. He didn't want to hand over the money."

"What? Was the quarrel over money?"

"Yes; and quite a small sum, too. But what did you think?"

"And you traveled forty miles for such trifles? You lost three days?"

"It's not trifles, Yelena Nikolaevna, when your fellow countrymen are involved. In that case to refuse would be a sin. I see that you, for instance, don't refuse help even to puppies, and I think you are fine. But as for the time I lost, that is not a misfortune, I can make it up. Our time does not belong to us."

"Then whom does it belong to?"

"To all who have need of us. I have told you all this so suddenly because I value your opinion. I can imagine how Andrei Piotrovich astonished you!"

"You value my opinion?" Yelena said in an undertone. "Why?" Insarov smiled again.

"Because you are a good young lady, not an aristocrat — that is all."

There was a brief silence.

"Dmitry Nikanorovich," she said, "do you know that this is the first time you have been so frank with me?"

"Is it? I have the feeling that I have always told you everything I was thinking."

"No, this is the first time, and I am very glad of it — and I, too, want to be frank with you. May I?"

He smiled and said: "You may."

"I warn you that I am very inquisitive."

"No matter, speak on."

"Andrei Piotrovich has told me a great deal about your life, about your youth. I know of one incident, one terrible incident — I know that you went back to your country later. . . . Don't answer me, for God's sake, if my question seems immodest to you, but one thought is tormenting me. Tell me, did you meet with that man — "

Yelena caught her breath. She felt both ashamed and frightened of her temerity. Insarov looked at her fixedly, narrowing his eyes a little and feeling his chin with his fingers.

"Yelena Nikolaevna," he began at last, and his voice was quieter than usual, a circumstance that almost terrified her. "I understand what man you have just referred to. No, I did not meet him, and God be thanked that I did not! I did not look for him. I did not look for him, not because I did not consider myself justified in killing him — I would have killed him with the utmost composure — but because there is no room for private revenge when it is a question of national, general vengeance — but no, that word is not suitable — when it is a question of the liberation of a nation. One thing would interfere with the other. In its own time the other, too, will not escape. The other will not escape," he repeated, and shook his head.

Yelena looked sidelong at him.

"Do you love your country very much?" she asked timidly.

"That is still unknown," he replied. "When any one of us dies for her, then it will be possible to say that he loved her."

"So that if you were deprived of the possibility of returning to Bulgaria," Yelena continued, "you would find life very oppressive in Russia?"

Insarov looked down.

"I feel that I could not endure it," he declared.

"Tell me," she began again, "is it difficult to learn Bulgarian?"

"Not in the least. It is shameful for a Russian not to know Bulgarian. A Russian should know all the Slavonic dialects. Would you like me to bring you some Bulgarian books? You will see how easy it is. What fine songs we have! Just as good as those of the Serbians. But wait a moment, I'll translate one of them for you. It tells of — But do you know anything at all about our history?"

"No, I don't," Yelena replied.

"Then wait, I'll bring you a book. You'll learn at least the main facts from it. And now listen to the song. But it would be better for me to bring you the translation written down. I am sure you will love us: you love everything that is oppressed. If only you knew how naturally rich our country is! But meanwhile it is trampled on, tortured," he exclaimed with an involuntary movement of the hand, and his face went dark. "They have taken everything from us, everything: our churches, our laws, our lands; the heathen Turks drive us like a herd, slaughter us — "

"Dmitry Nikanorovich!" Yelena exclaimed.

He stopped.

"Forgive me. I cannot talk about it with indifference. You have just asked me whether I love my country. But what else can one love on earth? What alone is immutable, what is beyond all doubts, what is impossible not to believe in, after God? And when that country has need of you — you must understand: the last peasant, the last beggar in Bulgaria, and I — we all desire one and the same thing. We all have the one aim. You can realize what confidence and strength that gives us!"

Insarov was silent for a moment, then once more he began to talk about Bulgaria. She listened to him with consuming, profound, and mournful attention. When he had ended, she asked him yet again:

"So you wouldn't remain in Russia for anything?"

When he went away, she gazed long after him. On that day he had become a different man to her. The man she saw go was not the man she had met two hours before.

From that day he began to call more and more often, but Berseniev more and more rarely. A strange feeling, of which they were both fully conscious, yet could not name, and which they were afraid to bring into the open, developed between the two friends. Thus a month passed.

15

Anna Vasilievna was fond of staying at home, as the reader already knows; but sometimes, quite unexpectedly, an invincible desire for something unusual, some astonishing *partie de plaisir*, arose within her, and the more difficulties this *partie de plaisir* involved, the more it called for preparations and arrangements, and the more she herself was agitated about it, the more enjoyable did she find it. If this mood took possession of her in wintertime, she would give orders for two or three boxes in a row to be taken, collected all her acquaintances, and went off to the theater, or even to a masquerade; if it was summertime she drove out of the town, the farther the better. The following day she would complain of a headache, would groan and remain in bed; but within a couple of months this thirst for the "unusual" would again flame up within her. And such a thirst developed now.

Someone happened to mention the beauties of Tsaritsino in her presence, and she abruptly announced that the day after tomorrow she intended to travel to Tsaritsino. An alarm was raised in the house. An urgent messenger galloped off to Moscow for Nikolai Artiomovich; the butler also galloped with him to purchase wine, meat pies, and all kinds of edible commodities; to Shubin went the order to hire a light carriage (one carette was not sufficient) and to arrange for relays of horses; the page ran twice to Berseniev and Insarov and took them two notes of invitation, written by Zoya first in Russian, then in French; Anna Vasilievna herself made arrangements for the young ladies' traveling attire. Meanwhile the *partie de plaisir* all but came to nothing: Nikolai Artiomovich arrived from Moscow in a sour and malevolent — *frondeur* — frame of mind (he was still in the sulks with Avgustina Khristianovna and, learning what was afoot, resolutely announced that he was not going — that to gallop from Kuntsevo to Moscow, and from Moscow to Tsaritsino, and from Tsaritsino back to Moscow, and from Moscow back to Kuntsevo, was absurd. "And in the last resort," he added, "let somebody first prove to me that one can be any happier in one spot on the earthly globe than in another, and then I'll go." Of course, nobody could prove that, and Anna Vasilievna, for the lack of a solid chaperon, was on the point of calling off the *partie de plaisir*, when she remembered Uvar Ivanovich. In her despair she sent to his room for him, remarking: "A drowning man clutches even at a straw." He was aroused; he came downstairs, listened silently to Anna Vasilievna's proposal, wriggled his fingers and, to the general astonishment, consented. She kissed him on the cheek and called him a dear; Nikolai Artiomovich smiled contemptuously and said: "*Quelle bourde!*" (he liked on occasion to use chic French words), and next morning, at seven o'clock, the carette and the light carriage, both packed to overflowing, rolled out of the yard of the Stakhovs' house. The ladies, the maid, and Berseniev were inside the carette, and Insarov mounted the box; in the light carriage were Uvar Ivanovich and Shubin. Uvar Ivanovich himself beckoned Shubin to join him with a wriggle of his fingers; he knew that the young man would tease him all the time, but a strange bond and a querulous frankness existed in the relations between the "black-earth force" and the young artist. On this occasion, however, Shubin left his fat friend in peace: he was taciturn, abstracted, and subdued.

The sun stood high in the cloudless azure when the carriages rolled up to the ruins of the Tsaritsino castle, a somber and sinister pile even at noonday. All the company climbed down on the grass and at once went into the garden. Yelena and Zoya walked in front with Insarov; behind them came Anna Vasilievna with an expression of perfect happiness on her face, arm in arm with Uvar Ivanovich. He panted and waddled; his new straw hat was cutting his forehead, and his feet were burning in his boots, but he, too, felt fine. Shubin and Berseniev completed the procession. "We shall be in reserve, brother, like veterans," Shubin whispred to Berseniev. "Bulgaria is there now," he added, indicating Yelena with his eyebrows.

The weather was marvelous. Everything everywhere was blooming, humming, and singing; the water of the lakes glittered in the distance; a festive, luminous feeling took charge of the soul. "Ah, it's good! Ah, it's good!" Anna Vasilievna incessantly declared. In reply to her exultant exclamations Uvar Ivanovich wagged his head affirmatively and once even remarked: "So you say!" Yelena exchanged a word or two with Insarov from time to time; Zoya held the edge of her broad hat with two fingers, coquettishly exhibited her little feet, shod in light-gray boots with squab toes, beneath her rose-colored barège gown, and looked sometimes to one side, sometimes behind her. "Aha!" Shubin suddenly exclaimed in an undertone, "Zoya Nikitishna is looking back. I'll go and join her. Yelena Nikolaevna despises me, and respects you, Andrei Piotrovich, and that amounts to the same thing. I'll go with Zoya, I'm sour enough. But I advise you to do a little botany, my friend: in your situation that is the very best thing you could think of; and it is of value scientifically. Good-by!" He ran up to Zoya, offered her his arm and, saying: "*Ihre Hand, madame*," took her by the arm and went on ahead with her. Yelena stopped, called Berseniev to her, and took his arm; but she continued to converse with Insarov. She asked him

the Bulgarian names for lilies of the valley, maples, oaks, limes.
. . . ("Bulgaria!" thought poor Andrei Piotrovich.)

Suddenly they heard a cry in front; they all raised their eyes.
Thrown by Zoya's hand, Shubin's cigar-case went flying into a
bush. "You wait, I'll pay you out for this!" he exclaimed. He
scrambled into the bush, found his cigar-case, and returned to
her; but before he quite reached her, she sent the case flying
again across the path! Five times this trick was repeated. He continually laughed and threatened her, but she only quietly smiled
and arched herself like a kitten. At last he caught her fingers and
squeezed them so hard that she squealed, and for long afterward
blew on her hand, pretending to be angry, while he sang something or other into her ear.

"They're full of play, the young people!" Anna Vasilievna
gaily remarked to Uvar Ivanovich.

He wriggled his fingers.

"What is Zoya Nikitishna up to?" Berseniev said to Yelena.

"And Shubin?" she replied.

Meanwhile the entire company approached an arbor known by
the name of Pleasant View, and halted to admire the spectacle of
the Tsaritsino lakes. The lakes extended, one after another, for
several miles; beyond them dense forests showed darkly. The
sward that covered all the slope of the hillside down to the main
lake gave the water an unusually clear, emerald tint. Nowhere
did a wave arise, even at the edge; nowhere did the surface
whiten with foam; not even a speckle of light ran over its placid
face. It was as though a congealed mass of glass had settled heavily
and lucidly in an enormous font, and the sky went to its very bottom, and the leafy trees gazed motionless into its transparent
depths. All the company stood long and silently admiring the
view; even Shubin was subdued, even Zoya grew pensive.

At last they all unanimously wanted to go for a row on the
water. Shubin, Insarov, and Berseniev raced one another headlong down the grassy slope. They found a large painted boat,
then two oarsmen, and called to the ladies, who went to them.
Uvar Ivanovich cautiously made his way down after the ladies.
The difficulty he had in getting into the boat and taking his seat
caused a good deal of laughter.

"Take care, master, don't sink us!" remarked one of the oarsmen, a young, snub-nosed lad in an Alexandrisk shirt.

471

"Now, now, no showing off!" Uvar Ivanovich remarked.

The boat was pushed out from the bank. The young men would have taken the oars, but Insarov was the only one who could row. Shubin suggested that they should sing some Russian song in chorus, and himself struck up: "Down the Mother Volga. . . ." Berseniev, Zoya, and even Anna Vasilievna took up the song (Insarov had no voice), but the result was discord. In the third verse the singers went astray; only Berseniev attempted to continue in a bass voice: "In the waves they could see nothing," but he also was soon put out of countenance. The oarsmen winked at each other and silently grinned.

"Well?" Shubin turned to them, "so the gentlemen don't know how to sing, you think?" The youngster in the Alexandrisk shirt only nodded his head. "Then you wait, snubnose," Shubin retorted, "and we'll show you. Zoya Nikitishna, sing us Niedermeyer's *Le Lac*. Stop rowing, you!"

The wet oars were raised into the air, like wings, and there they remained still, dripping with ringing drops of water. The boat floated a little farther and came to a stop, swinging gently in the water, like a swan. Zoya simpered.

"*Allons*," Anna Vasilievna said graciously.

Zoya threw off her hat and began to sing:

"*O, lac, l'année à peine a fini sa carrière. . . .*"

Her small but pure voice went speeding over the mirror of the lake. In the distant forests every word was echoed; it was as though there, too, someone were singing in a distinct and mysterious, but not a human, not a worldly voice. When she ended, a loud "Bravo" came from one waterside arbor, and several crimson-faced Germans who were on a visit to Tsaritsino, poured out of it. Some of them were in their shirt sleeves and without cravats, even without waistcoats, and they shouted "*Bis!*" so frantically that Anna Vasilievna ordered the oarsmen to row to the other end of the lake as quickly as possible. But before the boat touched the bank Uvar Ivanovich once more succeeded in surprising his friends; noticing that in one part of the forest the echo repeated every sound with particular clarity, he suddenly began to call like a quail. At first everybody started, but they at once thought it really amusing, especially as he imitated the quail's call very faithfully and realistically. This encouraged him, and he tried to miaow; but the miaowing was not so satisfactory. He called once more like a quail, looked round at them all, and was silent. Shubin rushed to kiss him; he pushed him away. At that moment the boat was moored, and all the company stepped onto the bank.

Meanwhile the coachman, the footman, and the maid had brought baskets from the carette and had prepared dinner on the grass beneath some old lime trees. They all seated themselves around the spread tablecloth and began on the meat pies and other food. They had excellent appetites, but from time to time Anna Vasilievna handed more food round and pleaded with her guests to eat a lot, assuring them that in the open air it was very healthful to do so. She said this even to Uvar Ivanovich. "Don't you worry!" he bellowed with his mouth stuffed full. "The Lord has given us such a lovely day!" she declared incessantly. One would not have recognized her: she seemed to have grown twenty years younger. Berseniev told her so. "Yes, yes," she said, "I, too, was good-looking in my time; I would have passed anywhere." Shubin attached himself to Zoya and continually poured out wine for her. She refused it, but he poured it out for her and ended by drinking it himself and then pouring out more for her. He also told her that he wanted to put his head on her knee; she flatly refused to allow him "such a great liberty." Yelena seemed to be the most serious of all, but in her heart there was a marvelous tranquillity, such as she had not known for long past. She felt infinitely happy, and she still continually wanted to have not only Insarov, but Berseniev also at her side. Andrei Piotrovich vaguely realized what that meant, and surreptitiously sighed.

The hours flew past; evening came on. Anna Vasilievna suddenly raised an outcry. "Ah, my goodness, how late it is!" she exclaimed. "You've eaten and drunk enough, gentlemen, time to wipe your beards." She began to fidget, and they all began to fidget, scrambled to their feet, and went back in the direction of the castle, where the carriages were waiting. As they passed the lake they halted once more, to admire Tsaritsino for a last time. Everywhere brilliant, late-afternoon colors were burning; the sky was glowing; the leaves were shining iridescently, stirred by the little breeze that had sprung up; the distant waters were gleaming like molten gold; the rust-colored turrets and arbors scattered about the garden stood out sharply against the dark green of the trees. "Good-by, Tsaritsino, we shall not forget this day's excursion!" Anna Vasilievna declared. . . . At that moment, as though in confirmation of this remark, a strange incident occurred that undoubtedly was not so easy to forget.

For Anna Vasilievna had not finished sending her farewell message to Tsaritsino when suddenly, a few paces away from her, behind a lofty bush of lilac, a hubbub of discordant exclamations, laughter, and shouts arose, and a whole horde of disheveled men, those same amateurs of the vocal art who had applauded Zoya so fervently, rushed out onto the path. The gentlemen amateurs seemed to be extremely merry. At the sight of the ladies they halted, but one of them, of enormous size, with a bull-neck, and eyes bloodshot like a bull's, stepped forward from the rest and, awkwardly bowing and swaying as he walked, approached Anna Vasilievna, who was petrified with fright.

"*Bon jour, madame*," he said in a hoarse voice. "How are you?"

Anna Vasilievna fell back a pace.

"But why," the giant continued in bad Russian, "you not wanted to sing *bis*, when our company shouted *bis*, and bravo, and *foro*?"

"Yes, yes, why?" several of the others asked.

Insarov was about to step forward, but Shubin stopped him and set himself in front of Anna Vasilievna.

"Allow me," he began, "worthy stranger, to express to you the unfeigned astonishment that you arouse in all of us by your behavior. So far as I can judge, you belong to the Saxon branch of the Caucasian race; consequently we must assume that you are acquainted with good society manners. Yet you are talking to a lady to whom you have not been introduced. Believe me, at any other time I in particular would be very glad to make your acquaintance, for I notice that you have such a phenomenal development of muscles — biceps, triceps and deltoids — that, as a sculptor, I would regard it as a genuine stroke of luck to have you as my model. But on this occasion leave us in peace."

The "worthy stranger" listened to all this speech with his head cocked contemptuously on one side and his arms akimbo.

"I not understand what you say," he said at last. "You think, perhaps, I am a cobbler, or a watchmaker? *Hein?* I am an officer, I am an official, yes."

"I have no doubt of that — " Shubin began.

"But what I say is," the stranger continued, with one powerful hand pushing Shubin aside as if he were a twig in his path, "I say:

why you not sing *bis* when we cried *bis*? But I will go now, this minute, only first it necessary is that this *Fräulein*, not this *madame*, no, she is not necessary, but that one, or that one" (he pointed to Yelena and Zoya), "gives me *einen Küss*, as we say in German, a little kiss, yes, well? Why, that is nothing."

"Nothing, *einen Küss*, that is nothing," the ranks of the company sounded again.

"Eh! *der Sakramenter!*" one completely drunk German said, choking with laughter.

Zoya clutched at Insarov's arm, but he tore himself from her grasp and placed himself right in front of the insolent giant.

"Be good enough to go away," he said to him in a low but harsh tone.

The German began to laugh ponderously.

"Go away? I like that! Can I not too take a walk? How mean you, 'go away'? Why go away?"

"Because you have dared to upset a lady," Insarov said, going suddenly pale. "Because you are drunk."

"What? I drunk? Do you hear? *Hören Sie das, Herr Provisor?* I am an officer, and he dares. Now I demand *satisfaction! Einen Küss will ich!*"

"If you take another step —" Insarov began.

"Well? What then?"

"I shall throw you into the water."

"Into the water? *Herr Je!* And is that all? Well, we shall see, it is very interesting, how into the water —"

The gentleman officer raised his hands and stepped forward; but suddenly something extraordinary occurred: he groaned, all his enormous carcass staggered, then was raised from the ground, his legs kicked in the air, and before the ladies could cry out, before anyone could understand how it had been done, all the gentleman officer's great bulk fell into the lake with a heavy splash and at once vanished beneath the water, sending it rolling in great waves.

"Ai!" the ladies squealed with one accord.

"*Mein Gott!*" came from the Germans.

A minute passed — then a round head, with dank, clinging hair, appeared above the water; it blew bubbles, did that head; two hands convulsively floundered close to the mouth.

"He'll drown! Save him, save him!" Anna Vasilievna cried to

Insarov, who was standing on the bank with straddled legs, breathing heavily.

"He'll float up," he said with contemptuous and merciless unconcern. "Let us go," he added, taking her by the arm. "Come along, Uvar Ivanovich, Yelena Nikolaevna."

"A — a — o — o — " the unfortunate German howled at that moment, as he successfully clutched at a waterside reed.

They all set off behind Insarov, and they all had to go past the "company." But, deprived of their leader, the revelers sobered down and did not utter a single little word; only one, the bravest of them all, shook his head and muttered: "Well, all the same, this — this is, God knows what — after this — " while another even took off his hat. Insarov looked very dangerous to them, and not without reason: something unpleasant, something dangerous, was indicated in his face. The Germans rushed to drag out their comrade, and as soon as he found himself on dry land he began lachrymosely to swear and shout after "those Russian swindlers" that he would make a complaint, that he would see His Excellency, Count von Kizeritz, himself.

But the "Russian swindlers" paid no attention to his shouts and hurried on to the castle as quickly as possible. They were all silent while they walked through the garden, only Anna Vasilievna ohed and ahed a little. But as they approached the carriages, they halted, and an irresistible, endless gust of laughter arose from them, as from Homer's heavenly inhabitants. First Shubin burst into a shrill guffaw, like a madman, then Berseniev began to drum like rattling peas, now Zoya split into a laugh like a string of beads, Anna Vasilievna also suddenly began to roll, even Yelena could not but smile, at last even Insarov could not resist. But loudest of all, and longest of all, and most violently of all roared Uvar Ivanovich: he laughed till he had the stitch, till he hiccuped, till he choked. He would quiet down a little and say through his tears: "I — wondered — what was that noise — but it was — he — smack — " And together with the last convulsively coughed-up word a new outburst of laughter would shake all his frame.

Zoya incited him still more. "I," she said, "saw his legs in the air — "

"Yes, yes," Uvar Ivanovich responded, "his legs — legs — and then, smack! And that was he falling flat!"

On the Eve

"Yes; and how did he manage to do it? Why, the German was three times as big as he!" Zoya asked.

"But I'll tell you," Uvar Ivanovich replied, wiping his eyes, "I saw him put one hand in the small of his back, one leg he put forward, and then, smack! I listen; what's that? — but it was he, falling flat. . . ."

Even after the carriages had been moving for some time and the castle at Tsaritsino was lost to sight, Uvar Ivanovich could not regain his composure. At last Shubin, who once more rode with him in the light carriage, shamed him into silence.

But Insarov was conscience-stricken. He sat in the carette opposite Yelena (Berseniev had taken the box seat) and was silent; she, too, was silent. He thought that she was condemning him, but she was not condemning him. She had been very frightened at first, then she was struck by the expression on his face, then she was lost in meditation. The subject of that meditation was not absolutely clear to her. The feeling she had felt all day had vanished, so much she realized; but it had been replaced by another, which for the moment she did not understand. The *partie de plaisir* had gone on too long; the evening passed imperceptibly into night. The carette bowled along swiftly, now past ripening cornfields, where the air was stifling and fragrant and eloquent of grain; now through broad meadows, and then sudden freshness beat in a gentle wave against their faces. The sky seemed to be smoking at its edges. At last the moon floated up, bleary and crimson. Anna Vasilievna dozed; Zoya leaned out of the window and gazed at the road. Finally it occurred to Yelena that she had not spoken to Insarov for more than an hour. She turned to him with some insignificant question; he at once answered joyfully.

Now vague, indefinite sounds were borne to their ears; it seemed as though thousands of voices were talking in the distance: Moscow was rushing toward them. In front tiny lights began to glimmer; they grew more and more; then stones rattled beneath the wheels. Anna Vasilievna awoke. Everybody in the carette began to talk, though now not one of them could hear what the others were saying, so noisily did the paved road thunder beneath the two carriages and the thirty-two horse-hoofs. Long and boring seemed the journey from Moscow to Kuntsevo; they all slept or at least were silent, their heads pressed into the various corners. Only Yelena did not close her eyes; she kept them fixed

477

on Insarov's vaguely outlined form. Shubin was overwhelmed with a feeling of sorrow; the breeze blew into his eyes and irritated him; he huddled into his greatcoat collar and all but burst into tears. Uvar Ivanovich snored felicitously, swaying to right and left.

At last the carriages stopped. Two footmen carried Anna Vasilievna out of the carette; she went completely to pieces and, as she said good-night to her companions, announced that she was only just alive. They began to thank her, but she simply repeated: "Just alive." Yelena (for the first time) squeezed Insarov's hand. For a long time she did not undress, but sat by the window.

Shubin seized an opportunity to whisper to the departing Berseniev:

"Well, and isn't he a hero? Throwing drunken Germans into the water!"

"But you didn't do it," Berseniev retorted, and went home with Insarov.

The dawn was beginning to gleam in the sky when the two friends returned to their house. The sun had not yet risen, but a cool breeze was beginning to play, a gray dew covered the grass, and the first larks were ringing high, high in the semi-crepuscular aerial abysm, whence, like a single eye, a large, belated star gazed down.

16

Soon after she had made Insarov's acquaintance Yelena began (for the fifth or sixth time) to keep a diary. Here are some passages from this diary:

"June. . . . Andrei Piotrovich brings me books, but I cannot read them. I am ashamed to tell him so, but I don't feel like giving back the books, and lying by saying that I have read them. I have a feeling that that would upset him. He notices everything I do. He seems to be very attached to me. He is a very good man, is Andrei Piotrovich.

" . . . What is it I want? Why does my heart feel so heavy, so languid? Why do I gaze so enviously at the birds flying by? I think I could fly with them, and fly — where to, I know not, only far from here. And is that not a sinful desire? I have my mother, my father, my family here. Do I not love them, then? No, I do not love them as I should like to love. It is a terrible thing for me to say, but it is true. Perhaps I am a great sinner; perhaps that is why I am so sad, why I have no peace. Someone's hand is lying on me, crushing me. It is just as though I were in a prison, and at any moment now the walls will fall in on me. Why is it that others do not feel this? Whom, then, shall I love, if I am cold to my own family? Evidently Papa is right: he reproaches me with loving only dogs and cats. I must think that over. I pray very little; I must pray. . . . But, seemingly, I would be capable of love!

" . . . I am still shy with Mr. Insarov. I know not why; I am not so young, surely? But he is so simple and good. Sometimes he has a very serious face. I suppose he cannot be bothered with us. I feel that, and I seem to feel ashamed to take up his time. Andrei Piotrovich is quite different. I am prepared to chatter away with him all day. But he, too, is always talking to me about Insarov. And in what terrible detail! I saw him last night with a dagger in his hand. And he seemed to be saying to me: 'I shall kill you and kill myself.' What rubbish!

" . . . Oh, that someone would say to me: this is what you should do! To be good is not enough; to do good — yes, that is the main thing in life. But how to do good? Oh, if I could only master myself! I do not understand why I think so often about Mr. Insarov. When he comes and sits and listens attentively, but himself makes no attempt to say anything, and does not fidget, I look at him, and I find it pleasant — but that is all. But when he has gone I am continually recalling his words, and I am vexed with myself and even agitated — I myself do not know why. (He speaks French badly, and is not ashamed of it — I like that in him.) But, after all, I always think a great deal about new faces. As I was talking to him I suddenly remembered our butler, Vasily, who dragged a legless old man out of a burning hut and himself all but perished. Papa called him a fine fellow, Mamma gave him five rubles, but I wanted to bow down at his feet. And he had a simple, even a stupid face, and afterward he took to drink.

" . . . Today I gave a groschen to a beggarwoman, and she said to me: 'why are you so sad?' But I had not even suspected that I looked sad. I think it is because I am alone, always alone, with all my good, with all my evil. I have no one to whom to reach out my hand. The one who comes to me I do not need; but the one I should like to come — passes by.

479

" . . . I do not know what is the matter with me today; my
head is in a turmoil, I am ready to fall on my knees and ask and
implore mercy. I do not know who and how, but it is as though
someone were killing me, and inwardly I cry out, and revolt. I
weep and cannot be silent. . . . O Lord! O Lord! subdue these
outbursts within me! Thou alone canst, all else is impotent;
neither my insignificant alms, nor occupations — nothing, nothing, nothing can help me. Really, I could go off somewhere as a
servant: I would find it easier.

"To what purpose is my youth, for what object am I living?
Why have I a soul, what is it all for?

" . . . Insarov — Mr. Insarov — really, I do not know what
form to use — continues to interest me. I want to know what he
has in his soul. He seems to be so open, so accessible, yet nothing
is visible to me. Sometimes he looks at me with such searching
eyes — or is that only my imagination? Paul is always teasing me
— I am angry with Paul. What is it he wants? He is in love with
me — but I do not need his love. He is in love with Zoya too. I am
unjust to him; he told me yesterday that I do not know how to be
half unjust — that is true. That is very bad.

"Ah, I feel that a man has need of misfortune, or poverty, or
illness; otherwise he at once begins to grow conceited.

" . . . Why did Andrei Piotrovich tell me about those two
Bulgars today? He appeared to tell me quite deliberately. What is
Mr. Insarov to me? I am angry with Andrei Piotrovich.

" . . . I take up my pen and know not how to begin. How unexpectedly he began to talk to me in the garden today! How affectionate and confiding he was! How suddenly this has come
about! It is just as though we were old, old friends and have only
just recognized each other. How was it I did not understand him
before? How close he is to me now! And this is the amazing thing:
I have grown much more tranquil now. I am silly; yesterday I
was angry with Andrei Piotrovich, and with him, and even called
him *Mr. Insarov*, but today — There, at last, is a true man, there
is someone upon whom one could depend. He does not flatter; he
is the first man I have met who does not flatter; all the others lie,
they all flatter. But Andrei Piotrovich, dear, kind, Andrei Piotrovich, what am I insulting you for? No! Andrei Piotrovich is possibly more learned than he, possibly he is even more intelligent.
. . . But, I don't know, somehow he is so small beside him. When

he talks of his country he grows and grows, and his face grows more handsome, and his voice like steel, and then it seems that there is no man on earth before whom he would lower his eyes. And he not only talks — he has acted and will act. I shall question him. . . . How he suddenly turned to me and smiled at me! Only brothers smile like that. Ah, how content I am! When he called on us the first time I never even thought we would become friends so quickly. But now I am even glad that on that first occasion I remained indifferent. Indifferent! Then am I not indifferent now?

"It is a long time since I have experienced such inward peace. So still am I within, so still. And there is nothing to write. I see him often, and that is all. What else is there to write?

" . . . Paul locks himself in his room, Andrei Piotrovich is visiting us more rarely — poor fellow. It seems to me he — However, that cannot be. I like to talk to Andrei Piotrovich: he never says a word about himself, always about something active, useful. Not like Shubin. Shubin is as elegant as a butterfly, and delights in his elegance; that is something butterflies do not do. For that matter, both Shubin and Andrei Piotrovich — I know what I want to say.

" . . . *He* likes to visit us, I can see that. But why? What has he found in me? True, we have similar tastes, he and I; neither of us likes poetry, neither of us knows anything about art. But how much better he is than I! He is composed, but I am in everlasting unrest; he has a road, he has an aim . . . but I, whither am I going, where is my nest? He is composed, but all his thoughts are far away. The time will come, and he will forsake us forever, he will go to his own home, thither, over the sea. Well, what of it! God speed him! But, all the same, I shall be happy that I knew him while he was here.

"Why is he not Russian? No, he could not be Russian.

"Mamma also likes him, she calls him a 'modest man.' Dear Mamma! She does not understand him. Paul is silent; he has guessed that I dislike his innuendoes, but he is jealous of him. The naughty boy! and what right has he? Have I ever —

"This is all nonsense! Why does all this come into my head?

" . . . And yet, none the less, it is strange that I have never loved anybody yet, down to my twentieth year. It seems to me that D (I shall call him D, I like that name: Dmitry) is so clear

Turgenev

of soul because he has given himself wholly to his cause, to his dreams. What need has he to get agitated? Anyone who has given himself wholly — wholly — wholly — he has few sorrows, he no longer has to answer for anything. Not *I* want: *it* wants. By the way, he and I like the same flowers. I picked a rose today. One petal fell off, he picked it up — I gave him all the rose.

" . . . For some time now I have been having strange dreams. What does that mean?

" . . . D calls on us frequently. Yesterday he stayed all the evening. He wants to teach me Bulgarian. I feel quite at home with him. Better than at home.

" . . . The days are flying past. . . . And I feel glorious, and for some reason awed, and I want to thank God, and tears are not far off. Oh, warm, shining days!

" . . . I still feel as light in my heart as ever, and only occasionally, only occasionally do I feel a little sad. I am happy. . . . Am I happy?

" . . . I shall not soon forget yesterday's excursion. What strange, new, terrible impressions! I was not frightened when he suddenly seized that giant and flung him, like a ball, into the water . . . but he frightened me. The way he said: 'He'll float up!' That turned my heart over. So I had not understood him. And afterward, when they all laughed, when I laughed, how hurt I felt for him! He was abashed, I felt that, he was abashed because of me. He told me so later, in the carette, in the darkness, when I tried to distinguish his face and was afraid of him. Truly, one cannot joke with him, and he knows how to defend himself. But why that anger, those trembling lips, that poison in his eyes? But perhaps it is not possible otherwise? It is not possible to be a man, a warrior, and to remain humble and gentle. Life is a rough business, he said to me recently. I repeated these words to Andrei Piotrovich; he did not agree with D. Which of them is right? But what a beginning the day had! How good it was for me to walk side by side with him, even in silence. . . . But I am glad of what happened. Evidently it was to be.

" . . . Once again anxiety. . . . I am not quite well.

" . . . All these past days I have not written anything in this book because I did not feel like writing. I felt that no matter what I wrote, it would always be something other than what is in my soul. But what is in my soul? I have had a long conversation with him, and it revealed a great deal to me. He told me of his plans. (By the way, I know now why he has a wound on his neck. . . . My God! when I think that he was already sentenced to death, that he only just escaped, that he was wounded. . . .) He has a presentiment that war will come and rejoices to think so. And, none the less, I have never seen D so sad. What can he — he! — be sad about? Papa came back from town, found us together, and gave us a strange look. Andrei Piotrovich arrived; I noticed that he has gone very thin and pale. He reproached me with being too cold and perfunctory with Shubin. But I had completely forgotten Paul. When I see him, I shall try to atone for my guilt. I have no time for him now — nor for anybody else in the world. Andrei Piotrovich talked to me with a kind of commiserating air. What does all this mean? Why is everything so dark around me and within me? It seems to me that around me and within me something enigmatic is going on, that I must find the word. . . .

" . . . I did not sleep last night, my head is aching. What is the point of writing? He went away so quickly today, and I had wanted to talk to him. . . . He seems to be avoiding me. Yes, he is avoiding me!

" . . . The word is found, light has flooded over me! God have mercy on me! . . . I am in love!"

17

On the very day Yelena wrote that last, fatal word in her diary, Insarov was sitting in Berseniev's room, and Berseniev was standing opposite him with an expression of bewilderment on his face. Insarov had just informed him of his intention to go back to Moscow the very next day.

"But for goodness' sake!" Berseniev exclaimed, "the finest time of all is just arriving. What will you do in Moscow? What a sudden decision! Or have you had some news?"

"I haven't received any news," Insarov replied. "I simply think I must not stay here."

"But how can you — "

"Andrei Piotrovich," Insarov said, "please do not insist, I ask you. It is just as painful for me to leave you, but it cannot be helped."

Berseniev gazed at him fixedly.

"I know there's no convincing you," he said at last. "And so the question is settled?"

"Absolutely settled," Insarov replied. He rose and went out.

Berseniev walked up and down the room, then picked up his hat and went off to the Stakhovs'.

"You have something to tell me," Yelena said to him the first moment they were alone.

"Yes; how did you guess?"

"That doesn't matter. Tell me, what is it?"

He told her of Insarov's decision.

She turned pale.

"What does it mean?" She uttered the words with difficulty.

"You know," Berseniev said, "that Dmitry Nikanorovich does not like giving any account of his actions. But I think — Let us sit down, Yelena Nikolaevna, you don't seem to be quite well. . . . I think I can guess the real reason for this abrupt departure."

"What, oh, what is the reason?" Yelena repeated, unconsciously squeezing his hand in her own suddenly cold hand.

"Well, you see — " he began with a mournful smile. "But how can I explain it to you? I must go back to last spring, to the time when I first came to know Insarov more intimately. I happened to meet him in the house of a fellow countryman of ours, who had a daughter, a very good-looking girl. I got the impression that Insarov was not altogether indifferent to her, and I told him so. He laughed and replied that I was mistaken, that his heart had not been affected at all, but that he would go away immediately if anything like that ever happened to him, as he does not wish — these were his very words — to betray his cause and his duty for the sake of satisfying personal feelings. 'I am a Bulgar,' he said, 'and I do not need Russian love.' . . ."

"Well — and what do — you now — " Yelena whispered, involuntarily turning her head aside like someone expecting a blow, but not releasing his hand.

"I think," he said, and he lowered his voice, "I think that what I then mistakenly assumed to have happened has now really come about."

"That is — you think — don't torture me!" the words burst from her.

"I think," he went on hurriedly, "that now Insarov has fallen in love with a Russian girl and, in accordance with his promise, has decided to go away."

Yelena squeezed his hand still more tightly and bowed her head still lower, as though seeking to hide from him the flush of shame that flooded all her face and neck with sudden crimson.

"Andrei Piotrovich, you're as kind as an angel," she said. "But surely he will come to say good-by?"

"Yes, I suppose so; he certainly will come, because he does not wish to go away. . . ."

"Tell him, tell — "

But now the poor girl could no longer control herself: the tears gushed from her eyes, and she ran out of the room.

"So she loves him as much as that," Berseniev thought as he slowly returned home. "I hadn't expected that; I hadn't expected that her feeling for him was already so strong. I am kind, she said," he continued his meditations. . . . "But who will say what feelings and impulses moved me to tell her all this? Certainly it was not out of kindness, not out of kindness. Was it simply the accursed desire to ascertain whether the dagger is still really in the wound? I should be satisfied — they love each other, and I have helped them. . . . 'A coming intermediary between learning and the Russian public,' Shubin calls me; evidently I was born to be an intermediary. But supposing I am mistaken? No, I am not mistaken. . . ."

Bitter was it for Andrei Piotrovich, and it did not even occur to him to pick up Raumer.

Next day, about two o'clock, Insarov called on the Stakhovs. As though by arrangement, at that hour a guest was sitting in Anna Vasilievna's reception room. It was their neighbor the archdeacon's wife, a very good and worthy woman, who, none the less, had had a little unpleasantness with the police because one very hot day she had taken it into her head to bathe in a lake close to a road along which some important general's family frequently drove. At first Yelena even found the visitor's presence a comfort, and not one drop of blood was left in her cheeks as soon as she heard Insarov's step. But her heart sank at the thought that he might say good-by without speaking to her alone. He, too, seemed embarrassed and avoided her eyes. "Surely he isn't going to say good-by at once?" she thought. In fact, Insarov turned to speak to Anna Vasilievna. Yelena hurriedly rose and called him aside, over to the window. The archdeacon's wife was astonished and attempted to turn round, but she was so tightly laced that her corset creaked with every movement she made. She remained immobile.

"Listen," Yelena hurriedly said, "I know what you have come for; Andrei Piotrovich has told me of your intention. But I ask you, I implore you not to say good-by to us today, but to come here tomorrow earlier in the day, about eleven o'clock. I must say a few words to you."

He silently bowed his head.

"I shall not keep you. . . . You promise me?"

He bowed again, but did not speak.

"Yelena, my dear, come here," Anna Vasilievna called. "Come and see what a marvelous reticule our visitor has."

"I embroidered it myself," remarked the archdeacon's wife.

Yelena stepped away from the window.

Insarov did not remain for more than fifteen minutes. Yelena surreptitiously watched him. He fidgeted as he stood, knew no more than before where to look, and made a strange departure, suddenly, as though he vanished.

That day passed slowly for Yelena, and still more slowly did the long, long night drag past. She sat on her bed, embracing her knees with her arms, and laying her head on them; then she went across to the window, set her burning brow against the cold glass, and thought, thought, thought one and the same thoughts till she was worn out. Her heart seemed to turn to stone within her, or to vanish from her breast altogether; she could not feel it, yet the blood beat heavily in her head, and her hair burned her, and her lips were parched. "He will come . . . he did not say good-by to Mamma, he will not deceive me. . . . Did Andrei Piotrovich really tell the truth? It cannot be. . . . He did not promise to come in so many words. . . . Have I really parted from him forever? . . ." Thoughts like these did not leave her head, literally did not leave her head; they did not come, did not return, they incessantly hovered within her, like a mist. "He loves me." The thought suddenly flamed up in all her being, and she gazed fixedly into the darkness; a secret, invisible smile parted her lips. . . . But she at once shook her head, placed her hands with interlocked fingers behind it, and again, like a mist, her former thoughts hovered within her. Toward morning she undressed and got into bed, but could not sleep. The first fiery rays of the sun penetrated into her room. . . . "Oh, if he loves me!" she suddenly exclaimed, and, unashamed of the light irradiating her, she opened wide her embrace. . . .

She rose, dressed, went downstairs. In the house no one was yet awake. She went into the garden. But in the garden it was so quiet and fresh, the birds twittered so trustfully, the flowers peeped so joyously, that she felt afraid. "Oh," she thought, "if it is true, then there is not one little blade of grass more happy than I. But is it true?" She returned to her room and, in order somehow to kill time, began to change her clothes. But everything dropped and slipped from her hands, and she was still sitting half undressed before her mirror when she was called to tea. She went downstairs.

Her mother noticed her pallor, but only said: "How interesting you look today!" and, running her glance over her, added: "That dress suits you very well; you should always wear it when you want to please someone." Yelena made no answer, and sat in a corner.

Meanwhile nine o'clock struck; eleven was still two hours away. She began to read, then to sew, then went back to the book; then she pledged herself that she would walk a hundred times along one avenue, and walked a hundred times; then she spent a long time watching her mother as she set out the cards for patience . . . and looked at the clock: it was not even ten. Shubin came into the reception room. She attempted to talk to him, and apologized to him, herself not knowing why. . . . Her every word not only cost her effort but aroused in her a feeling of bewilderment. Shubin leaned toward her. She expected a sneer, raised her eyes, and saw before her a sorrowful and good-natured face. . . . She smiled at that face. Shubin also smiled at her, silently, and quietly went out. She wanted to hold him back, but could not remember immediately how to call him.

At last eleven o'clock struck. She began to wait, to wait, to wait, and to listen. Now she could do nothing at all; she ceased even to think. Her heart awoke within her and began to beat louder, ever louder, and, strange to say, time also seemed to speed by more quickly. A quarter of an hour passed, half an hour passed, several more minutes passed, so she thought. And suddenly she started: the clock struck not twelve, but one. "He will not come, he will go away without saying good-by! . . ." This thought rushed with the blood to her head. She felt that her breath was failing her, that she was ready to burst into tears. . . . She ran to her room and fell on the bed, her face on her folded hands.

Half an hour she lay motionless; through her fingers the tears poured onto the pillow. She suddenly raised herself and sat up. Some strange thing had been accomplished within her: her face was changed, her moist eyes dried of themselves and began to glitter, her brows drew down, her lips pressed together. Another half-hour passed. For the last time Yelena listened intently: perhaps the well-known voice would reach her ears? She rose, put on her hat, her gloves, threw a mantle round her shoulders, and, slipping out unnoticed, walked at a brisk pace along the road leading to Berseniev's house.

18

Yelena walked with head bent and her eyes gazing fixedly ahead. She was afraid of nothing, she thought of nothing; she wanted only to see Insarov once more. She walked along without noticing that the sun had long since been hidden, veiled by heavy black clouds, that the wind was roaring impetuously among the trees and blowing her dress about, that the dust suddenly rose and rushed in a column along the road. . . . Large drops of rain began to fall. She did not notice them either; but they fell more and more rapidly, more and more heavily; lightning flashed, thunder pealed. Yelena stopped and looked about her. . . . Fortunately for her, not far from the place where the storm had overtaken her was a tumbledown, abandoned wayside chapel over a disused well. She ran to it and passed beneath its low roof. The rain lashed down in streams; the sky closed in above her. With dumb despair she gazed at the heavy sheets of swiftly falling rain. Her last hope of seeing Insarov vanished. An old beggar-woman entered the chapel, shook herself, curtsied as she said: "Out of the rain, my dear," and, groaning and moaning, sat down on the ledge by the well. Yelena put her hand into her pocket. The old woman noticed the movement, and her face, furrowed and yellow, but beautiful once, lit up. "Thank you, my bene-factress, thank you, my dear," she began. Yelena could not find her purse in her pocket, and the old woman was already holding out her hand. . . .

"I haven't any money, granny," Yelena said. "But here, take this, it may be of some use."

She gave her her handkerchief.

"Oh, my beauty," the beggarwoman said, "but what do I need your handkerchief for? Except perhaps to give to my little grandson when he takes a wife. God reward you for your kindness!"

There was a clap of thunder.

"Lord Jesus Christ!" the woman muttered, and crossed herself three times. "But surely I have seen you before," she added after a moment. "Surely you gave me Christian alms some time ago."

Yelena looked closely at the old woman and recognized her.

"Yes, granny," she replied, "and you asked me why I was so sad."

"Yes, my dear, so I did. I thought I recognized you. And now too you seem to be a living sorrow. The handkerchief you've given me is all wet, so it must be with tears. Oh, you young people, you're all nothing but sorrow, nothing but terrible misery!"

"But what sorrow, granny?"

"What sorrow? Ah, my kind young lady, you can't take me in, not an old woman like me. I know what you're grieving for, yours is not the sorrow of an orphan. You see, I have been young, too, my darling; I have passed through such trials too. Yes. But because of your goodness, this is what I tell you: if you have found a good man, not a featherbrain, you hold on to him firmly; hold on stronger than death. If it is to be, it will be; but if not, then evidently it is not pleasing to God. Yes. Why are you so surprised at me? I can tell fortunes too. If you wish, with your handkerchief I'll carry away all your sorrow! I'll take it away, and there'll be an end to it. Look, the rain is beginning to stop; you wait here a little longer, but I'll go. It won't be the first time I've got wet. But remember, my dear: you've had your sorrow, the sorrow's left you, and there will be no more thought of it. God be merciful!"

The beggarwoman rose from the ledge, left the chapel, and went her way. Yelena stared after her in bewilderment. "What does this signify?" she involuntarily whispered.

The rain slackened more and more, the sun began to shine fitfully. Yelena made ready to leave her refuge. Suddenly she saw Insarov, ten paces away from the chapel. Wrapped in a greatcoat, he was walking along the same road by which she had come; he appeared to be hurrying home.

She rested her arm on the infirm balustrade of the porch and tried to call him; but her voice betrayed her. . . . Insarov was already passing by without raising his head. . . .

"Dmitry Nikanorovich!" she said at last.

He abruptly stopped and looked back. . . . In that first minute he did not recognize her, but he at once turned back to her.

"You? You here?" he exclaimed.

She drew back, without speaking, into the chapel. He followed her.

"You here?" he repeated.

She continued silent and only looked at him with a long, tender look. He cast down his eyes.

"Have you been to see us?" she asked him.

"No — no, I haven't."

"No?" she repeated. and attempted to smile. "Is that the way you keep your promise? I waited for you all the morning."

"Remember, Yelena Nikolaevna, I did not make any promise yesterday."

She again smiled faintly and passed her hand over her face. Both her face and her hand were very pale.

"So you intended to go away without saying good-by to us?"

"Yes," he said harshly and gruffly.

"How could you? After our acquaintance, after those talks, after all that — So if I had not chanced to meet you here" (her voice began to rise, and she was silent for a moment), " . . . you would have gone away and would not have shaken my hand for the last time. And you would have felt no regret?"

Insarov turned away.

"Yelena Nikolaevna, please don't speak like that. As it is, I am far from happy. Believe me, my decision cost me much effort. If only you knew — "

"I don't want to know. Why are you going away?" she interrupted him in alarm. "Evidently it is necessary. Evidently we have got to part. You would not wish to make your friends unhappy without good reason. But do friends really part like that? For you and I are friends, aren't we?"

"No," Insarov said.

"What?" Yelena replied. Her cheeks went pink with a delicate flush.

"That is just why I am going away, because we are not friends. Do not force me to say something I do not wish to say, something I shall not say."

"You were frank with me in the past," she said with timid reproach. "Do you remember?"

"I could be frank then, I had nothing to conceal then; but now —"

"But now?" she queried.

"But now — but now I must go away. Good-by."

If at that moment Insarov had raised his eyes to Yelena, he would have seen that her face was growing more and more radiant as his own grew gloomier and darker. But he obstinately gazed at the ground.

"Well, good-by, Dmitry Nikanorovitch," she began. "But at least, as we have met, now give me your hand."

He was about to stretch out his hand.

"No, I cannot do even that," he declared, and turned his head away.

"You cannot?"

"I cannot. Good-by." And he went toward the chapel entrance.

"Wait just one moment longer," Yelena said. "You seem to be afraid of me. But I am braver than you," she added, with a sudden gentle tremor in all her body. "I can tell you — do you want me to? — Why you found me here. Do you know where I was going?"

Insarov stared at her in astonishment.

"I was coming to you."

"To me?"

She hid her face.

"You tried to force me to say that I love you," she whispered. "Well — I have said it."

"Yelena!" Insarov exclaimed.

She took the hands held out to her, glanced at him, and dropped on his chest.

He held her in a powerful embrace and was silent. He did not need to tell her that he loved her. By his very exclamation, by that immediate transformation of the entire man, by the rise and fall of his chest, on which she was so trustfully nestling, by the way the ends of his fingers played with her hair, Yelena could tell that she was loved. He was silent, and she did not need words. "He is here, he loves . . . and what more?" The stillness of bliss, the stillness of an inviolable haven, of an end achieved, that heavenly stillness which confers sense, and beauty, even on death, filled her with all its beatific wave. She did not wish for anything, because she possessed everything. "Oh, my brother, my friend, my dear . . . " her lips whispered, and she herself did not know whose heart it was, whether his or hers, that beat so delightfully and melted in her breast.

But he stood motionless; with his own strong embrace he surrounded this young life surrendered to him, on his chest he felt this new, infinitely precious burden; a feeling of deep emotion, a feeling of inexplicable gratitude, shattered his stern soul into dust, and tears he had never known before started to his eyes. . . .

But she did not weep; she only said: "Oh, my friend, oh, my brother!"

"So you will follow me everywhere?" he said to her fifteen minutes later, still surrounding and supporting her with his embrace.

"Everywhere, to the end of the world. Wherever you are, there shall I be."

"And you are not deceiving yourself, you know that your parents will never consent to our marriage?"

"I am not deceiving myself; I know that."

"You know that I am poor, almost a beggar?"

"I know."

"That I am not Russian, that I am not destined to live in Russia, that you will have to snap all your bonds with your own country, with your parents?"

"I know, I know."

"You know also that I have devoted myself to a difficult, an ungrateful task, that I — that we shall have to submit not only to dangers, but to deprivations, humiliations, perhaps?"

"I know, I know it all. . . . I love you."

"That you will have to give up all your present habits,

that there, alone among strangers, you, perhaps, will have to
work. . . ."

She laid her hand on his lips.

"I love you, my dear."

He began fierily to kiss her slender, rosy hand. Yelena did not
remove it from his lips, and she watched with a kind of childlike
delight, with laughing curiosity, as he covered that same hand of
hers, those fingers, with kisses. . . .

Suddenly she blushed and hid her face on his chest.

He caressingly lifted her head and gazed fixedly into her eyes.

"Then my greetings to you," he said to her, "my wife before
man and before God."

19

An hour later Yelena, her hat in one hand, her mantle in the other,
quietly entered the reception room of her home. Her hair had
broken loose a little, a small rosy spot was visible on either cheek,
the smile did not wish to go from her lips, her eyes were in a
reverie and, half-closed, were also smiling. In her weariness she
could hardly walk, and that weariness was pleasant to her. But
then, everything was pleasant to her. To her everything seemed
to be dear and gracious. Uvar Ivanovich was sitting by the window. She went up to him, laid her hand on his shoulder, yawned
a little, and involuntarily laughed.

"What is it?" he asked in astonishment.

She did not know what to say. She wanted to kiss him.

"Smack!" she uttered at last.

But Uvar Ivanovich did not even stir an eyebrow and continued to stare at her in astonishment. She dropped both her
mantle and her hat on him.

"Dear Uvar Ivanovich," she said, "I want to sleep, I am tired."
She smiled again and fell into a chair beside him.

"Hm!" Uvar Ivanovich croaked, and began to wriggle his
fingers. "In that case you should — yes. . . ."

But Yelena looked about her and thought: "With all this I
must part soon . . . and it is strange: I have no fear, nor doubts,
nor regrets. . . . No, I am sorry for Mamma." Then the chapel
again arose before her eyes, his voice again sounded in her ears,
she felt his arms round her. Her heart stirred joyously, but feebly;
the languor of happiness lay on it also. She recalled the old beg-

493

garwoman. "Truly, she has taken away my sorrow," she thought. "Oh, how happy I am! How undeservedly! How quickly!" It would have been good for her to give herself a little rein, and to let the sweet, endless tears well up within her. She restrained them only with her smile. Whatever position she adopted, it seemed to her that it was impossible to be better and more comfortable; always she felt as though she were being cradled. All her movements were slow and gentle; whither had her haste, her precipitancy, her angularity departed? Zoya entered; Yelena decided that she had never seen a more charming little face. Anna Vasilievna entered; something pricked Yelena, but with what tenderness she embraced her good mother and kissed her on the brow, just by the hair, which was already beginning to turn gray! Then she went to her room; how everything smiled at her there! With what a feeling of timorous exultation and humility she sat down on her bed, on that same bed where three hours previously she had spent such bitter moments! "And yet even then I knew that he loved me," she thought; "and even before — Ah, no, no! that is a sin. 'You are my wife' . . . " she whispered, covering her face with her hands, and she dropped to her knees.

Toward evening she grew more thoughtful. Sorrow took possession of her at the thought that now she would not be seeing Insarov for some time. He could not continue to live with Berseniev without arousing suspicion, and he and Yelena had decided that he was to return to Moscow, but would visit them once or twice as a guest between now and the autumn. For her part she had promised to write him letters and, if it were possible, to arrange meetings somewhere near Kuntsevo. Toward teatime she went into the reception room and there found all her family, including Shubin, who gazed at her keenly as soon as she appeared. She wanted to fall into friendly talk with him, as in the old days; but she was afraid of his perspicuity, was afraid of herself. It seemed to her that there must be some reason for his having left her in peace for more than two weeks.

Soon Berseniev arrived and gave Anna Vasilievna Insarov's greetings and conveyed his apologies for having returned to Moscow without paying his respects to her. It was the first time all day that Insarov's name had been pronounced in Yelena's presence; she felt herself turn crimson. She realized that she ought to express regret at the sudden departure of such a good acquaintance, but she could not force herself to act a part, and continued to sit motionless and speechless while her mother exclaimed and lamented. Yelena tried to keep close to Berseniev; she was not afraid of him, though he knew part of her secret; under his wing she took shelter from Shubin, who continued to gaze at her, not sarcastically, but attentively. Berseniev also was puzzled all the evening: he had expected to see Yelena more sorrowful. Fortunately for her, some argument about art arose between him and Shubin; she moved away and listened to their voices as though through her sleep. Little by little not only they, but all the room, everything surrounding her, seemed to be a kind of dream; everything — the samovar on the table, and Uvar Ivanovich's short waistcoat, and Zoya's polished nails, and the portrait in oils of the Grand Duke Konstantin Pavlovich on the wall — everything retreated, everything was concealed in a haze, everything ceased to exist. She felt only regret for them all. "What are they living for?" she thought.

"Are you sleepy, Yelena dear?" her mother asked her. She did not hear the question.

"A half-just insinuation, do you say? . . ." These words, which Shubin uttered sharply, suddenly aroused Yelena's attention. "Pardon me," he continued, "but that is precisely where taste is evinced. A just insinuation causes despondency — it is not Christian-like. To anything unjust a man is indifferent — it is stupid. But with the half-just a man feels vexation and impatience. For instance, if I say that Yelena Nikolaevna is in love with one of us, what kind of insinuation would that be, eh?"

"Ah, M'sieur Paul," Yelena said, "I should like to show that I am vexed, but really I cannot. I am very tired."

"Then why don't you go to bed?" Anna Vasilievna remarked. She herself always dozed of an evening, and so she readily sent others to bed. "Say good-night to me, and then off with you. Andrei Piotrovich will excuse you."

Yelena kissed her mother, bowed to the others, and went to her room. Shubin escorted her to the door.

"Yelena Nikolaevna," he whispered to her at the door, "you trample on M'sieur Paul; you mercilessly walk over him. But M'sieur Paul blesses you, and your little feet, and the shoes on your little feet, and the soles of your shoes."

Yelena shrugged her shoulders, reluctantly gave him her hand

— not the one Insarov had kissed — and, returning to her room, at once undressed, lay down, and fell asleep. . . . She slept a deep, undisturbed sleep — such as not even children sleep. Such sleep is known only by an infant restored from sickness to health, while the mother sits beside its cradle and watches it and listens to its breathing.

20

"Come into my room for a minute," Shubin said to Berseniev as soon as he had said good-night to Anna Vasilievna. "I have something I want to show you."

Berseniev went to Shubin's room in the wing. He was struck by the many studies, statuettes, and busts that, wrapped in damp rags, were scattered about the room.

"Why, I see you have been working in earnest," he observed.

"I have got to do something," Shubin answered. "If one thing isn't a success, I have to try another. For that matter, like the Corsicans, I am occupied more with a vendetta than with pure art. *Trema, Bisanzia!*"

"I don't understand," Berseniev remarked.

"Well, wait a moment. Now, please look, my dear friend and benefactor, at my vengeance number one."

Shubin uncovered one figure, and Berseniev saw a strikingly realistic, excellent bust of Insarov. Shubin had caught the facial features faithfully, down to the last detail, and had given them a magnificent expression: honest, noble, and bold.

Berseniev went into raptures.

"But it is absolutely enchanting!" he exclaimed. "I congratulate you. It ought to be exhibited! Why do you call that splendid work your vengeance?"

"Because, sir, I am intending to present this splendid work, as you are pleased to call it, to Yelena Nikolaevna on her name-day.[1] Do you understand the allegory? We are not blind, we see what is going on around us; but we are gentlemen, my dear sir, and we take vengeance in gentlemanly fashion."

"And now," Shubin added, unwrapping another figure, "as, according to the latter-day æsthetics, an artist enjoys the enviable

[1] The day assigned in the church calendar to the saint by whose name the child is christened, this day being annually observed rather than the birthday. (Tr.)

right of incarnating in himself all kinds of filth, transforming them into the pearl of creation, so we, in the creation of this pearl number two, have exacted vengeance not at all as a gentleman, but simply *en canaille.*"

He dexterously pulled away the canvas, and a statuette in the Dantan [1] style, also of Insarov, was presented to Berseniev's gaze. Anything more evil and cunning it would have been impossible to imagine. The young Bulgar was represented as a ram, rising on its hind legs and with horns ready to butt. Dumb seriousness, fervor, obstinacy, clumsiness, mental limitation, were all deeply impressed on the physiognomy of "the companion of the fine-fleeced sheep," yet the likeness was unquestionably so striking that Berseniev could not help bursting into a roar of laughter.

"What? Do you find it amusing?" Shubin said. "Do you recognize the hero? Do you advise sending this also to an exhibition? This, my brother, I shall present to myself on my own name-day. . . . Your worship, permit me to bow the knee!"

And Shubin sprang thrice into the air, kicking himself with his heels each time.

Berseniev picked up the canvas and threw it round the statuette.

"Oh, you great-hearted fellow!" Shubin began. "By the way, who was the historical personage who is regarded as particularly great-hearted? Well, it doesn't matter! But now," he continued, solemnly and mournfully unwrapping a third, quite large mass of clay, "now you will perceive something that will demonstrate to you that your friend is both humbly wise and sagacious. You will be convinced that he also, as a true artist, recognizes the necessity and benefit of boxing his own ears. Behold!"

The canvas unwound, and Berseniev saw two heads side by side and set close together, as though grafted to each other — he did not gather at first what they represented; but, looking more closely, he recognized that one of them was Annushka, the other, Shubin himself. They were rather caricatures than portraits, however. Annushka was presented as a good-looking, rather fat girl with a low brow, puffy eyes, and an audaciously upturned nose. Her swollen lips were simpering saucily; all her features expressed sensuality, unconcern, and insolence, yet not without good nature. Shubin had represented himself as a meager, emaciated *bon vivant*, with hollow cheeks, impotently hanging strands

[1] See note, p. 7. (Tr.)

of thin hair, a senseless expression in his faded eyes, and a nose peaked like that of a corpse.

Berseniev turned away in disgust.

"What a pair, brother!" Shubin remarked. "Wouldn't you like to compose a suitable inscription? I have already thought of inscriptons for the first two pieces. Beneath the bust will be: 'A Hero, planning to save his country.' Under the statuette: 'Beware, sausage-makers!' But under this piece — what do you think? — 'The future of the artist Pavel Yakovlevich Shubin.' Good?"

"That's enough!" Berseniev protested. "You shouldn't have wasted time on that — " He could not think of a suitable word immediately.

"Beastliness, you'd like to say? No, brother, forgive me, but if anything is to go to an exhibition, then it must be that group."

"Exactly, beastliness," Berseniev repeated. "And what rot it is! You haven't any of the prerequisites of such a development, though, unfortunately, our artists so far have been richly endowed with it. You're simply slandering yourself."

"Do you think so?" Shubin remarked gloomily. "If the prerequisites aren't in me and if they have been grafted on me, then the entire blame for it all will fall on — one person. Do you know," he added, wrinkling his face tragically, "that I have already attempted to become a drunkard?"

"You're lying!"

"I have, by God!" Shubin retorted, and he suddenly grinned and grew more cheerful. "But it doesn't taste nice, brother; it doesn't get down my throat, and afterward my head is like a drum. Even the great Lushchikhin — Kharlamy Lushchikhin, the leading soaker of Moscow, and even of all Great Russia — declared that I'd never make good at it. As he puts it, a bottle says nothing whatever to me."

Berseniev was about to bring his fist down on the group, but Shubin stopped him.

"Now, brother, don't smash it; it will serve as a lesson, as a warning."

Berseniev smiled.

"In that case perhaps I'll spare your warning," he said. "And hurrah for pure and eternal art!"

"Hurrah!" Shubin took up his words. "With it even the good is better, and the bad is no great woe!"

On the Eve

The two friends clasped each other's hands in a firm grip, and Berseniev went home.

21

When she woke up, Yelena's first feeling was one of joyous fear. "Is it really true, is it really true?" she asked herself, and her heart swooned with happiness. Memories swept over her . . . she was flooded with them. Then she was again enveloped in that blessed, rapturous stillness. But during the morning she was gradually eaten up with anxiety, and in the following days she grew languid and bored. True, she knew now what she wanted, but that did not make it any the easier. That unforgettable meeting had flung her out of her old groove once for all; she no longer stood still in that groove, she was far away. But meanwhile everything around her was accomplished in its normal order, everything went its own way, as though nothing had been changed; the former life went on as formerly, counting as formerly on her participation and co-operation. She attempted to write a letter to Insarov, but that, too, was not a success: the words that flowed on the paper seemed to be dead, or false. She had closed her diary; she drew a great line below the last sentence. That was the past; and with all her thoughts, with all her being, she had gone off into the future.

Life was difficult for her. To sit with her mother, who suspected nothing, to listen to her, answer her, talk to her, seemed a kind of crime; she felt the presence of something false in herself; she rebelled, though she had nothing to blush about; more than once the almost invincible desire arose in her soul to tell everything without reservation, no matter what followed. "Why didn't Dmitry take me straight from that chapel wherever he wished?" she thought. "Didn't he tell me that I was his wife before God? Why am I here?" She suddenly began to shun everybody, even Uvar Ivanovich, who was puzzled and wriggled his fingers more than ever. Now everything around her seemed no longer gracious, or dear, or even a dream. Like a nightmare everything crushed her breast with an immovable, dead weight; everything seemed to be both reproachful and indignant and did not want to know anything about her. . . . "You," said all her environment, "are ours none the less." Even her poor nurselings, the downtrodden birds and animals, looked at her — at least so she imagined —

499

distrustfully and inimically. She grew conscience-stricken and ashamed of her feelings. "After all, this is my home," she thought, "my family, my country. . . ." "No, this is no longer your country, no longer your family," another voice declared to her. Fear took possession of her, and she was angry at her pusillanimity. The trouble had only just begun, and she had already lost patience. . . . Was that what she had promised?

Not soon did she gain control of herself. But a week passed, and a second . . . she grew rather more composed and accustomed to her new situation. She wrote two little notes to Insarov and took them herself to the post; on no account — in her bashfulness and in her pride — could she bring herself to trust them to the maid. Now she began to look forward to seeing him himself. . . . But instead of him, one fine morning, Nikolai Artiomovich arrived.

22

No one in the house had ever seen the retired guards lieutenant Stakhov so sour and at the same time so overweening and important as he was that day. He walked into the reception room in his coat and hat, walked in slowly, placing his feet wide apart and clattering his heels; he went up to a mirror and stood a long time staring at himself, shaking his head with calm severity and biting his lips. Anna Vasilievna greeted him with outward agitation and secret joy (she never greeted him in any other fashion). He did not even remove his hat, did not greet her, and silently held out his hand in its chamois glove to Yelena to kiss. Anna Vasilievna began to question him concerning his course of treatment; he made no reply. Uvar Ivanovich made his appearance; he glanced at him and said: "Bah!" He always behaved coldly and arrogantly to Uvar Ivanovich, though he recognized in him "the traces of true Stakhov blood." It is a well-known fact that almost all the Russian noble families are convinced of the existence of exclusive, thoroughbred peculiarities proper only to them; more than once we have had occasion to hear talk "among themselves" about Podsalaskin noses and Perepreev napes. Zoya entered and curtsied to Nikolai Artiomovich. He groaned, dropped into a chair, demanded coffee for himself, and only then removed his hat. His coffee was brought; he drank a cupful and, looking in turn at them all, said between his teeth: *"Sortez, s'il vous plaît."* Turning to his wife, he added: *"Et vous, madame, restez, je vous prie."*

They all left the room except Anna Vasilievna. Her head began to shake with agitation. The solemnity of Nikolai Artiomovich's behavior alarmed her. She expected something out of the ordinary.

"What is the matter?" she exclaimed as soon as the door was shut.

Nikolai Artiomovich threw her an unconcerned glance.

"Nothing in particular; what is this habit you have of at once adopting a self-sacrificial air?" he began, quite unnecessarily drawing down the corners of his lips at every word. "I only wanted to warn you that a new guest will be dining with us today."

"Who is it?"

"Kurnatovsky; Yegor Andreevich Kurnatovsky. You don't know him. Over-secretary to the Senate."

"He will dine with us today?"

"Yes."

"And was it simply to tell me that that you ordered everybody to leave the room?"

Nikolai Artiomovich again threw her a glance, but this time it was ironical.

"Does that surprise you? You can keep your surprise for later."

He sat silent. She also was silent for a moment.

"I should like — " she began.

"I know, you always have regarded me as an 'immoral' man," Nikolai Artiomovich suddenly burst out. "And perhaps you are right. I do not wish to deny that in fact I have sometimes given you just cause for dissatisfaction" ("the gray horses!" the thought flashed through her head), "though you yourself must agree that, as you know, the state of your constitution — "

"But I don't blame you at all, Nikolai Artiomovich."

"*C'est possible.* In any case I have no intention of justifying myself. Time will justify me. But I consider it my duty to assure you that I know my duty and can labor for — for the benefit of the family entrusted — entrusted to me."

"What does all this mean?" Anna Vasilievna wondered. (She was not to know that the evening before, in one corner of the lounge in the English Club, an argument had broken out over the Russians' inability to make speeches. "Which one of us knows how to speak? Name anybody!" one of the parties to the argu-

Turgenev

ment had exclaimed. "Well, there's Stakhov, for instance," another had replied, pointing to Nikolai Artiomovich, who was standing close by and all but squealed with pleasure.)

"For instance," Nikolai Artiomovich continued, "my daughter, Yelena. Don't you consider that it really is time she stepped with a firm step along the path — got married, I mean to say? All this philosophizing and philanthropy are all very well, but only to a certain degree, only up to a certain age. It is time for her to leave her mists, to give up associating with all sorts of artists and scholars, and those Montenegrins, or whatever they are, and to become like everybody else."

"How am I to interpret your remarks?" Anna Vasilievna asked.

"Why, like this, if you will deign to listen," Nikolai Artiomovich said with always the same downward pull of his lips. "I tell you frankly, without equivocation: I have made the acquaintance of and become friendly with this young man, Mr. Kurnatovsky, in the hope of having him as my son-in-law. I dare to think that, when you have seen him, you will not accuse me of partiality or precipitancy of judgment." (As he spoke he admired his own eloquence.) "Of excellent education, he is a jurist, with superior manners, aged thirty-two, an over-secretary, a collegiate councilor,[1] and possesses the Order of St. Stanislav. You, I hope, will do me the justice of admitting that I am not to be numbered among those *pères de comédie* who rave only about rank; but you yourself have told me that Yelena Nikolaevna likes efficient, positive people. Yegor Andreevich is most efficient in his sphere. And, on the other hand, my daughter has a weakness for magnanimous deeds: so I must inform you that Yegor Andreevich, as soon as he achieved the possibility — you understand me — the possibility of existing comfortably on his salary, at once renounced in favor of his brothers the annuity that his father had allotted to him."

"But who is his father?" Anna Vasilievna asked.

"His father? His father also is a man well known in his way, of the very highest morality, *un vrais stoïcien*, a retired major, I think, steward to all the estates of the Counts B."

"Ah!" Anna Vasilievna exclaimed.

[1] The rank of councilor to the collegiate (or board) of a ministry or government department. Sixth from the top in the Czarist civil-service hierarchy. (Tr.)

On the Eve

"Ah! What d'you mean by 'ah'?" Nikolai Artiomovich seized on the word. "Are you also affected by prejudices, then?"

"But I didn't say anything—" she began.

"Yes, you did; you said: 'ah!' . . . But, in any case, I considered it necessary to advise you of my way of thinking, and I dare to think—I dare to hope that Mr. Kurnatovsky will be received *à bras ouverts*. He is not one of your Montenegrins."

"Of course; only we shall have to summon the cook and order a further dish to be added to the courses."

"You understand that I do not enter into that question," Nikolai Artiomovich said. He rose, put on his hat, and, whistling (someone had told him that one could whistle only in one's summer residence and in the *manège*), he went off to walk in the garden. Shubin took a look at him from the little window of his room and, silently, put out his tongue.

At ten minutes to four a hired carriage drove up to the veranda of the house, and a man still young, of good-looking appearance, and simply and exquisitely dressed, emerged from it and ordered his arrival to be announced. He was Yegor Andreevich Kurnatovsky.

Here is part of a letter Yelena wrote next day to Insarov:

Congratulate me, my dear Dmitry, I have a fiancé. He dined with us yesterday; Papa made his acquaintance, it appears, in the English Club and invited him to call. Of course, yesterday he did not call as a fiancé. But my kind mamma, to whom Papa had communicated his hopes, whispered into my ear what kind of guest he was. His name is Yegor Andreevich Kurnatovsky; he is an over-secretary to the Senate. First let me describe his appearance to you. He is not tall, but shorter than you, and well built: he has regular features, wears his hair cut short, and has large sidewhiskers. His eyes are small (like yours), brown, quick, his lips flat and broad; there is always a kind of official smile in his eyes and on his lips, just as though it were on duty all the time. He behaves very simply, talks distinctly, and everything about him is distinct: he walks, laughs, eats, just as though he were engaged in some business. "How closely she has studied him!" you may think as you read this. Yes, I have, in order to describe him to you. And how can one help studying one's fiancé! In him there is something of iron—both dull and empty at once, and honest; it

503

is said that he is indeed very honest. You also are iron, but not like him.

At table he sat next to me, Shubin sat opposite us. At first the conversation was about commercial enterprises; they say he knows all about them and all but resigned from the civil service in order to take over a large factory, but he didn't! Then Shubin began to talk about the theater; Mr. Kurnatovsky announced, and — I must admit — without any false modesty, that he had no understanding of art. That reminded me of you. But I thought: no, all the same, Dmitry and I have a different lack of understanding of art. He seemed to be trying to say: "I don't understand it, and besides it is unnecessary; but in a well-organized state it is permitted." However, to Petersburg and to the comme il faut *he is rather indifferent: once he even called himself a proletarian. We, he said, are manual workers! I thought: if you had said that I would not have liked it, but let him say it if he wishes, let him brag! He was very polite to me; but I continually had the feeling that I was being talked to by a very, very condescending head official. When he wants to praise anybody he says that so-and-so is a man of* principles, *that is his favorite word. He must be self-assured, industrious, capable of self-sacrifice (you see: I am impartial) — I mean, the sacrifice of his own advantage — but he is a great despot. It would be awful to get into his hands! At table there was some talk of bribes.*

"I quite understand," he said, "that in many instances the one who accepts the bribe is not to blame; he could not do otherwise. But, all the same, if he is caught he ought to be crushed."

I exclaimed: "Crush someone who is not to blame?"

"Yes," he said, "for the sake of principle."

"What principle?" Shubin asked.

Kurnatovsky was either confounded or surprised, and said: "That doesn't call for explanation."

Papa, who apparently worships him, added: "Of course not," and, to my regret, this subject was not discussed further.

In the evening Berseniev arrived and got into a terrible argument with him. I have never seen our good Andrei Piotrovich so excited. Mr. Kurnatovsky didn't at all deny the benefits of science, universities, and so on . . , but meanwhile I quite understood Andrei Piotrovich's indignation. Kurnatovsky regards all that sort of thing as a kind of gymnastics.

On the Eve

After dinner Shubin came up to me and said: "Now this man and a certain other" (he can never utter your name) "are both practical people, but look at the difference: that other man has a real, living ideal to which his life is devoted; but this one hasn't even a feeling of obligaton, but simply official integrity and soulless efficiency." Shubin is intelligent, and I have remembered his sensible words for you; but in my view what is there in common between you? You believe, but the other does not, because it is impossible to believe solely in oneself.

He left late, but Mamma managed to let me know that I had pleased him, that Papa was in raptures. . . . I wonder if he has already said of me that I, too, have principles? However, I all but told Mamma that I was very sorry, but I already had a husband. Why does Papa dislike you so much? With Mamma it would be possible somehow. . . .

Oh, my dear! I have described this gentleman to you in such detail in order to stifle my yearning. I do not live without you, I incessantly see you, hear you. . . . I expect you, only not here, as you wished — imagine how difficult and awkward that would be for us! — but you know, where I told you in my letter — in that coppice. . . . Oh, my dear! How I love you!

23

Some three weeks after Kurnatovsky's first visit Anna Vasilievna, to Yelena's great delight, removed to Moscow, to her large timber house near Prechistinka Boulevard. It was a house with columns, and with white lyres and wreaths above each window; it had a mezzanine, servants' offices, a fence, an enormous green yard, a well in the yard, and a dog-kennel by the well. Never before had Anna Vasilievna vacated her summer residence so early; but that year, as soon as the first autumn chill came on, she had an attack of gumboils. For his part, Nikolai Artiomovich, who had completed his course of treatment, was missing his wife; and in addition Avgustina Khristianovna had gone on a visit to her cousin in Reval. Some foreign family of performers exhibiting plastic poses, *des poses plastiques,* had arrived in Moscow, and when Anna Vasilievna read about them in the *Moscow News* her curiosity was greatly excited. In a word, further residence out of town proved to be inconvenient, and even, in Nikolai Artiomovich's words, incompatible with the fulfillment of his "designs"!

Turgenev

The last two weeks at Kuntsevo seemed very long to Yelena. Kurnatovsky visited them twice, on the Sundays; on other days he was occupied. He called to see Yelena, but he talked more with Zoya, who had taken a great fancy to him. *"Das ist ein Mann!"* she thought, looking at his swarthy and masculine face, listening to his self-assured, condescending speeches. In her opinion no one else had such a marvelous voice, no one else could pronounce: "I had the honorrr" or "I am highly saatisfied," so distinctively as he. Insarov did not call on the Stakhovs, but Yelena saw him once, surreptitiously, in a small coppice on the bank of the River Moskva, where she had arranged to meet him. They hardly had time to say more than a few words to each other. Shubin returned to Moscow with Anna Vasilievna; Berseniev came back some days later.

Insarov was sitting in his room, for yet a third time reading letters conveyed to him from Bulgaria "as occasion offered"; it was unwise to send them by post. He was deeply disturbed by them. Events were developing rapidly in the east; the occupation of the Danubian Principalities [1] by the Russian forces was agitating all minds; the threat was growing, already the murmur of the imminent, inevitable war could be heard. The conflagration was starting up all around, and no one could foresee where it would go, where it would halt; the old offenses, the former hopes, were all beginning to be revived. Insarov's heart beat violently: *his* hopes, too, were coming true. "But is it not rather early? Is it not in vain?" he thought, clenching his fists. "We are not ready yet. But so be it! I must go."

There was a light rustle from something outside the room, the door was flung open, and Yelena entered.

Insarov began to tremble all over his body; he rushed to her, fell on his knees before her, put his arms round her waist, and pressed his head against it.

"You didn't expect me?" she said, hardly getting her breath (she had run swiftly up the stairs). "My dear! My dear!" She put both her hands on his head and looked about her. "So this is where you live? I soon found you. Your landlord's daughter showed me the way. We returned to Moscow two days ago. I

[1] In July 1853, as a means of bringing pressure to hear on the Sultan of Turkey, during negotiations then in progress. (Tr.)

wanted to write to you, but I thought: better go myself. I can stay for fifteen minutes. Get up and lock the door."

He rose, swiftly locked the door, turned to her, and took her by the hands. He could not speak: his joy was choking him. She looked smilingly into his eyes — there was so much happiness in them. She felt abashed.

"Wait a moment," she said, gently releasing her hands. "Let me take my hat off."

She untied the ribbons of her hat, threw it down, slipped her mantle off her shoulders, tidied her hair, and sat down on the small old sofa. Insarov did not stir; he gazed at her as though enchanted.

"But sit down," she said, not raising her eyes to him and pointing him to her side.

He sat down, not on the sofa, but on the floor at her feet.

"Here, take my gloves off," she said in a nervous tone. She was beginning to feel apprehensive.

He set to work first to unbutton, then to draw off one glove; he drew it half off and avidly pressed his lips to her slender and delicate wrist, showing white beyond it.

Yelena shivered and tried to prevent him with the other hand; he began to kiss that other hand. She drew it away; he threw back his head, she gazed into his face, bent down — and their lips came together. . . .

The moment passed. . . . She tore herself away, rose, whispered: "No, no," and went swiftly across to the writing-table.

"After all, I am the mistress here, you should have no secrets from me," she declared, trying to appear unmoved and standing with her back to him. "What a lot of papers! What are these letters?"

Insarov frowned slightly.

"Those letters?" he said, rising from the floor. "You can read them."

She turned them over in her hand.

"There are so many of them and they are written in such small writing, and I must go in a minute. . . . Let them be! They're not from a rival? . . . But of course they're not in Russian," she added as she looked over the thin sheets.

He went to her and touched her waist. She suddenly turned

to him, smiled at him with a shining face, and leaned on his shoulder.

"These letters are from Bulgaria, Yelena; my friends are writing to me, they are calling me back."

"Now? There?"

"Yes — now. While there is still time, while it is still possible to travel."

She suddenly flung both arms round his neck.

"But of course you'll take me with you?"

He pressed her to his heart.

"Oh, my dear girl, oh, my heroine, the way you said that! But wouldn't it be sinful, wouldn't it be madness on my part, for me, homeless, solitary as I am, to drag you with me? . . . And where to, indeed!"

She closed his mouth.

"Ssh! — or I'll get angry and never come to your room again. Isn't everything decided, isn't everything settled between us? Am I not your wife? Does a wife part from her husband?"

"Wives do not go to war," he said with a half-mournful smile.

"True, when they can remain behind. But can I remain here?"

"Yelena, you are an angel! . . . But think, possibly I shall have to leave Moscow — within two weeks. I may no longer think about university lectures, or finishing my work."

"What of it?" she broke in. "You must go soon? Well, if you wish, I am ready now, immediately, this very minute, to remain with you, with you forever, and not return home, if you wish. We'll go off at once if you wish?"

He held her in his arms with doubled strength.

"Then may God punish me," he exclaimed, "if I am doing something evil! From this day onward we are united forever!"

"Do I remain?" Yelena asked.

"No, my pure girl; no, my treasure. Return home today, but be ready. This matter cannot be settled in a moment; we must think everything over well. We need money, a passport — "

"I have money," she interrupted; "eighty rubles."

"Well, that isn't much," he observed, "but it will be useful all the same."

"And besides, I can get more, I can borrow, I can ask Mamma — No, I won't ask her. . . . But I can sell my watch. . . . I have earrings, two bracelets — lace."

"It isn't a question of money, Yelena. The passport, your passport, how are we to manage that?"

"Yes, how are we to manage that? But is a passport absolutely necessary?"

"Absolutely."

She smiled wryly.

"A thought has just come into my head: I remember when I was still quite small — our maid ran away. She was caught, and pardoned, and she lived with us a long time after . . . but all the same we always called her 'Tatiana the runaway.' I didn't think then that I too, perhaps, might some day be a runaway like her."

"Yelena, how can you say such things?"

"Why, what of it? Of course, it would be better to travel with a passport. But if I cannot — "

"We'll arrange all that later, later; wait," he replied. "Only give me a chance to look round, a chance to think. We'll talk it all over together properly. But I have money."

With her hand she brushed back the hair fallen over his brow. "Oh, Dmitry! What fun it will be for us to travel together!"

"Yes," he said; "but there, when we arrive — "

"Well, and then," Yelena broke in, "won't it be fun to die together too? But no, why should we die? We shall live, we are young. How old are you, twenty-six?"

"Twenty-six."

"And I am twenty. There is a lot of time ahead of us yet. Ah! So you wanted to run away from me? You do not need Russian love, Bulgar! We'll see now how you succeed in getting away from me! But what would have happened to us if I hadn't come to you then?"

"Yelena, you know what was compelling me to go away."

"I know: you were in love and you were afraid. But did you really have no suspicion that you, too, were loved?"

"On my honor, Yelena, I swear I didn't."

She swiftly and unexpectedly kissed him.

"And that is just why I love you. But now good-by."

"So you cannot remain any longer?" he asked.

"No, my dear. Do you think it was easy for me to come out alone? The fifteen minutes have passed long since." She put on her mantle and hat. "But come and see us tomorrow evening. No, the day after tomorrow. It will be a strain, and boring, but it cannot be helped; at least we shall see each other. Good-by. Let me go." He embraced her for a last time. "Oh, look, you have broken my chain. Oh, my clumsy one! Well, it doesn't matter. So much the better. I shall go along Kuznetsky Most and hand it in to be repaired. And if anyone asks me, I shall say I have been to Kuznetsky Most." She took hold of the door handle. "By the way, I forgot to tell you: Monsieur Kurnatovsky will be proposing to me during the next few days, probably. But I shall give him —— look!" She set the thumb of her left hand to the tip of her nose and wriggled her fingers in the air. "Good-by. *Au revoir.* I know the way now. . . . But don't you lose any time. . . ."

She opened the door a little, stood listening, turned to Insarov, nodded, and slipped out of the room.

For a full minute he stood before the closed door and also listened. The downstairs door opening on the yard was banged. He went across to the sofa, sat down, and covered his eyes with one hand. Nothing like this had ever happened to him before. "What have I done to deserve such love?" he thought. "Isn't it a dream?"

But the delicate perfume of mignonette that Yelena had left in his poor, dark little room reminded him of her visit. It seemed that together with this perfume the air was still pervaded with the sounds of a youthful voice, and the noise of light, youthful steps, and the warmth and freshness of a youthful, maiden body.

24

Insarov decided to wait for still more definite news, but at the same time he began to prepare for departure. The matter was very difficult. For him personally there were no obstacles to be overcome: he had only to demand his passport. But what was to be done about Yelena? It was impossible to get her a passport by legal means. To marry her secretly, and then to present themselves to her parents . . . "Then they will let us go," he thought. "But if not? All the same, we shall leave. But if they lay a complaint — if . . . No, it would be better to get hold of a passport somehow."

He decided to discuss the question (of course, not mentioning any names) with a certain acquaintance of his, a retired or dis-

missed public prosecutor, an experienced and old expert on all
kinds of clandestine affairs. This worthy man did not live near at
hand: it took Insarov a whole hour in a shabby droshky to drive
to his place, and then he did not find him at home; and on the
return journey he was soaked to the skin by a sudden downpour.
Next morning, despite rather a bad headache, he went a second
time to see the retired prosecutor. The man listened to him
closely, taking snuff from a snuffbox decorated with a representation of a big-breasted nymph. Then, giving his visitor sidelong
glances with his crafty little eyes, also of snuff color, he demanded
"more definiteness in the exposition of the factual data." Noting
that Insarov was reluctant to enter into details (he had been reluctant even to visit the man), he confined himself to the advice
that Insarov should provide himself with "moneys," and asked
him to call again "when," he added, taking a pinch of snuff over
his open snuffbox, "you have more trust and have lost your distrust" (he did not broaden his "o's" into "a's," as is common in
Moscow). "But as for a passport," he continued, as though to
himself, "that is a work of human hands. You, for instance, are
traveling; well, who knows whether you are Maria Bredikhina or
Karolina Vogelmeyer?" Insarov had a feeling of repellence for
the prosecutor, but he thanked him and promised to return during
the next few days.

That same evening he went to call on the Stakhovs. Anna Vasilievna welcomed him graciously, reproached him gently for having completely forgotten them, and, noticing that he was pale,
asked after his health. Nikolai Artiomovich did not say one word
to him, only looked at him with a thoughtfully indifferent curiosity. Shubin treated him coolly. But Yelena amazed him. She was
expecting him, for him she had put on the dress she was wearing
when they had met in the chapel. But she greeted him so calmly
and was so amiable and so light-heartedly gay that, looking at
her, no one would have thought that this girl's destiny was already decided and that only the secret consciousness of happy
love gave animation to her features, lightness and charm to all
her movements. She poured out tea in place of Zoya, joked and
chattered. She knew that Shubin would be watching her and that
Insarov was incapable of donning a mask, incapable of appearing
unconcerned, so she had armed herself in advance. She was not

mistaken: Shubin did not take his eyes off her, while Insarov was very taciturn and gloomy all the evening. Yelena felt so happy that she was seized with a desire to tease him.

"Well, tell me," she suddenly asked him, "is your plan going ahead?"

He was disconcerted.

"What plan?" he said.

"Why, have you forgotten?" she replied, laughing into his face — he alone could understand the meaning of that happy smile. "Your Bulgarian anthology for Russians."

"*Quelle bourde!*" Nikolai Artiomovich muttered through his teeth.

Zoya sat down at the piano. Almost imperceptibly Yelena shrugged her shoulders and with her eyes directed Insarov to the door, as though giving him permission to go home. Then, with a short pause between the movements, she touched the table twice with her fingers and looked at him. He realized that she was arranging a meeting with him in two days' time, and she gave him a fleeting smile when she saw that he had understood her. He rose and began to take his leave: he felt unwell. Kurnatovsky arrived. . . . Nikolai Artiomovich jumped to his feet, raised his right hand above his head, and gently lowered it into the over-secretary's palm. Insarov remained a few minutes longer, in order to have a look at his rival. Yelena surreptitiously, craftily shook her head, the host did not consider it necessary to introduce them to each other, and Insarov went, exchanging a last glance with Yelena. Shubin reflected and reflected — and entered into a furious argument with Kurnatovsky over a juridical question of which he had no conception whatever.

Insarov did not sleep all night, and in the morning he felt very unwell. None the less, he occupied himself with putting his papers in order and writing letters. But his head was heavy and confused. Toward dinnertime he developed a fever; he could not eat anything. By evening his fever had risen rapidly; he had pains in all his joints and an agonizing headache. He lay on the same sofa on which Yelena had recently sat; he thought: "It serves me right; why did I drag across Moscow to see that old swindler?" and tried to sleep. . . . But now his illness mastered him. . . . His blood beat with terrible force, it burned fiercely, his thoughts circled round and round like birds. He lost consciousness. He lay flat on his back as though crushed, and suddenly had the impression that someone was quietly laughing and whispering above him. With some effort he opened his eyes; the light from a guttering candle struck at him like a knife. . . . What was that? The old prosecutor stood before him, in an Oriental silk gown belted with a foulard, as he had seen him the day before. ". . . Karolina Vogelmeyer," the toothless mouth muttered. As Insarov watched, the old man broadened, swelled, grew; now he was no longer a man, he was a tree. . . . Insarov had got to climb up its lofty boughs. He clung tightly, then fell chest-downward on a sharp stone. But Karolina Vogelmeyer in the form of a huckstress was squatting on her heels and babbling: "Pasties, pasties, pasties. . . ." And now blood was flowing, and sabers were glittering unbearably. . . . Yelena! Then everything vanished in a lurid chaos.

25

"Someone to see you, I don't know who it is, a locksmith or something," Berseniev's servant, who was strictly correct in his behavior to his master and had a skeptical turn of mind, told him the following evening. "He wants to see you."

"Send him in," Berseniev said.

The "locksmith" entered. Berseniev recognized him as the tailor, landlord of Insarov's room.

"What do you want?" he asked the man.

"I've come to you, sir," the tailor began, slowly shuffling his feet and waving his right arm from time to time, holding his cuff by the last three fingers. "We rather think our lodger is very ill."

"D'you mean Insarov?"

"That's the one, our lodger. You see, yesterday morning he was still up and about, and in the evening he only asked for a drink; my wife took him some water. But during the night he began to gabble away, we could hear him, for there's only a thin partition between us; and this morning he couldn't speak at all, and he was lying stretched out, and the heat that was coming from him, my goodness! I thought: 'I don't like this; if he dies it'll be bad for us, I ought to notify the police.' For, you see, he's all alone. But my wife, she says to me: 'Go,' she says, 'to that man who our lodger lived with outside Moscow: perhaps he'll tell you what to do or he may come himself.' So I came to your worship, because as things are we can't, I mean — "

Berseniev snatched up his hat, thrust a ruble into the tailor's hand, and drove hard with him back to the house where Insarov had his room.

He found his friend lying on the sofa, unconscious, and fully dressed. His face had changed terribly. Berseniev at once ordered the landlord and his wife to undress him and put him to bed, and rushed for a doctor, bringing one back with him. The doctor at once prescribed leeches, blisters, and calomel, and said that Insarov's blood must be let.

"Is he in any danger?" Berseniev asked.

"Yes, great danger," the doctor replied. "Severe inflammation of the lungs, double pneumonia well under way, possibly his brain is affected too, but the patient is young. His own strength is now being turned against him. You have called me in rather late; however, we will do all that science requires."

The doctor himself was still young, and he believed in science.

Berseniev remained with Insarov for the night. The landlord and his wife proved to be kind and even efficient people as soon as they had someone to tell them what to do. A lower-grade doctor arrived and put the patient through the medical tortures prescribed by his senior colleague.

Toward morning Insarov came round for a few minutes, recognized Berseniev, asked: "I am not well, apparently?" looked about him with the dull and sluggish bewilderment of a man seriously ill, and again lost consciousness. Berseniev drove home, changed his clothes, collected some books, and returned to the room. He had decided to stay there for a day or two at least. He shielded the sick man's bed with screens and made a small place for himself by the sofa. Far from cheerfully and far from rapidly did that day pass. Berseniev left the room only in order to eat. Evening came on. He lit a candle, set it in a shade, and began to read. Everything all around him was quiet. He could hear a restrained whisper, a yawn, and sometimes a sigh in the landlord's room beyond the partition. . . . One of them sneezed, and the others swore at him in a whisper. From behind the screens came a heavy and uneven breathing, occasionally broken by a faint groan, and the restless tossing of a head on the pillow. . . .

Strange were the thoughts that occurred to Berseniev. He was in the room of a man whose life hung by a thread, a man who, as he knew, was loved by Yelena. . . . He recalled the night when

Shubin had overtaken him and informed him that she loved him, him, Berseniev. But now . . . "What am I to do now?" he asked himself. "Let Yelena know about his illness? Or wait? This news will be even more mournful than that which I had to tell her once before; it is strange how fate is always making me an intermediary between them!" He decided that it would be better to wait a little. His gaze fell on the table, which was covered with piles of papers. . . . "Will he carry out his plan?" he thought. "Surely it will not all collapse?" He felt sorry for this young and fading life and promised himself that he would save him. . . .

The night was not a good one. Insarov wandered a great deal in his mind. Berseniev rose several times from his sofa, went across on tiptoe to the bed, and mournfully listened to the patient's incoherent babbling. Only once did he pronounce with sudden clarity: "I don't want that, I don't want that, you should not . . ." (here he used the feminine declension). Berseniev started and gazed at Insarov: his face, lined with suffering and deathly pale, was fixed, and his hands lay impotently. "I don't want that," he repeated almost inaudibly.

In the morning the doctor arrived, shook his head, and prescribed fresh medicine.

"He is still far from the crisis," he said as he put on his hat.

"But after the crisis?" Berseniev asked.

"After the crisis? There are two possibilities: *aut Cæsar, aut nihil.*"

The doctor departed. Berseniev walked up and down the street several times; he needed some fresh air. He returned and picked up his book. He had long since finished Raumer; now he was studying Grote.

Suddenly the door quietly creaked, and the landlord's daughter cautiously poked in her little head, covered, as usual, with a heavy kerchief.

"That young lady is here," she said in a whisper, "who gave me a kopek that other time. . . ."

The little head suddenly vanished, and Yelena appeared in its place.

Berseniev sprang up as though stung; but Yelena did not stir, did not cry out. . . . She seemed to understand everything in a single moment. A terrible pallor spread over her face; she walked across to the screens, glanced behind them, flung out her hands, and went rigid. In another moment she would have rushed to Insarov, but Berseniev restrained her.

"What are you doing?" he said in a quivering whisper. "You may kill him!"

She staggered back. He led her to the sofa and made her sit down.

She gazed into his face, then looked him up and down, then fixed her eyes on the floor.

"Is he dying?" she asked so coldly and calmly that he was frightened.

"For God's sake, Yelena Nikolaevna," he began, "why do you ask that? He's ill, truly — and quite dangerously ill. . . . But we shall save him: I guarantee you that."

"Is he unconscious?" she asked in the same manner as before.

"Yes, he is in a coma now. . . . That always occurs at the beginning of these illnesses, but it doesn't mean anything, it's nothing at all, I assure you. Take a drink of water."

She raised her eyes to him, and he realized that she had not heard his answers.

"If he dies," she said in exactly the same tone, "I shall die too."

At that moment Insarov quietly groaned. She started, clutched at her head, then began to untie her hat ribbons.

"What are you doing?" Berseniev asked her.

She did not answer.

"What are you doing?" he repeated.

"I shall remain here."

"What — for some time?"

"I don't know; perhaps all day, for the night, forever — I don't know."

"For God's sake, Yelena Nikolaevna, come to your senses. Of course I never expected to see you here; but all the same I — I assume that you came for only a short time. Remember, they may find out at home . . . "

"And what of it?"

"They will look for you. They will find you . . . "

"And what of it?"

"Yelena Nikolaevna! You see — he cannot defend you now."

She hung her head as though thinking, raised her handkerchief to her lips, and a convulsive sobbing suddenly burst with shattering violence from her breast. . . . She flung herself face-downward on the sofa and tried to choke back the sobbing, but all her body heaved and writhed, like a little bird only just caught.

"Yelena Nikolaevna! You see — he cannot defend you now." as he stood over her.

"Ah? What is that?" Insarov's voice suddenly called.

She straightened up, and Berseniev also stood rigid. . . . He waited a moment, then went across to the bed. Insarov's head was lying helplessly on the pillow as before; his eyes were closed.

"Is he delirious?" Yelena whispered.

"It seems so," Berseniev replied, "but that is nothing; they're always delirious too, especially if — "

"When did he fall ill?" she interrupted.

"Two days ago; I have been here since yesterday. Rely on me, Yelena Nikolaevna. I shall not leave him; everything possible will be done. If necessary, we will arrange for a consultation."

"He will die without me!" she exclaimed, wringing her hands.

"I give you my word to inform you each day of the course of his illness, and if any real danger should develop — "

"Swear to me that you will send for me at once, no matter when it is, day or night; write a note direct to me — it is all the same to me now. Do you hear? Do you promise to do that?"

"I promise, before God."

"Swear it."

"I swear."

She suddenly seized his hand and pressed her lips to it before he could snatch it away.

"Yelena Nikolaevna — what are you doing?" he stammered.

"No — no — don't do it — " Insarov uttered incoherently, and sighed deeply.

She went across to the screens, thrust her handkerchief between her teeth, and long, long gazed at the sick man. Silent tears flowed down her cheeks.

"Yelena Nikolaevna," Berseniev said to her, "he may come round and recognize you. God knows whether that will be good or not. Moreover, I am expecting the doctor at any moment. . . ."

She picked up her hat from the sofa, put it on, and stood still. Her gaze wandered mournfully round the room. She seemed to be recalling something. . . .

"I cannot go," she whispered at last.

Berseniev squeezed her hand.

"Pull yourself together," he said, "and calm yourself; you are leaving him in my care. I shall come and see you this very evening."

She glanced at him, said: "Oh, my good friend!" burst into tears, and rushed out.

Berseniev leaned against the door. A feeling grievous and bitter, yet not lacking in a strange consolation, crushed his heart. "My good friend!" he thought, and shrugged his shoulders.

"Who is there?" he heard Insarov's voice.

Berseniev went over to him.

"I am here, Dmitry Nikanorovich. What do you want? How do you feel?"

"Alone?" the sick man asked.

"Alone."

"But she?"

"What she?" Berseniev said almost in terror.

Insarov was silent.

"Mignonette," he whispered, and his eyes closed again.

26

For a full eight days Insarov hovered between life and death. The doctor called regularly, being interested, again as a young man, in a difficult case. Shubin heard of Insarov's serious condition and visited him; fellow countrymen, Bulgars, also turned up; among them Berseniev recognized both the strange figures who had amazed him by their unexpected visit to the house outside Moscow. They all expressed their sincere sorrow, and some offered to take Berseniev's place at the sick man's bedside; but, remembering the promise he had made to Yelena, he did not accept the offers. He saw her every day and surreptitiously passed on to her — sometimes by word of mouth, sometimes in a little note — all the details of the course of the illness. With what a sinking of heart she waited for him, how she listened to him and questioned him! She was continually wanting to rush to see the patient; but Berseniev implored her not to do that: Insarov was rarely alone.

The day she learned of his illness she herself all but fell ill. As soon as she returned home she locked herself in her room; but she was called to dinner, and she appeared in the dining-room with such a face that her mother was alarmed and wanted her to go to bed at once. Yelena succeeded in mastering herself, however. "If he dies," she repeated, "it will be the end of me." This thought soothed her and gave her the strength to appear indifferent. For that matter, no one greatly troubled her: Anna Vasilievna was preoccupied with her gumboils; Shubin was working furiously; Zoya had given herself over to melancholy and was preparing to read *Werther;* Nikolai Artiomovich was very dissatisfied with the "scholar's" frequent visits, especially as his own "designs" with regard to Kurnatovsky were developing slowly: the practical over-secretary was perplexed and took his time. Yelena did not even thank Berseniev: there are services for which it is dreadful and shameful to express gratitude. Only once, at her fourth meeting with him (Insarov had spent a very bad night, the doctor was hinting at a consultation), only during this meeting did she remind him of his oath. "Well, in that case, come along," he said to her. She rose and was about to go and dress. "No," he said, "all the same, we'll wait until tomorrow." Toward evening Insarov improved.

Eight days this torment continued. Yelena seemed to be calm; but she could eat nothing, she did not sleep at night. A dull pain possessed all her limbs; a dry, pungent smoke seemed to fill her head. "Our young lady is melting like a candle," her maid said of her.

At last, on the ninth day, a change occurred. Yelena was sitting in the reception room at her mother's side and, herself not understanding what she was doing, was reading the *Moscow News* to her. Berseniev entered. Yelena glanced at him (how swift, and shy, and penetrating, and anxious was the first glance that she gave him each time he called!) and at once guessed that he had brought good news. He smiled; he gave her a slight nod. She rose to meet him.

"He has come round, he is saved, in a week he will be quite well," he whispered to her.

Yelena stretched out her hands as though warding off a blow and said nothing; only her lips began to tremble, and a crimson flush suffused all her face. Berseniev turned to talk to Anna Vasilievna; but Yelena went to her room, fell on her knees, and began to pray, to thank God. . . . Light, happy tears flooded from her eyes. She suddenly felt an extreme weariness, laid her head on the pillow, whispered: "Poor Andrei Piotrovich," and at once fell asleep, with wet eyelashes and cheeks. It was long since she had last wept and slept.

27

Berseniev's words came true only in part: the danger was past, but Insarov's strength was restored slowly, and the doctor began to talk of a profound and general shock to his entire system. None the less the sick man rose from his bed and was able to walk about the room. Berseniev went back to his own home; but every day he visited his still weak friend, and every day, as before, he kept Yelena informed of the state of the patient's health. Insarov did not dare to write to her, and, in talks with Berseniev, only hinted obliquely at her; making a pretense of equanimity, Berseniev told him of his visits to the Stakhovs, at the same time endeavoring to convey that Yelena had been very upset and that now she was reassured. Yelena did not write to Insarov; she had something else in mind.

One day Berseniev informed her with a cheerful face that the doctor had now given Insarov permission to eat a cutlet, and that in all probability he would soon be going out. She was lost in thought and looked down. . . .

"Guess what I want to say to you," she said. He was embarrassed. He understood her.

"I suppose," he replied, looking away, "you want to tell me that you wish to see him."

Yelena crimsoned and said almost inaudibly:

"Yes."

"Well, what of it! That is very easy for you to manage, I think." "Pah!" he thought, "what a filthy feeling I have inside me."

"You are implying that I have been there — " Yelena said. "But I am afraid — he is rarely alone now, you say."

"That is an easy matter to arrange," Berseniev retorted, still not looking at her. "Of course, I cannot give him any notice; but let me have a note. Who can forbid you to write to him, seeing that he is a close acquaintance in whom you take some interest? There is nothing reprehensible in that. Make an assig — I mean, write and tell him when you are coming."

"I feel a little ashamed," Yelena whispered.

"Give me the note and I'll take it."

"That isn't necessary, but I wanted to ask you — don't be angry with me, Andrei Piotrovich — don't come and see him tomorrow."

Berseniev bit his lip.

"Ah! Yes, I understand; very well, very well." And after a few more words he hurriedly took his leave.

"So much the better, so much the better," he thought as he hastened home. "I haven't found out anything new, but so much the better, so much the better. Who wants to cling to the edge of someone else's nest? I do not regret anything, I have done what my conscience commanded, but now I have had enough. They can do as they like! Not without reason did my father often say to me: 'You and I, brother, are not sybarites, not aristocrats, not the spoilt children of destiny and nature, we are not even martyrs — we are toilers, toilers, and ever more toilers. Put on your leather apron, toiler, and stand to your work-bench, in your dark work-shop! But let the sun shine on others! Our dull life, too, has its pride and its happiness!' "

Next morning Insarov received a short note by the town post. "Expect me," Yelena wrote to him, "and give orders that nobody is to be allowed to see you. A. P. will not be coming."

28

Insarov read Yelena's note and at once began to tidy his little room, asked his landlady to take away the glasses of medicine, took off his dressing-gown, and dressed himself. His head swam and his heart beat with his weakness and joy. His legs bowed under him; he dropped on the sofa and began to look at his watch. "It is a quarter to twelve now," he told himself, "she simply cannot arrive before twelve. For the next quarter of an hour I shall think of something else; otherwise I shan't be able to stand it. She simply cannot arrive before twelve. . . ."

The door was flung open and Yelena entered in a light silk dress, looking very pale and very fresh and young and happy. With a feeble, joyous cry she fell on his chest.

"You are alive, you are mine," she declared, embracing and caressing his head. He stood stock-still, he panted with her proximity, with those caresses, with this happiness.

She sat down beside him and nestled against him and began to look at him with that smiling and caressing and tender gaze which shines only in a woman's loving eyes.

Her face suddenly turned mournful.

"How thin you have gone, my poor Dmitry," she said, passing her hand over his cheek, "and what a beard you have!"

"And you, too, have gone thin, my poor Yelena," he replied, catching her fingers with his lips.

She merrily shook her curls.

"That's nothing. You see how we'll recover! The storm came on just as it did the day we met in the chapel; it came on and now it has passed. Now we shall be living!"

He replied only with a smile.

"Ah, what days they have been, Dmitry, what cruel days! How can people survive those they love? I always knew in advance what Andrei Piotrovich would say to me, really I did: my life sank and rose together with yours. Greetings, my Dmitry!"

He did not know what to say to her. He felt like flinging himself at her feet.

"One other thing I have noticed," she continued, throwing her hair back. "I have made many observations during this time, in my leisure. When a person is very, very unhappy, with what stupid attention he watches everything that is going on all around him! Really, sometimes I stared at a fly; and yet there was such a chill and such horror in my own soul! But all that is past, is past, is it not? All is light before us, is it not?"

"You are before me," Insarov replied, "you are my light."

"But in that case for me too! Do you remember when I visited you — not the last time, no, not the last time," she repeated with an involuntary shudder, "but when you and I talked together and, ourselves not knowing why, we mentioned death. At that time I had not the least suspicion that it was watching over us. But now you are well again, are you not?"

"I am much better, I am almost well."

"You are well, you have not died. Oh, how happy I am!"

There was a brief silence.

"Yelena?" Insarov said interrogatively.

"What is it, my dear?"

"Tell me, did it never enter your head that this illness was sent us as a punishment?"

She glanced at him seriously.

"That thought did enter my head, Dmitry. But I thought: what am I to be punished for? What duty have I failed to perform, what have I sinned against? Perhaps I do not possess a conscience such as others have, for it was silent. Or perhaps I am to blame toward you? I am hindering you, I am halting you — "

"You will not halt me, Yelena, we shall go together."

"Yes, Dmitry, we shall go together, I shall follow you. . . . That is my duty. I love you — I know no other duty."

"Oh, Yelena," he said, "what inviolable chains your every word lays upon me!"

"Why speak of chains?" she caught him up. "You and I are free. Yes," she went on, thoughtfully gazing at the floor, while with one hand she continued to stroke his hair; "during these past few days I have experienced much that never before had I any conception of! If anyone had told me in advance that I, a young lady, well brought up, would go out alone from my house, under various invented pretexts, and go where! — to a young man's room — what indignation I would have felt! And it has all come true, and I don't feel any indignation at all. Really I don't!" she added, and turned to him.

He looked at her with such an adoring expression that she let her hand slip gently from his hair to his eyes.

"Dmitry!" she began again, "of course you don't know. You see, I saw you there, on that terrible bed, I saw you in the claws of death, unconscious — "

"You saw me?"

"Yes."

He was silent for a moment.

"And was Berseniev here?"

She nodded.

He leaned towards her.

"Oh, Yelena," he whispered, "I do not dare to look at you."

"Why not? Andrei Piotrovich is so good! I was not ashamed in front of him. And what had I to be ashamed of? I am ready to tell all the world that I am yours. . . . And I trust Andrei Piotrovich like a brother."

"He saved me," Insarov exclaimed. "He is the noblest, the kindest of men!"

"Yes. . . . And do you know that I owe everything to him? Do you know he was the first to tell me that you love me? And if I could reveal — Yes, he is the noblest of men."

523

Insarov gazed at Yelena fixedly.

"He is in love with you, is he not?"

She cast down her eyes.

"He loved me," she said in an undertone.

Insarov squeezed her hand strongly.

"Oh, you Russians," he said, "you have hearts of gold! And he, he looked after me, he did not sleep at night. . . . And you, you, my angel — Not one word of reproach, no hesitation . . . and all that for me, me. . . ."

"Yes, yes, all for you, because they love you. Ah, Dmitry! How strange it is! I think I have already spoken to you about it, but it doesn't matter, I like to repeat it, and you will like to hear it. When I saw you the first time — "

"Why are there tears in your eyes?" Insarov interrupted her.

"In my eyes? Tears?" She wiped her eyes with her handkerchief. "Oh, the stupid! He doesn't know even yet that one can cry with happiness too. Well, I was about to say that when I saw you for the first time I did not find anything different about you, really. I remember, at first I liked Shubin far more, though I had never loved him; and as for Andrei Piotrovich — oh, there was a minute when I thought: 'Surely this is the man!' But you — at first I felt nothing; but then — after — after — you just seized my heart with both hands and took it!"

"Spare me . . ." Insarov said. He tried to rise and fell back at once on to the sofa.

"What is the matter?" Yelena asked anxiously.

"Nothing — I am still a little weak. . . . This happiness is too much for my strength."

"Then sit quietly. Don't you dare to stir, don't get agitated," she added, threatening him with her finger. "And why have you taken off your dressing-gown? It is early yet for you to dress yourself up! Sit still, and I'll tell you fairy-stories. Listen and be silent. After your illness it is not good for you to talk much."

She began to tell him about Shubin, about Kurnatovsky, about all she had done during the last two weeks, of how, judging by the newspapers, war was inevitable, and so as soon as he was quite well it would be necessary, without losing a moment, to take steps to depart. . . . She said all this as she sat beside him, leaning against his shoulder. . . .

He listened to her, listened, now paling, now flushing . . . several times he tried to stop her, and suddenly he drew himself up.

"Yelena," he said in a strange and harsh voice, "leave me, and go."

"What?" she exclaimed in astonishment. "Do you feel unwell?" she added swiftly.

"No — I am all right — but, please, leave me."

"I don't understand you. Are you driving me away? . . . What are you doing?" she abruptly asked, for he bent from the sofa almost to the floor and pressed his lips to her feet. "Don't do that, Dmitry — Dmitry. . . ."

He half raised himself.

"Then leave me! You see, Yelena, when I fell ill, I did not lose consciousness at once and I knew that I was on the verge of death. Even in my fever, in my delirium, I realized, I vaguely felt, that this was death coming for me; I said farewell to life, to you, to all, I parted with all hope. . . . And suddenly this resurrection, this light after darkness, you — you — beside me, with me — your voice, your breath. . . . It is too much for my strength! I feel that I love you passionately, I hear you yourself saying you are mine, I cannot answer for anything. . . . Go!"

"Dmitry . . . " she whispered, and hid her head on his shoulder. Only now did she understand him.

"Yelena," he continued, "I love you, you know that, and I am ready to give my life for you . . . but why have you come to me now, when I am weak, when I am not master of myself, when all my blood is on fire? . . . You are mine, you say — you love me . . ."

"Dmitry," she repeated, and her face flamed and she pressed still more closely to him.

"Yelena, have pity on me — go, I feel that I might die — I shall not be able to resist these outbursts . . . all my soul is craving for you. . . . Think: death has all but parted us . . . and now you are here, you are in my arms — Yelena. . . ."

She began to throb all over.

"Then take me," she whispered almost inaudibly. . . .

29

With a scowl on his face Nikolai Artiomovich was pacing from end to end of his room. Shubin was sitting by the window and, with one leg crossed over the other, was calmly smoking a cigar.

"Do please stop walking from corner to corner," he said, flicking the ash off his cigar. "I am continually expecting you to say something, I follow you to and fro with my eyes, and my neck has begun to ache. And besides, there is something strained, something melodramatic in your bearing."

"All you think about is joking," Nikolai Artiomovich replied. "You're not prepared to enter into my position, you're not prepared to understand that I have grown used to this woman, that in the last resort I am attached to her, that her absence must torture me. Here it is October outside, and winter right under our noses. What can she be doing in Reval?"

"I expect she's knitting stockings — for herself, for herself; not for you."

"You laugh, you laugh; but I tell you that I don't know any woman like her. That honesty, that disinterestedness . . ."

"Did she give you her bills to pay?" Shubin asked.

"That disinterestedness," Nikolai Artiomovich repeated, raising his voice, "it is amazing. Let them tell me there are a million other women in the world; I say: show me those million; show me those million, I tell you: *ces femmes — qu'on me les montre!* And she doesn't write, that is what I find devastating!"

"You are as eloquent as Pythagoras," Shubin observed. "But do you know what I advise you?"

"What?"

"When Avgustina Khristianovna returns — you understand me?"

"Well, yes; what then?"

"When you see her — do you follow the development of my thought?"

"Why, yes, yes."

"Try thrashing her: what will come of it?"

Nikolai Artiomovich turned away indignantly.

"I thought he was really going to give me some useful advice! But what could you expect from him? An artist, a man without principles —"

"Without principles! But then, I hear your favorite, Mr. Kurnatovsky, a man with principles, won a hundred silver rubles from you yesterday. That is not exactly a delicate thing to do, you must agree."

"What of it? We were playing for stakes. . . . Of course, I

could have expected — But he is so poorly appreciated in this house — "

". . . that he thought: 'Where am I getting to?' " Shubin interrupted. " 'Whether he is to be my father-in-law or not is still concealed in the urn of destiny, but a hundred rubles is useful to a man who does not take bribes.' "

"Father-in-law! How the devil shall I be a father-in-law? *Vous rêvez, mon cher.* Of course, any other girl would have been delighted to have such a fiancé. Judge for yourself: a bold, intelligent man, made his own way in society, done military service in two provinces — "

"Led the Governor by the nose in —— province," Shubin observed.

"Very possibly. Evidently that was as it should be. A practical man, efficient — "

"And plays a good hand at cards," Shubin again observed.

"Well, yes, and he plays a good hand at cards. But Yelena Nikolaevna — Is it possible to understand her at all? I should like to know the man who would undertake to give her what she wants. One moment she is gay, the next she is bored; she suddenly goes so thin that you couldn't look at her, and then she suddenly recovers, and all this without any obvious reason. . . ."

An unpleasant-looking manservant entered with a cup of coffee, cream, and crackers on a tray.

"The father is satisfied with the prospective bridegroom," Nikolai Artiomovich continued, waving a cracker in the air, "but what has that to do with the daughter? That was all right in the former, patriarchal times, but now we have changed all that. *Nous avons changé tout ça.* Now a young lady talks with whom she pleases, she reads what she pleases; she goes off alone to Moscow without a manservant, without a maid, just as they do in Paris; and it is all accepted. The other day I asked: 'Where is Yelena Nikolaevna? They say, she has gone out. Where to?' No one knows. And do you call that order?"

"Do take your coffee and let the man go," Shubin said. "You yourself say that one shouldn't talk *devant les domestiques,*" he added in an undertone.

The lackey scowled at Shubin. But Nikolai Artiomovich took the cup, helped himself to cream, and collected nearly a dozen crackers.

"I simply wanted to say," he began as soon as the man had gone out, "that I don't mean a thing in this house. That is all. Because these days everybody judges by external appearances: for that matter, one man may be perfectly stupid, but he has an air of importance and they respect him; yet maybe another possesses talents that might — that might bring great benefit, but because of his modesty — "

"Are you a statesman, my dear Nikolai?" Shubin asked in an oily tone.

"Enough of your buffoonery!" Nikolai Artiomovich exclaimed angrily. "You forget yourself! There is a further proof for you that I don't mean a thing, not — a — thing, in this house!"

"Anna Vasilievna oppresses you, you poor fellow!" Shubin remarked, stretching himself. "Ah, Nikolai Artiomovich, you're not on the right path! You would do better to buy some little present for Anna Vasilievna. It is her birthday in a few days, and you know how she treasures the least sign of attention on your part."

"Yes, yes," Nikolai Artiomovich hurriedly replied, "I am very grateful to you for reminding me. Of course, of course, I simply must. And as it happens, I have got a little thing: a little clasp, I bought it at Rosenstrauch's the other day. Only I don't really know whether it is suitable."

"I suppose you bought it for that — for the Reval inhabitant?"

"That is — I — yes — I thought — "

"Well, in that case it certainly is suitable."

Shubin rose from his chair.

"Where could we go this evening, Pavel Yakovlevich, eh?" Nikolai Artiomovich asked him, affably looking him in the eyes.

"But you're going to the club."

"After the club — after the club."

Shubin stretched himself again.

"No, Nikolai Artiomovich, I have got to work tomorrow. Some other time." And he went out.

Nikolai Artiomovich knitted his brows, walked about the room, took a velvet-lined box containing the little clasp from his bureau, and spent a long time examining it and rubbing it with a foulard handkerchief. Then he sat down in front of a mirror and began diligently to comb his thick black hair, with a serious expression bending his head first to the right, then to the left, sticking his tongue in his cheek and keeping his eyes fixed on the parting. Behind him someone coughed; he looked round and saw the manservant who had brought his coffee.

"What do you want?" he asked.

"Nikolai Artiomovich," the man said, not without an air of solemnity, "you are our master!"

"I know; but what further?"

"Nikolai Artiomovich, please don't be angry with me; only as I have been in your worship's service ever since I was a boy, in my slavish zeal, so to speak, I should report to your honor —"

"But what is it?"

The man fidgeted as he stood.

"Just now you were pleased to say," he began, "that you did not know where Yelena Nikolaevna was pleased to go off to. I have happened to find out where she goes."

"Are you lying, you fool?"

"It is just as you wish; only three days ago I saw her deigning to enter a certain house."

"Where? What? What house?"

"In XXX Lane, off Povarskaya Street. Not far from here. And I asked the yardman who he had living there, what kind of residents."

Nikolai Artiomovich stamped his feet.

"Silence, you loafer! How dare you — ? Yelena Nikolaevna, out of the goodness of her heart, visits the poor, and you — Clear out, you fool!"

The terrified servant turned and rushed toward the door.

"Stop!" Nikolai Artiomovich exclaimed. "What did the yardman say to you?"

"Why, he said no — nothing. He said it was a stu — student."

"Silence, you drone! Listen, you scoundrel, if you say anything about this to anyone even in your sleep —"

"But, indeed, sir —"

"Silence! If you even hint — if anyone — if I discover — You won't find a place with me even under the ground! D'you hear? Take yourself off!"

The servant disappeared.

"Oh Lord my God! What does this mean?" Nikolai Artiomovich thought when the man had gone. "What did that blockhead tell me? Ah? All the same, I shall have to find out what that house is and who lives in it. I'll go myself. So that is what it has come to at last! . . . *Un laquais! Quelle humiliation!*"

And repeating aloud: "*un laquais!*" Nikolai Artiomovich locked the clasp away in the bureau and went to Anna Vasilievna's room. He found her in bed, with her cheek bound up. But the sight of her sufferings only irritated him, and he very quickly reduced her to tears.

30

Meanwhile the storm gathering in the East had burst. Turkey declared war on Russia; the date set for withdrawal from the principalities passed; the day of the defeat of the Turkish fleet at Sinop was not far off.[1] The last letters Insarov received importunately summoned him back to his country. His health was still not fully restored: he coughed, felt weak, and had slight feverish attacks; but he hardly ever remained at home. His soul was on fire, he no longer thought of his illness. He was continually driving about the city, having clandestine meetings with various persons; he wrote for nights on end, and vanished for days on end; he informed his landlord that he would be going away soon and presented him in advance with his few simple pieces of furniture. For her part, Yelena also made ready for the journey. One unpleasant evening she was sitting in her room, hemming handkerchiefs, and listening with involuntary dejection to the howling of the wind. Her maid entered and told her that her papa was in her mamma's bedroom and had sent for her. . . . "Your mamma is crying," she whispered after Yelena as she went out, "and your papa is angry. . . ."

Yelena slightly shrugged her shoulders and went to Anna Vasilievna's bedroom. Nikolai Artiomovich's good-hearted spouse was reclining in a folding chair and was sniffing at a handkerchief sprinkled with eau de Cologne; he himself was standing by the fireplace, buttoned to the top button, and wearing a high, stiff cravat and heavily starched collar, all his bearing vaguely reminiscent of some parliamentary orator. With an oratorical gesture he pointed his daughter to a chair, and when, not understanding his gesture, she looked at him interrogatively, he said with dignity, but without turning his head: "I ask you to sit down." (We may

[1] November 1853. (Tr.)

mention that Nikolai Artiomovich addressed his wife in the second person plural invariably, but his daughter only on extraordinary occasions.)

Yelena sat down.

Anna Vasilievna blew her nose tearfully. Nikolai Artiomovich thrust his right hand into the breast of his coat.

"I have summoned you, Yelena Nikolaevna," he began after a prolonged silence, "in order to have an explanation with you, or, to put it better, to demand an explanation from you. I am dissatisfied with you. No, that is too feebly said: your behavior grieves, affronts me — me and your mother — your mother, whom you see here."

Nikolai Artiomovich brought into play only the bass register of his voice. Yelena silently gazed at him, then at Anna Vasilievna, and turned pale.

"There was a time," he began again, "when daughters did not allow themselves to look down on their parents, and when the parental authority compelled the disobedient to shudder. That time is past, unfortunately; so, at least, many think. But believe me, we still have the existence of laws that do not permit — do not permit — in a word, laws still exist. I ask you to note that: laws exist."

"But, Papa dear —" Yelena began.

"I ask you not to interrupt me. We will return in thought to the past. I and Anna Vasilievna have done our duty. I and Anna Vasilievna have never spared anything for your upbringing: neither expense nor care. What benefit you have extracted from all these cares, these expenses, is another question; but I was entitled to think — I and Anna Vasilievna were entitled to think that you, at least, would sacredly observe those principles of morality which — which you, as our only daughter — *que nous vous avons inculqués*, which we have inculcated in you. We were entitled to think that no new 'ideas' whatever would affect that, so to speak, holy of holies. And what do we find? I will not even speak of the frivolity peculiar to your sex, to your age — but who could expect that you would forget yourself to such an extent —"

"Papa dear," Yelena said, "I know what you are trying to say —"

"No, you do not know what I am trying to say!" he cried in a falsetto voice, suddenly turning traitor to the majesty of his parliamentary bearing and the facile seriousness of his speech and his bass register. "You do not know, you brazen girl — "

"For God's sake, Nicolas," Anna Vasilievna stammered, *"vous me faites mourir."*

"Don't tell me *que je vous fais mourir*, Anna Vasilievna! You cannot imagine what you will hear in a moment! Prepare for the worst, I warn you!"

Anna Vasilievna was stupefied.

"No," Nikolai Artiomovich continued, turning to Yelena, "you do not know what I am trying to say!"

"I have done you a wrong — " she began.

"Ah, so at last!"

"I have done you a wrong," she repeated, "in that I haven't long since confessed — "

"Why, do you know," Nikolai Artiomovich interrupted her, "that I can annihilate you with a single word?"

Yelena raised her eyes to him.

"Yes, madame, with a single word! There is no point in looking like that!" (He folded his arms across his chest.) "Permit me to ask you whether you know a certain house in XXX Lane, off Povarskaya Street? Have you visited that house?" (He stamped his foot.) Answer me, you good-for-nothing, and don't attempt to prevaricate. The servants, the servants, a lackey, madame, *de vils laquais* have seen you, as you went in, to your — "

Yelena's face flamed, and her eyes began to flash.

"There is no need for me to prevaricate," she said. "Yes, I have visited that house."

"Excellent! You hear, you hear, Anna Vasilievna! And you, presumably, know who lives in that house?"

"Yes, I know: my husband."

Nikolai Artiomovich's eyes started out of his head.

"Your — "

"My husband," Yelena repeated. "I am married to Dmitry Nikanorovich Insarov."

"You — ? Married — ?" Anna Vasilievna could hardly get the words out.

"Yes, Mamma — forgive me. We were married secretly, two weeks ago."

Anna Vasilievna fell back in her chair; Nikolai Artiomovich fell back two paces.

"Married! To that ragamuffin, to that Montenegrin! The daughter of the hereditary noble Nikolai Stakhov has married a vagabond, a plebeian! Without her parents' blessing! And do you think that I shall leave it at that? That I shall not lay a complaint? That I shall allow you — that you — that — You to a nunnery, and he to penal servitude, into an army punitive company! Anna Vasilievna, be so good as to tell her at once that you cut her off from her heritage."

"Nikolai Artiomovich, for God's sake!" his wife groaned.

"And when and in what manner was this achieved? Who married you? Where? How? My God! What will all my acquaintances, what will all the world say now! And you, you shameless deceiver, could live beneath your parental roof after such behavior! You were not afraid — of thunder from heaven?"

"Papa dear," Yelena said (she was trembling from head to foot, but her voice was firm), "you are free to do with me whatever you like, but you have no reason to accuse me of being shameless, or of deceiving. I did not wish — to grieve you before, but in any case I would myself have told you everything during the next day or two, because I am leaving here next week with my husband."

"You're leaving? Where for?"

"For his country, for Bulgaria."

"To the Turks!" Anna Vasilievna exclaimed, and fainted.

Yelena rushed to her mother.

"Stand back!" Nikolai Artiomovich roared, and seized his daughter by the arm. "Stand back, you unworthy one!"

But at that moment the bedroom door was opened and a pale face with glittering eyes appeared. It was Shubin.

"Nikolai Artiomovich!" he shouted at the top of his voice. "Avgustina Khristianovna has arrived and has sent for you."

Nikolai Artiomovich turned round in a frenzy, shook his fist at Shubin, paused for a minute, then swiftly left the room.

Yelena fell at her mother's feet and put her arms around her knees.

Uvar Ivanovich was lying in bed. A shirt without a collar, held with a large stud, swathed his huge neck and parted in broad, flowing folds over his almost feminine breasts, exposing to view a large cross of cypress wood and a small amulet. A light blanket covered his expansive limbs. A candle burned smokily on the night table, beside a mug of kvass, and Shubin, his head between his hands, was seated on the bed at Uvar Ivanovich's feet.

"Yes," he said thoughtfully, "she is married and is intending to go away. Your dear gentle nephew roared and bawled for all the house to hear; for the sake of secrecy he locked the bedroom door, but not only the lackeys and maids, but even the coachman could hear every word! He's still raging and storming, he all but had a fight with me, he is going around burdened with his parental curse like a bear with a block; but he hasn't any real strength. It will be the death of Anna Vasilievna, but she is far more upset by her daughter's departure than by her marriage."

Uvar Ivanovich began to wriggle his fingers.

"She's a mother," he declared. "Well — and then — "

"Your nephew," Shubin continued, "is threatening to forward complaints to the Metropolitan, and the Governor General, and the Minister, but it will end with her going away. Who can find any pleasure in ruining his own daughter? He'll ride the high horse a little and then tuck in his tail."

"They have — no right," Uvar Ivanovich remarked, and he took a drink from the mug.

"That's true. But what a cloud of condemnation, of gossip, of tittle-tattle, will rise all over Moscow! She wasn't frightened by that. . . . For that matter, she is above it. She is going away, and where to! It is terrible even to think of! To what a distant, to what a remote spot! What awaits her there? I think of her as though she were on the point of driving out from some wayside tavern at night, in a blizzard, in zero weather. She will part from her country, from her family! But I understand why. Whom is she leaving behind here? Whom has she seen? Kurnatovskys, and Berseníevs and people like me; and that beats the lot. What has she to regret? One thing is bad: they say her husband — damn it, I find that word hard to get out — they say Insarov is coughing up blood; and that's bad. I saw him the other day. What a face! You could use him as a model for Brutus now. Do you know who Brutus was, Uvar Ivanovich?"

"Know what? A man."

"Exactly: 'this was a man.' Yes, it's a marvelous face, but unhealthy, very unhealthy."

"For fighting — that doesn't matter," Uvar Ivanovich declared.

"Exactly; for fighting it doesn't matter; you are pleased to express yourself with perfect justice today. But for living it does matter. And, you see, she wants to live a little longer with him."

"It's a youthful affair," Uvar Ivanovich commented.

"Yes, it's a youthful, glorious, audacious affair. Death, life, struggle, fall, triumph, love, freedom, country — good, good. God grant them to all! But that is not the same as sitting up to your neck in mud and trying to pretend that it doesn't matter to you, when in fact it really doesn't matter to you. But then — tautened strings sound out for all the world to hear, or snap!"

Shubin let his head fall on his breast.

"Yes," he continued after a long silence. "Insarov is worthy of her. But, on the other hand, what rot that is! No one is worthy of her. Insarov — Insarov — Why this false humility? Well, granted he is young, he stands up for himself, though hitherto he has no more than we sinners. But are we such utter rubbish after all? Take even me; am I rubbish, Uvar Ivanovich? Has God been so unkind to me in every respect? Has He given me no capacities, no talents? Who knows, perhaps someday the name of Pavel Shubin will be famous. You have a copper groschen lying on your table. Who knows, perhaps some day, after a century, that copper will go into a statue of Pavel Shubin, raised in his honor by grateful posterity."

Uvar Ivanovich rested on his elbow and fixed his eyes on the excited artist.

"A song of the distant future," he declared at last, with his usual wriggle of the fingers. "We're talking about others, but you — that — about yourself."

"Oh, great philosopher of the Russian earth!" Shubin exclaimed. "Your every word is pure gold, and not to me but to you should a statue be raised, and I shall undertake that task. Now, just as you are lying there, in that pose — of which one cannot be sure whether it expresses more indolence or strength. That is how I shall carve you. With just reproach have you struck at my egotism and my self-esteem! Yes! Yes! There is nothing to be said about me, nothing to boast of. We haven't anybody yet, we have no people, no matter where you look. Our Russians are all either small fry, rodents, petty Hamlets, Samoyeds, or subterranean

535

darkness and silence, or pushers, or idle talkers, and drumsticks! And then there are the others we often come across: men who have studied themselves to the point of an infamous fineness of detail, men who are incessantly feeling the pulse of their own sensations and reporting to themselves: 'That is what I feel, that is what I think.' A most useful, an efficient activity! No, if we had any decent people among us, that girl, that sensitive soul would not be leaving us, would not slip off like a fish into water! What does it all mean, Uvar Ivanovich? When will our time come? When will men be born among us?"

"When it is their time," Uvar Ivanovich replied, "they will come."

"They will come? Fundamental soil! Black-earth force! You said: 'They will come.' I warn you, I shall write down your words. But why are you putting out the candle?"

"I want to get to sleep. Good night."

31

Shubin had said the truth. The unexpected news of Yelena's marriage all but killed Anna Vasilievna; she took to her bed. Nikolai Artiomovich insisted that she should not allow her daughter to see her; he seemed delighted at the opportunity of showing that he was the master in the full sense of the word, as the family head in all his might; he incessantly roared and thundered at the servants, adding from time to time: "I'll show you who I am, I shall let you know — you wait!" So long as he was at home Anna Vasilievna did not see her daughter and contented herself with the presence of Zoya, who waited on her very zealously, but who thought to herself: *"Diesen Insarov vorziehen — und wem?"* But as soon as Nikolai Artiomovich had driven away (and this happened quite often: Shubin was right, Avgustina Khristianovna had returned), Yelena went to her mother; and Anna Vasilievna gazed at her fixedly, silently, with tears in her eyes. That mute reproach pierced Yelena's heart more than anything else; yet it was not contrition that she felt at such times, but a profound, infinite pity, resembling contrition.

"Mamma, my dear mamma!" she said, kissing her hand, "what else was I to do? I am not to blame, I have fallen in love with him, I could not act otherwise. Blame fate: it has linked my life with a man whom Papa doesn't like, and who will take me away from you."

"Oh!" Anna Vasilievna interrupted her, "don't remind me of that. When I recall where you are intending to go, my heart simply turns over!"

"My dear mamma," Yelena answered, "console yourself at least with the thought that it might have been worse: I might have died."

"But even so I have no hope of ever seeing you again. Either you will end your life there, somewhere in a hut, or I shall not survive the separation." Anna Vasilievna thought of Bulgaria as rather like the Siberian tundra.

"Don't say that, my dear mother, we shall see each other again, if God wills. And there are towns in Bulgaria just as there are here."

"What towns are there in Bulgaria! There's a war going on there now, and all over the country I expect they're firing cannon. . . . Do you intend to go away soon?"

"Soon — if only Papa — He wants to lay a complaint, he is threatening to force our divorce."

Anna Vasilievna raised her eyes to heaven.

"No, Yelena my dear, he will not lay any complaint. I myself would never have consented to this marriage for anything, I would rather have died; but you cannot undo what is done, and I shall not let shame be brought on my daughter."

Thus several days passed. Finally Anna Vasilievna summoned up courage, and one evening she was closeted with her husband in her bedroom. All the house hushed and listened tensely. At first nothing at all was to be heard; then Nikolai Artiomovich's voice began to boom out; then a quarrel developed, with shouting; someone even seemed to be groaning. . . . Shubin, the maid, and Zoya were all preparing to go to the rescue again, but the noise in the bedroom began to die down a little, passed into conversation, and nothing was to be heard. Only feeble sobbing was audible from time to time — and that, too, ceased. Keys were heard to rattle, there was the squeak of a bureau drawer being pulled out. . . . The door opened and Nikolai Artiomovich appeared. He stared harshly at everybody he met and went off to his club. But Anna Vasilievna sent for Yelena to come to her, gave her a vigorous hug, and, streaming with bitter tears, told her:

"Everything is settled, he will not cause any trouble, and there is nothing now to prevent your going — and abandoning us."

"You will permit Dmitry to come and thank you?" Yelena asked her mother when Anna Vasilievna was rather more composed.

"Wait a little, my soul, I cannot see the one who is parting us now. There will be time enough before your departure."

"Before our departure," Yelena said mournfully.

Nikolai Artiomovich had agreed "not to cause any trouble," but Anna Vasilievna did not tell her daughter what price he had set on his agreement. She did not tell her that she had promised to pay all his debts, and in addition to give him a thousand silver rubles in cash. In addition he had resolutely informed Anna Vasilievna that he did not wish to meet Insarov, whom he continued to call a Montenegrin, and on arriving at his club he quite unnecessarily fell to talking to his card partner, a retired general of engineers, about Yelena's marriage. "Have you heard," he said with dissembled unconcern, "that my daughter, through very great learning, has married some student?" The general stared at him through his spectacles, bellowed: "Hm!" and asked him what game he played.

32

But the day of departure was approaching. November was all but gone, the last days of the month were passing. Insarov had long since completed his preparations and was burning with desire to get away from Moscow as soon as possible. The doctor also hurried him. "You need a warm climate," he told him, "you'll never get better here." Impatience harassed Yelena too; she was alarmed by Insarov's pallor, his emaciation. She often looked at his changed features with involuntary terror. Her position had grown unbearable in her parents' house. Her mother lamented over her as though over the dead, but her father treated her with contemptuous coldness. The proximity of the parting secretly tortured him also, but he considered it his duty, the duty of an affronted father, to conceal his feelings, his weakness.

Anna Vasilievna did at last express a desire to see Insarov. When he entered her room she could not even bring herself to

538

look at him; he sat down by her armchair and waited with composed respect for her to speak. Yelena sat close by and held her mother's hand in her own.

At last Anna Vasilievna raised her eyes, said: "God be your judge, Dmitry Nikanorovich — " and stopped; the reproaches died on her lips.

"But you're ill!" she exclaimed. "Yelena, but he's ill!"

"I have been unwell, Anna Vasilievna," Insarov replied, "and even now I am not quite well again. But I hope my native air will restore me completely."

"Yes — Bulgaria!" Anna Vasilievna murmured, and thought: "My God, a Bulgar, dying, a voice that sounds as though it came from a barrel, eyes staring out of his head, his body nothing but a skeleton, with a coat looking like somebody else's, a face as yellow as camomile. And she's his wife, she loves him — it must be a dream. . . . " But she at once pulled herself together. "Dmitry Nikanorovich," she said, "you simply must — simply must go?"

"I simply must, Anna Vasilievna."

She looked at him.

"Oh, Dmitry Nikanorovich, God grant that you never have to go through what I am now suffering. . . . But you promise me to look after her, to love her. . . . You will not need for anything so long as I am alive!"

Tears choked her voice. She opened her arms, and Yelena and Insarov both clung to her.

The fatal day arrived at last. It was decided that Yelena should say farewell to her parents at home, but should set off on the journey from Insarov's room. The departure was fixed for twelve o'clock. Berseniev arrived fifteen minutes earlier. He thought he would find Insarov surrounded by fellow country-men, who would certainly wish to see him off; but they had all gone away before him. The two mysterious persons known to the reader had also gone (they had acted as witnesses at Insarov's wedding). The tailor welcomed the "good gentleman" with a bow. Presumably out of grief, or perhaps in his joy at acquiring the furniture, he had been drinking heavily; his wife soon bore him off. In the room everything was packed; a trunk, tied with rope, was standing on the floor. Berseniev was lost in thought: many were the memories that passed through his mind.

Twelve o'clock had long since passed, and the driver had already brought up his horses, but still the "young couple" did not put in an appearance. At last hurried steps were heard on the staircase, and Yelena entered, with Insarov and Shubin. Yelena's eyes were red: she had left her mother lying in a swoon; the parting had been very painful. Yelena had not seen Berseniev for more than a week, for during the latter days he had not called often on the Stakhovs. She had not expected to meet him, and cried out: "You, oh, thank you!" and threw her arms round his neck. Insarov also embraced him. An oppressive silence fell. What could these three human beings say, what did those three hearts feel? Shubin realized the need to put an end to this oppressive atmosphere by some living sound, by some remark.

"So our trio has gathered once more," he began, "for the last time! We will submit to the dictates of fate, we will think well of the past, and go with God to our new life! 'With God on the distant journey,'" he began to sing, and broke off. He suddenly felt ashamed and awkward. It was wicked to sing in the presence of the dead; and at that moment, in that room, the past of which he had spoken, the past of the people gathered in it, had died. It had died for the resurrection to a new life, let us grant . . . but none the less it had died.

"Well, Yelena," Insarov began, turning to his wife, "I think that is everything. Everything is paid, everything is arranged. Now there is only this trunk to be carried down. Landlord!"

The landlord, accompanied by his wife and daughter, entered the room. He listened, swaying a little, to Insarov's instructions, hoisted the trunk onto his shoulder, and swiftly ran down the stairs, his boots clattering.

"And now, according to the Russian custom, we must sit down," Insarov observed.

They all sat down. Berseniev sat on the old sofa, Yelena sat beside him; the landlady and her daughter settled down by the door. They were all silent; they all smiled tensely, and no one knew why he was smiling; each wanted to say something in parting, and each (with the exception, of course, of the landlady and her daughter: they only stared their eyes out), each felt that at such moments it was permissible to utter only banalities, that significant, or intelligent, or even simple heartfelt words would be incompatible, almost hypocritical. Insarov was the first to rise;

he began to cross himself. "Good-by, our little room!" he exclaimed.

Then there were kisses, the ringing but chilly kisses of parting, the farewell, half-unexpressed wishes, the promises to write, the last, half-suppressed parting words. . . .

Yelena, all in tears, had already seated herself in the heavy sleigh; Insarov solicitously covered her feet with a rug; Shubin, Berseniev, the landlord, his wife, the daughter, with the inevitable kerchief on her head, the yardman, a passing artisan in a striped gown — all were standing at the door, when suddenly a handsome light sleigh, harnessed to spanking trotting horses, dashed into the yard, and out of it, brushing the snow from his greatcoat collar, jumped Nikolai Artiomovich.

"Thank God you're still here!" he exclaimed, running across to the carriage. "Here, Yelena, here is our last parental blessing," he said, bending under the hood; taking a small icon wrapped in a velvet bag out of his coat pocket, he put it round her neck. She burst into tears and began to kiss his hands; but meanwhile his coachman brought out a bottle of champagne and three glasses from the front of the light sleigh.

"Well!" said Nikolai Artiomovich, while his tears dripped on the beaver collar of his greatcoat, "we have to see you off — and to wish — " He poured out the champagne; his hands were trembling; the froth rose over the rim and fell into the snow. He took one glass and handed the other two to Yelena and Insarov, who had already seated himself beside her. "God grant us — " Nikolai Artiomovich began, and could not finish; he drank down his wine; the others also drank. "Now you should too, gentlemen," he added, turning to Shubin and Berseniev; but at that moment the driver touched up his horses. Nikolai Artiomovich began to run beside the sleigh. "Don't forget, write to us," he said in a broken voice. Yelena put out her head and said: "Good-by, dear Papa, Andrei Piotrovich, Pavel Yakovlevich, good-by all, good-by Russia!" Then she threw herself back. The driver swung his knout and began to whistle; the sleigh, its runners grinding, turned to the right outside the gate and disappeared.

33

It was a bright April day. Over the broad lagoon separating Venice from the narrow strip of sandbank called the Lido slipped a narrow-prowed gondola, swinging measuredly as the gondolier pulled on the long oar. In its low cabin, seated on soft leather cushions, were Yelena and Insarov.

Yelena's features had changed little since the day of her departure from Moscow; but their expression was different: it was more thoughtful and severe, and her eyes had a bolder gaze. All her body had blossomed, and the hair seemed to be more exuberant and lay more luxuriantly along her marble forehead and fresh cheeks. Only around the lips, when they were not smiling, a hardly perceptible fold indicated the presence of a secret, constant anxiety. On the other hand, the expression of Insarov's face was the same as before, but the features had changed cruelly. He had gone thinner, older, paler, and was hunched up; he coughed almost incessantly with a curt, dry cough, and his sunken eyes glittered with a strange glitter. On the journey from Russia he had lain ill in Vienna for almost two months, and only at the end of March had he and Yelena arrived in Venice. Thence he hoped to make his way through Zara to Serbia and so into Bulgaria; all other roads were closed to him. War was already raging along the Danube; England and France had declared war on Russia; all the Slavonic lands were in turmoil and preparing for revolt.

The gondola touched ground on the inner edge of the Lido. Yelena and Insarov set off along the narrow sandy path, lined with consumptive little trees (they are planted every year, and they die every year), to the outer edge of the Lido, to the sea.

They walked along the shore. Before them the Adriatic rolled with turbidly turquoise waves; they foamed, hissed, came running on shore, and then, drawing back, left tiny shells and scraps of marine vegetation on the sand.

"What a mournful spot!" Yelena remarked. "I am afraid it may be too cold for you here; but I can guess why you wanted to come here."

"Cold!" Insarov protested with a swift but bitter smile. "A fine soldier I shall make if I am to be frightened of the cold. But I came here — I'll tell you why. When I look at this sea, I feel that from here I am nearer to my country. For it lies over there," he added, stretching his hand out toward the east. "And this wind is blowing from there."

"Isn't this same wind bringing the boat you are expecting?"

Yelena said. "Look, there's a sail showing white; perhaps that is it?"

Insarov gazed across the sea to where Yelena had pointed.

"Rendich promised to arrange everything for us within a week," he remarked. "I think one can rely on him. . . . Have you heard, Yelena?" he added with sudden enthusiasm. "They say that the poverty-stricken Dalmatian fishermen have sacrificed their leads — you know, those weights that make the nets sink to the bottom — for bullets. They hadn't any money, all they live by is fishing; but they gladly gave their last possessions and now they are starving. What a people!"

"*Aufgepasst!*" an arrogant voice shouted behind them. They heard the muffled thud of horse-hoofs, and an Austrian officer, in a short gray tunic and a green peaked cap, galloped past them. They had hardly time to step aside.

Insarov stared after him morosely.

"It's not his fault," Yelena said; "you know, this is the only spot in Venice where they can exercise their horses."

"It's not his fault," Insarov retorted; "but he has set my blood boiling with his shout, his mustaches, his cap, all the look of him. Let us go back."

"Yes, let us go back, Dmitry. And besides, it really does blow hard here. You did not take care of yourself after your Moscow illness, and you paid for it in Vienna. You need to be more careful now."

He was silent; only his previous bitter smile slipped over his lips.

"If you like," Yelena continued, "we'll row along the Grand Canal. You know, we haven't seen Venice properly since we arrived. And this evening we'll go to the theater; I have two tickets for a box. They say a new opera is to be performed. If you agree we'll give this day to each other; we'll forget politics, the war, and everything else; we will know only one thing: that we are alive together, that we are breathing, are thinking together, that we are united forever. . . . Would you like to?"

"You would like to, Yelena," Insarov replied, "and so would I like to also."

"I knew that," she remarked with a smile. "Come on, then; come on."

They returned to the gondola, seated themselves, and ordered the gondolier to row them, without hurrying, along the Grand Canal.

Venice has to be seen in April for one to appreciate all the inexpressible charm of that magic city. The mildness and gentleness of spring are as fitting to Venice as the brilliant sun of summer to magnificent Genoa, as the gold and purple of autumn to that great and ancient city, Rome. Like the spring, the beauty of Venice is not only deeply moving: it quickens a feeling of longing; it wearies and troubles the inexperienced heart like the promise of an intimate, lucid, yet mysterious happiness. Everything in Venice is light, is intelligible, and everything is wrapped in the drowsy haze of an infatuated stillness; everything in her is silent, and everything is welcoming; everything in her is feminine, beginning with the very name: not for nothing has she alone been called "the Beautiful." The palaces, the churches, rise lightly and miraculously, like the harmonious dream of a youthful god; there is something fabulous, something captivatingly strange in the greenish-gray gleam and the silky iridescence of the silent waters of the canals, in the noiseless movement of the gondolas, in the absence of harsh city sounds, of harsh knocking, clatter, and hubbub. "Venice is dying, Venice is desolated," her inhabitants tell you; but perhaps that final delight, the delight of withering in the very moment of blossoming and the triumph of beauty, has been denied her. Those who have not seen her do not know her; neither Canaletto nor Guardi (not to mention later painters) was capable of conveying that silvery tenderness of the air, that fleeting and intimate perspective, that amazing consonance of most graceful outlines and melting colors. The man who has outlived his time has been broken by life, has no reason to visit Venice: she will be bitter to him, like the memory of the unachieved dreams of his earliest days. But sweet will she be to those in whom all their forces are still seething, who feel themselves fortunate; let such bring their happiness beneath its enchanted skies and, no matter how radiant that happiness may be, she will gild it still more with an untarnishable refulgence.

The gondola in which Insarov and Yelena were sitting floated gently past the Riva degli Schiavoni, the Doges' Palace, the

Piazzetta, and entered the Grand Canal. On both sides extended marble palaces; they seemed to slip quietly by, hardly allowing the gaze to take in and comprehend all their beauty. Yelena felt profoundly happy. In the azure of her heaven hung one dark little cloud — and it, too, was passing into the distance: today Insarov was very much better. They floated along to the steep arch of the Rialto and then turned back. Yelena was afraid of the effect the chilly churches might have on Insarov; but she remembered the Accadèmia delle Belle Arti and ordered the gondolier to go there. They had soon passed through all the halls of that small museum. Being neither experts nor dilettantes, they did not halt before every picture, did not place any constraint on themselves: a light-hearted gaiety had unexpectedly come upon them. Suddenly everything seemed very amusing to them. (Children know this feeling very well.) To the great scandalizing of three English visitors, Yelena laughed to tears at Tintoretto's St. Mark, jumping down from heaven like a frog into water in order to save a tortured slave. Insarov, for his part, went into raptures over the back and the calves of the energetic man in a green cloak in the foreground of Titian's *Ascension*, raising his hands to the Madonna. But the Madonna herself, a splendid, powerful woman, calmly and majestically aspiring to the bosom of God the Father, impressed both Insarov and Yelena; and they also liked the severe and sacred picture of old Cima da Conegliano.

As they left the Accadèmia they looked back once more at the Englishmen with long hare-teeth and hanging side-whiskers who were just behind them — and laughed; they saw their gondolier, with his short-cut jacket and short pantaloons — and laughed; they noticed a huckstress with a little knot of gray hair on the very crown of her head — and they laughed more than ever; they looked each other in the face at last — and overflowed with laughter. And as soon as they had taken their seats in the gondola they strongly, strongly squeezed each other's hand. They arrived at the hotel, ran to their room, and ordered dinner for themselves. Their gaiety did not leave them even at the table. They toasted each other, drank to the health of their Moscow friends, applauded the *camerière* for bringing them a tasty dish of fish, and again and again demanded that he should serve them with live *frutti di mare*. The *camerière* grimaced, and fidgeted with his feet, and as he left them he shook his head, and once even whispered with a sigh: *"Poveretti!"* After dinner they went to the theater.

The theater was presenting a Verdi opera, a rather banal one, to tell the truth, but it had already been successfully performed all over Europe and was well known to all Russians: it was *La Traviata*. The season was over in Venice, and none of the singers rose above the level of the mediocre; they all shrieked at the top of their voices. The part of Violetta was played by an artist who had no great reputation and, judging by the public's frigidity toward her, she was not a popular favorite, but she was not lacking in talent. She was a young, not very beautiful, black-eyed girl with a voice not altogether even and already ruined. She was dressed in clothes motley and poor to the point of naïveté: a crimson snood covered her hair, a gown of faded azure satin constrained her bosom, thick Swedish gloves were drawn right up to her angular elbows. And in any case how was she, the daughter of some Bergamo shepherd, to know how Parisian camellias dress? Nor did she even know how to deport herself on the stage; but there was much truth and artless simplicity in her acting, and she sang with that peculiar temperament of expression and rhythm which is found only in the Italians. Yelena and Insarov sat alone in the darkened box, right by the stage; the playful mood that had come upon them at the Accadèmia di Belle Arte had not yet passed. When the father of the unfortunate youth who has been caught in the temptress's net appeared on the stage in a pea-green frock coat and a disheveled white peruke, opened his mouth crookedly, and, himself already out of countenance, gave vent to a despondent bass tremolo, they all but burst into laughter. . . . But Violetta's performance affected them.

"They're hardly clapping that poor girl at all," said Yelena, "yet I greatly prefer her to some self-assured second-rate celebrity who would pose and grimace and do everything for effect. This artist seems to have some sorrow of her own; she doesn't even notice the audience."

Insarov leaned against the edge of the box and gazed fixedly at Violetta.

"Yes," he said, "she's not playing a part; she has the smell of death."

Yelena lapsed into silence.

The third act began. The curtain rose. . . . Yelena shivered at the sight of that bed, those curtains hung about it, the glasses of medicines, the shielded lamp. . . . It recalled something that had only recently occurred. . . . "But the future? But the present?" flashed through her head. As though arranged, in response to the actress's simulated coughing Insarov's thick, unfeigned cough sounded in the box. . . . Yelena glanced at him surreptitiously and at once set her features in an imperturbable and tranquil expression. He understood and began to smile and very quietly to hum the music.

But he soon stopped. Violetta's performance grew steadily better, continually freer. She threw off all the extrinsic, all the unnecessary, and *found* herself: she achieved that rare, that highest happiness for an artist! The audience stirred, stared, and was amazed. The plain-looking girl with her ruined voice began to gather them all into her hand, to possess them. But now even her voice no longer sounded as though it had been ruined, it grew warm and strong. Alfredo appeared; Violetta's joyous cry all but aroused that storm whose name is *fanatismo* and compared with which all our northern ravings are as nothing. . . . Another moment — and the audience again died into silence. Now came the duet, the finest number in the opera, in which the composer has succeeded in expressing all the feeling of regret for a madly wasted youth, all the last struggle of a desperate and impotent love. Carried away, caught up by the atmosphere of general sympathy, with tears of artistic joy and genuine suffering in her eyes, the singer gave herself over to the emotion that moved her; her face was transformed and, confronted with the sinister specter of suddenly approaching death, with such a cry of supplication did the words "*Lascia mi vivere . . . morir si giovine*" burst from her to storm all heaven that the theater began to rattle with a frenzy of clapping and rapturous shouts.

Yelena turned cold. She felt with her hand for Insarov's hand, found it, and squeezed it strongly. He responded to her pressure; but she did not look at him, nor he at her. This squeeze of the hand had no resemblance to that with which they had greeted each other in the gondola a few hours previously.

They floated back to their hotel once more along the Grand Canal. Night had already fallen — a luminous, gentle night. The same buildings came to meet them, but now they seemed different. Those that were lit up by the moon gleamed a golden white, and in that very whiteness the details of the decoration and the outlines of the windows and balconies seemed to have disappeared; they stood out more distinctly on the buildings flooded with a tenuous haze of even shadow. The gondolas with their little red lights seemed to speed along even more inaudibly and swiftly; their steely prows glistened mysteriously, the oars rose and fell mysteriously above the silvery little scales of the agitated water; here and there the gondoliers called curtly and softly (they never sing, these days); hardly any other sounds were audible. The hotel in which Insarov and Yelena were staying was on the Riva degli Schiavoni; they left the gondola before it reached the hotel and walked several times round the Piazza of St. Mark, under the arches, where there were throngs of festive people outside the tiny cafés. To walk together with the beloved being through a strange town, among strangers, is peculiarly pleasant: everything seems to be splendid and significant, you wish everybody well, you wish them peace and the same happiness with which you yourself are filled. But now Yelena could no longer surrender unconcernedly to her feeling of happiness; her heart, shaken by its recent impressions, could not find reassurance; and as they passed the Doges' Palace, Insarov pointed without speaking to the muzzles of the Austrian guns peering out from below the arches and pulled his cap down over his eyes. Then he felt tired — and, taking one last look at the Cathedral of St. Mark, at its dome, where, beneath the rays of the moon, patches of phosphorescent light were burning on the bluish-colored lead, they slowly returned home.

Their little room looked out on the broad lagoon stretching from the Riva degli Schiavoni to the Giudecca. Almost opposite their hotel rose the pointed spire of St. George's; to the right, high in the air, glittered the golden ball of the Dogana, and the church of the Redentore, the most beautiful of Palladio's creations, stood adorned like a bride; to the left the masts and yards of ships, the funnels of steamers emerged blackly; here and there a half-furled sail hung like a great wing, and the pennants hardly stirred. Insarov sat down by the window, but Yelena would not allow him to admire the view for long; he suddenly developed a fever, he was overcome by a wasting debility. She put him to bed and waited until he had fallen asleep, then quietly returned to the window.

Oh, how quiet and gracious was the night, with what dovelike humility did the azure air respire, how all suffering, all sorrow should have been silenced and lulled to sleep beneath this clear sky, beneath these sacred, innocent rays! "O God," Yelena thought, "why is there such a thing as death, why is there parting, sickness, and tears? Or otherwise why is there this beauty, this sweet feeling of hope, why the reassuring consciousness of a firm refuge, of constant defence, immortal protection? What is the meaning of this smiling, benedictory heaven, this happy, quietly resting earth? Or is it all really only within us, while outside us is eternal cold and silence? Are we really alone — alone — and out there, everywhere, in all those inaccessible abysses and depths — everything, everything is alien to us? But in that case what is the point of our desires and the joy of prayer?" (*"Morir si giovine"* was still ringing in her soul.) ". . . Surely one may implore, to avert, to save — O God, surely one may believe in a miracle?" She laid her head on her clenched hands. "Enough?" she whispered; "surely not already enough? I have been happy, not only in single minutes, not in hours, not in whole days — no, but for whole weeks at a time. But by what right?" She grew afraid of her own happiness. "But if this is not permissible?" she thought. "If this is not given for nothing? For this was heaven . . . but we are human beings, poor, sinful human beings. . . . *Morir si giovine.* . . . O gloomy phantom, depart! Not to me alone is his life necessary!"

"But supposing this is punishment," she thought again, "supposing we are now to make full payment for our guilt. My conscience was silent, it is silent now; but is that, after all, any proof of innocence? O God, surely we are not so criminal! Surely Thou, who created this night, this sky, cannot wish to punish us for having loved? But if that is so, if he is to blame, if I am to blame," she added with an involuntary outburst, "then grant him, O God, grant us both to die at least an honest, glorious death, there, on his native fields, and not here, not in this lonely room."

"But the grief of a poor, lonely mother?" she asked herself, and was abashed, and found no reply to her question. She did not know that every man's happiness is founded on another's unhappiness, that even his advantage and comfort require the disadvantage and discomfort of others, as a statue requires a pedestal.

"Rendich!" Insarov murmured in his sleep.

Yelena tiptoed across to him, bent over him, and wiped the perspiration from his face. He tossed about a little on the pillow and then was still.

She went again to the window, and again her thoughts took possession of her. She began to argue with herself and to assure herself that there was no reason to be afraid. She even felt ashamed of her weakness. "Is there really any danger, isn't he better?" she whispered. "After all, if we hadn't been at the theater today, none of this would have come into my head." At that moment she saw a white gull high above the water; probably it had been started up by a fisherman; and it flew silently, with an uneven flight, as though surveying a place where it could settle. "If it flies this way," Yelena thought, "that will be a good sign." The gull circled in one spot, folded its wings — and, as though shot, with a mournful cry it dropped somewhere far beyond the dark outline of a ship. Yelena shuddered, but then she felt ashamed that she had shuddered and, without undressing, she lay down on the bed beside Insarov, who was breathing heavily and rapidly.

34

Insarov awoke late, with a dull pain in his head, and with a feeling, as he put it, of disgusting weakness in all his body. None the less he got up.

"Rendich hasn't arrived, has he?" was his first question.

"Not yet," Yelena answered, and handed him the latest issue of the *Osservatore Triestino*, in which there was a great deal about the war, about the Slavonic lands, about the Principalities. Insarov began to read; she occupied herself with getting some coffee ready for him. . . . Someone knocked at the door.

"Rendich," they both thought, but someone called out in Russian: "May I come in?" Yelena and Insarov exchanged looks of astonishment. Without waiting for their answer, an elegantly dressed man with small, sharp features and spirited little eyes entered the room. He was beaming as though he had just won an enormous sum of money or had heard some very pleasant news.

Insarov rose from his chair.

"You don't recognize me?" the stranger began, walking up to him jauntily and bowing affably to Yelena. "Lupoyarov; d'you remember, we met at the E.'s' in Moscow."

"Oh yes, at the E.'s'," Insarov confirmed.

"Of course, of course. Will you introduce me to your wife? Madame, I have always felt profound respect for Dmitry Vasilievich — " (he corrected himself) "Nikanor Vasilievich, and I am very glad to have the honor at last of making your acquaintance. Just imagine," he continued, turning to Insarov, "I heard only yesterday that you are here. I am staying in this hotel too. What a city this is, this Venice! It is poetry, sheer poetry! One thing is horrible: the accursed Austrians at every step. I've had enough already of those Austrians. By the way, have you heard that a decisive battle has been fought on the Danube? — three hundred Turkish officers killed, Silistra captured, Serbia has already declared herself independent. You, as a patriot, should be delighted, shouldn't you? My Slavonic blood is boiling even in me. None the less, I advise you to be careful; I am confident that you are being watched. The spy system here is fearful! Yesterday some suspicious individual came up to me and asked me: 'Are you a Russian?' I told him I was a Dane. . . . But surely you are not well, dear Nikanor Vasilievich? You need treatment; madame, you should look after your husband. I ran round the palaces and the churches yesterday like a madman — of course you have visited the Doges' Palace? What wealth everywhere! Especially that large hall, and the place where Marino Faliero was executed — there he stands: *decapitati pro criminibus*. And I've been in the celebrated prisons; and that was where my soul rose in revolt — I, as you may remember, was always interested in social problems and revolted against the aristocracy. That is where I'd put the defenders of aristocracy: in those prisons. Byron said truly: 'I stood in Venice, on the Bridge of Sighs'; for that matter, he, too, was an aristocrat. I was always for progress. The younger generation is all for progress. But what do you think of the Anglo-French? We'll see whether Boustrapas[1] and Palmerston can do much. You know, Palmerston has become Prime Minister. But say what you like, the Russian fist is no joke! That Boustrapas is a terrible scoundrel! If you like I'll give you Victor Hugo's *Les Chatiments* — it's amazing! '*L'avenir le gendarme de Dieu*' — rather daringly put, but strong, strong. And Prince Vyazemsky put it well: 'Europe conforms Basha-Kadik-Lar, not turning its eyes from Sinope.' I am fond of poetry. I've got Proudhon's

[1] A contemptuous nickname for Napoleon III. (Tr.)

latest book too, I've got everything. I don't know about *you*, but I am glad of the war — so long as I am not wanted back at home, for I plan to go on from here to Florence, to Rome. France is out of the question, so I am thinking of going to Spain — the women there, they say, are marvelous, only there is a lot of poverty and insects. I'd dash off to California, it is all nothing to us Russians, but I have given my word to an editor to study in detail the question of trade in the Mediterranean. You'll say it is not an interesting and rather a special subject, but we need, we need specialists; we have done enough philosophizing, now we need practice, practice. . . . But you are very unwell, Nikanor Vasilievich, I may be exhausting you, but all the same I'll sit a little longer. . . ."

Lupoyarov crackled away for a long time in the same fashion, and when he went, he promised to devote much more time to them.

Worn out by the unexpected visit, Insarov lay down on the divan.

"There," he said bitterly, glancing at Yelena, "there is your younger generation! There are others who look big and put on airs, but in their souls they're just as much empty windbags as that gentleman."

Yelena made no reply to her husband: at that moment she was far more disturbed about Insarov's weakness than the state of the entire younger generation of Russia. . . . She sat down beside him and took up some work. He closed his eyes and lay motionless, very pale and thin. She glanced at his sharply outlined profile, at his outstretched arms and hands, and a sudden fear clutched at her heart.

"Dmitry — " she began.

He started.

"What? Has Rendich arrived?"

"Not yet. But what do you think? You are in a fever; you really are not at all well; wouldn't it be better to send for a doctor?"

"That windbag has frightened you. There's no need for a doctor. I shall have a little rest and it will all pass. After dinner we shall have another ride — somewhere."

Two hours passed. . . . Insarov was still lying on the divan, but he could not get to sleep, though he did not open his eyes. Yelena did not leave him; she dropped her work on her knees and did not stir.

"Why don't you sleep?" she asked him at last.

"Ah yes, wait a moment." He took her hand and laid it beneath his head. "There now — that's good. Wake me up as soon as Rendich arrives. If he says the boat is ready, we'll set off at once. . . . We'll have to pack everything."

"It won't take long to pack," she replied.

"What did that fellow say about a battle, about Serbia?" he asked a little later. "I expect he made it all up. But we must, we must go. We mustn't lose time. . . . Be prepared."

He fell asleep, and the room grew quiet.

Yelena leaned her head against the back of her armchair and gazed long out of the window. The weather had changed for the worse; a wind had risen. Great white clouds were tearing across the sky, a slender mast swayed in the distance, a long pennant with a red cross incessantly fluttered, fell and fluttered again. The pendulum of an ancient clock knocked oppressively, with a mournful wheeze. She closed her eyes. She had slept poorly all night; little by little she, too, fell asleep.

Strange was the dream she dreamed. It seemed that she was sailing in a boat over the Tsaritsino lake with some strangers. They were silent and sat motionless; no one was rowing; the boat floated on of itself. Yelena was not afraid, but bored; she was curious to know who these people were, and why she was with them. She looked, and the lake widened, the banks disappeared — now it was no longer a lake, but a restless sea: enormous, azure, silent waves majestically rocked the boat; something thundering, threatening, rose from the bottom, her unknown fellow travelers suddenly jumped up, shouted, waved their arms. . . . Yelena recognized their faces; among them was her father. But a white whirlwind came flying over the waves . . . everything whirled, everything was mingled in confusion. . . .

She looked about her: everything all around was white as before; but it was snow, snow, never ending snow. And now she was no longer in a boat, she was riding, as when she left Moscow, in a sleigh. She was not alone: beside her was sitting a little creature wrapped in a very old cloak. She looked closely at her companion: it was Katya, her poor little friend. Yelena was possessed with a feeling of horror. "But didn't she die, then?" she thought.

"Katya, where is it you and I are going?"

Katya did not reply and wrapped herself in her cloak; she was freezing. Yelena, too, felt cold. She looked away along the road; a town was visible in the distance amid the fine dust of the snow. Lofty white towers with silvery cupolas . . . "Katya, Katya, is that Moscow?" "No," thought Yelena, "that is the Solovietsky Monastery; in it are many, very many and narrow cells, like a hive; it is stifling, close, in there — Dmitry is shut away there. I must free him. . . ." Suddenly a gray, yawning abysm opened up before her. The sleigh fell into it. Katya laughed. "Yelena, Yelena!" came a voice from the abysm.

"Yelena!" sounded really in her ears. She swiftly raised her head, looked round, and was stupefied: Insarov, as white as snow, as the snow of her dream, had half risen from the divan and was gazing at her with dilated, gleaming, terrible eyes. His hair was scattered over his brow, his lips were parted strangely. Horror, mingled with a yearning emotion, was expressed on his suddenly transformed features.

"Yelena!" he said; "I am dying."

She fell with a cry to her knees and huddled against his breast.

"It is all over," he repeated, "I am dying. . . . Good-by, my poor little one. Good-by, my country! . . ."

He fell back on the divan.

She ran out of the room and called for help, the *camerière* rushed for a doctor. She dropped to the ground beside her husband.

At that moment a broad-shouldered, sunburnt man in a thick baize greatcoat and a sou'wester drawn over his eyes appeared at the door. He halted in astonishment.

"Rendich!" Yelena exclaimed. "Is it you? Look, for God's sake, he's in a bad way! What's the matter with him? My God, my God! We went for a ride only yesterday, he was talking to me only a moment ago. . . ."

Rendich did not speak and only stepped aside. A little figure in a peruke and spectacles slipped nimbly past him: it was a doctor who lived in the same hotel. He went across to Insarov.

"Signora," he said after a few moments, "the foreign gentleman is dead — *il signore forestiere e morto* — of aneurism, and collapse of the lungs."

35

Next day Rendich was standing by the window in the same room while Yelena, wrapped in a shawl, sat in front of him. Insarov was lying in a coffin in the next room. Yelena's face looked both terrified and lifeless; two fine furrows had appeared on her forehead, between the eyebrows; they gave a strained expression to her immobile eyes. On the window sill lay an opened letter from Anna Vasilievna. She had written to call her daughter back to Moscow, if only for a month; she complained of her loneliness, of Nikolai Artiomovich, sent her greetings to Insarov, inquired after his health, and asked him to let his wife go.

Rendich was a Dalmatian, a fisherman whom Insarov had come to know during his previous journey to his own country and had sought out again in Venice. He was a stern, rough, audacious man, and devoted to the Slavonic cause. He despised the Turks and hated the Austrians.

"How long will you have to remain in Venice?" Yelena asked him in Italian. And her voice was as lifeless as her face.

"A day, to take on cargo and to avoid arousing suspicions; and then straight to Zara. I shall not rejoice our fellow countrymen. They had long been waiting for him; they had set their hopes in him."

"They had set their hopes in him," Yelena repeated mechanically.

"When will the funeral be?" Rendich asked.

She answered, but not at once: "Tomorrow."

"Tomorrow? I shall stay; I would like to cast a handful of earth into his grave. And I must help you too. But best of all would be for him to lie in Slavonic earth."

She looked at him.

"Captain," she said, "take me and him and carry us to the other side of the sea, away from here. Is that possible?"

He thought for a moment.

"It is possible, only it is difficult. It will be necessary to bother the accursed local authorities here. But supposing we manage all that, and we bury him there; how am I to get you back?"

"You won't have to get me back."

"What? But where will you stay?"

"I shall find myself a place somewhere; only take us, take me."

Rendich scratched the nape of his neck.

"As you wish, but it is all very difficult. I'll go and try. But you be waiting here for me in a couple of hours' time."

He went off. Yelena passed into the other room, leaned against the wall, and stood there a long time, as though petrified. Then she dropped to her knees, but she could not pray. In her soul there were no reproaches; she did not dare to ask God why He had not spared, had not pitied, had not protected, why He had punished beyond the measure of the guilt, if there had been any guilt. Every one of us is guilty by the very fact that we are alive; and there is no thinker so great, no man such a benefactor to humanity, that he could hope to be entitled to live because of the benefit he has conferred. . . . Yelena could not pray: she was petrified.

That same night a broad boat cast off from the hotel where the Insarovs had lived. Yelena and Rendich were sitting in the boat, and a long box covered with black cloth was lying in it. They rowed for about an hour, and at last floated up to a small two-masted ship anchored at the very entrance to the harbor. Yelena and Rendich boarded the ship; sailors hoisted up the box. About midnight a storm sprang up, but in the morning the ship sailed past the Lido. During that day the storm raged with terrible violence, and the experienced mariners in the Lloyds offices shook their heads and did not expect any good to come of it. The Adriatic Sea between Venice, Trieste, and the Dalmatian coast is extremely dangerous.

Three weeks after Yelena's departure from Venice, Anna Vasilievna received the following letter in Moscow:

My dear parents, I am saying good-by to you forever. You will never see me again. Dmitry died yesterday. Everything is finished for me. I shall bury him, and I don't know what will happen to me. But now I have no other country than D.'s country. A rising is in preparation there, the people are getting ready for war; I shall go as a nurse; I shall care for the sick and wounded. I do not know what will happen to me, but though D. is dead I shall remain faithful to his memory, to his life task. I have learned Bulgarian and Serbian. In all probability I shall not survive all this — so much the better. I have been led to the edge of the abyss and

*must fall. Fate did not unite us for nothing. Who knows, perhaps
I killed him; now it is his turn to drag me after him. I have sought
happiness — and I find, perhaps, death. Evidently that was to be;
evidently there was guilt. . . . But death covers all and reconciles
all — is that not so?*

*Forgive me all the affliction I have caused you: that was not
within my power to avert. But to return to Russia — to what end?
What is to be done in Russia?*

Accept my last embraces and blessings and do not condemn me.

E.

Some five years have passed already since that day, and no
further news whatever has come of Yelena. All letters and in-
quiries have been fruitless. In vain did Nikolai Artiomovich himself travel to Venice and Zara when peace was concluded. In
Venice he learned what the reader already knows, but in Zara no
one could give him any positive information concerning Rendich
and the ship he had chartered. There were obscure rumors that
apparently some years previously the sea, after a violent storm,
had flung a coffin up on the shore, and in it was a man's corpse.
. . . According to other, more reliable reports, this coffin was not
flung up by the sea at all, but was brought and buried near the
shore by a foreign lady who arrived from Venice. Some added
that this lady was afterward seen in Herzegovina among the
troops that were then being assembled; they even described her
costume, black from head to foot. Whether this was so or not, all
traces of Yelena vanished forever and irrevocably, and no one
knows whether she is still alive, is hiding somewhere, or whether
that little play of life is already ended, her gentle ferment has
ended, and death's turn has come. Sometimes it happens that a
man, on awakening, asks himself in involuntary alarm: "Am I
really already thirty — forty — fifty years old? How is it life has
passed so swiftly? How is it death has approached so close to
me?" Death is like a fisherman who has caught a fish in his net
and leaves it for the time being in the water; the fish still swims,
but the net is around it, and the fisherman will drag it out — when
he so wishes.

What has happened to the other characters in our story?
Anna Vasilievna is still alive; she aged considerably after the

blow that fell upon her, and she complains less, but grieves far more. Nikolai Artiomovich also has grown older and grayer, and has parted from Avgustina Khristianovna. He now reviles everything foreign. His housekeeper, a beautiful woman of about thirty, a Russian, goes about in silk gowns and wears gold rings and earrings. Kurnatovsky, as a man with temperament, and as an energetic representative of the dark-haired men who admire amiable blondes, has married Zoya; she is completely his slave and has even ceased to think in German. Berseniev is in Heidelberg. He was sent abroad at government expense; he has visited Berlin and Paris, and is not wasting his time; an efficient professor will come of him. The scientific world has drawn attention to his two articles: "On Certain Peculiarities of Ancient German Law in the Matter of Judicial Punishment" and "On the Importance of the Urban Element in the Problem of Civilization." But it is a pity that both articles were written in a rather ponderous style and are sprinkled with foreign words. Shubin is in Rome; he has devoted himself entirely to his art and is regarded as one of the most remarkable and highly promising of the younger sculptors. The strict purists consider that he has not studied the ancients sufficiently, that he has no "style," and allocate him to the French school. He is getting enormous numbers of commissions from the English and the Americans. Of recent days his *Bacchante* has caused much excitement; the Russian Count Boboshkin, well known as a wealthy man, intended to purchase it for a thousand scudi, but preferred to give three thousand to another sculptor, a Frenchman *pur sang*, for a group representing "a young peasant woman, dying of love on the breast of the Genius of Spring." Shubin occasionally corresponds with Uvar Ivanovich, who alone has not changed in the least or in any way. "Do you remember," Shubin wrote to him recently, "what you said to me that night when we heard the news of poor Yelena's marriage, when I sat on your bed and talked to you? You remember, I asked you then whether we would ever have the men, and you answered that 'they would come.' Oh, black-earth force! So now too, I, from hence, from my 'beautiful distance,' again ask you: well, what now, Uvar Ivanovich, will they come?"

Uvar Ivanovich wriggled his fingers and gazed into the distance with his enigmatic gaze.

Rudin

1855

I

IT was a quiet summer morning. The sun was already fairly high in the clear sky, but the fields were still glistening with dew; a fragrant freshness breathed from the recently awakened valleys, and in the forest, still damp and soundless, the little early birds were singing merrily. On the crest of a rolling hill, which was covered from crest to foot with newly ripened rye, was a small village. Toward this village a young woman in a white muslin gown and a round straw hat, and carrying a parasol, was making her way along a byroad. A page followed a little distance behind her.

She was walking leisurely, and seemed to be enjoying her walk. All around her, over the tall supple rye, long waves ran with a gentle rustle, speckling it with successive silvery-green and reddish patches; skylarks were singing away high above her. The young woman was walking from her own village, which was not quite a mile from the little hamlet for which she was making; her name was Alexandra Pavlovna Lipina. She was a widow, childless and reasonably rich, and she lived with her brother, a retired cavalry captain named Sergei Pavlich Volintsiev, who was unmarried, and administered her estate.

Alexandra Pavlovna reached the hamlet, stopped outside the first hut, a very ramshackle and humble one, and, calling her page to her, ordered him to go in and ask after the woman's health. He soon returned, accompanied by a senile peasant with a white beard.

"Well, what is the news?" Alexandra Pavlovna asked.

"She's still alive . . ." the old man said.

"May I come in?"

"Why not? Of course."

Alexandra Pavlovna entered the hut. It was close and stuffy and

559

smoky inside. . . . Someone began to stir and groan on the stove sleeping-place. Alexandra Pavlovna looked about her, and through the murk saw an old woman's yellow and furrowed face, framed in a checkered shawl. A peasant's heavy overcoat covered her up to her neck; she had difficulty in getting her breath and moved her thin arms feebly.

Alexandra Pavlovna went up to the old woman and touched her forehead with her fingers; it was burning hot.

"How do you feel, Matriona?" she asked, bending over the sleeping-place.

"O-oh!" the old woman groaned, fixing her eyes on Alexandra Pavlovna. "Bad, bad, my dear! My time has come, my lady!"

"God is merciful, Matriona: perhaps you'll get better. You've taken the medicine I sent you?"

The old woman groaned miserably and did not answer. She had not caught the question.

"She's taken it," said the old man, who had halted at the door. Alexandra Pavlovna turned to him.

"Isn't there anybody to look after her except you?" she asked.

"There's a girl, her granddaughter, but she's always out. She can't sit for long, she's so fidgety. It's too much trouble for her even to give her granny a sip of water. And I'm old myself — what can I do?"

"Why not have her taken to my hospital?"

"No; why take her to hospital? She'll die in any case. She's had a long life; it must be God's will. She'll never get down from the stove. What's the good of sending her to the hospital? As soon as they try to lift her up she'll die."

"Oh!" the sick woman groaned; "beautiful lady, don't leave my little orphan; our masters are far away, but you — "

The old woman was silent. She had exhausted her strength in saying so much. "Don't worry," Alexandra Pavlovna said; "everything will be attended to. Look, I've brought you some tea and sugar. If you feel like it, you have a good drink — of course you have a samovar," she added, glancing at the old man.

"Samovar, did you say? We haven't got a samovar, but we can get one."

"Then get one, or I'll send you one of mine. And tell your granddaughter that she's not to run off and leave her. Tell her she ought to be ashamed."

The old man made no answer, but he took the packet of paper containing tea and sugar with both hands.

"Well, good-by, Matriona," said Alexandra Pavlovna; "I'll come again soon, and don't you worry, and you take the medicine regularly. . . ."

The old woman raised her head and drew herself toward Alexandra Pavlovna.

"Give me your little hand, lady," she murmured.

Alexandra Pavlovna did not take her hand, she bent over her and kissed her on the forehead.

"Now mind!" she said to the old man as she went out, "be sure to give her the medicine, as it says. And give her tea to drink. . . ."

The old man again said nothing and only bowed.

Alexandra Pavlovna breathed freely when she found herself in the fresh air. She opened her parasol and was about to set off for home when a man about thirty years of age, in an old coat of coarse gray linen and a cap of the same material, suddenly drove round the corner in a low racing sulky. Seeing Alexandra Pavlovna, he at once reined in his horse and turned his face toward her. His face was broad, and with no color in the cheeks, with its small, pale gray eyes and fair whiskers, it matched the hue of his clothes.

"Good morning," he said with a sleepy smile; "what are you doing here, may I ask?"

"I've been visiting a sick woman. . . . But where have you come from, Mikhaïl Mikhaïlich?"

The man named Mikhaïl Mikhaïlich gazed into her eyes and again smiled.

"It's kind of you to visit the sick woman," he went on, "only wouldn't it be better if you took her to the hospital?"

"She's too weak; she can't be moved."

"So you're not intending to close down your hospital, then?"

"Close it down? What ever for?"

"Why, just to close it down."

"What a strange idea! What made you think of that?"

"Why, you're always going about with Lasunskaya, and she seems to have some influence over you. And according to her, hospitals and schools are all nonsense, they're all unnecessary inventions. Philanthropy ought to be personal, and education too;

561

it is all a work of the soul — that is how she puts it, I think. Who makes her talk like that, I'd like to know."

Alexandra Pavlovna laughed.

"Daria Mikhailovna is an intelligent woman; I like and respect her very much; but even she can be mistaken, and I don't believe every word she says."

"And very wise of you," Mikhail Mikhailich retorted, still remaining seated in his sulky, "because she herself doesn't believe much in what she says. But I'm very glad I've met you."

"Why are you?"

"What a fine question! As though it were not always pleasant to meet you! Today you are as fresh and delightful as the morning."

Alexandra Pavlovna laughed again.

"What are you laughing at?"

"You may well ask! If only you could see the limp and chilly manner in which you paid your compliment! My only wonder is that you didn't yawn over the last word."

"A chilly manner. . . . You're always looking for fire, but fire is good for nothing. It flames up, begins to smoke, and then goes out."

"But it warms," Alexandra Pavlovna caught him up.

"Yes — and it burns."

"Well, what if it does burn! That's no misfortune. At any rate it is better than — "

"But I'll be interested to see what you say once you've been well burned," Mikhail Mikhailich interrupted her in an annoyed tone, and slapped his horse with the reins. "Good-by!"

"Mikhail Mikhailich, wait a moment!" Alexandra Pavlovna called to him; "when are you coming to see us?"

"Tomorrow; my regards to your brother."

And the sulky dashed off.

Alexandra Pavlovna stared after Mikhail Mikhailich.

"What a sack!" she thought. Hunched up, dusty, with his cap on the back of his head and strands of yellow hair poking untidily from under the cap, he certainly did look like a large sack of flour.

Alexandra Pavlovna quietly made her way back home. She walked with downcast eyes. The clatter of a horse's hoofs close at hand caused her to stop and raise her head. . . . Her brother was riding to meet her; walking beside him was a young man of medium height, in a light unbuttoned coat, a light cravat, and a light gray hat, with a light cane in his hand. He had smiled at Alexandra Pavlovna long before, though he saw that she was walking in a reverie, not noticing anything; and as soon as she halted he went up to her and said joyfully, almost tenderly:

"Good morning, Alexandra Pavlovna, good morning!"

"Ah! Konstantin Diumidich! Good morning!" she replied. "Has Daria Mikhailovna sent you?"

"Precisely so, precisely so," the young man answered with beaming face. "Daria Mikhailovna has sent me to you; I preferred to walk. . . . The morning is so beautiful, and it is only three miles. When I reached the house you were not at home. Your dear brother told me you had gone to Semionovka village, and he himself was intending to go out to the fields; and so I came along with him, to meet you. Ye-es. How pleasant it is!"

The young man spoke pure and correct Russian, but with a foreign accent, though it was difficult to determine what exactly the accent was. There was an Asiatic quality in the features of his face. The long hooked nose, the large, slanting, immobile eyes, the thick crimson lips, the retreating forehead, hair as black as pitch — everything in his face indicated an Eastern origin, yet the young man was named Pandalevsky and said his native town was Odessa, though he had been educated somewhere in Byelorussia, at the expense of a philanthropic and wealthy widow. Another widow had obtained him a position. All together, middle-aged ladies were fond of patronizing Konstantin Diumidich; he was clever at seeking them out and making a hit with them. Even now he was living with a wealthy woman landowner, Daria Mikhailovna Lasunskaya, as an adopted son or a hanger-on. He was very affectionate, complaisant, sensitive, and secretly sensual, he had a pleasant voice, played the piano well, and had the habit, when talking to anybody, of staring at them. He dressed very neatly and cleanly and wore his clothes an extraordinarily long time, shaved his broad chin very assiduously, and brushed his hair very flat and smooth.

Alexandra Pavlovna heard him to the end, then turned to her brother.

"I'm having nothing but meetings today; I've just been talking to Lezhniov."

"Ah, to Lezhniov? Was he going somewhere?"

"Yes; and just imagine, he was driving a sulky, and wearing a kind of canvas sack all covered with dust. . . . What a queer fellow he is!"

"Yes, maybe; but he's a fine fellow."

"Whom did you say? Mr. Lezhniov?" Pandalevsky asked, as though surprised.

"Yes, Mikhailo Mikhailich Lezhniov," Volintsiev retorted. "But good-by, sister; it's time I was off to the fields; they're sowing your buckwheat. Mr. Pandalevsky will escort you home. . . ."

And he rode off at a trot.

"With the greatest of pleasure!" Konstantin Diumidich exclaimed, and he offered Alexandra Pavlovna his arm.

She took it, and they walked along the road leading to her house.

Evidently it gave Konstantin Diumidich great pleasure to walk arm in arm with Alexandra Pavlovna; he took little steps, smiled, and his Oriental eyes even went moist, which, however, was no rare occurrence with him: it cost him no effort to be moved and to shed tears. And who would not find it pleasant to have a beautiful, young, and well-favored woman on his arm? All the province of —— declared unanimously that Alexandra Pavlovna was charming; and the province of —— was not mistaken. Just her straight, very slightly turned-up little nose was sufficient to send any man frantic, not to speak of her velvety hazel eyes, her golden auburn hair, the dimples in her rounded little cheeks, and her other beauties. But best of all was the expression of her charming face; trusting, good-natured, and modest, it was touching and attractive. Alexandra Pavlovna looked and smiled like a baby; other young ladies found her rather simple. . . . Could one wish for anything else?

"You said Daria Mikhailich sent you to me?" she asked Pandalevsky.

"Ye-es, she sent me," he answered, pronouncing the letter "s" like the English soft "th"; "they categorically desired and commanded me to ask you earnestly to have dinner with them today. . . . They" (when he was referring to a third person, especially a lady, Pandalevsky strictly observed the plural number) "are expecting a new guest, to whom they categorically wish to introduce you."

"Who is it?"

"He is a Baron Muffel, of Petersburg, and a gentleman in waiting. Daria Mikhailovna recently made his acquaintance at Prince Harin's house, and they speak very highly of him as an amiable and educated young man. The Baron also occupies himself with literature, or, I should say — ah, what a charming butterfly! Let me draw your attention to it. — I should say, political economy. He has written an article about some very interesting question, and wishes to submit it to Daria Mikhailovna's judgment."

"An article on political economy?"

"From the literary aspect, Alexandra Pavlovna, from the literary aspect. I think you know that Daria Mikhailovna is an expert on that subject. Zhukovsky has sought her advice, and a benefactor of mine who lives in Odessa, the invaluable old man Roksolan Mediarovich Ksandrika — of course you know the name?"

"Not at all, I haven't even heard it before."

"Not heard of such a man? Amazing! I was about to say that Roksolan Mediarovich also has always had a very high opinion of Daria Mikhailovna's knowledge in the sphere of the Russian language."

"But isn't this Baron a pedant?" Alexandra Pavlovna asked.

"Not in the least; Daria Mikhailovna says that, on the contrary, one can recognize him at once as a man of the world. He talked of Beethoven with such eloquence that even the old Prince went into raptures. . . . That, I admit, even I would readily listen to; for that is within my province. Allow me to offer you this beautiful wild flower."

Alexandra Pavlovna took the flower, but, after walking a few steps, let it fall on the road. . . . Now they were only some two hundred paces, no more, from her house. Of recent construction and newly limewashed, with its broad, clear windows it looked out hospitably from a dense green of old limes and maples.

"So what do you command me to report to Daria Mikhailovna?" Pandalevsky spoke again, a little offended by the fate of the flower he had offered. "Will you come to dinner? She invites your brother too."

"Yes, we'll come, without fail. But what of Natalia?"

"Natalia Alexeevna is well, thank God! . . . But we've already passed the road to Daria Mikhailovna's estate. Permit me to take my leave of you."

Alexandra Pavlovna halted. "But aren't you going to call on us?" she asked in an uncertain tone.

"I would be sincerely delighted, but I am afraid of being late. Daria Mikhailovna wishes to hear a new étude by Thalberg, so I must prepare and study it. Moreover, I confess that I doubt whether my conversation can give you any pleasure."

"But, indeed — why do you — ?"

Pandalevsky sighed and expressively cast his eyes down.

"Good-by, Alexandra Pavlovna," he said after a momentary silence; he bowed and dropped back.

Alexandra Pavlovna turned and went home.

Konstantin Diumidich also went home. All the sweetness at once vanished from his face. A self-confident, almost harsh expression appeared on it. Even his gait was changed: now he took longer strides and trod more heavily. He walked a mile or so, jauntily swinging his cane, and suddenly smirked again: by the roadside he saw a young, quite good-looking peasant girl driving calves away from a field of oats. Konstantin Diumidich went up to the girl as cautiously as a cat and fell into conversation with her. At first she was silent, flushing and smiling, but at last she covered her mouth with her sleeve, turned away, and said:

"Go along, sir; I really — "

Konstantin Diumidich threatened her with his finger and ordered her to gather him some cornflowers.

"What do you want cornflowers for? Going to twine garlands?" the girl retorted; "now, do get along, really — "

"Listen, my dear — my little beauty," Konstantin Diumidich began.

"Oh, do go along!" the girl interrupted. "Here come the young masters."

Konstantin Diumidich looked round. He saw Vania and Piotya, Daria Mikhailovna's sons, running along the road, with their teacher, Basistov, a young man of twenty-two, a recent graduate of the university, walking behind them. Basistov was well built, with a simple face, a large nose, big lips, and little pig's eyes, he was an ugly and clumsy, but decent, honest, and straightforward man. He dressed carelessly and did not have his hair cut — not out of any desire to be different, but because he was lazy; he was fond of eating, fond of sleeping, but was also fond of good books and exciting conversation, and he hated Pandalevsky with all his soul.

Daria Mikhailovna's children worshipped Basistov and were quite unafraid of him; with everybody else in the house he was on good terms, which was not altogether to the mistress's liking, no matter how much she maintained that she was entirely without prejudices.

"Good morning, my dear boys," said Konstantin Diumidich; "how early you are out walking this morning! But I," he added, turning to Basistov, "have been out for a long time; it is a passion of mine to enjoy nature."

"We saw you enjoying nature!" Basistov muttered.

"You're a materialist: even now God knows what you are thinking. I know you!"

When talking to Basistov or similar people Pandalevsky always grew a little irritated and then pronounced the letter "s" cleanly, even with a slight whistle.

"Well, I suppose you were asking that girl the way?" Basistov said, shifting his gaze to right and left. He felt that Pandalevsky was staring him straight in the face, and he found that extremely unpleasant.

"I repeat, you are a materialist and nothing more. You always try to see only the prosaic side in everything. . . ."

"Boys!" Basistov suddenly commanded. "Do you see that willow in the meadow? Let's see who reaches it first — one! two! three!"

And the two boys tore off headlong toward the willow. Basistov rushed after them.

"The peasant!" thought Pandalevsky; "he's spoiling those lads. . . . He's an absolute peasant!"

And, casting a satisfied glance over his own trim and elegant little figure, Konstantin Diumidich brushed his outspread fingers over his coat sleeve a couple of times, then brushed his collar and went on. When he reached his room he put on an old dressing-gown and sat down thoughtfully at the piano.

2

The house owned by Daria Mikhailovna Lasunskaya was regarded as all but the finest in all the province of ——. A huge brick building constructed according to Rastrelli sketches in the taste of the last century, it rose majestically on the crest of a low hill, at the foot of which flowed one of the largest rivers of central Russia. Daria Mikhailovna herself was a wealthy lady of quality, the widow of a privy councilor. Though Pandalevsky was in the habit of saying of her that she knew all Europe, and all Europe knew her! — in fact, Europe knew her very little, and she played no important role even in Petersburg; on the other hand, everybody in Moscow knew her and called on her. She belonged to the highest society and was reputed to be a rather strange, not altogether good, but extraordinarily intelligent woman. In her youth she had been very beautiful. Poets had written poems to her, young men had fallen in love with her, important gentlemen had dangled around her. But twenty-five or thirty years had passed since that time, and not a trace of her former charms was left. "Surely," anyone who saw her for the first time involuntarily asked himself, "surely that little, thin, yellowish, peaknosed, and still by no means old woman was never a beauty? Surely she is not the one for whom lyres were strummed?" And everybody mentally wondered at the mutability of all earthly things. True, Pandalevsky considered that Daria Mikhailovna had kept her magnificent eyes amazingly; but then Pandalevsky also declared that all Europe knew her.

Daria Mikhailovna and her children spent every summer at her country home (she had three children; her daughter Natalia, aged seventeen, and her two sons, aged ten and nine), and she kept open house; in other words, she welcomed male visitors, especially bachelors; she could not endure the provincial ladies. But how much she suffered in consequence from those ladies! According to them, Daria Mikhailovna was arrogant, and immoral, and a terrible tyrant; but, worst of all, she allowed herself such freedom in conversation that one was shocked! Certainly Daria Mikhailovna did not like to put any constraints on herself in the country, and in the free simplicity of her behavior one could distinguish some suggestion of a metropolitan lioness's contempt for the rather obscure and petty creatures around her. . . . She was very free and easy with her town acquaintances also and even derisive; but there was no hint of contempt in her attitude to them.

By the way, reader: have you ever noticed that a man may be unusually abstracted in a circle of subordinates, but is never abstracted with his superiors? Why should that be? However, such questions do not get us anywhere.

When Konstantin Diumidich had at last learned the Thalberg étude by heart and went down from his clean and cheerful room into the reception hall, he found all the household already gathered. The salon had begun. The mistress was arranged on a broad couch, with her feet tucked under her, and was turning over the leaves of a new French brochure in her hands; sitting by the window, at embroidery frames, were Daria Mikhailovna's daughter on one side, and Mlle Boncourt on the other; Mlle Boncourt was the governess, a withered old maid of sixty years, with a wig of black hair under a varicolored mobcap, and cotton wool in her ears; Basistov had placed himself in the corner by the door and was reading a newspaper; beside him Piotya and Vania were playing checkers, while the gentleman of rather stocky build, with hair tousled and gray, a swarthy face, and black, shifty little eyes, who was leaning against the stove with his hands behind his back, was named Afrikan Semionich Pigasov.

A strange man was this Mr. Pigasov. He was always in a temper with all and everything, but especially women, and fumed at everything from morn till night, sometimes very much to the point, sometimes quite stupidly, but always to his own satisfaction. He was cantankerous almost to the point of childishness; his laugh, the sound of his voice, all his being seemed to be soaked in bile. Daria Mikhailovna gave him a ready welcome to her house: he diverted her with his sallies. They certainly were quite amusing. It was a passion of his always to exaggerate. For instance, no matter what misfortune was mentioned in his presence — if someone told him that a village had been burned down after being struck by lightning, water had carried away a mill, a peasant had chopped off his own hand with an axe — he always asked with concentrated spleen: "And what is her name?" — in other words, who was the woman who had caused this misfortune, for he was convinced that all misfortunes were due to some woman or other, if you only got to the bottom of the affair. One day he flung himself down on his knees before a young lady almost unknown to him, who had pestered him with an invitation, and began lachrymosely but with a furious look to implore her to spare him, he had not done her any wrong and never would in the future either. One day a horse dashing downhill ran into one of Daria Mikhailovna's washerwomen, flung her into a ditch, and all but killed her. After that he always spoke of this horse as a "good, kind little horse," and regarded the hill and the ditch as very picturesque spots. He had not made a success of life, and that was why he affected this nonsense.

He was of poor parents. His father had occupied various petty positions, was barely literate, and did not trouble about his son's education; he fed and clothed him, and that was all. His mother had spoiled him, but she died early. Pigasov educated himself, obtained his own place in the county school, then in a high school, learned French, German, and even Latin, and, leaving the high school with an excellent certificate, went to Dorpat University, where he continually struggled with want, but attended the three-year course to the end. His capacities were not above the ordinary; he was distinguished by patience and persistence, but he had a particularly strong sense of ambition, a desire to move in good society, and not to be left behind, in despite of fate. He studied diligently, and entered Dorpat University out of ambition. Poverty annoyed him and developed in him a gift of observation and cunning. He always had an original way of expressing himself; but from youth up he developed a peculiar kind of splenetic and provocative eloquence. His thoughts did not rise above the general level; but his manner of speaking was such that he appeared to be not only an intelligent, but even a very intelligent man.

Having gained a Bachelor's degree, he decided to devote himself to learning; he realized that in any other career he could not keep up with his companions (he endeavored to choose them from a higher circle and was ready to ingratiate himself with them, even to fawn on them, though he fulminated against everything). But, to put it simply, he lacked the material for the savant's life. He had gained himself an education not because he had any love of knowledge, and fundamentally he knew too little. He failed miserably in debate, whereas the student who shared a room with him, whom he continually laughed at, a man of very restricted mind but with a sound and solid education, achieved complete triumph. This failure infuriated Pigasov: he flung all his primers and exercise books into the fire and entered the civil service.

At first he did not do badly: though he was not particularly good as an official, he was efficient; but he was also extremely self-confident and audacious; however, he wanted to rise in the world too quickly — he got involved in difficulties, made a mistake, and had to retire. He spent some three years at home in a little villa he had acquired, and suddenly married a rich, half-educated woman landowner, whom he caught on the hook of his free and easy and scoffing manners. But now all his conduct was too splenetic and sour; he was oppressed by family life. . . . After living with him for several years, his wife secretly went off to Moscow and sold her estate to some clever speculator, though Pigasov had only just built a house on it. Shaken to his foundations by this last blow, he planned to go to law with his wife, but failed to win. . . . Now he was living out his life in loneliness; he called on his neighbors, whom he reviled behind their backs and even to their faces, and who received him with a forced half-laugh, though he did not inspire them with any serious alarm — and never picked up a book. He possessed about a hundred souls; his peasants were not badly off.

"Ah! Konstantin!" Daria Mikhailovna said as soon as Pandalevsky entered the reception hall. "Will Alexandrine be coming?"

"Alexandra Pavlovna bade me thank you and regards it as a particular pleasure," Konstantin Diumidich reported, amiably bowing in all directions and touching his beautifully coiffured hair with a plump but white little hand with pointed nails.

"And will Volintsiev also be coming?"

"Yes, they will be coming too."

"Well then, Afrikan Semionich," Daria Mikhailovna continued, turning to Pigasov, "so in your view all young ladies are unnatural?"

Pigasov's lips writhed to one side, and he nervously tugged at his elbow.

"I say," he began in an unhurrying voice — even in his most violent attacks of spleen he always spoke slowly and distinctly — "I say that young ladies generally — of course I am silent in regard to company present — "

"But that doesn't prevent your thinking of them too," Daria Mikhailovna interrupted.

"I am silent in regard to them," Pigasov repeated. "All young ladies generally are unnatural to the highest degree — unnatural in the expression of their feelings. If a young lady is frightened, for instance, or delighted with something, or sad, she always first gives her body some elegant twist like this" (and Pigasov hideously twisted his waist and stuck out his fingers rigidly) "and then cries 'Ah!' or begins to laugh or cry. However, I did once succeed" (and here he smiled self-satisfiedly) "in obtaining a genuine, sincere expression of her sensations from one remarkably unnatural young lady."

"And how did you do that?"

Pigasov's eyes began to sparkle.

"I came up behind her and whacked her with an ash stake on her side. You should have heard her squeal! But I said to her: 'Bravo! Bravo! Now, that is the voice of nature, that was a natural cry. . . . And you behave like that in the future!'"

Everybody in the room laughed.

"What rubbish you do talk, Afrikan Semionich!" Daria Mikhailovna exclaimed. "Am I to believe that you could hit a girl in the side with a stake?"

"It's the very truth, I hit her with a stake, quite a large stake, the kind they use in defense of a fortress."

"*Mais c'est une horreur ce que vous dites là monsieur,*" Mlle Boncourt cried out, giving the laughing children a menacing look.

"Don't you believe him," Daria Mikhailovna said; "don't you know him yet?"

But the indignant Frenchwoman would not be appeased for a long time and went on muttering something to herself.

"You may not believe me," Pigasov continued in an unconcerned tone, "but I assert that I have said the absolute truth. Who should know if not I? After that I don't suppose you will believe that our neighbor Chepuzova, Yelena Antonovna herself — note that, herself — told me how she tortured her own niece."

"Now for some more imagination!"

"Excuse me, excuse me! Listen and judge for yourselves. Note that I have no desire to slander her, I am even fond of her, in so far, that is, as one may be fond of a woman: in all her house she hasn't a single book except annuals, and she cannot read except aloud — and that exercise puts her in a perspiration and afterward she complains that her eyes are popping out. . . . In a word, she's a fine woman, and she has some fat maids. Why should I slander her?"

"Well!" Daria Mikhailovna remarked, "Afrikan Semionich has mounted his hobbyhorse; now he won't dismount till evening."

"My hobbyhorse! But women have no less than three, from which they never dismount — except when they're asleep."

"And what are those three hobbyhorses?"

"Condemnation, insinuation, and reprobation."

"Do you know what, Afrikan Semionich?" Daria Mikhailovna began; "there must be some reason why you hate women so much. Some woman must have — "

"Done me some wrong, are you going to say?" Pigasov interrupted her.

Daria Mikhailovna was a little embarrassed; she remembered his unfortunate marriage . . . and only nodded.

"One woman certainly did do me a wrong," Pigasov said, "though she was a good woman, very good. . . ."

"And who was she?"

"My mother," he said, lowering his voice.

"Your mother? And how did she do you any wrong?"

"By giving birth to me. . . ."

Daria Mikhailovna knitted her brows.

"It seems to me," she said, "that our conversation is taking a mournful turn. . . . Konstantin, play that new étude of Thalberg to us. Perhaps the sounds of music will tame Afrikan Semionich. For Orpheus tamed wild beasts."

Konstantin Diumidich sat down at the piano and played the étude very satisfactorily. At first Natalia Alexeevna listened attentively, then she turned again to her embroidery.

"*Merci, c'est charmant*," Daria Mikhailovna said, "I am fond of Thalberg. *Il est si distingué.* What are you thinking about, Afrikan Semionich?"

"I was thinking," Pigasov began slowly, "that there are three categories of egotists: the egotists who live themselves and let others live: the egotists who live themselves and do not let others live; and finally the egotists who do not live themselves and will not let others live either. The majority of women belong to the third category."

"How very kind of you! Only one thing surprises me, Afrikan Semionich, and that is the self-confidence you have in your judgments, as though you can never be wrong."

"Who says so! I can make mistakes too; even a man can make

mistakes. But do you know the difference between the mistakes we men make and those of a woman? You don't? It's this: a man can say, for instance, that twice two are not four, but five, or three and a half; but a woman will say that twice two is a wax candle."

"I think I have heard that from you before. . . . But may I ask what connection there is between your idea of the three kinds of egotists and the music we have just listened to?"

"No connection at all, and I didn't even listen to the music."

"Well, 'thou, father, I see, art incorrigible, so drop it,' " Daria Mikhailovna retorted, slightly twisting Griboyedov's line. "Then, what do you like, if you don't like music? Literature, I suppose?"

"I am fond of literature, but not the present-day kind."

"Why not?"

"I'll tell you why not. I recently crossed the Oka on a ferry with a certain gentleman. The ferry put in at a steep part of the bank, the carriages had to be pulled up by hand. The gentleman had a particularly heavy carriage. While the ferrymen were straining themselves to drag the carriage onto the bank, the gentleman groaned so bitterly as he stood on the ferry that one even felt sorry for him. . . . There, I thought, is a new application of the system of division of labor! And that's like our current literature: others haul and do all the work, but it does the groaning."

Daria Mikhailovna smiled.

"And that is called the reproduction of contemporary existence," the indefatigable Pigasov went on; "profound sympathy for social questions, and I don't know what else. . . . Oh, how I dislike those high-flown words!"

"But then the women whom you're always attacking, they at any rate don't use high-flown words."

He shrugged his shoulders.

"They don't use them because they don't know them."

Daria Mikhailovna reddened a little.

"You're beginning to be insolent, Afrikan Semionich!" she remarked with a forced smile.

There was a hush in the room.

"Where is this Zolotonosha?" one of the boys suddenly asked Basistov.

"In Poltava province, my boy," Pigasov hastened to answer;

"in the heart of Khokhlandia." [1] (He was glad of an opportunity to change the conversation.) "Now, we were talking about literature," he went on; "if I had money to spare I'd at once become a Little Russian poet."

"And what next? A fine poet!" Daria Mikhailovna retorted. "Do you know Little Russian, then?"

"Not in the least; nor is it necessary."

"Why isn't it?"

"Why, it just isn't! You only have to pick up a sheet of paper and write at the top: 'Thoughts,' and then begin: 'Ah, thou lot of mine, thou lot of mine!' or 'The little Cossack Nalivaiko sits on a mound,' or 'Down the hill, down the green, play, play, la-de-hey, hop hop!' or something of that sort. And you've done the trick! Print and publish! The Little Russian will read it, will rest his cheek on his hand, and will surely weep, he is such a sensitive soul!"

"Excuse me," Basistov exclaimed, "why do you talk like that? That doesn't correspond with the truth. I have lived in Little Russia, I love it, and I know its language; 'play, play, la-de-hey,' is absolute nonsense."

"Maybe, but the Khokhol will cry all the same. You call it a language. But is there such a thing as a Little Russian language? I once asked a certain Khokhol to translate the following phrase, the first that came into my head: 'Grammar is the art of correct reading and writing.' Do you know how he translated it? Into exactly the same words, only with a slightly different pronunciation. . . . Well, and do you call that a language? A separate language? Why, rather than agree I am ready to let my best friend be pounded in a mortar. . . ."

Basistov was about to make some retort.

"Let him be," Daria Mikhailovna said, "you know you will never hear anything but paradoxes from him."

Pigasov smiled venomously. A footman entered and reported that Alexandra Pavlovna and her brother had arrived.

Daria Mikhailovna rose to meet her guests.

"Good afternoon, Alexandrine," she said, going up to her; "how very sensible of you to come! . . . Good afternoon, Sergei Pavlich!"

[1] Khokhlandia, the land of the Khokhols. "Khokhol" is a Russian nickname universally used for Ukrainians. (Tr.)

Volintsiev squeezed Daria Mikhailovna's hand and went across to Natalia Alexeevna.

"Tell me, is that Baron, your new acquaintance, coming today?" Pigasov asked.

"Yes, he's coming."

"They say he's a great philosopher: he oozes Hegel."

Daria Mikhailovna made no reply; she seated Alexandra Pavlovna on the couch and sat down beside her.

"Philosophy," Pigasov continued, "is a higher viewpoint! But take my death: that is a higher viewpoint too. And what can you see from above? I believe that when you want to buy a horse you don't look it over from the top of a watchtower."

"The Baron intended to bring you some article, didn't he?" Alexandra Pavlovna asked.

"Yes, an article," Daria Mikhailovna replied with exaggerated unconcern, "on the relations between trade and industry in Russia. . . . But don't be afraid: we shan't stop to read it here — I haven't invited you for that. *Le Baron est aussi aimable que savant.* He speaks Russian so well! *C'est un vrai torrent — il vous entraîne.*"

"He talks Russian so well," snorted Pigasov, "that he is deserving of praise in French."

"Snort away, Afrikan Semionich, snort away! . . . It suits your disheveled coiffure very well. . . . All the same, why hasn't he arrived yet? Do you know what, *messieurs et mesdames,*" Daria Mikhailovna added, glancing around her, "let us go into the garden. . . . There is still an hour or so to dinner, and the weather's glorious. . . ."

All the company rose and went into the garden.

Daria Mikhailovna's garden ran right to the edge of the river. In it there were many old lime avenues, deep golden and scented, with emerald vistas at the ends, and many arbors of acacia and lilac.

Volintsiev went with Natalia and Mlle Boncourt into the very heart of the garden. He walked at Natalia's side, without speaking. Mlle Boncourt followed a little way behind.

"What have you been doing today?" he asked at last, tugging at the ends of his handsome brown whiskers.

In features he was very like his sister; but there was less play and life in their expression, and his eyes, handsome and kindly, had a mournful look.

"Why, nothing," Natalia answered. "I've listened to Pigasov abusing everything, I've done some frame embroidery, and I've been reading."

"And what did you read?"

"I've been reading — the history of the crusades," Natalia said with some hesitancy.

Volintsiev looked at her.

"Ah!" he said at last, "that should be interesting."

He broke off a twig and began to swish it through the air. They walked on another twenty paces.

"Who is this Baron your mother has made acquaintance with?" Volintsiev asked again.

"He's a gentleman in waiting, a visitor to these parts; *maman* speaks very highly of him."

"Your mother is easily carried away."

"That shows that she is still very young in heart," she remarked.

"Yes. I'll be sending you your horse soon. It is almost perfectly broken in now. I want her to go straight into a gallop, and I'll train her to do it!"

"*Merci.* . . . All the same, I feel a little unhappy. You're breaking her in yourself; they say that is very difficult."

"You know, Natalia Alexeevna, to give you the least pleasure I am ready — I — and not such little things. . . ."

He began to stammer.

She gave him a friendly look and said once more: "*Merci.*"

"You know," he went on after a long silence, "that there isn't a thing — But what am I saying that for? You know it quite well!"

At that moment a bell began to sound in the house.

"Ah, *la cloche du dîner!*" Mlle Boncourt exclaimed; "*rentrons.*"

"*Quel dommage,*" the old Frenchwoman thought as she followed Volintsiev and Natalia up the steps of the veranda, "*quel dommage que ce charmant garçon ait si peu de ressources dans la conversation.* . . ." Which can be translated as: "You're very nice, my dear, but you're rather slow."

The Baron did not arrive in time for dinner. They waited half an hour for him. At the table conversation failed to develop. Sergei Pavlich only gazed at Natalia, beside whom he sat, and zealously kept her glass filled with water. Pandalevsky vainly tried to arouse the interest of his neighbor, Alexandra Pavlovna: he simply effervesced with sweetness, yet she all but yawned. Basistov rolled balls of bread and thought of nothing at all; even Pigasov was silent, and when Daria Mikhailovna remarked to him that he was very unamiable today, he morosely replied: "And when am I ever amiable? That isn't my business. . . ." Smiling bitterly, he added: "Be a little patient. You see I'm kvass, just simple Russian kvass, but your gentleman in waiting, now — "

"Bravo!" Daria Mikhailovna exclaimed. "Pigasov is jealous, he's prematurely jealous!"

But Pigasov made no answer and only scowled.

Seven o'clock struck, and they all assembled again in the reception hall.

"Evidently he's not coming," said Daria Mikhailovna.

But at that moment they heard the sound of a carriage, a small tarantass drove into the yard, and a few moments later a footman entered and handed Daria Mikhailovna a letter on a small silver salver. She read it through, then turned to the footman and asked:

"But where is the gentleman who brought this letter?"

"He's sitting in the carriage. Am I to receive him?"

"Ask him in."

The footman went out.

"Just imagine, what a nuisance!" Daria Mikhailovna continued. "The Baron has received instructions to return at once to Petersburg. He's sent me his article by the hand of a certain Mr. Rudin, his friend. The Baron wanted to introduce him to me, he spoke very highly of him. But how provoking this is! I had hoped the Baron would stay here. . . ."

"Dmitry Nikolaevich Rudin!" the footman announced.[1]

---

[1] Turgenev admitted that the character of Rudin was drawn from life, the prototype being Bakunin. Several of the students portrayed in Chapter VI were also drawn from life. (Tr.)

Rudin

3

The man who entered was about thirty-five, tall, rather stooping, curly-haired, swarthy, with a face irregular but expressive and intelligent, a watery gleam in his quick, dark-blue eyes, a straight, broad nose, and finely curved lips. His clothes were not new and they fitted him tightly, as though he had outgrown them.

He walked swiftly up to Daria Mikhailovna and, bowing slightly, told her that he had long wanted to have the honor of being introduced to her, and that his friend, the Baron, greatly regretted that he could not say good-by to her in person.

The thin tone of Rudin's voice was in strong contrast to his height and broad chest.

"Sit down . . . very glad," Daria Mikhailovna said. After introducing him to the rest of the company, she asked whether he lived in the district or was a visitor.

"My estate is in T— province," he answered, holding his hat on his knees; "and I have been here only a short while. I have come on business and am staying for the time being in your provincial town."

"With whom?"

"With the doctor. He was a colleague of mine at the university."

"Ah! With Dr. X. People speak well of him. They say he understands his business. But have you known the Baron long?"

"I met him last winter in Moscow, and have just spent about a week with him."

"He's a very intelligent man, is the Baron."

"Yes."

Daria Mikhailovna sniffed at the corner of her handkerchief, which was soaked in eau de Cologne.

"Are you in the civil service?" she asked.

"Who? I?"

"Yes."

"No — I'm retired."

There was a brief silence. The general conversation was resumed.

"Pardon my curiosity," Pigasov began, turning to Rudin. "Do you know the contents of the article the Baron sent?"

"Yes."

"That article deals with the relations of trade — or rather of industry to trade in our country. That is how you were pleased to express it, I think, Daria Mikhailovna?"

"Yes, that's what it is about," Daria Mikhailovna said, and put her hand to her brow.

"I, of course, am a poor judge in such matters," Pigasov went on, "but I have to admit that I think the very title of the article extraordinarily — how can I put it delicately? — extraordinarily obscure and confused."

"Why do you think so?"

Pigasov smiled and glanced sidelong at Daria Mikhailovna.

"But is it clear to you?" he said, again turning his foxy little face to Rudin.

"To me? Quite clear."

"Hm. Of course, you know best."

"Have you a headache?" Alexandra Pavlovna asked Daria Mikhailovna.

"No. It's just my usual — *C'est nerveux.*"

"Permit me to inquire," Pigasov again said in a rather thin, nasal tone, "is your acquaintance, Baron Muffel — that is his name, I think?"

"Quite right."

"Is Baron Muffel specially studying political economy, or does he only devote to that interesting science the hours of leisure remaining after worldly pleasures and service occupations?"

Rudin stared at him fixedly.

"In this question the Baron is a dilettante," he answered, flushing slightly; "but there is much that is sound and interesting in his article."

"Not knowing the article, I cannot argue with you. . . . But I venture to ask, I suppose your friend Baron Muffel's composition is concerned more with general observations than with facts?"

"It contains facts, and observations based on those facts."

"Yes-s; yes-s. I confide to you that in my opinion — and if necessary I can express my opinion; I lived three years in Dorpat — all these so-called general observations, hypotheses, systems — pardon me, I am a provincial, I go straight to the point — are no good for anything. It is all mental acrobatics — it only mystifies people. Pass on the facts, gentlemen, and you will have done enough."

"Do you really think so!" Rudin retorted. "Well, but should one pass on the sense of the facts?"

"General observations!" Pigasov went on, "All these general observations, surveys, conclusions will be the death of me. It is all based on so-called convictions; any man can talk about his convictions, and then will even demand respect for them, will make a great to-do about them. . . . Ugh!"

And he shook his fist. Pandalevsky burst into laughter.

"Excellent!" Rudin said. "So in your view there aren't any such things as convictions?"

"No, they don't exist."

"Is that your conviction?"

"Yes."

"Then how can you say that they don't exist? You have just given us one to begin with."

Everybody in the room smiled and exchanged glances.

"Pardon me, pardon me, however — " Pigasov began.

But Daria Mikhailovna clapped her hands, exclaimed: "Bravo, bravo, Pigasov's demolished, demolished!" and gently took Rudin's hat from his hands.

"You can wait a little before you rejoice, madame, you'll have plenty of time!" Pigasov said with chagrin. "It is not enough to utter one smart retort with an air of superiority; you have to prove, to refute. . . . We have got away from the subject of discussion."

"Excuse me," Rudin remarked unconcernedly, "it is a very simple matter. You don't believe in the value of general observations, you don't believe in convictions — "

"I don't believe, I don't believe, I don't believe in anything."

"Very good! You're a skeptic."

"I don't see any necessity to use such a pedantic word. For that matter — "

"Now, don't interrupt!" Daria Mikhailovna intervened.

"Snap, snap, snap!" Pandalevsky said to himself at that moment, and grinned broadly.

"That word expresses my thought," Rudin continued. "You understand it, so why not use it? You don't believe in anything. So why do you believe in facts?"

"What do you mean? Now, that's first-rate! Facts are well known, anyone knows what facts are. . . . I judge of them by experience, by my own feelings!"

"But do you suggest that your senses cannot deceive you? Your senses tell you that the sun goes round the earth — or, perhaps you do not agree with Copernicus? You don't believe in him either?"

A smile again slipped over all the others' faces, and all eyes were fixed on Rudin. "But he's no fool!" each of them thought.

"You're still pleased to jest," Pigasov began. "Of course, that is very original, but it doesn't get us anywhere."

"In all that I have said so far," Rudin retorted, "there is unfortunately very little of originality. It has all been known a long time and has been said a thousand times. That's not the point."

"Then what is?" Pigasov asked not without insolence. In the course of the argument he had begun with banter, then he had turned rude, but finally he grew sulky and lapsed into silence.

"This is," Rudin continued; "I, I have to admit, cannot but feel sincere regret when I hear intelligent people attack — "

"Systems?" Pigasov interrupted.

"Yes, if you like, even systems. Why should that word frighten you so much? Any system is based on knowledge of fundamental laws, the elements of life."

"But they cannot be known, or discovered — if you don't mind my saying so!"

"Pardon me. Of course, they are not accessible to everybody, and it is man's weakness to err. None the less you will probably agree with me that Newton, for instance, discovered some at least of these fundamental laws. He was a genius, I grant; but the discoveries made by geniuses are great precisely because they become the property of all. The endeavor to discover the general elements in the individual phenomena is one of the radical qualities of the human mind, and all our education — "

"Now where are you going!" Pigasov interrupted in a drawling tone. "I am a practical man, and I cannot go into all these metaphysical subtleties and don't want to."

"Excellent! That is as you wish. But note that your very desire to be exclusively a practical man is itself a kind of system, a theory — "

"Education, you say!" Pigasov took him up; "now you've

thought of something else to astonish us with! It is so very necessary, your boasted education! I wouldn't give a brass farthing for it!"

"But really, how stupidly you argue, Afrikan Semionich!" Daria Mikhailovna remarked; inwardly she was well satisfied with the composure and exquisite courtesy of her new acquaintance. "*C'est un homme comme il faut,*" she thought, looking at Rudin's face with benevolent interest. "I must take him up"; she mentally said these last words in Russian.

"I am not proposing to defend education," Rudin went on after a moment's silence; "it has no need of my defense. You don't like it — every man to his taste. Besides, it has taken us too far from the point. Allow me only to recall the old saying: 'Jupiter, you are angry; therefore you must be guilty.' I only wanted to say that all these attacks on systems, general observations, and so on are particularly distressing because, with the systems, people reject all knowledge, science, and faith in science generally, and so they reject faith in themselves too, in their own strength. But people need that faith: they cannot live simply by impressions, it is a sin for them to be afraid of thought and not trust it. Skepticism has always been distinguished by barrenness and impotence. . . ."

"That's all talk!" Pigasov muttered.

"Maybe. But allow me to point out that when we say 'that's all talk' we are often ourselves trying to avoid the necessity of saying something more vital than mere words."

"But what?" Pigasov asked, looking at him quizzically.

"You understood what I tried to say to you," Rudin retorted with involuntary but immediately restrained impatience. "I repeat, if a man has no strong basis in which he believes, has no ground on which he stands firmly, how can he have any comprehension of the needs, the significance, the future of his nation? How can he know what he himself should do, if — "

"I retire in your honor!" Pigasov burst out, bowing and falling back, without looking at anybody.

Rudin looked at him, smiled faintly, and said no more.

"Aha! He's turned to flight!" Daria Mikhailovna said. "Don't be alarmed, Dmitry — Excuse me," she added with a friendly smile; "what is your patronymic?"

"Nikolaich."

"Don't be alarmed, dear Dmitry Nikolaich. He didn't deceive any of us. He wants to give the impression that he does not *wish* to go on arguing. . . . But he feels that he *cannot* argue with you. Come and sit down by us, and we'll have a little talk."

Rudin shifted his chair nearer to her.

"How is it we haven't met before?" Daria Mikhailovna continued. "That surprises me. . . . Have you read this book? *C'est de Tocqueville, vous savez.*"

She held out a French brochure to him.

He took the thin little book in his hand, turned over several pages, and then, putting it back on the table, replied that he hadn't actually read this work of de Tocqueville, but he had often thought about the question the writer raised. Conversation began to flow. Rudin seemed at first to hesitate, could not bring himself to express his opinions, could not find words; but finally he caught fire and began to talk. Within fifteen minutes only his voice was to be heard in the room. They all crowded in a circle round him. Pigasov alone remained apart, in a corner by the fireplace.

Rudin talked sensibly, ardently, to the point; he revealed a great deal of knowledge and much reading. No one had expected to find him at all remarkable — he was dressed so simply, there had been so little talk about him. They all thought it strange and incomprehensible that such an intelligent man could turn up so suddenly in the countryside. So much the more did he surprise and, one might say, enchant everybody, beginning with Daria Mikhailovna. . . . She was proud of her discovery and was already thinking of how she would show him off to the world. There was much that was almost childish in her first impressions, despite her years. Alexandra Pavlovna, to tell the truth, understood little of what Rudin said, but she was greatly astonished and delighted; her brother also was astonished; Pandalevsky watched Daria Mikhailovna and was jealous; Pigasov thought: "For five hundred rubles I'll get an even better nightingale. . . ." But Basistov and Natalia were astounded most of all. Basistov could hardly catch his breath; he sat with gaping mouth and goggling eyes and listened, listened as he had never listened to anyone before. Natalia's face was tinged with a crimson flush, and her eyes, fixed immutably on Rudin, now darkened, now glittered. . . .

Rudin

"What wonderful eyes he has got!" Volintsiev whispered to her.

"Yes, they're fine eyes."

"It's a pity he has such large red hands."

Natalia made no answer.

Tea was brought in. The conversation grew more general, but by the very abruptness with which everybody lapsed into silence the moment Rudin opened his mouth, it was possible to tell the impression he had made. Suddenly Daria Mikhailovna was moved with a desire to tease Pigasov. She went over to him and said in an undertone: "Why are you silent and only smiling venomously? Make another attempt to take him on!" Without waiting for his answer, she beckoned Rudin across.

"There's one other thing you don't know about him," she said to Rudin, pointing to Pigasov. "He is a terrible woman-hater, he's always attacking them; please put him on the right road."

Rudin looked at Pigasov — and involuntarily looked down at him, for he was two heads higher. Pigasov all but shriveled with malice, and his yellowish face turned white.

"Daria Mikhailovna is mistaken," he began in an uncertain tone; "I don't attack women only; I am no great lover of the human race at all."

"How is it you have such a poor opinion of humanity?" Rudin asked.

Pigasov looked him straight in the eyes.

"Probably through study of my own heart, in which every day I discover more and more rubbish. I judge of others by myself. Maybe that is unjust and I am much worse than others, but what am I to do? It's just a habit!"

"I understand you and sympathize with you," Rudin replied. "What noble soul has never experienced the thirst for self-abasement? But it is not wise to remain in that hopeless state."

"I humbly thank you for giving my soul a certificate of nobility," Pigasov retorted. "But my state isn't bad; in fact, it's quite good, so that even if there is a way out of it, who cares? I shan't bother to look for it!"

"But that means — pardon my saying so — preferring the satisfaction of one's own selfish ambition to the desire to be and live in truth. . . ."

585

"Oh, rather!" Pigasov exclaimed. "Selfish ambition, that's something I understand, and you, I hope, understand it, and anyone understands it; but truth — what is truth? Where is it, this truth of yours?"

"I warn you, you are repeating yourself," Daria Mikhailovna remarked.

Pigasov shrugged his shoulders.

"Well, and is that any misfortune? I ask: where is truth? Even the philosophers do not know what it is. Kant says it is one thing; but Hegel says oh no, you're lying, it is something else."

"But do you know what Hegel does say about it?" Rudin asked without raising his voice.

"I repeat," continued Pigasov, who had grown excited, "that I cannot understand what truth is. In my opinion it doesn't exist at all in this world; I mean, of course there is the word 'truth,' but the thing itself doesn't exist."

"Fie! Fie!" Daria Mikhailovna exclaimed, "aren't you ashamed to say such a thing, you old sinner? Truth doesn't exist? Then what is there left to live for in the world?"

"Well, you know, I think, Daria Mikhailovna," Pigasov retorted in a vexed tone, "that you, at any rate, would find it easier to live without truth than without your cook Stepan, who is such a master at making bouillon! And what do you want truth for, I'd like to know? You can't make a bonnet out of it!"

"A joke is no answer," Daria Mikhailovna observed, "especially when it verges on slander. . . ."

"I don't know about truth, but obviously verity stings the eyes," Pigasov muttered, and angrily walked away.

But Rudin began to talk about ambition, and talked very much to the point. He proved that without ambition man is insignificant, that ambition is the Archimedean lever with which the earth can be shifted from its place, but that at the same time only he is worthy to be called a man who knows how to control his ambition as a rider does a horse, who brings his personality in sacrifice to the common good. . . .

"Self-love," he concluded, "is suicide. The selfish man dries up like a lone, barren tree; but ambition, being an active striving for perfection, is the source of everything great. . . . Yes, man needs to overcome the obstinate egotism of his personality in order to give it the right to express itself!"

"Could you lend me a pencil?" Pigasov turned to Basistov.

Basistov did not at first understand what Pigasov had asked him.

"What do you want a pencil for?" he asked at last.

"I want to write down that last sentence of Mr. Rudin's. If you don't write it down you'll forget it, and that would be a pity! And you must agree that such a phrase is just like a grand slam in whist."

"There are some things that it is sinful to laugh at and make fun of, Afrikan Semionich!" Basistov said hotly, and he turned his back on Pigasov.

Meanwhile Rudin had gone over to Natalia. She rose; her face expressed her embarrassment.

Volintsiev, who was sitting beside her, also rose.

"I see you have a piano here," Rudin began as softly and graciously as a traveling prince. "It isn't you who plays it, by any chance?"

"Yes, I do play," Natalia said, "but not very well. Konstantin Diumidich plays much better than I do."

Pandalevsky thrust his face forward and bared his teeth. "You mustn't say that, Natalia Alexeevna; you play just as well as I can."

"Do you know Schubert's Erlkönig?" Rudin asked.

"He does, he does!" Daria Mikhailovna broke in. "Sit down at the piano, Konstantin. . . . So you like music, Dmitry Nikolaich?"

Rudin only slightly inclined his head and ran his hand over his hair, as though preparing to listen. . . . Pandalevsky began to play.

Natalia stood by the piano, opposite Rudin. At the first note his face took on a beautiful expression. His dark-blue eyes slowly wandered, occasionally resting on Natalia. Pandalevsky finished playing.

Without speaking, Rudin went across to the open window. A fragrant mist lay like a soft shroud over the garden; the near-by trees exuded a drowsy freshness. The stars were faintly shining. The summer night was tender in its tenderness. Rudin looked out into the dark garden and turned round.

"That music and this night," he said, "remind me of my student days in Germany: our meetings, our serenades. . . ."

"So you've been in Germany?" Daria Mikhailovna asked.

"I spent a year at Heidelberg and about a year in Berlin."

"And did you dress as a student? They say they have a special dress of their own there."

"In Heidelberg I wore large boots with spurs and a Hungarian hussar coat with braid, and let my hair grow right down to my shoulders. . . . In Berlin the students dress just like anyone else."

"Tell us something about your student life," Alexandra Pavlovna said.

Rudin began to tell about it. He was not quite successful in the attempt. His descriptions lacked color. He had no gift for provoking laughter. From stories of his foreign adventures, however, he soon passed to general observations on the importance of education and science, about universities and university life in general. In broad and bold outlines he sketched an enormous picture. Everybody listened to him with deep attention. He spoke in masterly fashion, absorbingly, not altogether clearly . . . but that very lack of clarity conferred especial charm on his remarks.

The very profusion of his thoughts prevented him from expressing himself definitely and precisely. Pictures were replaced by pictures; comparisons, sometimes unexpectedly bold, sometimes strikingly true, followed comparisons. Not the self-satisfied artifice of the experienced talker, but inspiration breathed through his impatient improvisation. He did not seek words: they themselves came obediently and freely to his lips, and every word seemed to be poured straight from his soul, and flamed with all the fire of conviction. Rudin possessed what is perhaps one of the highest secrets — the music of eloquence. By striking certain strings of the heart, he was able to make all the others tremble and vaguely echo. One or another listener, perhaps, did not exactly understand what the talk was about; but even so his breast heaved, curtains parted before his eyes, something radiant shone out before him.

All Rudin's thoughts seemed to be turned toward the future; this conferred on them an impetuous and youthful quality. . . . He stood at the window, not looking at anyone in particular, and talked; and, inspired by the general sympathy and attention, the proximity of young women, the beauty of the night, carried away by the flood of his own sensations, he was exalted to eloquence, to poetry. . . . The very sound of his voice, concentrated and quiet, increased the fascination; his lips seemed to be uttering something higher, unexpected even to himself. . . . Rudin spoke of that which gives eternal significance to man's temporal life.

"I remember a certain Scandinavian legend," he ended. "A King was sitting with his warriors in a dark, long shed, around the fire. It was nighttime, and in the winter. Suddenly a little bird flew in at one open door and flew out at another. The King remarked that this bird was like man in the world: it had flown in out of the darkness and had flown out into the darkness, and had not remained long in the warmth and light. . . . 'O King,' the very oldest of the warriors retorted, 'the bird is not lost even in the darkness, and it finds its nest. . . .' In the same way our life is swift and insignificant; but everything great is achieved by human beings. The consciousness that he is the instrument of these higher forces should replace all man's other joys; in death itself he finds his life, his nest. . . ."

Rudin stopped and lowered his eyes with a smile of involuntary embarrassment.

"*Vous êtes un poète*," Daria Mikhailovna declared in an undertone.

And all inwardly agreed with her — all except Pigasov. Not waiting for the end of Rudin's long discourse, he had quietly picked up his hat and, as he went out, had whispered malevolently to Pandalevsky, who was standing by the door:

"I've had enough, I'm going off to the fools."

No one restrained him, however, or even noticed his absence.

The servants brought in supper, and half an hour later everybody had departed and driven off. Daria Mikhailovna coaxed Rudin into remaining for the night. As Alexandra Pavlovna returned home with her brother in the carette, she several times expressed her wonder and astonishment at Rudin's uncommon intellect. Volintsiev agreed with her, but he remarked that Rudin sometimes expressed himself rather obscurely. . . . "I mean not altogether intelligibly," he added, probably wishing to clarify his thought. But his face clouded over, and his gaze, fixed on one corner of the carette, seemed even more sorrowful.

As Pandalevsky went to bed and took off his silk-embroidered braces, he said aloud: "A very cunning man!" Suddenly, giving his page-valet a harsh glance, he ordered him to go out. Basistov did not sleep all night and did not undress: until morning light he sat writing a long letter to a comrade of his in Moscow. And though Natalia did undress and did get into bed, she, too, did not sleep for a minute and did not even close her eyes. Resting her head on her hand, she gazed fixedly into the darkness; her blood beat feverishly, and again and again a deep sigh caused her breast to heave.

4

Next morning Rudin had only just had time to dress when a manservant called on him from Daria Mikhailovna with an invitation to present himself to her in her private room and take tea with her. Rudin found her alone. She greeted him very amiably, inquired whether he had slept well, herself poured a cup of tea for him, even asked whether it was sweet enough, offered him a cigarette, and again repeated more than once that she was amazed that she had not made his acquaintance long before. Rudin went to seat himself some little way off, but Daria Mikhailovna pointed him to a small pouffe placed beside her chair and, bending a little toward him, began to inquire about his family, his intentions and plans. She talked heedlessly and listened abstractedly; but Rudin realized quite well that she was paying attention to him and all but adulated him. Not for nothing had she arranged this early morning meeting, not for nothing had she dressed herself simply, but elegantly, à la Mme Rècamier.

She soon ceased to ply him with questions, however; she began to tell him about herself, about her youth, and the people she had known. Rudin listened sympathetically to her prolix chatter, though, strange to say, no matter whom Daria Mikhailovna spoke about, she, she alone, was always left in the foreground, while the other person seemed to steal away and disappear. On the other hand, he learned in detail that she had talked to a certain well-known dignitary, that she had had a certain influence on a well-known poet. Judging from her stories, one would have thought that all the remarkable people in the past twenty-five years had dreamed only of getting an opportunity to meet her and of winning her favor. She talked of them quite simply, without any particular enthusiasm or glorification, as members of her own class, and called some of them eccentrics. She talked of them and, like a rich setting to a precious stone, their names were built up into a brilliant frame around the chief name — around Daria Mikhailovna. . . .

But Rudin listened, smoking a cigarette, and was silent, only interjecting brief remarks into the garrulous lady's speech. He could and liked to talk; it was not beyond his powers to lead the conversation, but he could listen too. Those whom he did not immediately intimidate trustfully blossomed out in his presence, so readily and approvingly did he follow the thread of their conversation. There was much geniality in him, that special geniality which is possessed by people accustomed to feeling that they are superior to others. In argument he rarely allowed his opponent to express his opinion, and crushed him with vehement and passionate dialectic.

Daria Mikhailovna expatiated upon herself in Russian. She was distinguished by her knowledge of her native tongue, though she frequently employed Gallicisms and French words. She deliberately used simple, popular turns of speech, but not always successfully. Rudin's ear was not affronted by the strange variety of speech that came from her mouth, and indeed it is doubtful whether he had any ear — for that.

At last she grew weary and, leaning her head against the back of the armchair, fixed her eyes on him and lapsed into silence.

"Now I understand," he began in a deliberate tone, "I understand why you come to the country every summer. You need that rest: the country stillness, after the life of the capital, freshens and strengthens you. I am sure that you must feel profound sympathy for the beauties of nature."

She gave him a sidelong look.

"Nature — yes — yes — of course. . . . I'm terribly fond of it; but do you know, Dmitry Nikolaich, even in the country one cannot be without people. But here there is almost nobody. Pigasov is the most intelligent man in the district."

"Yesterday's ill-tempered old man?" he asked.

"Yes, that's the one. . . . In the country, however, even he is of use — at least he makes one laugh sometimes."

"He is not a stupid man," Rudin objected, "but he is on a false road. I don't know whether you will agree with me, Daria Mikhailovna, but in negation — in complete and universal negation — there is no grace whatever. Deny everything and you may

Turgenev

easily gain the reputation of a sage; that is a well-known trick. Good-natured people are ready at once to conclude that you are superior to that which you deny. But often that is not true. To begin with, one can find spots on all things; and secondly, even if you are speaking to the point, so much the worse for you; directed only to negation, your mind grows poorer and withers. In satisfying your self-esteem, you deprive yourself of the true satisfaction of contemplation; life — the very essence of life — slips beyond your shallow and splenetic observation, and you end by railing and ridiculing. The right to deny, to upbraid, belongs only to him who loves."

"*Voilà Monsieur Pigasov enterré*," said Daria Mikhailovna. "What a master you are at delineating a man! For that matter, in all probability Pigasov would not understand you. But the only person he loves is himself."

"And he decries himself in order to have the right to decry others," Rudin followed up her thought.

She smiled.

"From the sick — what is the saying? — from the sick to the hale. By the way, what do you think of the Baron?"

"The Baron? He's a fine man, with a good heart, and he knows a great deal . . . but he is lacking in character . . . and all his life he will remain half a savant, half a man of the world; in other words, a dilettante; in other words, speaking without circumlocution — nothing. . . . And that is a pity!"

"I am of the same opinion," Daria Mikhailovna replied. "I have read his article: '*Entre nous . . . cela a assez peu de fond.*'"

"Whom else have you here?" Rudin asked after a silence.

Daria Mikhailovna brushed the ash from her cigarette with her little finger.

"Why, there is hardly anyone else. Alexandra Pavlovna Lipina, whom you saw yesterday: she is very nice — but that's all. Her brother, too, is a splendid man, *un parfait honnête homme*. You know Prince Harin. And that is the lot. We have two or three neighbors, but they're just hopeless. They either put on airs, with terrible affectations, or they are unsociable, or they're ridiculously free and easy. I never invite the young ladies, you know. We have one other neighbor; they say he is very well educated, and even a learned man, but he's a terrible eccentric, a visionary. Alexandrine knows him, and I think she is not indifferent to him.

. . . Now you should interest yourself in her, Dmitry Nikolaich: she's a dear creature; she only needs to be developed a little, she simply must be developed!"

"She is very likable," Rudin remarked.

"An absolute child, Dmitry Nikolaich, a real baby. She was married, *mais c'est tout comme* — if I were a man, I'd fall in love only with women like her."

"Really?"

"Undoubtedly. Such women are at least fresh, and it is impossible to counterfeit freshness."

"But you can counterfeit everything else?" Rudin asked and smiled, which was a very rare occurrence with him. When he smiled, his face took on a strange, almost aged expression, his eyes shriveled, his nose wrinkled. . . .

"And who is this eccentric, as you described him, to whom Madame Lipina is not indifferent?" he asked.

"A man named Lezhniov, Mikhailo Mikhailich, a local landowner."

Rudin was amazed and looked up.

"Mikhailo Mikhailich Lezhniov?" he asked. "Is he a neighbor of yours, then?"

"Yes. Why, do you know him?"

He was silent.

"I used to know him — a long time ago. He is a rich man, I believe?" he added, plucking at the fringe of the chair with one hand.

"Yes, he's wealthy, though he dresses terribly and goes about in a racing sulky, like a steward. I wanted to entice him over here: they say he is intelligent; and I have some business to settle with him. . . . You know, I manage my estate myself."

Rudin inclined his head.

"Yes, myself," Daria Mikhailovna went on, "I haven't introduced any of the stupid foreign ideas, I keep to our Russian ways, and, as you see, affairs don't go badly, apparently," she added, describing a circle with her hand.

"I have always been convinced," Rudin remarked politely, "that those people who deny that women have any practical capacities are quite wrong."

Daria Mikhailovna smiled amiably.

"You are very condescending," she said; "but what was I trying to say? What were we talking about? Oh yes! About Lezhniov. I have some business to settle with him in regard to land boundaries. I have invited him over here several times, and I'm even expecting him today; but he won't come, God knows . . . he's such an eccentric!"

The curtain before the door was quietly drawn aside, and the butler entered — a tall man, gray and bald, in a black frock coat, white cravat, and white vest.

"What do you want?" Daria Mikhailovna asked. Half turning to Rudin, she added in an undertone: *"N'est-ce pas, comme il ressemble à Canning?"*

"Mikhailo Mikhailich Lezhniov has arrived," the butler reported; "am I to show him in?"

"Ah! My goodness!" Daria Mikhailovna exclaimed; "speak of the devil — Ask him in."

The butler went out.

"He's such an eccentric; he's come at last, and then at an inopportune moment: he has interrupted our conversation."

Rudin rose from his seat, but Daria Mikhailovna stopped him.

"But where are you going? We can talk just as well in front of you. And I would like you to define him, as you did Pigasov. When you speak, *vous gravez comme avec un burin.* You remain."

He was about to say something, but he thought better of it and remained.

Mikhailo Mikhailich, who is already known to the reader, entered the room. He was wearing the same gray coat, and in his sunburnt hands he held the same old cap. He bowed composedly to Daria Mikhailovna and went up to the tea table.

"So you've come to see us at last, M'sieur Lezhniov!" Daria Mikhailovna said. "Please sit down. I hear you are acquaintances," she continued, pointing to Rudin.

Lezhniov took one look at Rudin and smiled queerly.

"I know Mr. Rudin," he said with a slight bow.

"We were at the university together," Rudin remarked in an undertone, and cast his eyes down.

"We met later, too," Lezhniov said coldly.

Daria Mikhailovna stared in some astonishment at them both and asked Lezhniov to sit down. He sat down.

"You wished to see me," he began, "in regard to the boundaries?"

"Yes, in regard to the boundaries, but I wanted to see you apart from that. After all, we are near neighbors and all but kin."

"I am very grateful to you," Lezhniov retorted; "as for the boundaries, we have completely settled the matter with your steward: I agree to all his proposals."

"I knew that."

"Only he told me that the documents couldn't be signed without my personally seeing you."

"Yes; that is a rule I have made. By the way, you must excuse my asking, but all your peasants are on a rental basis, aren't they?"

"Precisely."

"And yet you are attending to the question of boundaries yourself? That is very praiseworthy."

Lezhniov made no comment.

"And so I have turned up for that personal interview," he said.

Daria Mikhailovna smiled.

"I see you have turned up. You said that in such a tone — apparently you were very reluctant to visit me."

"I never visit anyone," he remarked phlegmatically.

"Not anyone? But you visit Alexandra Pavlovna, don't you?"

"I have known her brother a long time."

"Her brother! However, I force no one — But excuse me, Mikhailo Mikhailich, I am older than you and I may reprove you. What makes you want to live such an unsociable life? Or is it just *my* house that you don't like? Don't you like me?"

"I don't know you, Daria Mikhailovna, and so I can't not like you. You have a very fine house; but, I confess to you frankly, I do not like formalities. I haven't even a decent frock coat; I have no gloves; and besides, I don't belong to your circle."

"You belong to it by birth, and by education, Mikhailo Mikhailich! *Vous êtes des nôtres.*"

"We'll put birth and education aside, Daria Mikhailovna! That's not the point. . . ."

"A man has to live with other people, Mikhailo Mikhailich! What a queer desire, to sit like Diogenes in his barrel!"

"To begin with, he found his barrel very satisfactory, and secondly, how do you know that I do not mix with people?"

Daria Mikhailovna bit her lip.

"That's another matter! I can only regret that I have not been deemed worthy of inclusion among the people with whom you are acquainted."

"M'sieur Lezhniov," Rudin intervened, "seemingly exaggerates the highly praiseworthy feeling of a love of freedom."

Lezhniov did not answer and only glanced at him. There was a brief silence.

"Well then," Lezhniov began, rising, "I can regard our business as settled and can tell your steward to send me the documents."

"You may — though, I have to confess, you are so unamiable — I ought to refuse you."

"But the boundaries as drawn up are far more advantageous to you than to me."

Daria Mikhailovna shrugged her shoulders.

"So you are not prepared even to have breakfast with me?" she asked.

"I humbly thank you: I never eat breakfast, and besides I am in a hurry to get home."

She rose.

"I do not detain you," she said, going over to the window; "I do not presume to detain you."

He began to take his leave.

"Good-by, M'sieur Lezhniov! Forgive me for troubling you."

"Oh, please, it's nothing!" he retorted, and left the room.

"What do you think of him?" Daria Mikhailovna asked Rudin. "I had heard that he was eccentric, but he is quite impossible!"

"He suffers from the same disease as Pigasov," Rudin said, "the desire to be original. Pigasov pretends to be Mephistopheles, and this man a cynic. In such people there is much egotism, much self-esteem, and little truth, little love. You see, there is a kind of calculation in it too; the man has donned a mask of indifference and laziness, in the hope that someone will think: what a man, and what talents he has ruined in himself! But if you look more closely you find he has no talents whatever."

"*Et de deux!*" Daria Mikhailovna said. "You're a terrible man at hitting people off. There's no hiding from you."

"Do you think so?" he said. "For that matter," he continued, "really I ought not to have spoken to Lezhniov; once I was fond of him, I loved him as a friend — but then, owing to various misunderstandings — "

"You quarreled?"

"No. But we parted, and parted, it seems, forever."

"Yes, I noticed that all the time he was here you did not seem to be yourself. . . . However, I am deeply grateful to you for this morning . . . I have spent the time extraordinarily pleasantly. But one must have regard to one's dignity. I release you till tomorrow, and I shall go to occupy myself with affairs. My secretary, you have seen him — *Konstantin, c'est lui qui est mon secrétaire* — should be waiting for me already. I recommend him to you: he is a very fine, very willing young man, and absolutely enthusiastic about you. Good-by, *cher* Dmitry Nikolaich! How grateful I am to the Baron for making me acquainted with you!"

And Daria Mikhailovna stretched out her hand to Rudin. He squeezed her hand, then raised it to his lips. Then he went into the hall, and from the hall onto the terrace. On the terrace he met Natalia.

5

Daria Mikhailovna's daughter, Natalia Alexeevna, might not have seemed attractive at first glance. She had not had time to mature; she was thin and swarthy and carried herself with a slight stoop. But the features of her face were beautiful and regular, though too large for a girl of seventeen. Especially fine was her clear and level brow above delicate eyebrows that seemed to be cloven in the middle. She talked little, but listened and watched attentively, almost fixedly — as though she wanted to be quite sure she understood everything. She often sat perfectly still and lost in thought, with her hands dropped at her side; at such times her face expressed the internal workings of her mind. . . . An almost imperceptible smile would suddenly appear on her lips and vanish; her large, dark eyes would slowly look up. . . . "*Qu' avez-vous?*" Mlle Boncourt would ask her, and even scold her, saying that it was unbecoming for a young girl to sit thinking and to adopt an abstracted air. But Natalia was not abstracted: on the contrary, she studied diligently; she read and worked willingly. She felt deeply and strongly, but secretly; even in childhood she had rarely wept, and now she even sighed but rarely, and only turned rather pale when something upset her. Her mother regarded her as a well-mannered, sensible girl, and jokingly called her *mon honnête homme de fille*, but had no

great opinion of her mental capacities. "Fortunately my dear
Natalia is cold," she would say, "she doesn't take after me; and
so much the better. She will be happy." Daria Mikhailovna was
mistaken. For that matter, it is a rare mother who understands
her own daughter.

Natalia loved Daria Mikhailovna, but did not give her all her
confidence.

"Hide nothing from me," her mother said to her one day, "or
you may become secretive: you know your own mind so
much . . ."

Natalia looked her mother in the face and thought: "But why
shouldn't I know my own mind?"

When Rudin met her on the terrace, she was going with Mlle
Boncourt to her room to put on her hat for a walk in the garden.
Her morning studies were already finished. Her mother had
ceased to treat her as a girl; Mlle Boncourt had long since stopped
giving her lessons on mythology and geography; but every morning she had to read historical books, travels, and other edifying
works in the Frenchwoman's presence. Daria Mikhailovna selected
them, as though she had a special system of her own. In reality
she simply passed on to Natalia everything the French bookseller
in Petersburg sent her, excluding, of course, the novels of Dumas
fils and company. These she read herself. Mlle Boncourt stared
even more strictly and sourly through her spectacles when Natalia
read history books. According to the old Frenchwoman's ideas, all
history was filled with impermissible happenings; though, for
some unknown reason, of all the great men of antiquity the only
one she had ever heard of was Cambyses; while her knowledge
of the great of modern times was confined to Louis XIV and
Napoleon — a man she could not endure.

But Natalia also read books of which Mlle Boncourt did not
even suspect the existence: she knew all Pushkin by heart. . . .

When she saw Rudin, Natalia blushed a little.

"Are you going for a walk?" he asked her.

"Yes. We're going into the garden."

"May I come with you?"

Natalia looked at Mlle Boncourt.

"*Mais certainement, monsieur, avec plaisir,*" the old maid hurriedly replied.

Rudin fetched his hat and went with them.

At first as she walked with Rudin along the one path, Natalia felt awkward; but after a time she grew a little easier. He began to question her about her studies, and whether she liked the country. She answered not without some bashfulness, but without that precipitate timidity which is so often presented, and accepted, as pudency. Her heart beat.

"You're not bored in the country?" he asked, giving her a side-long glance.

"How can one be bored in the country? I am very glad we are here. I am very happy here."

"You are happy — that is a great word. However, that is under-standable: you are young."

He pronounced that last word with a curious inflection: as though he were envious of Natalia, or else felt sorry for her.

"Yes! Youth!" he added. "All the aim of learning is to achieve consciously what to youth is given freely."

Natalia looked at him attentively; she did not understand what he meant.

"I have talked with your mother all the morning," he went on; "she is an unusual woman. I understand why all our poets valued her friendship. And do you like poetry?" he added after a mo-mentary silence.

"He's putting me through an examination," Natalia thought, and said: "Yes, very much."

"Poetry is the language of the gods. I, too, love poems. But poetry is not to be found only in verse: it is spread everywhere, it is all around us. . . . Look at these trees, this sky — all things breathe beauty and life; and where there is beauty and life, there is poetry.

"Let us sit down here, on this bench," he continued. "That's right. For some reason I have the feeling that when you grow used to me" (and he looked into her face with a smile) "you and I will be friends. What do you think?"

"He's treating me as if I were a girl," Natalia again thought and, not knowing what to say, asked him whether he intended to re-main in the country for long.

"All the summer, the autumn, and perhaps the winter. I am a very poor man, you know; my affairs have all gone to pieces, and besides I have already grown bored with dragging from place to place."

She was astonished.

"Surely you don't think it's time you rested?" she asked diffidently.

He turned to face Natalia.

"What did you mean by that?"

"I meant," she answered with some embarrassment, "that others can rest; but you — you should labor, should strive to be of benefit to others. Who if not you — "

"I thank you for your flattering opinion," he interrupted her. "To be of benefit to others — that is easy to say!" (He passed his hand over his face.) "To be of benefit!" he repeated. "Even if I had a firm conviction of how I could be of benefit — even if I believed in my strength — where is one to find sincere, sympathizing souls? . . ."

And he waved his hand so hopelessly and hung his head so miserably that Natalia involuntarily asked herself: was it this man's speeches, those exalted speeches, breathing with hope, that she had listened to the previous evening?

"But no," he added, suddenly shaking his leonine mane, "that is nonsense, and you are right. I thank you, Natalia Alexeevna, I thank you sincerely." (Natalia had no idea whatever what he was thanking her for.) "One single word from you has reminded me of my duty, has pointed out my path to me. . . . Yes, I must act. I must not conceal my talent, if I have any; I must not expend my forces simply on idle chatter, useless chatter, simply on words. . . ."

And his words flowed like a river. He talked beautifully, fervently, persuasively — of the shame of pusillanimity and laziness, of the necessity to do something. He heaped reproaches on himself, argued that to consider in advance what one wants to do is just as detrimental as to prick a ripening fruit with a pin, that it was only a useless waste of energy and powers. He assured her that there was no noble thought which would not arouse someone's sympathy, that only those people would go misunderstood who either do not themselves know what they want or are not worth understanding. He talked a long time, ended by once more thanking her, and quite unexpectedly squeezed her hand, saying: "You are a splendid, noble creature!"

This liberty astounded Mlle Boncourt, who, though she had lived in Russia for forty years, had difficulty in understanding

Rudin

Russian and was only amazed at the rapidity and fluency of the speech that came from Rudin's mouth. For that matter, she regarded him as a kind of virtuoso or artist; and in her view it was impossible to require such people to observe decorum.

She rose and, energetically adjusting her dress, informed Natalia that it was time to go home, the more so as Monsieur Volinsoff (as she called Volintsiev) was intending to arrive for lunch.

"And there he is!" she added, glancing down one of the avenues leading from the house.

Volintsiev was in fact not far off.

He came up with an irresolute step, bowing to them all when some distance away. Turning to Natalia with a miserable expression on his face, he asked her:

"Ah! So you're out for a walk?"

"Yes," Natalia answered, "we were just on our way home."

"Ah!" Volintsiev said. "Well, let us go, then."

And they all walked toward the house.

"How is your sister's health?" Rudin asked Volintsiev in a particularly gracious tone. The previous evening also he had been very amiable to Volintsiev.

"Thank you very much, she is quite well. She may be coming today. . . . I think you were discussing something when I came up?"

"Yes, Natalia Alexeevna and I were having a conversation. She said one word to me that had a very strong effect upon me. . . ."

Volintsiev did not ask what that one word was, and they all returned to Daria Mikhailovna's house in profound silence.

A further salon was held before dinner. Pigasov, however, did not arrive. Rudin was not in form; he continually insisted on Pandalevsky playing Beethoven. Natalia did not leave her mother's side and sat lost in thought for some time, then turned to her embroidery. Continually expecting Rudin to let fall some sapient remark, Basistov did not take his eyes off him. Thus about three hours passed rather monotonously. Alexandra Pavlovna did not arrive for dinner, and as soon as Volintsiev rose from the table, he ordered his carriage to be brought and slipped away without taking leave of anyone.

He felt unhappy. He had long loved Natalia and was always on the point of proposing to her. . . . She was gracious to him—

but her heart remained undisturbed: he saw that clearly. Nor did
he hope to inspire her with a more tender feeling, and he only
waited for the moment when she would grow quite used to him,
would draw close to him. So what could have agitated him now?
What change had he noticed during the past two days? Natalia
treated him exactly as before.

Whether it had occurred to him that perhaps he did not know
Natalia's disposition at all, that she was even more a stranger to
him than he had thought, or whether jealousy had awakened
within him, or whether he had a vague presentiment of some misfortune . . . certain it is that he suffered, though he tried hard to
reason with himself.

When he entered his sister's room, he found Lezhniov sitting
with her.

"Why have you come back so early?" Alexandra Pavlovna
asked.

"Oh, I was just bored."

"Was Rudin there?"

"Yes."

Volintsiev threw off his cap and sat down.

She turned to him energetically:

"Please, Sergei, help me to convince this obstinate man" (she
pointed to Lezhniov) "that Rudin is unusually intelligent and
eloquent."

Volintsiev muttered something.

"Why, I don't dispute that in the least," Lezhniov began; "I
have no doubt whatever of Mr. Rudin's intelligence and eloquence. I only say that I don't like him."

"But have you seen him, then?" Volintsiev asked.

"I saw him this morning, with Daria Mikhailovna. You see *he*
is her grand vizier now. When the time comes, she will part from
him too — only with Pandalevsky will she never part — but now
Rudin reigns. I've seen him, of course I've seen him! He was sitting there, and she pointed me out to him: 'Look, my dear sir,
what strange creatures we have in our district!' I'm not a race-
horse, I'm not used to having my paces shown off. I got up and
went."

"But why were you there at all?"

"On a boundary question. But that was nonsense: she simply

wanted to have a look at my physiognomy. The lady is well known!"

"You are upset by his superiority, that's what it is!" Alexandra Pavlovna said with some heat. "That is something you cannot forgive him. But I am sure that besides being intelligent, he must be very good-hearted. You look at his eyes when he — "

" — is speaking of lofty integrity," Lezhniov said for her.

"You make me angry and I shall cry. I sincerely regret that I didn't go to Daria Mikhailovna's, but remained with you. You're not worth it. I have had enough of your teasing me," she added in a miserable tone. "You had better tell me about his youth."

"About Rudin's youth?"

"Why, yes. You did tell me that you know him well and have known him a long time."

Lezhniov rose and strode about the room.

"Yes," he began, "I know him well. Do you want me to tell you about his youth? Very good. He was born at T—, the son of poor landowners. His father died when he was very young. He was left alone with his mother. She was a very good woman and did not expect much from him; she lived entirely on oatmeal, and all the money she had she spent on him. He was given an education in Moscow, first at the charge of some uncle, and then, when he grew up and was fully fledged, at the expense of a certain wealthy princess with whom he had an arrangement — well, forgive me, I won't — with whom he became friendly. Then he entered the university. It was at the university I came to know him, and we became very close friends. I'll tell you of our life and habits at that time some other day. I can't now. Then he went abroad. . . ."

Lezhniov continued to walk about the room; Alexandra Pavlovna followed him with her eyes.

"From abroad," he went on, "Rudin wrote very rarely to his mother, and visited her only once, for some ten days. . . . The old woman died in his absence, in the care of strangers; but right to the moment of her death she never took her eyes off his portrait. I used to visit her when I was living at T—. She was a good woman and hospitable; she always regaled me on cherry jam. She loved her Dmitry obliviously. The gentlemen of the Pechorin school will tell you that we always love those who themselves have little capacity for love; but it seems to *me* that all mothers love their children, especially those who are away. Later I came across Rudin abroad. Some lady had got attached to him, one of our Russians, some bluestocking, no longer young and beautiful, and so just what a bluestocking should be. He went about with her for quite a long time, and finally threw her over — but no, I'm wrong: she threw him over. And then I threw him over. And that's all."

Lezhniov stopped speaking, passed his hand over his forehead, and dropped into a chair as though tired.

"But do you know what, Mikhailo Mikhailich?" Alexandra Pavlovna began; "I see you are an ill-natured man; really, you're no better than Pigasov. I am sure that all you have said is true, that you haven't made any of it up; and yet in what an unfriendly light you have presented it all! That poor old woman, her devotion, her lonely death, that lady — what is it all aimed at? . . . You know you can paint the lives of the finest of men in such terrible colors — and adding nothing, note — that anyone would be horrified! And you know that's a form of slander, after all!"

Lezhniov rose and again walked about the room.

"I had no desire whatever to make you feel horrified, Alexandra Pavlovna," he said at last. "I am not a slanderer. But really," he added after a moment's thought, "there is indeed a grain of truth in what you say. I did not slander Rudin, but — who knows? — maybe since then he has changed — maybe I am being unjust to him."

"Ah! So you see. . . . Then promise me that you will renew your acquaintance with him, will get to know him properly, and then tell me your final opinion about him."

"If you wish. . . . But why are you silent, Sergei Pavlich?"

Volintsiev started and raised his head as though he had been aroused from sleep.

"What can I say? I don't know him. And besides I have a headache today."

"You certainly do look pale today," Alexandra Pavlovna remarked. "Are you well?"

"My head aches," he repeated, and went out.

Alexandra Pavlovna and Lezhniov gazed after him and exchanged glances, but did not say anything. Neither he nor she was unaware of what was going on in Volintsiev's heart.

6

Two months and more passed. During all that time Rudin was almost continuously Daria Mikhailovna's guest. She could not do without him. To tell him about herself, to listen to his observations, became a necessity of her being. One day he did express a desire to leave, on the pretext that he had spent all his money; she gave him five hundred rubles. He also borrowed two hundred rubles from Volintsiev. Pigasov visited Daria Mikhailovna much more rarely than formerly: Rudin oppressed him with his presence. For that matter, Pigasov was not the only one who felt oppressed.

"I don't like that clever fellow," he would say; "he expresses himself unnaturally, he's the very image of a character out of a Russian novel; he says: 'I,' and pauses with emotion. 'I, you know, I —' And all the words he uses are so long. If you sneeze, he at once begins to demonstrate to you why it was you sneezed and didn't cough. . . . If he praises you, it's just as though he were promoting you in rank. . . . If he begins to upbraid himself, to throw mud at himself — well, you think, now he won't dare to show himself in the light of day. But not on your life! He even grows more cheerful, as though he had drunk plenty of strong vodka."

Pandalevsky was afraid of Rudin and handled him carefully. Volintsiev's relations with him were peculiar. Rudin called Volintsiev a knight, extolled him to his face and behind his back; but Volintsiev could not get to like him, and always felt involuntary impatience and vexation when Rudin began to analyze his virtues in his presence. "Isn't he laughing at me?" he thought, and his heart quickened inimically within him. He tried to master himself, but he was jealous of Rudin's friendship with Natalia. And Rudin also, though he always gave Volintsiev a boisterous welcome, though he called him a knight and borrowed his money, hardly felt well disposed toward him. It would be difficult to determine what exactly these two men did feel when, squeezing each other's hands in a friendly grip, they looked into each other's eyes. . . .

Basistov continued to worship Rudin and to catch his every word in its flight. Rudin paid little attention to him. He did happen to spend a whole morning with him once, talking with him about the most important world problems and tasks, and rous-

ing the younger man to vivid rapture. But then he dropped him.
. . . Evidently he sought pure and devoted souls only in words.
With Lezhniov, who began to call on Daria Mikhailovna, he did
not even enter into argument, and appeared to avoid him. Lezhniov for his part treated him coldly, but did not express his final
opinion about him — a circumstance that greatly troubled Alexandra Pavlovna. She admired Rudin, but she also believed Lezhniov. Everybody in Daria Mikhailovna's house submitted to
Rudin's whims: his least wish was fulfilled. The order of the
daily occupations depended on him. Not one *partie de plaisir* was
made up without him. He was not a great lover of all kinds of un-
premeditated excursions and undertakings, however, and he took
part in them like a grown-up in children's games, with a gracious
and slightly bored benevolence. On the other hand, he entered
into everything about the house: with Daria Mikhailovna he discussed arrangements on the estate, the education of the children,
the farm management, and business affairs generally; he listened to
her suggestions, was not even bored by the details, and suggested
changes and innovations. She expressed herself as delighted with
them, but that was all. In the management of her estate she continued to follow the advice of her steward, an elderly one-eyed
Little Russian, a good-natured and cunning rogue. "The old is fat,
the new is thin," he used to say, calmly grinning and winking his
single eye.

After Daria Mikhailovna herself, Rudin talked to no one so
often and so long as to Natalia. He secretly gave her books, confided his plans to her, read her the first pages of proposed articles and works. Their purport was often unintelligible to her.
For that matter, apparently he did not make any great effort to
ensure that she understood him, so long as she listened to him.
His friendship with Natalia was not entirely to Daria Mikhailovna's liking. "But," she thought, "let her chatter away with him
in the country. As a girl she amuses him. There's no great harm
done, and she will learn a little in any case. . . . In Petersburg I
shall change all that. . . ."

Daria Mikhailovna was mistaken. Not as a girl did Natalia
talk to Rudin: she greedily drank in his words, she tried to get
to the heart of their meaning; she submitted her own thoughts,
her doubts, to his judgment; he was her preceptor, her leader. For

the time being, only her head seethed, but a young little head does not seethe alone for long. What sweet moments Natalia experienced when, on a bench in the garden, in the pallid shadow cast by an ash, Rudin began to read Goethe's *Faust* to her, or Hoffmann, or Bettina's letters,[1] or Novalis, continually stopping to explain those passages that seemed obscure to her! She talked German badly, like almost all our young ladies, but she understood it well, and Rudin was thoroughly steeped in German poetry, in the German romantic and philosophical world, and drew her with him into those forbidden lands. Unknown, beautiful, they opened before her attentive gaze; from the pages of the book Rudin held in his hand amazing pictures, new, luminous thoughts, poured in a ringing stream into her soul; and in her heart, shaken by the noble joy of great sensations, the sacred spark of rapture quietly shone out and burst into flame. . . .

"Tell me, Dmitry Nikolaich," she began one day as she was sitting at her embroidery frame by the window, "you're going to Petersburg for the winter, aren't you?"

"I don't know," Rudin replied, letting the book he was fingering drop to his knees. "If I can manage the means, I shall."

He spoke lifelessly; he felt tired and had done nothing all day.

"It seems to me that you could find the means."

He shook his head. "That's how it seems to you!" And he looked away significantly.

Natalia was about to say something, but stopped.

"Look," Rudin began, pointing to the window; "do you see that apple tree? It is broken down with the weight and quantity of its own fruit. A faithful emblem of genius. . . ."

"It is broken down because it didn't have any support," she retorted.

"I understand you, Natalia Alexeevna; but it is not so easy for a man to find it — that support."

"It seems to me that others' sympathies — in any case, loneliness . . ."

She was a little confused, and she blushed.

"And what will you do in wintertime in the country?" she hastily added.

---

[1] Bettina von Arnim, authoress of *Goethe's Briefwechsel mit einem Kinde* (1835). (Tr.)

"What shall I do? I shall finish my long article — you know it — on the tragic in life and in art — I told you my plan three days ago — and I'll send it to you!"

"And will you print it?"

"No."

"Why not? Then whom will you perform all that labor for?"

"At least for you."

Natalia cast down her eyes.

"It is beyond my understanding, Dmitry Nikolaich!"

"What is the article about, if I may ask?" Basistov, who was sitting a little way off, modestly inquired.

"On the tragic in life and in art," Rudin repeated. "And of course Mr. Basistov will read it. In any case, I haven't yet properly formulated the main idea. I haven't yet sufficiently defined in my own mind the tragic meaning of love."

Rudin readily and often talked about love. At first when she heard the word "love," Mlle Boncourt started and pricked up her ears like an old regimental charger hearing a trumpet; but later she grew accustomed to it and only used to purse her lips and deliberately take a pinch of snuff.

"It seems to me," Natalia remarked diffidently, "that the tragic in love is unhappy love."

"Not at all," Rudin protested; "that is rather the comic side of love. . . . The problem needs to be posed in quite a different fashion . . . one has to draw from deeper sources. . . . Love!" he continued. "In it everything is a mystery: how it comes, how it develops, how it disappears. Sometimes it appears suddenly, indubitable, joyous as the day; sometimes it smolders a long time, like fire under ashes, and bursts into flame in the soul when everything is already consumed; sometimes it creeps into the heart like a snake, or suddenly slips out of it. . . . Yes, yes; that is a serious problem. And besides, who loves, these days, who dares to love?"

And he was lost in thought.

"Why haven't we seen Sergei Pavlich for such a long time?" he suddenly asked.

Natalia flamed up and bent her head over her frame.

"I don't know," she whispered.

"What an excellent, what a noble man!" Rudin said, rising. "He is one of the finest examples of the true Russian courtier. . . ."

Mlle Boncourt gave him a sidelong look with her French eyes. Rudin walked about the room.

"Have you ever noticed," he said, turning sharply on his heels, "that on an oak — and the oak is a strong tree — the old leaves only fall off when the young leaves are beginning to break through?"

"Yes," Natalia slowly replied, "I have."

"Exactly the same thing happens with old love in a strong heart: it has died right out, but it still holds on; only another, new love can revive it."

Natalia made no answer.

"What is he getting at?" she thought.

He stood for a moment, shook back his hair, and walked away.

But Natalia went to her own room. Long she sat in bewilderment on her bed, long she pondered over Rudin's last words, then suddenly clenched her fists and fell to bitter weeping. What she was weeping about, God knows! She herself did not know why the tears had so suddenly started to flow. She wiped them away; but they flowed again, like water from a long-accumulating source.

That very same day Alexandra Pavlovna had a talk about Rudin with Lezhniov. At first he refused to say anything, but she had decided to achieve her end.

"I see," she said to him, "that you still don't like Dmitry Nikolaevich any more than before. Hitherto I have deliberately refrained from questioning you; but now you have had time to ascertain whether any change has occurred in him, and I want to know why you don't like him."

"As you wish," Lezhniov replied with his customary phlegmatism, "as you are so impatient; only, I ask you not to be angry —"

"Well, begin, begin!"

"And to let me have my say to the end."

"By all means, by all means; begin!"

"Well then," he began, slowly dropping on the divan, "I confess to you that I certainly do not like Rudin. He's an intelligent man —"

"I should say so!"

"He is a remarkably intelligent man, though he is essentially empty —"

"That is easy to say!"

"Though he is essentially empty," he repeated. "But that in itself is nothing: we're all empty. I do not even reproach him with the fact that he is a despot in his soul, and lazy, not too well versed — "

Alexandra Pavlovna threw out her hands.

"Not too well versed! Rudin!" she exclaimed.

"Not too well versed," he repeated in exactly the same tone; "he likes to live at other people's expense, to play a role, and so on — that is all in the order of things. But the real trouble is that he is as cold as ice."

"He cold — that ardent spirit cold?" Alexandra Pavlovna interrupted.

"Yes, as cold as ice, and he knows it, and pretends to be an ardent spirit. The trouble is," Lezhniov continued, gradually growing more excited, "that he is playing a dangerous game, dangerous not for him, of course; he doesn't stake a kopek, not even a hair, on the card, but others stake their souls — "

"Whom and what are you referring to? I don't understand you," said Alexandra Pavlovna.

"The trouble is that he is not honorable. After all, he is an intelligent man: he ought to know the value of his own words; but he says them as though they really do cost him something. . . . There is no denying the fact that he is eloquent; only his eloquence is not Russian. Yes, and finally it is forgivable in a youngster to talk eloquently, but at his age it is shameful for a man to console himself with the sound of his own speeches, it is shameful for a man to show off as he does!"

"It seems to me, Mikhailo Mikhailich, that to the listener it makes no difference whether you are showing off or not."

"Excuse me, Alexandra Pavlovna, but it does make a difference. One man may say something to me and I accept everything he says; but another may say the same words, or even more eloquent ones, and I do not even prick up my ears. Why is that?"

"You mean, *you* will not prick up your ears," she interrupted.

"Yes, I will not," Lezhniov retorted, "though perhaps I have big ears. The whole point is that Rudin's words remain only words and never become deeds; and yet those very words can disturb, can ruin, a youthful heart."

"But of whom, of whom are you speaking, Mikhailo Mikhailich?"

He paused.

"Do you wish to know whom I refer to? I refer to Natalia Alexeevna."

Alexandra Pavlovna was disconcerted for a moment, but she smiled almost at once.

"Dear me," she began, "what strange thoughts you always have! Natalia is still a child; and besides, if there was anything, do you really think that Daria Mikhailovna — "

"Daria Mikhailovna, to begin with, is an egotist and lives for herself; secondly, she is so convinced of her ability to bring up children that it does not even occur to her to be anxious about them. 'Fie! How could it happen! One moment, one majestic glance, and everything will pass like water off a duck's back.' That is what that lady thinks; she regards herself as a female Mæcenas, and a clever woman, and God knows what else; but in reality she is no more than an old society dame. But Natalia is no child; believe me, she reflects more often and more profoundly than you and I. And then such an honest, passionate, and ardent nature must needs come into contact with such an actor, such a coxcomb! For that matter, that, too, is in the order of things!"

"A coxcomb? Are you calling *him* a coxcomb?"

"Of course I am. . . . But tell me yourself, Alexandra Pavlovna, what is his role in Daria Mikhailovna's house? To be the idol, the oracle in the house, to intervene in domestic arrangements, in family slanders and quarrels — is that worthy of a man?"

She stared at him in amazement.

"I don't recognize you, Mikhailo Mikhailich," she said. "You've gone quite red, you're quite agitated. Really, there must be something else concealed behind all this."

"You're right, there is! You talk to a woman seriously, with conviction, but she will not rest until she has invented some petty, extraneous reason for your speaking as you do and not otherwise."

Alexandra Pavlovna grew angry.

"Bravo, M'sieur Lezhniov! You are getting to run down women just as regularly as Mr. Pigasov does. But say what you like, I don't care how astute you are, all the same it is difficult for me to believe that you could understand everybody and everything in such a short time. It seems to me you are mistaken. According to you, Rudin is a kind of Tartuffe."

"That is just the point, that he is not even a Tartuffe. Tartuffe did at least know what he was aiming at; but, with all his intelligence, this man --"

"Well, what of him, what of him? Finish your sentence, you unjust, loathsome man!"

Lezhniov rose.

"Listen, Alexandra Pavlovna," he began, "it is you who are unjust, not I. You condemn me for my harsh judgment of Rudin, but I have every right to speak harshly of him! Possibly I bought that right at no cheap price. I know him well: I lived a long time with him. Remember, I promised to tell you of our life in Moscow some time or other. Evidently I have got to do it now. But will you have the patience to hear me to the end?"

"Speak on, speak on."

"Very well, then."

He began to walk with slow paces about the room, occasionally halting and thrusting his head forward.

"You know, perhaps," he began, "or perhaps you don't know, that I was left an orphan when still young, and at the age of seventeen I had no one to look after me. I lived in my aunt's house in Moscow and did as I pleased. As a boy I was rather futile and self-ish, I was fond of showing off and bragging. When I entered the university I behaved like a schoolboy and soon got myself into a scrape. I shan't stop to tell you about it, it isn't worth it. I lied, and lied rather scurvily. . . . I was caught in my lies, was shown up publicly and put to shame. . . . I lost control of myself and cried like a child. This happened in an acquaintance's apartment, in the presence of many of my colleagues. They all started to laugh at me, all except one student, who, note, had been even more indignant with me than the others so long as I stood out and did not admit that I was lying. I don't know whether he felt sorry for me or what, but he linked his arm in mine and took me to his home."

"And was he Rudin?" Alexandra Pavlovna asked.

"No, it was not Rudin; it was a man — he is dead now — it was a man out of the ordinary. His name was Pokorsky. I am not capable of describing him in a few words, but if I begin to talk about him I shan't want to talk about anybody else. He was a clear, lofty spirit, and I have never since met a mind like his. Pokorsky lived in a low-ceilinged little room, in the mezzanine of a little old wooden house. He was very poor and kept himself going somehow by giving lessons. There were times when he could not even offer his guests a cup of tea, and his only couch was so broken down that it was beginning to look like a rowboat. But despite these inconveniences a large number of people used to visit him. Everybody loved him, he drew all hearts to him. You will not believe how pleasant and cheerful it was to sit in his poor little room! It was there I made Rudin's acquaintance. He had already parted from his Princess then."

"But what was there unusual about this Pokorsky?" Alexandra Pavlovna asked.

"How can I tell you? Poetry and truth, that is what attracted everybody to him. With a clear and spacious mind, he was yet as pleasant and amusing as a child. Even now I can hear his ringing laughter in my ears, and yet at the same time —

He burned a little midnight lamp
Before the shrine of good —

as one half-mad and very dear poet of our little circle said of him."

"But how did he talk?" Alexandra Pavlovna asked again.

"He talked well when he was in the mood, but not so as to astonish you. Even then Rudin was twenty times more eloquent than he."

Lezhniov halted and folded his arms.

"Pokorsky and Rudin had no resemblance to each other. There was far more glitter and crackle about Rudin, finer phrases, and perhaps more enthusiasm. He seemed to be far more talented than Pokorsky, but in reality he was a beggar by comparison. Rudin could develop any thought superbly, could argue with masterly power; but his thoughts were not born in his own head, he took them from others, especially from Pokorsky. Pokorsky was quiet and gentle to look at, even weak — and he loved women madly, he loved to carouse, and could stand up for himself. Rudin seemed to be full of fire, daring, life, but in his soul he was cold and all but timorous until his self-esteem was touched; then he went mad. He was always trying to make others subservient to him, but he conquered them in the name of general elements and ideas, and in fact he had a strong influence over many. True, no one liked him; only I, perhaps, was attached to him. They bore his yoke. . . . Everybody gave himself to Pokorsky of his own choice. On the other hand, Rudin never refused to discuss and argue with anyone who came along. . . . He did not read so very many books, but in any case he read far more than Pokorsky and all the rest of us; and in addition he had a systematic mind, a marvelous memory, and you know that has its effect on youth! Give youth conclusions, results, even though unsound, yet results! A perfectly conscientious person will not agree to doing that. You try to tell any youngster that you cannot give him the full truth because you yourself do not possess it . . . he will not stop to listen to you. But nor can you fool him. You must at least half believe that you possess the truth. . . . And that is why Rudin had such a strong influence on us fellows.

You see, I have just told you that he did not read so very much, but he had read books of philosophy, and his head was so arranged that he at once extracted all the general purport from what he had read, seized the very root of the matter, and then from it deduced luminous, sound threads of thought in all directions; he opened up mental prospects. To tell the truth, our little circle consisted of boys, and boys who had not completed their education. Philosophy, art, science, even life itself — all these were only words to us, or perhaps even conceptions, alluring, beautiful, but scattered, disintegrated. We had no understanding, no grasp of the general connection between all these concepts, the general law of the world, though we vaguely talked about it, endeavored to get some clear idea of it. . . . Listening to Rudin, we thought at first that we had at last clutched at it, that general connection, that at last the curtain had been raised! Granted, he did not speak his own thoughts, but what did that matter! He introduced a harmonious order into everything we knew, all the scattered was suddenly united, was composed, grew before our eyes like an edifice, everything shone, spirit breathed everywhere. . . . Nothing remained senseless, fortuitous; in everything there was intelligent necessity and beauty, everything gained a clear meaning, and, at the same time, a mysterious meaning; every separate phenomenon of life sounded in accord, and we ourselves, in a kind of sacred, horrific veneration, with a pleasant flutter of the heart, felt ourselves, so to speak, living vessels of the eternal truth, its instruments, called to something great. . . . This doesn't sound absurd to you?"

"Not in the least!" Alexandra Pavlovna slowly replied; "why

do you think it would? I don't entirely understand you, but I don't think it absurd."

"Of course, since then we have had time to grow wiser," he continued; "all that may seem childish to us now. . . . But I repeat, at that time we were indebted to Rudin for a great deal. Pokorsky was incomparably higher than he, indisputably; Pokorsky breathed fire and strength into us all; but sometimes he felt lifeless and was silent. He was highly strung, and had poor health; on the other hand, when he spread his wings — God! Where he flew to — into the very depths and azure of heaven! But in Rudin, in that handsome and well-built lad, there were many pettinesses; he even gossip-mongered; it was his passion to interfere in everything, to resolve and elucidate everything. His fussy activity never grew weary. . . . His was a political nature! I speak of him as I knew him then. For that matter, he has not changed, unfortunately. On the other hand, he has not changed in his beliefs either — at the age of thirty-five! . . . Not everyone can say that of himself."

"Sit down," Alexandra Pavlovna said. "What are you swinging about the room for, like a pendulum?"

"It is easier for me to talk when I walk about," he replied. "Well, having entered Pokorsky's circle, I confess to you, Alexandra Pavlovna, that I was completely transformed; I grew more humble, I inquired into things, I studied, I rejoiced, I venerated — in a word, it was as though I had entered some temple. And in very deed, as I recall our meetings, well, by God, there was much in them that was good, even moving. You imagine: some five or six lads come together, one tallow candle burning, tea of the filthiest taste is handed round, and the lumps of sugar provided with it are old, very old; but you should have seen all our faces, you should have heard our speeches! In all eyes there was rapture, and cheeks burned, and hearts beat, and we talked of God, of truth, of the future of humanity, of poetry — sometimes we talked nonsense, we were enthusiastic over trifles; but what of that? . . . Pokorsky would sit with his legs tucked under him, resting his pale cheek on his hand; and his eyes would shine, would shine. Rudin would stand in the middle of the room and talk, talk eloquently, just like a young Demosthenes before a raging sea; from time to time the tousle-haired poet Subbotin would give off explosive exclamations, as if in his sleep; a forty-year-old

Bursch named Scheller, the son of a German pastor, famous among us as the profoundest of thinkers because of his everlasting, quite inviolable silence, would be observing his silence with a special rapture; even the merry Shchitov, the Aristophanes of our meetings, would lapse into silence and only grin; two or three novitiates would be listening with exultant delight. . . . And the night would fly past quietly and smoothly, as though on wings. And now the dawn would be graying, and we would disperse, moved, merry, honest, sober (at that time we did not even think of wine), with a kind of pleasant weariness in our souls . . . and you looked even at the stars with a kind of trustfulness, as though they had grown closer, and more intelligible. . . . Ah! They were great times then, and I don't like to think that they went for nothing! Nor did they, not even for those who afterward were vulgarized by life. . . . How often have I happened to meet men who were my former comrades! You would think the man had become quite an animal, but you had only to mention the name of Pokorsky in his presence and all the last remnants of nobility within him began to stir, as though in a dark and dirty room you had unstoppered a forgotten phial of perfume. . . ."

He lapsed into silence; his colorless face flushed.

"But then why and when did you quarrel with Rudin?" Alexandra Pavlovna said, looking at Lezhniov in perplexity.

"I did not quarrel with him; I parted from him when I got to know him thoroughly, abroad. But even in Moscow I had reason to quarrel with him. He played a dirty trick on me even then."

"What did he do?"

"I'll tell you. I — how shall I say it? — it doesn't accord with my general appearance — but I have always been capable of falling in love."

"You?"

"Yes, I. That is strange, isn't it? But meanwhile, it is so. Well, then too I fell in love with a certain very nice little girl. But what are you staring at me like that for? I could tell you something much more astonishing about myself!"

"But what, I should like to know?"

"Why, just this. During those Moscow days I used to go off nights to an assignation — whom do you think with? With a young lime tree at the end of my garden. I would embrace her slender and shapely trunk, and I felt that I was embracing all na-

Rudin

ture, and my heart would expand and would be moved as though all nature really were pouring into it. . . . That is what I was like then! . . . But that's not all! I suppose you think I never wrote poetry? But I did, and I even wrote a complete play, in imitation of *Manfred*. Among the characters was a specter with blood on its breast, and not its own blood, please note, but the blood of humanity generally. . . . Ye-es, ye-es, you mustn't be surprised. . . . But I had begun to tell you about my love. I made the acquaintance of a certain girl — "

"And you stopped going to assignations with the lime?" Alexandra Pavlovna asked.

"I did. This girl was an exceedingly nice and exceedingly good-looking creature, with merry, clear eyes and a ringing voice."

"You describe her well," she remarked with a smile.

"But you're a very harsh critic," he retorted. "Well, this girl lived with her old father. . . . But I won't go into details. I will only tell you that she really was exceedingly nice; she would pour you out three quarters of a glass of tea when you had asked for only half a glass! . . . By the third day after my first meeting with her I was on fire, and on the seventh day I could control myself no longer and confessed everything to Rudin. It is impossible for a young man in love to avoid talking; and I confessed myself in every detail to him. At that time I was completely under his influence, and I will admit without equivocation that in many respects his influence was beneficial. He was the first man who was not fastidious about me, he rough-hewed me. I was passionately fond of Pokorsky and was afraid of his spiritual purity; but I was closer to Rudin. When he learned of my love he went into indescribable raptures: he congratulated me, embraced me, and at once set to work to enlighten me, to explain to me all the seriousness of my new situation. I pricked up my ears. . . . Well, but you know yourself how he can talk. His words had an unusual effect on me. I suddenly felt an amazing respect for myself, I adopted a serious look and ceased to smile. I remember I even began to walk more cautiously, as though in my breast I bore a vessel filled with precious fluid, which I was afraid of spilling. . . . I was very happy, the more so as I was obviously regarded with favor. Rudin expressed the wish to make the acquaintance of my girl; and for that matter I myself rather insisted on introducing him."

617

"Well, I see, I see now what happened," Alexandra Pavlovna interrupted. "Rudin won your girl from you, and to this very day you are unable to forgive him. . . . I am prepared to wager that I am right!"

"And you would lose your wager, Alexandra Pavlovna: you are wrong. Rudin did not win my girl from me, nor did he even want to win her; but all the same he destroyed my happiness, though now, judging cold-bloodedly, I am prepared to say thank-you to him for doing so. But at the time I all but went out of my mind. Rudin had no desire whatever to injure me — on the contrary! But through his accursed habit of pinning down every movement of life, both his own and others', with a word, like a butterfly with a pin, he set to work to explain to both of us our own selves, our relationships, and how we ought to behave, despotically forced us to report our thoughts and feelings to him, praised us, chided us, even entered into correspondence with us, imagine that! . . . Well, he completely knocked us off our course! I would hardly have married my young lady (so much sound sense was still left to me), but at the least I would have spent a few months very happily with her, like Paul and Virginia; but now misunderstandings cropped up, the atmosphere grew strained — in a word, there was trouble! It ended with Rudin, one fine morning, arguing himself into the conviction that it was his sacred duty as a friend to inform her old father of all that was going on — and so he did."

"Really!" Alexandra Pavlovna exclaimed.

"Yes, and, note, he did it with my permission — that was the marvel of it! . . . I remember to this day what a chaos I had in my head at the time: everything was simply going round and round, making me feel I was in a camera-obscura; white seemed to be black, black white; falsehood seemed to be truth, imagination a duty. . . . Ah! even now I am ashamed to think of it! Rudin — he never despaired — I should say not! And he used to soar amid all kinds of misunderstandings and entanglements like a swallow above a lake."

"And so you parted from your girl?" Alexandra Pavlovna asked, naïvely bending her little head on one side and raising her eyebrows.

"We parted — and our parting was unpleasant, humiliatingly awkward, public, and unnecessarily public. . . . I myself wept, and she wept, and the devil knows what happened. . . . Somehow a Gordian knot had been tied, and it had to be cut, and that was painful! However, everything in the world is for the best. She married a good man and is now flourishing. . . ."

"But confess, you've never been able to forgive Rudin, even so," Alexandra Pavlovna began.

"What?" he interrupted her. "I wept like a baby when I saw him over the frontier. But to tell the truth, the seed had been sown in my soul even then. And when I met him again abroad — well, I was older too then. . . . I saw Rudin in his true light."

"But what exactly did you discover in him?"

"Why, all that I told you an hour ago. But enough of talking about him. Perhaps everything will pass off satisfactorily. I only wanted to prove to you that if I am harsh in my judgment of him, it isn't because I don't know him. . . . As for Natalia Alexeevna, I shan't waste words unnecessarily; but you keep an eye on your brother."

"On my brother? But what about him?"

"Why, look at him. Haven't you noticed anything?"

She cast down her eyes.

"You're right," she said; "you know — for some time now — it's just as though — I don't recognize my brother. . . . But surely you don't think — "

"Quiet! I think this is he coming," Lezhniov said in a whisper. "But Natalia is not a child, believe me, though unfortunately she is as inexperienced as a child. You see, that girl will surprise us all."

"How?"

"Why, like this — do you know that it's that kind of girl who drowns herself, takes poison, and so on? Don't you believe that she's so quiet; there are strong passions in that girl, and she has character — my goodness, she has!"

"Now it seems to me that you are going off into poetry. To such a phlegmatic man as you, I suppose even I seem like a volcano."

"Well, hardly!" he said with a smile. "And as for character, thank goodness you haven't any at all."

"Well, of all the impudence!"

"Impudence? Excuse me, but that is the greatest of compliments."

Volintsiev entered and looked suspiciously at his sister and

Lezhniov. He had grown thinner of recent days. They both began to talk to him, but he hardly smiled at their jests and looked, as Pigasov had once said of him, like a miserable hare. In all probability, however, there has never yet been a man on earth who hasn't looked even worse than that at least once in his life. Volintsiev felt that Natalia was slipping away from him, and so he felt that the earth also was slipping from under his feet.

7

The next day was Sunday, and Natalia was late in rising. All the previous day she had been very taciturn, secretly she was ashamed of her tears, and she slept very badly. Sitting, half dressed, before her small piano, she played chords, almost inaudibly in order not to disturb Mlle Boncourt, then set her brow against the chilly keys and remained a long time without stirring. She thought continually, not of Rudin himself, but of something he had said, and was completely buried in her thoughts. Occasionally she recalled Volintsiev to mind. She knew that he loved her. But her thoughts at once turned from him. . . . She felt a strange agitation. In the morning she hurriedly dressed, went downstairs, and, after greeting her mother, seized an opportune moment and went out into the garden.

The day was hot; it was a bright, a radiant day, though there had been a few fine showers. Low, smoky clouds floated smoothly across the sky, not veiling the sun, and occasionally dropped the copious floods of a sudden and momentary downpour over the fields. The large, glittering drops were scattered rapidly, with a dry patter, as though they were diamonds; the sun played through their glittering tracery; the grass, recently troubled by the wind, now did not stir as it avidly drank in the moisture; the freshened trees languidly rustled all their leaves; the birds did not cease singing, and it was a joy to hear their fussy twittering against the fresh roar and rattle of the onward speeding rain. The dusty roads smoked and were lightly speckled with the sharp blows of the frequent sprinkles. But now the little cloud passed over, a breeze sprang up, the grass began to be flooded with emerald and gold . . . clinging to one another, the leaves of the trees grew translucent. . . . A pungent scent arose from everything . . .

The sky was almost clear when Natalia went into the garden.

It was vivid with freshness and stillness, that modest and happy stillness to which the heart of man responds with a sweet languor of secret sympathy and indefinite desire. . . .

Natalia walked beside the lake, down a long avenue of silver poplars; suddenly Rudin appeared before her, as though he had sprung out of the ground.

She was disconcerted. He gazed into her face.

"Are you alone?" he asked.

"Yes, I am alone," Natalia replied; "I just slipped out for a moment. . . . I ought to be going back now."

"I'll walk back with you."

And he walked along at her side.

"You seem to be sad?" he said.

"I? . . . But I was about to remark that I think you are not yourself."

"Maybe — I have these moods sometimes. It is more excusable in me than in you."

"But why? Surely you don't think I have nothing to be sad about?"

"At your age you should delight in life."

Natalia took a few steps without speaking.

"Dmitry Nikolaevich!" she said.

"Yes?"

"Do you remember — the comparison you made yesterday — do you remember — with the oak?"

"Why, yes, I remember. What about it?"

Natalia took a surreptitious glance at him.

"Why did you . . . what were you trying to suggest by that comparison?"

He bent his head and fixed his gaze on the distance.

"Natalia Alexeevna!" he began, with his own restrained and significant emphasis, which always made the listener think he had not given utterance to even a tenth of what was oppressing his soul; "Natalia Alexeevna, you may have noticed that I talk little about my past. There are certain strings that I do not touch at all. My heart — who has any need to know what has gone on within it? It has always seemed a sacrilege to exhibit it for show. But with you I am frank: you arouse my trust. . . . I cannot conceal from you that I, too, have loved and suffered, like everybody else. . . . When and how? It is not worth talking about that; but my heart has experienced many joys and many sorrows. . . ."

He was silent for a moment.

"What I said to you yesterday," he went on, "can to a certain extent be applied to me, to my present position. But again it is not worth talking about that. That side of life has already passed for me. All that remains to me now is to drag along a sultry and dusty road, from post stage to post stage, in a rattling cart. . . . When I shall arrive, and whether I shall ever arrive, God knows. . . . Let us rather talk about you."

"But, Dmitry Nikolaevich," Natalia interrupted him, "do you really expect nothing of life?"

"Oh, no! I expect a great deal, but not for myself. . . . I shall never renounce activity, the blessedness of activity, but I have renounced all pleasure. My hopes, my dreams — and my own personal happiness have nothing in common. Love" (at this word he shrugged his shoulders), "love is not for me; I — am not worthy of it; the woman who loves has the right to demand all the man, but I cannot now surrender myself wholly. Moreover, to please is the task of youth; I am too old. How am I to turn others' heads! God grant that I can keep my own on my shoulders!"

"I understand," Natalia said. "Anyone who aims at a great end should not think about himself; but isn't it possible for a woman to appreciate such a man? On the contrary, it seems to me that a woman turns more readily from an egotist. . . . All young people, all youngsters, in your view, are egotists, they are all occupied only with themselves, even when they love. But believe me, a woman is not only capable of understanding self-sacrifice: she is capable of sacrificing herself."

Natalia's cheeks flushed a little, and her eyes glittered. Before her acquaintance with Rudin she would never have uttered so long a speech and uttered it with such fervor.

"You have more than once heard my opinion on woman's vocation," Rudin replied with a condescending smile; "you know that in my view only Joan of Arc could have saved France. . . . But that is not the point. I wanted to talk about you. You are standing on the threshold of life. . . . To reflect on your future is pleasant, nor is it fruitless. . . . Listen: you know I am your friend; I take almost a family interest in you. . . . And so I hope you will not find my question immodest: tell me, has your heart remained completely undisturbed hitherto?"

Natalia flamed up and did not say a word. Rudin halted, and she halted.

"You are not angry with me?" he asked.

"No," she said; "but I simply did not expect — "

"In any case," he continued, "you need not answer me. Your secret is known to me."

Natalia looked at him almost with fear.

"Yes — yes; I know whom you are fond of. . . . And I must say you could not make a better choice. He is a splendid man; he will know how to appreciate you; he is not trampled on by life — he is simple and clear of soul . . . he constitutes your happiness."

"Whom are you referring to, Dmitry Nikolaich?"

"Don't you understand whom I'm referring to? To Volintsiev, of course. Why? Isn't it true, then?"

Natalia turned a little away from him. She was dumbfounded.

"Isn't he in love with you? Of course he is! He never takes his eyes off you, he follows your every movement; and besides, is it possible to conceal love? And aren't you, for your part, favorably disposed toward him? So far as I have been able to observe, your mother likes him too. . . . Your choice — "

"Dmitry Nikolaich," Natalia interrupted him, in her confusion stretching her hand out to a bush standing close by, "really it is very awkward for me to talk about it, but I assure you — you are mistaken."

"I am mistaken?" he repeated. ". . . I don't think so. I have only recently made your acquaintance, but I already know you well. What is the meaning of the change I see in you, and see so clearly? Are you the same girl I first met six weeks ago? . . . No, Natalia Alexeevna, your heart is not at rest."

"Maybe," Natalia replied hardly audibly. "But none the less you are mistaken."

"How do you mean?" Rudin asked.

"Leave me, don't question me!" she replied, and with swift steps went back toward the house.

She was feeling frightened at all that she was suddenly experiencing within herself.

Rudin overtook and halted her.

"Natalia Alexeevna," he began, "this conversation cannot end in this fashion: it is too important for me, too. . . . How am I to understand what you have said?"

"Leave me!" she repeated.

"Natalia Alexeevna, for God's sake!"

His face expressed agitation. He turned pale.

"You understand everything, you must understand me too!" said Natalia, tearing her hand away from his; and she went on without looking back.

"Only one word!" he cried after her.

She stopped, but did not turn round.

"You asked me what I was trying to convey by yesterday's comparison. Then know, I don't wish to deceive you. I was talking about myself, about my past — and about you."

"What? About me?"

"Yes, about you; I, I repeat, do not wish to deceive you. . . . You know now what feeling, what new feeling I was talking about then. . . . Until today I would never have resolved upon — "

Natalia suddenly covered her face with her hands and ran toward the house.

She was so disturbed by the unexpected end to her conversation with Rudin that she did not even notice Volintsiev as she ran past him. He was standing motionless, with his back against a tree. He had arrived fifteen minutes previously to make a call on Daria Mikhailovna and had found her in the reception hall; he had said a couple of words, had withdrawn unnoticed, and had gone off to look for Natalia. Guided by that sense peculiar to people in love, he went straight into the garden and came upon her and Rudin just as she tore her hand away from his grasp. The world went dark before him. Following Natalia with his gaze, he broke away from the tree and took a few steps, himself not knowing whither or why. Rudin noticed him when they drew level. They gazed into each other's eyes, bowed, and parted in silence.

"It will not end here," they both thought.

Volintsiev walked to the very end of the garden. He felt bitter and nauseated; but his heart felt like lead, and from time to time his blood rose angrily. Rain again began to fall. Rudin returned to his room. He, too, was not easy in his mind: thoughts whirled in his head like a whirlwind. The trustful, unexpected contact of a young, honest soul would disturb anybody.

At the table everything seemed to go awkwardly. Natalia was very pale, could hardly keep in her chair, and did not raise her eyes. Volintsiev sat, as usual, beside her and from time to time talked to her forcedly. It so happened that that day Pigasov was dining with Daria Mikhailovna. He was the most talkative of all at the table. Among other things he began to argue that people, like dogs, can be divided into the short- and the long-tailed kinds. People are dock-tailed, he said, both from birth and by their own fault. Things go badly for the dock-tailed — they never are successful in anything, they have no self-confidence. But the man who has a long fluffy tail, he's the favorite of fortune. He can be both worse and weaker than the dock-tailed, but he is sure of himself, he waves his tail — and everybody admires him. And yet the thing to be wondered at is that, after all, the tail is quite a useless part of the body, you must agree; what use is a tail? But everybody judges your merits by your tail.

"I," he added with a sigh, "belong to the dock-tailed group and, most annoying of all, I myself cut off my tail."

"In other words, you are trying to say," Rudin remarked perfunctorily, "something that La Rochefoucauld said long before you: have confidence in yourself, and others will believe you. Why you had to drag the tail in I don't understand."

"Please let everyone," Volintsiev remarked sharply, and his eyes began to burn, "please let everyone express himself as he thinks best. Talk of despotism — in my view there is no worse despotism than that of the so-called intelligent people. The devil take them all!"

They were all amazed at his outburst, and there was a hush. Rudin tried to look at him, but could not withstand his gaze; he turned away, smiled, and did not open his mouth.

"Aha! And you're dock-tailed too!" thought Pigasov; but Natalia's soul froze with terror. In her astonishment Daria Mikhailovna gave Volintsiev a long stare and finally was the first to speak; she began to talk about some extraordinary dog owned by her friend, the Minister XX.

Volintsiev drove away soon after dinner. As he took leave of Natalia he could not resist saying to her:

"Why are you so abashed, as though you had done something wrong? You cannot do wrong to anybody! . . ."

She did not understand a word of what he said and only gazed after him. Just before tea Rudin came across to her. Bending over the table as though sorting out the newspapers, he whispered:

"It's all like a dream, isn't it? I simply must see you alone — if only for a minute." He turned to Mlle Boncourt. "Here it is," he said to her, "here is the *feuilleton* you were looking for." He leaned across to Natalia again, adding in a whisper: "Try to be by the terrace in the lilac arbor about ten o'clock. I shall be waiting for you. . . ."

Pigasov was the hero of the evening. Rudin yielded the field of battle to him. He greatly amused Daria Mikhailovna: first he told about one of his neighbors who, having been under his wife's thumb for thirty years, had become such a woman himself that one day, as he was stepping across a little puddle, Pigasov saw him put his hand behind him and draw the folds of his frock coat aside, just as women do with their skirts. Then Pigasov turned to another landowner who had been first a mason, then a melancholiac, and finally wanted to be a banker.

"How did you come to be a mason, Filip Stepanich?" Pigasov asked him.

"It's well known how: I grew a long nail on my little finger."

But Daria Mikhailovna laughed most of all when Pigasov turned to expatiating on love and declared that women had pined for him too, that one passionate German woman had even called him an "appetizing African" and "dear little hoarse-voice." Daria Mikhailovna laughed, but Pigasov was not lying: in fact he had every right to brag of his conquests. He asserted that there was nothing easier than to make any woman you like fall in love with you: you had only to tell her ten days in succession that she had paradise between her lips, and bliss in her eyes, and that all other women were simply old rags compared with her, and on the eleventh day she herself would say that there was paradise between her lips and bliss in her eyes and would fall in love with you. All kinds of things do happen in the world. Who knows, perhaps Pigasov is right.

Rudin

Rudin was in the arbor as early as half past nine. In the distant and pallid depths of the sky the stars were only just beginning to shine; the west was still crimson — there the horizon seemed clearer and purer; the crescent moon was gleaming golden through a black latticing of weeping birches. The other trees either stood like morose giants with a thousand chinks resembling eyes or were blended in compact, somber masses. Not one little leaf was stirring; the upper branches of the lilacs and acacias seemed to be listening to something and stretched themselves in the warm air. The house emerged darkly close at hand; the long, lighted windows showed as patches of reddish light. Mild and still was the evening, but a restrained and passionate sigh was lurking in that stillness.

Rudin stood with his arms folded on his chest and listened with strained attention. His heart was beating violently, and he involuntarily held his breath. At last he heard light, hurrying steps, and Natalia entered the arbor.

He rushed to her and took her by the hands. They were as cold as ice.

"Natalia Alexeevna!" he began in a quivering whisper, "I wanted to see you — I could not wait till tomorrow. I must tell you what I did not suspect, what I did not confess to myself even this morning: I love you!"

Natalia's hands feebly trembled in his hands.

"I love you," he repeated, "and how could I so long deceive myself, how is it I did not guess long ago that I love you! . . . But you? . . . Natalia Alexeevna, tell me, you? . . ."

Natalia hardly breathed.

"You see, I have come here," she said at last.

"No, tell me, do you love me?"

"I think I — do . . ." she whispered.

Rudin squeezed her hands even more firmly and tried to draw her toward himself. . . .

She gave a swift glance behind her.

"Let me go — I am frightened — I have the feeling that someone is listening to us. . . . For God's sake, be careful. Volintsiev guesses."

"Who cares! You saw that I did not answer him today. . . . Ah, Natalia Alexeevna, how happy I am! Now nothing whatever will separate us!"

She glanced into his eyes.

"Let me go," she whispered, "it is time I was going."

"One moment," Rudin began.

"No, let me go, let me go. . . ."

"You seem to be afraid of me?"

"No; but it is time I — "

"Then do repeat at least once more . . ."

"You say you are happy?" Natalia asked.

"I? There is not a man in all the world more happy than I! Surely you don't doubt that?"

Natalia raised her head. Beautiful was her pale face, noble, youthful, and agitated, in the mysterious shadow of the arbor, by the feeble light falling from the nocturnal sky.

"Then know," she said, "I will be yours."

"Oh, God!" Rudin exclaimed.

But Natalia slipped from his grasp and went out. He stood there a little longer; then, slowly, he left the arbor. The moon clearly lit up his face; a smile was hovering on his lips.

"I am happy," he uttered in an undertone. "Yes, I am happy," he repeated, as though wishing to convince himself.

He drew himself up, shook his curls, and walked briskly into the garden, swinging his arms merrily.

But meanwhile the bushes forming the lilac arbor very quietly parted, and Pandalevsky appeared. He looked about him cautiously, shook his head, pursed his lips, and said significantly: "Well, indeed! It will be necessary to bring this to Daria Mikhailovna's notice," and disappeared.

8

On his return home Volintsiev was so despondent and moody, replied so reluctantly to his sister, and so quickly shut himself away in his room that she resolved to send a messenger for Lezhniov, to whom she turned at all moments of difficulty. He sent the reply that he would come the next day.

Volintsiev was no more cheerful next morning. After drinking tea he thought of going off to work, but he remained at home, lay down on the divan, and turned to reading a book, which was a rare occurrence with him. He felt no attraction to literature and was simply afraid of poetry. He used to say: "That's incomprehensible as poetry," and in confirmation of his

words he would quote the following lines from the poet
Aibulat: [1]

And to the end of the mournful days
Neither proud experience nor prudence
Will ever shatter with their hands
The bloody lives of forget-me-nots.

Alexandra Pavlovna watched her brother anxiously, but did
not trouble him with questions. A carriage drove up to the door.
'Well,' she thought, 'thank goodness, Lezhniov. . . .' A servant
entered and reported Rudin's arrival.

"Who has arrived?" he asked.

"Dmitry Nikolaich Rudin," the servant repeated.

Volintsiev got up.

"Ask him in," he said. "And you, sister, leave us," he added,
turning to Alexandra Pavlovna. "Leave us."

"But why — " she began.

"I know why," he interrupted vehemently. "I ask you."

Rudin entered. Standing in the middle of the room, Volintsiev
bowed coldly to him and did not hold out his hand.

"You didn't expect me, did you?" Rudin began, and put his hat
on the window sill.

His lips were quivering slightly. He felt awkward, but he endeavored to conceal his confusion.

"You're right, I did not expect you," Volintsiev retorted. "After
yesterday, I would rather have expected someone to arrive —
with a challenge from you."

"I understand what you are trying to say," Rudin said, sitting
down, "and I am very glad of your frankness. It is far better so.
I have myself come to you, as you are a man of magnanimity."

"Can't you leave out the compliments?" Volintsiev remarked.

"I wish to explain to you why I have come."

"You and I are acquainted: why shouldn't you call on me? Besides, this is not the first time you have honored me with a visit."

"I have called on you as one magnanimous man to another
magnanimous man," Rudin repeated. "I want now to refer to
your judgment. . . . I trust you completely. . . ."

"But what is it you want?" Volintsiev said, still standing in the

[1] Pseudonym of K. M. Rozen, a Russian minor poet of the early nineteenth century. (Tr.)

same position and gazing morosely at Rudin, with an occasional tug at the ends of his mustaches.

"Allow me — I have come in order to make an explanation, of course; but, all the same, that cannot be done all at once."

"But why can't it?"

"A third person is involved — "

"What third person?"

"Sergei Pavlich, you understand me."

"Dmitry Nikolaich, I don't understand you in the least."

"As you wish — "

"I wish you to speak without circumlocutions," Volintsiev broke in. He was beginning to be angry in earnest.

Rudin's face clouded.

"Excuse me — we are alone — I must tell you — for that matter, you probably guess already" (Volintsiev impatiently shrugged his shoulders) — "I must tell you that I love Natalia Alexeevna, and am entitled to presume that she loves me in return."

Volintsiev went pale, but made no answer; he crossed to the window and turned his back.

"You understand, Sergei Pavlich," Rudin continued, "that if I were not confident — "

"Excuse me!" Volintsiev hurriedly interrupted him, "I haven't any doubt whatever. . . . Well, and congratulations! I am only wondering what the devil made you take it into your head to call on me with this news. . . . Where do I come in? What has it to do with me whom you love and who loves you? That I simply cannot make out."

He continued to stare out of the window. His voice sounded muffled.

Rudin rose to his feet.

"I will tell you, Sergei Pavlich, why I resolved to call on you, why I did not consider I had even the right to conceal from you my — our mutual dispositions. I have too deep a respect for you — that is why I have called; I did not want — neither of us wanted to play out some comedy in your presence. I knew of your feeling for Natalia Alexeevna. . . . Believe me, I know my worth: I know how little worthy I am to take your place in her heart. But if that has been fated to occur, surely it is better not to be cunning, to resort to deceit, to make a pretense? Surely it is better not to submit to misunderstandings or even the possibility of such a scene as occurred at the dinner table yesterday? Sergei Pavlich, surely you agree?"

Volintsiev folded his arms on his chest, as though attempting to subdue himself.

"Sergei Pavlich!" Rudin continued; "I have distressed you, I feel that — but understand us — understand that we had no other means of proving our respect for you, of proving that we can appreciate your straightforward nobility. With any other man frankness, complete frankness, would be incompatible; but with you it becomes a duty. It is pleasant for us to think that in your hands our secret — "

Volintsiev burst into a forced laugh.

"Thank you for your confidence!" he exclaimed, "Though, I ask you to note, I did not desire either to know your secret or to betray my own to you; but you dispose of it as if it were your own property. But allow me: you speak as if you are acting for others besides yourself. So I can assume that Natalia Alexeevna knows of your visit to me, and the purpose of this visit?"

Rudin was a little disconcerted.

"No, I have not informed Natalia Alexeevna of my intention; but I know she shares my manner of thought."

"All this is very fine," Volintsiev said after a moment's silence, and he began to drum his fingers on the window-glass, "though I must admit it would be far better if you respected me less. To tell the truth, I haven't any need whatever of your respect. But what is it you want of me now?"

"I want nothing — or rather I want just one thing: I want you not to regard me as a cunning and artful man, I want you to understand me. . . . I hope that now you can no longer have any doubt of my sincerity. I want us to part as friends, Sergei Pavlich. . . . I want you to hold out your hand to me as before — " And he came toward Volintsiev.

"Pardon me, my dear sir," Volintsiev said, turning and falling back a pace, "I am ready to do full justice to your intentions; this is all very fine, shall we say, even exalted. But we are simple people, we eat our cake without icing, we are not in a condition to follow the struggle of such great minds as yours. . . . What seems sincere to you seems obtrusive and immodest to us. . . . What to you is simple and clear is confused and dark to us. . . . You boast of that which we conceal; so how can we understand you? Pardon me! I cannot regard you as a friend, nor can I give you my hand. . . . That, perhaps, is petty, but then, I myself am petty."

Rudin picked up his hat from the window sill.

"Sergei Pavlich," he said in a mournful tone, "good-by; I have been deceived in my expectations. My visit is indeed rather odd; but I hoped that you — " (Volintsiev made an impatient movement). "Forgive me, I shall not say any more about that. Taking everything into consideration, I see clearly that you are right and could not act otherwise. Good-by, and allow me at least once more, for the last time, to assure you of the purity of my intentions. . . . I am convinced of your discretion. . . ."

"But this is too much!" Volintsiev exclaimed, and he shook with anger. "I didn't in the least solicit your confidence; and so you have no right whatever to count on my discretion!"

Rudin was about to say something more; but he only threw out his hands, bowed, and withdrew, and Volintsiev flung himself on the divan and turned his face to the wall.

"May I come in?" Alexandra Pavlovna's voice came from outside the door.

He did not reply at once, and he stealthily passed his hand over his face. "No, sister," he said in a rather changed tone. "Wait a little longer."

Half an hour later Alexandra Pavlovna again came to the door. "Mikhailo Mikhailich has arrived," she said; "would you like to see him?"

"Yes," he answered, "send him here."

Lezhniov entered.

"What, aren't you well?" he asked, seating himself in an armchair by the divan.

Volintsiev half raised himself, rested on his elbow, gazed long, long into his friend's face, and at once told him of all his conversation with Rudin, from beginning to end. He had never before even hinted to Lezhniov of his feelings for Natalia, though he guessed that they were not a secret to him.

"Well, brother, you have astonished me," Lezhniov said as soon as Volintsiev had finished his story. "I expected many singularities of him, but this — Though even in this I recognize him."

"Excuse me," said the agitated Volintsiev, "but it was simply insolence! Why, I all but flung him through the window! Was it that he wanted to brag in front of me, or was he afraid? But why should he be? How can one bring oneself to drive and call on a man — "

Volintsiev flung his hands behind his head and lapsed into silence.

"No, brother, that's not the reason," Lezhniov calmly replied. "I know you won't believe me, but he did it from a good impulse. Really. . . . You see, it is noble, and frank, and then it provides an opportunity to talk, to bring his eloquence into play; and, you see, that is just what he needs, that is what he is not in a condition to live without. . . . Oh, his tongue is his enemy. . . . Yes, but on the other hand it is his servant."

"You cannot imagine the exultantly solemn air with which he entered and spoke! . . ."

"Ah, but you see he can't do without it! He buttons up his coat as though he were fulfilling a sacred duty. I would set him on an uninhabited island and watch around the corner how he began to arrange his life there. And he talks of simplicity!"

"But tell me, for God's sake," Volintsiev asked, "what is it all — philosophy, or what?"

"That is difficult to answer; on the one hand, perhaps it is simply philosophy; but on the other it is anything but that. We mustn't put any old rubbish to the charge of philosophy."

Volintsiev gave him a glance.

"But wasn't he lying? What do you think?"

"No, my son, he was not lying. But all the same, do you know what? Enough of discussing this matter. Let's light our pipes and ask Alexandra Pavlovna to join us. . . . With her around it is easier to talk, and easier to be silent. She'll give us some tea."

"If you like," Volintsiev replied. "Come in, sister," he called.

Alexandra Pavlovna entered. He seized her hand and pressed it firmly to his lips.

Rudin returned home in a vague and singular state of mind. He was annoyed with himself, and upbraided himself for his unforgivable impetuosity, for his childishness. Not without reason has someone said: there is nothing more oppressive than the realization of a stupidity just committed.

Regret gnawed at Rudin.

"The devil drove me," he whispered between his teeth, "to

go and call on that landowner! A fine idea to have! Simply asking for insolence. . . ."

But in Daria Mikhailovna's house something unusual was occurring. The mistress herself had not put in any appearance all the morning, and she did not come down to dinner. According to Pandalevsky, the only person allowed to see her, she had a headache. Nor did Rudin achieve more than a sight of Natalia: she remained in her room with Mlle Boncourt. . . . Meeting him in the dining-room, she looked at him so mournfully that his heart trembled. Her features were changed, as though since yesterday misfortune had overwhelmed her. The yearning of an indefinite presentiment began to torment him. In order to amuse himself somehow, he occupied himself with Basistov, talked a great deal to him, and found him to be an enthusiastic, lively youngster with exalted hopes and still unscathed faith. Toward evening Daria Mikhailovna put in an appearance for a couple of hours in the reception hall. She was amiable to Rudin, but seemed to keep herself at a distance, and one moment was laughing, the next frowning; she talked haughtily and mostly in innuendos . . . she bore herself with all the airs of a court lady. She seemed now to have cooled off a little in regard to Rudin. "What is this mystery?" he thought, looking sidelong at her head flung back.

He did not have to wait long for the solution to the mystery. Returning, about midnight, to his room, he passed along a dark corridor. Suddenly someone thrust a note into his hand. He looked around: a girl was retreating in the distance, he thought she looked like Natalia's maid. He reached his room, dismissed his man, opened the note, and read the following lines, written in Natalia's hand:

Come tomorrow morning, at seven, not later, to Avdiukhin Pond, beyond the oak wood. Any other time is impossible. This will be our last meeting, and everything will be ended, if — Come. We shall have to reach a decision. . . .

PS. If I don't arrive, it means we shall not see each other again; then I shall let you know. . . .

Rudin sat thinking, then he turned the note over in his hands, laid it beneath his pillow, undressed, and got into bed. But he did not fall asleep for a long time; then he slept lightly, and it was not yet five o'clock when he awoke.

Rudin

9

The Avdiukhin Pond, where Natalia had proposed to meet Rudin, had long since ceased to be a pond. It had burst its banks some thirty years before, and so it had fallen into neglect. Only by the flat and shallow bottom of the ravine, once covered with oily slime, and by the remnants of the dam, could one have guessed that a pond had once been here. And here, too, a farmstead had existed. It had disappeared long since. Two great pines stood as a reminder of the farmstead; the wind everlastingly roared and howled gloomily among their lofty, meager green. . . . Among the people of the district mysterious rumors circulated of a terrible crime that was said to have been committed at the feet of these pines; it was also said that neither of them would fall without causing someone's death; that formerly a third pine had stood here, but it had been overthrown by a storm and had crushed a girl beneath it. All the area around the former pond was regarded as an unclean spot; empty and bare, but lonely and gloomy, even on a sunny day, it seemed even more gloomy and lonely because of the proximity of a senile oak wood that had long since withered and died. The scanty gray shells of the enormous trees hovered like despondent phantoms over the low, bushy undergrowth. They were a dreary sight: they looked as though wicked old men had come together to ponder on some evil design. A narrow, hardly worn track wound from side to side. No one ever went past Avdiukhin Pond without special need. Natalia had deliberately chosen this isolated spot. It was not half a mile from Daria Mikhailovna's house.

The sun had long risen when Rudin arrived at the pond; but it was not a cheerful morning. Compact masses of milky-colored cloud veiled all the sky; whistling and howling, the wind drove them along rapidly. Rudin began to walk backward and forward over the dam, which was covered with clinging burs and blackened nettles. He was not at ease. These meetings, these new sensations interested, but they also agitated him, especially since yesterday's note. He saw that the denouement was at hand, and secretly was confused in mind, though no one would have thought so, seeing with what concentrated resolution he folded his arms on his chest and looked about him. It was not without justification that Pigasov had once said of him that his head was continually hanging like that of a Chinese idol. But no matter how powerful a head may appear to be, it is difficult to tell what is going on inside it. . . . Rudin, the intelligent, sagacious Rudin, was not in a position to say for certain whether he loved Natalia, whether he was suffering, or whether he would suffer if he parted from her. Then why, not even playing the Lovelace — we have to do him that justice — had he swept the poor girl off her feet? Why was he waiting for her with a secret flutter of the heart? To that there is one answer: no one is so easily carried away as a man lacking in passion.

He walked about the dam, but Natalia hastened to him straight across the fields, through the wet grass.

"Miss! Miss! you'll get your feet wet," her maid, Masha, said to her, hardly able to keep up behind her.

Natalia did not hear her and ran without looking back.

"Ah, I hope we haven't been seen!" Masha declared. "It's amazing that we managed to get out of the house. If only Mam'-selle doesn't wake up. . . . Thank goodness it isn't far. . . . And there he is already waiting," she added, suddenly catching sight of Rudin's stately figure as he stood picturesquely on the dam. "Only it's silly of him to stand like that in the open, he ought to go into the ravine."

Natalia halted.

"Wait here, Masha, by the pines," she said, and went down to the pond.

Rudin advanced to meet her, but stopped in amazement. He had not seen such an expression on her face before. Her brows were knitted, her lips pressed together; her eyes had a firm and stern gaze.

"Dmitry Nikolaich," she began, "we haven't any time to waste. I have come for five minutes. I must tell you that my mother knows everything. Mr. Pandalevsky was watching us the night before last and told her of our meeting. He has always been Mother's spy. She summoned me to her room yesterday."

"My God!" Rudin exclaimed; "this is terrible. . . . But what did your mother say?"

"She wasn't angry with me, didn't scold me, only reproached me a little for my thoughtlessness."

"Is that all?"

"Yes, and she informed me that she would rather consent to see me dead than married to you."

"Did she really say that?"

"Yes; and she added that you yourself have no desire whatever to marry me, that you're only doing it out of boredom, you're just making love to me, and that she didn't expect it of you; but, for that matter, she was herself to blame, why did she let me see you so often? . . . that she counts on my being sensible, that I have greatly surprised her . . . and really I don't remember what else she said to me."

Natalia said all this in an even, almost toneless voice.

"But you, Natalia Alexeevna, what did you reply?" Rudin asked.

"What did I reply?" she repeated. "What do *you* intend to do now?"

"My God! My God!" he exclaimed. "This is cruel! So soon — such an unexpected blow! . . . And your mother was so indignant as all that?"

"Yes — yes, she will not listen to a word about you."

"This is terrible! So there is no hope whatever?"

"None whatever."

"Oh, why are we so unfortunate? That odious Pandalevsky! . . . You ask me, Natalia Alexeevna, what I intend to do? My head is going round and round — I cannot think of a thing. . . . I feel only my own unhappiness. . . . I am astonished that you can be so composed! . . ."

"Do you think I find it easy?" she said.

He began to walk up and down the dam. Natalia did not take her eyes off him.

"Your mother didn't question you, then?" he said at last.

"She asked me if I love you."

"Well — and what did you say?"

Natalia was silent for a moment before answering: "I did not lie."

Rudin took her by the hand.

"Always, in all things, noble and magnanimous! Oh, the heart of a maid is pure gold! But did your mother really declare so resolutely that our marriage was impossible?"

"Yes, quite resolutely! I've already told you: she is convinced that you yourself have no thought of marrying me."

Turgenev

"So she regards me as a deceiver! What have I done to deserve that?" And he clutched his head.

"Dmitry Nikolaich!" Natalia said, "we are wasting time. Remember, I am seeing you for the last time. I have come here not to weep, not to complain — you see that I am not weeping — I have come for advice."

"But what advice can I give you, Natalia Alexeevna?"

"What advice? You are a man; I have become accustomed to trusting you, I shall trust you to the end. Tell me, what are your intentions?"

"My intentions? Your mother will probably refuse to have me in her house."

"Possibly. Even yesterday she told me that she will have to break off her acquaintance with you. . . . But you are not answering my question."

"What question?"

"What do you think we must do now?"

"What must we do?" Rudin replied: "naturally, submit."

"Submit," Natalia slowly repeated, and the blood fled from her lips.

"Submit to fate," he continued. "What else can we do? I know all too well how bitter that is, how heavy, how unbearable; but judge for yourself, Natalia Alexeevna, I am poor. . . . True, I can work; but even if I were rich, would you be able to endure the violent break with your family, and your mother's anger? . . . No, Natalia Alexeevna; we may not even think of it. Evidently we are not fated to live together, and the happiness of which I dreamed is not for me!"

Natalia suddenly covered her face with her hands and burst into tears. Rudin drew closer to her.

"Natalia Alexeevna! Dear Natalia!" he said ardently; "don't weep, for God's sake; don't torment me, be comforted. . . ."

She raised her head.

"You tell me to be comforted," she began, and her eyes flashed through her tears. "I am not crying for the reason you think. That is not what hurts me; what hurts me is that I have been deceived in you. . . . And how much! I come to you for advice, and at such a moment, and your first word is: submit — submit! So that is how you put into practice your talk of freedom, of sacrifices that —"

638

Her voice broke.

"But, Natalia Alexeevna," the disconcerted Rudin began, "remember — I do not go back on my words — only — "

"You ask me," she continued with new strength, "what I replied to my mother when she informed me that she would rather see me dead than married to you. I replied that I would rather die than marry another. . . . And you say: submit! So she was right: so you were just playing with me, because you had nothing to do, out of boredom. . . ."

"I swear to you, Natalia Alexeevna — I assure you — " Rudin declared.

But she did not listen to him.

"But why didn't you stop me? Why did you yourself — Or didn't you think that there might be obstacles? I feel ashamed to talk about it — but then, it is all over now."

"You must calm down, Natalia Alexeevna," he began; "we must both of us think what measures — "

"You have spoken so often of self-sacrifice," she interrupted; "but, do you know, if you were to say to me today, this minute: 'I love you, but I cannot marry you, I will not answer for the future, give me your hand and come with me,' do you know, I would follow you, do you know that I would be ready for all things? But, truly, it is a long way from words to deeds, and you are now showing cowardice, just as you did the day before yesterday, at dinner, in front of Volintsiev."

The color rushed into Rudin's face. Natalia's unexpected exaltation had dumbfounded him, but her last words stung his self-esteem.

"You are too worked up now, Natalia Alexeevna," he began, "you cannot understand how grievously you insult me. I hope that with time you will do me justice; you will understand how much it cost me to renounce a happiness that, as you yourself say, would not impose any obligations upon me. Your tranquillity of spirit is the most precious thing in the world to me, and I would be the meanest of men if I decided to take advantage — "

"Maybe, maybe," Natalia interrupted; "maybe you are right, I do not know what I am saying. But hitherto I have trusted you, I have believed every word you said. . . . Please weigh your words in future, don't cast them to the wind. When I told you I love you, I knew what that word meant: I was ready for anything. . . . Now it remains for me to thank you for the lesson — and to say good-by."

"Stop, for God's sake, Natalia Alexeevna, I implore you! I am not deserving of your contempt, I swear to you. Now put yourself in my place. I am answerable for you and for myself. If I did not love you with the most devoted love — yes, by God! — I would myself at once propose that you should run away with me. Sooner or later your mother would forgive you — and then — But before thinking of my own happiness — "

He stopped. Natalia's gaze, fixed straight on him, embarrassed him.

"You are trying to prove to me that you are an honest man, Dmitry Nikolaich," she said. "But I have no doubt of that. You are not capable of acting calculatingly; but do you think that I wished to be convinced of that, do you think that that was why I came here?"

"I did not expect, Natalia Alexeevna — "

"Ah! that was your true self speaking then! No, you did not expect all this — you did not know me. Don't be anxious — you do not love me, and I shall never force myself on anyone."

"I do love you!" Rudin exclaimed.

Natalia drew herself up.

"Maybe; but how do you love me! I remember all your words, Dmitry Nikolaich. Do you remember what you said to me: without complete equality there is no love? . . . You are too high for me, you are no mate to me. . . . I am justly punished; before you lie tasks more worthy of you. I shall not forget this day. . . . Good-by. . . ."

"Natalia Alexeevna, are you going? Must we part like this?"

He stretched out his hands to her. She halted. Apparently his imploring voice had shaken her.

"No," she said at last; "I feel that something has snapped within me. . . . I came here, I talked with you just as if I were in a fever; now I must come to my senses. That is not to be, you yourself have said that it will not be. My God, as I came here I was mentally saying good-by to my home, to all my past — and then what? Whom did I meet here? A man of faint heart. . . . And how did you know that I am not capable of enduring the parting from my family? 'Your mother does not consent. . . . This is terrible!' That is all I have heard from you. Is that you, is that you, Rudin? No! Good-by! . . . Ah, if you loved me I would feel it now, at this moment. . . . No, no, good-by!"

She turned swiftly and ran to Masha, who for some time had been growing anxious and was making signs to her.

"It is *you* who are a coward, and not I!" Rudin shouted after her.

She no longer paid any attention to him and hastened home across the fields. She reached her bedroom safely; but as soon as she crossed the threshold her strength betrayed her, and she fell senseless into Masha's arms.

But Rudin remained standing on the dam for a long time after. At last he started, made his way with slow steps to the path, and slowly walked along it. He was deeply shamed . . . and chagrined. "What a girl!" he thought. "At the age of eighteen! . . . No, I did not know her. . . . She is a remarkable girl. What strength of will! . . . She is right; she is worthy of more than the love I felt for her. . . . Felt?" he asked himself. "Do I then no longer feel love? If so, that is how it was all bound to end! How miserable and petty I was to her!"

The light rattle of a sulky made him raise his eyes. Lezhniov was driving toward him behind his invariable trotting horse. Rudin silently exchanged bows with him, and, as though struck by a sudden thought, turned off the road and went swiftly in the direction of Daria Mikhailovna's house.

Lezhniov gave him time to retreat, gazed after him, and, after a little thought, also turned his horse round — and drove back to Volintsiev, with whom he had spent the night. He found him still asleep and did not ask for him to be disturbed. While waiting for tea, he seated himself on the balcony and lit his pipe.

10

Volintsiev got up about ten o'clock. Learning that Lezhniov was sitting on his balcony, he was greatly surprised and told a servant to ask him in.

"What has happened?" he asked him. "I thought you were going back home."

"Yes, I was, but I met Rudin. . . . He was striding alone over the fields, and he had a very discomposed expression on his face. So I changed my mind and came back."

"You came back because you had met Rudin?"

"Well, to tell the truth, I myself don't really know why I came back. Probably because he reminded me of you; I wanted to have a little longer with you; and I can have plenty of time to get back home."

Volintsiev smiled bitterly.

"Yes, one cannot think of Rudin now without thinking of me too. . . ." He called to his servant: "Bring us some tea."

Over the tea Lezhniov turned to talking about agricultural matters, about a new method of roofing granaries with paper. . . .

Suddenly Volintsiev jumped up from his chair and struck the table with such force that the cups and saucers clattered.

"No!" he exclaimed. "I am not able to bear this any longer! I'll challenge that clever fellow, and then he can shoot me, or else I'll do my best to put a bullet into his learned brow!"

"Steady now, steady now, old man!" Lezhniov muttered. "What made you shout like that? I've dropped my pipe. . . . What's the matter with you?"

"Why, I can't hear his name mentioned and remain unmoved. It makes my blood boil."

"Enough, brother, enough! Aren't you ashamed?" Lezhniov protested as he picked up his pipe from the floor. "Drop it! Ignore him! . . ."

"He has insulted me," Volintsiev continued, striding about the room. "Yes, he has insulted me. You must agree that that is so. I didn't take it in at first: he put me in a fix; and besides, who would have expected it? But I'll show him that he can't joke with me. . . . I'll shoot him like a partridge, the damned philosopher!"

"And much you'll gain by that, of course! I won't say anything about your sister. We know you are carried away by passion, so how could you stop to think of your sister! But in regard to someone else, do you think that by killing the philosopher you will amend your own affairs?"

Volintsiev flung himself into a chair.

"Then I'll go away somewhere! For here I'm just eating my heart out: I just can't find a place for myself."

"You'll go away — now, that is another matter! Now, that I agree with. And do you know what I suggest? Let's all go off together — to the Caucasus, or simply to Little Russia, to eat dumplings.[1] That's a splendid idea!"

[1] The dumplings made by the Ukrainians are famous all over Russia. (Tr.)

Rudin

"Yes; but whom shall we leave my sister with?"

"But why shouldn't Alexandra Pavlovna go with us? I tell you it will be first-rate. I'll take on the job of looking after her! She shan't lack for anything; if she wishes, I'll arrange a serenade under her window every evening; I'll scent up all the post drivers with eau de Cologne, and plant flowers along the roads. And then you and I, my boy, we'll simply be reborn; we'll get such a lot of pleasure out of it, we'll come back such fatguts that love will never find its way into our hearts again!"

"You must have your joke, Misha!"

"I'm not joking at all. It's a brilliant idea you've had."

"No! It's stupid!" Volintsiev again shouted. "I want to fight him, fight him! . . ."

"Again! You are in a state of *colere* today, my boy!"

A man entered with a letter.

"Who is it from?" Lezhniov asked.

"From Dmitry Nikolaevich Rudin. Madam Lasunskaya's man brought it."

"From Rudin?" Volintsiev repeated. "For whom?"

"For you."

"For me? . . . Give it to me."

He seized the letter, swiftly unsealed it, and began to read. Lezhniov watched him closely: a strange, almost joyous astonishment was expressed on his friend's face; he let his hands fall.

"What is it?" Lezhniov asked.

"Read it," Volintsiev said in an undertone, and held out the letter.

Lezhniov began to read. This is what Rudin had written:

To Sergei Ivanovich!
Dear Sir:

I am departing from Daria Mikhailovna's house today, and departing forever. That in all probability will astonish you, especially after what occurred yesterday. I cannot explain to you what exactly is compelling me to behave in this manner; but for some reason I have the feeling that I should inform you of my departure. You do not like me, and even consider me a bad man. I have no intention of justifying myself: time will justify me. In my opinion, it is unworthy of a man, and indeed useless, to attempt to demonstrate to a prejudiced man the injustice of his prejudices.

Anyone who wishes to understand me will excuse me, but anyone who does not wish to or is unable to understand me, such a man's accusations do not affect me. I have been mistaken in you. In my eyes you will still remain a noble and honest man; but I had assumed that you were capable of rising above the milieu in which you have developed. . . . I was mistaken. There is nothing to be done about it! It is not the first, nor will it be the last time. I repeat to you: I am departing. I wish you happiness. You must agree that this wish is completely disinterested, and I hope that you will now be happy. Perhaps in time you will change your opinion of me. Whether we shall ever meet again I do not know, but, in any case, I remain, with sincere respect for you,

D. R.

PS. The two hundred rubles I owe you I shall send as soon as I arrive at my village, in T— province. I also ask you not to say anything about this letter in front of Daria Mikhailovna.

PPS. Yet one last but important request: as I am now going away, I hope you will not make any mention to Natalia Alexeevna of my visit to you.

"Well, what do you say to that?" Volintsiev asked as soon as Lezhniov had finished the letter.

"What is there to say," the other retorted, "but to exclaim in the Oriental fashion: 'Allah! Allah!' and stick your thumb in your mouth with surprise — that is all one can do. He is departing. . . . Well, pleasant journey and smooth road! But here is the curious thing: even this letter he wrote as a matter of *duty*, and he called on you out of his feeling of duty. . . . These people find duty at every step, and it's nothing but duty — and debts!" [1] Lezhniov added, pointing with a smile to the postscript.

"But the phrases he puts to paper!" Volintsiev exclaimed. "He is mistaken in me; he expected me to rise above some milieu or other. . . . Goodness, what a lot of rot! Worse than poetry!"

Lezhniov did not answer; only his eyes smiled. Volintsiev rose.

"I intend to drive over to Daria Mikhailovna's," he said; "I want to find out what it all means. . . ."

"Wait a bit, my boy: give him a chance to clear off. What point is there in your coming into collision with him again? He's disappearing, what more do you want? Better go and lie down and

[1] A play on words: *dolg* = "duty" and "debt." (Tr.)

644

have a good sleep; I expect you did nothing but turn over from side to side all night. But now your affairs will improve."

"How do you deduce that?"

"That's how it seems to me. Really, go and get some sleep; and I'll go and spend a little while with your sister."

"I have no desire whatever for sleep. What on earth am I to sleep for? . . . I'd rather go and have a look at the fields," said Volintsiev, pulling down the ends of his coat.

"And that's a good idea too. Go, my boy, go and have a look at the fields. . . ."

And Lezhniov went off to Alexandra Pavlovna's part of the house.

He found her in the reception hall. She welcomed him graciously; she was always glad to see him. But her features remained sorrowful. She was disturbed by Rudin's visit of the previous day.

"Have you just seen my brother?" she asked Lezhniov. "How is he today?"

"He's all right, he's gone off to look at the fields."

Alexandra Pavlovna was silent for a moment or two.

"Please tell me," she began, attentively studying the hem of her handkerchief, "do you know why —"

"Why Rudin called yesterday?" he took her up. "I do: he came to say good-by."

Alexandra Pavlovna raised her head.

"To say good-by?"

"Yes. Haven't you heard? He is leaving Daria Mikhailovna."

"Leaving her?"

"Forever; at least, so he says."

"But, excuse me, how are we to understand that, after all that has —"

"That's another question! It is impossible to understand, but it is so. Something must have happened there. He pulled the string too tight, and it snapped."

"Mikhailo Mikhailich!" Alexandra Pavlovna began; "I don't understand one little bit; I think you are laughing at me."

"No, really I'm not. I tell you he is going away, and he is even writing and informing his acquaintances of his intention. It isn't a stupid step, if you think, in certain aspects; but his departure has hindered the realization of one extraordinary plan that your brother and I had begun to discuss."

"What do you mean? What was the plan?"

"Why, just this. I had proposed to your brother that we should go off and travel, for our own pleasure, and take you with us. As for looking after you personally, I undertook that. . . ."

"Very fine!" Alexandra Pavlovna exclaimed. "I can imagine how you would look after me. Why, you would starve me to death."

"You say that, Alexandra Pavlovna, because you don't know me. You think I am a chump, an absolute chump, just a wooden block; but do you know that I am capable of melting like sugar, and spending all day on my knees?"

"Now, I'd really like to see it, I must admit!"

He suddenly stood up. "Then take me as your husband, Alexandra Pavlovna, and you will see it all."

She blushed right to her ears.

"Why did you say that, Mikhailo Mikhailich?" she said again and again in her confusion.

"Why," he answered, "I simply said something that has been a long time and a thousand times on the tip of my tongue. I have spoken out at last, and you can do as you wish. But in order not to impose any restraint upon you, I will go now. If you wish to be my wife — But I shall leave you now. If the idea is not repugnant to you, simply send for me: by that act I shall understand. . . ."

Alexandra Pavlovna was about to detain him, but he had already briskly left the room; going hatless into the garden, he leaned on a wicket gate and began to gaze into the distance.

"Mikhailo Mikhailich!" the maid's voice sounded behind him, "please come to the mistress. She ordered me to call you."

Mikhailo Mikhailich turned round, astonished the girl by seizing her head with both hands, kissed her on the forehead, and went to Alexandra Pavlovna.

II

Returning home immediately after his meeting with Lezhniov, Rudin locked himself in his room and wrote two letters: one to Volintsiev (its contents are already known to the reader) and the other to Natalia. He sat very long over this second letter, crossing out and rewriting a great deal of it, and then, carefully copying it on a sheet of thin postal paper, folded it as small as possible and put it in his pocket. With a look of sorrow on his face he walked backward and forward about the room several times, sat down on a chair in front of the window, and rested his head on his hand; the tears slowly oozed onto his eyelashes. . . . He rose, buttoned himself up tightly, called his man, and ordered him to ask Daria Mikhailovna whether he could see her.

The man soon returned and reported that Daria Mikhailovna had ordered him to ask Rudin to come. He went to her.

She received him in her private room, as on the first occasion, two months before. But now she was not alone: with her was Pandalevsky, as modest, fresh, clean, and amiable as ever.

Daria Mikhailovna welcomed Rudin affably, and Rudin bowed affably to her, but after one glance at their smiling faces anybody with the least experience would have realized that something unpleasant had occurred between them, even if it had not been expressed in words. Rudin knew that Daria Mikhailovna was angry with him. Daria Mikhailovna suspected that he already knew all.

Pandalevsky's report had greatly upset her. The worldly arrogance in her began to awaken. Rudin, a poor man with no official post and at present unknown in the world, had had the impudence to make an assignation with her daughter, the daughter of Daria Mikhailovna Lasunskaya!

"Assuming he is clever, that he is a genius!" she said. "But what does that prove? After this anyone may hope to be my son-in-law."

"For long I did not believe my eyes," Pandalevsky joined in. "I am amazed that he doesn't know his place!"

Daria Mikhailovna was greatly upset; she gave Natalia a serious lecture.

She asked Rudin to sit down. He sat down, but now no longer as the old Rudin, almost the master of the house, and not even as a close acquaintance, but as a guest, and not an intimate guest. All this change had occurred in a single moment. So water is suddenly turned into solid ice.

"I have come to you, Daria Mikhailovna," Rudin began, "to thank you for your hospitality. I have received certain news from my little village this morning, and I must travel there without fail this very day."

Daria Mikhailovna gazed at Rudin fixedly.

"He has forestalled me; evidently he guesses," she thought. "He is saving me the trouble of explanations; so much the better. Hurrah for intelligent people!"

"Really?" she said aloud. "Ah, what unpleasant news! Well, it cannot be helped! I hope to see you this winter in Moscow. We ourselves shall be leaving here soon."

"I don't know, Daria Mikhailovna, whether I shall succeed in getting to Moscow; but if I can manage the resources, I shall consider it my duty to call on you."

"Aha, brother!" Pandalevsky thought in his turn; "is it so long since you were behaving like the master here? And now listen to the way you have to talk!"

"So you have received unsatisfactory news from your village?" he asked with his usual drawl.

"Yes," Rudin dryly replied.

"A failure of the harvest, perhaps?"

"No — something else. . . . Believe me, Daria Mikhailovna," Rudin added, "I shall never forget the time I have spent in your house."

"And I, Dmitry Nikolaich, shall always recall our acquaintance with you with pleasure. . . . When are you leaving?"

"Today, after dinner."

"So soon? . . . Well, I wish you a good journey. And perhaps, if your affairs do not detain you, perhaps you will still find us here."

"I doubt whether I shall manage that," Rudin retorted, and rose to his feet. "Excuse me," he added, "I cannot repay my debt to you at once; but as soon as I arrive in my village —"

"Enough, Dmitry Nikolaich!" Daria Mikhailovna interrupted him. "Aren't you ashamed? . . . But what time is it?" she asked.

Pandalevsky took a gold and enameled watch from his waist-coat pocket and looked at it, cautiously resting his rosy cheek against his hard white collar.

"Thirty-three minutes past two," he said.

"Time to dress," Daria Mikhailovna remarked. "Good-by, Dmitry Nikolaich!"

Rudin rose. All the conversation between him and Daria Mikhailovna had borne a peculiar impress. So actors rehearse their parts, so diplomats at conferences exchange previously formulated phrases.

Rudin left the room. Now he knew by experience how society people do not even throw out, but simply drop anyone who has become unnecessary to them, like a glove after a ball, like a bag emptied of sweets, like an out-of-date lottery ticket.

He hastily packed and began to wait impatiently for the moment of departure. On learning his intentions everybody in the house was greatly astonished; even the servants looked at him in amazement. Basistov did not conceal his regret. Natalia obviously avoided Rudin; she tried to avoid meeting his eyes. None the less, he managed to slip his letter into her hand. At dinner Daria Mikhailovna again repeated that she hoped to see him before their departure for Moscow, but he made no answer. Pandalevsky talked most to him. Rudin felt more than once like throwing himself on him and punching his shining, ruddy face. Mlle Boncourt looked at Rudin again and again with a crafty and peculiar expression in her eyes; one can sometimes notice a similar expression in old, very intelligent setters. . . . "Ehee!" she seemed to be saying to herself, "so you've got it!"

Six o'clock arrived at last, and Rudin's tarantass was brought to the door. He hurriedly began to take leave of them all. He felt very down-in-the-mouth. He had not expected to leave this house in such a fashion: almost as though he were being turned out. . . . How had it all happened? And what was the hurry for? But in any case the end would have been the same; so he was thinking as, with an artificial smile, he bowed in all directions. He glanced for the last time at Natalia, and his heart was moved: her eyes were fixed on him with a mournful, parting reproach.

He briskly ran down the steps, jumped into the tarantass. Basistov offered to accompany him as far as the first posthouse and got in with him.

"Do you remember," Rudin began, as soon as the tarantass had driven out of the courtyard onto the broad fir-lined road, "do you remember what Don Quixote says to his man as they drive out of the Duchess's palace? 'Freedom, my friend Sancho,' he says, 'is one of man's most precious gifts, and happy is he whom heaven has given a piece of bread, who does not need to be indebted to another for it.' What Don Quixote felt then, I feel now. . . . God grant that you too, my good Basistov, may experience that feeling some day!"

Basistov squeezed Rudin's hand, and the honest young fellow's heart beat strongly in his deeply agitated breast. All the way to the posthouse Rudin talked about the dignity of man, the meaning of true freedom — he talked ardently, nobly, and justly — and when the moment of parting arrived, Basistov could not control himself; he flung his arms around Rudin's neck and burst into tears. Rudin also shed tears; but he did not weep because he was parting from Basistov, and his tears were tears of self-esteem.

Natalia went to her room and read Rudin's letter.

Dear Natalia Alexeevna [he had written]:
I have decided to go away. There is nothing else I can do. I have decided to go away before I am told plainly to remove myself. My departure will put an end to all misunderstandings; and I don't suppose anyone will feel regret for me. So why wait? . . . That is all true; but why should I write to you?

I am parting from you, probably, forever, and to leave with you a memory of me even worse than the one I deserve would be too bitter. That is why I am writing to you. I do not wish either to justify myself or to accuse anyone whatever, except myself: I want so far as possible to explain. . . . The events of the last few days have been so unexpected, so sudden. . . .

Today's meeting will serve me as a memorable lesson. Yes, you are right: I did not know you, I only thought I knew you! In the course of my life I have met all kinds of people, I have been friendly with many women and girls; but when I met you I, for the first time, met a soul absolutely *honest and direct. I was not used to that, and I was unable to appreciate you. I felt an attraction toward you from the first day of our acquaintance — you may have noticed that. I spent hour after hour with you, and I did not recognize you; I hardly even tried to recognize you — and I could imagine that I loved you! For that sin I am now punished.*

I have loved one woman in the past also, and she loved me. . . . My feeling for her was complex, just as was hers for me, but as she herself was not simple, that happened to suit us perfectly. The truth was not revealed to me then; nor did I recognize it now, when it arose before me. . . . I have recognized it at last, but too late. . . . One cannot recall the past. . . . Our lives might have come together — and now they never will. How can I prove to you that I could have loved you with a true love — with love of the heart, not of the mind — when I myself do not know whether I am capable of such love?

Nature has given me much — I know that, and I shall not be mock-modest with you out of a false sense of shame, especially now, at a moment for me so bitter, so shameful. . . . Yes, nature has given me much; but I shall die without accomplishing anything worthy of my powers, without leaving any beneficent trace behind me. All my riches will be wasted; I shall not see the fruits of my seeds. I lack — I myself cannot say what exactly it is I lack — I probably lack that without which it is impossible to move the hearts of people or to possess the heart of a woman; but domination over minds alone is both unstable and useless. My fate is strange, almost comic: I give myself wholly, avidly, completely — and cannot give myself. I shall end by sacrificing myself for some trifle in which I shall not even believe. . . . My God! At the age of thirty-five I am still continually making ready to do something! . . .

I have never before expressed myself like this to anyone — this is my confession.

But enough of me. I want to talk about you, to give you some advice: I am no good for anything more. . . . You are still young; but, no matter how long you live, always follow the inspiration of your heart, never submit yourself either to your own or to another's mind. Believe me, the simpler and narrower the circle within which one's life is passed, the better; it is not a matter of seeking and finding new sides in life, but of ensuring that all its transitions are accomplished betimes. "Blessed is he who has been young from youth. . . ." But I must remark that that advice applies far more to me than to you.

I confess to you, Natalia Alexeevna, that I am very depressed. I have never deceived myself as to the nature of the feeling I inspired in Daria Mikhailovna; but I did hope that I had found at least a tempororay harborage. . . . Now I have again to go tossing about the world. What can take the place for me of your conversation, your presence, your attentive and intelligent look?

. . . I am myself at fault; but you must agree that fate seems to have deliberately laughed at us. A week ago I myself hardly guessed that I loved you. Only the day before yesterday, in the garden, I heard for the first time from you — but why recall to you what you said then? — and now, today, I am already going away, going away in shame, after a cruel explanation with you, not bearing any hopes with me. . . . And you do not yet know how deeply I am guilty in regard to you. . . . I have a kind of stupid frankness, a kind of garrulity. . . . But why speak about that! I am going away forever.

(Here Rudin had intended to tell Natalia of his visit to Volintsiev. But he thought better of it and struck out all this passage, and added a second postscript to his letter to Volintsiev.)

I remain alone in the world in order to devote myself, as you said to me this morning with a cruel sneer, to other tasks for which I am more suited. Alas, if I only could devote myself to these tasks, could overcome my own inertia at last! . . . But no! I shall remain the same unfinished creature I have been hitherto. . . . At the first obstacle I have crumbled completely; this incident with you has shown me that. If I had at least sacrificed my love to my future work, to my calling! But I was simply frightened of the responsibility that had fallen on me, and so I am, in fact, not worthy of you. I am not worthy that you should tear yourself away from your sphere for me. . . . But in any case all this may be, is for the best. Out of this trial I may, perhaps, emerge cleaner and stronger.

I wish you perfect happiness. Good-by! Think of me sometimes. I hope that you will yet hear of me.

Rudin

Natalia dropped the letter on her knees and sat long motionless, her gaze fixed on the floor. This letter demonstrated to her more clearly than any other possible proofs how right she had been when, on parting from Rudin that morning, she had involuntarily exclaimed that he did not love her! But that did not make it any easier for her. She sat without stirring; she had the feeling that dark waters had closed without a splash over her head, and she was going to the bottom, going stiff and numb.

Rudin

For anyone the first disillusionment is oppressive; but for a sincere soul who does not wish to be self-deceived, who is alien to frivolity and exaggeration, it is almost unbearable. Natalia recalled her childhood, when on her evening walk she had always tried to go in the direction of the lighted rim of the sky, toward the spot where the sunset was burning, and not toward the dark side. Dark was the life that now lay before her, and she turned her back on the light. . . .

Tears started to her eyes. Not always are tears beneficial. They are comforting and salutary when, having long accumulated in the heart, they flow out at last, first impetuously, then more and more easily, more and more sweetly; the dull languor of yearning is resolved by them. . . . But there are chilly tears, meagerly flowing tears; they are expressed from the heart drop after drop by the heavy and motionless burden of grief lying on it; they are comfortless and do not bring relief. Necessity weeps with such tears, and the one who has not shed them has not yet been unhappy. Natalia knew them that day.

A couple of hours passed. She took herself in hand, rose, wiped her eyes, lit the candle, burned Rudin's letter in it to the end, and flung the ashes out of the window. Then she opened Pushkin at random and read the first lines she came to (she often resorted to this method of prognostication). This is what she read:

> He who has felt, who has been disturbed
> By the spectre of irrevocable days . . .
> For him no longer is there enchantment,
> He is gnawed by the serpent of recollection
> He is corroded by remorse. . . .

She stood a moment, gazed with a chilly smile at herself in the mirror, and, making a little gesture with her head in a downward direction, went into the reception hall.

As soon as Daria Mikhailovna saw her she led her into her own room, seated her beside herself, and graciously patted her cheek. But meanwhile she looked attentively, almost inquisitively into her eyes. Daria Mikhailovna was secretly bewildered: it occurred to her for the first time that she really did not know her daughter. When Pandalevsky told her of Natalia's meeting with Rudin she was not so much indignant as astonished that the in-

Turgenev

telligent Natalia could resolve on such a step. But when she sent for her and began to upbraid her — not in the least in the manner one would expect from a European woman, but rather vociferously and quite inelegantly — Natalia's firm replies, the resolution of her looks and movements, bewildered and even alarmed her.

Rudin's sudden and not entirely comprehensible departure had removed a great load from her heart; but she had expected tears, attacks of hysteria. . . . Natalia's superficial composure again took her aback.

"Well now, my child," she began, "how are you today?"

Natalia gazed at her mother.

"Well, he's gone away — your affair. I suppose you don't know why he took himself off so quickly?"

"Mamma dear!" Natalia began in a quiet tone, "I give you my word that if you don't mention him, you will never hear anything from me."

"So you confess that you were to blame toward me?"

Natalia drooped her head and repeated:

"You will never hear anything from me."

"Well, then see to it!" Daria Mikhailovna retorted with a smile. "I trust you. But the day before yesterday, do you remember how — Well, I won't. Of course, it is dead and done with. Isn't it? Now I recognize you again; for I was completely at a loss about you. Well, now kiss me, my clever girl!"

Natalia raised Daria Mikhailovna's hand to her lips, but her mother kissed her on her bowed head.

"Always listen to my advice, don't forget that you are a Lasunskaya and my daughter," she added, "and you will be happy. And now you can go."

Natalia went out without speaking. Daria Mikhailovna gazed after her and thought: "She's just like me — she too will have her fun; *mais aura moins d'abandon.*" And she was buried in memories of the past, of the long past. . . .

Then she sent for Mlle Boncourt and sat a long time with her, locked in close discussion. Dismissing her, she sent for Pandalevsky. She simply had to know the true reason for Rudin's departure . . . but Pandalevsky completely reassured her. That was in his province.

Next day Volintsiev and his sister arrived for dinner. Daria Mikhailovna was always very amiable to him, and on this occasion she was particularly gracious. It was unbearably difficult for Natalia; but Volintsiev was so respectful, and talked to her so diffidently, that in her soul she could not but thank him.

The day passed quietly, rather boringly, but as they dispersed, everybody felt that they had found again their old paths; and that means much, very much.

Yes, they had all found their old paths . . . all except Natalia. When at last she was alone, she dragged herself with difficulty to her bed and, weary, shattered, fell with her face in the pillow. It seemed so bitter, and repellent, and banal for her to live, she felt so ashamed of herself, her love, her sorrow, that at that moment she would probably have been ready to die. . . . Many yet were the oppressive days, the sleepless nights, the exhausting agitations that lay before her, but she was young — life had only just begun for her, and life sooner or later has its way. No matter what blow may fall on a man, he will eat something that very same day, and a great deal the next day — forgive the coarseness of my expression — and there you have the first consolation. . . .

Natalia suffered torments, she was suffering for the first time. . . . But the first sufferings like first love, are not repeated — and thank God for that!

12

Some two years later, one day early in May, Alexandra Pavlovna was sitting on the balcony of her house. Now her name was not Lipina, but Lezhniova; she had married Mikhailo Mikhailich more than a year since. She was as pleasant-looking as before, only she had filled out recently. Below the balcony, from which stairs led down into the garden, a foster-mother was strolling about, carrying a crimson-cheeked baby in a little white jacket and with a white pompon on its hat. From time to time Alexandra Pavlovna glanced down at the child. It did not whimper, but sucked its finger seriously and looked about calmly. It was already showing itself to be a worthy son of Mikhailo Mikhailich.

Beside Alexandra Pavlovna an old acquaintance, Pigasov, was sitting on the balcony. He had grown perceptibly grayer since we last met him; he stooped, was thinner, and whistled as he spoke, for one of his front teeth had fallen out; the hissing made his remarks even more venomous. . . . His rancor had not diminished with the years, but his witticisms had lost their point, and he repeated himself more than formerly. Mikhailo Mikhailich was not at home; he was expected by teatime. The sun had already set; in the west where it had gone down, a streak of pale golden lemon hue extended along the horizon; in the opposite quarter of the sky there were two such streaks: one, lower, dove-blue, and the other, higher, crimson and lilac. Small, light clouds were melting in the zenith. Everything promised a spell of fine weather.

Suddenly Pigasov burst into a laugh.

"What are you laughing at, Afrikan Semionich?" Alexandra Pavlovna asked.

"Just thoughts. . . . Yesterday I heard a peasant say to his wife — and she apparently had been talking rather a lot — 'Don't creak!' . . . I was delighted with the expression. Don't creak! Really, when you think of it, what is a woman capable of passing judgment on? You know I always except present company. Our fathers were wiser than we. In their legends the beauty sat by the window, a star in her forehead, and not a sound came from her lips. And that's how it ought to be. And you judge for yourself: the day before yesterday our marshal's wife shot at me as though putting a bullet into my brow: she said she didn't like my *tendency!* Tendency! Well, wouldn't it be better for her and for everybody else if by some beneficent dispensation of nature she were suddenly deprived of the use of her tongue?"

"But you're always the same, Afrikan Semionich; you're always attacking us poor women. . . . Do you know, that is really a kind of misfortune for you. I feel sorry for you."

"Misfortune? What makes you say that? To begin with, in my view there are only three misfortunes in the world altogether: to live in a cold house in winter, to wear tight boots in summer, and to spend the night in a room with a squawling infant that cannot be put to sleep with insect powder. And secondly, you must pardon me, but I have become the most peaceable of men now. You could use me as a copybook! That is how morally I behave now!"

"You behave well, there's no gainsaying that! Yelena Antonovna was complaining to me about you no longer ago than yesterday."

"You don't say! And what did she say to you, if I may know?"

"She told me that all the morning you had replied to her questions with nothing but 'What?' 'What?' and that in such a squeaky voice."

He smiled.

"But it was a good idea, you must agree, Alexandra Pavlovna — wasn't it?"

"Astonishing! How can you be so impolite to a woman, Afrikan Semionich?"

"What? Do you regard Yelena Antonovna as a woman?"

"Well, what is she, in your opinion?"

"A drum, if you like, an ordinary drum, the kind they beat with sticks — "

"Ah, yes!" she interrupted him, desiring to change the conversation. "I hear you are to be congratulated."

"What on?"

"On the conclusion of the case. The Glinov meadows have been left with you."

"Yes, I've won," Pigasov gloomily replied.

"All the years you've been fighting for them, and now you seem dissatisfied."

"I confess to you, Alexandra Pavlovna," he said slowly, "that there can be nothing worse and more insulting than happiness that comes too late. It cannot give you any satisfaction in any case, and on the other hand it deprives you of the right, the most precious right, to rail and curse your fate. Yes, madame, it is a bitter and shameful thing, is belated happiness."

Alexandra Pavlovna only shrugged her shoulders.

"Nurse," she called, "I think it is time Mishka was put to bed. Give him to me."

And she occupied herself with her son, while Pigasov snorted and went to another part of the balcony.

Suddenly, not far off, along the road at the bottom of the garden, Mikhailo Mikhailich appeared in his sporting sulky. In front of his horse two enormous yard dogs, one yellow, the other gray, were running; he had recently acquired them. They snapped at each other incessantly and lived in inseparable friendship. An old shaggy mongrel went out of the gate to meet them, opened its mouth as though intending to bark, and ended by yawning and turning back, amiably wagging its tail.

"Look, Alexandra," Lezhniov called to his wife when still some distance away, "look whom I've brought to see you. . . ."

At first Alexandra Pavlovna did not recognize the man sitting behind her husband.

"Ah! Mr. Basistov!" she exclaimed at last.

"Yes, Basistov!" Lezhniov replied; "and what glorious news he has brought! Wait a moment, you'll soon hear."

And he drove into the yard.

A few seconds later he and Basistov came onto the balcony.

"Hurrah!" Lezhniov exclaimed, embracing his wife. "Sergei is getting married!"

"To whom?" Alexandra Pavlovna asked agitatedly.

"To Natalia, of course. . . . Our friend has brought this news from Moscow, and there's a letter for you. . . . Do you hear, Mishka?" he added, seizing his son by the arm. "Your uncle's getting married; . . . What villainous phlegmatism! Even at that news he only blinks his eyes!"

"He wants to go to sleep," the nurse observed.

"Yes," Basistov said, going up to Alexandra Pavlovna, "I arrived from Moscow today, with a commission from Daria Mikhailovna, to examine the estate accounts. And here is the letter."

Alexandra Pavlovna hurriedly unsealed her brother's letter. It consisted of a few lines. In his first outburst of joy he informed his sister that he had proposed to Natalia, had gained her consent and Daria Mikhailovna's agreement, promised to write more by the first post, and sent all his embraces and kisses. It was obvious that he had written in a kind of fever.

Tea was brought, Basistov was made welcome. Questions were fired at him in a fusillade. Everybody, even Pigasov, was delighted with the news he had brought.

"Please tell me," Lezhniov said in passing. "We heard rumors of a certain Mr. Korchagin. So it was all nonsense?"

(Korchagin was a handsome young man, a society lion, extraordinarily inflated and important; he carried himself with

Rudin

unusual majesty, as though he were not a living man, but his own statue, erected by public subscription.)

"Well, no, not altogether," Basistov replied with a smile. "Daria Mikhailovna was very favorable to him, but Natalia Alexeevna would not even hear of it."

"Why, I know him," Pigasov joined in; "he's an arrant blockhead, a cracking blockhead — absolutely! Why, if everybody were like him, you'd have to give me large sums to get me to remain alive — just imagine!"

"Maybe," Basistov rejoined, "but he plays by no means a minor role in society."

"Well, it doesn't matter!" Alexandra Pavlovna exclaimed. "Forget him! Ah, how glad I am for my brother! And Natalia, is she cheerful and happy?"

"Yes. She's as self-contained as ever — you know her — but she seems to be satisfied."

The evening passed in pleasant and lively conversation. They sat down to supper.

"Ah, by the way," Lezhniov asked Basistov as he poured out wine for him, "do you know where Rudin is these days?"

"I don't know for certain now. He stayed in Moscow for a short time last winter, then went with a certain family to Simbirsk; he and I corresponded for some time: in his last letter he informed me that he was leaving Simbirsk — he didn't say where he was going — and since then I haven't heard a word."

"He won't hurt!" Pigasov remarked; "he's sitting and preaching somewhere or other. That gentleman will always find two or three devotees who will listen to him with gaping mouths and give him money in exchange. You see, he'll end by dying somewhere in Tsarevokokshaisk or in Chukhloe, in the arms of some ancient old maid in a wig, who will think of him as the greatest genius in the world. . . ."

"You are very harsh on him," Basistov said in a low, dissatisfied tone.

"Not at all!" Pigasov retorted. "I am being perfectly just. In my view, he is simply nothing but a lickspittle. I forgot to tell you," he went on, turning to Lezhniov, "I happened to make the acquaintance of a man named Terlakhov, with whom Rudin traveled abroad. And really, really! The things he told me about him, you cannot imagine — absolutely side-splitting! It is a notable fact that in time all Rudin's friends and followers become his enemies!"

"Please exclude me from the list of such friends!" Basistov interrupted him heatedly.

"Well, you — you're different! I'm not talking about you."

"And what did Terlakhov tell you?" Alexandra Pavlovna asked.

"Why, a great deal: I can't remember everything. But he told me an amazing story of what happened to Rudin once. In the course of his continual development (these gentlemen are always developing: others just sleep, or eat, for instance, but they are always at a stage of development of sleeping or eating; isn't that so, Mr. Basistov?" Basistov made no answer.) ". . . And so, continually developing, Rudin came, by way of philosophy, to the intellectual conclusion that he ought to fall in love. He began to look for a person worthy of such an astonishing intellectual conclusion. Fortune smiled on him. He made the acquaintance of a certain little Frenchwoman, a superlatively beautiful little modiste. The affair occurred in a certain German town on the Rhine, you must note. He began to call on her, to take her books of different kinds, to talk to her about nature and Hegel. Can you imagine the modiste's position? She regarded him as an astronomer. But, you know, he isn't bad-looking in himself, and he was a foreigner, a Russian — and she liked him. Well, finally he makes an assignation, and a very poetic assignation: in a gondola on the river. The Frenchwoman agreed, dressed herself in her best, and went with him in the gondola. And they boated about for a couple of hours. And what do you think he occupied himself with all that time? He stroked the girl on the head, thoughtfully gazed up at the sky, and repeated several times that he felt a paternal tenderness for her. The French girl returned home furious, and she herself told Terlakhov all about it afterward. That's the kind of man he is!" He laughed.

"You're an old cynic!" Alexandra Pavlovna remarked in a vexed tone, "and I am coming more and more to the conclusion that even those who run Rudin down cannot say one bad word about him."

"Not one bad word? Excuse me, but his everlasting living at

Rudin

other people's expense, his loans — Mikhailo Mikhailich! I am sure he borrowed from you, too?"

"Listen, Afrikan Semionich!" Lezhniov began, and his face took on a serious expression; "listen: you know, and my wife knows, that recently I have not felt particularly benevolently disposed toward Rudin, and even frequently condemned him. With all that" (he poured more champagne into the glasses), "this is what I now propose to you: we have just drunk the health of our dear brother and his bride; I propose that we now drink to the health of Dmitry Rudin!"

Alexandra Pavlovna and Pigasov both gazed at him in amazement, while Basistov gave a violent start, went red with pleasure, and stared wide-eyed.

"I know him well," Lezhniov went on, "his defects are well known to me. They come to the surface all the more because he himself is not a shallow man."

"Rudin has the nature of a genius," Basistov joined in.

"There is a touch of genius in him, I think," Lezhniov replied, "but nature — That is all his trouble, that he really has no nature. . . . But that's not the point at the moment. I want to talk of what is good in him, and rare. He has enthusiasm; and that, believe me, who am a phlegmatic kind of man, is the most precious quality in our time. We have all become intolerably judicious, imperturbable, and flabby; we have dozed off to sleep, we have gone cold, and our thanks to anyone who can move us and warm us for even a moment! And high time too! Do you remember, Alexandra, I once talked to you about him and accused him of being cold? Well, I was both right and wrong. That coldness of his is in his blood — that is not his fault — but not in his head. He is not an actor, as I called him, not a windbag, not a cheat; he lives on others not like a pushing parasite, but like a child. . . . Yes, he certainly will die somewhere in poverty and need; but is that really anything to justify us in throwing stones? He himself will never achieve anything just because there is no nature, no blood in him; but who is justified in saying that he will not bring, has not already brought, benefit to others? That his words have not scattered many good seeds in youthful souls to whom nature has not denied, as it has to him, the strength of activity, the ability to exploit their own designs? Why, I myself, I was the first to experience that. . . . My wife knows what Rudin meant to me in my youth. I remember I also declared that Rudin's words cannot have any effect on people; but then I was speaking about people like myself, people of my own age, people who have already seen a little of life and have been overcome by life. One false note in a speech, and for us all its harmony has gone; but fortunately a young man's hearing is not so well developed, not so spoilt. If the essence of what he hears seems excellent to him, why should he be concerned with the tone? He will find the tone in himself."

"Bravo! Bravo!" Basistov exclaimed. "What a true remark! And as for Rudin's influence, I swear to you that that man was capable not only of moving you; he shifted you from your place; he would not let you halt, he turned you upside down from your very foundations, he set you on fire!"

"Do you hear that?" Lezhniov went on, turning to Pigasov. "What other proof do you require? You attack philosophy; when you talk about it you cannot find words contemptuous enough. I myself don't think overmuch of it and I don't understand it well; but our chief misfortunes don't arise from philosophy! Philosophic word-spinning and nonsense can't be inculcated in the Russian: he has too much common sense for that; but on the other hand one cannot allow honest striving for the truth and for conscience to be attacked under the name of philosophy. Rudin's misfortune consists in the fact that he does not know Russia, and that is indeed a great misfortune. Russia can manage without each of us, but not one of us can manage without her. Woe to him who thinks he can, woe twice over to him who actually does manage without her. Cosmopolitanism is nonsense; the cosmopolite is a cipher, and worse than a cipher; apart from nationality there is neither art nor truth, nor life; there is nothing. Without a distinctive physiognomy there is no such thing as even an ideal face; only a banal face is conceivable without a distinctive physiognomy. But again I say that that is not Rudin's fault: that is his fate, a bitter and heavy fate, and we can't reproach him with that. It would carry us very far if we tried to analyze why we have the Rudins among us. But for what there is good in him, let us be grateful to him. That is easier than to be unjust to him — and we have been unjust to him. To punish him is

Rudin

not our business, nor is it necessary: he has punished himself far more harshly than he deserved. . . . And God grant that misfortune may eradicate all the evil from him and leave behind only the good! I drink to Rudin's health! I drink to the health of the comrade of my finest years, I drink to youth, to its hopes, to its strivings, to its trustfulness and honesty, to all that made our hearts beat at the age of twenty. After all, we have never known anything better, and never shall. . . . I drink to thee, golden time, I drink to the health of Rudin!"

They all clinked glasses with Lezhniov. In his fervor Basistov all but broke his glass, and tossed off the toast at one gulp, while Alexandra Pavlovna squeezed her husband's hand.

"I never suspected, Mikhailo Mikhailich, that you could be so eloquent," Pigasov remarked; "why, it was almost worthy of Rudin himself: it moved even me."

"I am not at all eloquent," Lezhniov retorted, not without a touch of acerbity, "but I think it is difficult to move you. In any case, enough of Rudin; let us talk about something else. . . . Well — what is his name? — Pandalevsky, is he still staying with Daria Mikhailovna?" he added, turning to Basistov.

"Of course, he's still with her! She has obtained him a very good position."

Lezhniov laughed sarcastically.

"Now, there's a man who won't die in poverty, one can guarantee that."

Supper ended, the guests dispersed. Left alone with her husband, Alexandra smilingly gazed into his face.

"How fine you were today, Misha!" she said, caressing his brow with her hand. "How intelligently and nobly you spoke! But confess that you have been drawn a little to Rudin's side, just as previously you were turned against him. . . ."

"Don't kick a man when he's down . . . but at that time I was afraid he might turn your head."

"No," Alexandra Pavlovna replied artlessly, "he always seemed too learned to me, I was afraid of him and didn't know what to say in his presence. But that Pigasov sneered at him very viciously today, don't you agree?"

"Pigasov?" Lezhniov said. "That was just why I spoke so hotly in favor of Rudin, because Pigasov was here. He dare call Rudin

663

a lickspittle! In my view his behavior, Pigasov's behavior, is a hundred times worse. He has an independent fortune, he sneers at everything, but how he toadies to the eminent and the wealthy! Do you know that that same Pigasov who runs down everybody and everything so rancorously, who attacks philosophy, and women — do you know that when he was an official he took bribes, and what bribes! Ah! That's the issue!"

"Really?" Alexandra Pavlovna exclaimed. "I would never have suspected it! . . . Listen, Misha," she added after a moment, "I want to ask you something."

"Well?"

"What do you think? Will my brother be happy with Natalia?"

"What can I answer? There is every probability. . . . She will be in command — there's no point in our keeping that a secret from each other — she is more intelligent than he; but he's a fine fellow and he loves her with all his heart. And what else do you want? After all, we love each other and are happy, aren't we?"

Alexandra Pavlovna smiled and squeezed his hand.

On the very day that the events we have just related were happening in Alexandra Pavlovna's home, in one of the remote provinces of Russia a shabby little basket wagonette, to which a troika of villagers'[1] horses was harnessed, was dragging along a highway in the heat of the day. On the driver's seat, with his feet resting sideways on the shaft, was perched a gray-headed little peasant in a ragged coat, who tugged at the rope reins and occasionally waved his little knout; in the wagonette a tall man, in a forage cap and an old, dusty light coat, was sitting on a small, shabby trunk. This man was Rudin. He sat with his head hanging and the peak of his cap drawn over his eyes. The uneven jolts of the wagonette flung him from side to side; he seemed completely senseless, as though dozing. At last he straightened up.

"When on earth shall we reach the post station?" he asked the peasant sitting in the driver's seat.

[1] Horses hired from the peasants were poorer than those kept by the posthouses. (Tr.)

"Why," the peasant began, giving the reins a still stronger tug, "when we get to the top of the rise, less than a couple of miles will be left, that's all. . . . Now you, think — I'll make you think," he added in a piping voice, turning to whip up the right-hand horse.

"You seem to drive very badly," Rudin remarked; "we've been dragging along ever since first thing this morning and we haven't arrived yet. You might at least sing something."

"Ah, what can I do? You can see for yourself, the horses are worn out . . . and then it's so hot. And as for singing, we can't: we're not coachmen. . . . Hi, you ram, you ram!" the peasant suddenly shouted, addressing himself to a man in a short brown coat and well-patched bast shoes who was just passing, "out of the way, you ram!"

"What a —— coachman!" the pedestrian muttered after him, and halted. "Moscow swine!" he added in a voice strong with reproach, shook his head, and trudged on.

"Now where are you going?" the peasant said in a deliberate tone, tugging on the shaft-horse. "Ah, you artful! Really artful. . . ."

The emaciated horses managed somehow or other to drag up to the posthouse at last. Rudin climbed out of the basket body, settled with the peasant (who did not bow to him and tossed the money about in his palm — evidently little would be left for vodka), and himself carried his trunk into the posthouse waiting-room.

A certain acquaintance of mine, who in his time has traveled much about Russia, has observed that if the walls of the post-house waiting-room are adorned with pictures representing scenes from the *Caucasian Prisoner* or portraying Russian generals, you can get horses quickly; but if the pictures depict the life of the well-known gamester Georges Germany,[1] the traveler need not hope for an early departure: he will have time to admire the curling peruke, the white double waistcoat, and the extraordinarily narrow and short pantaloons of the gamester in his youth, and his frenetic physiognomy when, as an old man, he kills his son, swinging a chair high above him in a garret with a steep roof. The room Rudin entered was hung with these very pic-

[1] The hero of a melodrama by Victor Ducange (1827). (Tr.)

tures from *Thirty Years, or The Life of a Gamester*. At his shout the postmaster appeared, sleepy-eyed (by the way, has anyone ever seen a postmaster not sleepy-eyed?), and, without even waiting for Rudin's question, announced in a languid voice that there were no horses.

"How can you say there aren't any horses," Rudin said, "when you don't even know where I'm going? I've arrived here with villagers' horses."

"We never have any horses," the postmaster replied. "But where are you going?"

"To —sk."

"There aren't any horses," the postmaster repeated, and left the room.

Rudin vexedly went over to the window and flung his cap on the table. He had changed little, but he had grown yellow during the past two years; threads of silver shone here and there among his curls, and his eyes, still handsome, seemed to have grown dim; fine lines, the traces of bitter and anxious feelings, lay round the lips, on the cheeks, in the temples.

His clothes were worn and old, and he showed no linen at all. Evidently he was past his prime; as gardeners put it, he had gone to seed.

He turned to reading the inscriptions on the walls — the well-known diversion of bored travelers. Suddenly the door creaked, and the postmaster entered.

"There aren't any horses to —sk, and won't be any for a long time," he said; "but there are horses going back to —ov."

"To —ov?" Rudin said. "But, pardon me, that is right off my track. I'm traveling to Penza, and —ov lies, I think, on the road to Tambov."

"What of it? You can get there from Tambov, or you can turn off somehow from —ov."

Rudin thought for a moment.

"Well, all right," he said at last, "order the horses to be harnessed. It's all the same to me; I'll go to Tambov."

The horses were soon brought round. Rudin carried out his trunk, climbed into the peasant's cart, seated himself, and looked as dejected as before. There was something impotent and mournfully humble about his huddled figure. . . . And the troika dragged along at an unhurrying trot, with the bells ringing spasmodically.

EPILOGUE

Several more years passed.

One cold autumn day a carriage drove up to the veranda of the main hotel in the provincial town of S—; out of it, stretching and groaning a little, climbed a gentleman who, though not yet elderly, had acquired that fullness of body which we are accustomed to calling respectable. Going up the stairs to the second floor, he halted at the entrance to a wide corridor and, failing to find anyone about, called in a loud voice for a room. A door banged somewhere, a lanky menial came running out from behind low screens, and went on ahead with a brisk, sidelong step, his shiny back and rolled-up sleeves glimmering in the twilit corridor. When he was shown into his room, the traveler at once flung off his greatcoat and scarf, sat down on the sofa, and resting his fists on his knees, first looked about him as though half awake, then ordered his servant to be summoned. The menial made a noncommittal movement and went out. This traveler was none other than Lezhniov. He had been called from his estate to S— on questions connected with the recruiting levy.

Lezhniov's servant, a curly-haired, red-faced youngster, wearing a gray greatcoat belted with a blue girdle, and soft felt boots, entered the room.

"Well, my boy, so we've arrived," Lezhniov remarked. "Yet you were continually afraid the tire would come off the wheel."

"We've arrived," the servant rejoined, trying to smile through the upturned collar of his greatcoat, "but just why the tire didn't come off — "

"Is there no one here?" came a voice from the corridor.

Lezhniov started and began to listen.

"Hey! Anyone there?" the voice repeated.

Lezhniov rose, went to the door, and swiftly opened it.

Before him stood a tall man, almost completely gray-headed and stooping, in an old velveteen coat with bronze buttons. Lezhniov recognized him at once.

"Rudin!" he exclaimed in an agitated tone.

Rudin turned. He could not distinguish the other man's features, for Mikhailo Mikhailich was standing with his back to the light; and he stared at him in astonishment.

"Don't you recognize me?" Lezhniov asked.

"Mikhailo Mikhailich!" Rudin exclaimed, and stretched out his hand; but suddenly he looked embarrassed and made to draw it back. . . . Lezhniov hurriedly seized it with both his hands.

"Come in, come into my room!" he said to Rudin, and drew him into the room.

"How you have changed!" he said after a moment's silence, involuntarily lowering his voice.

"Yes, so they say!" Rudin retorted, while his gaze wandered round the room. "The years . . . but you, now, hardly at all. How is Alexandra — your wife?"

"Thank you, she is well. But what fate has brought you here?"

"Me? That is a long story. To be exact, I arrived here by chance. I was looking for a certain acquaintance. . . . But I am very glad — "

"Where are you dining?"

"I? I don't know. Somewhere in an inn. I must leave here today."

"Must?"

Rudin smiled meaningly.

"Yes, must. I am being consigned to my own village, to compulsory residence."

"Have dinner with me."

Rudin for the first time looked straight into Lezhniov's eyes.

"You are proposing that I should dine with you?" he said.

"Yes, Rudin, for old times' sake, as comrades. Will you? I didn't expect to meet you, and God knows when we shall see each other again. And you and I can't part like this!"

"Very well, I agree."

Lezhniov squeezed Rudin's hand, called his servant, ordered dinner, and gave instructions for a bottle of champagne to be placed on ice.

All through the dinner, as though by mutual agreement, Lezhniov and Rudin talked only about their student days, recalling many incidents and many, both dead and living, people. At first Rudin talked reluctantly, but he drank several glasses of wine, and the blood began to heat up in him. At last the waiter brought in the last dish. Lezhniov rose, locked the door, and, returning to the table, sat down right opposite Rudin and quietly rested his chin in both hands.

"Well, now," he began, "tell me all that has happened to you since I last saw you."

Rudin gazed at him.

"My God!" Lezhniov thought again, "how he has changed, the poor wretch!"

Rudin's features had changed but little, especially since we saw him at the post station, though the imprint of approaching age was already upon them. But their expression was different. His eyes had a different look; all his being, his movements, now sluggish, now incoherently impulsive, his cooler, half-broken speech, expressed an ultimate weariness, a secret and quiet sorrow, far different from that half-feigned sadness which formerly had distinguished him, as it generally distinguishes a youth who is filled with hopes and confident ambition.

"Tell you all that has happened to me?" he began. "I can't tell you all, nor is it worth it. . . . I've suffered a great deal, I've wandered not only in body, but in soul too. My God, in what and in whom haven't I been disillusioned! And with whom haven't I been friends! Yes, with whom!" Rudin repeated, noticing that Lezhniov was looking into his face with a look of peculiar commiseration. "How many times have I been repelled by my own words — I do not mean coming from my own lips, but from the lips of people who have shared my views! How often have I passed from the impatience, the irritability of a child to the dull insensibility of a horse, which doesn't even twitch its tail when it is whipped! . . . How often have I rejoiced, hoped, felt enmity and despondency, in vain! How often have I flown up like a hawk — and returned on all fours, like a snail with its shell crushed! . . . Where haven't I been, along what roads haven't I walked! . . . But some roads are muddy," Rudin added, and he turned away a little. "You know — " he continued.

"Listen!" Lezhniov interrupted him. "At one time you and I used to 'thee' and 'thou' each other. Would you like to — renew our old terms? . . . Let's drink to 'thou'!"

Rudin started, half rose, and in his eyes flickered something that words cannot express.

"Let us drink," he said; "I thank thee, brother, let us drink!"
They both tossed off their glasses.

"*Thou* knowest," Rudin began again, emphasizing the "thou"
and smiling, "that inside me there is a kind of worm, which gnaws
at me and nibbles and will never let me have perfect rest. It drives
me up against people — first they submit to my influence, and
then — "

Rudin swept his hand through the air.

"Since I saw you — saw thee — last, I have re-experienced and
relearned a great deal. . . . I have begun to live again, have
turned to something new a score of times — and now — thou
seest!"

"You never had any stamina," Lezhniov said, almost to himself.

"As thou sayest, I have never had any stamina! . . . I never
had the capacity to construct; and besides, brother, it is difficult
to construct when you have no firm ground under your feet, when
you yourself have to establish your own foundation! I shall not
describe all my adventures — that is, to be exact, all my failures.
I'll relate two or three instances — those instances from my life
when, it seemed, success was beginning to smile on me, or rather
when I was beginning to hope for success — which is not quite
the same thing. . . ."

Rudin flung back his gray and now thinning hair with the same
sweep of the hand with which he had once flung back his dark,
thick curls.

"Well, listen," he began. "In Moscow I made the acquaintance
of one very queer gentleman. He was very rich and possessed
extensive properties; he was not in the Czar's service. His main,
his only passion was love of science, of science and learning generally. Even to this day I cannot make out why he had this passion. It fitted him as a saddle does a cow. He kept himself abreast
of intellectual activity only with effort and could hardly talk at
all, only rolled his eyes expressively and shook his head significantly. I, brother, have never met a nature less talented and more
poverty-stricken than his. . . . There are places like him in
Smolensk province, just sand and nothing more, with only scanty
grass, and that such as no animal will eat. Nothing came to his
hand — everything slipped out of his grip, the farther the better;
and he was mad also in the sense of making everything easy difficult. If it had depended on him, his servants would have eaten

with their heels, really they would! He worked, wrote, and read indefatigably. He paid court to learning with a kind of obdurate persistence, with a terrible patience; he had enormous ambition and an iron character. He lived alone and had the reputation of being an eccentric. I made his acquaintance — well, and he took a fancy to me. I must confess I soon got to the bottom of him, but his fervor touched me. Besides, he possessed such resources, so much good could be done through him, so much essential benefit could be achieved. . . . I went to live with him and finally traveled with him to his estate. I had enormous plans, brother: I dreamed of all kinds of improvements, innovations — "

"As you did with Lasunskaya, remember?" Lezhniov remarked with a good-natured smile.

"How! There I knew in my heart of hearts that nothing would come of my words; but here — here quite a different field was opened before me. . . . I took agricultural books with me — true, I didn't read a single one of them to the end — well, and I set to work. At first things didn't go as I had expected, but then they did seem to move well. My new friend continually said nothing, just watched, but didn't interfere with me — that is, to a certain extent he didn't. He accepted my proposals and carried them out, but with some obstinacy, stiffly, with secret distrust, and he continually pursued his own plans. He valued his every thought extraordinarily highly. He would come at it with effort, like a ladybird getting to the end of a grass blade; and he would sit and sit on it, always seeming about to unfold his wings and fly off — and suddenly he would topple down and start climbing up again. . . . Don't be surprised at all these comparisons: I thought of them even then. And so two years passed. The work made poor progress, despite all my efforts. I began to grow tired, I grew fed up with my friend, I began to taunt him, he smothered me like a feather bed; his distrust passed into a dull irritability, an inimical feeling took possession of both of us, we reached the stage when we could not talk to each other about anything; he surreptitiously but incessantly endeavored to demonstrate that he was not subject to my influence, he either modified my arrangements or canceled them altogether. . . . I realized at last that my position in relation to this worldly landowner was that of a sponger in the field of intellectual exercise. I began to feel regret at wasting my time and strength in vain, regret at the feeling that again and

again I was deceived in my expectations. I knew very well what
I was losing by going away; but I could not control myself, and
one day, as the result of a painful and shocking scene of which
I was witness, and which showed up my friend to me in an altogether too unpleasant light, I quarreled finally with him and departed, I threw over this landowner pedant molded out of steppe
flour with an admixture of German treacle. . . ."

"In other words, you threw away your daily bread," Lezhniov
observed, and set both hands on Rudin's shoulders.

"Yes, and once more found myself light and naked in empty
space. Fly where you like — Oh, let's drink!"

"To your health!" Lezhniov declared, and he rose and kissed
Rudin on the brow. 'To your health and in memory of Pokorsky!
. . . He, too, had it in him to choose poverty."

"And there you have the first episode in my adventures," Rudin
began after a pause. "Shall I go on?"

"Please do."

"Ah, but I don't feel like talking. I've grown tired of talking,
brother. . . . Well, all the same, so be it. I knocked about a
number of places after that — and, by the way, I could tell how
I obtained a post as secretary to a well-meaning high dignitary
and what came of it; but that would take us too long. . . . After
knocking about a bit, I decided to become, at last — please don't
laugh — a practical man of business. A certain opportunity came
my way; I came into contact with a man — you may have heard
of him — with a man named Kurbeyev — do you know him?"

"No, I've never heard of him. But excuse me, Rudin, how
could you, with your intellect, fail to see that it was anything but
your business to become — excuse the play on words — a man of
business."

"I know it isn't, brother; but then, what is my business? . . .
But if you had seen Kurbeyev! Please don't think of him as some
empty-headed talker. They say I was eloquent once. Compared
with him I am as nothing. He was a man extraordinarily learned,
knowledgeable, an intellect, a creative intellect, brother, an intellect in the field of industry and commercial enterprises. His
mind simply bubbled with the most audacious, the most unexpected of projects. I joined him, and we decided to devote our
energies to a socially valuable work."

"What was it, may I ask?"

Rudin

Rudin looked down. "You'll laugh."

"But why should I? No, I shan't laugh."

"We decided to make a certain river in K— province navigable," Rudin declared with an awkward smile.

"You don't say! So this Kurbeyev was a capitalist?"

"He was poorer than I," Rudin retorted, and he let his gray head slowly sink.

Lezhniov burst into a roar of laughter; but he suddenly stopped and took Rudin by the hand.

"Please forgive me, brother," he said, "but I hadn't in the least expected that. Well, and what happened, did your enterprise remain only on paper?"

"Not entirely. We saw the beginning of its achievement. We hired workers — and set to work. But then we came up against all kinds of difficulties. To begin with, the mill-owners simply refused to understand what we were doing; and moreover we couldn't manage the water without machinery, and we hadn't money for machinery. Six months we lived in dugouts. Kurbeyev lived on nothing but bread, and I, too, never ate my fill. Not that I regret that; nature in those parts is amazing. We struggled and struggled, persuaded merchants, wrote letters, circulars. It ended by my throwing my last farthing into the plan."

"Well," Lezhniov remarked, "I don't suppose it was difficult for you to spend your last farthing."

"You're right, it wasn't."

Rudin looked out of the window.

"But I assure you the plan wasn't at all a bad one and could have been of tremendous benefit."

"And what happened to Kurbeyev?" Lezhniov asked.

"Him? He's in Siberia now, he's become a gold prospector, and you see, he'll make himself a fortune; he won't fail."

"Maybe not; but as for you, you certainly won't make yourself a fortune now."

"I? It can't be helped! For that matter, I know that in your eyes I have always been a useless sort of fellow."

"You? Enough of that, brother! . . . There was a time, truly, when my eyes were open only to your bad qualities; but now, believe me, I have learned to appreciate you. You won't make yourself a fortune — but for that very reason I like you — forgive me!"

Rudin smiled wanly.

"Really and truly?"

"I respect you for it!" Lezhniov repeated; "do you understand me?"

They were both silent for a while.

"Well, shall I pass on to episode three?" Rudin asked.

"By all means."

"Then listen. The third episode, and the last. This episode I have only just completed. But I haven't bored you?"

"Speak on, speak on."

"Well, you see," Rudin began, "one day I was thinking at a moment of leisure — I always had plenty of leisure — I was thinking: 'I've got sufficient knowledge, good intentions' — listen, even you won't deny that I had good intentions?"

"Anything but!"

"In all other respects I had failed more or less — so why shouldn't I become a pedagogue, or, in simple language, a teacher — why go on living in vain?"

Rudin stopped and sighed.

"Why go on living in vain, wouldn't it be better to try to pass on to others what I know? Perhaps they would derive at least a little benefit from my knowledge. After all, my abilities were no ordinary ones, I am good at talking. . . . Well, so I decided to devote myself to this new task. I had trouble in getting a position; I didn't want to give private lessons; there was nothing for me in the primary schools. Finally I succeeded in obtaining a post as teacher in the local high school here."

"Teaching what?" Lezhniov asked.

"Teaching Russian literature. I tell you I had never flung myself into any other task with such fervor. The thought of having influence on youth inspired me. I sat three weeks over the composition of my introductory lecture."

"You haven't it with you?" Lezhniov asked.

"No — it's been mislaid somewhere. It didn't turn out at all badly, and I liked it. Even now I can see the faces of my audience — good faces, young faces, with expressions of open attention, sympathy, even astonishment. I went to the desk and read my lecture in a fever; I thought I had written sufficient to last an hour, but I finished it in twenty minutes. The inspector was sitting there too, a dry old man, with silver spectacles and a close-cut wig — occasionally he stretched his head out toward me. When I had finished and jumped out of my chair, he told me: 'Very good, only rather lofty, rather obscure, and you said very little about the actual subject.' But the students followed me with a respectful gaze — really they did! That is what makes youth so precious! My second lecture I also wrote out, and the third too — but then I began to speak extempore."

"And were you successful?" Lezhniov asked.

"I had a great success. I passed on to my audience all that I had in my soul. Among them were two or three really outstanding lads; the others didn't understand me too well. For that matter, I have to admit that even those who understood me sometimes embarrassed me with their questions. But I did not despair. They all loved me; in the examinations I gave them all perfect marks. But then an intrigue was started against me — or rather, there wasn't really an intrigue, but I just hadn't got into my right sphere. I was a constraint on others, and was in turn constrained. I lectured to high-school pupils in a manner not always adopted toward students; my listeners gained little from my lectures. . . . I myself didn't know the facts at all well. Moreover, I was not satisfied with the circle of activity that was allotted to me — as you know, that is my weakness. I wanted radical transformations, but, I swear to you, those transformations would have been both efficient and easy. I hoped to carry them through by means of the director, a good and honest man, on whom I had influence at first. His wife helped me. I, brother, have not met many such women in my lifetime. She was nearly forty; but she believed in the good, loved everything that's fine just like any fifteen-year-old girl, and was not afraid of expressing her convictions in front of anybody, no matter whom. I shall never forget her noble exaltation and purity. On her advice I drew up a plan. . . . But then they began to undermine me, to blacken me in her eyes. The mathematics master did me particular injury — he was a petty man, vinegary, splenetic, and with no faith in anything, a kind of Pigasov, only far more efficient than he. By the way, how is Pigasov, still alive?"

"Yes, and, just imagine, he's married a bourgeois woman who, they say, beats him."

"With good cause! Well, and is Natalia Alexeevna in good health?"

"Yes."

"And happy?"

"Yes."

Rudin was silent for a moment.

"What was I talking about — ah, yes: the mathematics master. He hated me; he compared my lectures with fireworks, seized upon every not perfectly clear phrase I uttered, and once even took me down a peg over some memorial of the fifteenth century . . . but most of all he suspected my intentions; my last soap bubble came up against him as if he were a pin and burst. The inspector, whom I had failed to get on with from the first, set the director against me; there was a scene; I wouldn't give way, I got worked up, the affair came to the knowledge of the authorities; I was forced to hand in my resignation. I didn't stop there, I wanted to prove that they couldn't treat me like that . . . but they were able to treat me how they liked. . . . Now I have to leave this town altogether."

There was a silence. Both the friends sat with hanging heads. Rudin was the first to speak.

"Yes, brother," he began; "now I can say with Koltsov: [1] 'To what hast thou brought me, O my youth, what hast thou lived to see, that I cannot take one step! . . .' And yet was I really good for nothing after all, was there really no work for me to do on earth? I often asked myself that question and, no matter how much I tried to depreciate myself in my own eyes, I could not but feel the presence in me of forces not given to all men. So why have those forces remained without fruit? And one other thing: do you remember when you and I were abroad, I was so presumptuous and false? . . . As though at that time I didn't clearly realize what I wanted, I was intoxicated with words and believed in phantoms; but now, I swear to you, I can say what I want aloud, in front of anybody. I have absolutely nothing to conceal: I am a man of good intentions — fully and in the very essence of the words; I am reconciled, I wish to achieve an easy end, to be of at least some little benefit. But no, it can't be done! What is the meaning of it all? What prevents my living and behaving like other people? . . . That is the only thing I dream of now. But hardly have I managed to achieve a definite position, to halt at a certain point, when fate sends me flying down from it. . . . I

[1] Alexis Koltsov, a Russian poet (1809-42). (Tr.)

have begun to be afraid of it — of my fate. . . . Why should all this be? Can you resolve me that problem?"

"Problem!" Lezhniov repeated. "Yes, that is the right word. You were always a problem even to me. Even in our youth, when after some petty escapade you would suddenly begin to talk to such effect that the heart trembled, and then — you'd begin again — well, you know what I am trying to say — even then I didn't understand you; and that is why I stopped liking you. . . . The powers you possess are so many, your striving for the ideal so indefatigable — "

"Words, all words! There were never any deeds!" Rudin interrupted.

"Never any deeds? But what deeds — "

"What deeds? You remember how Pryazhentsev kept his blind grandmother and all her family. . . . Now, there's a deed for you."

"Yes, but a fine word is also a deed."

Rudin gazed silently at Lezhniov and quietly shook his head.

Lezhniov was about to say something, but he passed his hand over his face.

"And so you're going to your village?" he asked at last.

"Yes, to my village."

"But do you still possess a village, after all you have gone through?"

"Something is left. Two and a half souls. I have a corner where I can die. Perhaps you are thinking at this minute: 'And even now he can't do without fine words.' Truly, words have ruined me; they have eaten into me, to the end I could not free myself of them. But what I have just said was not phrase-mongering. These white hairs, these lines, brother, are not empty phrases, these ragged elbows are not empty phrases. You were always hard on me, and you were right; but this is not the moment to be hard, when everything is finished, and there is no oil in the lamp, and the lamp itself is shattered, and at any moment now the wick will burn out. . . . Death, brother, must reconcile me in the end."

Lezhniov jumped to his feet.

"Rudin!" he exclaimed, "why do you say that to me? How have I deserved this of you? What sort of judge am I, and what sort of man would I be if, at the sight of your sunken cheeks and lined face, the very word 'phrase-mongering' could enter my head? Do you want to know what I think about you? Very good! I think: there goes a man — with his abilities, what couldn't he have achieved, what earthly advantages would he not have possessed today, if he had wished! . . . but I find him hungry, without anchorage. . . ."

"I arouse your pity," Rudin said thickly.

"No, you are mistaken. You inspire me with respect, that's what! Who prevented your spending year after year with that landowner, your friend, who, I am fully convinced, if only you had been ready to toady to him, would have made your position secure? Why couldn't you settle down in the high school; why is it, you queer fellow, that no matter what the intentions with which you begin a thing, it must always end by your sacrificing your own personal advantage, by your not sending roots down into uncongenial soil, no matter how fertile it be?"

"I was born a rolling stone," Rudin continued with a despondent flicker of a smile. "I cannot stop."

"That is true; but you cannot stop, not because there is a worm living within you, as you said at the beginning. It is not a worm living within you, not the spirit of vacuous restlessness — the fire of love for the truth burns in you, and it is obvious that, despite all your petty foibles, it burns in you more strongly than in many who do not even regard themselves as egotists, but who probably would call you an intriguer. Yes, and I would have been the first, in your place, to silence that worm within me long since and would have reconciled myself to everything; but you haven't even grown more embittered, and I am sure you are ready this very day, this very minute, to turn again to new work. like any youngster."

"No, brother, I am tired now," Rudin declared. "I've had enough."

"Tired! Another man would have died long ago. You say death reconciles; but do you think that life doesn't reconcile? Anyone who has lived his years without growing forbearing to others is himself not deserving of forbearance. You have done what you could, have fought as long as you could. . . . What more can one expect? Our roads parted — "

"You are quite a different man from me, brother," Rudin interrupted with a sigh.

Rudin

"Our roads parted," Lezhniov continued, "perhaps just because, owing to my position, my cold blood, and other fortunate circumstances, nothing prevented my sitting at home and remaining a spectator, with folded arms; but you had to go out into the field, with your sleeves rolled up, to toil, to work. Our roads parted — but see how close we are to each other. Why, you and I are talking to each other almost in the same language, we understand each other at the slightest hint; we have grown up with the same feelings. Why, there are few of us left now, brother; you and I are the last of the Mohicans! We could be at loggerheads and even hostile to each other in the old years, when we still had a large part of our lives before us; but now that the crowd is growing thin around us, when the new generations are going past us and not even toward our aims, we need to hold on firmly to each other. Let's clink glasses, brother, and let us sing as in the old days: *Gaudeamus igitur!*"

The friends clinked glasses and sang the ancient students' song in broken and falsetto, entirely Russian voices.

"So now you're going to your village," Lezhniov began again. "I don't think you will remain there for long, and I can't imagine, brother, how, where, and in what way you will end. . . . But remember: no matter what happens to you, there is always a place for you, there is one nest where you can take refuge. I mean my house — do you hear, old comrade? The intellect also has its casualties, and there needs to be a refuge for them too."

Rudin rose.

"Thank you, brother," he continued, "thank you! I shall not forget you for that. Only I am not worth giving refuge. I have spoiled my life, and I have not served thought as I should."

"Silence!" Lezhniov continued. "Every man remains what nature has made him, and more cannot be demanded of him! You have called yourself the Wandering Jew! . . . But how do you know? Possibly it is your assignation to wander everlastingly, possibly in doing so you are fulfilling a higher destiny that is unknown to you yourself; popular wisdom does not declare for nothing that we all walk under God. You are going?" Lezhniov went on, seeing that Rudin had picked up his cap. "Won't you stay the night?"

"I'm going! Good-by. Thank you. . . . But I shall come to a bad end."

Turgenev

"That only God knows. . . . Are you determined to go?"

"I am going! Good-by. Don't think badly of me."

"Well, but don't think badly of me either . . . and don't forget what I have just told you. Good-by. . . ."

The friends embraced. Rudin walked swiftly out of the room.

Lezhniov long walked backward and forward in his room, then halted before the window, lost in thought. He muttered half aloud: "Poor wretch!" and, seating himself at the table, began to write a letter to his wife.

But outside the wind was rising and howling with a sinister howl, striking hard and rancorously at the ringing windowpanes. The long autumnal night came on. Happy he who on such nights sits beneath his house roof, he who has a warm corner for himself. . . . And may God help all homeless wanderers!

In the sultry noonday of June 26, 1848, in Paris, when the rising of the National Workshops was all but crushed, in one of the narrow alleys of the Saint-Antoine faubourg, a battalion of troops of the line was taking a barricade. Several gunshots had already shattered it, those of its defenders left alive were abandoning it and thinking only of their own salvation, when suddenly on its very crest, on the shattered body of an overturned omnibus, appeared a tall man in an old coat belted with a red scarf, and with a straw hat on his gray, disheveled hair. In one hand he held a red flag, in the other a blunt and crooked saber, and he shouted something in a tense, thin voice, clambering upward and waving both flag and saber. A Vincennes sharpshooter took aim at him — fired. . . . The tall man dropped the flag and, like a sack, tumbled headlong face-downward, as though bowing down at someone's feet. . . . The bullet had passed right through his heart.

"*Tiens!*" said one of the fleeing insurgents to another. "*On vient de tuer le Polonais.*"

"*Bigre!*" the other replied, and they both rushed into the cellar of a house, where all the shutters were closed and the walls were pitted with the traces of bullets and cannon balls.

That *Polonais* was — Dmitry Rudin.

A Quiet Spot
(*The Backwater*)

1854

I

IN a quite large, recently whitewashed room in the master's apartments of a country house at the village of Sasov, in XXX county, T— province, a young man in an overcoat was sitting at an old warped table examining accounts. He was working by the light of two tallow candles, in silver traveling candlesticks; in one corner an open hamper had been placed on a bench, in another a servant was setting up an iron bedstead. Beyond a low partition a samovar was gushing and hissing; a dog shifted restlessly on some hay just put down. A peasant in a new home-made overcoat belted with a crimson girdle was standing at the door; he had a big beard and an intelligent face, and by all the signs was the headman of the village; he kept his eyes fixed on the young man. By one wall stood a small, very decrepit piano, next to as ancient a commode, with holes where the locks should have been; between the windows was a tarnished mirror; on the partition hung an old, almost completely peeling portrait of a woman with powdered face, in a *robe ronde* and with a narrow black ribbon round her slender neck. Judging by the obvious crookedness of the ceiling and the slope of the floor, with its many chinks between the boards, the room to which we have introduced the reader had existed for many, many years; no one lived in it permanently, it was used only when the master arrived. The young man seated at the table was the owner of the village of Sasov. He had arrived only the evening before from his main estate, which was about sixty miles away, and he intended to leave again the very next day, when he had completed his examination of the condition of the estate, had heard the peasants' requests and verified all the documents.

"Well, but that will be enough for today," he said, raising his head. "I'm tired. You can go now," he added, turning to the headman, "but come as early as possible tomorrow, and bring the peasants for a meeting early in the morning, d'you hear?"

"Yes."

"And tell the secretary to let me have the report for the past month. But you have done well to whitewash the walls," the master continued, looking about him. "It makes everything seem cleaner."

The headman also silently looked at the walls.

"Well, now you can go."

The peasant bowed and went out.

The master stretched himself.

"Hey!" he cried, "bring me some tea. . . . Time for bed!"

The servant went behind the partition and soon returned with a glass of tea, a bunch of shop-made cracknels, and a cream jug, on an iron tray. The young man began to drink the tea; but before he had had time for more than a couple of sips he heard someone entering the next room, and a squeaky voice asked:

"Is Vladimir Sergeich Astakhov at home? Can I see him?"

Vladimir Sergeich (for that was the name of the young man in the overcoat) looked at his man in astonishment and said in a hurried whisper:

"Go and find out who it is."

The man went out, slamming the badly fitting door behind him.

"Report to Vladimir Sergeich," the same squeaky voice said, "that his neighbor Ipatov wishes to see him, if it is no trouble to him; and with me is another neighbor, Ivan Ilich Bodryakov, who also desires to express his respects."

Vladimir Sergeich made an involuntary gesture of vexation. None the less, when his man entered the room he told him:

"Ask them in."

And he rose to welcome the guests.

The door opened and they appeared. The one who entered first was a solid-looking, gray-haired old man with a small round head and small gleaming eyes; he was followed by a tall, gaunt man of about thirty-five, with a long, swarthy face and untidy hair and a rolling gait. The little old man was wearing a neat gray coat with large mother-of-pearl buttons; a rose-colored cravat, half covered by the turn-down collar of his white shirt,

loosely enfolded his neck, his feet were adorned with cloth button shoes, the variegated checks of his Scottish pantaloons were
pleasant to see, and he made a pleasant impression altogether. His
companion, on the contrary, aroused a less satisfactory feeling
in the beholder: he was wearing an old black frock coat, tightly
buttoned up; his trousers, of thick winter woolens, matched the
color of his frock coat; neither around his neck nor at his wrists
was any linen to be seen. The old man was the first to speak;
bowing affably, he began in the same piping voice:

"I have the honor to introduce myself — Mikhail Nikolaich
Ipatov, your nearest neighbor and even a distant relation. I have
been wanting to have the pleasure of making your acquaintance
for a long time. I hope I have not disturbed you."

Vladimir Sergeich replied that he was very glad and had himself desired to meet him, and that he had not been disturbed in
the least and wouldn't they be pleased to sit down . . . and have
some tea.

"And this nobleman," the old man continued, listening to
Vladimir Sergeich's broken remarks with a friendly smile and
pointing to the gentleman in the frock coat, "is also a neighbor
of ours — and my close acquaintance Ivan Ilich. He too greatly
wanted to meet you."

The gentleman in the frock coat, who, to judge by his face,
could hardly have been thought to have any great desire for
anything at all, so abstracted and simultaneously sleepy was its
expression — the gentleman in the frock coat bowed awkwardly
and wearily. Vladimir Sergeich bowed in reply and repeated his
invitation to sit down.

The guests sat down.

"I am very glad," the old man began, affably waving his hands,
while his companion, with mouth a little open, turned to gazing
at the ceiling. "I am very glad that I have at last the honor of
meeting you personally. Though you live and have your permanent residence in a county quite a distance from these parts,
none the less we include you among our own root-and-branch
proprietors, so to speak."

"That is very flattering," Vladimir Sergeich replied.

"Flattering or not, it is so. You must excuse us, Vladimir Sergeich, we here, in —— county, are a plain-spoken people; we

live in simple fashion; we say what we think, without ambiguity. I must tell you that among ourselves, we call on one another only in morning coats, even on name-days. Really! That is just our established habit. For this reason the neighboring counties call us morning-coaters, and even accuse us of having bad taste; but we don't pay any attention to them! Why, are we to live in the country and stand on ceremony into the bargain?"

"Of course, what could be better — in the country — than such natural relations?" Vladimir Sergeich observed.

"But all the same," the old man rejoined, "even among us of this county you will find intelligent people, one may say people of European education, though they do not wear frock coats. Take our historian, Stepan Stepanich Yevsiukov, for example; he studies Russian history from the very earliest times and is known in Petersburg, he is a very learned man! In our county town there is an ancient Swedish cannon ball, you know — it is set up in the middle of the square — and he was the one who discovered it. Yes indeed! And there's Anton Karlich Tsentelier — he's studied natural history; but I know they say science comes easily to all Germans. When some ten years ago a runaway hyena was killed in our parts, it was Anton Karlich who discovered that it really was a hyena, because of the peculiar arrangement of its tail. And then there is the landowner Kaburdin: he devotes himself more to writing light articles; he has a very daring pen, his articles are printed in *Galatea*. And Bodryakov — not Ivan Ilich, no, Ivan Ilich does not bother his head with that sort of thing — but another Bodryakov, Sergei — now, what is his patronymic, Ivan Ilich? What is it?"

"Sergeich," Ivan Ilich responded.

"Oh yes, Sergei Sergeich — now, he writes poetry. Of course, he's not a Pushkin, but sometimes his thrusts are so keen that he might be a Petersburg poet. Do you know his epigram on Agei Fomich?"

"Which Agei Fomich?"

"Ah, pardon me! I continually forget that you are not really a local resident. He's the chairman of our local court. The epigram was very funny. Ivan Ilich, I think you remember it?"

"Agei Fomich," Bodryakov began phlegmatically:

A Quiet Spot

> " — we all respect,
> And made him a justice by election."

"I must tell you," Ipatov interrupted, "that he was elected almost by a unanimous vote, for he is the most worthy of men."
"Agei Fomich," Bodryakov repeated,

> " — we all respect,
> And made him a justice by election.
> At table he is most correct,
> So should he not dispense correction?"

The old man smiled.
"He-he-he! It isn't bad, is it? Ever since then, will you believe it, whenever we say 'good morning,' for instance, to Agei Fomich, we always invariably add: 'so should he not dispense correction?' And do you think Agei Fomich is at all angry? Not in the least; no, that is not our way. You ask Ivan Ilich."
Ivan Ilich only rolled his eyes.
"Be angry over a joke — why, how could we? Take Ivan Ilich himself: we all call him 'Adaptable Soul' because he so readily agrees to everything. And what of it? Does Ivan Ilich take offense at the name? Never!"
Ivan Ilich gazed, slowly blinking first at the old man, then at Vladimir Sergeich.
The name "Adaptable Soul" certainly fitted him very well. He had not even a suggestion of what we call will or character. Anyone who wished could lead him where he liked; one had only to say to him: "Ivan Ilich, come along," and he picked up his hat and went. But if someone else happened to turn up at that moment and said to him: "You stay behind, Ivan Ilich," he put down his hat and stayed behind. He was of a peaceable and quiet disposition, all his life he had been a bachelor, he did not play cards, but he liked to sit beside the players and look into each of their faces in turn. He could not live without company, could not endure seclusion; at such times he grew despondent; however, that was very rarely his lot. He happened to have one other peculiarity: when rising from bed of a morning, he always began to sing in an undertone the very old ballad:

Turgenev

Once a baron in the country
Lived with rustic simplicity. . . .

Because of this idiosyncrasy Ivan Ilich was also called the "finch," for it is well known that a caged finch sings only once in the day, early in the morning. Such was Ivan Ilich Bodryakov.

The talk between Ipatov and Vladimir Sergeich continued for quite a time, but no longer in its previous somewhat speculative direction. The old man questioned Vladimir Sergeich about his estate, about the condition of his timber and other outgoings, about the improvements he had already introduced or was only intending to introduce in his husbandry; he imparted certain of his own observations; he advised him, among other things, to scatter oats all around meadow mounds in order to get rid of them, as this apparently would encourage the pigs to root them up with their snouts; and so on. At last, however, observing that Vladimir Sergeich's eyelids were sticking together and that he was showing signs of hesitation and even incoherence in his remarks, the old man rose and, bowing amiably, announced that he did not intend to constrain his host any further by his presence, but he hoped to have the pleasure of seeing Vladimir Sergeich as an honored guest in his own house not later than the next day, at dinner.

"And in my village," he added, "except for the very little children, I dare to say the first person you meet, even a chicken or a woman, will show you the road as soon as you ask for Ipatovka. The horses will take you there of themselves."

Vladimir Sergeich replied with rather a stammer, which, however, was a habit of his, that he would endeavor — that if nothing came up to hinder —

"Now, now, we shall be expecting you without fail," the old man graciously interrupted him; he squeezed his hand firmly and went out briskly, half turning at the door and exclaiming: "Without ceremony!"

Adaptable Soul Bodryakov bowed without speaking and vanished behind his companion, after a preliminary stumble at the door.

After seeing his unexpected guests to the door, Vladimir Sergeich at once undressed, got into bed, and fell asleep.

Vladimir Sergeich Astakhov was one of those people who,

having cautiously tried his powers in two or three different careers, say of themselves that they have decided finally to regard life from the practical aspect and to devote their leisure to the multiplication of their receipts. He was not stupid, was quite miserly and very sober-minded, he liked reading, society, music, but everything in moderation . . . and he behaved very decorously. He was only twenty-seven years old. Of recent times many young people have developed on similar lines. He was of average height, well built, his features were pleasant, but banal; their expression hardly ever changed, his eyes always had one and the same hard and clear gaze; only rarely was that look softened by a faint nuance of sorrow, or maybe of boredom; a polite smile hardly ever left his lips. His hair was beautiful, fair, silky, and hung in long curls. His fortune was reputed to consist of some six hundred souls on a good estate, and he was thinking of marriage — a marriage of inclination, but at the same time advantageous. He particularly wanted to find a wife with connections. He considered that he did not have sufficient connections. In a word, he deserved the term "gentleman," which had recently come into fashion.

Rising next morning very early, as usual, our *gentleman* occupied himself with affairs and, to do him justice, occupied himself with them quite efficiently, which cannot always be said of practical young people in our Russia. He listened patiently to the peasants' confused requests and complaints, satisfied them as far as he could, investigated the disputes and disagreements that had arisen within families, shamed some, shouted at others, verified the secretary's report, exposed two or three of the headman's swindles; in a word, he arranged matters so that he was left satisfied with himself, while on their way home after the meeting the peasants spoke well of him. Despite his promise to Ipatov the previous evening, Vladimir Sergeich had decided to dine at home and had even ordered his traveling cook to prepare his favorite rice soup with giblets. But suddenly, perhaps as the result of the feeling of satisfaction that had filled his soul ever since the morning, he halted in the middle of the room, struck his hand against his forehead and, with some feeling of temerity, exclaimed aloud: "But I'll drive over to call on that old chatterer." No sooner said than done; within the half-hour he was seated in his fairly new tarantass, to which four good peasant horses were harnessed, and was driving to Ipatovka, which was reckoned to be no more than eight miles of good road away.

2

Mikhail Nikolaich Ipatov's farmstead consisted of two separate small houses for the masters, built opposite each other, on either side of a great lake of running water. A long dam, lined with silver poplars, closed one end of this lake; almost level with it the red roof of a small water-mill was visible. Built to an identical plan, painted with the same lilac paint, with the gleaming glass of their small, clean windows the little houses seemed to be exchanging glances across the broad stretch of water. A semicircular terrace jutted from the center of each house, and above the façade was an acute-angled pediment supported on four closely spaced white columns. All around the lake ran an old-world garden; limes extended along it in avenues or stood in compact groups; here and there tough old pines with pale yellow trunks, dark oaks, and magnificent ashes raised their lofty, solitary crowns; a dense greenery of spreading lilacs and acacias grew right up to the sides of both houses, leaving bare only their fronts, from which winding paths of brick ran down the slopes. Varicolored ducks and white and gray geese were swimming in separate flocks over the gleaming water of the lake; it was never overgrown with weed, for it was fed from copious springs rising from the bottom of a steep and stony gulley at its "head." The farmstead had an excellent situation, friendly, solitary, and beautiful.

Mikhail Nikolaich himself lived in one of the two houses; his mother, a withered old woman over seventy years of age, lived in the other. When Vladimir Sergeich drove onto the dam he did not know which house to make for. He looked about him — and saw a yard boy fishing, standing barefoot on a half-rotten trunk lying in the water. Vladimir Sergeich called to him.

"But who do you want, the old mistress or the master, her son?" the boy retorted without taking his eyes off the float.

"What mistress?" Vladimir Sergeich replied; "I want Mikhail Nikolaich."

"Ah, the young master! Well, then you drive to the right."

And the boy pulled up his line and dragged a small silvery carp out of the still water. Vladimir Sergeich drove to the right.

Mikhail Nikolaich was playing checkers with Adaptable Soul when he was informed that Vladimir Sergeich had arrived. He was highly delighted, jumped up from his armchair, ran into the vestibule, and there kissed his visitor thrice.

"You find me with my constant friend, Vladimir Sergeich," the garrulous old man remarked. "I am with Ivan Ilich, who, I may say in passing, is perfectly enchanted with your amiability" (Ivan Ilich silently stared into one corner). "He was so kind as to remain to play checkers with me; all my family have gone out to walk in the garden, but I shall send for them at once."

"But why trouble them?" Vladimir Sergeich began.

"What trouble is it, for mercy's sake! Hey, Vanka, run quickly for the young ladies — tell them I said a guest has arrived. But how do you like this locality — not at all bad, is it? Kaburdin has written some verse about it — "Ipatovka, lovely refuge," that's how it begins, and it goes on very well, too, only I don't remember it all. The garden is enormous, there's the rub: it's too big for our resources. But these two houses, which are so like each other, as perhaps you have been pleased to observe, were built by two brothers, my father, Nikolai, and my Uncle Sergei. It was they who developed the garden; they were exemplary friends — Damon and — well, I never! I've forgotten how the other was called."

"Pythias," Ivan Ilich interposed.

"Really, was it? Well, it doesn't matter" (at home the old man talked far more bluntly than when visiting). "Probably you are not unaware, Vladimir Sergeich, that I am a widower; I have lost my wife. My older daughters are in state educational institutions, and I have staying with me only the two younger girls and a sister-in-law, my wife's sister — you'll see her in a moment. But what am I thinking of? I haven't shown you any hospitality. Ivan Ilich, my friend, just go and see about some hors d'œuvres. . . . What vodka would you prefer?"

"I never drink before dinner."

"Really, how can you say that! But it is just as you wish. The guest's choice, to the guest be the honor. We live quite simply here. What we have here, I dare say, is not merely a quiet little spot, but a rural retreat, absolutely a rural retreat, a secluded little corner, that's what it is! But why don't you sit down?"

Turgenev

Vladimir Sergeich sat down, still holding his hat.

"Allow me to relieve you of your hat," Ipatov said. Delicately taking it from him, he carried it to a corner. Then he returned, looked with an amiable smile into the guest's eyes, and, not knowing what to say to please him most, asked him very cordially whether he liked playing checkers.

"I play all games badly," Vladimir Sergeich replied.

"And very sensible of you," Ipatov said. "However, checkers is not a game, but rather an amusement, a passing of empty time, isn't that so, Ivan Ilich?"

Ivan Ilich gave Ipatov an indifferent look, as though thinking: "The devil knows whether it is a game or an amusement." Then, after pausing a moment, he said:

"Yes; checkers is all right."

"Now, they say chess is another matter," Ipatov went on; "they say it is a very difficult game. But in my view — ah, here are my family coming!" he interrupted himself, glancing through the half-open glass door leading to the garden.

Vladimir Sergeich rose, turned, and saw two girls about ten years of age, pink in cotton dresses and large hats, nimbly running up the steps of the terrace. Soon after, they were followed by a young woman of twenty, tall, of full and shapely figure, in a dark dress. They all came into the room; the children sedately curtsied to the visitor.

"Now I must introduce my daughters," said the host. "This one is named Katya, and this is Nastya. And this is my sister-in-law, Maria Pavlovna, whom I have already had the pleasure of mentioning. I would ask you to be gracious to her."

Vladimir Sergeich bowed to Maria Pavlovna; she replied with a barely perceptible inclination of the head.

Maria was holding a large clasp-knife open in her hand; her mass of fair hair was rather untidy, a small green leaf was entangled in it, the braid was breaking away from the comb, her swarthy face was flushed, and her crimson lips were parted; her dress appeared to be crumpled. She was breathing rapidly and her eyes were sparkling; evidently she had been working in the garden. She at once left the room; the children ran after her.

"They've gone to tidy their toilet a little," the old man remarked, turning to Vladimir Sergeich. "They mustn't appear in company without attending to that."

A Quiet Spot

Vladimir Sergeich smirked at him in reply and grew rather abstracted. Maria Pavlovna had greatly impressed him. It was long since he had seen such a straightforwardly Russian steppe beauty. She soon returned, sat down on a sofa, and did not stir. She had tidied her hair, but had not changed her dress and had not even donned cuffs. Her features expressed not so much pride as harshness, almost roughness; her brow was broad and low, her nose short and straight; a sluggish and dilatory smile occasionally twisted her lips; her straight eyebrows were knitted contemptuously. She almost constantly kept her large, dark eyes half-closed. "I know," her *unfriendly* young face seemed to be saying, "I know you are all looking at me; well, look on, I'm fed up!" But when she raised her eyes, there was something wild, beautiful, and dumb in them, a look reminiscent of the gaze of a doe. She was superbly built. A classic poet would have compared her with Ceres or Juno.

"What have you been doing in the garden?" Ipatov asked her desiring to draw her into the conversation.

"We have been cutting off the dead twigs and hoeing the rows," she replied in a rather low but pleasant and melodious voice.

"And why have you got so tired?"

"The children are tired; I am not."

"I know," the old man retorted with a smile, "you are a real Bobalina[1] to me! And have you been to see Granny?"

"Yes; she is resting."

"Do you like flowers?" Vladimir Sergeich asked her.

"I do."

"Why don't you put your hat on when you go out?" Ipatov remarked. "Look how flushed and sunburnt you are."

She passed her hand over her face without answering. Her hands were small, but rather broad and quite red. She did not wear gloves.

"And do you like gardening?" Vladimir Sergeich asked her again.

"Yes."

Vladimir Sergeich began to tell them about a neighbor of his, the wealthy landowner N., who had a beautiful garden. Among

[1] Perhaps the Greek heroine of this name in the wars of independence, in the 1820's. (Tr.)

other things he mentioned that the head gardener, a German, received two thousand rubles in silver as salary alone.

"What is this gardener's name?" Ivan Ilich suddenly asked.

"I don't remember, Meyer or Miller, I think. But why do you ask?"

"Oh, nothing. I just wanted to know the name," Ivan Ilich replied.

Vladimir Sergeich continued his story. The children, Mikhail Nikolaich's daughters, entered, quietly sat down, and quietly began to listen. . . .

A servant appeared at the door and reported that Yegor Kapitonich had arrived.

"Ah! Ask him in! Ask him in!" Ipatov exclaimed.

Yegor Kapitonich was a stocky, fat old man, one of the breed of men called shorties or stumpies, with a bloated yet furrowed little face rather like a baked apple. He was wearing a gray Hungarian cloak with black strings and a standing collar; his broad velveteen trousers, of coffee color, ended far above the ankles.

"Good evening, worthy Yegor Kapitonich," Ipatov exclaimed, going to meet him. "It's ages since we saw you last."

"Why, what d'you expect?" Yegor Kapitonich retorted in a guttural and lachrymose voice, after bowing to all the others present. "You know quite well, Mikhail Nikolaich, that I am not a free man."

"But how aren't you a free man, Yegor Kapitonich?"

"Why, you know very well, Mikhail Nikolaich; my family, my affairs — And then there is Matriona Markovna." And he waved his hand.

"But what of Matriona Markovna?"

Ipatov gave a little wink to Vladimir Sergeich as though desiring in advance to ensure his attention.

"Why, everybody knows," Yegor Kapitonich retorted, seating himself, "she's always dissatisfied with me, as if you didn't know. No matter what I say, it's always wrong, it's not delicate, not seemly. But why it isn't seemly the Lord only knows. And the young ladies, my daughters, I mean, take their example from their mother. I do not say that Matriona Markovna is not a very fine woman, but really she is very strict in regard to conduct."

A Quiet Spot

"But how is your conduct unsatisfactory, Yegor Kapitonich, for goodness' sake?"

"That's just what I think myself, but evidently it is difficult to please her. Yesterday, for instance, I said at the table: 'Matriona Markovna'" (and Yegor Kapitonich put a very wheedling tone into his voice), "'Matriona Markovna,' I said, 'why is it Aldoshka doesn't look after the horses, she doesn't know how to ride,' I said. 'The raven stallion has been ridden to death.' And she, Matriona Markovna, how she flared up, how she set to work to shame me! 'You,' she said, 'don't know how to talk properly in ladies' society.' The young ladies jumped up from the table at once, and the next day it was all known to the Biriulevsky young ladies, my wife's nieces. But what had I said that was so bad? Judge for yourself. And no matter what I say — and sometimes of course I am a little imprudent, who isn't, especially at home? — the Biriulevsky young ladies know all about it the very next day. You simply don't know what is going to happen next. Sometimes I am sitting like this, thinking in my own way — I, as perhaps you know, breathe rather deeply — and Matriona Markovna again sets to work to shame me. 'Don't wheeze like that,' she says, 'who wheezes nowadays?' 'What are you scolding me for, Matriona Markovna?' I answer; 'really you should feel sorry for me, but you scold me.' And now I no longer think when I'm at home. I sit and look at my feet all the time, really I do! And then only the other night, when we went to bed, 'Matriona Markovna,' I said, 'what are you up to, my dear? You've spoilt your page so much he's just like a little pig; he might wash his face on Sundays at least.' And what is there in that remark? After all, you must admit I said it gently, I only made a hint, but once more I missed the mark. Once more Matriona Markovna began to put me to shame. 'You don't know how to behave in ladies' society,' she says, and the next day it was all known to the Biriulevsky young ladies. And how can a man think of paying visits in such circumstances, Mikhail Nikolaich?"

"What you are saying surprises me," Ipatov replied. "I hadn't expected that of Matriona Markovna; I think she — "

"Is a very fine woman," Yegor Kapitonich caught him up; "a model wife and mother, one may say. She is strict only in regard to manners. She says *ensemble* is necessary in everything, and apparently I haven't got it. You know, I don't talk French, I only understand it. But what is the ensemble that I haven't got?"

Ipatov, who himself was not particularly good at French, only shrugged his shoulders.

"And what about your children, the sons, I mean?" he asked Yegor Kapitonich after a moment.

Yegor Kapitonich gave him a sidelong look.

"As for my sons, they're all right. I'm satisfied with them. The young ladies have got right out of hand, but I am satisfied with my sons. Lolia is doing well in the service, the authorities approve of him; Lolia is a clever boy. But Mikhets, he's not like Lolia; he's turned into a kind of philanthropist."

"Why a philanthropist?"

"The Lord knows, he never talks to anybody, he's unsociable. Matriona Markovna is always making him feel uncomfortable. 'What,' she says, 'taking your example from your father? You can show him respect, but in your manners you must imitate your mother.' When he pulls up a bit he will go too."

Vladimir Sergeich asked Ipatov to introduce him to Yegor Kapitonich. A conversation developed between them. Maria Pavlovna took no part in it; Ivan Ilich sat down beside her, but he, too, only said a couple of words to her altogether. The children went over to him and began to tell him something in a whisper. . . . The housekeeper, a gaunt old woman with her head tied in a dark kerchief, entered and announced that dinner was ready. They all went to the dining-room.

The dinner went on for some time. Ipatov kept a good cook, and his wines were not at all bad, though he ordered them not from Moscow, but from the provincial town. Ipatov lived in comfort, as the saying is. He possessed not more than three hundred souls, but he was completely free of debts and had put the estate in order. Over the table the host himself talked most; Yegor Kapitonich seconded him, but at the same time he did not forget himself: he ate and drank magnificently. Maria Pavlovna was constantly silent, only rarely replying with a half-smile to the two girls' hurried chatter as they sat one on each side of her; they were obviously very fond of her. Several times Vladimir Sergeich attempted to talk to her, but without any particular success. Adaptable Soul Bodryakov even ate sluggishly and flabbily. After dinner they all went onto the terrace to drink coffee. The weather was beautiful; the delicious scent of the limes, which were now in full blossom, reached them from the garden; the summer air, slightly chilled by the heavy shadow of the trees and the humidity of the near-by lake, respired with a gracious warmth. Suddenly they caught the clatter of horse-hoofs from beyond the poplars of the dam, and a moment later a horse-woman appeared in a long riding-habit and a round gray hat, sitting a bay horse. She was riding at a gallop; a page was gallop-ing along behind her on a small white nag.

"Ah!" Ipatov exclaimed, "here comes Nadiozhda Alexeevna; now, that's a pleasant surprise."

"Alone?" asked Maria Pavlovna, who until that moment had been standing perfectly still at the door.

"Yes — evidently something has detained Piotr Alexeich."

Maria Pavlovna looked up from under knitted brows, her cheeks were suffused with color, and she turned away.

Meanwhile the horsewoman rode through a wicket gate into the garden, galloped up to the terrace, and lightly vaulted to the ground, waiting neither for her page nor for Ipatov, who had gone to meet her. Briskly gathering up the hem of her habit, she ran up the steps and, springing onto the terrace, exclaimed merrily:

"And here I am!"

"And very welcome!" Ipatov said. "Now, this is unexpected, this is a pleasure! Allow me to kiss your little hand."

"By all means," the visitor replied, "only you must take my glove off. I cannot." As she held out her hand to him she nodded to Maria Pavlovna. "Maria dear, just imagine, my brother will not be coming today," she said with a little sigh.

"I can see for myself that he hasn't come," Maria Pavlovna re-plied in an undertone.

"He told me to tell you that he is busy. Don't be angry. Good evening, Yegor Kapitonich; good evening, Ivan Ilich. Good eve-ning, children. . . . Vasia," the new arrival continued, turning to her page, "tell them to give Beauty a good walk up and down, do you hear? Maria dear, please give me a pin, to pin up my train. . . . Mikhail Nikolaich, come here."

Ipatov moved closer to her.

"Who is the new face?" she asked in quite a loud voice.

"He is a neighbor, Vladimir Sergeich Astakhov; you know, the owner of Sasovo. Would you like me to introduce him to you?"

"All right — later on. Ah, what wonderful weather!" she went

Turgenev

on. "Yegor Kapitonich, tell me, surely Matriona Markovna doesn't grumble even in such weather?"

"Matriona Markovna never grumbles in any kind of weather, madame, she is only strict in regard to manners. . . ."

"But what are the Biriulevsky young ladies up to? They know everything the very next day, don't they?" And she laughed a ringing and silvery laugh.

"You're always ready to laugh," Yegor Kapitonich retorted. "But when should one laugh, if not at your age?"

"Yegor Kapitonich, my dear, don't be angry! Ah, I am tired, may I sit down? . . ."

She dropped into an armchair and playfully drew her hat right down over her eyes.

Ipatov led Vladimir Sergeich over to her.

"Allow me, Nadiozhda Alexeevna, to introduce our neighbor, Mr. Astakhov, whom you have probably heard a great deal about."

Vladimir Sergeich bowed, but Nadiozhda looked up at him from under the brim of her round hat.

"Nadiozhda Alexeevna Veretieva, a neighbor of ours," Ipatov continued, turning to Vladimir Sergeich. "She lives not far away with her brother, Piotr Alexeich, a retired lieutenant of the guards. She is a great friend of my sister-in-law and is generally partial to our house."

"A complete letter of recommendation," Nadiozhda Alexeevna said with a smile, still gazing up at Vladimir Sergeich from under her hat.

But meanwhile Vladimir Sergeich was thinking: "Why, this one's very good-looking, too." And truly, Nadiozhda Alexeevna was a very good-looking young woman. Slender and shapely, she seemed much younger than she really was. She was already past her twenty-seventh year. She had a round face, a small head, fair, fluffy hair, a sharp, almost impudently turned-up little nose, and merry, rather crafty little eyes. There was such a gleam of mockery in those eyes, and they sparkled and lit up so! Her features, extraordinarily vivacious and mobile, sometimes adopted an almost amusing expression; humor peered through them. Occasionally, more often than not quite suddenly, a hint of reflection fled across her face — and then it grew mild and kindly; but she was

696

not of a reflective nature. She quickly saw the funny side of people and was good at drawing caricatures. From the day of her birth everybody had spoilt her, and that was evident at first glance: people spoilt in childhood retain the distinguishing marks to the end of their lives. Her brother was fond of her, though he declared that she stung not like a bee, but like a wasp, because a bee stung and died, but when a wasp stung, it made no difference to it. This comparison annoyed her.

"Have you arrived for a long stay?" she asked Vladimir Sergeich, lowering her eyes and twisting the riding-whip in her hands.

"No, I intend to leave again tomorrow."

"Where for?"

"For home."

"Home? What for, if I may dare to ask?"

"I don't understand. I have business awaiting me at home that will not brook delay.

Nadiozhda Alexeevna looked at him.

"Are you such a — regular man, then?"

"I endeavor to be a man of regular habits," Vladimir Sergeich retorted. "In our positive times any man of probity *should* be positive and regular."

"That is absolutely right," Ipatov remarked. "Isn't it, Ivan Ilich?"

Ivan Ilich only looked at Ipatov, but Yegor Kapitonich said: "Yes, that is so."

"Pity!" said Nadiozhda Alexeevna; "a *jeune premier* is just what we need. Of course you can play comedy?"

"I have never tested my powers in that field."

"I am sure you would make a good actor. You have such a — serious deportment, and that is indispensable to a *jeune premier* these days. My brother and I are planning to start a theater here. For that matter, we shall not confine ourselves to comedies, we shall play everything — drama, ballet, and even tragedy. Why shouldn't Maria play Cleopatra or Phèdre? Just look at her!"

Vladimir Sergeich turned round. . . . Resting her head against the door and standing with folded arms, Maria Pavlovna was thoughtfully gazing into the distance. . . . At that moment her harmonious features recalled those of some classic sculpture. She did not catch Nadiozhda Alexeevna's last words but, noticing that everybody's eyes were suddenly fixed on her, she at once guessed the reason, blushed, and turned to go into the reception room. . . . Nadiozhda Alexeevna nimbly seized her by the arm and, with the playful affection of a kitten, drew her to herself and kissed her almost masculine hand. Maria Pavlovna flamed still more vividly.

"You're always up to some trick or other, Nadia," she said.

"Didn't I speak the truth about you, then? I am prepared to appeal to everybody. . . . Well, all right, all right, I won't. But I repeat," Nadiozhda Alexeevna continued, turning to Vladimir Sergeich, "it is a pity you are going. True, we have one *jeune premier*, he forces himself on us; but he is very bad."

"Who is he? May I ask?"

"Bodryakov, the poet. And how can a poet be a *jeune premier*? To begin with, he dresses horribly; secondly, he writes epigrams, but he is quite shy when any woman is around, and even with me, would you believe it! He lisps, he has one hand always raised above his head, and I don't know what else. Tell me, please, M'sieur Astakhov, are all poets like that?"

Vladimir Sergeich drew himself up a little.

"I have never known any of them personally, and I must admit that I have never sought their acquaintance."

"True; of course you are a positive man. There's nothing else for it, we shall have to have Bodryakov. Other *jeunes premiers* are still worse. He will at least learn his part by heart. In addition to playing tragic roles, Maria will act as our prima donna. You haven't heard how well she sings, M'sieur Astakhov?"

"No," Vladimir Sergeich replied with a smirk, "I didn't even know — "

"What is the matter with you today, Nadia?" Maria Pavlovna began in a dissatisfied tone.

Nadiozhda Alexeevna jumped to her feet.

"For goodness' sake, Maria dear, sing something to us, please. . . . I shan't stop worrying you till you sing us something, Maria, my soul. I would sing myself in order to amuse the guest, but you know what a poor voice I have. But on the other hand, see how splendidly I shall accompany you!"

Maria Pavlovna remained silent for a moment.

'There's no denying you," she said at last. "You're like a spoilt child, you're always governed by your caprices. I will sing if you wish."

"Bravo, bravo," Nadiozhda Alexeevna exclaimed, and clapped her hands. "Gentlemen, let us go into the reception room. But as for caprices," she added, smiling, "that will be remembered against you. How can you expose my weaknesses in the presence of strangers? Yegor Kapitonich, does Matriona Markovna shame you like *that* in front of strangers?"

"Matriona Markovna is a very worthy lady," Yegor Kapitonich muttered; "only in regard to manners — "

"Well, come on, come on!" Nadiozhda Alexeevna interrupted him, and went into the reception room.

They all followed her. She threw off her hat and sat down at the piano. Maria Pavlovna stood by the wall, some distance away from her.

"Maria dear," Nadiozhda said, after thinking for a moment, "sing us 'Peasant, sow the corn.' "

Maria Pavlovna began to sing. She had a pure and strong voice, and she sang well — simply and without affectation. They all listened to her with deep attention, and Vladimir Sergeich could not conceal his astonishment. When she ended he went up to her and began to assure her that he had never expected —

"You wait a moment, there may be more!" Nadiozhda Alexeevna interrupted him. "Maria, I will comfort your Khokhol [1] soul; now sing us 'In the oak wood.' "

"Are you Little Russian, then?" Vladimir Sergeich asked Maria.

"I was born in Little Russia," she replied and began to sing "In the oak wood."

At first she sang the words without feeling; but gradually the mournfully passionate national melody began to move her, her cheeks flushed, her eyes glittered, her voice acquired a fervent tone. She sang the song to the end.

"My goodness, how well you sang it!" Nadiozhda Alexeevna said, bending over the keys. "What a pity my brother was not here!"

Maria Pavlovna at once cast down her eyes and smiled her usual bitter smile.

"But you must sing something more," Ipatov remarked.

[1] Common nickname for Ukrainians. (Tr.)

"Please do, if you would be so kind," Vladimir Sergeich added.

"Forgive me, but I shall not sing any more today," she declared, and she left the room.

Nadiozhda Alexeevna gazed after her, thought for a moment, then smiled, began to play "Peasant, sow the corn" with one finger, then suddenly struck up a brilliant polka and, without finishing it, struck a thunderous chord, slammed down the piano lid, and got up.

"Pity there's nobody to dance with," she exclaimed. "That would be just the thing."

Vladimir Sergeich went across to her.

"What a marvelous voice Maria Pavlovna has!" he remarked. "And with what feeling she sings!"

"Do you like music, then?"

"Yes — very much."

"Such a learned man, and you like music?"

"But what makes you think I am learned?"

"Ah, of course! Pardon me, I am continually forgetting, you are a positive man. But where has Maria gone off to? Wait a moment, I'll go after her."

And she fluttered out of the reception room.

"A flirt, as you can see," Ipatov said, going over to Vladimir Sergeich. "But very good-hearted. And the education she has had, you cannot imagine! She can make herself understood in all languages. Well, but they are people of fortune, so that is understandable."

"Yes," Vladimir Sergeich said abstractedly. "A very pleasant girl. Pardon my asking, but was your wife also born in Little Russia?"

"Exactly! My late wife was a Little Russian, like her sister, Maria Pavlovna. To tell the truth, my wife did not even have a perfectly pure Russian accent; though she had a perfect command of the Russian language, none the less her pronunciation was not quite correct; as you know, they have a longer 'i,' and a more guttural 'h' in Little Russia. Maria Pavlovna left her native land when she was still quite young. But the Little Russian blood is very obvious, don't you think?"

"Maria Pavlovna sings amazingly well," Vladimir Sergeich observed.

"Yes, not at all badly. But, by the way, why don't they bring in the tea? And where have the young ladies gone off to? It is time for tea."

The young ladies did not return for a long time. Meanwhile the samovar was brought in and the table was laid for tea. Ipatov sent for them, and they came back together. Maria Pavlovna sat at the table to pour out the tea, but Nadiozhda Alexeevna went over to the terrace door and began to gaze into the garden. After the bright summer day a clear and still evening was coming on: the sunset was flaming; flooded with purple over half its expanse, the broad lake was a motionless mirror, majestically reflecting all the aerial depths of the sky, and the upside-down, blackened trees, and the house, in the silvery mistiness of its deep bosom. Everything around was hushed in silence. There was not a sound to be heard anywhere.

"Look, how good it is!" said Nadiozhda Alexeevna to Vladimir Sergeich as he went over to her. "Look, down there, in the lake a star has lit up just by that little fire in the house; the star is red, and the fire is golden. And here is Granny coming," she added in a loud voice.

A small carriage pulled along by two men appeared from behind a lilac bush. In it was an old woman wrapped from head to foot, completely doubled up, with her head sunk right on her breast. The fringe of her white mobcap almost entirely covered her withered and shriveled face. The carriage halted in front of the terrace. Ipatov emerged from the reception room, and his daughters ran out after him. All the evening they had scurried continually from room to room like little mice.

"I wish you good evening, dear Mother," Ipatov said, going up to the old woman and raising his voice. "How do you feel?"

"I've driven over to have a look at you," his mother said throatily and with effort. "What a wonderful evening it is! I slept during the day, but now my legs are aching. Oh, these legs of mine! They don't serve me, they only hurt me."

"Mother, let me introduce our neighbor, Mr. Vladimir Sergeich Astakhov."

"Very glad," the old woman replied, looking at him with her large black but faded eyes. "Please be nice to my little son. He is a good man; I gave him what education I could; you know, that's the woman's task. He is still a little faint-hearted, but God grant he will settle down, though it is about time; it is time I

701

handed over affairs to him. Is that you, Nadia?" she added, glancing at Nadiozhda Alexeevna.

"Yes, Granny."

"And is Maria pouring out the tea?"

"Yes, Granny, she is pouring out the tea."

"And who else is there?"

"Ivan Ilich and Yegor Kapitonich."

"Matriona Markovna's husband?"

"Yes, Granny."

The old woman chewed her lips.

"Well, good! But, by the way, Mikhail, I simply cannot get hold of the headman; order him to come to see me early tomorrow. I have a good deal of business with him. I see that without me you still can't manage things properly. Well, that's enough, I'm tired, take me away, you. . . . Good-by, my dear sir, I don't remember your name and patronymic," she added, turning to Vladimir Sergeich. "You must excuse an old woman. But you needn't accompany me, my little grandchildren. There's no need. You want to do nothing but run about. You sit and sit, and learn your lessons, do you hear? Maria is spoiling you. Well, take me back."

The old woman's head, which she had raised with difficulty, again fell forward on her breast.

The little carriage started off and quietly rolled away.

"How old is your mother?" Vladimir Sergeich asked.

"She has passed her seventy-third year. But it is now twenty-six years since she lost the use of her legs; it occurred soon after my late father's death. Yet she was a beauty once."

They were all silent for a moment.

Suddenly Nadiozhda Alexeevna started.

"What is that? A bat flew past, didn't it? Oh, how horrible!" And she hurriedly returned to the reception room.

"Time I rode home. Mikhail Nikolaich, order my horse to be saddled."

"Time I was off, too," Vladimir Sergeich remarked.

"But where are you off to?" Ipatov said. "Stay the night here. Nadiozhda Alexeevna has only just over a mile to ride, but you have a good seven. And in any case what are you hurrying off for, Nadiozhda Alexeevna? Wait for the moon, it will be up soon, and then there will be more light to ride by."

"Certainly," said Nadiozhda Alexeevna; "it is long since I had a ride by moonlight."

"And will you stay the night?" Ipatov asked Vladimir Sergeich.

"Really, I don't know. . . . However, if it is not any trouble — "

"Not in the least, it will be a pleasure. I'll give orders at once for a room to be prepared for you."

"But it really is lovely to ride horseback by moonlight," Nadiozhda Alexeevna began as soon as candles had been brought in, tea had been handed round, and Ipatov and Yegor Kapitonich had sat down to play preference together, while Adaptable Soul silently seated himself beside them. "Especially through the woods, between hazel bushes. It is horrific, and pleasant, and there is such a strange play of light and shade, you're thinking all the time that someone is stealing behind you or before you. . . ."

Vladimir Sergeich smiled indulgently.

"And there's another thing," she continued; "have you ever chanced to sit close by a forest on a warm, dark, still night? It always seems to me as though just behind me, quite close, right by my ear, a couple is arguing furiously in an almost inaudible whisper."

"That is your blood beating," Ipatov declared.

"You describe things very poetically," Vladimir Sergeich observed.

Nadiozhda Alexeevna looked at him.

"Do you think so? . . . In that case, my descriptions would not please Maria."

"Why not? Doesn't she like poetry, then?"

"No. She considers that it is all made up, all untrue, and she doesn't like that."

"A strange reproach!" Vladimir Sergeich exclaimed. "Made up! But how could it be otherwise? What else are authors for?"

"Well, there you are! But, by the way, you shouldn't like poetry, either."

"On the contrary, I like good poems, when they are really good and melodious and — how can I put it? — present ideas, thought. . . ."

Maria Pavlovna rose.

Nadiozhda Alexeevna swiftly turned to her.

"Where are you going, Maria?"

"To put the children to bed. It will be nine soon."

"Can't they get into bed without you?"

But Maria Pavlovna took the children one by each hand, and left the room with them.

"She is out of spirits today," Nadiozhda Alexeevna observed. "And I know why," she added in an undertone. "But it will pass."

"Permit me to ask," Vladimir Sergeich began, "where do you intend to spend the winter?"

"Perhaps here, perhaps in Petersburg. But I think I shall be bored in Petersburg."

"In Petersburg? Of course you won't! How could you be?"

And Vladimir Sergeich began to describe all the conveniences, all the advantages and attractions, of life in the capital. She listened to him attentively, not taking her eyes off him. It was as though she were learning his features by heart, and occasionally she smiled to herself.

"I see you are very eloquent," she said at last. "I shall have to spend the winter in Petersburg."

"You will not regret it," he remarked.

"I never regret anything; it isn't worth the labor. If you have done something stupid, try to forget it as soon as possible, that's all."

"Permit me to ask," Vladimir Sergeich began again in French after a brief silence, "have you known Maria Pavlovna for long?"

"Permit me to ask," she retorted with a swift smile, "why you asked me that particular question in French?"

"Well — for no particular reason."

She again smiled sarcastically.

"No, I haven't known her very long. But she is a remarkable girl, don't you agree?"

"She is very original," Vladimir Sergeich said noncommittally.

"Well, and coming from your lips, from the lips of positive people, is that praise? I don't think so. Perhaps I, too, seem original to you. All the same," she added, rising and glancing through the open window, "the moon appears to have risen; that is its light shining above the poplars. Time I was off. . . . I'll go and order them to saddle Beauty."

"He's already saddled," said her page, emerging from the shadow of the garden into the stream of light falling across the terrace.

"Ah! Well, that's excellent! Maria, where are you? Come and say good-by to me."

Maria Pavlovna came in from the next room. The men rose from the card-table.

"And so you're going already?" Ipatov asked.

"Yes, it's time I was off."

She approached the door leading to the garden.

"What a night!" she exclaimed; "come and turn your faces to it; can you feel how it seems to be breathing? And what a scent! All the flowers have awakened now. They have awakened, but we are getting ready for sleep. . . . And that reminds me, Maria," she added, "I've just told Vladimir Sergeich that you do not like poetry. But now good-by . . . they're just bringing up my horse."

She ran briskly down the steps of the terrace, lightly climbed into the saddle, said: "Till tomorrow," and, striking the horse's neck with her whip, galloped toward the dam. The page set off at a trot behind her.

They all gazed after her. . . .

"Till tomorrow!" her voice sounded yet again from behind the poplars.

The drumming of horse-hoofs could be heard for a long time in the silence of the summer night. At last Ipatov suggested that they should return to the house.

"It certainly is fine in the open air," he said, "but we must finish our game."

They all obeyed him. Vladimir Sergeich began to question Maria Pavlovna why she didn't like poetry.

"I don't like poems," she replied with seeming reluctance.

"But perhaps you have read very few poems?"

"I haven't read any myself, but others have read them to me."

"And wasn't there really one that you liked?"

"Not one."

"Not even Pushkin's poems?"

"Not even Pushkin's."

"Why not?"

Maria Pavlovna did not reply, but Ipatov, craning his head over the back of his chair, remarked with a good-natured laugh that she disliked not only poems but sugar; in fact, she could not stand anything sweet.

"But there are some poems that are not sweet," Vladimir Sergeich objected.

"For instance?" Maria Pavlovna asked him.

He scratched himself behind the ear. . . . He himself knew very few poems by heart, especially such as were not sweet.

"Why, of course," he exclaimed at last, "do you know Pushkin's 'Upas'? No? Now, that is a poem that you simply could not call sweet."

"Say it to us," Maria Pavlovna said, and looked down.

He stared at the ceiling for a moment, knitted his brows, muttered a little to himself, and finally declaimed "The Upas."

After the first four verses Maria Pavlovna slowly raised her eyes, and when he had ended, she said as slowly:

"Please say it again."

"So you like those verses?" Vladimir Sergeich asked.

"Say it again."

He repeated "The Upas." She rose, went into another room, and returned with a sheet of paper, an inkpot, and a pen.

"Please write it out for me," she said to him.

"Certainly, with pleasure," he replied, setting to work. "But I must confess that I wonder why you have taken such a liking to that poem. I said it simply in order to show you that not all verses are sweet."

"I grant that!" Ipatov exclaimed. "What do you think of it, Ivan Ilich?"

Ivan Ilich, as was his custom, only glanced at Ipatov and did not utter a word.

"There, it's ready," Vladimir Sergeich said as he set an exclamation mark at the end of the last verse.

Maria Pavlovna thanked him and carried the sheet with the poem written on it to her room.

Half an hour later supper was served, and within an hour all the guests scattered to their rooms. Vladimir Sergeich talked to Maria Pavlovna more than once, but it was difficult to carry on conversation with her, and his stories did not seem to interest her very much. When he lay down to sleep he would in all probability have dropped off quite quickly if his neighbor, Yegor Kapitonich, had not disturbed him. After completely undressing and getting into bed, Matriona Markovna's husband talked for a very long time to his man, lecturing him continually. Every word he uttered clearly reached Vladimir Sergeich's ears; only a thin partition separated them.

"Hold the candle in front of your chest," Yegor Kapitonich said in a complaining tone. "Hold it so that I can see your face. You have worn me out, you shameless fellow; you have quite worn me out."

"Forgive me, how have I worn you out, Yegor Kapitonich?" came the man's thick and sleepy voice.

"How? I'll tell you how. How often have I told you, Mitka, have I said to you: when you go anywhere with me on a visit, always take two of every article of dress, especially — hold the candle in front of your chest — especially underwear. But what did you do to me today?"

"Well, what did I do?"

"What did you do? What shall I put on tomorrow?"

"Why, the same as you put on today."

"You've worn me out, you rogue, you've worn me out. Even today I didn't know what to do with myself because of the heat. Hold the candle in front of your chest, I tell you, and don't sleep when your master is talking to you."

"But Matriona Markovna said it was sufficient, she asked what you were taking all that lot with you for. It only gets worn out unnecessarily."

"Matriona Markovna — is that anything to do with a woman? You've worn me out. Oh, you've worn me out!"

"And besides, Yakhim said the same."

"What did you say?"

"I say, Yakhim said the same."

"Yakhim! Yakhim!" Yegor Kapitonich said reproachfully. "Ah, you've worn me out, you scoundrel, you don't even know how to talk Russian properly. Yakhim! What is Yakhim? 'Yefim,' now, that isn't so bad, you can say that, because Yefim is a real Greek name; you understand me? — hold the candle in front of your chest — so if you are in a hurry, perhaps you can say Yefim, but never Yakhim on any account. Yakhim!" Yegor Kapitonich added, putting all the emphasis on the first syllable. "You've worn me out, you thief! Hold the candle in front of your chest!"

And for a long time after, Yegor Kapitonich continued to teach his servant sense, despite the sighs, coughs, and other indications of impatience emitted by Vladimir Sergeich. . . .

At last he dismissed his Mitka and fell asleep; but this did not make things any easier for Vladimir Sergeich. Yegor Kapitonich snored so noisily and heavily, with such playful transitions from high notes to the very lowest, with such whistling and even smacking of his lips, that it seemed as though the very partition were quivering in response. Poor Vladimir Sergeich all but cried. It was very stuffy in the room assigned to him, and the feather bed on which he was lying wrapped all his body in a kind of creeping heat.

In despair he got out of bed at last, opened the window, and greedily began to breathe in the fragrant nocturnal freshness. The window overlooked the garden; the sky was clear; one moment the round disk of the full moon was reflected clearly in the lake, then was drawn out into a long golden shaft of slowly modulating gleams. On one of the paths in the garden Vladimir Sergeich descried a figure in woman's attire. He looked more attentively: it was Maria Pavlovna; by the moonlight her face seemed pale. She was standing perfectly still, and suddenly she began to speak. . . . He cautiously stretched out his head. . . .

> *"But with commanding glance a lord*
> *His servant to the Upas sent . . ."*

came to his ears.

"What an effect those few lines have had!" he thought. And he began to listen more closely. . . .

But soon she lapsed into silence and turned her face still more directly toward him; he could distinguish her dark, large eyes, her severe brows and lips. . . .

Suddenly she started, turned round, passed into the shadow cast by a solid wall of lofty acacias, and vanished. He remained standing for quite a long while by the window, but went back to bed at last, though he did not drop off to sleep for some time.

"A strange creature!" he thought as he turned over from side to side. "And they say one never finds anything striking in the provinces. . . . Evidently that is false. A strange creature! I shall ask her tomorrow what she was doing in the garden."

But Yegor Kapitonich was still snoring away as before.

A Quiet Spot

3

Next morning Vladimir Sergeich awoke rather late, and after tea with the others and breakfast in the dining-room he at once drove home to complete his economic arrangements, despite old Ipatov's attempts to detain him. Maria Pavlovna also was present at tea. Vladimir Sergeich, however, did not deem it necessary to question her about her belated walk of the evening before; he was one of those people who find it difficult to concentrate on any unusual thought or conjecture for two days in succession. He would have had to talk about poetry, and the so-called "poetic" mood very quickly wearied him. He spent all day till dinnertime in the fields, then ate with a big appetite, dozed off, and on awakening was about to turn to the secretary's report. But without finishing the first page he ordered his tarantass to be brought round and drove off to Ipatovka. Evidently not even positive people have stony hearts within their breasts, nor do they like being bored any more than other, ordinary mortals.

As he drove onto the dam he heard voices and the sounds of music. At Ipatov's house Russian songs were being sung in chorus. He found gathered on the terrace all the company he had left in the morning; they were all, including Nadiozhda Alexeevna, sitting in a circle round a man of about thirty-two years of age, swarthy, black-haired, and black-eyed; he was wearing a velvet jacket, had a red handkerchief carelessly knotted round his neck, and held a guitar in his hands. He was Piotr Alexeevich Veretiev, Nadiozhda Alexeevna's brother. On seeing Vladimir Sergeich, old Ipatov came to meet him with an exclamation of delight, led him to Veretiev, and introduced them to each other. Having exchanged the usual greetings with his new acquaintance, Astakhov bowed respectfully to Veretiev's sister.

"We're singing songs, country-fashion, Vladimir Sergeich," Ipatov began. Pointing to Veretiev, he added: "Piotr Alexeevich is our soloist, and how he can sing! You should hear him."

"That will be very pleasant," Vladimir Sergeich replied.

"Wouldn't you like to join in the chorus?" Nadiozhda Alexeevna asked him.

"I would be delighted to, but I haven't any voice."

"That doesn't matter! Look, Yegor Kapitonich is singing too,

709

and I am singing. You only have to join in. Sit down. And you begin, brother."

"What song shall we sing now?" Veretiev asked, strumming the strings of the guitar. Stopping suddenly, he looked at Maria Pavlovna, who was sitting beside him. "Now I think it is your turn," he said to her.

"No, you sing," she replied.

"Well, there's the song 'Floating down the Mother Volga,' " Vladimir Sergeich said portentously.

"No, we're saving that for the end," Veretiev answered. Striking the strings, he began the song "The sun is setting."

He sang magnificently, bravely and merrily. His masculine face, already expressive enough, grew still more animated as he sang; occasionally he twitched his shoulders, suddenly muted the strings with his palm, raised his hand, threw back his curls, and glanced around him like a hawk. He had seen the celebrated Ilia in Moscow more than once, and he imitated him. The chorus bravely joined in. Maria Pavlovna's voice rose in a melodious stream above all the others; she seemed to be drawing them behind her. But she did not wish to sing by herself, and Veretiev remained the soloist to the end.

They sang many other songs too.

Meanwhile, together with the evening, a storm came on. It had been steaming hot ever since midday, and thunder had rumbled continually in the distance. But now a broad cloud, which had long been lying like a leaden shroud on the very line of the horizon, began to grow and appear above the summits of the trees, the stifling air began more perceptibly to quiver, shaken more and more mightily by the approaching thunder; a wind arose and whistled impetuously among the leaves, died away, then again began to whistle protractedly, to howl; a somber twilight sped over the earth, swiftly driving away the last reflection of the sunset; massive clouds suddenly began to float, to course over the sky, as though they had broken loose; a fine rain sprinkled down, lightning flashed with a crimson fire, and the thunder rumbled heavily and angrily.

"Let's go in," said old Ipatov. "Otherwise I'm afraid we'll get wet through."

They all rose.

"In a minute!" Veretiev exclaimed; "one last song. Listen:

A Quiet Spot

Ah, my home porch, my dear home porch,
Porch of mine, so new, so new . . ."

he began to sing in a loud voice, nimbly running all his fingers
over the strings of the guitar. "Porch of mine, of maple new,"
they took up the chorus, as though involuntarily carried away.
Almost at the same moment the rain started to lash down in
streams; but Veretiev sang "My Porch" to the end. Drowned from
time to time by the crashes of thunder, the audacious song seemed
even more daring to the accompaniment of the patter and gurgle
of the rain. At last the final burst of the chorus sounded out, and
all the company ran laughing into the reception room. The girls,
Ipatov's daughters, laughed especially loudly as they shook the
rain from their dresses. None the less, as a precautionary measure
Ipatov closed the window and locked the door, and Yegor Kapitonich praised him for it, remarking that Matriona Markovna
also always ordered everything to be shut and locked during a
storm, because electricity functions more effectively in an open
space. Ivan Ilich gazed into his face, moved away, and knocked
over a chair. Similar petty misfortunes were constantly happening
to him.

The storm passed very quickly. The doors and windows were
opened once more and the rooms were filled with the smell of
dampness. Tea was brought in. After tea the old men again
sat down to play cards. Ivan Ilich attached himself to them, as
usual. Vladimir Sergeich went to join Maria Pavlovna, who
was sitting at the window with Veretiev, but Nadiozhda
Alexeevna called him across to herself and at once entered into
a fervent conversation with him about Petersburg and Petersburg life. She attacked it; Vladimir Sergeich began to defend
it. It seemed as though she was attempting to keep him at her
side.

"What are you arguing about?" Veretiev asked, rising and
coming over to them.

He rolled slowly as he walked; in all his movements was manifest negligence, or perhaps weariness.

"Continually about Petersburg," Nadiozhda Alexeevna answered. "Vladimir Sergeich cannot praise it sufficiently."

"It's a fine city," Veretiev remarked, "but in my view it is fine
everywhere. I do really think so. So long as there are two or

three women and, pardon my frankness, wine, really a man has nothing left to wish for."

"That surprises me," Vladimir Sergeich retorted. "Do you really think that there is nothing else for an educated man but — "

"Maybe — indeed — I agree with you," Veretiev interrupted him, for with all his politeness he had developed the habit of never listening to objections to the end. "But that is outside my province, I am not a philosopher."

"Nor am I a philosopher," Vladimir Sergeich replied, "and I haven't the least desire to be one. But now we are talking about something quite different."

Veretiev looked abstractedly at his sister; and she, smiling a little, bent toward him and whispered under her breath:

"Piotr, my dear, do us a favor, imitate Yegor Kapitonich for us."

In a moment Veretiev's face changed and, God knows by what miracle, became extraordinarily like the face of Yegor Kapitonich, though there was absolutely nothing in common between the two men's features, and Veretiev only wrinkled his nose and drooped the corners of his lips.

"Of course," he began to whisper in a voice that perfectly recalled that of Yegor Kapitonich; "Matriona Markovna is a very strict lady in regard to manners, but she is a model spouse. Really, no matter what I say — "

"It is all known to the Biriulevsky young ladies," Nadiozhda Alexeevna joined in, hardly able to restrain her laughter.

"Everything is known to them the very next day," Veretiev replied with such a ludicrous grimace, with such an embarrassed, sidelong glance, that even Vladimir Sergeich burst into laughter.

"I see you have a great gift of mimicry," he observed.

Veretiev passed his hand over his face, his features recovered their customary expression, and Nadiozhda Alexeevna exclaimed:

"Oh, yes! He can imitate everybody, anybody he likes. . . . He's a master of mimicry."

"And could you mimic me, for instance?" Vladimir Sergeich asked.

"I should say so!" Nadiozhda Alexeevna retorted; "of course he could."

"Ah, then do me the favor, take me off," Astakhov said, turning to Veretiev. "I ask you not to stand on ceremony."

A Quiet Spot

"But did you believe her?" Veretiev replied, very slightly closing one eye and giving his voice the tone of Astakhov's voice, but so discreetly and faintly that only Nadiozhda Alexeevna noticed it, causing her to bite her lips. "Please don't believe her, she'll tell you worse things than that about me."

"And what an actor he is, if you only knew!" Nadiozhda Alexeevna continued. "He can play every conceivable role. So marvelously! He is our producer, and prompter, and everything else. Pity you are going away so soon!"

"Sister, your partiality blinds you," Veretiev said in a serious tone, but with the same nuance. "What will Mr. Astakhov think of you? He will regard you as a provincial woman."

"But really!" Vladimir Sergeich began.

"Piotr, do you know what?" Nadiozhda Alexeevna broke in. "Please show us how a drunken man simply cannot get his handkerchief out of his pocket; or, even better, show us a boy catching a fly on the window, and how it buzzes under his fingers."

"You're a perfect child," Veretiev replied.

None the less, he rose and, going over to the window by which Maria Pavlovna was sitting, began to run his hand over the glass and to imitate a boy catching a fly. The fidelity with which he imitated its mournful buzz was simply astonishing. There really seemed to be a living fly struggling beneath his fingers. Nadiozhda Alexeevna laughed, and little by little everybody in the room began to laugh. Only Maria Pavlovna's face did not change, her lips did not even twitch. She sat with downcast eyes. But she raised them at last and, giving Veretiev a serious look, said through clenched teeth:

"A fine ambition, to turn yourself into a clown!"

He at once turned away from the window and, after standing for a moment in the middle of the room, went out on the terrace and thence into the garden, which was not completely dark.

"He's an amusing fellow, is Piotr Alexeevich," Yegor Kapitonich exclaimed, slapping a seven of trumps down on his opponent's ace. "Really amusing!"

Nadiozhda Alexeevna rose and went hurriedly to Maria Pavlovna, asking her in an undertone:

"What did you say to my brother?"

"Nothing," she replied.

"How, nothing! You must have said something!"

She waited a moment, then added: "Come on," took Maria Pavlovna by the arm, and made her rise and go with her into the garden.

Vladimir Sergeich stared after them not without astonishment. They were not absent for long, however; a quarter of an hour later they returned, and Piotr Alexeevich came with them.

"What a beautiful night!" Nadiozhda Alexeevna exclaimed as she entered. "How lovely it is in the garden!"

"Ah, yes, that reminds me," Vladimir Sergeich said. "May I ask, Maria Pavlovna, was it you I saw last night in the garden?"

She glanced swiftly into his eyes.

"And so far as I could catch the words, you were reciting Pushkin's 'Upas.' "

Veretiev knitted his brows slightly and stared at Astakhov.

"Yes, it was I, you're quite right," Maria Pavlovna said. "Only I wasn't reciting anything; I never recite."

"Perhaps I simply had the impression," Vladimir Sergeich began. "None the less — "

"You simply had the impression," Maria Pavlovna pronounced coldly.

"What is this 'Upas'?" Nadiozhda Alexeevna asked.

"But don't you know?" Astakhov retorted. "A poem by Pushkin: 'On soil stunted and meager'; don't you remember it, then?"

"I don't seem to remember. The upas is a poisonous tree, isn't it?"

"Yes."

"Like the datura," said Nadiozhda Alexeevna. "Do you remember, Maria, how good our daturas looked, on the balcony, by moonlight, with their long white flowers? Do you remember the scent that poured out of them, sweet, surreptitious, and insidious?"

"An insidious scent?" Vladimir Sergeich exclaimed.

"Yes, insidious. Why are you astonished? They say it is dangerous, but it is very attractive. How can something evil be attractive? Evil shouldn't be beautiful, should it?"

"Oho! What speculations!" Piotr Alexeevich remarked. "How far from poetry we have got!"

"I read that poem to Maria Pavlovna yesterday," Vladimir Sergeich broke in, "and she liked it greatly."

"Ah, then read it to us, please," Nadiozhda Alexeevna said.

"If you like."

And he recited "The Upas."

"Too bombastic," Veretiev declared, apparently with some reluctance, as soon as Vladimir Sergeich had finished.

"The poem is too bombastic?"

"No, not the poem. Excuse me, but it seems to me that you do not recite it simply enough. The thing speaks for itself. However, I may be mistaken."

"No, you are not mistaken," Nadiozhda Alexeevna said with emphasis.

"Oh, but then, everybody knows that in your eyes I am a genius, the most talented of men, who knows everything, who could do everything, only laziness, unfortunately, gets the better of him. Isn't that so?"

She only shook her head.

"I won't argue with you, you should know better than I," Vladimir Sergeich observed, and he pouted a little. "That isn't in my province."

"I am mistaken; forgive me," Veretiev hurriedly replied.

Meanwhile the game had finished.

"Ah, that reminds me, Vladimir Sergeich," Ipatov began as he rose. "A local landowner, a neighbor, a very fine and worthy man named Gavrila Stepanich Akilin, has commissioned me to ask you whether you will do him the honor of being present at a ball he is giving. Or, rather, I call it a ball for the sake of euphony, but it is really a soirée with dancing, and no ceremony. He would infallibly have called on you himself, but he was afraid of disturbing you."

"I am very grateful to the landowner," Vladimir Sergeich retorted, "but I must infallibly go home . . ."

"But what are you thinking of, when there's going to be a ball? Why, the ball is tomorrow. It is Gavrila Stepanich's name-day tomorrow. What difference does one day make? And how delighted he will be to see you! And it is only six miles from here. If you will allow us, we will take you there in our carriage."

"I really don't know," Vladimir Sergeich began. "But are you going?"

"All the family! And Nadiozhda Alexeevna, and Piotr Alexeevich, they're all going!"

Turgenev

"If you wish, you can ask me for the fifth quadrille this very minute!" Nadiozhda Alexeevna remarked. "The first four are already taken."

"You are very kind; but are you already engaged for the mazurka?"

"I? Let me think — no, I don't think I am."

"In that case, if you will be so good, I should like to have the honor . . ."

"So you will go? Excellent. With pleasure."

"Bravo!" Ipatov exclaimed. "Well, Vladimir Sergeich, you have put me in your debt. Gavrila Stepanich will be simply over-whelmed. Won't he, Ivan Ilich?"

Ivan Ilich wanted to say nothing, as was his invariable habit, but he considered it better to utter an approving sound.

"What on earth made you," Piotr Alexeevich said to his sister an hour later as he sat with her in the light chaise that he himself drove, "what on earth made you tie yourself up to that moper for the mazurka?"

"I have my own plans," Nadiozhda Alexeevna retorted.

"And what are they, if I may be permitted to know?"

"That is my secret."

"Oho!"

He brought his whip down lightly on the horse, which had begun to prick up its ears, to snort and jib. It had been startled by a shadow falling from a large willow bush across the road, which was dimly lit by the moon.

"And will you dance with Maria?" Nadiozhda Alexeevna asked her brother in turn.

"Yes," he said unconcernedly.

"Yes! Yes!" she repeated reproachfully. "You men," she added after a moment's silence, "you are simply not worth being loved by decent women."

"Do you think so? Well, and that Petersburg moper, is he worth it?"

"More than you are."

"Is that so!" and he added with a sigh:

" *'What a commission, O Creator,*
To be — a grown-up sister's brother!' "

716

Nadiozhda Alexeevna broke into a laugh.

"I do give you a lot of trouble, there's no denying. And now I have a commission to you."

"Really? I hadn't the least suspicion of that."

"I'm speaking in regard to Maria."

"And in what regard?"

Her face turned a little sorrowful.

"You know quite well," she said quietly.

"Ah, I understand! It cannot be helped, Nadiozhda Alexeevna, I do love drinking with a good friend, sinful man that I am! I do love it."

"Be quiet, brother, don't talk like that! . . . It's not a joking matter."

"Tarara-boom . . ." Piotr Alexeevich muttered through clenched teeth.

"It is your ruin, but you joke . . ."

" 'Peasant sow the rye, the little wife is a poppy,' " Piotr Alexeevich sang out loud. He struck the horse with the reins, and she dashed off at a fast trot.

4

When he reached home Veretiev did not undress, and two hours later — the dawn had only just begun to flush the sky — he was out of the house again.

Halfway between his estate and Ipatovka, on the slope of a broad ravine, was a small birch "reserve." The young trees grew very close together, no ax had ever touched their shapely trunks; a light but almost unbroken shade fell from their delicate foliage over the soft, fine grass, which was speckled with the golden heads of celandines, the white dots of woodland harebells, and the raspberry crosses of gillyflowers. The recently risen sun flooded all the grove with strong, though not brilliant light; everywhere dewdrops were glistening, here and there large drops suddenly caught fire and glowed; everything had a breath of freshness, of life, and that innocent exaltation of the first moments of the morn, when everything is already so luminous and still so soundless. The only sounds to be heard were the skylarks' voices, strewn over the distant fields, and in the grove itself two or three smaller birds leisurely tried out their little flourishes and then seemed to be listening to see how they had gone. From the damp earth came a strong, healthy scent; the pure, light air was flooded with cooling breezes. Morning, the glorious summer morning, was evident in everything; everything looked and smiled with the morning, like the crimson, freshly washed little face of an awakened infant.

Not far from the ravine, in the middle of a small meadow, Veretiev was sitting on a raincoat spread over the grass. Maria Pavlovna was standing beside him, leaning against a birch tree, with her hands folded behind her.

They were both silent. She gazed fixedly into the distance; a white scarf fell from her head over her shoulders; the running breeze stirred and lifted the ends of her hastily tidied hair. Veretiev sat with bowed back, lashing at the grass with a twig.

"Well," he began at last, "so you are angry with me?"

She did not reply.

He glanced at her.

"Maria, are you angry?" he repeated.

She gave him a swift look, turned a little away from him and said:

"Yes."

"What for?" he asked, and threw away the twig.

Again she did not reply.

"But you certainly are entitled to be angry with me," he began after a brief silence. "You must regard me as not only a frivolous, but even — "

"You don't understand me," she broke in. "I am not in the least angry with you for my own sake."

"Then for whose sake?"

"For yours."

He raised his head and smiled wryly.

"Ah! I understand!" he said. "Once more, once more you are beginning to be disturbed by the thought: why don't I do anything with myself? Do you know what, Maria? — you're an extraordinary creature, really you are! You worry so much about others and so little about yourself. You have no egotism in you whatever, really you haven't! There isn't another girl like you in all the world. The only misfortune is that I simply am not worthy of your affection; I say that not in jest."

"So much the worse for you. You feel that and yet you do nothing about it."

He again smiled wryly.

"Maria, come out from behind my back; give me your hand," he said with an affectionately wheedling tone in his voice.

She only shrugged her shoulders.

"Give me your beautiful, honest hand, I want to kiss it reverently and tenderly. Just as a featherbrained pupil kisses the hand of his indulgent teacher."

And he stretched his hand out to her.

"Stop it!" she said. "You're always laughing and joking, and you will joke away all your life."

"Hm! Joke away all your life! That's a new expression! For I hope, Maria Pavlovna, you did use the verb 'to joke' in its active sense?"

She knitted her brows.

"Stop it, Veretiev!" she repeated.

"To joke away a life!" he continued, and half rose. "But you are disposing of yours even more stupidly; you are sobering away all your life. Do you know, Maria, you remind me of a certain scene in Pushkin's *Don Juan*. You haven't read Pushkin's *Don Juan*, have you?"

"No."

"Ah, of course, I had forgotten that you never read poetry. In it a girl named Laura is visited by guests, but she turns them all away except one, named Carlos. They both go onto the balcony, it is a marvelous night. Laura admires the night, but Carlos suddenly starts to show her that as time passes she will grow old. 'What of it?' Laura replied. 'There may be rain and cold in Paris now, but here the night of lemons and laurel is scented.' Who can foretell the future? Look about you, Maria; isn't it beautiful here too? Look how everything is rejoicing in life, how young everything is. And aren't we young too?"

He drew closer to her; she did not draw away from him, nor did she turn her head toward him.

"Smile, Maria," he continued; "only with your good smile, and not with your usual little sneer. I love your good smile. Raise your proud, stern eyes. What is the matter? You turn away. Do at least stretch out your hand to me."

"Ah, Veretiev," she began, "you know I have no gift of speech. You have just told me about that Laura. But then she is a woman. It is forgivable for a woman not to think about the future."

"When you speak, Maria," he answered, "you continually flush with self-consciousness and bashfulness, the blood flows in a crimson flood to your cheeks. I love that trait in you terribly."

She glanced right into his eyes.

"Good-by," she said, and flung the scarf round her head. He held her back.

"Now, now, wait a moment!" he exclaimed. "Well, what exactly do you want? Command me! Do you want me to enter the civil service, to become an agriculturist? Do you want me to publish ballads with guitar accompaniment, to print a collection of poems, or drawings, to engage in painting, sculpture, tight-rope dancing? I'll do everything, everything you command, so long as you are satisfied with me! Now, really and truly, Maria, do believe me!"

She glanced at him again.

"All that is only words, and not deeds. You assure me that you will pay heed to me — "

"Of course I will."

" — pay heed to me, and how many times have I asked you — "

"What have you asked?"

She hesitated.

"Not to drink wine," she said at last.

He laughed.

"Ah, Maria, Maria! You, too, on that subject? My sister also is grieving over that. But, to begin with, I am not a drunkard at all; and secondly, do you know why I drink? Look at that swallow there — do you see how boldly it controls its little body, casting it wherever it wishes? Now it is wheeling up, now it has dropped, and it even gave a little squeak of joy, did you hear it? And that is just why I drink, Masha, to experience the same sensations that that swallow experiences. . . . Fling yourself wherever you wish, carry yourself wherever you think to — "

"Yes, but what is it all for?" she interrupted.

"What do you mean? What else should one live for?"

"But is it really impossible to achieve all that without wine?"

"It is impossible: we are all perverted, spoilt. Now, passion — passion produces the same effect. That is why I love you."

"Like wine — I humbly thank you."

"No, Maria; I do love you, but not like wine. Wait and I shall prove that to you some day, when we are married and go abroad.

A Quiet Spot

Do you know, I am already thinking even now how I shall take you to see the Venus of Milo. And then indeed it will be to the point to say:

> *Stand you with a serious eye*
> *Before Milo's Cypria?*
> *Two there are, and at your sight*
> *The marble seems to lose its might.*

Why am I continually quoting poetry today? It must be the morning having an effect on me. What air! It's just like drinking wine."

"Wine again!" Maria remarked.

"Well, what of it! Such a morning, and you with me, and not feel intoxicated? 'With a serious eye . . .' Yes," he continued, gazing fixedly at her, "that is so. . . . But you see I remember, I have seen, oh, rarely, but I have seen those dark, magnificent eyes — I have seen them with a tender look! And how beautiful they are then! Please don't turn away, Maria, do at least smile — show me your eyes at least with a merry look, if they do not wish to vouchsafe me a tender glance."

"Do stop it, Veretiev!" Maria Pavlovna said. "Let me go, it is time I went home."

"But now I am really making you laugh," he caught her up; "really, I am making you laugh. And, by the way, look, there is a hare running — "

"Where?" she asked.

"Over there, beyond the ravine, across the oatfield. Someone must have startled him; they never go running in the morning. If you like I'll make him stop at once." And he gave a loud whistle. The hare at once squatted down, pricked up its ears, drew in its forelegs, straightened up, began to nibble, sniffed at the air, and nibbled again. Veretiev nimbly squatted down on his heels in imitation of the hare and began to wrinkle his nose, to sniff and nibble like it. The hare passed its paws over its face a couple of times, shook itself — its paws must have been wet with dew — set back its ears, and ran on. Veretiev rubbed his hands over his cheeks and shook himself too. . . . Maria Pavlovna could not help bursting into a laugh.

"Bravo!" Veretiev exclaimed, and he jumped up. "Bravo! There, that proves it, you are not a flirt. Do you know that if any society young lady had teeth like yours she would be smiling all the

time! But that is why I love you, Maria, because you are not a
society young lady, you do not smile unnecessarily, you do not
wear gloves on those hands which it is so cheerful to kiss, because
they are sunburnt and one can feel the strength in them. . . . I
love you because you do not pretend to be clever, because you
are proud, and taciturn, do not read books, do not like poetry — "

"But would you like me to say some poetry to you?" she interrupted him, with a peculiar expression on her face.

"Poetry?" he asked in astonishment.

"Yes, poetry, the poetry that Petersburg gentleman read yesterday evening."

" 'The Upas' again? . . . So it was true, you did recite it in
the garden at night? That is just like you. . . . But do you really
like it so much?"

"Yes, I do."

"Say it to me."

She was a little abashed . . .

"Say it, say it!" Veretiev repeated.

Maria Pavlovna began to say the poem aloud. Veretiev stood in
front of her, his arms folded on his chest, and listened. At the first
line she slowly raised her eyes to heaven: she did not want to
meet his gaze. She recited the poem in her even, gentle voice,
reminiscent of the sounds of a violoncello; but when she reached
the lines:

And the wretched slave expired at the feet
Of the invincible lord. . . .

her voice quivered, her immobile, haughty brows were raised
naïvely, like a girl's, and her eyes rested on him with involuntary
devotion. . . .

He suddenly flung himself at her feet and embraced her knees.

"I am thy slave," he exclaimed. "I am at thy feet, thou art my
lord, my divinity, my wide-eyed Hera, my Medea. . . ."

She tried to thrust him away, but her hands came to rest on his
thick curls, and, with a smile of embarrassment, she let her head
fall on her breast. . . .

5

Gavrila Stepanich Akilin, who was giving the ball, was one of
those landowners who arouse the astonishment of their neighbors

A Quiet Spot

by their art of living well and hospitably on insignificant resources. Though he possessed no more than four hundred peasant
souls, he received all the province in an enormous, palatial, brick-
built house with columns, a tower, and a flag on the tower, all of
which he himself had had erected. He had inherited this estate
from his father, and it had never been distinguished by its good
management. Gavrila Stepanich had been a long time absent from
it, in service at Petersburg; at last, some fifteen years before the
time of our story, he had returned to his country home with the
rank of collegiate assessor,[1] with a wife and three daughters, had
simultaneously set to work to reorganize the estate and to build
the house, had immediately established a private band, and had begun to give dinners. At first everybody prophesied for him rapid
and inevitable ruin; more than once the rumors spread that Gavrila
Stepanich's estate was to be sold under the hammer. But the years
passed, dinners, balls, banquets, concerts followed one after another in customary order, new buildings grew out of the earth
like mushrooms, and Gavrila Stepanich's estate was not sold under
the hammer, and he himself went on living on the same scale as before, and had even grown fatter recently. Then the neighbors'
gossip took another direction; they began to hint at certain important, apparently secret sums; they began to talk of a mortgage.
. . . "And if he were only a good manager!" so the nobles
reflected among themselves; "but he isn't, not in the least! That
is indeed amazing; in fact, it is incomprehensible." Whatever the
secret of his manner of life, everybody visited Gavrila Stepanich
very readily; he made guests very welcome and played cards for
any stakes. He was a little, rather gray-haired man with a small,
angular head, a yellow face, and yellow eyes, and was always
meticulously shaved, and scented with eau de Cologne. On week-
days and holidays he wore an ample blue frock coat, buttoned
right up, with a large cravat, in which he had the habit of concealing his chin, and his linen was dazzling. He screwed up his eyes
and pouted his lips when he took snuff, and he talked very affably and softly, continually interlarding his remarks with polite
expressions. To look at, he was not at all impressive, did not inspire respect, and did not appear to be clever, though cunning
sometimes twinkled in his eyes. He had made advantageous ar-

[1] A titular rank in the czarist civil-service hierarchy, being the eighth
class. The lowest rank was the fourteenth class. (Tr.)

rangements for his two older daughters; the youngest was still at
home, but was engaged. Gavrila Stepanich also had a wife, an
insignificant and speechless creature.

Dressed in a frock coat and white gloves, Vladimir Sergeich
arrived at the Ipatovs' house at seven o'clock in the evening. He
found them all quite ready; the girls were sitting primly, afraid
of crumpling their very white, starched dresses; old Ipatov, seeing Vladimir Sergeich in a frock coat, gently chided him and
pointed to his own morning coat; Maria Pavlovna was wearing a
deep rose muslin gown, which greatly suited her. Vladimir Sergeich paid her a few compliments. Her beauty attracted him,
though she obviously avoided him; he liked Nadiozhda Alexeevna
too, but the unconstraint of her behavior rather embarrassed him.
Moreover, there was often open derision in her speech, her looks,
even in her smiles, and that disturbed his metropolitan and well-
bred soul. He would not have been averse to joining with her in
deriding others, but it was unpleasant for him to think that she
was capable, perhaps, of laughing at him.

The ball had already begun; quite a number of guests had
arrived, and the home-made band was blaring, whining, and
whistling in chorus when the Ipatov family and Vladimir Sergeich entered the hall of Akilin's house. The host met them at the
very door, thanked Vladimir Sergeich warmly for so sensitively
giving him a pleasant surprise — as he put it — and, taking Ipatov
by the arm, led him into the reception room, to the card-tables.
Gavrila Stepanich had not had a good upbringing, and everything in his house — the music, and the furniture, and the food,
and the wine — not only was less than first-class, but was not even
eligible for the second class. On the other hand, everything was
without stint, and he himself did not put on airs, did not swagger
. . . nor did the nobles demand any more of him; they were perfectly satisfied with his hospitality. At supper, for instance, caviar
cut into pieces and heavily salted was handed round; but no one
objected to taking it in his fingers and washing it down with
whatever drink he liked; truly, the wine was rather cheap, but
none the less it was genuine grape wine and not some other con-
coction. Certainly the springs in Gavrila Stepanich's furniture
were rather troublesome because of their inflexibility and stiffness;
but, ignoring the fact that many of the sofas and armchairs had no
springs at all, anyone could set a woolen cushion beneath his

head; and there were innumerable such cushions, all knitted by Gavrila Stepanich's wife with her own hands, lying about everywhere. And then, indeed, one had nothing left to wish for.

In a word, Gavrila Stepanich's house could not have been more in accord with the free and easy and unceremonial ways of thought of the inhabitants of XXX county. And if he had not been so modest, they would have elected him to the position of marshal at the noblemen's assemblies, and not the retired Major Podpekin, who was a very worthy and respected man, though he did comb his hair over the right temple from behind the left ear, did dye his mustaches a lilac color, and went into a melancholia after dinner because he suffered from asthma.

Well, the ball had already begun. Ten couples were dancing a quadrille. The male partners consisted of officers of a regiment quartered near by, young (and sometimes not so young) landowners, and two or three officials from the county town. Everything was as it should be, everything took its normal course. The marshal was playing cards with a retired senior civil councilor [1] and a wealthy gentleman, the owner of three thousand souls. The senior civil councilor wore a diamond ring on his forefinger, talked very quietly, did not shift the heels of his feet, which were set together in the position adopted by dancers of former times, and did not move his head, which was half covered by an excellent velvet collar. The wealthy gentleman, on the other hand, continually smiled, raised his eyebrows, and showed the gleaming whites of his eyes. The poet Bodryakov, a man of awkward and wild appearance, was talking in one corner with the learned historian Yevsiukov; they held each other by the coat button. Next to them a nobleman with unusually long waist was expounding some daring opinions to another nobleman, who timidly gazed at his brow. The dear mammas in variegated mobcaps sat along the wall; the gentlemen of low degree huddled together at the door, the young with embarrassed, the old with humble countenances. But one cannot describe it all. We repeat: everything was as it should be.

Nadiozhda Alexeevna had arrived even before the Ipatovs: Vladimir Sergeich caught sight of her dancing with a young man of handsome appearance and expressive eyes, thin black mustaches, and dazzling teeth and wearing an elegant frock coat; a gold

[1] Fourth class in the civil-service hierarchy. (Tr.)

chain hung in a half-circle across his vest. Nadiozhda Alexeevna was wearing a dove-blue gown with white flowers; a small chaplet of the same flowers encircled her curly head; she smiled, played with her fan, looked about her gaily; she felt that she was the queen of the ball. Vladimir Sergeich went up to her, bowed, and, with a gallant look, asked her whether she remembered yesterday's promise.

"What promise?"

"Why, you are going to dance the mazurka with me."

"Yes, of course I am."

The young man standing beside Nadiozhda Alexeevna suddenly went red.

"You, mademoiselle, must have forgotten," he began, "that you had already given me your promise for today's mazurka."

Nadiozhda Alexeevna was put to confusion.

"Ah, my goodness, now what shall we do?" she said. "Forgive me, please, Monsieur Stelchinski, I am so forgetful; really, I feel so conscience-stricken — "

M. Stelchinski made no answer and only lowered his eyes. Vladimir Sergeich drew himself up a little.

"Do be so kind, Monsieur Stelchinski," Nadiozhda Alexeevna continued. "After all, you and I are old acquaintances, but M'sieur Astakhov is a stranger to these parts; don't put me in a difficult position, permit me to dance with him."

"As you wish," the young man retorted. "However, it's your turn to begin."

"I am very grateful," Nadiozhda Alexeevna said, and fluttered off to meet her opposite partner.

Stelchinski glanced after her, then looked at Vladimir Sergeich. Vladimir Sergeich looked at him in his turn and walked away.

The quadrille was soon over. Vladimir Sergeich walked about the hall for a few moments, then made his way to the reception room and halted by one of the card-tables. Suddenly he felt someone touch his arm from behind; he turned and saw Stelchinski standing before him.

"I must have a couple of words with you in the next room, if you will allow me," he said in French very politely and with a non-Russian accent.[1]

Vladimir Sergeich followed him.

---

[1] Stelchinski — as the name indicates — is Polish. (Tr.)

A Quiet Spot

Stelchinski halted by the window.

"In the presence of a lady," he began in the same language, "I could not say anything but what I did say. But you, I hope, are not under the impression that I really intend to forgo my right to the mazurka with Mademoiselle Veretiev."

Vladimir Sergeich was astonished.

"What do you mean?" he asked.

"What I say," Stelchinski calmly replied; he set his hand in his breast and dilated his nostrils. "I have no such intention, and that is that."

Vladimir Sergeich also set his hand in his breast, but he did not dilate his nostrils.

"Allow me to remark to you, my dear sir," he began, "that by your behavior you may involve Mademoiselle Veretiev in some unpleasantness; and I assume — "

"It would be extremely unpleasant for me myself. But no one prevents your withdrawing, saying that you are unwell, or going away. . . ."

"That I shall not do. Whom do you take me for?"

"In that case, I am compelled to demand satisfaction of you."

"In what sense do you mean — satisfaction?"

"You know in what sense."

"Are you challenging me to a duel?"

"Precisely, if you do not renounce the mazurka."

Stelchinski tried to say these words in a very calm tone. Vladimir Sergeich's heart throbbed. He stared his undreamed-of and unguessed-at opponent in the face. "Pah, my goodness, what lunacy!" he thought.

"You're not joking?" he said aloud.

"I am not in the habit of joking," Stelchinski answered gravely, "especially with people who are strangers to me. You do not renounce the mazurka?" he added after a moment's silence.

"No, I do not," Vladimir Sergeich retorted in a reflective tone.

"Excellent! We shall fight tomorrow."

"Very good."

"My second will call on you first thing tomorrow morning."

And, bowing courteously, Stelchinski walked away, obviously pleased with himself.

Vladimir Sergeich remained at the window for some moments longer.

"Here's a fine thing!" he thought. "Here's the result of your new acquaintances! Of course, I had to come! Fine! Glorious!"

At last he recovered, however, and went into the hall.

In the hall a polka was being danced. Maria Pavlovna flashed past his eyes, with Piotr Alexeevich, whom he had not noticed before; she seemed pale and even sorrowful. Then Nadiozhda Alexeevna swept by, all beaming and joyous, with some little bowlegged but fiery artillery officer; on the second round she passed with Stelchinski. As he danced he shook his hair violently.

"Well, my boy," Vladimir Sergeich suddenly heard Ipatov's voice behind him, "only watching and not dancing? But you must surely admit that for our quiet little spot, so to speak, it isn't at all bad, is it?"

"A devilish quiet little spot!" Vladimir Sergeich thought and, muttering something in reply, he went off to another corner of the hall.

"I shall have to find a second," he continued his meditations, "but where the devil am I to find one? I can't ask Veretiev, and I don't know anybody else; this is a devilish awkward situation to be in!"

When he was angry Vladimir Sergeich liked to mention the devil.

At that moment his eyes fell on the Adaptable Soul, Ivan Ilich, standing inactive by a window.

"Perhaps he would do?" he thought, and, shrugging his shoulders, added almost aloud: "It will have to be he."

He went across to him.

"A very queer thing has just happened to me," our hero began with a forced smile. "Just imagine, some strange young man has challenged me to a duel; to refuse is out of the question; I've got to have a second; wouldn't you like to act?"

Though Ivan Ilich was distinguished, as we know, by imperturbable tranquillity, such an extraordinary proposition astonished even him. He stared at Vladimir Sergeich in utter bewilderment.

"Indeed," Vladimir Sergeich added, "I would be greatly obliged to you. I don't know anybody here. You alone —"

"I cannot," Ivan Ilich muttered, as though awaking from sleep, "I simply cannot."

"But why not? Perhaps you are afraid of some unpleasantness; but I hope it will all be kept secret. . . ."

A Quiet Spot

As he said these words Vladimir Sergeich felt himself turn red, and he was put to confusion.

"How stupid! How terribly stupid it all is!" he was mentally asseverating even as he spoke.

"Excuse me, I simply cannot," Ivan Ilich repeated; he shook his head and fell back, once more overturning a chair as he did so.

For the first time in his life he had had to refuse a request; but then, what a request it was!

"At least," Vladimir Sergeich continued in an anxious tone, taking him by the arm, "at least you will do me the favor of telling nobody what I have told you. I most humbly ask you that."

"That I can do, that I can do," Ivan Ilich hurriedly replied. "But as for the other, I'm very sorry, I simply am not in a position to act."

"Well, good, good!" Vladimir Sergeich said. "But don't forget, I rely on your discretion. . . . Tomorrow I shall inform that gentleman," he muttered angrily to himself, "that I could not find a second, and he can arrange things as he knows best. I am a stranger here. And the devil prompted me to turn to this gentleman! But what else was I to do?"

Vladimir Sergeich was feeling very, yes, extremely depressed.

Meanwhile the ball continued. He would have been very glad to depart at once, but until the mazurka was finished there could be no thought of his leaving. How could he let his opponent triumph! Unfortunately for him, the master of ceremonies was a young and jaunty gentleman with long hair and sunken chest, over which a black satin cravat wound like a little waterfall, though it was pierced with an enormous gold pin. This young gentleman was famous all over the province as knowing to the last detail all the manners and rules of high society, though he had lived only six months in Petersburg and had not succeeded in penetrating higher than the homes of the collegiate councilor [1] Sandaraka and his son-in-law, the civil councilor [2] Kostandaraka. He was the master of ceremonies at all the balls; he gave signals to the musicians by clapping his hands; amid the blare of the trumpets and the whine of the violins he shouted: *"En avant deux!"* or *"Grande chaîne!"* or *"A vous, mademoiselle!"* and from

[1] Sixth class rank in civil service. (Tr.)
[2] Fourth-class rank in civil service. (Tr.)

time to time flew impetuously, slipping and scraping, pale and perspiring, through the hall. He never began the mazurka before midnight. "And that is a favor," he would say. "In Petersburg I would have kept you going till two in the morning." Very long did that ball seem to Vladimir Sergeich. He wandered like a shade from the hall to the reception room, occasionally exchanging chilly glances with his rival, who did not sit out a single dance. He would have asked Maria Pavlovna for a quadrille, but she was already engaged; and a couple of times he exchanged remarks with the fussy host, who seemed to be disturbed by the look of boredom engraved on the new guest's features. At last the long-desired mazurka thundered out. Vladimir Sergeich found his lady, brought two chairs, and sat with her as the last couple, almost opposite Stelchinski.

As one might expect, the young master of ceremonies led the way in the first couple. The expression with which he began the mazurka, the way he dragged his lady after him, the way he stamped his little foot on the floor and twitched his head as he did so — to describe all this is surely beyond a human pen.

"I have the impression, M'sieur Astakhov, that you are bored?" Nadiozhda Alexeevna began, suddenly turning to her partner.

"I? Not in the least. Why have you got that impression?"

"Why, just from the expression on your face. You haven't smiled once since we arrived. I hadn't expected that of you. It doesn't become you positive people to be unsociable and knit your brows à la Byron. Leave that to the authors."

"I observe, Nadiozhda Alexeevna, that you frequently call me a positive man, apparently in sarcasm. You must regard me as a very cold and reasonable being, incapable of anything like — But do you know what I have to tell you? A positive person often has a very heavy heart, but he does not consider it necessary to reveal to others what is going on inside him; he prefers to be silent."

"What is behind that remark?" Nadiozhda Alexeevna asked, glancing at him.

"Nothing," Vladimir Sergeich retorted with assumed unconcern, and adopted a mysterious look.

"All the same — ?"

"Really, nothing. . . . You'll find out some day, after."

Nadiozhda Alexeevna would have liked to follow up her questions, but at that moment a girl, the host's daughter, led Stelchinski and another gentleman in blue spectacles up to her.

"Life or death?" she asked her in French.

"Life!" Nadiozhda Alexeevna exclaimed. "I don't want death yet awhile."

Stelchinski bowed; she went off with him.

The gentleman in blue spectacles, whose name was Death, went with the host's daughter. Both the names had been proposed by Stelchinski.

"Please tell me who that Mr. Stelchinski is," Vladimir Sergeich asked Nadiozhda Alexeevna as soon as she returned to her seat.

"He is in the Governor's service; he is a very pleasant young man. He's not a local man. A bit of a fop, but that is in the blood of all Poles. I hope you haven't had any words with him over the mazurka?"

"None at all, why should I?" he retorted after a momentary hesitation.

"I am so forgetful! You cannot imagine!"

"I ought to be glad of your forgetfulness; it has afforded me the pleasure of dancing with you this evening."

She looked at him with eyes narrowed a little.

"Really? Do you like dancing with me?"

He replied with a compliment. Gradually his tongue loosened. Nadiozhda Alexeevna was very charming always, and especially that evening; to Vladimir Sergeich she seemed enchanting. The thought of tomorrow's duel played on his nerves and gave glitter and vivacity to his speech; under its influence he allowed himself some slight exaggeration in the expression of his feelings. . . . "Who cares!" he thought. Through all his words, through his suppressed sighs, through his suddenly moody glances emerged something mysterious, involuntarily sorrowful, something exquisitely hopeless. At last he let his tongue wag to the point of deliberating on love, on women, on his own future, on his conception of happiness and what he demanded of fate. . . . He expressed himself allegorically, allusively. On the eve of his possible death Vladimir Sergeich flirted with Nadiozhda Alexeevna.

She listened to him attentively, laughing, shaking her head, sometimes arguing with him, sometimes pretending to be distrustful. . . . The conversation, frequently interrupted by gentlemen approaching with their ladies, began toward the end to take a rather strange turn. . . . Now he began to question her about herself, about her character, about her sympathies. . . . At first she retorted with jests, then suddenly, quite unexpectedly to him, asked him when he was going.

"Where to?" he asked in bewilderment.

"To your home."

"To Sasovo?"

"No, home to your estate, sixty miles away."

He gazed down at his feet.

"The sooner the better," he said with a preoccupied look on his face. "I think tomorrow — provided I am still alive. For I have business to attend to! But what made you suddenly think of asking me about that?"

"I just did!" she retorted.

"All the same, what was the reason?"

"I just did!" she repeated. "I am amazed at the inquisitiveness of a man who is going away tomorrow, but who today wishes to know my character. . . ."

"But excuse me — " he began.

"Ah, here, just the thing — read it," she interrupted him, laughing as she handed him a card from a sweetmeat she had just taken from a near-by table, while she rose to meet Maria Pavlovna, who with another lady had come to a halt in front of her.

Maria Pavlovna was dancing with Piotr Alexeich. Her face was deeply flushed, it was burning, but it did not look gay.

Vladimir Sergeich glanced at the card; on it was printed in poor French:

"Qui me néglige, me perd."

He raised his eyes and met Stelchinski's gaze fixed directly on him. Vladimir Sergeich smiled forcedly, rested his elbow on the low back of his chair, and crossed one leg over the other.

"So much for you!"

The fiery artillery officer whirled Nadiozhda Alexeevna to her chair, gently spun round with her in front of it, bowed, clicked his spurs, and walked away. She sat down.

"Allow me to inquire," Vladimir Sergeich began with emphasis, "how I am to understand this card — "

"But what was on it, by the way?" she asked. "Ah, yes! '*Qui me néglige, me perd.*' Why, that is an excellent worldly rule,

which can be applied at every step. In order to succeed in anything whatever, one must not neglect anything . . . One must
strive to achieve everything: maybe at least something will fall to
one. But I feel so silly: I — I am talking to you, a practical man,
about worldly rules. . . ."

She laughed, and in vain did Vladimir Sergeich continually try
through all the rest of the mazurka to renew their previous conversation. She evaded it with the wilfulness of a capricious infant.
He talked to her about his feelings, but she either did not reply to
him at all or drew his attention to the ladies' dresses, to other
men's ludicrous faces, to the dexterity with which her brother
danced, to Maria Pavlovna's beauty. She began to talk about
music, about yesterday, about Yegor Kapitonich and his wife,
Matriona Markovna . . . and only at the very end of the mazurka, when he was taking his leave of her, did she say with an
ironical smile on her lips and in her look:

"And so you definitely are going off tomorrow?"

"Yes, and perhaps a long distance," he said significantly.

"I wish you a pleasant journey."

She went swiftly over to her brother, merrily whispered something into his ear, then asked aloud:

"Are you grateful to me? Don't you agree? Otherwise he would
have asked *her* for the mazurka."

He shrugged his shoulders and said:

"All the same, nothing will come of it."

She led him into the reception room.

"The flirt!" Vladimir Sergeich thought. Picking up his hat, he
slipped unnoticed from the hall, found his valet, whom he had
previously ordered to be ready, and was putting on his coat when,
to his extreme astonishment, the valet reported that they could
not depart, their driver had in some unknown manner drunk himself dead drunk and it was quite impossible to arouse him. Vladimir Sergeich cursed the driver unusually tersely, but extremely
vigorously (they were standing in the vestibule, and there were
strangers present) and informed the valet that if the driver was
not in a fit state as soon as dawn came, no one in the world could
imagine what might come of it. Then he returned to the hall and,
without waiting for supper, which was already prepared in the
reception room, asked the butler to let him have a room. The host
suddenly seemed to spring up through the floor right by his elbow

(Gavrila Stepanich wore shoes without heels and consequently walked without making any noise) and tried to detain him, assuring him that there would be caviar of the finest quality at supper. But he pleaded that he had a headache. Half an hour later he was lying beneath a short blanket on a small bed and trying to sleep.

But he did not sleep. Turn from side to side as he might, strive as he did to think of something else, Stelchinski's figure importunately arose before him. . . . Now he's taking aim . . . now he has fired . . . "Astakhov's killed," someone says. Vladimir Sergeich could not call himself a brave man, nor for that matter was he a coward; but the very thought of a duel, no matter with whom, had never entered his head. . . . To fight a duel! With his common sense, his peaceable disposition, his respect for the decencies, his dreams of future prosperity and an advantageous match! If he personally had not been involved he would have laughed aloud, so stupid and absurd did the whole business seem to him. To fight a duel! Whom with and what about?

"Pah, the devil! What lunacy!" he involuntarily exclaimed aloud. "Well, but supposing he really does kill me," he continued his meditations; "I must, in any case, take the necessary steps, make arrangements. . . . Who will grieve for me?"

And he angrily closed his widely staring eyes, drew the blanket around his neck. . . . But all the same he could not get to sleep.

The dawn was already gushing over the sky and, exhausted by the fever of sleeplessness, he was going off into a doze when he suddenly felt a weight on his feet. He opened his eyes. . . . Veretiev was sitting on his bed.

Vladimir Sergeich was extremely astonished, especially when he noticed that Veretiev was not wearing a coat, that his bare breast was revealed beneath his unbuttoned shirt, his hair had fallen over his forehead and his very face seemed changed. Vladimir Sergeich half rose from the bed.

"Permit me to ask — " he began, throwing out his hands.

"I've come to see you," Veretiev began in a hoarse voice. "Excuse my appearance — we have been drinking a little. . . . I wanted to reassure you. I said to myself: 'A gentleman is lying there who, in all probability, is unable to sleep. We shall help him.' Listen: you are not fighting a duel tomorrow, and you can sleep."

Vladimir Sergeich was even more astonished.

"What did you say?" he muttered.

"Yes, it is all settled," Veretiev continued. "That gentleman from the banks of the Vistula — Stelchinski — apologizes to you . . . tomorrow you will receive a letter. . . . I repeat: it is all over. Snore away!"

He rose and made his way with uncertain steps toward the door.

"But pardon me, pardon me," Vladimir Sergeich began, "how could you know, and how can I believe — ?"

"Ah. You think that I — that — " (he swayed forward a little) — "I tell you — he will send you a letter tomorrow. . . . You do not arouse any particular sympathy in me, but magnanimity is my weakness. And besides, what is there to explain? After all, it is a mere nothing. . . . But confess," he added, winking one eye, "you were funking it a little, weren't you?"

Vladimir Sergeich grew angry.

"But pardon me, indeed, my dear sir — " he began.

"Well, all right, all right," Veretiev interrupted with a good-natured smile. "Don't take offense. After all, you are not to know that we never have a ball without this happening. It is the established custom. It never has any consequences. Who would wish to present his forehead to a bullet? But, on the other hand, why not play the big bully a little? With a visitor, for instance? *In vino veritas.* However, neither you nor I know Latin. But I see by the look of you that you want to get to sleep. I wish you a good night, Mr. Positive Man, you well-intentioned mortal. Accept the good wishes of another mortal, one who is not worth a brass farthing. *Addio, mio caro!*"

And Veretiev left the room.

"This is the devil knows what!" Vladimir Sergeich exclaimed after a moment, and struck his fist on the pillow. "This is simply unlike anything on earth! . . . This will have to be cleared up! I shall not stand this!"

None the less, five minutes later he was already sleeping a profound and beneficent sleep. He grew easier at heart. . . . An averted danger fills a man's soul with sweetness and assuages it.

Now to tell what had happened before Veretiev's unexpected nocturnal visit.

Among the inhabitants of Gavrila Stepanich's house was his second cousin's son, who occupied a bachelor apartment on the ground floor. Whenever balls were held, the young men ran down to him to have a hurried smoke between the dances, and after supper they gathered in his apartment for a friendly drink. That night quite a number of guests dropped in. Among them were Stelchinski and Veretiev. Ivan Ilich Adaptable Soul also wandered down in the wake of the others. They made some hot punch. Though Ivan Ilich had promised Astakhov not to tell anyone about the forthcoming duel, none the less, when Veretiev happened to ask him what he had been discussing with that moper (as Veretiev invariably called Astakhov), Adaptable Soul could not restrain himself and repeated all his conversation with Vladimir Sergeich word for word.

Veretiev laughed, but then was lost in thought.

"But whom is he going to fight with?" he asked.

"That I cannot say," Ivan Ilich replied.

"At any rate, whom had he talked to?"

"With several people. . . . With Yegor Kapitonich. Surely he isn't going to fight him?"

Veretiev walked away.

And so they made punch and began to drink. Veretiev sat in the most prominent place; gay and dissolute, he took the lead wherever young men were gathered. He threw off his coat and cravat. They asked him to sing; he picked up a guitar and sang several songs. Little by little their heads began to grow hot; they began to propose toasts. Stelchinski, with crimson face, suddenly jumped onto the table and, raising his glass high above his head, exclaimed in a loud voice:

"To the health of —— and I know whom." He hurriedly took charge of himself, drank off his wine, dashed the glass on the floor, and added: "And may my enemy be smashed into fragments like that this very morrow!"

Veretiev, who had long been watching him, swiftly raised his head.

"Stelchinski," he said, "to begin with, get down off that table. It is unbecoming, and your shoes are perfectly appalling. And secondly, come over here; I want to tell you something."

He led him aside.

"Listen, brother, I know you are going to fight a duel tomorrow with that gentleman from Petersburg."

"How — who told you?"

A Quiet Spot

"I'm telling you. And I also know whom you are fighting over."

"Namely? I would be curious to know."

"Ah, you old Talleyrand! Why, over my sister, of course. Now, now, don't pretend to be surprised. It makes you look like a goose. I cannot imagine how all this has come about, but it is so. Enough, brother," Veretiev continued, "what's the point of all this pretense? I know you have long been setting your cap at her."

"But even so, that does not prove — "

"Oh, do stop it! Now listen to what I am going to say to you. Not in any form shall I permit this duel. D'you understand? All this nonsense will have extremely serious consequences for my sister. You must forgive me, but so long as I am alive that is not going to happen. If you and I go to the devil, that is as it should be, but she has a right to live a long time yet, and to live in happiness. Yes, I swear," he added with sudden energy, "I will betray all others, even those who would be prepared to sacrifice everything for me; but I won't allow anyone to touch a hair of her head!"

Stelchinski forcedly roared with laughter.

"You're drunk, my friend, and you're raving — that's all."

"And you aren't, I suppose? But whether I am drunk or not doesn't make one iota of difference. I am speaking to the point. You shall not fight that gentleman, I guarantee that. It was a fine idea of yours to get mixed up with him! Jealous, I suppose? Well, there's the truth at last; infatuated people are fools! And she only danced with him so that he shouldn't think of asking — Well, that's a different question. But this duel is not coming off."

"Hm! I should like to know how you are going to prevent me."

"Why, like this: if you don't give me your word this minute to call off this duel, I shall fight a duel with you myself."

"Indeed?"

"My dear friend, you needn't have any doubt about it. I shall insult you, my dear fellow, this very moment, in front of everybody, in the most fantastic fashion, and then we'll fight at once if you like. I think you will find that unpleasant for many reasons, won't you?"

Stelchinski flared up, declared that this was *intimidation*, that he would never allow anyone to interfere in his affairs, that no matter what happened he . . . and ended by submitting and forgoing any kind of attempt on Vladimir Sergeich's life. Veretiev embraced him, and before half an hour had passed they were drinking *"Bruderschaft"* together — in other words, with clasped hands. . . . The young master of ceremonies also drank *Bruderschaft* with them and at first clung to them like a leech; but at last he fell asleep like any innocent, and lay long on his back in a state of complete stupefaction. The expression of his small, pallid face was both amusing and pitiful. Goodness, what would the society ladies of his acquaintance have said if they had seen him in such a humiliating state? But, fortunately for him, he did not know any society ladies.

Ivan Ilich also distinguished himself that night. To begin with, he astonished the guests by suddenly striking up: "A baron once lived in a village."

"The finch has begun to sing," everybody cried. "Who has ever known a finch to sing at night?"

"Why, anyone would think I knew only one song," retorted Ivan Ilich, who was excited with wine. "I know others too."

"Now, now, now, let us have a demonstration of your art."

Ivan Ilich was silent for a moment, then abruptly began in a bass voice: "Crambabuli, legacy of our fathers," but so incoherently and queerly that a general outburst of laughter at once drowned his voice and he lapsed into silence.

When they dispersed, Veretiev went to Vladimir Sergeich and had the brief conversation we have already related.

Next day Vladimir Sergeich drove off very early to his own house at Sasovo. He spent all the morning in a state of agitation, all but mistook a visiting merchant for Stelchinski's second, and breathed easily only when his valet brought him a letter from the Pole. He read this letter several times — it was very artfully written. . . . Stelchinski began with the words: *"La nuit porte conseil, monsieur"*; he made no apology for anything, because, in his opinion, he had not insulted his opponent in any way. However, he confessed that he had been unnecessarily heated the evening before, and ended by announcing that he was entirely at Mr. Astakhov's (*de M. Astakhof*) disposition, but that he himself no longer demanded satisfaction. Having composed and dispatched an answer, in which courtesies that bordered on playfulness were combined with a note of dignity, which, however, was lacking in braggadocio, Vladimir Sergeich rubbed his hands and sat down to dinner, ate with great satisfaction, and immediately on rising from the table went off home, not even sending relays of horses in advance. The road he took passed less than three miles from Ipatov's estate. . . . Vladimir Sergeich gazed at it.

"Good-by, quiet little spot!" he said with a wry smile.

The images of Nadiozhda Alexeevna and Maria Pavlovna momentarily arose in his mind. He shrugged his shoulders, turned away, and dropped off into a doze.

6

Three months and more passed. Autumn had arrived long since: the seared forests had been stripped bare, the tomtits had arrived, and, sure sign of the proximity of winter, the wind began to howl and moan. But still no heavy rains had fallen, and the roads had not yet dissolved into mud. Taking advantage of this circumstance, Vladimir Sergeich set off to settle certain affairs in the provincial town. He spent the morning paying various visits and in the evening drove to the club. In the enormous, gloomy hall of the club he met several acquaintances and, among others, an old retired cavalry captain named Fleech, a well-known businessman, wit, card-player, and gossip. Vladimir Sergeich fell into conversation with him.

"Ah, and by the way," the retired captain suddenly exclaimed, "an acquaintance of yours passed through here the other day, and she asked me to convey her good wishes to you."

"What acquaintance?"

"A Madame Stelchinskaya."

"I don't know any Madame Stelchinskaya."

"You knew her when she was single. She was born a Veretieva — Nadiozhda Alexeevna. Her husband was on our Governor's staff. You must have seen him too, at various times — a lively little fellow, with mustaches. . . . He picked up a fine little piece, with a fortune too."

"You don't say!" Vladimir Sergeich remarked. "So she married him. . . . Hm! And where have they gone off to?"

"To Petersburg. She asked me also to remind you about some card from confectionery. . . . What was it, if I may be so inquisitive?"

And the old gossip thrust out his pointed nose.

"Really, I don't remember; some joke or other," Vladimir Sergeich replied. "But may I ask where her brother is now?"

739

"Piotr? Well, he's in a bad way."

Mr. Fleech turned his little foxy eyes upward and sighed.

"Why, what do you mean?" Vladimir Sergeich asked.

"He's gone completely to the dogs! He's a lost soul."

"But where is he now?"

"No one knows where he is. He went off somewhere after the gypsies, that is the most likely. He's nowhere in the province, I'll guarantee that."

"But old Ipatov, is he still living there?"

"Mikhail Nikolaich? The old eccentric fellow? Yes, he's still there."

"And everybody in his house just the same as before?"

"Of course, of course. Why, you're not thinking of marrying his sister-in-law, surely? Why, she's not a woman, she's a monument, really she is! Hee hee! Why, we're already beginning to say — that she, we say, you see . . ."

"You don't say!" Vladimir Sergeich retorted, narrowing his eyes.

At that moment someone proposed a game of cards to Fleech, and the conversation was broken off.

Vladimir Sergeich had intended to return home at once, but unexpectedly he received a report by courier from the headman that six peasants' huts at Sasovo had been burned down, and he decided to drive over there. It was thirty-seven miles from the provincial capital to Sasovo. Toward evening Vladimir Sergeich arrived in the room with which the reader is already familiar. He at once ordered the headman and the secretary to be sent for, and berated them to good purpose; next morning he surveyed the scene of the fire and took the necessary measures. And after dinner, after some vacillation, he set out to call on Ipatov. Vladimir Sergeich would have remained at home if Fleech had not told him about Nadiozhda Alexeevna's departure. He had no desire to meet her, but he was not averse to having another look at Maria Pavlovna.

As on his first visit, he found Ipatov playing checkers with Adaptable Soul. The old man was delighted to see him, but it seemed to him that Ipatov had a careworn face, and his speech did not flow freely and readily, as formerly.

Vladimir Sergeich exchanged glances with Ivan Ilich without

speaking. They were both a little embarrassed; however, they soon recovered their composure.

"Are all your people well?" Vladimir Sergeich asked as he sat down.

"All well, praise be, I thank you humbly," Ipatov replied. "Only Maria Pavlovna isn't quite — she spends most of her time in her room."

"Caught a cold?"

"No — not exactly. She'll be down for tea."

"And Yegor Kapitonich? What is he doing these days?"

"Ah! Yegor Kapitonich is devastated. His wife has died."

"Surely not!"

"She died of cholera in twenty-four hours. You wouldn't recognize him now, he is quite unlike himself. 'Without Matriona Markovna,' he says, 'my life is a burden. I shall die,' he says, 'and praise to God!' he says; 'I don't wish to live,' he says. Yes, the poor wretch is gone to pieces."

"Oh, my goodness, how unpleasant!" Vladimir Sergeich exclaimed. "Poor Yegor Kapitonich!"

They were all silent for a moment or two.

"I hear your neighbor has taken a husband," Vladimir Sergeich began, reddening a little.

"Nadiozhda Alexeevna? Yes, she's married." Ipatov looked sidelong at him. "Of course, of course, she has married and already gone away."

"To Petersburg?"

"To St. Petersburg."

"I suppose Maria Pavlovna misses her? I think they were very close friends, weren't they?"

"Of course she misses her. It couldn't be otherwise. But, for that matter, so far as friendship is concerned, I tell you that girls' friendships are even worse than men's. So long as they can see each other, all is well; but out of sight, out of mind."

"Do you think so?"

"Yes, I swear it is so. Take Nadiozhda Alexeevna, for instance. She hasn't written a single letter to us since she left, and yet she absolutely promised and even swore she would. Though, truly, she has other matters to concern herself with now."

"Has she been gone long?"

"Yes, it will be about six weeks ago. She galloped off the very day after the wedding, in the foreign fashion."

"They say her brother also has gone away?" Vladimir Sergeich remarked after a brief pause.

"Yes, he's gone too. You see, they're used to living in the capital; they wouldn't remain long in the country!"

"And no one knows where he's gone to?"

"No one."

"He's gone without leaving a trace," Ivan Ilich remarked.

"He's gone without leaving a trace," Ipatov repeated. "Well, and what about you, Vladimir Sergeich? What have you been doing?" he added, turning in his chair.

Vladimir Sergeich began to tell of his own doings. Ipatov listened to him, listened, and at last exclaimed:

"But why doesn't Maria come down? Ivan Ilich, you might go for her."

Adaptable Soul left the room. On returning he announced that Maria Pavlovna would be coming immediately.

"Why, has she a headache?" Ipatov asked in an undertone.

"Yes," Ivan Ilich replied.

The door opened and Maria Pavlovna entered. Vladimir Sergeich rose, bowed, and in his astonishment could not utter a word, so changed was she since he had seen her last. The color had gone from her sunken cheeks; broad black rims surrounded her eyes, her lips were compressed bitterly; all her face, immobile and dark, seemed petrified.

She raised her eyes, and there was no light in them.

"How do you feel?" Ipatov asked her.

"I am well," she replied, and sat down at the table, on which the samovar was already hissing.

Vladimir Sergeich was thoroughly bored that evening. And indeed they were all out of sorts. The conversation continually took a cheerless turn.

"Why, just hark to the notes it is producing!" Ipatov said in passing, after listening to the howling of the wind. "The summer has gone long since; and now the autumn is going, now winter is at hand. And there will be heavy drifts all around. If the snow would only fall soon! But now if you go into the garden you're filled with misery. . . . It's just like some ruin. The trees knocking with their branches. . . . Yes, the beautiful days are past!"

"They're past," Ivan Ilich repeated.

Maria Pavlovna silently gazed through the window.

"God grant they'll return!" Ipatov remarked.

No one made any response.

"But do you remember how beautifully we sang songs here then?" said Vladimir Sergeich.

"And what of it?" the old man replied with a sigh.

"But you could sing," Vladimir Sergeich continued, turning to Maria Pavlovna. "You have such a beautiful voice."

She did not reply.

"And how is your mother?" Vladimir Sergeich asked Ipatov, not knowing what else to talk about.

"God be praised, she gets about a little with all her infirmities. She came across in her carriage only today. I must say she is like a tree half snapped, she creaks and creaks; but then, you see some other, younger tree go toppling over, while she goes on standing and standing. Ah, dear, dear!"

Maria Pavlovna let her hands drop on her knees and bowed her head.

"But, all the same, her life is hard," Ipatov spoke again. "It's a true saying: 'old age is no pleasure.'"

"But in youth too there is no pleasure," Maria Pavlovna said as though to herself.

Vladimir Sergeich wanted to return to Sasovo for the night, but it grew so dark outside that he could not bring himself to undertake the drive. He was given the same room upstairs in which he had spent a disturbed night, through Yegor Kapitonich's kindness, three months before. . . .

"Does he still snore?" he thought, and remembered Kapitonich's exhortations to his servant, remembered Maria Pavlovna's unexpected appearance in the garden. . . .

He went across to the window and set his brow against the cold glass. His own face looked back dimly at him as though his eyes were fixed on a dark curtain, and only after some moments was he able to distinguish the branches of trees, outlined against the starless sky, impetuously tossing amid the gloom. They were tousled by the unresting wind.

Suddenly he had the impression that he saw something white glimmering over the ground. . . . He stared, smiled wryly, shrugged his shoulders, and, exclaiming half aloud: "What imagination can do!" got into bed.

He fell asleep very quickly, but once more he was not fated to spend a quiet night. He was aroused by the sound of running feet in the house. . . . He raised his head from the pillow. . . . He heard anxious voices, exclamations, hurried steps; doors were banged; now a woman's weeping was heard; there were shouts in the garden; other shouts replied, farther off. . . . The noise in the house grew more tumultuous with every moment. . . . "Fire!" the thought flashed through his head. He took alarm, jumped out of bed, and rushed to the window. But there was no glare; only crimson points of fire scurried along the garden paths, past the trees — people were running with lanterns. He went swiftly to the door, opened it, and ran into Ivan Ilich. Pale, disheveled, half dressed, Adaptable Soul was rushing he himself knew not where.

"What's the matter? What has happened?" Vladimir Sergeich asked agitatedly, violently clutching him by the arm.

"She's gone, she's drowned, she's thrown herself in the water," Ivan Ilich replied in a panting voice.

"Who's thrown herself into the water, who's gone?"

"Maria Pavlovna! Who else but Maria Pavlovna? He's ruined her, the poor girl! Come, help! Come, let's hurry! Quicker, run quicker, everybody!"

And Ivan Ilich rushed headlong down the stairs.

Somehow or other Vladimir Sergeich managed to draw on his shoes; he flung his greatcoat round his shoulders and hurried after him.

He met no one at all in the house, they had all run out into the garden. He came across only the two girls, Ipatov's daughters, in the corridor, by the vestibule. Half dead with fright, they were standing in their white dresses, with linked hands and bare feet, beside a night light set on the floor. Through the reception room, past an overturned table, he ran out on the terrace. Beyond the thicket, in the direction of the dam, lights, shadows flickered. . . .

"Fetch boathooks! Hurry for boathooks!" he heard Ipatov's voice.

"A net, a net, a boat!" other voices shouted.

A Quiet Spot

He ran toward the shouts. He found Ipatov on the bank of the lake; a lantern hanging from a bough brilliantly lit up the old man's gray head. He was wringing his hands and staggering about as though drunk; close by him a woman, lying on the grass, was writhing and sobbing; people were bustling all around. Ivan Ilich had already waded up to his knees in the water and was groping about the bottom with a pole; a coachman undressed, shivering all over his body; two men dragged a boat down the bank; the sharp clatter of horse-hoofs sounded along the street of the village. . . . The wind tore past with a howl, as though attempting to blow out the lanterns, and the lake splashed and seethed, a sinister black.

"What's this I hear?" Vladimir Sergeich exclaimed, running up to Ipatov. "Is it possible?"

"Boathooks, fetch some boathooks," the old man groaned in answer.

"But you may be mistaken, surely, Mikhail Nikolaich — "

"No, how can there be any mistake?" the woman lying on the grass, who was Maria Pavlovna's maid, spoke up in a tearful voice. "I myself, unhappy wretch, heard her, heard my little one fling herself in the water. I heard her struggling in the water, I heard her cry out: 'Save me!' and then once more: 'Save me!' "

"But why didn't you stop her, for goodness' sake?"

"Why, sir, how could I? Why, when I looked, she had already left the room. But my heart seemed to know; during the last few days she was continually grieving and never saying a word. And so I knew. I ran straight out into the garden, as though someone had told me. Suddenly I heard something bubbling in the water. 'Save me,' I heard her shouting. . . . 'Save me.' . . . Oh, my dear! Oh, my darling!"

"But you may have imagined it all?"

"How could I imagine it? And where is she, then? Where has she got to?"

"So that is the white I thought I saw in the darkness," Vladimir Sergeich remembered.

Meanwhile men ran up with boathooks, others dragged along a net and began to open it out over the grass, a great crowd of people gathered, fussing and bustling . . . jostling. . . . The coachman snatched up one boathook, the headman another. They both jumped into the boat, cast off, and began to probe in the

745

water with the boathooks; the people on the bank held up lanterns for them to see by. Strange and terrible seemed their movements and their shadows in the haze, above the troubled lake, by the vague and uncertain gleam of the lanterns.

"I've hooked in something!" the coachman suddenly shouted. They all froze still where they stood.

The coachman hauled the boathook toward himself, bent down. . . . Something branching, black, slowly floated up. . . .

"An old log," the coachman said, and jerked the boathook free.

"Come back, come back," some shouted from the bank. "You'll never do anything with boathooks, you need the net."

"Yes, yes, the net," others took up the cry.

"Wait a bit," the headman said; "I've hooked in something now — something soft, I think," he added after a moment.

A white patch appeared beside the boat.

"It's our lady!" he suddenly shouted. "It's she!"

He was not mistaken. . . . The boathook had caught in the sleeve of Maria Pavlovna's dress. The coachman at once seized her and dragged her out of the water. With two strong punts the boat was at the bank. . . . Ipatov, Ivan Ilich, Vladimir Sergeich, all rushed to Maria Pavlovna, raised her, carried her in their arms to the house, at once undressed her, began to pump the water out of her, to warm her. . . . But all their efforts, all their endeavors were fruitless. . . . Maria Pavlovna did not come around. . . . Life had already departed from her.

Vladimir Sergeich left Ipatovka early next morning; before he left he went to take a last farewell of the dead girl. She was lying on the table in the reception room, in a white dress. . . . Her heavy tresses were still not quite dry, a look of mournful bewilderment was impressed on her pale face, which had not had time to be distorted; the parted lips seemed to be attempting to speak and to ask something . . . the hands folded tightly, as though in yearning, were pressed to her breast. . . . But no matter what the mournful thoughts with which the poor drowned unfortunate had perished, death had laid on her the impress of his everlasting speechlessness and reconciliation . . . and who can understand what a dead face expresses in those few moments when it meets the gaze of the living for the last time before it disappears forever and disintegrates in the grave?

A Quiet Spot

Vladimir Sergeich stood for a few seconds, in decorous meditation, before Maria Pavlovna's body, crossed himself three times, and went out, not noticing Ivan Ilich, who was crying quietly in one corner. . . . And not he alone wept that day; all the servants in the house wept bitterly: Maria Pavlovna had left behind her a good memory.

A week later old Ipatov wrote the following letter in reply to one that had come at last from Nadiozhda Alexeevna:

A week ago, dear Madame Nadiozhda Alexeevna, my unfortunate sister-in-law, your acquaintance, Maria Pavlovna, put an end to her own life, throwing herself at night into the lake, and we have already committed her body to the earth. She decided on this grievous and terrible step without saying good-by to me, without leaving a letter or even a little note in order to reveal her last will. . . . But you know best of all, Nadiozhda Alexeevna, on whose soul must fall this great and mortal sin! God be your brother's judge, but my sister-in-law could not cease to love him, nor survive the parting. . . .

Nadiozhda Alexeevna received this letter in Italy, where she had traveled with her husband, Count de Stelchinski as he was called in all the hotels. For that matter, he did not confine his visits to hotels; he was frequently to be seen at the gaming-tables, in the pump-rooms, at the waters. At first he lost a great deal of money, then he ceased to lose, and his face acquired a peculiar expression, suspicious or insolent, such as is worn by a man to whom adventures occur quite unexpectedly. . . . He saw his wife rarely. Nadiozhda Alexeevna, however, was not bored in his absence. She developed a passion for the arts. She made more and more acquaintances among artists and liked discussing the beautiful with young men. Ipatov's letter greatly upset her, but it did not prevent her going off the same day to the Dogs' Cave to watch the death of the poor creatures overcome by sulphur fumes.

She did not go alone. She was accompanied by various escorts. Among them the most affable was a certain M. Popelien, an unsuccessful French painter with a little beard, and wearing a check jacket. He sang the latest ballads in a piping voice, was very free with his witticisms, and, although he was of meager build, he ate a great deal.

7

It was a sunny, frosty January day; a large number of people were out walking on the Nevsky Prospekt. The clock in the Duma tower said three o'clock. Among those walking along the broad flagstones sprinkled with fine yellow sand was our old acquaintance Vladimir Sergeich Astakhov. He had grown much more mature since we parted with him, had surrounded his face with side-whiskers, and his body had filled out; but he had not aged. He moved with the crowd, unhurriedly, and occasionally looking about him. He was expecting his wife; she intended to drive up in the carriage together with her mother. Five years had passed since Vladimir Sergeich got married exactly as he had always desired: his wife was wealthy and had the very best of connections. Affably raising his superlatively polished top hat as he met innumerable acquaintances, Vladimir Sergeich continued to advance with the easy gait of a man satisfied with fate, when suddenly, right outside the Passage, a gentleman in a Spanish cloak and a peaked cap, with a face already showing considerable signs of wear, with dyed whiskers, and large eyes encircled by rather bloated flesh, all but ran into him. Vladimir Sergeich stepped aside with dignity, but the gentleman in the peaked cap stared at him and suddenly exclaimed:

"Ah, Mr. Astakhov! Good afternoon!"

Vladimir Sergeich made no answer and halted in astonishment. He could not understand how his name was known to this gentleman who was daring to walk along the Nevsky Prospekt in a peaked cap.

"You don't recognize me," the gentleman in the peaked cap continued. "I saw you some eight years ago, in the country, in T— province, at the Ipatovs'. My name is Veretiev."

"Ah! My goodness! Forgive me!" Vladimir Sergeich exclaimed. "But how you have changed since then!"

"Yes, I've grown older," Piotr Alexeich retorted, and passed his hand, which was ungloved, over his face. "But you haven't changed."

Veretiev had not aged so much as gone thin and lost grip of himself. Fine furrows covered his face, and when he spoke, his lips and cheeks twitched a little. By all the signs it was evident that he had experienced much.

"Where have you been all this while, that no one has seen you?" Vladimir Sergeich asked him.

"I've wandered about a bit. But have you been continually in Petersburg?"

"Chiefly in Petersburg."

"Married?"

"Yes."

And Vladimir Sergeich looked rather severe, as though desiring to convey to Veretiev: "Don't think of asking me to introduce you to my wife, my fine fellow."

Apparently Veretiev understood him. An unconcerned smile flickered over his lips.

"But what of your sister?" Vladimir Sergeich asked. "Where is she?"

"I cannot tell you for certain. She is probably in Moscow. I haven't had a letter from her for a long time."

"Is her husband still alive?"

"Yes."

"And Mr. Ipatov himself?"

"I don't know; I expect he's alive too; or he may be dead."

"And that gentleman, what was his name, Bodryakov, wasn't it?"

"The one you asked to be your second, d'you remember, when you were in such a funk? How the devil should I know?"

Vladimir Sergeich was silent for a moment, with a serious look on his face.

"I have always remembered that evening with pleasure," he said at last, "when I had the occasion" (he all but said "honor") "to meet your sister and you. She was a very pleasant person. And do you still sing so delightfully?"

"No, I've lost my voice. . . . Yes, they were good times then!"

"I paid one other visit to Ipatovka later," Vladimir Sergeich added, mournfully raising his brows; "for that is what the place was called, wasn't it? On the very day of a certain terrible occurrence — "

"Yes, yes, it was terrible, it was terrible," Veretiev hurriedly broke in. "Yes, yes. But do you remember how you all but fought a duel with the man who is now my brother-in-law?"

"Hm! I remember!" Vladimir Sergeich retorted with emphasis.

"But I must confess that it is so long ago that sometimes it all seems like a dream to me."

"Like a dream," Veretiev repeated, and his pale cheeks flushed. "Like a dream — no, it was not a dream; at least, not for me. It was the time of youth, of gaiety and happiness, the time of infinite hopes and invincible powers; and if it was a dream, it was a beautiful dream. But now you and I have grown older, have grown more stupid, and we dye our mustaches, and we wander along the Nevsky, and we have become good for nothing, like brokendown nags; we're played out; we've been buffeted about, but we try to look important and put on airs, and we idle about and, I'm afraid, drink rivers of wine — now, that is more like a dream, and a most hideous dream. Life is spent, and spent in vain, stupidly, trivially — that's the bitterness of it! Now, if we could shake that off like a dream, if we could only wake up from that! . . . And then, everywhere, always, one horrible memory, one specter — However, good-by."

Veretiev walked swiftly away. But as he drew level with the door of one of the leading confectioners on the Nevsky Prospekt, he halted, went in, and, after drinking a glass of orange bitters at the buffet, passed through the billiard room, foggy and dim with tobacco smoke, into a back room. There he found several acquaintances, former comrades of his: Piotia Lazurin, Kostya Kovrovsky, Prince Serdiukov, and two other gentlemen, who were known simply as Vasiuk and Filat. They were all no longer young, though they were bachelors; some of them had lost a little hair, others were going gray; their faces were covered with furrows, they had double chins; in a word, all these gentlemen had long since passed the period of growth, as we say. They all continued to regard Veretiev, however, as an unusual sort of man, destined to astonish the universe; and the only reason why he was wiser than they was that he himself fully realized his own utter and fundamental uselessness. Even outside his circle there were people who thought that if he had not ruined himself, something would have come of him, the devil knows what. . . . Those people were mistaken: nothing ever comes of the Veretievs.

Piotr Alexeich's friends welcomed him with their usual greetings. At first he perplexed them by his gloomy features and splenetic remarks, but he soon grew more composed, waxed merry, and affairs took their usual course.

A Quiet Spot

As soon as Veretiev had left him, Vladimir Sergeich knitted his brows and drew himself up. Piotr Alexeich's unexpected sally had greatly embarrassed, had even affronted him.

" 'We've grown more stupid, we dye our mustaches' . . . *parlez pour vous, mon cher*," he said at last, almost aloud, and snorting a couple of times in an excess of involuntary indignation, he prepared to continue his walk.

"Who was that talking to you?" a loud and self-confident voice sounded behind him.

Vladimir Sergeich turned and saw one of his good acquaintances, a certain M. Pomponsky. This M. Pomponsky, a tall and stout man, occupied a rather important position, and never since the days of his youth had he had any doubts of himself.

"Oh, some eccentric fellow," Vladimir Sergeich replied, taking M. Pomponsky by the arm.

"Pardon me, Vladimir Sergeich, but, really, is it permissible for a respectable man to talk in the street with an individual who is wearing a peaked cap? It is not done! I am amazed! Where could you have made acquaintance with such a creature?"

"In the country."

"In the country. . . . One doesn't recognize country neighbors in town — *ce n'est pas comme il faut*. A gentleman should always behave like a gentleman, if he wishes — "

"There is my wife," Vladimir Sergeich hurriedly interrupted him. "Let us go to her."

And the two gentlemen made their way to a low, elegant carriage, where the pale, weary, and fretfully haughty little face of a still young, yet already faded woman was peering through the window.

Behind her could be seen another lady, also apparently indignant — her mother. Vladimir Sergeich opened the carriage door and offered his wife his arm. Pomponsky went with the mother-in-law, and the two couples set off along the Nevsky, followed by a short, black-haired lackey in pea-green boots and with a large cockade in his hat.

The Diary of
a Superfluous Man

Lambswater Hamlet, March 20, 18 —

1850

THE DOCTOR has just left me. At last I have gained my point! With all his cunning, he had to tell me in the end. Yes, I shall die soon, very soon. The rivers will be freed of ice again, and I, with the last snows probably, will float away — whither? God knows! Also down to the sea. Well, what of it! If death has to come, then let it be in the spring. Yet isn't it absurd to begin a diary perhaps two weeks before one's death? But what of it? And in what respect are fourteen days less than fourteen years, or fourteen centuries? In face of eternity, they say, everything is a mere nothing; and that is true; but then, eternity itself is a mere nothing. I appear to be embarking on speculation; that is a bad sign — I'm not already funking it, surely? It would be better if I started to write about something more concrete. It is raw and windy outside, I am forbidden to go out. So what can I write about? A decent man doesn't talk about his ailments, and surely to write a story is not my line; deliberations on exalted subjects are beyond my powers; a description of the life surrounding me cannot interest even me. And yet to do nothing is boring; to read is being lazy. I know! I'll tell myself all my own life. An excellent idea! On the eve of my death that is only right, and it cannot offend anyone. I begin.

I was born, some thirty years ago, to quite wealthy landowners. My father was a passionate gambler; my mother was a lady of character — a very virtuous lady. Only I have never known any woman whose virtue caused me less satisfaction. She staggered beneath the burden of her qualities and tortured everybody, beginning with herself. During all the fifty years of her life she never rested once, never folded her arms; she was everlastingly bustling and fussing like an ant — and without any benefit, which

753

cannot be said of an ant. An indefatigable worm gnawed at her day and night. Only once did I see her completely at rest, and that was the first day after her death, in her coffin. As I looked at her I, to tell the truth, had the feeling that her face expressed a quiet astonishment; the half-open lips, the sunken cheeks and benignly motionless eyes, seemed to be uttering the words: "How good it is not to stir!" Yes, it is good, it is good to be severed at last from the exhausting consciousness of life, from the importunate and restless feeling of existence! But that is away from the point.

I was brought up badly and not at all cheerfully. My father and mother both loved me; but that did not make things any the easier for me. As a man openly devoted to a shameful and ruinous failing, my father had no authority whatever in his own house and carried no weight at all; he was conscious of his downfall and, not having the strength to renounce his beloved passion, tried at least, by his affectionate and modest demeanor, by his evasive meekness, to deserve the indulgence of his exemplary wife. My mother did, indeed, bear his misfortune with that magnificent and sumptuous long-suffering of the virtuous, in which there is so much selfish pride. She never reproached my father in any respect, silently handed him her last money, and paid his debts. He exalted her to her face and behind her back, but he did not like staying at home and caressed me by stealth, as though he himself were afraid of infecting me by his very presence. But when he was with me his distorted features looked so kindly, the feverish sneer on his lips was replaced by such a touching smile, his hazel eyes, with their meshes of fine furrows, beamed with such love, that I involuntarily pressed my cheek against his cheek, which was damp and warm with tears. With my handkerchief I wiped away those tears; and they flowed again, without effort, like water from an overfilled glass. I too began to cry, and he comforted me, stroked me on the back with his hand, kissed me all over my face with his trembling lips. And even now, more than twenty years after his death, when I recall my poor father, a mute sobbing rises in my throat, and my heart beats, beats so hotly and bitterly, is fretted with such yearning pity, as though he still had a long time to struggle and there were still something to pity!

My mother, on the other hand, was always consistent in the

way she treated me, kindly, but coldly. One often finds such mothers, moralizing and just, in children's books. She loved me, but I did not love her. Yes, I shunned my virtuous mother and passionately loved my sinful father.

But that will be enough for today. The beginning is made; and as for the end, no matter what it may be, I have no need to worry. That is for my disease to attend to.

March 21

Today the weather is remarkably fine. Warm and clear; the sun is playing merrily on the thawing snow; everything is glittering, steaming, melting; the sparrows are chattering like mad around the dark sweating fences; the humid air is sweetly and fearfully tickling my chest. Spring, spring is coming! I am sitting by the window and gazing across the little stream into the open field. O nature, nature! I love you so much, and from your womb I have emerged not even viable. Look, a male sparrow is hopping about with outspread wings; it calls — and every sound of its voice, every bristling little feather on its tiny body, is quivering with health and strength. . . .

What deduction follows from that? None whatever. It is healthy and has the right to call and to bristle its feathers; but I am ill and must die — that is all. It is not worth saying any more about it. And in nature lachrymose harangues are exhaustingly funny. Let us return to our story.

I was brought up, as I have already said, very badly and not at all cheerfully. I had no brothers and sisters. I was educated at home. And besides, what would my mother have had to occupy herself with if she had put me into a boarding school or a government educational institution? That is what children are for: to save their parents from being bored. We lived mostly in the country, but from time to time we went to Moscow. I had teachers and tutors, as is proper; I particularly remember one cachectical and lachrymose German named Rikman, an unusually mournful, woebegone creature, vainly consumed with an exhausting fretting for his distant native land. My unshaven old male nurse, Vasily, nicknamed "the Goose," used to sit by the stove in the terrible stuffiness of the crowded anteroom, which was heavy with the sour smell of stale kvass. He would sit in his everlasting cossack-style coat of blue sacking, playing cards with the coachman Potap, who wore a new foamy-white sheepskin greatcoat and everlasting greased boots, while Rikman sang on the other side of the partition:

> *"Herz, mein Herz, warum so traurig?*
> *Was bekümmerts dich so sehr?*
> *S'ist ja schön im fremden Lande —*
> *Herz, mein Herz, — was willst du mehr?"*

After my father's death we went to Moscow to live. I was now twelve years old. My father died in the night from a stroke. I shall never forget that night. I was sleeping soundly, as all children commonly sleep; but I remember that even in my sleep I thought I heard a heavy and measured snoring. Suddenly I felt someone take me by the shoulder and shake me. I opened my eyes: I saw Vasily. "What's the matter?" "Get up, get up, Alexei Mikhailich is dying!" I jumped like a madman out of my bed and ran into their room. I looked and saw my father lying with his head flung back, his face all crimson, and snoring stertorously. Servants with terrified faces were crowded at the door; in the ante-room someone asked in a hoarse voice: "Have they sent for the doctor?" In the yard a horse was brought out from the stables, the gate creaked. A tallow candle was burning on the floor in the room; my mother was there lamenting, but without losing either her decorum or the consciousness of her own worth. I flung myself on my father's breast, embraced him, stammered: "Daddy, Daddy! . . ." He lay motionless and with his eyes queerly screwed up. I glanced into his face — an unbearable horror caught my breath. I began to howl with fear; like a bird seized with rough hands, I was dragged off and led away. Only the evening before, he had caressed me so ardently and despondently, as though he had a presentiment of his imminent death.

A rough and sleepy doctor, smelling strongly of herb vodka, arrived. My father died under his lancet, and the very next day, completely numb with grief, I stood with a candle in my hand before the table on which the body was lying, and listened senselessly to the deacon's guttural drone, occasionally interrupted by the priest's feeble voice. The tears streamed again and again down my cheeks, over my lips, my collar, my shirt-front; I cried my eyes out. I stared fixedly, I attentively stared at my father's immobile face, as though I expected him to do something. But meanwhile my mother slowly bowed herself again and again to the ground, slowly rose, and, crossing herself, pressed her fingers firmly to her forehead, her shoulders, and her belly. I had no thoughts whatever in my head; I was completely leaden; but I felt that something terrible was being done to me. . . . That day death looked me in the face and noted me.

We moved to Moscow after my father's death for a very simple reason: all our estate was sold under the hammer to pay the debts — absolutely everything except one little hamlet, the very one in which I am now living out my magnificent existence. I confess that though I was young then, I was saddened by the sale of our nest; or rather, in reality I was sad only about our garden. Almost my only happy memories are connected with that garden. There one gentle spring evening I buried my best friend, an old dog with docked tail and crooked paws, named Trixy. There I used to hide in the long grass to eat stolen apples, the red, sweet, Novgorod kind. And there, finally, between bushes of ripe raspberries I first saw the maid Klavdia, who, despite her snub nose and habit of laughing into her handkerchief, aroused such a tender passion in me that in her presence I barely breathed, my heart stopped beating, and I was speechless. But one Easter Sunday, when it was her turn to kiss my hand as her young master, I all but flung myself down to kiss her patched kidskin shoes. My God! Was all that really twenty years ago? It does not seem all that time since I rode my little shaggy chestnut horse along by the old wattle fence of our garden and, rising in the stirrups, picked the two-colored leaves of the poplars. So long as man is living he is not conscious of his own life: like sound, it becomes perceptible to him only when a little time has passed.

O my garden, O you overgrown paths beside the shallow pond! O sandy little spot beneath the crumbling dam, where I caught gudgeon and loaches! And you, lofty birches, with long, hanging branches, beyond which, along the byroad, rose a peasant's dreary song, unevenly broken by the jolts of his cart — I send you my last farewell. . . . As I part with life, to you alone do I stretch out my hands. I should like once more to breathe in the bitter freshness of the wormwood, the sweet smell of the reaped buckwheat in the fields of my native parts. I should like once more to hear in the distance the modest tinkle of the cracked bell in our parish church; to lie once more in the cool shade beneath an oaken bush on the slope of the well-known ravine, once more to follow with my gaze the mobile tracks of the wind, running in a darker stream over the golden grass of our meadow. . . .

Ah, to what purpose is all this? But I cannot write any more today. Till tomorrow.

March 22

Today it is cold and overcast again. Such weather is far more suitable. It is in accord with my task. Yesterday quite ineptly aroused in me a multitude of unwanted feelings and memories. That will not happen again. Sentimental outpourings are just like liquorice: when you first begin to suck it, it doesn't seem at all bad, but then it tastes quite unpleasant. I shall simply and calmly tell my life story.

And so we went to live in Moscow. . . .

But now the thought occurs to me — is it really worth while telling my life story?

No, it simply is not worth it. . . . My life has been in no way different from that of many other people. The parental home, the university, service in minor positions, retirement, a small circle of acquaintances, honest poverty, modest pleasures, humble occupations, moderate desires — for goodness' sake, who doesn't know all that? And so I shall not bother to tell my life story, especially as I am writing for my own satisfaction. And as my past does not suggest anything either excessively cheerful or even excessively sad even to me, it cannot contain anything worthy of consideration. I would do better to analyze my character for my own benefit.

What sort of man am I? . . . Someone may remark that no one inquires into that either. Agreed. But then I am dying; don't you see, I am dying; and before one's death surely the desire to know what sort of bird I have been would seem excusable?

Having given some little thought to this important question and, for that matter, having no need whatever to be excessively bitter in regard to myself, as is the manner of people who are strongly convinced of their own virtues, I must confess one thing: in this world I have been a completely superfluous man, or better, a completely superfluous bird. And I intend to demonstrate this tomorrow, because today I am coughing like an old sheep, and my nurse, Terentievna, will not give me any peace. "Lie down," she says, "my master, and have a drink of tea. . . ." I know why she is so persistent: she wants some tea herself. Well, all right! Why not let the poor old woman extract every possible benefit from her master? — while it is not too late.

March 23

Winter again. Snow is falling in great clumps.

Superfluous, superfluous . . . I have thought of an excellent word. The farther I penetrate into myself, the more closely I examine all my past life, the more am I convinced of the stern truth of that expression. Superfluous — precisely. To other people that word is not applicable. People are bad, good, intelligent, stupid, pleasant, and unpleasant; but superfluous . . . no. Yet understand me: even without these people the universe could manage quite well — of course; but uselessness is not their main quality, not their distinctive characteristic, and when you speak of them the word "superfluous" is not the first to come to the tongue. But I — about me it is not possible to say anything else: I am superfluous, and that is all there is to it. A supernumerary man, and nothing more. Evidently nature did not reckon on my turning up, and so she treated me as an unexpected and uninvited guest. Not without reason did one wit, a great lover of the game of preference, say of me that my mother had forfeited a trick. I am writing of myself calmly, without any spleen. . . .

The question is settled. All my life I continually found my place occupied, perhaps because I sought that place where I should not have sought it. I was mistrustful, shy, peevish, like all ailing people; and, moreover, probably owing to excessive self-esteem or in consequence of some unsatisfactory allocation of my being between my feelings and thoughts — and the expression of those feelings and thoughts — I came up against a senseless, incomprehensible, and invincible obstacle. And when I decided to conquer that obstacle by force, to break down that barrier, my movements, the expression of my face, all my being acquired a look of agonizing strain. I not only seemed to be, I actually became unnatural and tense. I myself felt that and hastened to return to my normal state. At such moments a terrible fear arose within me. I analyzed myself down to the last tiny thread, compared myself with others, recalled the least glances, smiles, and words of the people before whom I desired to display myself, interpreted everything in a bad sense, laughed venomously at my own pretensions to "be like everybody else"; and suddenly, in the middle of the laugh, sadly let myself go quite flat, fell into an absurd despondency. And then I returned myself to my previous state. In a word, I spun around like a squirrel in a wheel. Whole days were passed in this agonizing, fruitless activity. Well, now, please tell me, tell me yourself, who and what has any need of such a man? Why this happened to me, what was the cause of this painstaking fussing with my own self — who knows? Who can say?

I remember, one day I left Moscow in the diligence. The going was good, yet to the four-in-hand the driver harnessed yet a fifth horse. This unfortunate, this fifth, this quite useless horse, fastened untidily to the singletree by a thick, short rope, which mercilessly chafes its flank, rubs its tail, forces it to run in a very unnatural manner, and makes all its body look like a comma, always arouses my profound sympathy. I remarked to the driver that surely on this occasion it would have been possible to do without the fifth horse. . . . He was silent for a moment, wagged his head, lashed the animal a dozen times in succession across its meager back and under its swollen belly — and said, not without a sneer: "Why, but there it is; it's been tied on! And what the devil for?"

I too have simply been tied on! . . . But, thank goodness, the posthouse is not far away now.

Superfluous . . . I promised to demonstrate the justice of my opinion, and I shall keep my promise. I do not consider it necessary to recall a thousand details, everyday incidents and events, which, for that matter, in the eyes of any thinking man would serve as irrefutable proofs in my favor — I mean in favor of my view. It would be better for me to begin directly with one quite important event, after which I think no doubt whatever will remain of the exactitude of the word "superfluous." I repeat: I have no intention of going into details, but I cannot pass over in silence one quite curious and remarkable circumstance: namely, my friends' (even I had friends) strange behavior toward me whenever I happened to meet them or even when I called on them. They seemed to be made to feel awkward. When they advanced to welcome me they smiled not quite naturally, looked not into my eyes, nor at my feet, as some do, but more often at my cheeks, hurriedly pronounced: "Ah! Good morning, Chulkaturin!" (Fate has favored me with such a name) or "Ah! and here's Chulkaturin," and at once stepped away or even remained motionless for a time, as though trying to recall something.

I noticed all this because I am not lacking in penetration and the gift of observation; I am not at all stupid; quite amusing, and not quite ordinary thoughts sometimes enter my head. But as I am a superfluous man and have imposed an internal constraint on myself, it is fearful for me to express my thoughts, especially as I know in advance that I shall express them very badly. I sometimes wonder how people can talk, and so simply, so easily. . . . What audacity, you know! I mean, I have to confess it, even I, despite my constraint, quite often had an itching tongue. But really I gave vent to speech only in my youth, and in my more mature years I almost always succeeded in checking myself. I would say in an undertone: "Well now, we would do better to be silent for a moment," and I would calm down. We are all clever at silence; our women especially have been greatly taken by it. Some exalted Russian maiden will be so potently silent that even in a man prepared for such a spectacle it is capable of producing a slight shiver and a cold sweat. But this is not my subject, and it is not for me to criticize others. I set about the story I promised.

Some years ago, owing to a combination of quite insignificant, but for me highly important circumstances, I had to spend about six months in the county town of O—. This town is built entirely on a slope, and is built very inconveniently. It has about eight hundred inhabitants, of more than usual poverty, and the little houses are like nothing on earth. Along the main street, as a pretext for a roadway, here and there menacing slabs of unhewn limestone show whitely, with the result that even the peasants' carts drive round them. In the very center of the astonishingly untidy square is a tiny, yellow erection with dark holes, and in the holes people wearing large peaked caps sit and pretend to be trading. Right outside it is an extraordinarily tall multicolored pole, and by this pole, for order's sake, on the instructions of the authorities, a cart of yellow hay stands and one official chicken struts about. In a word, in the town of O— life is excellent. During the first few days of my stay in this town I all but went out of my mind with boredom. I must say of myself that although, of course, I am a superfluous man, it is not by my own choice. I am sickly myself, but I cannot stand anything sickly. . . . I would not be at all averse to happiness, I have even tried to approach it from one side and another. . . . And so it is not surprising that I too can be bored, like any other mortal. I was in the town of O— on official business. . . .

Terentievna is absolutely determined to wear me out. Here is a specimen of our conversation:

Terentievna: "Oh, sir! what are you always writing for? It isn't good for you to write."

I: "But I'm bored, Terentievna."

She: "You have a drink of tea and lie down. If God wills, you'll have a little sweat and get a little sleep."

I: "But I don't want to sleep."

She: "Ah, master, what are you saying? For the Lord's sake! Lie down now, lie down; it's better that way."

I: "I shall die in any case, Terentievna!"

She: "God preserve and forgive! . . . Well, will you order some tea?"

I: "I shan't live through the week, Terentievna!"

She: "Oh, master, what are you saying? . . . Then I'll go and get the samovar going."

O decrepit, yellow, toothless creature! So am I not a human being even to you?

March 24. A cracking frost

On the very day of my arrival in the town of O— my above-mentioned official business made it necessary for me to call on a certain Kirila Matveevich Ozhogin, one of the chief officials in the county. But I made his acquaintance, or, as we say, made friends with him, only two weeks later. His house was on the main street and was distinguished from all the others by its size, its painted roof, and two lions at the gates, of the species that look uncommonly like the unfortunate dogs whose habitat is Moscow. These lions in themselves showed that Ozhogin was a man of affluence. And in fact he owned four hundred peasant souls. He received all the best people of the town of O— and had the reputation of being hospitable. He was also called on by the town governor, an unusually bulky man who looked as though cut from long-lying material, who drove in a two-horse ginger-colored droshky. And he was called on by other officials: by the lawyer, a jaundiced and malevolent creature; by the surveyor, a wit, of German extraction, with a Tatar face; by the officer of communications, a tender soul, a singer, but a gossip; and by the former marshal of the county, a gentleman with dyed hair, a swelling shirt-front, tight-fitting pantaloons, and that most noble expression which is peculiar to people who have been submitted to trials. He was also called on by two landowners, friends inseparable, both of them no longer young and even showing signs of wear. The younger of these landowners constantly annihilated the elder, and always closed his friend's mouth with the same protest: "Do stop it, Sergei Sergeich, where are you getting to? Why, you write the word 'cork' with a 'k.' . . . Yes, gentlemen," he would go on with all the fire of conviction, turning to the others present, "Sergei Sergeich writes not 'cork,' but 'kork.' " And everybody present laughed, although in all probability not one of them was distinguished by any particular gift for spelling. But the unfortunate Sergei Sergeich lapsed into silence and bowed his head with a fading smile. But I forget that my days are numbered, I am describing things too minutely. And so, without further circumstantial details, Ozhogin was married, he had a daughter, Yelizaveta Kirillovna, and with this daughter I fell in love.

Ozhogin himself was a commonplace sort of man, neither bad nor good, and his wife was like a perennial chickling; but their daughter did not take after her parents. She was very good-looking, vivacious, and of a gentle character. Her gray, gleaming eyes beamed good-naturedly and frankly below her childishly raised eyebrows; she smiled almost continually, and laughed too, quite often. Her fresh voice sounded very pleasant; she moved easily, swiftly, and blushed merrily. She did not dress with any excess of elegance; only simple dresses suited her. In general I was not quick at making acquaintances, and if I found myself at ease with anyone from the beginning — a thing that, I may mention, hardly ever happened — I confess that this was greatly in favor of the new acquaintance. Toward women I did not know how to behave at all, and in their presence I either scowled and adopted an infuriated look, or bared my teeth in the most stupid manner and grew tongue-tied in my embarrassment. With

Yelizaveta Kirillovna, on the other hand, I felt completely at home from our very first meeting. This is how it came about.

I went one day to see Ozhogin before dinner, asked if he was at home, and was told: "He's at home, dressing; please come into the hall." I went into the hall and saw a girl in a white dress standing at the window with her back toward me, holding a cage in her hand. As usual, I felt a little awkward; none the less I did nothing, only coughed for the sake of decorum. The girl turned round swiftly — so swiftly that her curls struck her in the face. She saw me, bowed, and with a smile showed me a little box half filled with seed. "May I go on?" I, of course, as is correct in such circumstances, first bent my head and simultaneously swiftly bent and straightened my knee (just as though someone had struck me from behind in the hock, a movement that, as is known, is a sign of excellent breeding and affable ease of manners). Then I smiled, raised my hand, and passed it cautiously and gently through the air a couple of times. The girl at once turned away, pulled a little board out of the cage, began to scrape it vigorously with a knife, and suddenly, without changing her position, said the following words:

"This is Papa's bullfinch. . . . Do you like bullfinches?"

"I prefer siskins," I replied, not without effort.

"And I like siskins too; but look at him, what a nice little bird he is! Look, he's not afraid." (What amazed me was that I was not afraid.) "Come closer. His name is Popka."

I went up to her and bent to look at the bird. "He is a dear, isn't he?" She turned her face to me; but we were standing so close to each other that she had to throw her head back a little in order to look at me with her gleaming eyes. I looked at her: all her youthful, rosy face was smiling with such friendliness that I too smiled and all but laughed with pleasure.

The door opened; Mr. Ozhogin entered. I at once went to him and began to talk to him very easily. I myself don't know how it came about that I remained to dinner, sat on all the evening, and the next day Ozhogin's footman, a lanky and purblind fellow, even smiled at me as a friend of the family while he relieved me of my greatcoat.

To find a shelter, to build oneself at least a temporary nest, to know the comfort of everyday relations and habits — this happiness I, a superfluous man, without family memories, had not ex-

perienced hitherto. If anything about me had the least reminis-
cence of a flower, and if that comparison were not so trite, I
would have dared to say that from that day I blossomed in my
soul. Everything in me and around me changed in an instant. All
my life was irradiated with love — absolutely all my life, down to
the smallest details, like a dark, neglected room into which a
candle has been carried. I lay down to sleep and rose again, I
dressed, I breakfasted, I smoked a pipe, all differently from before. I even danced a little as I walked, really I did, as though
wings had suddenly sprouted from my shoulders. I, I remember,
was not for a single moment unaware of the feeling that Yelizaveta Kirillovna inspired in me; and from the first day I loved her
passionately, and from the very first day I knew that I was in
love. During the following three weeks I saw her every day.
Those three weeks were the happiest time in my life; but the
memory of them is oppressive. I cannot think of them in isolation: I involuntarily recall what followed them, and a venomous
sorrow slowly takes possession of the heart that a moment before
was moved with tenderness.

When a man is very happy his brain, as is well known, functions very little. A calm and joyous feeling, a feeling of satisfaction, penetrates into all his being; he is engulfed by it; his
consciousness of personality vanishes — he felicitates, as badly educated poets say. But when, at last, this "enchantment" passes, a
man sometimes feels annoyed and regretful that amid his happiness he studied himself so little, that by way of meditation and
memory he did not double, did not continue his enjoyment — as
though a "felicitating" man has any time, and even finds it worth
while, to meditate on his feelings. A happy man is like a fly in the
sunlight. And so I too, when I recall those three weeks, find it
almost impossible to retain an exact, definite impression, especially
as during all this time nothing of any note occurred between us.
. . . Those twenty days are to me something warm, young, and
scented, a lighter streak in my dim and gray little life. My memory suddenly grows inexorably faithful and clear only from the
moment when, to use the words of those same badly educated
authors, the blows of fate fell upon me.

Yes; those three weeks. . . . For that matter, they were not
entirely without lasting impress on my mind. Sometimes, when I
happen to think for long about that time, other memories sud-

denly float up from the gloom of the past — just as stars unexpectedly emerge in the evening sky to meet the attentive gaze. One walk especially, in a wood outside the town, has remained in my memory. There were four of us: old Mrs. Ozhogina, Liza, myself, and a certain Bizmionkov, a petty official of the town, a flaxen-haired, kind, and quiet little man. I shall have more to say about him later. Mr. Ozhogin himself had remained at home: he had a headache through oversleeping. The day was marvelous, warm and still. It has to be observed that pleasure-gardens and social walks are not to the mind of the Russian. In the so-called public gardens of the provincial towns you will never meet a living soul at any season of the year, except perhaps some old woman, who sits down with a groan on a sun-baked green bench close to a large tree, and even then only if there is no greasy seat under a near-by gateway. But if there happens to be a scraggy little birch wood in the proximity of the town, on Sundays and holidays the merchants and sometimes the officials readily drive out to it with samovars, pasties, and watermelons; they set out all this profusion of good things on the dusty grass right by the road, sit down in a circle, and eat and drink tea in the sweat of their faces until the very evening. It was exactly this type of wood that existed just over a mile from the town of O—.

We drove there after dinner, drank our fill of tea, as is usual, and then set out, all four of us, to stroll through the wood. Bizmionkov took old Mrs. Ozhogina by the arm, I took Liza. The day was now declining toward evening. At that time I was in the very zenith of my first love (not more than two weeks had passed since the day of our first acquaintance), in that state of passionate and attentive adoration when all your soul innocently and involuntarily follows every movement of the beloved being; when you can never be satiated with her presence, or listen too much to her voice; when you smile and look like a child restored to health, and the least experienced of men can see at one glance a hundred paces away what is happening to you. Until that day I had never had the chance to hold Liza by the arm. I walked beside her, quietly strolling over the green grass. A light breeze literally fluttered around us, between the white trunks of the birches, occasionally flinging her hat ribbon into my face. I persistently watched her gaze until, at last, she gaily turned to me, and we smiled at each other. The birds twittered approvingly above us, the blue sky shone graciously through the delicate foliage. My head was swimming with an excess of delight. I hasten to remark that Liza was not in the least in love with me. She liked me; she never shunned anybody; but not I was destined to disturb her childlike tranquillity. At this period she was seventeen. . . . And meanwhile, in my very presence, this very same evening that gentle internal ferment began within her which portends the child's transformation into a woman. . . . I witnessed that transformation of all her being, that innocent bewilderment, that anxious meditation; I was the first to observe that sudden gentleness of gaze, that ringing uncertainty of voice, and — O fool, O superfluous man! — for a whole week after I was not ashamed to assume that I, I was the cause of the change!

This is how it happened.

We walked for quite a long time, until evening had set in, and we talked little. I was silent, like all inexperienced lovers, and in all probability she had nothing to say to me. But she seemed to be meditating on something and shook her head in a peculiar way, thoughtfully biting a leaf she had plucked. From time to time she started off in front, with such resolution . . . and then she suddenly halted, waited for me, and looked about her with raised eyebrows and an abstracted smile. The evening before, she and I had read *The Caucasian Prisoner* [1] together. With what avidity she had listened to me, resting her little face in both hands and leaning her breast against the table! I began to talk about that reading; she reddened, asked me whether I had given the finch some hempseed before our departure, began to sing some song aloud, and suddenly fell silent. On one side the wood ended in quite a steep and lofty cliff; at the bottom flowed a winding little river, and beyond it endless meadows, here and there intersected with gulleys, and now slightly rising, like waves, then broadly spreading like a tablecloth, stretched into the boundless distance. Liza and I were the first to reach the edge of the wood; Bizmionkov was left behind with the mother. We came out at the edge, halted, and both involuntarily screwed up our eyes: directly in front of us, amid an incandescent haze, the livid, enormous sun was setting. Half the sky was burning and reddening; crimson rays struck across the meadows, casting a lurid reflection even on the shady sides of the gulleys, lying like molten lead on the river wherever

[1] A narrative poem by Pushkin. (Tr.)

it was not concealed beneath overhanging bushes, and seeming to be pressing into the heart of the cliff and the wood. We stood flooded with the burning refulgence. I am not capable of communicating all the passionate exultation of that picture. They say that a blind man once imagined the color of red as a trumpet sound. I don't know how far this comparison is just, but certainly there was something challenging in that flaming gold of the evening air, in the purple gleam of the sky and the earth. I cried out with rapture and turned at once to Liza. She was gazing straight at the sun. I remember the conflagration of the sunset was reflected as tiny points of fire in her eyes. She was overwhelmed, was profoundly moved. She made no response to my exclamation; for long she did not stir; she stood with head hanging. . . . I stretched out my hand to her; she turned away from me and suddenly burst into tears. I looked at her with a secret, almost joyous amazement. . . .

Bizmionkov's voice sounded a couple of paces away. Liza swiftly wiped away her tears and looked at me with an irresolute smile. Her mother, resting on her fair-haired escort's arm, came out of the wood; they too admired the spectacle. Liza's mother asked her something, and I, I remember, involuntarily trembled when she answered in a broken voice, like a cracked glass. Meanwhile the sun set, the glow began to fade. We walked back. I again took Liza by the arm. It was still light in the wood, and I could distinguish her features clearly. She was embarrassed and did not raise her eyes. The blush that had suffused all her face did not vanish: it was as though she were still standing in the radiance of the setting sun. . . . Her hand gently touched mine. For long I could not say anything, so violently was my heart beating within me. In the distance the carriage appeared through the trees; the coachman was driving to meet us at a walking pace along the crumbling sandy road.

"Lizaveta Kirillovna," I said at last, "why did you weep?"

"I don't know," she replied after a brief silence, and looked at me with her mild, still moist eyes — I thought their look seemed changed — and she was silent again.

"I see you love nature. . . ." I continued. That was not what I had wanted to say at all, and even that phrase I could hardly stammer out. She shook her head. I could not say another word

The Diary of a Superfluous Man

. . . I was waiting for something . . . not an avowal — how could I! I was waiting for a trustful glance, a question. . . . But Liza gazed at the ground and was silent. I repeated yet again in an undertone: "Why?" and did not get an answer. I could see that she was feeling awkward, almost ashamed.

Fifteen minutes later we were sitting in the carriage and approaching the town. The horses moved at a fast trot; we sped swiftly through the darkening, humid air. I suddenly began to talk a great deal, incessantly addressing myself first to Bizmionkov, then to Mrs. Ozhogina, and did not look at Liza. But I was able to observe that her gaze rested on me from time to time as she sat in the corner of the carriage. On arriving home she roused herself; she did not want to read with me, however, and soon retired to bed. The change, that change of which I have spoken, had been accomplished in her. She had ceased to be a girl, she too had begun to wait — like me — for something. She did not wait long.

But that night I returned to my apartments completely enchanted. The vague, was it presentiment or suspicion? — that had stirred within me had vanished. The sudden constraint in Liza's behavior toward me I ascribed to maidenly bashfulness, timidity. . . . Had I not read a thousand times in innumerable works that the first arrival of love always agitates and frightens a maiden? I felt extremely happy, and was already mentally making various plans. . . .

If anyone had said into my ear: "You're lying, my friend! Something quite different awaits you, brother. You are to die in loneliness, in a wretched little house, to the unbearable grumbling of an old woman who can hardly wait for your death in order to sell your boots for a trifling sum. . . ."

Yes, involuntarily one says with a certain Russian philosopher: "How to know what you don't know?" Till tomorrow.

March 25. A white winter's day

I have reread what I wrote yesterday, and all but tore up the whole book. It seems to me that I am telling my story too expansively and too fondly. For that matter, as all my other memories of this time are without joy, except that peculiar kind of joy which Lermontov had in mind when he said that it is pleasurable and painful to disturb the sores of old wounds, why shouldn't I indulge myself? But one should have respect for one's honor too. And so I continue without any display of fondness.

For a whole week after that walk outside the town my position did not show any essential improvement, though the transformation in Liza grew more obvious with every day. I, as I have said, interpreted this change in the manner most favorable to myself. . . . The misfortune of lonely and shy people — shy from self-esteem — consists just in the circumstance that, although they have eyes and even stare those eyes out, they see nothing, or see everything in a false light, as if through tinted spectacles. Their own thoughts and observations hinder them at every step. At the beginning of our acquaintance Liza turned to me trustfully and easily, like a child; perhaps in her attitude to me there was even something still more simple, something of childish attachment. . . . But when that strange, almost abrupt transformation was accomplished within her, she, after a brief bewilderment, felt constrained in my presence, she involuntarily turned away from me, and at the same time grew sad and thoughtful. . . . She waited — for what? She herself did not know, but I . . . as I have said, I rejoiced in this transformation. By God, I all but swooned, as they say, with rapture. For that matter, I am prepared to agree that in my place any other man might have been deluded. . . . Who is without self-esteem? I need not say that all this became clear to me only when I had to fold my broken wings, which were weak enough already.

The misunderstanding that arose between me and Liza continued a whole week — and there is nothing surprising in that: I have had to be witness of misunderstandings that lasted for year after year. And, indeed, who was it who said that the truth is the only reality? A lie is just as viable as truth, if not more so. Certainly, I remember that even during that week a worm occasionally stirred within me. . . . But a man like me, a solitary individual, I will say again, is just as incapable of understanding what is going on inside him as of that which is being accomplished before his eyes. And besides, is love a natural feeling? Is it inherent in man to love? Love is a sickness; and no law has been laid down for sickness. Granted that at times my heart constricted unpleasantly; but then, everything within me was turned upside down. In such a case how can you demand that a man should

The Diary of a Superfluous Man

recognize what is satisfactory and what not, or the cause, the meaning of every separate sensation?

But in any case all these misunderstandings, presentiments, and hopes were resolved in the following manner.

One day, it was in the morning, about twelve o'clock, as I entered Mr. Ozhogin's vestibule I heard an unknown, ringing voice in the hall. Then the door was thrown open and, accompanied by the master, a tall and well-built man of about twenty-five appeared, swiftly flung round his shoulders his military greatcoat, which had been lying on a bench, took an affectionate leave of Kirila Matveich, carelessly touched his peaked cap as he passed me, and disappeared with a jingle of spurs.

"Who is that?" I asked Ozhogin.

"Prince N.," he answered with a preoccupied air. "He's been sent from Petersburg to take over the recruits. But where have all the servants vanished to?" he continued crossly. "No one handed him his coat."

We entered the hall.

"Has he been here long?" I asked.

"They say he arrived yesterday evening. I offered him a room with us, but he refused. But he seems to be a very charming fellow."

"Has he spent long with you?"

"About an hour. He asked me to introduce him to Olimpiada Nikitinichna."

"And did you?"

"Of course."

"And to Lizaveta Kirillovna — ?"

"He made her acquaintance too, of course."

I was silent.

"Is he going to stay here long, do you know?"

"Yes; I think he will have to remain here a couple of weeks and more."

And Kirila Matveich hurried off to dress.

I walked up and down the hall several times. I don't remember that Prince N.'s arrival made any special impression on me at the time, apart from that unpleasant feeling that customarily takes possession of us when a new face appears in our domestic circle. Possibly with this feeling went a touch of the jealousy felt by a shy and obscure Moscow man for a brilliant Petersburg

771

officer. "The Prince," I thought, "is a man from the capital; he will look down on us. . . ." I had not seen him for more than a minute, but I had been able to note that he was good-looking, adroit, and free and easy. After walking about the hall for some time I finally halted before a mirror, took a comb out of my pocket, gave my hair a look of picturesque negligence, and, as sometimes happens, was suddenly sunk in contemplation of my own features. I remember my attention was anxiously concentrated on my nose; its rather soft and indefinite outline did not give me any special satisfaction — when suddenly, in the dark depths of the sloping glass, which reflected almost all the room, a door was opened and Liza's graceful figure appeared.

I don't know why, but I did not stir and did not change the expression on my face. Liza craned her neck, stared at me attentively, and, raising her eyebrows, biting her lips, and holding her breath, like someone who is glad he has not been noticed, cautiously fell back and quietly drew the door open behind her. The door creaked a little. She started and froze still. . . . I did not move. . . . She reached for the handle again and vanished. There could be no possibility of doubt: the expression on her face at the sight of me, an expression that indicated nothing but a desire to retire unnoticed, to avoid an unpleasant meeting, the sudden flash of satisfaction that I managed to catch in her eyes when she thought she had succeeded in slipping away unobserved — all these things said only too clearly: this girl does not love me. For long, long I could not remove my gaze from the dumb, immobile door, which again appeared as a white patch in the depths of the mirror. I felt like smiling at my own strained figure. I drooped my head, returned home, and flung myself on the sofa. I felt unusually disheartened, so disheartened that I could not weep. . . . And what was there to weep over? . . . "Surely not?" I affirmed incessantly as I lay like a corpse on my back, with my hands folded on my chest. "Surely not?" How do you like that "Surely not?"

March 26. A thaw

When next day, after much vacillation and with sinking heart, I entered the Ozhogins' familiar reception hall, I was no longer the man they had known for the past three weeks. All my former habits, which under the influence of a new feeling I had begun to live down, reappeared and took possession of me, like masters returning to their homes. People like me are guided in general not so much by positive facts as by their own impressions. I, who no longer ago than yesterday had been dreaming of "the raptures of mutual love," now had no doubt whatever of my own "unhappiness," and was in utter despair, though even I could not find any sensible pretext for my despair. I could hardly be jealous of Prince N., and no matter what qualities he abounded with, his arrival was not in itself sufficient to put an end to Liza's predilection for me all at once. . . . But then, had any such predilection ever existed? I recalled the past. "But what of the walk in the wood?" I asked myself. "But what of her expression in the mirror?" "But," I continued, "the walk in the wood, I think . . ." "Pah, my God, what an insignificant creature I am!" I exclaimed aloud at last. This was the kind of half-expressed, half-formulated thought that, returning a thousand times, circled in my head like a monotonous whirlwind. I repeat, when I called on Ozhogin next day, I was the same mistrustful, suspicious, strange person I had been since childhood. . . .

I found all the family in the reception hall; Bizmionkov also was sitting there, in a corner. They all seemed in good spirits; Ozhogin especially beamed, and with his very first words he informed me that Prince N. had spent all the previous evening with them. Liza greeted me calmly. "Well," I said to myself, "now I understand why you are in good spirits." I confess that this second visit of the Prince rather puzzled me. I hadn't expected it. In general, people like me expect everything in the world except that which should happen in the natural order of things. I sulked and adopted the air of an injured but magnanimous man; I wanted to punish Liza with my disfavor, from which, by the way, it should follow that none the less I had not completely given up hope. They say that in certain cases, when you are really loved, it is quite helpful to torment the adored being. But in my position that would have been inexpressibly stupid: in her utter innocence Liza did not pay any attention to me. Only Mrs. Ozhogina noticed my solemn taciturnity and anxiously inquired after my health. Of course I replied with a bitter smile that, thank God, I was quite well. Ozhogin continued to expatiate on his guest. But, noticing that I replied reluctantly, he addressed himself more to Bizmionkov, who was listening to him with greater attention. While he was talking, a manservant entered and announced Prince N.'s arrival. Ozhogin jumped up and ran to meet him; Liza, on whom I at once fixed an eagle gaze, reddened with delight and fidgeted on her chair. The Prince entered, perfumed, gay, gracious. . . .

As I am not composing a novel for a benevolent reader, but am writing simply for my own satisfaction, there is no reason why I should resort to the usual stratagems of the littérateurs. I shall say at once, without further procrastination, that from the first day she met him Liza fell passionately in love with the Prince; and the Prince took a fancy to her, partly because he had nothing to do, partly through a habit he had of turning women's heads, but also partly because Liza was in fact a very pleasant creature. There was nothing surprising in the circumstance that they fell in love with each other. In all probability he had not expected to find such a pearl in such a filthy shell (I am referring to the God-forsaken town of O—), and even in her dreams she had never seen anything in the least resembling this brilliant, intelligent, captivating aristocrat.

After the first greetings Ozhogin introduced me to the Prince, who was very courteous to me. Indeed, he was always courteous to everybody and, despite the immeasurable chasm between him and our obscure county circle, he had the gift not only of setting people at ease, but even of appearing as though he were our equal and only happened to live in St. Petersburg.

That first evening. . . . Oh, that first evening! In the happy days of our childhood our teachers taught us to admire and imitate the valiant endurance of that young Lacedæmonian who, having stolen a fox and concealed it beneath his garment, allowed it to devour all his entrails without once crying out, so preferring death itself to dishonor. . . . I cannot find any better comparison to convey my inexpressible sufferings during all that evening, when I first saw the Prince at Liza's side. My constantly strained smile, my agonizing keenness of observation, my stupid silence, my yearning and futile desire to leave, all these were probably very remarkable in their kind. More than one fox devoured my entrails: jealousy, envy, the sense of my own insignificance, and helpless anger, all gnawed at me. I could not but admit that the Prince was indeed a very charming young man. . . . I watched him with consuming eyes; in truth, I think I forgot to blink as

The Diary of a Superfluous Man

I gazed at him. He did not talk only to Liza, but of course he talked only for her. I must have greatly bored him. . . . In all probability he quickly guessed that he had to do with an eliminated lover; but, out of pity for me, and profoundly conscious of my complete impotence, he treated me with unusual mildness. You can imagine how that affronted me!

During the evening, I remember, I attempted to make amends; I (do not laugh at me, whoever you may be whose eyes chance to fall on these lines, especially as this was my last dream) — I, believe me, in the midst of my many and varied torments, suddenly imagined that Liza was trying to punish me for my haughty coldness at the beginning of my visit, that she was angry with me and was flirting with the Prince only out of pique. I seized a suitable moment and, going up to her with a humble but gracious smile, muttered: "Enough, forgive me. . . . Besides, I'm not behaving like this because I'm afraid." And then, without waiting for her reply, I abruptly adopted an extremely animated and jaunty expression, smiled wryly, stretched my arm above my head in the direction of the ceiling (I remember I wanted to adjust my neckerchief), and even prepared to spin round on one leg, as though wishing to say: "It's all over, I'm in good spirits, let's all be in good spirits." However, I didn't spin round on one leg, for I was afraid of falling, owing to some unnatural petrifaction of my knees. . . . Liza did not understand me at all, stared into my face in amazement, hurriedly smiled as though wanting to get away from me as quickly as possible, and went back to the Prince. With all my blindness and stupidity, I could not but confess to myself that she had not been angry at all and had not been vexed with me at that moment: she simply hadn't even been thinking of me. The blow was decisive; my last hopes collapsed with a crash, just as a sheet of ice caught in the spring sunlight suddenly disintegrates into little pieces. I was completely overwhelmed at the very first pressure, and, like the Prussians at Jena, lost everything at once, in one day. No, she had not been angry with me. . . .

Alas, quite the reverse! She herself — I could see that — was being washed around as by a wave. Like a young tree already half cut off from the bank, she avidly leaned over the torrent, ready to yield to it forever not only the first blossoms of her spring, but all her life. Anyone who has happened to be the witness of such an infatuation has known some bitter moments, if he loved and was not loved in return. I shall always remember that consuming attention, that tender gaiety, that innocent self-oblivion, that gaze, still childlike and already womanly, that happy, blossoming smile, which never left the parted lips and the crimsoned cheeks. . . . Everything of which Liza had had a vague presentiment during our walk in the wood had now come to pass. And she, yielding herself entirely to love, at the same time grew completely still, and shone like young wine that has ceased to ferment because its time has come. . . .

I had the patience to sit through that first evening and all the following evenings — right to their end! I could have no hope in anything. With every day Liza and the Prince grew more and more attached to each other. But I had absolutely lost all sense of my own dignity and could not tear myself away from the spectacle of my own unhappiness. I remember one day I attempted to refrain from going; in the morning I gave myself my word of honor to remain at home. And at eight o'clock in the evening (usually I went out at seven) I jumped up like a madman, put on my hat, and, panting, ran to Kirila Matveich's reception room. My position was extremely awkward: I was stubbornly silent; sometimes I did not utter a sound for days at a time. As I have already said, I was never distinguished by eloquence; but now all the sense I had in me seemed to fly out in the Prince's presence, and I was left as bare as a falcon. And with it all, when alone I forced my unfortunate brain to work so hard, pondering over all that I had observed or noticed during the previous day, that when I returned to the Ozhogins', I hardly had the strength to continue my observations. As a sick man I was shown mercy; I saw that. Every morning I made a new, final decision, usually agonizingly hatched out during the past sleepless night; at one time I prepared to have an explanation with Liza, to give her friendly advice. . . . But when I chanced to find myself alone with her, my tongue suddenly ceased to function, as though it had gone stiff, and both of us anxiously looked for the arrival of a third person. Then I wanted to flee, forever, of course, leaving a letter behind for the object of my devotion, a letter filled with reproaches; and one day I even began that letter. But my sense of justice had not completely faded; I realized that I had no right to reproach anybody with anything, and I threw my missive into the fire.

The Diary of a Superfluous Man

At one moment I magnanimously offered all myself in sacrifice, blessed Liza in her happy love, and from my corner smiled at the Prince mildly and amiably. But the hard-hearted lovers not only did not thank me for my sacrifice; they did not even notice it and evidently had no need of either my blessings or my smiles. . . . Then, in my chagrin, I abruptly passed to the exactly contrary state of mind. I promised myself that, wrapping myself in my cloak like a Spaniard, I would strike down the fortunate rival from around a corner, and took a bestial delight in imagining Liza's despair. . . . But, to begin with, there were very few such corners in the town of O—, and, secondly, a plank fence, a lantern, a policeman in the distance . . . no, at that sort of corner it was somehow more decent to trade in doughnuts than shed human blood. I must confess that among other means for effecting my salvation, as I very indefinitely expressed my thoughts when I talked with myself, I did even think of speaking to Ozhogin — in order to draw this nobleman's attention to his daughter's dangerous situation, to the mournful consequences of her frivolity. . . . One day I even began to talk to him about a certain ticklish subject, but I spoke so cunningly and obscurely that he listened and listened to me and suddenly, as though just waking up, rubbed his hand vigorously and swiftly all over his face, not sparing his nose, then snorted and walked away. I need not say that, having taken this decision, I assured myself that I was acting from the most disinterested of motives; I desired the general good, I was performing the duty of a friend of the family. . . . But I venture to think that even if Kirila Matveich had not cut short my outpourings I would not have had the courage to finish my harangue. Sometimes, with the gravity of an ancient merchant, I took to weighing up the Prince's qualities; sometimes I comforted myself with the hope that it was only temporary, that Liza would come to herself, that her love was not real love. . . . Oh, no! In a word, I cannot think of a single thought that I did not play with at that time. Only one resource, I confess openly, never entered my head: namely, not once did I think of taking my own life. Why I didn't think of that I don't know. . . . Perhaps even then I had a presentiment that in any case I was not to live long.

It is understandable that in such unpropitious circumstances my conduct, my treatment of other people, were more than ever

777

distinguished by unnaturalness and strain. Even old Mrs. Ozhogina — that innately stupid creature — began to shun me and
at times did not know how to approach me. Bizmionkov, who
had always been polite and ready to do services, avoided me.
Even then I had the impression that in him I had a fellow sufferer,
that he too was in love with Liza. But he never responded to my
hints, and in general talked with me only reluctantly. The Prince
treated him very amiably; the Prince, one may say, respected
him. Neither Bizmionkov nor I hindered the Prince and Liza;
but he did not grow antagonistic to them as I did, did not look
like a wolf or a sacrifice, and readily joined them when they
desired him to. True, in such cases he was not distinguished by
any jocularity, but his cheerfulness had always been of a quiet
kind.

Thus about two weeks passed. The Prince was not only good-
looking and intelligent; he played the piano, sang, could draw
quite well, and could tell a story. His stories, drawn from the
higher circles of life in the capital, always made a strong impression on the listeners, all the stronger because he did not appear
to attach any special significance to them. . . .

The consequence of this simple artifice of his, if you like to
call it so, was that during his brief residence in the town of O—
he absolutely enchanted all the local society. It is always very
easy for a man from a higher circle to enchant our steppe nobility.
The Prince's frequent visits to the Ozhogins (he spent whole
evenings with them) of course aroused the jealousy of the other
noblemen and officials. But the Prince, who was a man of the
world and intelligent, did not overlook a single one of them,
visited them all, said at least one kindly word to all the ladies
and young ladies, allowed them to feed him on monstrously
heavy dishes and to give him wretched wines with high-sounding
names to drink — in a word, he behaved excellently, prudently,
and adroitly. Prince N. was in general a man of gay disposition,
convivial, amiable by nature, and also, be it added, by calculation;
so how could he fail to be a complete success, and in every respect?

From the moment of his arrival everybody in the house found
that time flew past with extraordinary speed; everything went
well; old Ozhogin, though he pretended that he noticed nothing,
in all probability rubbed his hands in secret at the thought of
having such a son-in-law. The Prince himself was managing the

whole affair very quietly and decorously. When suddenly, one unexpected occurrence . . .

Till tomorrow. I am tired now. These memories irritate me even on the edge of the grave. Terentievna decided today that the tip of my nose is already peaked; and that, they say, is a bad sign.

March 27. The thaw continues

Affairs had reached the position above described, the Prince and Liza were in love with each other, the old Ozhogins were waiting for something to happen, Bizmionkov was present at all this — more could not be said of him — I was struggling like a fish against the ice, and watching so far as was in my power. I remember I now set myself the task of at least not allowing Liza to perish in the toils of a seducer and so had begun to pay special attention to the maids and the fateful "back door." Though, on the other hand, sometimes I dreamed all night of how in due course I would stretch out my hand with touching magnanimity to the deluded victim and say to her: "The crafty fellow has betrayed you; but I am your faithful friend . . . we will forget the past and will be happy!" When suddenly all through the town spread the joyous news: in honor of the distinguished visitor the county marshal was intending to give a grand ball, to be held at his personal estate of Gornostayovka, also known as Gubnyakovo. All the officials and authorities of the town of O— received invitations, from the town governor down to the druggist, who was an unusually carbuncular German with stern pretensions to the ability to talk pure Russian, as the result of which he constantly and by no means aptly used strong expressions, such as "I, may the devil take me to himself, am an absolute lad today. . . ."

As usual, fearful preparations were undertaken. One shopkeeper who stocked cosmetics sold sixteen dark-blue boxes of pomade with the inscription "*A la jesmin*" and with a specifically Slavonic letter after the "n." The young ladies made themselves tight-fitting dresses with agonizing waists, and promontories jutting out at the front. On their own heads the mothers erected menacing embellishments in lieu of mobcaps. The bustling fathers were run off their hind legs, as the saying is. . . .

The longed-for day arrived at last. I was among those invited. It was reckoned to be six miles from the town to Gornostayovka.

Kirila Matveich offered me a place in his carriage, but I refused.
. . . In like manner punished children refuse their favorite food
at table, in order to have a good revenge on their parents. Moreover, I felt that my presence would be irksome to Liza. Bizmionkov took my place. The Prince drove in his own calashe, and I in
a wretched droshky that I hired at great expense for the solemn
occasion.

I shall not stop to describe that ball. Everything was as it
should be: the musicians playing in chorus, with trumpets more
than usually out of tune, the stupefied landowners with their inveterate families, the lilac ice, the slimy orgeat, the servants in
patched boots and knitted cotton gloves, the provincial lions with
convulsively grimacing faces, etc., etc. And all this little world
revolved around its sun, around the Prince. Lost in the crowd,
not noticed even by the forty-eight-year-old maidens with red
pimples on their foreheads and blue flowers on their crowns, I
constantly watched first the Prince, then Liza. She was very
nicely dressed and looked very beautiful that evening. They
only danced twice with each other (true, he had the mazurka
with her!),[1] but at least to *me* it seemed that some secret, unbroken communication existed between them. Not even looking at
her, not talking to her, he seemed continually to be turning to
her, to her alone; he was kind, and brilliant, and affable to others
— for her alone. She obviously regarded herself as the queen of
the ball — and of the beloved; her face simultaneously beamed
with childish joy and innocent pride, and then was abruptly lit
up with another, more profound feeling. She radiated happiness.
I noticed all this. . . . It was not the first time I had had the opportunity to observe them. . . . At first it greatly afflicted me,
then it seemed to move me, and finally it infuriated me. I suddenly
felt extremely angry and, I remember, was extremely delighted
at this new sensation and even conceived a certain respect for
myself. "We'll show them that we've not perished yet," I said
to myself.

When the first challenging sounds of the mazurka thundered
out I looked about me calmly, coldly and jauntily went up to
one long-faced young lady with a red and shining nose, a mouth
opened awkwardly as though left unbuttoned, and a scraggy
neck, like the neck of a double-bass — went up to her and, dryly

[1] The mazurka would last an hour or more. (Tr.)

clicking my heels, invited her to be my partner. She was wearing a rose-colored dress that looked as though it had only recently, and still not completely, faded; over her head quivered a discolored, despondent fly on an excessively broad copper spring, and all together this maiden was, if one may put it so, saturated with a kind of sour boredom and inveterate failure. All the evening she had not stirred from her place: no one had thought of asking her to dance. In the absence of any other lady, one sixteen-year-old fair-haired youngster was about to turn to this maiden, and did take a step toward her, but he thought better of it, looked about for a moment, and briskly vanished into the crowd. You can imagine the joyous astonishment with which she accepted my invitation! I triumphantly led her right through the hall, found two chairs, and sat down with her in the ring of the mazurka, as the tenth couple, almost opposite the Prince, who, of course, had been assigned the first place. The Prince, as I have said, had Liza for his partner. Neither I nor my lady was troubled with invitations to dance, so we had ample time for conversation. To tell the truth, my partner was not distinguished by any capacity for uttering words in coherent speech; she used her mouth more for executing a peculiar smile downward, which I had not previously observed, in the course of which she turned her eyes upward, as though some invisible force were elongating her face. But I had no need of her eloquence. Fortunately, I felt angry, and my partner did not inspire me with any feeling of timidity. I began to criticize everybody and everything in the world, especially attacking the youth of the metropolis and the Petersburg *mirliflores,* and finally let myself go so much that my partner gradually ceased to smile and, instead of turning her eyes up, began suddenly — out of astonishment, I suppose — to squint, and so queerly too, as though she had only just noticed that she had a nose on her face. The gentleman next to me, one of those lions I have already mentioned, threw glances at me more than once, and even turned to me with the expression of an actor who is supposed to awaken in an unknown country and has to convey: "You here too?"

For that matter, even while I sang away like a nightingale, as the saying is, I went on watching the Prince and Liza. They were continually being asked for a turn in the dance; but I suffered less when they were both dancing. And even when they were sitting side by side and talking to each other, smiling that gentle smile which never wishes to leave the faces of happy lovers, even then I was not troubled so much. But when Liza fluttered through the hall with some dashing fop, and the Prince, with her azure gauze scarf on his knees, thoughtfully followed her with his eyes as though enjoying his conquest — then, oh, then I felt unendurable torments and in my fury gave vent to such malicious remarks that both my partner's pupils were fixed on her nose! Meanwhile, the mazurka was drawing to an end. The dancers began to perform the figure known as *"la confidante."* In this figure a lady sits in the middle of the ring, chooses another lady as a confidante, and whispers into her ear the name of the gentleman with whom she wishes to dance. A gentleman leads other gentlemen up to her one after another; but the confidante rejects them all until, at last, the previously chosen lucky man arrives. Liza sat in the middle of the ring and selected the host's daughter, a maiden to be reckoned among those of whom one says: "God help them!" The Prince began to seek the chosen one. Having vainly presented at least ten young men (the host's daughter rejected them all with the pleasantest of smiles), he at last turned to me. Something extraordinary occurred within me at that moment; I literally blinked with all my body and wanted to refuse, but I got up and went. The Prince led me to Liza. . . . She did not even look at me. The host's daughter shook her head; the Prince turned to me and, presumably stimulated by the gooselike expression on my face, made me a deep bow. This derisive bow, this rejection, conveyed to me by a triumphant rival, his negligent smile, Liza's unconcerned inattention — all these things carried me away. . . . I drew closer to the Prince and whispered furiously: "You appear to be taking the liberty of laughing at me?"

He looked at me with contemptuous astonishment, took me by the arm again, and, acting as though he were escorting me to my seat, coldly replied: "What?"

"Yes, you, you!" I continued in a whisper, submitting to him none the less — in other words, going with him to my seat. "You; but I have no intention of allowing any vacuous Petersburg upstart . . ."

The Prince smiled coldly, almost condescendingly, squeezed my arm, and whispered: "I understand you; but this is not the

The Diary of a Superfluous Man

place; we'll talk about it later." He turned away, went up to Bizmionkov, and led him to Liza. The pale-faced petty official proved to be the chosen one. Liza rose to meet him.

Sitting beside my lady with the despondent fly on her head, I felt myself almost a hero. My heart was beating violently, my breast was heaving nobly beneath my starched shirt-front, I breathed deeply and rapidly. And suddenly I looked so grandly at the adjacent lion that he involuntarily twitched one little foot that he had turned toward me. Having dealt with this person, I ran my eyes round the circle of dancers. . . . I had the impression that two or three gentlemen were looking at me in some astonishment; but, generally speaking, my talk with the Prince had not been observed. . . . My rival was already sitting on his chair, perfectly calm and with his former smile on his face. Bizmionkov led Liza to her seat. She bowed to him amiably and at once turned to the Prince, with some anxiety, it seemed to me. But he smiled to her in reply, graciously waved his hand, and evidently said something very pleasant to her, for she crimsoned deeply with pleasure, drooped her eyes, and then fixed them on him again with affectionate reproach.

The heroic mood that had suddenly developed in me did not vanish until the mazurka was ended; but I no longer uttered sarcasms and did not criticize. I only looked from time to time moodily and sternly at my lady, who was evidently beginning to be afraid of me and was reduced to stuttering and blinking incessantly when I returned her to the natural fortress of her mother, a very fat woman with a red toque on her head. Entrusting the terrified maiden to her rightful ownership, I walked away to the window, folded my arms, and began to wait for what would happen next. I waited quite a long time. The Prince was continually surrounded by the host — literally surrounded, just as Britain is surrounded by the sea — not to speak of the other members of the county marshal's family and other guests. And besides, he could not go up and begin to talk to such an insignificant person as I without arousing general astonishment. I remember that this insignificance of mine even gave me cause for joy. "Have a good time!" I thought, watching as he courteously turned first to one, then to another worthy person who had achieved the honor of being noticed by him if only for the "twinkling of an eye," as the poets say. "Have a good time, my boy — you'll come up to me at last, for, after all, I have insulted you." Finally the Prince, neatly escaping from the crowd of his adorers, passed by me, glanced perhaps at the window, or at my hair, turned back, and suddenly halted, as though he had remembered something.

"Ah, yes!" he said, turning to me with a smile. "That reminds me, I have a little business with you."

Two landowners, among the most importunate, who had persistently followed the Prince, must have thought that the "little business" was of an official nature, for they respectfully fell back. The Prince took me by the arm and led me aside. My heart knocked in my chest.

"I think you," he began, drawling the word "you" and gazing at my chin with a contemptuous expression, which, strangely enough, could not have accorded better with his fresh and handsome face, "you made some impertinent remark to me."

"I said what I thought," I retorted, raising my voice.

"Sssh! Quieter!" he remarked. "Gentlemen don't shout. Perhaps you would like to fight a duel with me?"

"That is your business," I replied, drawing myself up.

"I shall be compelled to challenge you," he said carelessly, "if you do not withdraw your expression."

"I have no intention of withdrawing anything," I retorted proudly.

"Really?" he observed, not without a sarcastic smile. "In that case," he continued after a moment's silence, "I shall have the honor to send my second to you tomorrow."

"Very good!" I said in a voice as unconcerned as possible.

He bowed slightly.

"I cannot forbid your regarding me as vacuous," he added, arrogantly narrowing his eyes, "but the Princes N. cannot be upstarts. Good-by, Mr. — Mr. Stuccoturin."

He swiftly turned his back on me and went back to the host, who was beginning to get agitated.

Mr. Stuccoturin! . . . My name is Chulkaturin. . . . I could not think of anything to say to him in reply to that last affront and only stared after him furiously. "Till tomorrow!" I whispered, clenching my teeth, and at once sought out an officer of my acquaintance, an Uhlan captain named Koloberdayev, a desperate reveler and a splendid fellow. I briefly told him about my quarrel with the Prince and asked him to be my second. Of course he agreed at once, and I went home.

I could not sleep all night — out of agitation, not cowardice. I am not a coward. In fact, I thought very little about the possibility that I might be deprived of life, of that highest good on earth, as the Germans call it. I thought only of Liza, of my shattered hopes, of what I ought to do. "Should I attempt to kill the Prince?" I asked myself; and of course I wanted to kill him, not for the sake of vengeance, but in my desire for Liza's good. "But she will not survive that blow," I continued. "No, better that he should kill me!" I confess I also found it pleasant to think that I, an obscure local individual, should have compelled such an important person to fight with me.

Morning came upon me during these meditations; and the morning was immediately followed by Koloberdayev.

"Well," he asked me as he clattered into my bedroom, "and where is the Prince's second?"

"Give him a chance," I replied crossly; "it is only eight o'clock. I expect the Prince is still asleep."

"In that case," the indefatigable captain retorted, "order some tea for me. I've got a headache from yesterday. . . . I haven't even undressed. For that matter," he added with a yawn, "I very rarely do undress."

Tea was brought for him. He drank six glasses with rum, smoked four pipes, told me that the previous day he had bought a horse for almost nothing after the coachmen had rejected it, and that he planned to break it in, tying up one foreleg. And he fell asleep, without undressing, on the sofa, with a pipe in his mouth. I got up and put my papers in order. One note of invitation from Liza, the only note I had ever received from her, I was about to put in my breast; but I thought better of the idea and threw it into my box. Koloberdayev snored quietly, his head hanging half off the leather upholstery. . . . I remember I spent a long time examining his crumpled, audacious, carefree, good-natured face. At ten o'clock my servant announced the arrival of Bizmionkov. The Prince had chosen him as his second.

Together we aroused the captain, who was dead asleep. He rose, stared at us with glassy eyes, asked in a hoarse voice for vodka, pulled himself together, and, bowing to Bizmionkov, went with him into the next room for a conference. The seconds' con-

ference did not last long. Fifteen minutes later they both came
to me in the bedroom. Koloberdayev informed me: "We shall
fight this very day, at three o'clock, with pistols." I silently
nodded my agreement. Bizmionkov at once took his leave and
departed. He was rather pale and inwardly agitated, like a man
unaccustomed to such activities; but he was very courteous and
cold. I felt rather conscience-stricken in his presence, I did not
dare to look him in the eyes. Koloberdayev again began to tell
me about his horse. This conversation was very much to my mind.
I was afraid he might make some mention of Liza. But my good
captain was not a gossip, and moreover he was contemptuous of
all women, calling them salads, God knows why. At two o'clock
we had something to eat, and at three were already on the scene
of action — in that same birch wood where I had once walked
with Liza, two paces from that cliff.

We were the first to arrive. But the Prince and Bizmionkov did
not keep us waiting long. Without exaggeration, the Prince was
as fresh as a rose; his hazel eyes gleamed with extraordinary
affability beneath the peak of his cap. He was smoking a cigar,
and when he saw Koloberdayev he shook his hand warmly. Even
to me he bowed very amiably. I, on the contrary, felt that I was
pale, and my hands, to my great chagrin, were trembling a little
. . . my throat was dry . . . I had never fought a duel before.
"Oh, God!" I thought, "so long as this derisive gentleman doesn't
take my agitation for nervousness!" I mentally consigned my
nerves to all the devils; but glancing, at last, straight in the Prince's
face and catching an almost imperceptible sneer on his lips, I
suddenly grew angry again and at once recovered my equanimity. Meanwhile our seconds were arranging the details, measur-
ing off the paces, loading the pistols. Koloberdayev was the more
active; Bizmionkov mostly watched him. The day was excellent
— no worse than that of the unforgettable walk. As then, the
deep azure of the sky was peering through the gilded green of
the leaves. Their murmur seemed to irritate me. The prince
continued to smoke his cigar, leaning his back against the trunk
of a lime tree. . . .

"Please take up your positions, gentlemen; all is ready," Koloberdayev said at last, handing us the pistols.

The Prince walked away a few paces, halted, and, turning his
head round, asked me across his shoulder: "So you don't take

back your words?" I wanted to reply, but my voice betrayed me, and I contented myself with a contemptuous gesture. The Prince again smiled sarcastically and took up his position. We began to approach each other. I raised my pistol, intending to aim at my enemy's breast — at that moment he was indeed my enemy — but suddenly I elevated the barrel, as though someone had jogged my elbow, and fired. The Prince staggered and put his left hand to his left temple; a little stream of blood flowed down his cheek from beneath his white chamois glove. Bizmionkov rushed to him.

"It's nothing," he said, taking off his cap, which had been holed by the bullet. "As it didn't enter the head it must be a scratch."

He calmly took a batiste handkerchief out of his pocket and pressed it against his blood-soaked curls. I stared at him as though petrified and did not stir.

"Please go to the line!" Koloberdayev said to me severely.

I obeyed.

"Is the duel to continue?" he added, turning to Bizmionkov.

Bizmionkov made no answer. But the Prince, without removing his handkerchief from the wound and not even giving himself the pleasure of torturing me as I stood, retorted with a smile: "The duel is ended," and fired into the air. I all but burst into tears with chagrin and fury. With all his magnanimity this man had finally trodden me into the mud, had disposed of me. I wanted to object, wanted to demand that he should fire at me. But he came up to me and held out his hand.

"Now everything is forgotten between us, isn't it?" he said in a kindly tone.

I glanced at his white face, at that bloodstained handkerchief, and, completely unmanned, ashamed, and annihilated, I squeezed his hand. . . .

"Gentlemen," he added, turning to the seconds, "I hope that everything will be kept secret?"

"Of course!" Koloberdayev exclaimed. "But, Prince, allow me. . . ."

And he himself tied up the Prince's head.

As the Prince departed he bowed to me once more; but Bizmionkov did not even glance at me. Shattered — morally shattered — I returned home with Koloberdayev.

"Why, what's the matter with you?" the captain asked me. "Don't be alarmed; the wound isn't dangerous. He'll be able to dance even tomorrow, if that's what you want. Or are you sorry you didn't kill him? In that case you're wrong; he's a fine fellow."

"Why did he spare me?" I muttered at last.

"Well, there's a fine thing!" the captain calmly replied. "Oh, these authors!"

I have no idea why it occurred to him to call me an author.

I flatly refuse to describe my sufferings during the evening that followed this unfortunate duel. My self-esteem suffered beyond all my powers of explanation. It was not that I was tormented by conscience; it was the realization of my stupidity that devastated me. "I have myself administered the last, the final blow to my hopes!" I declared as I walked about my room with great strides. "The Prince, wounded by me and forgiving me. . . . Yes, Liza is his now. Now nothing can save her, can hold her back on the edge of the precipice." I knew quite well that our duel could not remain a secret, despite the Prince's words; in any case, it could not remain a secret to Liza. "The Prince isn't so stupid," I whispered in my rage, "as not to exploit it. . . ." But meanwhile I was mistaken. All the town learned about the duel and its real cause, and the very next day, of course; but it was not the Prince who talked too much; on the contrary. When, with bandaged head and with an explanation already formulated, he presented himself to Liza, she knew everything before he spoke. . . . I cannot say whether it was Bizmionkov who betrayed me or whether the news reached her through other channels. But in any case is it possible to keep anything a secret in a small town?

You can imagine how Liza received him, how all the Ozhogin family received him! As for me, I immediately became the object of general indignation, of abomination. I was a monster, a crazy, jealous fool, and a cannibal. My few acquaintances turned from me as from the plague. The town authorities immediately approached the Prince with the proposal to punish me exemplarily and severely; only the Prince's own insistent and urgent requests averted the disaster that hung over my head. That man was fated to annihilate me in every respect. With his magnanimity he slammed me down as if with a coffin lid. I need not say that the Ozhogin house was at once closed to me. Kirila Matveich even returned an ordinary pencil that I had forgotten to bring away with me. In reality, he in particular had no good reason to be angry with me. My "crazy" jealousy, as it was called in the town, defined, elucidated, so to speak, the Prince's relations with Liza. The old Ozhogins themselves, and all the other citizens began to regard him almost as a fiancé. In fact, this could not have been altogether pleasant for him. But he liked Liza very much; moreover, he had not yet gained his end. . . . With all the adroitness of an intelligent man of the world he adapted himself to his new situation and at once entered into the spirit, as one says, of his new role . . .

But I! . . . Now I turned my back on my hopes, on all the hopes of my future. When one's sufferings reach the point of causing all one's entrails to crack and groan like an overloaded cart, it would be desirable for those sufferings to cease being laughable. . . . But no! Laughter not only accompanies tears to the end, to the point of exhaustion, the impossibility of shedding any more — no, it goes on ringing and echoing even when the tongue is petrified and lamentation itself dies away. . . . And so, firstly because I have no intention of seeming ludicrous even to myself, and secondly as I am terribly tired, I postpone the continuation and, if God wills, the end of my story until tomorrow. . . .

March 29. A light frost. Yesterday it thawed.

Yesterday I did not have the strength to continue my diary; like Poprishchin, I spent most of the day lying in bed and talking to Terentievna. Now there's a woman! She lost her first husband with the plague sixty years ago, she has survived all her children, she is herself unforgivably old, she drinks as much tea as you like, she is well fed, warmly clothed; but what do you think she talked to me about all day yesterday? I had given orders that the half-moth-eaten collar of some outworn livery was to be given to another completely plucked old woman for a waist-coat (she wears breastplates in the form of a waistcoat). . . . And what do you think? — Terentievna wanted to know why she couldn't have it. "I am your nurse, I believe. . . . Oh, my dear master, it's a sin on your part. . . . And what did I look after you so tenderly for, I'd like to know? . . ." and so on.

The merciless old woman completely wore me out with her reproaches. . . . But to return to the story.

And so I suffered like a dog that has had its hind parts run
over. Only then, only after my final banishment from the Ozhogins' house, did I fully realize how much satisfaction a man
may draw from contemplation of his own unhappiness! O human-
kind, truly thou art a wretched generation! But all the same,
away with philosophic reflections! . . . I spent the days in utter
loneliness and only by the most roundabout and sneaking ways
discovered what was happening in the Ozhogin family and what
the Prince was doing: my servant had made the acquaintance of
his coachman's first cousin once removed. This acquaintance
afforded me some relief, and, as the result of my hints and little
presents, my servant quickly guessed what he should talk about
when he was dragging off his master's boots each evening. Sometimes I happened to meet one of the Ozhogin family, or Bizmionkov, or the Prince, in the street. . . . I bowed to the Prince and
Bizmionkov, but did not enter into conversation with them. I
saw Liza only three times all together: once with her mother
in a fashionable shop; once in an open carriage, with her father,
mother, and the Prince; and once in church. I need not say that
I did not have the temerity to go up to her, and I gazed at her
only from afar. In the shop she was very preoccupied, but gay.
She was ordering something for herself and was fussily measur-
ing out ribbons. Her mother stood watching her, her arms folded
over her belly, her nose tilted up, and smiling with that stupid
and devoted smile which is permissible only to loving mothers.
In the carriage with the Prince, Liza was— I shall never forget
that meeting! The old Ozhogins were sitting on the back seat of
the carriage, the Prince and Liza in front. She was paler than
usual; the two rosy patches were hardly visible on her cheeks.
She was half turned to him; resting on her outstretched right
hand (she was holding an umbrella in the left) and languidly
bending her little head, she was gazing straight into his face with
her expressive eyes. At that moment she was entirely his, she
trusted him irrevocably. I did not have a good chance of observing his face — the carriage dashed by too quickly — but it seemed
to me that he too was deeply moved.

The third time I saw her in church. Not more than ten days
had passed since I had met her in the carriage with the Prince,

not more than three weeks since the day of my duel. The business on which the Prince had come to O— was now completed, but he continued to procrastinate with his departure; he reported to Petersburg that he was unwell. The town was every day expecting him to make a formal proposal to Kirila Matveich. I myself was only waiting for this last blow in order to go away forever. I had taken a violent dislike to the town of O—. I could not remain indoors, and I wandered about its neighborhood from morning till evening. One gray unpleasant day, returning from a walk interrupted by rain, I went into the church. Evening service had only just begun, there were very few people present. I looked about me, and suddenly, close to a window, noticed a familiar figure. I did not recognize her at first; that pale face, that faded glance, those sunken cheeks — surely that was not the same Liza whom I had seen two weeks before? Wrapped in a cloak, hatless, half illuminated by the cold light falling from a broad clear window, she gazed fixedly at the altar screen and seemed to be trying to pray, trying to shake off a despondent torpor. Behind her a red-faced, fat little page with yellow cartridge pockets across his chest [1] was standing with his hands folded behind his back and gazing at his mistress with sleepy bewilderment. I trembled all over and was about to go up to her, but I stopped. An agonizing presentiment crushed my heart. Liza stood without moving in the least till the end of the service. Everybody else had left, the verger began to sweep the church, and still she did not stir from the spot. The page went up to her, said something to her, touched her dress. She looked round, passed her hand over her face, and went out. I followed her home, keeping some little distance behind, then returned to my house.

"She is lost!" I exclaimed as I entered my room.

To this day I, as a man, do not know what my sensations were at that moment; I remember that, folding my arms, I flung myself on the sofa and fixed my gaze on the floor; yet I don't know, but in the midst of my misery I seemed to have a feeling of satisfaction. . . . I would not have admitted this feeling for anything if I had not been writing this only for my own pleasure. . . . Truly, I was racked by terrible, agonizing presentiments . . . and, who knows, perhaps I would have been greatly em-

---

[1] A page's traditional dress was a cossack coat, with cartridge pockets as ornamentation. (Tr.)

barrassed if they had not been fulfilled. "Such is the human heart!" some middle-aged Russian moralizer would exclaim in an expressive voice at this point, raising his fat forefinger adorned with a carnelian ring. But what do we care for the opinion of a Russian moralizer with an expressive voice, and a carnelian ring on his finger?

Rightly or wrongly, my presentiments were justified. Suddenly the news spread through the town that the Prince had gone, apparently as the result of an order received from Petersburg; that he had gone without making any proposal either to Kirila Matveich or to his wife, and that Liza was left to weep over his infidelity to the end of her days. The Prince's departure was quite unexpected, because only the previous evening his coachman, so my servant assured me, had had no suspicions whatever of his master's intentions. This news put me in a fever; I dressed at once and was about to hurry to the Ozhogins'. But after thinking it over, I deemed it decorous to wait till the next day. For that matter, I did not lose anything by remaining at home. That same evening a man named Pandopipopulo, a Greek who had chanced to get stranded in O— on his way to somewhere else, a gossip of the first magnitude, who had surpassed all others in his indignation with me because of my duel with the Prince, came to see me. He did not even give my servant time to report his arrival, but burst into my room, squeezed my hand vigorously, apologized to me a thousand times, called me a model of magnanimity and daring, described the Prince in the blackest of colors, and did not spare the old Ozhogins, whom, in his opinion, fate had justly punished; in passing he had a smack at Liza also and then ran off, after kissing me on the shoulder. Among other things, I learned from him that the Prince, *en vrai grand seigneur*, on the eve of his departure, had reacted to Kirila Matveich's delicate hint with the cold reply that he did not intend to deceive anybody and had no thought of getting married, then had risen, bowed himself out, and was such a . . .

Next day I went to call on the Ozhogins. At my appearance the purblind valet jumped up from the bench with the speed of lightning. I ordered him to announce my visit; he ran off and returned at once. "Please," he said, "the master has ordered me to ask you in." I went into Kirila Matveich's private room — Till tomorrow.

The Diary of a Superfluous Man

March 30. A frost

And so I entered Kirila Matveich's room. I would have given a handsome reward to anyone who could have shown me my own face as this worthy official, hurriedly flinging his Bokharan gown around him, came up to me with outstretched hands. I must have beamed with modest triumph, condescending sympathy, and boundless magnanimity. . . . I felt myself to be something after the style of Scipio Africanus. Ozhogin was obviously embarrassed and afflicted; he avoided my gaze and fidgeted where he stood. I noted also that he spoke in an unnaturally loud voice and all together expressed himself very indefinitely; he indefinitely but fervently begged my pardon, indefinitely referred to the departed guest, added a few general and indefinite remarks about the delusory and transient nature of earthly blessings, and suddenly, feeling a tear in his eyes, hurried to take a pinch of snuff, probably in order to deceive me in regard to the cause of his tearfulness. . . . He used Russian green tobacco, and it is well known that that plant makes even old men shed tears, so that the human eye looks dull and meaningless for several moments. I, of course, handled the old man very carefully, asked after the health of his wife and daughter, and at once neatly turned the conversation to the interesting question of crop rotation. I was dressed in normal attire, but the feeling of gentle decorum and mild condescension that filled me gave me a fresh and holiday feeling, as though I were wearing a white waistcoat and white tie. One thing agitated me: the thought of seeing Liza. . . . Finally Ozhogin himself offered to take me to his wife. On seeing me, that good but stupid woman was at first terribly disconcerted; but her mind was incapable of retaining one and the same impression for any length of time, and so she soon calmed down. Finally I saw Liza. She entered the room. . . .

I expected to find her a shamed and contrite sinner and had in advance given my features the most gracious and encouraging of expressions. . . . Why lie? I really did love her and was athirst for the happiness of forgiving her, of stretching out my hand to her. But, to my inexpressible amazement, in reply to my significant bow she laughed coldly, carelessly remarked: "Ah, so it's you?" and at once turned away from me. Truly, I thought her laugh seemed forced, and in any case it did not match her terribly wasted features in the least . . . but, all the same, I had not ex-

793

pected such a reception. . . . I stared at her in astonishment. What a transformation had been wrought in her! There was nothing in common between the former child and this woman. She seemed to have grown up, to have taken herself in hand; all the features of her face, especially the lips, seemed to have acquired definition . . . her gaze had grown deeper, firmer, and darker.

I stayed on with the Ozhogins until dinnertime; she rose, left the room, and returned, calmly answered questions, and deliberately paid no attention to me. She — I saw that — she wanted to make me feel that I was not worth even her anger, though I had all but killed her lover. At last I lost patience: a venomous innuendo burst from my lips. . . . She started, gave me a swift glance, rose, and, going over to the window, said in a voice that quivered a little: "You can all say what you like, but understand this: I love that man, and shall always love him, and I do not in the least regard him as having wronged me; on the contrary. . . ." Her voice began to break, she paused. . . . She tried to master herself, but could not; she burst into tears and left the room. . . . Her old parents were upset. . . . I squeezed their hands, sighed, turned my eyes up, and retired.

I am too weak, the time left to me is too short, I am not in a state to describe with my previous detail the new series of tormenting ideas, resolute intentions, and other fruits of so-called inward struggle that I experienced after the renewal of my acquaintance with the Ozhogins. I had no doubt that Liza still loved and would for long go on loving the Prince. . . . But as a man who has been tamed by circumstances and has tamed himself, I did not even dream of her love. I desired only her friendship; I desired to win her trust, her respect, which, so experienced people assure us, is regarded as the most reliable basis for happiness in marriage. . . . Unfortunately, I left out of calculation one rather important circumstance — namely, that ever since the day of the duel Liza had hated me. I began to visit the Ozhogins' home as in past days; Kirila Matveich showed me more affection and favor than ever before. I even have reason to think that now he would gladly have given his daughter to me, though I was not a groom to be proud of; public opinion was persecuting him and Liza, while it exalted me, on the contrary, to the very heavens. Liza's treatment of me did not change. She was silent for the most part, obeyed when she was summoned to a meal, showed no out-

The Diary of a Superfluous Man

ward signs of grief whatever, but none the less she melted like a candle. I must be just to Kirila Matveich: he spared her in every way; his old wife only bristled up as she looked at her poor little child. One man Liza did not shun, though she did not talk much to him either, and that was Bizmionkov. The old Ozhogins treated him harshly, even roughly; they could not forgive him for acting as the Prince's second; but he continued to visit them, as though he did not notice their unkindness. With me he was very cold and — strange to say — I seemed to be afraid of him.

This went on for about two weeks. At last, after one sleepless night, I decided to clear up my position with Liza, to reveal my heart to her, to tell her that despite all the past, despite all the possible rumors and slanders, I would regard myself as only too happy if she would bestow her hand on me, would again give me her trust. Really, I seriously imagined that I would be displaying an incomparable example of magnanimity, as the textbooks put it, and that she would agree even if it was only in her astonishment. In any case, I wanted to clear my position with her and to free myself, finally, of uncertainty.

Behind the Ozhogins' house was quite a large garden, ending in a small, neglected, and overgrown lime grove. In the middle of this grove was an ancient arbor in Chinese style; a board fence separated the garden from a blind alley. Sometimes Liza wandered for hours in the garden. Kirila Matveich knew this and had forbidden her to be disturbed, to be watched; leave her to overcome her sorrow. When she was not to be found indoors, it was only necessary to ring a bell on the porch before dinner for her to appear at once, with the same stubborn silence on her lips and in her gaze, with a crumpled leaf in her hand. One day, observing that she was not in the house, I pretended that I was going, said good-by to Kirila Matveich, put on my hat, and went out into the yard and from the yard into the street. But I at once slipped back through the gate very quickly and made my way past the kitchen into the garden. Fortunately, no one noticed me. Not stopping to think, I went with hurried steps into the grove. Ahead of me on the path I saw Liza. My heart beat violently. I halted, sighed deeply, and was just about to go up to her when suddenly, without turning round, she raised her hand and began to listen. . . .

From beyond the trees, in the direction of the alley, came the

795

clear sound of two blows, as though someone were knocking on the fence. Liza clapped her hands, I heard the faint creak of a wicket gate, and Bizmionkov came through the trees. I nimbly concealed myself behind a trunk. Liza silently turned to him. . . . She silently took him by the arm, and they both went quietly along the path. I gazed after them in astonishment. They halted, looked about them, vanished behind some bushes, came into sight again, and finally entered the arbor. This arbor was a little circular erection, with one door and one small window; in the middle was an old one-legged table, overgrown with delicate green moss; two old benches made of boards stood, one on either side, a little distance from the damp and darkened walls. Here on unusually hot days, and then only once a year, and then only in past days, the family had drunk tea. The door could not be closed at all; the frame had long since come away from the window and, held by one corner, hung mournfully, like the broken wing of a bird. I stole up to the arbor and cautiously peered through the window chink. Liza was sitting on one of the benches, with her head hanging; her right hand was lying on her knees, her left hand Bizmionkov was holding in both his hands. He was looking at her commiseratively.

"How do you feel today?" he asked her in an undertone.

"Just the same," she replied, "neither worse nor better. Emptiness, a terrible emptiness!" she added, raising her eyes mournfully.

He did not answer her.

"What do you think?" she continued. "Will he write to me again?"

"I don't think so, Lizaveta Kirillovna!"

She was silent. Then she said:

"And besides, what is there for him to write about? He told me everything in his first letter. I could not be his wife; but I was happy — for a brief while — I was happy. . . ."

Bizmionkov shrank into himself.

"Ah!" she continued with animation, "if only you knew how loathsome that Chulkaturin is to me! . . . Whenever I see that man's hands, I still imagine I can see — his blood." (I turned cold behind my chink.) "For that matter," she added thoughtfully, "who knows? If it hadn't been for that duel, perhaps — Ah, when I saw him wounded, I at once felt that I was entirely his."

The Diary of a Superfluous Man

"Chulkaturin is in love with you," Bizmionkov remarked.

"And what is that to me? Do I need anyone's love?" She paused and then slowly added: "Except yours. Yes, my friend, your love is indispensable to me: without you I would perish. You have helped me to endure the terrible minutes. . . ."

She was silent. . . . He began to stroke her hand with paternal tenderness.

"It can't be helped, it can't be helped, Lizaveta Kirillovna," he repeated several times in succession.

"Yes, and even now," she said thickly, "I would die without you, I think. You alone are a support to me; and besides, you remind me of him — for you knew everything. Do you remember how fine he was that day? . . . But forgive me: it must be painful for you — "

"Speak on! Speak on! Why do you say that? You mustn't!" he broke in.

She squeezed his hand.

"You are very good, Bizmionkov," she continued; "you are as good as an angel. It can't be helped! I feel that I shall love him even to my grave. I have forgiven him, I am grateful to him. God grant him happiness! God grant him a wife to his heart!" and her eyes filled with tears. "So long as he doesn't forget me, so long as he thinks of his Liza, if only occasionally. Let us go," she added after a brief silence.

Bizmionkov raised her hand to his lips.

"I know," she began fervently, "that everybody is reproaching me now, everybody is throwing stones at me. Let them! All the same, I would not exchange my unhappiness for their happiness. . . . No! No! . . . He did not love me long, but he did love me! He never deceived me: he did not tell me that I would be his wife; I myself never thought of that. Only poor Papa hoped for it. And even now I am not altogether unhappy: I still have the memory, and, no matter how terrible the consequences — I am stifled here — it was here I saw him for the last time. . . . Let us go out."

They rose. I had hardly time to spring aside and hide behind a stout lime tree. They emerged from the arbor and, so far as I could judge by the noise of their footsteps, went into the grove. I don't know how long I remained standing there, not moving from the spot, sunk in senseless bewilderment, when suddenly

Turgenev

I heard footsteps again. I started and cautiously peered out from my ambush, to see Bizmionkov and Liza returning along the same path. They were both deeply agitated, especially Bizmionkov. He seemed to be crying. Liza halted, looked at him, and clearly uttered the following words: "I consent, Bizmionkov. I would not consent if you wished only to save me, to get me out of a terrible situation; but you love me; you know everything — and you love me. I shall never find a more reliable, faithful friend. I will be your wife."

He kissed her hand; she smiled at him miserably and went toward the house. He rushed into the grove, and I went home. As he had probably said exactly what I had intended to say to Liza, and as she had replied with the very answer I had desired to hear from her, there was no need for me to worry my head any longer. Two weeks later she married him. The old Ozhogins were glad of any groom.

Well, tell me now, am I not a superfluous man? In all this story haven't I played the part of a man who is superfluous?

The role played by the Prince — there is no need to dilate on it. Bizmionkov's role also is comprehensible. . . . But I? Why was I mixed up in it all? What a stupid fifth wheel to a cart! Ah, I feel bitter, bitter! . . . But now, just as the haulers say: "One more heave, just one more little heave" — so in another little day, or two, it will no longer be bitter for me, nor sweet.

March 31

I'm bad. I am writing these lines in bed. The weather changed suddenly yesterday evening. Today it is hot, almost a summer's day. Everything is melting, falling, running. The scent of furrowed earth is in the air: a heavy, strong, stifling scent. Everything is steaming. The sun strikes so hard, flames so fiercely. I'm in a bad way. I feel that I am disintegrating.

I thought I would keep a diary, and instead what have I done? Told just one incident from my life. I have let my pen run away with me; the faded memories awoke and carried me off. I have written unhurriedly, in detail, as though I still had years before me; but now, now I haven't time to continue. Death, death is coming. I can already hear its menacing crescendo. . . . Time . . . time!

Well, and what does it matter? Did it make any difference

what I told? In face of death the last earthly anxieties disappear. I feel that I am sinking; I am growing simpler, clearer. Rather late have I clutched at sense! A strange thing! I am sinking — definitely, and at the same time I am afraid. Yes, I am afraid. Half bent over the silent, yawning abysm, I shudder, I turn away, I survey all around me with avid attention. The least article is doubly dear to me. I cannot tire of looking at my poor, cheerless room as I say farewell to every tiny spot on my walls! Satiate yourselves for the last time, eyes of mine! Life is retreating; it is quietly and steadily running away from me, like the shore from the gaze of a seafarer. My nurse's old yellow face tied up in a dark kerchief, the hissing samovar on the table, the little pot of geranium on the window sill, and you, my poor dog Treasure, the pen with which I write these lines, my own hand, I see you now — there you are, there. . . . Is it really possible that — today, maybe — I shall never see you again? It is hard for a living creature to part from life! What are you fawning on me for, poor dog? What are you resting your breast against the bed for, convulsively tucking in your docked tail and not removing your kind, mournful eyes from me? Are you sorry for me? Or do you already feel that soon your master will be no more? Ah, if I could but pass in thought over all the other articles in my room! I know that these memories are cheerless and insignificant, but I have no others. Emptiness, a terrible emptiness! As Liza said.

Oh, my God, my God! So I am dying. . . . A heart able and ready to love will soon cease to beat. . . . And will it really grow still forever, without once having tasted happiness, without even once expanding beneath the pleasurable burden of joy? Alas! That is impossible, impossible, I know. . . . If, at the least, now, before my death — for death, after all, is a sacred thing, it does exalt any creature — if some dear, sad, friendly voice could sing a farewell song of my own sorrow over me, I might, perhaps, reconcile myself to it. But to die stupidly, stupidly. . . .

I think I am beginning to wander.

Good-by, life, good-by, my garden, and you, my limes! When summer comes, don't forget to be covered from top to foot with flowers . . . and let it be good for people to lie in your perfumed shade, on the fresh grass, beneath the murmuring whisper of your leaves gently stirred by the wind. Good-by, good-by! Good-by, everything and forever!

Turgenev

Good-by, Liza! As I wrote those two words I all but smiled. That exclamation seems bookish to me. I would appear to be composing a moving story and ending a desperate letter. . . .

Tomorrow is the 1st of April. Surely I shall not die tomorrow? That would even be indecent, somehow. And yet it fits me. . . .

How the doctor babbled away today! . . .

April 1

Finish. . . . Life is finished. I definitely shall die today. It is hot outside — almost stifling — or is it my breast that is refusing to breathe already? My little comedy is played out. The curtain falls.

In my annihilation I shall cease to be superfluous. . . .

Ah, how hot this sun is! Those mighty rays breathe of eternity. . . .

Good-by, Terentievna. . . . This morning, as she sat by the window, she burst into tears . . . over me, perhaps — but perhaps over the fact that she herself will have to die soon. I made her promise "not to hurt" Treasure.

It is difficult for me to write . . . I throw down the pen. . . . Time! Death is already approaching with a rising thunder, like a carriage along the road at night. It is here, it is fluttering round me, like that gentle wafting which caused the hair of the prophet to stand on end. . . .

I am dying. . . . Live on, the living!

> *And round the dark tomb's chilly entrance*
> *Let the young life, the children, play;*
> *And let indifferent nature's radiance*
> *With beauty infinite array.*

Publisher's note. Beneath these last lines is the profile of a head with a large forelock and mustaches, with the eyes *en face* and radiating eyelashes; and under the head someone has written the following words:

> *This manuscript was read*
> *And Its Contents were not Approved*
> *by Piotr Zudoteshin*
> *M   M   M   M*

The Diary of a Superfluous Man

Dear Sir
Piotr Zudoteshin
My dear Sir.

But as the handwriting of these lines is nothing like that in which all the rest of the book is written, the publisher feels justified in concluding that the above-mentioned lines were added later, by someone else, especially as it has come to his (the publisher's) knowledge that Mr. Chulkaturin did in fact die during the night of April 1, 18—, on his hereditary estate, Lambswater.

A NOTE ON THE TYPE IN WHICH
THIS BOOK IS SET

This book was set on the Linotype in Janson, a recutting made direct from the type cast from matrices (now in possession of the Stempel foundry, Frankfurt am Main) made by Anton Janson some time between 1660 and 1687.

Of Janson's origin nothing is known. He may have been a relative of Justus Janson, a printer of Danish birth who practised in Leipzig from 1614 to 1635. Some time between 1657 and 1668 Anton Janson, a punch-cutter and type-founder, bought from the Leipzig printer Johann Erich Hahn the type-foundry which had formerly been a part of the printing house of M. Friedrich Lankisch. Janson's types were first shown in a specimen sheet issued at Leipzig about 1675. Janson's successor, and perhaps his son-in-law, Johann Karl Edling, issued a specimen sheet of Janson types in 1689. His heirs sold the Janson matrices in Holland to Wolffgang Dietrich Erhardt.

The book was composed, printed, and bound by The Plimpton Press, Norwood, Massachusetts. Typography and binding designs are by W. A. Dwiggins.